DOORS OF THE CHURCH ARE OPEN:

SMOKE & MIRRORS: GRACE and the GREY AREA

SONYA SHERRELL SHUMAN
Atlanta, Georgia
September 10, 2014

PREFACE

Acts 17:24-28 (NIRV)

[24] "He is the God who made the world. He also made everything in it. He is the Lord of heaven and earth. He doesn't live in temples built by hands. [25] He is not served by human hands. He doesn't need anything. He himself gives life and breath to all people. He also gives them everything else they have. [26] From one man he made all the people of the world. Now they live all over the earth. He decided exactly when they should live. And he decided exactly where they should live. [27] God did this so that people would seek him. Then perhaps they would reach out for him and find him. They would find him even though he is not far from any of us. [28] 'In him we live and move and exist.' As some of your own poets have also said, 'We are his children.'

This book was written with the reader in mind. This book was a lifetime in the making and a labor-intensive dedication to everyone out there who has been confused, let down, rejected and compartmentalized by religion and all of its polarizing effects.

Religion stifles us. It embalms and castrates us. It buries us alive. Religion is tradition and tradition at some point, is rendered in effective because times change and people, their needs and their views change along with the times. We are ever evolving individuals with varying looks, likes and locations. All with some basic innate necessities and/or desires in common: Love, validation and understanding. Those are just a few to say the least.

We all want to be loved where we are, for who we are even when we don't know why we are. It is a base craving that goes neglected by the people called to love beyond the way things appear; like Jesus did. There are so many souls being lost. So many people being misunderstood and rejected because of religion. The habit. The practice. The tradition. The prison. There are people who attend the same church each week, because it is traditional to do so, that are not growing/evolving, who read the word of God but don't know how to practice godly principles beyond the callousness and rigidity of religion. People with callings that don't know what service is about; all it encompasses. In this day and age, maybe now more than ever, it seems as if believers are still picking and choosing who to love and serve. Sticking with old recipes and forced formulas that are past practice. People don't come to a restaurant or dinner table a soup kitchen or food pantry just to leave hungry. They come to get filled, have their needs met. If we are going to serve people, in love, the way Jesus did, we must begin by meeting them where they are. We also cannot afford to keep losing precious souls and lives unnecessarily by keeping the Good News inside of a building while there are starving people on the other side of the door. And sometimes, no matter how hungry people are, they will not come to a place of refreshment and restoration if they feel there is no place for them. If they feel they don't look/act the part. Religion not only turns people off, it intimidates people.

The people behind the doors of the church too often forget that they were once the people on the other side of the door they now ignore and walk past. Every believer was once a sheep without a shepherd. Every believer, still has issues nobody knows about but them and God. Some, only God know about because they are buried that deep. We cover up with big hats and sharp suits. We scream Hallelujah! From the mountain tops. The people on the other side of the door can hear you, their curious to know what that's all about, but we never invite them in. Even worse, we leave them thinking we have the market cornered on love and understanding, when obviously, we do not. Many of us still, after years of being saved, struggle with their same issues because deliverance isn't always instantaneous. It is a fact. Yet, we live in fear thinking if we own up to our short comings, form behind the pulpit to the back pew, we will be judged; harshly. See, same fears and issues the people on the people on the other side of the door have. Thin line isn't it.

On another hand, we tend to save all of our good loving and good deeds for the people in the building (just a building mind you. We the people, are the church. The believers. The body of Christ. Imperfect, yet to apprehend or acquiesce if we're going to be totally honest. Every blood-washed believer is a work in progress). We forget about the people on the other side of the door. We forget where we came from, how we got to where we are. We surround ourselves with the safety of religion and forget to go back and get one. We forget about truth in the testimony. We negate the "out" in outreach when we fail to reach out. "Lord thank you that I'm saved. Thank you for my church family. Lord thank you from where you have brought me from. Thank you for where you're taking me to. Thank you for my pastor and his wife and for my family. Thank you Jesus my kids ain't like those kids out there. Thank you Jesus." Now, is that a right or wrong way to pray? Wrong attitude? Maybe. Depends on perception. Depending on perspective. With all of that being said, there is no condemnation to them that are in Christ. We only do what comes naturally to us. Keeping in mind, so many natural tendencies go against spiritually healthy and mature things. We do what we know how until we know better.

Matthew 5:46 (NLT)

46 If you love only those who love you, what reward is there for that? Even corrupt tax collectors do that much.

There are many more people who are not attending church services traditionally than are not. There are many reasons why. There are endless reasons as to why people would rather stay at home and enjoy the message of the televangelist than to get up, get dressed and go outside to a house of worship i.e. a building, filled with people they are unsure of. Comfort, laziness, no risk of insult or injury involved. People fear rejection and judgment. That all stems from what it all begins with, reception and perception. I wrote this book in attempts to bridge the gap between the churchgoers and the people in the preferred seating, private pews at home. To bring understanding to the religious and the rejected. I wrote this book to remind everyone that tradition is of no effect. Tradition can be a shackle; am obstacle. In hindsight, it has historically been at times, a more of a hindrance as opposed to it being a help. There are people behind prison bars in maximum security settings that enjoy much more liberty than religious people. Even sinners seem to enjoy more freedom. They are not bound to rules. Something to think about. Not that I am in support of a sinful lifestyle. Not that I even encourage it. I've been there….I don't! I am merely stating the obvious.

There is a hurting, hungry world out here that is being picked over and passed by each and every day. From the reality televisions cast members who display their most intimate and personal issues before millions weekly for viewers to consume and criticize. To the abusive spouse, the hustler n the trap house, the drug-addicted single mother, the promiscuous teen girls and the boys and men that feast on their insecurities to their own delight, that have insecurities of their own they mask by overcompensating by being sexually promiscuous themselves. Even the homosexual that walks around labeled like a leper; an invisible "G" on their chest. Some who don't even know why they are the way they are; many who did not choose to "be" and for the many that do. The millions in the LGBT community that are not looking for a cure, but they have a cause. The people who are not looking to be "fixed", so to speak…but, looking to be loved. Not necessarily understood, but loved. Branded, scorned. Each and every one. All of the aforementioned plus the millions more who may not even know why or how. Even if they do. The commandment is to love. God never gave us a command to judge. He is the Righteous Judge. Something the religious forget. It is the believer's responsibility to love. Not even to understand, just to love.

Matthew 22:34-40 (KJV)

34 But when the Pharisees had heard that he had put the Sadducees to silence, they were gathered together.

35 Then one of them, which was a lawyer, asked him a question, tempting him, and saying,

36 Master, which is the great commandment in the law?

37 Jesus said unto him, Thou shalt love the Lord thy God with all thy heart, and with all thy soul, and with all thy mind.

38 This is the first and great commandment.

39 And the second is like unto It, Thou shalt love thy neighbor as thyself.

40 On these two commandments hang all the law and the prophets.

I wrote this book for the masses. For me. For you. Pastor, prophet, parishioner, passer-by, pimp, prostitute, politician and pusher, poser, etc. We have so much in common. The line between the believer and the non-believer is so very thin. Christ, salvation makes the difference. Love, well, believer or not, we all still have that in common as human beings. We all desire it whether we admit it or not. People act out in the most criminal of ways for lack of it or lack of understanding of what it means or looks like. It is painful to see how many of us still don't know love. Believer and non-believer alike. Truth be told, many people outside of the traditional church seem to be more "loving" and charitable at heart than many believers even today. We still tend to base love on feeling when love is a conscious choice.

Love is never about how we feel. Love surpasses emotion on a grand scale. Love is action. Love is power. Love is not fleeting and inconsistent. Love understands even when we don't. Love is aware and never confused. Love is our lawyer in the court of law. Love is our surgeon in the operating room. Love gives selflessly. Love is concerned for our every need. Love looks past the obvious. Love loves those that are hard to love with ease. Love loves even when we don't love it back. Loves is unconditional. Loves has nothing to do with religion. Love has everything to do with relationship. God is love. God longs for a deeply personal relationship with each and every one of us. It is not His will that any of us perish. He can get to us any way he chooses at any given time, under any given circumstances, by Christ Jesus. Love, God is not unlimited. Nor is He reduced to be housed in a building. Nor does he only make himself available to certain people. That's religious belief. That's man's interpretation. That is a lack of faith in the Creator of the universe who is the Alpha and the Omega. The beginning and the end. Omnipresent. Omniscient. He can be everywhere all at once. He is. That is how He is able to meet every need. He is God. Religion is the thing that places limits on an infinite God. Only a finite mind would think so small. He know how to reach us and His avenues and methods are not always conventional. They are as diverse as the whole of His masterful creation. Salvation is ours for the taking in the way we will we receive it. He knows His creation intimately. How great is our God?!

Psalm 139:1-17(KJV)

139 O lord, thou hast searched me, and known me.

² Thou knowest my downsitting and mine uprising, thou understandest my thought afar off.

³ Thou compassest my path and my lying down, and art acquainted with all my ways.

⁴ For there is not a word in my tongue, but, lo, O Lord, thou knowest it altogether.

5 Thou hast beset me behind and before, and laid thine hand upon me.

6 Such knowledge is too wonderful for me; it is high, I cannot attain unto it.

7 Whither shall I go from thy spirit? Or whither shall I flee from thy presence?

8 If I ascend up into heaven, thou art there: if I make my bed in hell, behold, thou art there.

9 If I take the wings of the morning, and dwell in the uttermost parts of the sea;

10 Even there shall thy hand lead me, and thy right hand shall hold me.

11 If I say, surely the darkness shall cover me; even the night shall be light about me.

12 Yea, the darkness hideth not from thee; but the night shineth as the day: the darkness and the light are both alike to thee.

13 For thou hast possessed my reins: thou hast covered me in my mother's womb.

14 I will praise thee; for I am fearfully and wonderfully made: marvelous are thy works; and that my soul knoweth right well.

> 15 My substance was not hid from thee, when I was made in secret, and curiously wrought in the lowest parts of the earth.

16 Thine eyes did see my substance, yet being unperfect; and in thy book all my members were written, which in continuance were fashioned, when as yet there was none of them.

I wrote this book for everyone struggling to connect like I used to. Struggling to connect the dots in life, in relationships, in these streets, in the church, in their minds, spirits and hearts. This is for the judgmental who rule the houses of worship and for the judgmental people who may never step foot inside of said establishment. This is for all of the ones who need a fresh perspective. Blind people who need to take a walk in someone else's shoes that their eyes may be opened.

This work, is for everyone imprisoned within, as I used to be. I did the work. I continue to do the work, moving through the process. I have spent valuable time taking a hard, cold look at myself when there was no one else around to distract me. No job, children leaving the nest, done with sex, drugs and rock n' roll (For the most part anyway. I still have a great affinity for different types of music thanks to my parents). No outlet. No cable TV. Often no electricity, no gas, no hot water; sometimes no running water. Nobody who understood where I was spiritually in my dawning, awakening, becoming and being. No well to draw from. Now template to trace. No example to follow. No illustration. Nowhere to run. No friends. No release, besides the mirror, ever constant before me. The Holy Spirit was my constant companion. The only things I had to rely on were the Word of God, the ugly truth that I had work to do and ugly truths to face about myself. Yep! Even after having received Christ over 15 years prior in the gymnasium of Weequahic High School (Thank you Ronnette Smith for introducing me to Christ.)

I was saved and in the throes of transformation, still becoming; not yet apprehended; not yet delivered from everything. Still wrestling with my past. Still wanting what used to be when I didn't know how to cope with what was and I couldn't see beyond the "what is" into the what "could be". I was saved and very religious. Judgmental, preaching hard, spitting all of the fire that was shut up in my bones, being led by the Holy Spirit, but still a work in progress. I had something. Something deep down inside of me that the Lord was going to use. A thing or two He had placed deep, down inside that was climbing its way up into my belly from only God knows where. Something I did not pray for or see coming. A fire, a passion. An unbridled passion. I had it. I had what it takes. Yet, there was no compassion, understanding or wisdom to harness it. No finesse, no humility, not enough experience, not enough refinement to bring it all together and smooth it out. No attention to detail. No concern for the audience. I was crass and calcified. I had no love. I had so much going in the way of ministry. But I had no love, so really, I was nothing. Little did I know, the Lord would use everything about me; good, bad and unbridled, to bring glory to His name.

In denial. Defeated by my limited view of life, love, the Lord and people. Prideful, I thought I was doing alright. But, God in all of His infinite wisdom, knew something drastic would have to happen for me to begin to get it. Get what? In all of my "getting", I needed to "get" understanding. Wisdom and knowledge where not going to be enough.

If the Lord had not shut every door in that season in my life, I would have died spiritually, emotionally, mentally, financially, relationally. The sum of all of those deaths can be greater than the pain and void left by a physical death. Physical death, in a sense, in my mind at the time, would have been more freeing. I actually prayed no to wake up to see another day, many a night in my suffering. He did not honor my request obviously. Anything less than forging ahead in the muck and mire would have been weak. A punk out so-to-speak (back in the day slang). I can truly say, the Lord is my strength. His word was and still is a lamp to my feet and a light to my path. I was truly groping in the darkness. I wanted to give up. He was offering me a new perspective on life, love, people, myself, and himself. The work was just too hard. I was done. I just wanted Him to leave me alone. "Why don't you leave me alone?" I would gripe day after miserable day. "Is that really what you want?" I heard Him say time and time again. No that's is not what I had wanted. In my mind's eye, I just didn't want to do the hard work. I was good at walking away from people, places and things. Giving up, had always been the easiest thing for me to do. It was the obvious choice I am today, so glad I did not make. It wasn't that I held on. It was that God in all of His faithfulness, held on to me. He is faithful. Thank you Jesus.

Psalm 103 (NIV)

[1] Praise the Lord, my soul;
   all my inmost being, praise his holy name.
[2] Praise the Lord, my soul,
   and forget not all his benefits—
[3] who forgives all your sins
   and heals all your diseases,
[4] who redeems your life from the pit

and crowns you with love and compassion,
⁵ who satisfies your desires with good things
    so that your youth is renewed like the eagle's.

⁶ The Lord works righteousness
    and justice for all the oppressed.

⁷ He made known his ways to Moses,
    his deeds to the people of Israel:
⁸ The Lord is compassionate and gracious,
    slow to anger, abounding in love.
⁹ He will not always accuse,
    nor will he harbor his anger forever;
¹⁰ he does not treat us as our sins deserve
    or repay us according to our iniquities.
¹¹ For as high as the heavens are above the earth,
    so great is his love for those who fear him;
¹² as far as the east is from the west,
    so far has he removed our transgressions from us.

¹³ As a father has compassion on his children,
    so the Lord has compassion on those who fear him;
¹⁴ for he knows how we are formed,
    he remembers that we are dust.
¹⁵ The life of mortals is like grass,
    they flourish like a flower of the field;
¹⁶ the wind blows over it and it is gone,
    and its place remembers it no more.
¹⁷ But from everlasting to everlasting
    the Lord's love is with those who fear him,
    and his righteousness with their children's children—
¹⁸ with those who keep his covenant
    and remember to obey his precepts.

¹⁹ The Lord has established his throne in heaven,
    and his kingdom rules over all.

²⁰ Praise the Lord, you his angels,
    you mighty ones who do his bidding,

who obey his word.
21 Praise the Lord, all his heavenly hosts,
    you his servants who do his will.
22 Praise the Lord, all his works
    everywhere in his dominion.

Praise the Lord, my soul.

To give up suicide on every level. The lack of being
challenged to grow is cancerous. Death is eminent and slow.
We do our children a grave disservice by catering to their
every whim.

It is truly bad to merely float in the abyss of just existing,
never gaining the strength, wisdom, tenacity and desire to
crawl from amongst the carbs in the barrel. Walk until you can
run. Run until you gain the speed and enough wind beneath
your wings at just the right moment…giving you the
momentum to fly. Taking advantage of the momentum,
looking down at where you have been lifted away from, you
soar. Not without falling sometimes of course. Falling doesn't
mean failure. It just means try again. Failure is when you just
refuse to get up and try it another way.

Psalm 37:23-24 (KJV)

23 The steps of a good man are ordered by the Lord: and he
delighteth in his way.

24 Though he fall, he shall not be utterly cast down: for the
Lord upholdeth him with his hand.

You soar with the eagles. Away from mediocrity, stagnation
and limitations…I slowly began to soar. If I had not traveled

through the wilderness season of my life, I would not know what a relationship with God, myself and people could even be like. The truth. The possibilities. The love.

My eyes, my heart, my spirit would not have been opened, not even available to love. Did God force me out of the confines of religion by boxing me in? No. I had been praying for a heart like His. His eyes to see. I prayed for His will to be done. I prayed boldly for brokenness. I believe I had been led by the Holy Spirit to do so. Just as I had been led into the wilderness by the Spirit of the Lord (another story). I had no idea what I was asking for. But, it helped me in ways I could not have ever imagined and let me tell you, my imagination is vivid. I prayed for greater anointing, godly wisdom and understanding. I pray to be more like Jesus every day and that does not come without a price. I am still learning that nothing that is worth it comes on a flowery bed of ease. No relationship, no goal, dream or even strain of ministry. If it didn't for Jesus, it will not for us. It all takes sacrifice from parenting to preaching.

There were so many different prayers. So many requests of God on this journey. So much more to unfold, know; so much more to be re-educated on. To rethink and explore. So much more evolution. I'm only at the halfway mark in my life. I don't want to spend the rest of my life as blind as I was in the first half. I pray His will be done in my life, the life He has granted me, daily. My desire is to live, walk, run, fly, soar, explore and expound upon, under the anointing of His Holy Spirit, by His grace, for His glory with purpose in mind, heart and spirit. For that is the abundant life to me.

This book is about purpose in connection. Depth of character, love and relationship. Growth, wisdom, knowledge, understanding and the process of becoming. This book is not just a case for ministry. I pray the reader finds it practical for everyday life and every relationship. This book, is for the whole of humanity. This book was not written to build a case or make excuse for sin or irresponsibility. Nor was it strictly written in the format it was, objecting to the rules of writing and religion for the sake of rebellion or just in the name of creative license. I truly believe in creative license and ministry is my life. I believe more so in people and love. I believe in the abundance of life and all that may mean beyond the obvious. I believe in God and seeing through His eyes. I believe in His agenda.

This work was not a preconceived notion though now, looking back, I truly believe, via personal experiences, it has been, thus far, a lifetime in the making. In my mind, I believe there a story behind everything. That's how my mind works. In that vein, I believe as a writer, now an author that this book is a byproduct of God's calling on my life. A calling, a life I did not ask for. A calling I fought. Not what I wanted. His will. This work is set in place to set the captives free. Free from the chains that contain.

Luke 4:18-19 (NIV)

[18] "The Spirit of the Lord is on me,
    because he has anointed me
    to proclaim good news to the poor.
He has sent me to proclaim freedom for the prisoners
    and recovery of sight for the blind,
to set the oppressed free,
[19]   to proclaim the year of the Lord's favor."[a]

Jesus came to give us life and more abundantly. A limited view will allow you to think of material possessions or longevity of years. Not so, the abundant life, since Jesus assures us that life, itself does not consist of the abundance of things…

Luke 12:15 (ESV)

[15] And he said to them, "Take care, and be on your guard against all covetousness, for one's life does not consist in the abundance of his possessions."

Life, and the abundance thereof must be about deeper more meaningful, more purposeful things. Like love, truth, connection, freedom, etc. The Apostle Paul wrote:

Colossians 2 (KJV)

2 For I would that ye knew what great conflict I have for you, and for them at Laodicea, and for as many as have not seen my face in the flesh;

[2] That their hearts might be comforted, being knit together in love, and unto all riches of the full assurance of understanding, to the acknowledgement of the mystery of God, and of the Father, and of Christ;

[3] In whom are hid all the treasures of wisdom and knowledge.

[4] And this I say, lest any man should beguile you with enticing words.

⁵ For though I be absent in the flesh, yet am I with you in the spirit, joying and beholding your order, and the steadfastness of your faith in Christ.

⁶ As ye have therefore received Christ Jesus the Lord, so walk ye in him:

⁷ Rooted and built up in him, and stablished in the faith, as ye have been taught, abounding therein with thanksgiving.

⁸ Beware lest any man spoil you through philosophy and vain deceit, after the tradition of men, after the rudiments of the world, and not after Christ.

⁹ For in him dwelleth all the fullness of the Godhead bodily.

¹⁰ And ye are complete in him, which is the head of all principality and power:

¹¹ In whom also ye are circumcised with the circumcision made without hands, in putting off the body of the sins of the flesh by the circumcision of Christ:

¹² Buried with him in baptism, wherein also ye are risen with him through the faith of the operation of God, who hath raised him from the dead.

¹³ And you, being dead in your sins and the uncircumcision of your flesh, hath he quickened together with him, having forgiven you all trespasses;

¹⁴ Blotting out the handwriting of ordinances that was against us, which was contrary to us, and took it out of the way, nailing it to his cross;

¹⁵ And having spoiled principalities and powers, he made a shew of them openly, triumphing over them in it.

¹⁶ Let no man therefore judge you in meat, or in drink, or in respect of a holyday, or of the new moon, or of the Sabbath days:

¹⁷ Which are a shadow of things to come; but the body is of Christ.

¹⁸ Let no man beguile you of your reward in a voluntary humility and worshipping of angels, intruding into those things which he hath not seen, vainly puffed up by his fleshly mind,

¹⁹ And not holding the Head, from which all the body by joints and bands having nourishment ministered, and knit together, increaseth with the increase of God.

²⁰ Wherefore if ye be dead with Christ from the rudiments of the world, why, as though living in the world, are ye subject to ordinances,

²¹ (Touch not; taste not; handle not;

²² Which all are to perish with the using ;) after the commandments and doctrines of men?

²³ Which things have indeed a shew of wisdom in will worship, and humility, and neglecting of the body: not in any honor to the satisfying of the flesh.

I encourage you to let the Spirit of the True and Living God lead you as you read this work. I pray it blesses the reader. May you live the abundant life, crawling, walking, running and flying and soaring, eyes wide open, seeing through His with your heart?

May God bless you richly and keep you.

Matthew 9:10-13(NIV)

[10] While Jesus was having dinner at Matthew's house, many tax collectors and sinners came and ate with him and his disciples.
[11] When the Pharisees saw this, they asked his disciples, "Why does your teacher eat with tax collectors and sinners?"

[12] On hearing this, Jesus said, "It is not the healthy who need a doctor, but the sick. [13] But go and learn what this means: 'I desire mercy, not sacrifice.'[a] for I have not come to call the righteous, but sinners."

DOORS OF THE CHURCH ARE OPEN:
Smoke and Mirrors
GRACE AND THE GREY AREA by
Sonya S. Shuman

WHAT A MAN. WHAT A MIGHTY
GOOD MAN.

"On that daggone game again huh boy? How you manage to spend so much time on that game in this nasty room is beyond me. You don't notice you lodging in a war zone boy? How do you maneuver in this pig sty? You live in this beautiful home, in this beautiful neighborhood, without so much as a concrete care in this world thus far and you can't even show me a thanks of gratitude or a grain of respect by just cleaning up your room? How long you think this gon' go on for? Greg? Gregory Jonah... G! Boy you hear me?!" He yells from the doorway to his room. His father then walks over to his inattentive son as his back remains turned with his over-head, name-brand headphones on. He bobs his head to the A.S.A.P Rocky playing in his ear. His father snatches the headphones from his ears abruptly," And see, this mess, this is the problem...the problem with your grades, the problem with your chores, the problem with your attitude! This music! That game! Now how many times do I have to remind you that what you feed will dominate? Boy, you changing before my very eyes. What's up for real G? Why can't you put this controller down and turn this music off long enough to get yourself together man?"

Gregory laughs, "Pop you stay buggin' man. Pssshhh... Man it's nothin'" aight? It's not harming me. I'm ok, this is the music I like. Don't sweat the small stuff pop. It ain't never that serious.
Be buggin man. Word up."

His dad pulls him up from the floor by his collared, uniform shirt, "Boy what you think I'm one of your ignorant wannabe friends, huh? You think I'm a joke G? Do you see me as a game or you just lookin' for a challenge this afternoon? May I remind you of just who is the buck and who is the bull round here?! Disrespect me again, it's gon' be somethin'...somethin' a young buck like you ain't got enough strength, stamina or skill to handle. Don't push me G! Lil' boy, you ain't ready! You don't want what you're asking' for. Now be a nice young man clean up this third world country you call a room, turn off that garbage, watch your mouth, check your ego and oh yeah partner, no gaming for a month! And no cell phone, no iPod...Oh wait, and no socializing! Straight home after school man until I see a change in attitude, responsibility and grades. See, respect goes a long way. Next time check yaself before you wreck yaself son." Greg's dad eases him back down to the floor leaving the room exhausted from the conflict with a simmering headache. He had just arrived home from a long day. He hadn't had a chance to wash it away.

"Joker stay preachin' a sermon man. Get to the point dog and be boutcha business." The boy mumbles as he cleans his room.

"Speak up." his father beckons.

"Nothin' man dang. Psssshhh... This joker wit' his bionic ears." Shaking his head. He knows not to push his father too far.

Barker. Barker Golden is G's dad's name. Barker Golden is a prestigious lawyer. An ambitious, over-achieving partner at a top law firm in New Jersey. Barker had everything that hard work afforded, education and focus rewarded; all that success seemed to epitomize, depending on your view of just what success really is.

Barker was quite a unique name. A name his mother had given him in efforts to increase his chances of success outside of the world she had known most of her life. A peculiar name it was as far as the African American community was concerned. His peers had teased him about his name most of his life. Barker's mom had envisioned her children growing to be greater than their impoverished upbringing would statistically allow them to. His parents had been small business owners as well as leaders in a mega-church in the city of Newark. In every aspect of life, the Goldens had paid their dues, rising through the ranks to become outstanding pillars of the community. Newark is the largest city in NJ so that had over time, yielded the Goldens a huge congregation as well as a noteworthy social media following.

God had rewarded them for their faithfulness and diligence. Their business and ministry had taken off and everybody saw it. Everybody wanted to be the Goldens. From the outside, they had a great life and always seemed to be on the up-swing financially. They were genuinely good people that did all they could to uplift the community. They had worked really hard for everything they had and didn't mind giving back to the same community that had given so much to them. Barker's parents had grown up within that very community and had witnessed so much oppression. They were some of the few who had believed they could use the oppression they were in as an opportunity. Their faith, their vision had served them well.

Reverend and Mrs. Golden had counseled many in that community through much sorrow, hurt, lack, fear and brokenness. Barker and his siblings had grown up for the most part, in that same community. At least until Barker had turned 15. That's when the ministry and business had really begun to bloom, allowing the Goldens to be able to move outside of that community. They wanted to ensure their children had a quality life before it had seemed too late. Barker in turn had wanted better for his son and despite being the son of a preacher and a teenaged father by the age of 16 himself, Barker moved forward with his parents support and had educated himself to make that dream and many more for himself and his son come true. Yes, Mr. Golden was quite the local hero and success story. Everybody in the community looked up to the Goldens. True pillars of the community.

Gregory was Barker's only child via his high school sweetheart Stacey. Stacey and Barker were in separable in high school. Typical American high school love story. She, the head of the cheer leading team. He the star quarter back at one of the local high schools; He was prom king...Her queen. Both had parents in ministry, both raised in church and both sexually active in the name of teenage love at very tender ages, thus Gregory. That classic all-American love story had become a classic all- American tragedy as Stacey began abusing drugs after Barker had gone off to college.
Stacey had fallen in with the wrong crowd as she believed she had lost her sense of self, worth and identity when Barker had left. She had made no plans to leave the

community and the community had made no plans to leave Stacey.

Stacey had big problems at home even though her parents were in ministry. Her parents were abusive towards one another. Her mother had a boyfriend in the church, he was the head Deacon. It was a tiny little secret in their tiny little church. Her father was the Pastor but he had a drinking problem. That didn't make things any better. Her parents had lost interest in one another ages ago but for appearances sake, would clean up their act in front of outsiders in efforts of keeping their scandals to a minimum and holding on to what few parishioners they had left. They lost interest in Stacey. They hadn't noticed how she slowly started to fall through the cracks before their very eyes. It had become the deepest layer of pain in her life.

The Goldens had taken the liberty of gaining custody of and caring for G. He was the joy of their lives. They did all they could to help Stacey when they could but, to no avail. Stacey was a different person now. Stacey did not want to be helped. Barker had become a single parent at the tender age of 18. Just two short years later Mrs. Golden would be diagnosed with breast cancer. After a five year uphill battle, much prayer, fasting, many tears and endless chemotherapy treatments, Mrs. Golden had succumb to the illness. The Golden family would weather the storm. They would survive the loss but they would never be the same. Especially Pastor Golden. Barker had secretly idolized his mother. He wanted to someday marry a woman just like Carla Marie Golden. His mother was the queen of his heart. He would defend her honor in life and in death. They didn't make 'em like Carla Golden anymore.

Though for various reasons Barker had grown weary of love and relationships for a season, impatient with the female psyche and bored with the lack of challenge from the young women in his age group, there would never be a shortage of bountiful, bouncy beauties willing and waiting to bed Barker. He was educated, an athlete, health conscious, successful, independent, funny and a Minister of the Gospel. After law school he had decided to fully give himself over to the Lord to be used. Not only was he a lawyer, Barker was a Junior Pastor. Dividing his time between his work caseloads, being a dedicated father, mentoring inner-city youth and being devoted to ministry, he juggled everything well on the surface. He seemed extremely successful at it all. With all of that responsibility, many were beginning to wonder where he got the time and energy from to be so seamless; so perfectly balanced. It was like he never broke a sweat. He always appeared to be cool, calm, collected; in control of everything; nothing lacking. Nothing too hard for good old' Barker Golden. The golden boy from the golden family. There was no such thing as pressure as far as Barker was concerned. He had spent most of his life being everything to everybody. The good guy doing all he could to live up to everyone's expectations.

At 33, Barker stood a towering 6'3", 220lbs of shiny, mahogany skin. Teeth as bright as stars in the midnight sky. A smile as wide the keys on a Baby Grand piano; Barker was just as smooth as the finish on that lovely instrument. Barker was rich, by his parents design. He and his brothers never wanted for anything. The world and all of its goods were at his disposal. He had made sound financial investments early on as taught by his father that would ensure the security of both his and Gregory's future for many years to come.

 Alpha male. He looked good in a suit and he knew it. His eyes, emerald green. Toned and chiseled, he worked out religiously each morning, four days a week, two hours at a time; that had been his regiment since he was in high school. Barker was the number one stunner; a consistent head turner everywhere he showed his face. Yet to the naked eye he would appear as gracious as he could be which did not mirror his Type A personality, achievements and good looks. As expected though, and to those who truly knew him; as he is a man, a successful man from a successful family. His ego sometimes got the best of him.

Everywhere he went, he was the man every other man wanted to be; Barker Golden was the one to beat. Most of the time, he never had allowed anything as superficial as education, status or looks to go to his head nor inflate his ego. He knew he wasn't perfect, but he continually mounted up the massive amount of pressure from the onlookers who did. So as pressure in some way, shape or form, has to be relieved/released before the vessel housing said pressure explodes, things were inevitably bound to occur.

He did all he could to keep his ego in check most times. But with all that he had going for him, not to mention The Lord being on his side, there were many times where containing his ego proved to be an uphill battle. Nevertheless, all a man can do is try. Barker knew deep down inside that he wasn't God. Barker Golden was just a man. He had wished others around him would get the memo, especially the women.

After using his good looks and effortless charm to land himself endless meaningless sexual conquests, Barker had come to the end of himself as he found no challenge in his extracurricular activities of the past. Barker was ready at last to straighten up and fly right. He was called to ministry and now he was ready to accept the challenges of that calling, or so he thought. Challenges were right up his alley, after all, Barker had been a star athlete all throughout high school and college. It was in his blood. But, he had known for some time that besides being a Minister of the Gospel, he had always wanted to practice law. He couldn't figure out how to make the two extremes co-exist, but, again, challenges were right up his alley and Barker believed that no matter the cost or the loss, he indeed, was born to win. Still, at the age of 33, Newark's golden boy had yet to figure out whether that was a matter of ego or a matter of faith. Nevertheless his motto was LET'S GET IT! And he meant it. He went after what he wanted with ferocious tenacity to be rivaled and true to form, he got it.

He truly belonged to Christ now. The Junior Pastor knew life was more than sex, achievements, accolades and money. But the women in the church had begged to differ for so many years. Though seasons were changing, he had once again, little by little begun to develop the desire for companionship and connection. He had passing thoughts of wedding a holy woman. Barker had even prayed on several occasions for a godly woman that could be a wife to him; a surrogate mother to G, he had felt as if his prayers had fallen on deaf ears so very often as pickings were slim by his standards.

He had begun to view the women in his church as desperate she wolves with no standards that were all posers just playing church. Women that were looking at him like he was the score of lifetime; Barker knew they were on the come up. He wasn't having it. He could see right through 'em all; "Game recognize game. These women man...I'm from Bricks just like them. They must have forgotten. Won't catch ya boy slippin'. No sir." he often thought to himself as he chuckled on the inside as he watched them bend over backwards to get his attention.

As of late, due to his devotion to God and his ever increasing dissatisfaction with the opposite sex, Barker had taken a personal and very spiritual vow of prolonged celibacy. It had become an added factor in his strict health and wellness regiment. For a young red-blooded All-American male like the likes of Barker Golden, exercise was a tension and stress reliever; celibacy would prove to be the exact opposite. His mind and heart were in the right place but, his body had failed to align itself. Doing the right thing isn't always the easy thing, even if it is the best thing.

Inside, he longed for someone with a mature, quiet, nurturing spirit; she didn't have to be perfect. He knew there was no such thing. Yet, Barker seemed to not be able to help himself. The man had unrealistically high standards. He had looked through the older women. Now they could cook and clean in their sleep! Those women were independent. Superficially it appeared as if they even rellshed being single. As if they were less than eager to give up those gratuitous liberties they held so dearly without a fight. They seemed happy and content in their own skin. They had their own, they were seasoned and experienced; Older women had an opinion. They could hold a conversation. But, after careful consideration, the truth was that they were all just too old, not energetic enough, and too gossipy, settled in their own ways, not flexible enough, non-submissive and bitter about many a thing in life. They had just given up on their looks. Many had forgotten how to treat a man; how talk to a man because they had spent most, if not all of their lives being single. Those women had grown comfortable in their zones. Far be it from him to crash their party. At a time he had wondered why, soon he had begun to wonder no more. The writing was on the wall. Spiritually, on the outside they appeared fruitful. But, upon closer inspection, he found them to be too religious. "Do they have a real relationship with God or are they addicted to the routine of church going? I think they just goin' through the motions." he said to himself.

They attended every church event. They were pillars. Chairs of committees and such. Yet, outside of the pomp and circumstance, beyond the borders of the church walls, where they felt most comfortable and safe, he saw no real evidence of evolution. They seemed to have a form of godliness and but no power, but what good was it if it didn't extend beyond tradition?

Then there were the blossoming beauties in his age group. They seemed ok by his finicky standards. Problem is, they were just as ambitious, as driven as he was. They weaved in and out of the church pews like rambunctious children on a sugar bender before their afternoon power nap. The heel-clicking boss ladies kept full dance cards, busy schedules; sharp minds and even sharper tongues. Unachievable standards that matched their over-achieving socio-economical statuses; enviable by all means. He judged them harshly not taking note that they mirrored who he was in many areas.

 Leaders in their field, they were too independent for his taste. Physically they fit the bill. Fashionistas who ruled the gym and who could rock any runway. Trophies that had no plans to be kept. Completely goal oriented, plus vastly self-sufficient, they believed they didn't need men. Some of them were single moms who were so meticulous in their planning, their calendars for the next two years were filled to capacity. The married ones rushed their children in and out of service while their spouses lagged behind slavishly in obedience. "Gotta be kidding me. Not ya boy." boasted to himself. Each time he looked at them, he could hear Beyoncé singing that infamous line from her song Diva playing in heavy rotation in his head, "Tell me somethin'? Where yo boss at? Where my ladies up in here that like to talk back?" He wasn't havin' none of that.

They gave money all of the time it seemed, as if to make-up for their lack of enthusiasm towards the word of God. They weren't religious, nor were they spiritual. The combine shone nonchalant. He found out most of them only attended service to appease their parents or due to the urging of a spouse or in-law. At the very least, church had become an activity to them for the family to attend; A networking engagement. Sanctioned appearances would also prove rewarding on the children's college applications. The children that always occurred unaffected and stoic. During service they were allowed to text and play Candy Crush. "Reminds me....I need to have a meeting with the ushers this week. They need to be more aware. When did church become a pastime or social event?" Never mind him sizing up the fairer sex while the choir sang.

Barker seemed to grow increasingly annoyed in the pulpit week after week. Not just with the women. With the flock. It was a huge flock. Although the faces in the pews seemed to change, the mood and activity or lack thereof, in the pews had not. From the pulpit he had a panoramic spiritual view he really didn't want. Being in tune with the Holy Spirit wasn't always as rewarding as one might assume. Oh the things he knew. The things he saw in the spirit. How lonely, having no spouse to connect to. Who would help shoulder the burden of leadership inside, outside, away from ministry? She would have to show herself durable, patient, tenacious. "She has to be creative and spiritual." he said to himself.

Loneliness deepened by the day. Secretly he guessed the women in his demographic might prove be too much of a challenge for him. Something his pride would never allow him to admit openly. Barker welcomed challenges only, he figured for these women to be submissive would be equal to the Taming of the Shrew. "They got it goin' on. But I don't need no woman competing with me. Looks ain't everything. Not my thing. I need a partner; A gentle giant on the inside who's willing to compromise. Sacrifice...be by my side. Take time. How are we ever going to build if you're out here crafting your own blueprints?" contemplated the Pastor.
Beyond, the golden boy desired a feminine specimen that would illuminate his manhood in every way. Typical of a Type A personality, he needed to lead. As a consequence, he needed to be depended on. "I'm a simple man...don't ask for much."

He glanced at the younger women from time to time, after all, he wasn't dead. Just practicing abstinence in obedience to God and in frustration with how desperate the women all around him were when he knew very well, as most men do, they need not be. The ball was in their court but they didn't have a clue; they weren't even patient enough to get a clue. The young women were physically right up his alley. They were pleasing to the eye and in just the right light, some of them even still held an attractive innocence about them that many men find endearing; even sexy. They could be submissive and flexible. Those girls could be molded. "But how manipulative would that be? And who has that kind of time?" he thought so often. He knew they wouldn't be enough of a challenge for him. "That might be too easy to conquer. Been there." He reasoned on and on doing the math over and over.

What he found attractive about them was that the lasses didn't appear jaded. They kept themselves looking attractive at all costs. They weren't that independent or successful by any means. But that didn't matter to Barker as he was traditional about a lot of relationship roles; that's the way he was raised; Husbands provide and protect. Wives keep the home and care for the children. The dominant and the submissive made for a great formula he believed. "What could go wrong? My parents had a perfect marriage." he reminisced. "If it ain't broke..?"

   It was 2013 and though he delighted in the thought of a woman that might mirror his mother. He also knew he had to step out of the Stone Age into the new age to deal accordingly. Yet in all of the promise he had seen in the young women at his church, he had taken the time to dig deeper in getting to know the few that attended regularly. Much to his chagrin, surprisingly, though they were regular attendees/faithful church goers, they lacked substance. Beneath the surface they were obviously no different than the young women in world. They held no standards nor the challenge he had longed for.

The young women came to church late most of the time. They didn't know how to mother their children; they could not control them. They would usually sashay into the sanctuary with their cleavage overly exposed, dresses too short, too much make-up, the "do me" hair perfectly done and have a seat in bunches as to outdo one another in lost efforts to gain his attention. They couldn't cook or clean or maintain their own identity and independence outside of a relationship which led to them racking up baby-daddies like mob bosses rack up charges upon indictments at federal courthouses. They really had issues. They were broken and looking for love because they didn't have it for themselves. Most of them had yet to even begin to know what it was to receive and embrace the love of God. The young women came to the church house to hear the word not to obey. "Do they even understand what's being fed to them?" he wondered too many times. "How do they even know if what the Man of God is saying is true? This could all be a sham for all they know! Do they even study the word at home?" He had imagined that the inexperienced lot could be led astray by any wolf in sheep's clothing. Many of them only held a mental concept of God; the same one they had from their time in youth group. It disappointed them they hadn't grown. He was impatient with them.

Before the watchful eyes of mothers and ministers, they praised God with one eye open, the other closed. Jumping up and down at every sermon, he often believed they weren't even absorbing what thus saith the Lord. "They goin' thru the motions too." he chided.

 Much like the older women, they presented themselves sanctified and knowledgeable at first glance. They were adult in age and body, infantile in spirit. "They're still drinking' milk." he shook his head. "How much milk can you drink before you become lactose intolerant? Jesus!" They didn't have to be biblical scholars. Barker didn't expect them to be able to keep his spiritual pace or be well versed in scripture or the inner workings of the behind the scenes affairs of church business. He resolved that what needed to be taught could be learned. The pastor just needed to be able to have a conversation and be understood. He wanted someone to connect to from the inside out. The Holy Spirit had to abound.

He became unjustly critical; bored. Barker was tired of church routine; frustrated with the hunt. Looking for a worthy potential he could muster up the energy to chase. Where were the unconventional women with traditional values that would make him sit up and wag his tail?

He thirsted for more. The Junior Pastor hungered for a teachable spirit in which the lessons would not be so labor intensive to extol upon. See, that was too much work for him. Sadly for Barker, it was a repeat of Stacey post high school and that, he refused to attach himself to ever again. Barker had standards even if the women around him didn't. He wanted the best for himself and for his son; He wouldn't settle for less. He was trying his best to be a great example for his son in every area. "Maybe I want too much? Nah...I don't wanna settle." he winced.

LOST AND TURNED OUT

"Ya'll come on down here and get this breakfast while it's hot now!" yelled Liza.

"Girl those kids comin', they know the routine, have patience honey...you young mothers need patience. They're children not robots. Give them time to get dressed baby. I know you're tired. I know." says Liza's mother with a soothing voice.

Her name is Connie Lilac Debril. Not only Liza's mother and grandmother of three, she's Liza's right hand and rock. Where would Liza be without good old Connie Debril? That's a question Liza never wanted to know the answer to. Her mother and children were all she had. Her home life was her world outside of work. And that was good enough for her. Her small family was what kept her going. They were her motivation. They were her reason for getting out of the bed each night. Liza's family was her reason for living. They gave her a reason to pray and a reason to believe in God. Other than that, she found no other reason to. If Connie had taught her nothing else that was positive, she at least had taught little Liza Rose how to be independent of a man. She too, taught Liza how to pray. Connie taught her child that God was real. She taught her daughter what she knew about Jesus, the Good Shepherd. Jesus, the Lord over all.

Connie was a single mother who had raised Liza the best she could. Connie never knew exactly who Liza's father was; she never tried to find out; she wasn't interested. Connie didn't care. Too much water under the bridge. Too much pain and suffering to rehearse. Too many mistakes and bad choices to recall, all in the name of securing a future for her most prized possession, her anchor and rock...her beautiful lone child, Liza Rose Debril. Liza was everything to Connie as Connie was everything to Liza. A more tightly knit union between mother and daughter could not have been imagined nor rivaled. Even that of Cissy and Whitney, Whitney and Bobbi Kristina or Joan and Melissa were incomparable. They were closer to the likings of Naomi and her daughter in-law Ruth. They were dedicated to one another come hell or high water and true to form, both hell and high water would come to test their relationship. They just appeared to be naturally resilient as such a bond could never be broken. Liza and Connie loved one another unconditionally. In many ways their relationship had even grown co-dependent. Connie and Liza had never lived apart; always under the same roof. They couldn't find it within themselves to live separately. Two peas in a pod.

Connie Debril had grown up in a neighborhood brothel in the South Ward in Newark, NJ. Her mother was an uneducated field worker who had migrated from the South. Unlearned and illiterate, one thing she had never forgotten how to do was to count money and use her body. She had been abused and mistreated by men all of her life as she too had been raised in a brothel in the backwoods of Tupelo, Mississippi by an uneducated mother who only knew how to do two things: Count money and use her body. It was the family business. Use what you got to get what you want could have been the mantra of those times for the Debrils. They knew how to use what they had and the Debrils women were local bombshells. Legends who had what every man wanted. The Debrils were industrious in their trade ensuring they would never be without. As long as they had good product, kept creative and consistent, those women could meet the demand with their supply.

Connie used to go to church regularly do to the urging of a good friend. But, Connie had heard of generational curses through another source. Many a night she lie silently wondering as her mind wandered aimlessly if her profession was just that or was it just everybody was doing what it was they knew? She reasoned within herself time and time again, "Well how wrong can it be? It's tax free money for my sweet honey. Which means I'm in control of my own bank roll. I guess it don't hurt to give up my body when I know Jesus still has my soul." Connie had been doing what she knew all of her life even if she wasn't quite certain of just how right it was, she on the other hand was just as uncertain of just how wrong it was. She had been taught that there was nothing wrong with using what she had to get not only what she wanted but, what she had needed like the widow with the jar of oil in the Bible or the single mother with the son that used a portion of the little flour and oil she had left to feed the prophet Elijah in the Bible. In her limited view of the Biblical stories she read, there was little difference in the way she provided for her child. All Connie Debril knew is all she knew. All she had to work with was what she had. She somehow believed that the Lord had blessed her with gifts. And those gifts made room for her. At least that what men and her momma had told her all of her life.

Much of the people in the neighborhood looked down on the Debrils because of their choices. They judged from the outside. Her neighbors never stopped to ask her who she really was. No one was interested in her story. She was worthless to so many; especially the wives in the area. Connie did her best to pay that no never-mind. She figured they couldn't be that much better than she was in her twisted reasoning. In her mind, they were getting paid to provide the same service she was in a way. Only difference was the circumstance; the format. An exchange of promises and rings and a signed piece of paper made it legal for them to do what she was doing illegally.

Maybe they didn't have an imaginary sign that flashed above their heads everywhere they went that read: OVER A BILLION SERVED. Maybe they were educated, sophisticated, reared better. Maybe they had just chosen to make better choices. But in her mind, the differences between the wife and whore were minimal. They served one man daily but for the same reason…needs had to be met. The man provided goods; the woman provided services. One hand washed the other. It was the way she was taught. That's what Rose had drilled into her head from the cradle. Being raised in the Honey Pot, that mindset was all she knew.

On weekly trips to the beauty salon, she heard the wives complain about what a chore it was to be intimate with their husbands; sexually and otherwise. The wives had lost interest. Life had become mundane behind the glare of the carats on their fingers. The rings no longer symbolized commitment. The rings seemed to symbolize status, imprisonment and duty. They had lost sight of everything. Everything women like Connie had imagined love, marriage and relationship to be. The wives kept their hair done but paid no attention to anything below the neck. "He better be glad I'm still married to his sorry ass." She heard one of them say.

She thought, "Maybe if you stop thinking of him as a sorry ass, he'll stop being a sorry ass. Be positive for once! Did you ever stop to think that maybe he's just as sorry as his wife? Lawd ha' mercy. Jesus said it himself: 'How can two walk together unless they agree?' Oh wait that's right.....I been knowing your husband since high school. Yeah, Thomas. That's right. Y'all don't even agree that's why y'all don't ever walk together. Y'all ain't never on the same page except when y'all bein' sorry as hell. Sad."

Connie saw these men leave for work each morning looking more and more beaten down as the years passed. She also noticed that as the years passed they arrived home later and later. They attended church with their wives and children less and less. Some of the husbands would arrive home and sit in the car and talk on the phone for a whole hour before entering the house. Some would take a swig out of a fifth before they took the keys out of the ignition. Others would drive around the block just looking at young girls remembering yesterday; wanting to be desired. Fantasizing about having passionate sex in crazy positions and places. A few would think for a moment as they looked into the window from the outside. Hearing all of the noise from the unruly children, smelling the same dishes wafting through the air Monday thru Friday. Knowing how she's gonna look and what she's gonna say; not up for a nagging lecture, those few would drive off to places unknown until the wee hours of the morning. Off some place where they could find adventurous sex, no expectations, no responsibilities. Peace, quiet, a full stomach and lap to lay their heads in. The husbands longed for the atmosphere they used to come home to. Things had changed. People had changed. There weren't too many loving couples walking together in agreement in the neighborhood. Connie spent a lot of time wondering what happened to their happily ever after, after those fairytale wedding ceremonies she heard about on her front stoop that she had never been invited to. "Good for you." she gasped.

The wives yelled at their husbands a lot over the phone for small things. Maybe they didn't realize how that tore their men down. Yet, Connie knew. After all, she had a front row seat to much of the drama as she lie next to many a husband, many a night, listening to many a wife bark through the speaker as the man lay quiet. Cell in one hand, thigh in the other. "Hear this nonsense I gotta put up with?" she recalled a client whispering to her. "My wife... wife... Hmm... She don't even know how to talk to a man. I never heard my mother talk crazy to my father like that. They had their share of problems. But man, she respected my father. My father loved her because of that. I remember me and my dad had a private conversation. Man to man, over a few brews. I asked him if he ever cheated on my mom. He was honest. He said he had been tempted a few times. Women don't make it easy. Especially when y'all goin through stuff. Seem like the wrong one show up at the right time when you and you baby at odds. I wasn't ready for that much truth but he gave it to me so I took it like a man. He told me what hindered him from cheating on her was the way she responded to him. Consistently respectful; no matter how angry he made her or how hurt she was over something dumb he did. My mother had this calm tone. Even when she was being authoritative, she wasn't threatening, cruel or harsh to him he said. The way she treated him, even when he knew his ego was way outta control...that right there Nene. That's what stopped him from straying when ish hit the fan. He wanted to honor because she honored him. She gave my father peace Nene." he stroked her thigh, "Woman won't give me no peace. I can't even beat my chest in my own house. Where I MAKE IT HAPPEN. She always wanna go toe-to-toe wit' me like a raging bull. That ain't attractive. That ain't sexy. She don't even know me enough to just let me blow my wind and give me my space.

She talk too much. Where the old school women at that just let a man be sometimes? Let me make love to you when I'm stressed. Gimme some space when I don't wanna talk about it just yet. Don't ask me a million questions when you see I don't wanna talk. Let me relax and let it off the way I know how. Hear ya man! Learn when to let me be. Let me have you when I want you. That's when I really need you." He rolled over after he made his speech. He buried his face deep in Connie's plush pillows and plunged into her aggressively. Connie let out a loud sigh. He covered her mouth with his hand. As he pounded, she begged him to stop pushing him away. "Please stop." she cried faintly biting his hand. He uncovered her mouth to push her thighs farther apart. He breathed in her ear as if he couldn't catch his breath, "Please don't tell me to stop. I need you." He rewarded her handsomely at dawn for her ear and her time. He became a regular overtime. She walked him to the door. He kissed her on the cheek, "Call you. Alright?" While he stood there staring at Connie his phone rang, "Yeah..."
It was his wife again.

"Where are you? I've only been calling you all night long! Where you been?" she blasted.

Calmly he replied, "Nowhere. Nowhere, man. What? No. I ain't got time right now. I'll see you after work. I gotta go." He waved goodbye to Connie as he walked down the stairs.

She noticed how the wives forced themselves to care about how their husband's days were going. They had let themselves go over the years. The jealous wives had become bitter, insatiable, and rigid. Many religious and stiff. They judged her from afar not knowing she had a few keys. Keys that would unlock some hidden doors in their marriages. Their husbands often used women like her as therapists and paid them accordingly. Every night had not been ripe with musk of lust. She knew what the wives needed to know that they didn't know they did.

She shook her head at them because she had the answers they sought to the problems in their marriages. After all, where were many of them spending their time? Not with Connie per say. But she knew all too well, those dissatisfied husbands that had grown bored, tired; weary of routine...they were most likely keeping company somewhere across town with a woman just like her. A woman with nothing to lose and everything to gain that listened, fed his ego, kept in satisfied. A woman who was energetic, loose, lively, fun with a youthful appearance yet, with grown woman experiences and wit. A woman whose bed had a lot of secrets. A kept woman, yes! Just like them. A woman who had served a billion. A billion of unsatisfied men who were driven into her arms by wives who just stopped caring enough to notice or just plain didn't get the memo. Wives who looked the part that had over time just gotten so used to the role that they had taken It for granted. Wives that just refused to show up to the theater anymore and put on a Tony winning performance for their men. Women who had forgotten to please the bad boy boyfriend that was still alive inside of the good guy husband. Taking everything for granted, the spotlight was now on the understudy.

Connie couldn't believe her ears sometimes as she listened on in complete amazement at how these women, in her same age bracket, just didn't enjoy sex with their husbands anymore. Many complained of not having enough time because of the children or being tired from work. They were all young wives. Never having had experience in that area, Connie couldn't understand how women could not be desirous towards their husbands. Sex was her business. She was always ready. Even when she wasn't, Rose had schooled her on how to put on her game face and get ready. It had become second nature to her.

"Why they always got excuses?" she wondered walking home from the salon. "What's wrong with givin' ya man sex when he want it? However he want it? Chicks is crazy. I'm carrying damn bags. I wish I did have a good man to worry about instead of a billion no good ones, that ain't mine that don't give a damn about me and mine. Shoot! Get tired of that there. Dumb broads don't even realize what they got. And shucks," she paused to stomp out her cigarette. "If it ain't all that, let the joker go so he can stop tippin'. Let him be with somebody who want him. Jesus! Selfish, stupid, blind women. Make me sick. Oh so what his feet stink. So what he leave his drawers on the floor and his mama call too much for dumb stuff. Lawd if that's the only problems you got... Take him to a podiatrist or buy him some foot powder. Teach him to pick up after himself. Answer the phone, tell his momma he sleep, give him some, put him to sleep and next time she call just hand him the phone and just say thank you Jesus. What on Earth is the problem?"

She was looking at their issues from the outside of the bubble. For the wives, the answers ran just as deep as the problems. As deep as the Mississippi River. It wasn't that simple. That was just surface. Connie and the women like her only got half of the story. All they knew was what they heard and thought they were seeing. They weren't living in their houses or suffering through those broken marriages. Just the same, the judgmental wives looked down on women like Connie, never having had their experiences, lived their realities. Never caring enough to seek out information on the hurt beyond the hype. Many of the wives envied the freedom they believed the ones they deemed whores had. They often fantasized that the life was glamorous; problem free; free of pressure and responsibility. They were blind to the fact that those women too had sex, most of the time out of duty or obligation. They too were leaders in their homes. Mothers, just trying to make it. They tired of men and sex too. Yet, they didn't show it. It was more business than pleasure. They had so much in common that would go unspoken.

Many of the women like Connie secretly wanted the life they thought they knew everything about but had no idea of. They didn't know that it took more than open legs and minds, a closed mouth and a clean house to keep a marriage afloat for a lifetime. All they knew was the physical aspect of relation between a male and a female. They knew nothing of the work, disappointments, compromise, sacrifice the wives were all too familiar with. The wives knew nothing of the loneliness, the pain, the backstory, the abuse, the lack of self-worth that came with the so-called liberty of doing with your body whatever you please. Connie knew first hand that everything that is permissible was not profitable. Ships passing in the night the twain. It is a stamp of severe ignorance on humanity to always want what is not yours or what you cannot have. Fearing what we don't understand or know too well to reveal to others; our dirty little secrets. The past revisited in another. Judging it too harshly; a common thread of the same. All of those women insecure and comparing themselves unjustly. "Look at her old stupid self. Just like her old nasty mother. Probably can't even read." She heard one woman comment to another as they passed her on the sidewalk leading up to her steps.

"Yeah I can. I can hear too!" Connie dropped her bags and went walking towards the women, "I can fight too! And oh yeah, I'm good at math. I can count money. Matter of fact, I counted your man money this mornin' before he went to work! If I am nasty, it's because ya man like it like that. Oh but you wouldn't know cause you ain't nasty enough! Better ask somebody! If you was more like me maybe he would stay home and keep some money in his pocket. Tell him I'll see him payday cause I damn sure don't wanna see his ass no other time. I'll be wearing the red panties he brought me back last week from his business trip. The lace ones wit' his name on the front! Getcha predictable asses on!" Connie was from the streets without apology and she gave as good as she got. If they talked to Connie, they made sure to walk while they did it. She knew who God was. Yet, that didn't lessen her issues. She was a work in progress like everyone else. The Lord knew who she was and why she was. He was patient.

Even if she made poor choices, some she couldn't help at the time, she was not was ashamed of who she was. What she was not, was stupid. Oh Connie Debril wasn't at all illiterate! No sir! See although she had been raised in a Newark brothel, although she had succumb to generational curses, Connie's mother had refused to at least allow one generational curse to go unabolished. Connie had to get a high school education at the very least. And for all intended purposes; for lack of motivation beyond expectation, that was all she had done. "Shucks man....Better than nothin'! I ain't as dumb as a lot of these dummies out here so it's good enough. I hope my momma is proud of me...all that matters." She often thought as she pulled on one of her five her afternoon Newports during her scheduled reflections.

After high school Connie remained local, moved out of the brothel and kept the family business alive from her own place on a much smaller scale. After her mother had passed away, the house she was raised in became run down as Connie refused to take care of it. Too many memories. Too much pain. Too much to deal with. Beyond the pain of her mother introducing her to the family business by manipulating her with the trappings of the lifestyle, Connie drew most of the pain of her dreaded memories from the fact that her first sexual experience was with a John. She was raped. She was only ten years old. She had already seen and heard too much at such an impressionable tender age. But it was the exact age when her mother was introduced to the oldest profession by her mother and well, it was all Connie's mother had known. The beat went on.

Round and round and round we go, where we stop, heaven only knows.

BACK DOWN
MEMORY LANE

"Uh-huh....and how you doin' today?" Connie mumbles, cigarette in mouth, hand on hip, one eye squinted from the rising smoke, speaking to a regular passer-by. She always ventured out to the front porch about twelve-ish each afternoon after helping Liza get the children off to school and a morning briefing about last night's events from Liza. After Liza settled in for a daily routine of sleep during the day, rise-n-grind at night, Connie would enjoy a bit of left over breakfast with a side order of wake-n-bake on the back porch before venturing through the house and out the front door to take in the day's gossip and last night's criminal mishaps on the front stoop. It was her routine. It was her lifestyle. "Who got shot last night? Where? See, I knew it! Hangin' round those boys...Tried to tell Cat to talk to her son. But hey, you can lead somebody to water can't make 'em drink it. Whatchu gon' do huh? Now where Cat at wit her tore up sad behind self? Sick'nin! Say what you want about me, I ain't never been on no drugs or been that into to somethin' else that I just gave my child to the street or fed my baby to the wolves like that! Hell no! Child, ask me if I get it? Do I get it? You damn right I don't! What's to get?" Connie barks to the small group of regulars that gather on the stoop to decipher the overnight goings on in the immediate area.

 "You ever goin' back to ya momma house Nene?" asks a young woman at the foot of the stoop.   The neighbors called Connie "Nene" for short...that's what her mother called her. Her mother had given birth to a daughter two years after she had given birth to Connie, the baby lived only three years which was longer than the doctors had even anticipated due to a rare brain disease. Her name was Lisa, she was Liza's name sake and she never could pronounce the name "Connie" so she would just call her Nene. Sometimes when people would call Connie 'Nene', her eyes would well up with tears and she'd whisper a faint, inaudible, "Yes baby", as if she was responding to her baby sister Lisa.

Lisa's death was something Connie and her mother had never quite gotten over. They had never gained real closure or had taken the time to console one another. They completely mourned the loss. The pain was too great. Connie's mother had been impregnated by several men several times after the birth and death of Lisa, but she had chosen to abort each pregnancy as her hopes of ever having a healthy child again had dissipated. Also, mothering children would require too much of her attention and time and time was money. Plus she could not bear the prospect of losing another beautiful child. It was all too much. Connie's mother had thrown herself and Connie into their work. There would be no looking back after that. Their relationship became more of a business relationship, less than amorous, the gap had widened as they both aged. Connie did not even attend her mother's funeral. On the day of the funeral she sat on her couch, Liza in arm, cigarette burning in the ash tray just out of reach. As she rocked her beloved to sleep, the child seemed inconsolable.

Finally the mother looks down at her child, "Shh... Oh baby. Shh... Why can/'t you go to sleep? I know, I know my baby....you havin' a hard time. Probably mourning ya Grandma, huh? Yeah I am too. But nobody will ever know that but us and Jesus. You know who Jesus is baby? Jesus is the Lord. He's over everybody and in charge of everything. And I know He's here (tears streaming down her face). Shh... Yes, yes, momma knows He's here. He will always be here, even when it don't feel like it baby. I'm not perfect, but I won't let you forget the Him, if that's all I can give you good, I will give you Jesus. Now since Grandma is gon' on, He all we got. It's just Him and us Lil' Liza. We couldn't go to see Grandma off because she probably wouldn't want me there. I can't be there even if she did. Hurts too much. I was five when we said goodbye to ya Aunt Lisa...can't say no more goodbye's baby. You're all I got besides The Lord. I hope me and you don't never, ever have to say goodbye."

Still rocking her baby to sleep she wipes her eyes, "Thank you Jesus. I know I ain't right. I've even had people over at the church tell me you don't love or accept me. I guess they forgot about the woman all the men was about to stone 'til you came to the rescue in the Bible. I'm just like her. And see some of those men in that church, well, they just like the men in that story. But nobody believes you would ever come to my rescue. That's funny, they're judging' me while all of the while they Pastor, the Good Reverend comin' to my place with his gin and cigar in one hand and his Bible in the other, right after service sometimes! Him and his wife but I guess they better than me huh? Crazy, sometimes how they beat me to my own daggone door! They my friends so I guess they alright. But I know them people at that little church far from perfect. They just don't think I know. Funny how things go behind the scenes ain't it Jesus? Oh, how people find ways to reach past all of the skeletons in they own darn closet just to get that old trusty latter they keep within reach, and use that same latter they don't want nobody usin' on them to get up on they high horses and judge. Then they run down the latter quicker then they got up there and bury with the shovel they keep hidden behind that latter. Church people get up there in front of everybody, sang them good ol' songs, holla out Hallelujah, run and jump all over the church makin' people think they in so good wit' God but when the show over, they show they true colors 'cause they don't know how to love nobody. Instead of lovin' on you and gettin' to know you, they steady scrutinizin' everything they think they know about you just from lookin' at you or hearin' about you instead of talkin' to you, not about you and prayin' for you.

Laawwddd Jesus, you know how many of those Deacons and 'Good Husbands' I done turned away from here over the years? If them righteous people only knew! But far be it from me to bust anybody's bubble or to kill anybody's 'fantasy life' or 'perfect family'. They just don't know. Let the church say amen if they can handle the truth Jesus! That's what I'm waitin' for and maybe then I'll go back. I'll go back when they learn how to treat somebody and when they can handle the truth! Ha! Ha! Yes Lawd they got work to do!"

Connie continues, "That's why I stopped goin' a long time ago man. Yeah I know I ain't right or so I hear. But you still see fit to hold me anyway like a child when I need you to, just like I'm holding mine. 'Cause she need me to. Speaking of right. What is right anyway? God, if somebody's right ain't my right and my right ain't they right, then who right and who wrong? All of my life I've been hearin' people say what me and Rose was doin' wasn't right. But if that's all we knew, just like the drug dealers, how can we be wrong God? Just how?" Finally Liza is sound asleep. As Connie lays the child down in her bedroom, decorated with all of the pink, frilly things little girls dream of, she takes a deep breath and looks down at her child, "Well, baby, I don't guess Imma be takin' you to church. Jesus gon' have to do house calls. It's safer for us here. I don't want my baby there anyway. Ain't no need for her to go there! Church gon' be filled with sugar daddies, pimps, ho's, lyin', cheatin' husbands, corrupt cops and drug dealers. Man, I see them same guys out here every day outside of their Sunday best. I know all of 'em. Yep Liza, the same ones who look at me like I'm dirt when I go to church. Yes ma'am, they all came to momma's Honey Pot, that's what they used to call momma's house. That's where they all came to get somethin' sweet. I've seen it all little lady. I've seen it all. When you're old enough I tell you all about it. Now baby, I used to hear my momma float this "generational curses" thing around from time to time, she would mumble it under her breath sometimes in her sleep. She would kick and cry as if she was fightin' for her life. I would always have to run to her side and wake her up to calm her down. I used to ask her what a 'generational curse' was but she would only say, 'It's somethin' bad child. It's a Bad circle that don't never end until somebody brave and smart get the gall to break it up bit by bit is all. To break it up you gotta be strong as an ox child. To break it up, you gotsta have a talk with the Good Shepherd. He the only one can help. He the only one can keep you. But you gotta want it. Sometimes you just don't know how to want it. Scared to let go of what you know is all. Can't be scared to let go. That's what Rose said. But as strong as she was, I guess she was scared. She was always scared to do new stuff. Sometimes I felt like she was preachin' to herself when she was talkin' to me after them bad dreams. Anyway, sweet dreams Liza Rose. I never want you to be afraid of new stuff."

   She walked away in her tight, black, chiffon, see-through slip clickin' her 5 inch heels all of the way from Liza's room back to the couch in the living room. Even on the day of her mother's funeral Connie was ready for action. Time is money she remembered her mother teaching her and wasting time was wasting money and wasting any of it was bad for the lifestyle her time and her business had afforded her. Connie had to keep working what she had while she still had it. After all, nobody has it forever.

Whatever she stood to lose, whenever she stood to lose it, she prayed that Liza wouldn't find it. Not fully understanding what a generational curse was, she knew it was a bad circle that had no ending unless somebody decided to some new stuff and end it. That was all of the information she believed she needed to begin new stuff with Liza. The last thing she wanted was for her daughter to pick it up what she was putting down, the way she had been trained to put it down, just as it had happened with her mother Rose and her mother before her. Her great grandmother's name was Hyacinth. Hyacinth was Rose's favorite flower. Rose wanted Connie to be different, but eventually, those 'generational curses' got in the way. Rose lived and died with very little hope, faith and love. She would only teach her daughter what she knew. It had haunted Rose until the day she died. She died alone, in the Honey Pot, lamenting she hadn't taught her daughter anything new. She was wrong, the newness had come in the way Connie reared her child. Her lack of newness birthed a hunger for greater things for her daughter. She wanted new stuff for Liza. She did her best. She had taken some small steps away from what she had been taught. Very protective of her child, wanting to be a better mother than Rose, she did new stuff with Liza. Rose would've been proud.

"Nene!" yelled the young woman at the foot of the stoop. "Nene...,"

"That's Ms. Nene to you young girl and don't you forget it!" as Connie's reflections resend, she is brought back to present day. "Mind your manners. I know ya mother and I know she taught you better than that. And no! Hell no ain't nobody goin' back to that damn house! For what?! Rose is dead ok!? Now if you so curious, you go! Hell, I'm sick of people talkin' to me about that damn house..." Frowning in anger as she blows out the last of her cigarette smoke. She plucks the butt into the grass as she opens the front door, "Yous about a nosy ass! Unbelievable..", she slams the front door and goes back the way that she came, back through the house, to the back porch to light up and calm down. Connie was having a hard enough time letting go of her past, the last thing she needed were reminders.

Liza and those children were all she had besides her prayers and the Good Shepherd to keep her looking ahead. "The Queen is dead. Been dead a long time." she speaks to herself as she puffs on her joint tears fill her eyes. As they run down her face like rain on a window pane, she can be heard in the near distance singing, "Somebody Loves You" a Patti LaBelle tune that always kept her in memory of the Queen, Rose Debril from Tupelo, Mississippi. "Long live the Queen." she whispers as she turns to go back inside.

SOMEBODY BETTER PRAY FOR ME

 "Father, what on Earth is wrong with me? It's three in the morning on a Friday. Why am I still awake? I'm not happy Lord. I'm not satisfied. I mean, I'm so thankful for the life you and my parents have given me, but boy am I in need of something more. Am I selfish for wanting more? I know King Solomon said all was vanity and that, I don't doubt. I believe it more and more as time passes. I just don't know... I have a successful career, a good son, a loving family and a blossoming ministry. God my plate is full. But, there still seems to be something missing. The routine is getting to me now. You know, the daily schedule, high demands. I've been trying to carry all of the weight of me and those around me for so long, all by myself. I thought that's what men were supposed to do. I never saw my father cry or complain God, not even when my mom passed away. Alvin Golden was the pillar of strength for everyone around him at that time. Not even while she was sick did I see him lose control or even his faith or temper. He was such a rock for the family. I could not have asked for a stronger man to be my example. I just don't know how he got through it alone. I guess it's safe to say he depended on you."

He prayed, "Man! How on Earth did he spend so many years alone after my mom passed after being with her for so long? He is really strong. How is it the pressures of ministry never broke him or made him want to run away and hide? And he's the Senior Pastor and founder of the church, I'm just the Junior Pastor and right now, I'm tired of it. There are even times I hide behind my smile because I don't want to let people down. Lord as Pastors and fathers, basically as leaders and men, everything inside and outside, everything in history and in the present tells us that we are supposed to be strong ALL OF THE TIME. But reality is, that is becoming increasingly more difficult for me. Does that mean I am less of a man because I'm admitting that I am tired and that this walk is hard? I hope not. I guess what I'm trying to say Lord, while it is just me and you here, is that I can't take it no more. Maybe from somebody else's perspective, I look weak. But I am willing to risk it in this hour of honesty."

"LORD!" he yells. "I'm tired! I'm tired of playing hero. I'm tired of being a single parent. I'm tired of everybody putting me on this pedestal that I am struggling to stay on! I am angry! I feel over-worked, pulled and yanked on every side!" "LORD, NOBODY KNOWS! LORD MY GOD, NOBODY CARES! LORD MY GOD, WHERE ARE YOU? JESUS, WHO AM I ANY MORE?! JESUS I AM DESPERATE FOR RELIEF. LORD! I AM THIRSTY! I AM HUNGRY! WHO IS GOING TO FILL ME UP? I'm on E."

 He slides off of the bed and down on to cold hardwood floor, he falls to his knees, "Jesus, I am drowning. Help me. I am malnourished in every possible way but spiritually.... Spiritually overwhelmed. Physically too! This may be less than holy conversation Father, but I will take my chances because with you, I know I can. I am but a man. A man of God, a man of faith, but a man nonetheless. Lately I've been feeling amorous. The desire to connect with a woman is growing by the day. I haven't been with a woman in a long time. Uh-huh... I had to say it! I am backed all the way up to the wall Lord. I need release! WHY IS IT THAT NOBODY IS TALKING ABOUT THIS SIDE OF MINISTRY AND MANHOOD AT THE PASTORS CONFERENCES AND MINISTERS MEETINGS? ARE WE ALL JUST A BUNCH OF PRIDEFUL LIARS? WHY IS IT SUCH A CRIME FOR US TO

OPENLY ADMIT HOW FLAWED WE ARE? LORD GOD! WE ARE MEN!!! Father, I am a man. I have man needs tonight.

I am tense and moody. I feel like I'm about to explode! Now, I know very well I have my pick of the litter in that church, but I don't see anything that suits me.   Church girls...either tryin' to hard or they're aloof. Either focused on all the wrong things or they're bitter; broken. After all of these years, some of them have been ridin' with the ministry longer than I've have, before it even blew up, and they still haven't healed!! Lord if I'm wrong, forgive me. That's just the way I see it. I don't see wife potential in that crowd. Ain't nothing there for a brother.

God, my wife ain't gotta be perfect. She just has to be different... Her own woman, in her own right. I want someone that poses a challenge. I have to be able to know she's mine from the inside out on sight; Lord, I desire a woman of purpose that can submit who exudes femininity, power and strength. There has to be something that leaps in my spirit when I see her that will let me know. I don't want a yes woman. I want a yes and amen woman. But she must pose a challenge, be different and have her own mind. There has to be a woman out there that I can learn something from. I want a partner for life in my wife.

God, I just need a break. A break from everything and everybody. I'm not superman. And I need a woman who can see that and accept me flaws and all. I can't put on any more heirs. I don't want a church girl Lord, I want a real woman that hasn't been tainted by religion. Please send me a saved, sound-minded, spiritual, smart, sexy, sometimes sarcastic someone who knows who she is. Somebody I can just be 'Boom' in front of. Not always Pastor, father or Esquire. God, I'm dying inside and nobody knows it. I can't even show it. I am just a man on a mission, with a message and a plan. Jesus, I need a friend."

As Barker knows full well prayer is a naked, open, honest-to-goodness conversation with God, he remains positioned at the base of his bed clutching his pillow. A voice whispers:

"SON I KNOW YOUR ISSUES. I KNOW YOUR FEARS. I KNOW YOUR SHORT COMINGS. I KNOW YOU'RE EXPECTATIONS. I KNOW WHO YOU ARE AND WHY YOU ARE. I APPROVE YOUR TESTINGS AND TRIALS AND I AM VERY WELL VERSED IN YOUR TEMPTATIONS AND TURMOIL. I KNOW WHEN MY CHILDREN NEED REST. I ALSO KNOW THAT TRYING TO HANDLE EVERYTHING ON YOUR OWN AND DOING EVERYTHING HUMANLY POSSIBLE TO LIVE UP TO THE EXPECTATIONS OF OTHER PEOPLE IS NOTHING MORE THAN PRIDE IN DISGUISE. BEFORE PRIDE GOES DESTRUCTION. YOU MUST MAKE THE CHOICE TO LAY THINGS DOWN. YOU CAN DO ALL THINGS THROUGH CHRIST. SON, YOU HAVE BEEN TRYING TO DO ALL THINGS THROUGH YOU...I AM GOD. BUT, I DRAW THE LINE AT CONTROLLING EACH AND EVERY SINGLE DETAIL OF PEOPLE'S LIVES; THAT I WILL NOT DO. I WILL GLADLY TAKE THE WHEEL WHEN YOU INVITE ME TO. BUT, IF YOU DON'T INVITE TO, I WILL NOT.

YOUR WIFE, YOUR FUTURE, ALL IN MY HANDS, MY WAY, MY TIMING FOR MY PURPOSE. I AM GOD. I CREATED THE UNIVERSE AND EVERYTHING IN IT. I AM IN CONTROL. I KNOW WHAT TO DO AND HOW TO DO IT WITHOUT YOUR HELP. YOU CAN WRECK A BLESSING BY HOLDING ON TO UNJUST EXPECTATIONS AND REFUSING TO LET GO OF YESTERDAY. YOU SAY YOU'RE JUST A MAN... WELL, I HAVE CALLED YOU TO COME OUT FROM AMONG THEM TO BE MORE THAN THAT. LET THIS SAME MIND THAT WAS IN CHRIST BE IN YOU BARKER. SEEK ME FIRST. YOU WRESTLE WITH PRIDE. JESUS WAS FREE OF PRIDE. YOU WERE CALLED TO SERVE. NOT TO LIVE FOR YOU. JESUS DIDN'T EVEN TRY TO PLEASE HIMSELF. I AM GOD SON.

YOU KNOW THE WORD SON, IT'S INSIDE OF YOU. I HAVE CHOSEN YOU. I HAVE PLACED IT THERE. NOT BECAUSE YOU WERE PERFECT, BUT BECAUSE I KNEW YOU WOULD DO

WHAT I CALLED YOU TO DO...NOT PERFECTLY, BUT EFFECTIVELY. BARKER YOU ARE STILL VERY YOUNG YET AND YOU HAVE A WAYS TO GO TO CHANGE AND GROW. I HAVE CALLED YOU AND HAVE PUT MY WORDS IN YOUR MOUTH. AT THE APPOINTED TIME, I WILL USE YOU AND YOUR FAMILY TO BRING GLORY TO ME. BUT THINGS MUST CHANGE FIRST IN ORDER FOR THAT TO HAPPEN. ALL IS IN MY HANDS. I DON'T EXPECT PERFECTION. YOU NEED MORE LOVE AND LESS PRIDE. DEAL WITH YOUR PRIDE BEFORE IT DEALS WITH YOU. ALWAYS REMEMBER THIS SON, YOU CAN MISS A BLESSING IF YOU ARE TOO FOCUSED ON LOOKING FOR IT TO COME THE WAY YOU THINK IT IS SUPPOSED TO. FOR WHO CAN KNOW THE MIND OF GOD? I LOVE YOU. JUST BE STILL AND KNOW THAT I AM GOD."

His conversation with God would prove to offer him temporary relief. He was in his flesh, frustrated and resistant. It would be a restless night for the young Pastor.

WRECKING BALL

"POP!" screams Gregory from the living room.

"What man?! If you want me come to me! Don't raise your voice to me in my house boy! Respect! Now what man? What?!" barks Barker.

Laughing loudly from the bathroom doorway, "Ay, who you gettin' fresh for Pop? Let a brother find out you got you a ill lil' dip you ain't tell me about....." G continues, "You gotta consult ya boy on all things feminine and fine Pop. Know why?"

"No, I don't know why. I'm not even sure I want to know why but, I'm sure you'll take the time to enlighten me even when it's so obvious that a brother is not beat."

"Pssshhhhh Pop?!" laughs Gregory holdin' his chest. "What do you mean you're not sure you wanna know why man?"

"Like I said..." Barker said sarcastically.

"I'm that nig...."

"Watch that mouth boy! You know better."

"Oh my bad. But Pop! That's why! Just like you used to be in back in your day man..."

He puts down his razor, "Boy what?! What do you mean 'Back in my day'? Don't get it twisted son! It's still my day! You see me and you know where I'm from! Don't let the smooth taste fool you kid! You better go down the way and ask somebody. I'M THAT MAN! And you...You....Oh you best believe YOU ARE WHO YOU ARE BECAUSE OF ME!" boasts Barker as he pokes his finger into G's chest while slowly exiting the Master Bathroom. Continuing as he makes his way to the closet of the Master Bedroom, "Your name, your fame and your game is ALL because of Boom baby boy, and don't you EVER forget it!" Barker mumbling as he rifles through his neatly hung collection of posh casual wear, "Back in my day...pssshhh...sucka! Who he talkin' to? See that's what I'm talkin' about Lord, I'm a man and everybody just sees me as a functioning title. Burns me up!"

"Old man who you in there talkin' to? You seein' dead people man?"

His father steps out of his walk-in closet, "Yeah man. I see dead people and you're one of them! Now get ghost!"

"Corny as hell man..." snickers Greg as he leaves the Master Bedroom.

"Watch that mouth before I check that chin joker!"

"Awwwww man! Look at you pop... all swaggy. Where you goin' buddy?" G asks as Barker gallops down the winding stair case and enters the foyer.

Barker again poking his son firmly in the chest, "First of all KID, you're playing with me way too much these days and I don't like it so quit before things get realer than they have to in here. Second of all, I'm goin' to a place your lil' young behind has not dared to boldly go before. Third of all, don't wait up. And for four, you and ya lil' homies better not tear up my house or..."

G and his friends in unison, "Things gon' get realer than they have to get to in here."   "Sir yes sir!" Echoes a voice from the background of the young mob.

He shakes his head as they break out into laughter, "Jesus, I feel sorry for you guys' parents. They must be real proud... Here boy, money for pizza. No girls. No drugs. No alcohol. No fighting. No noise. No extra company. No pool. No loud music. No complaints from the neighbors. We are one of the few affluent minority families within this community and in all of these years of being here, not one complaint has been registered in my name or against you or me. Let's try to keep it that way shall we?"

"Yes sir."

"Boy don't patronize me witcha 'Yes sir' bull. I'm out!"

Gregory's friends in boy band unison, "Night Boom!" As they cackle and jump up in laughter Barker chuckles and yells as he exits, "Nighty night ladies! Try not to pee the bed girls."

"I WANNA SEE MY SON YOU BASTARD!" screeches a crackling voice from just beyond the manicured lawn.

"Oh my goodness....No! No! No! Please God no. What is she doing here? Am I being punched? Man, I don't need this tonight. I don't need this ever. Stacey? Stacey, just what in the hell are you doing here?" He whispers as he runs toward the mother of his son and hushes her.

"Oh you uppity Negro, don't play me! Why you keep challengin' my motherhood Boom?! Huh? Oh 'cause I ain't perfect like ya momma?! Huh? Mrs. Carla 'GOLDEN GIRL' Golden. She wasn't perfect Boom! Don't you know that? Ain't nobody perfect boy. I think it's real messed up how you been weighin' me against her on the justice scale all of this time Boom. I'll never be her I promise you. But I also promise you this: We more alike than you think. You know how it go, guys be attracted to females that remind them of they momma. So with that being said..."

"HEY! HEY! LAY OFF MY MOTHER GIRL. MY MOTHER WAS A SAINT AND TWICE THE MOTHER YOU COULD EVER HOPE TO BE! SHE WAS EVERYTHING THAT WAS GOOD AND RIGHT WITH THE WORLD FROM THE CRADLE TO THE GRAVE, OK? YOU GOT THAT! DON'T YOU EVER TARNISH HER NAME OR MAKE AN ATTEMPT TO TARNISH HER REPUTATION...EVER! AS A MATTER OF FACT STACEY, DON'T YOU EVEN THINK ABOUT MY MOTHER! AND AIN'T NOBODY ATTRACTED TO YOU BUT THE DOPE MAN. AIN'T NOBODY I KNOW EVEN REMOTELY ATTRACTED TO YOU. THAT TOILET YOU CALL A MOUTH IS THE INSURANCE ON THAT! STOP DISRESPECTIN' MY MOTHER STACEY. I'M NOT GONNA KEEP TELLIN' YOU! WHAT YOU BEEN SMOKIN' TONIGHT THAT WOULD HAVE YOU THAT HIGH THAT YOU THINK YOU COULD EVER STEP TO ME ABOUT MY MOTHER? HUH? MY MOTHER WAS A SAINT! YOU GOT THAT GIRL?"

"First off, your MOTHER wasn't no saint! We all got a past. Just because you ain't privy to the drop on the 'GOLDEN GIRL' that don't mean I'm not."

"Watch ya mouth girl I just fired my second warning shot...best be careful." he barks clinching his teeth, staring angrily.

"Awwwwwww you miss your mother? I feel you. I never really got a chance to tell you how sorry I am for your loss. I feel bad for that. I'm so sorry Boom. Really, she was good people man. But on the flip side, MY SON MUST BE MISSIN' HIS MOTHER TOO! DONTCHA THINK? DON'T YOU EVER THINK THAT HE COULD BE MOURNING A LOSS B?!"

"Please Stacey. You know full well that it is not the same. You didn't die physically, you just died spiritually. You still floatin' around in the atmosphere like a money man in the summer time, just floatin' by, lookin' to get caught by the next low-life that wanna rub up on you for a dollar or two. All Greg gotta do is go down the way and hit the greasiest street corner in the Bricks and find you girl. You full of it and you know it. I ain't comin' between you and your son. YOU ARE! And even if I was, I would be well within my rights as a parent, barring breaking the law; I will always do whatever I can to protect my son. EVEN FROM YOU! Now as for you, you can just get a grip man. Stacey you don't even want that boy. If you did, you would be somewhere tryin' to get it together and we wouldn't be having this time wasting conversation right now; Man, I could be well into my evening by now. Jeez..."

"Oh no the hell you did not!"

"Seeing is believing and yes I did! I'm prayin' for you baby." he rebuts prideful.

"Never mind all dat prayer foolishness. Wait! As a matter of fact, truth be told, I'm actually prayin' for you PASTOR!!!!! And why you in my business? BOY WHERE IS MY   SON?! Pssshhhh...Askin' me what am I doin' here...Please! ...could care less about ya lil' neighbors in ya lil' gated community. Where ever my son at is where Imma be. Whatchu mean what am I doin' here? Question is whatchu doin' here without me? Barker why you doin' this? Why you hidin' G from me? Huh? He the only thing I got that's right. Why you take that from me Boom?" she cries.

 "Awww man. No, no, no...C'mon, shhh, C'mon. You know I always hated to see you cry." he consoles his son's mother. Holding her tightly wiping her tears, "Stace, you need to get clean. I'm not keeping him from you. Stace, I don't want G to see you like this. You're better than this. C'mon girl..... I don't want war with you ma. You already know what it is. Nothing I do is ever to hurt you. You gave me my son. What would I gain from hurting his mother, huh?! Come on girl now..."

Stacey pulls back, "C'mon girl? C'mon girl? You come on! You left me Boom. You left me. Why couldn't you see there wasn't ever gonna be a me without you?"

He rolled his eyes, "Yep. There it is. Ok, here we go. Welcome to the Stacey James blame game everybody. Pull up a chair, get comfy. It's gonna be a long night folks."

Girl! I ain't God. Who am I? Go on with your life man please. You don't need nobody but Jesus man."

She cuts him off, "You ain't get the memo B? QB and the Lead Cheerleader, the American dream, 2.5 kids, cute house in the burbs, white picket fence, dog and a mini-van. Boom, I was supposed to be a soccer mom and you the lawyer husband. Remember that?"

"Yeah Stace, I remember, but when you gonna let go? We were children. C'mon babe, let me take you home. You hungry?".

"Ok. Ok. Ok. But what about G Boom? When you gon' let me see G?" she begs.

"Real soon baby. Real soon. Let's get you well first, k?" Barker consoles his high school sweetheart. "Let's get goin' babe, get you some food...get you home."

Stacey, "What kinda food Boom?"

"Whatever you want sweetie. Whatever you want."

As they get into the car and drive off, G emerges from the dimly lit doorway, cell phone in hand, "Yoooooooo, I swore I heard my Pop talkin' to my Mom...that's ill. I hope I'm not losin' it. What? Am I seein' dead people? Ha! Ha! Yeah...uuumm, No! Not even...but I would love to see what you wearin' though sexy. Shoot me a pic real quick aight? What? Nah, don't worry about them. What? No I ain't gon' show nobody. I promise." he laughs and winks at his boys.

"Alright, we are here. You are home. Safe and sound. Did you get enough to eat?"

"Yeah, I did B. Thank you. You still can be sweet when you wanna be."

He smiled, "I never changed Stacey, Still me. I like being nice. You just can't see that because you..."

Stacey interrupts Barker sharply, "NO YOU DON'T BROTHER! NO THE HELL YOU DON'T! DON'T GO THERE BIBLE BOY! DON'T YOU DARE! WHATEVER CONDITION I'M IN YOU GOT ME HERE WHEN YOU ABANDONED ME AND YOUR SON. THEN YOU HAD THE NERVE TO TAKE HIM FROM ME! BOOM PLEASE ALRIGHT...JUST PLEASE."

"You're seeing it wrong Stacey, and for the life of me I can't figure out why you are so stuck in the past. Get on with your life already! What is wrong with you besides the obvious? All of these years I have been praying for you but yet, no change. Now I know the prayers of the righteous avail much but c'mon ma, you gotta want to change. And not for me, for our son or anybody else; Stacey gotta want to change for Stacey. C'mon now, you grew up in the church just like me, and yeah, alright so we were rebellious and hot in the pants and made our mistakes, but, babe you gotta get past that."

"Prayers of the righteous do what now? Knock it off! I know you Boom. You got a form of godliness and no power. That's why your prayers tank son."

"Yeah aight. Whatever. And I ain't your son. SON! You just focus on getting some help aight? Now, if there's nothing more…"

Arrogant ass! So, oh what now you a drug counselor huh? Boy miss me with that nonsense."

"WOULD YOU PLEASE LISTEN!!?" Barker begs.

"Listen to you preach to me? I'm not one of your parishioners or shall I say, adoring fans, so I think not. And for the love of God, please don't mention church to me ever again. Please. Brother you ain't got a clue, ok? Why the let you of all people be a Pastor is beyond me. If the only knew…you ain't nothing special child."

"Lady, and I use the term loosely, may I please continue? May I state my case without being rudely interrupted?"
As G's mother sits silently looking straight ahead, Barker continues, "For the last time, I went off to college to secure our future like a man is supposed to, for our family so we could live out the dream. How else was it gonna come true Stacey? I was being responsible Stace. I really was tryin'. I really tried…" he grabs her hand as she opens the passenger side door to exit.

She wept, "I don't know if whatchu sayin' is good enough B, verdict is out on that right now. That ain't gonna make it right and that ain't gonna get me back. So save it".

Annoyed Barker explains with one eye brow raised, he firmly grasps her chin in efforts to force her to look him straight in the eye, "Look at me Stacey. Baby girl, nobody's here holdin' out hope for reconciliation. I've moved on a thousand times over. So girl go head aight?! I'm just givin' you some truth to help you gain your footing and sleep at night. Believe when I say I sleep well and as far as anything else goes I AM GOOD. And please Miss, don't flatter yourself. You are definitely not that hot chick from high school that everybody wanted a piece of anymore, so let's keep it in perspective shall we? Don't be offended sweetheart just a little dose of reality for you. Seems you need clarity.".

"LET MY HAND GO YOU POMPOUS ASS! JUST A POMPOUS ASS! WHY IN THE HELL DO ANYBODY ATTENDED THAT BIG ASS CHURCH? HOW CAN ANYBODY EVEN GET INSIDE WHEN YA BIG ASS HEAD AND YA BIG ASS EGO IS TAKIN' UP SO MUCH DAMN SPACE! BOY YOU A PIECE OF WORK. OH SO YOU BETTER THAN ME RIGHT? AMAZIN'! YEAH YOU GOT IT GOIN' ON; ON THE SURFACE, BUT YOU DAMN SHO' AIN'T GOT THE LOVE OF GOD UP IN YOU. DON'T FORGET THE LORD GIVETH AND THE LORD TAKETH AWAY. YOUS A MESS! YOU CAN'T EVEN BE NICE TO THE MOTHER OF YOUR CHILD.

"Shut up Stacey."

She refuses, "YOU SWEET ALL OF THE TIME...WHEN? WHERE? AND TO WHO? PSSSHHHH BROTHER PLEASE ALRIGHT? BOOM YOU MAY GOT ALL THESE PEOPLE FOOLED BUT BOY OH BOY, DO YOUR TRUE COLORS BEGIN TO SHOW WHEN YOU GET UPSET. BOY YOU GET FUNKY! AND GUESS THE HELL WHAT?! YOU JUST RAN INTO

SOMEBODY WHO AIN'T GOT TIME FO' DAT. BOY BYE."
Stacey slams the car door.

He lowers the window, "Stacey, I'm sorry I talked to you
that way. I'm so sorry. I'm not perfect. You know that Stace.
You know that better than anyone else. I'm just a man and
Imma make mistakes. Girl, you be makin' me lose it! I
meant no real harm. I promise you..."

"Save ya promises B and all dat drama. What kind of fool am I? I
been in love with you all of these years. Maybe I was too blind
to see what was really good. You are not who I thought you
were. Or was it that I chose not to see it? You know what?
Imma take your sound advice. Imma move on. But you need to
do the same and let ya mother go. And while you doin' that, let
ya fantasy about y'all perfect little life go, ok? If you gonna dish
it out, taste it first before you start makin' plates PASTOR. Check
the stats and the facts boss!"

"You on ya last leg 'bout my mother aight?! Don't push
me Stacey. Find yourself ma."

"Boy please! Find deez! And, trust mother, IF I WAS
CLEAN, AFTER HOW YOU SHOWED YO' ASS TONIGHT, I
WOULDN'T WANT YOU BACK IF WE WERE THE LAST TWO
PEOPLE STANDING. Witcha' has been athlete, part time
preachin'; one foot in the world, one in the word;
lukewarm, hypocritical ass. Get it together!"

Oh and by the way Bible Boy, I ain't as educated or as
classy as you are your highness, but I know when I'm being
insulted and manipulated, I ain't been out survivin' these
mean Brick City streets all this time for nothin' Jack! I heard
you man, you said 'NO REAL HARM', now that implies,
some harm, ain't that right counselor?"

Barker puts his head down quietly.

"The prosecution rests its case your honor. Court adjourned Bible boy! AND I WANNA SEE MY SON SOONER THAN LATER AND I MEAN IT BOOM!".

"Stop calling me 'Bible Boy'! And by the way how did you get on to the property? Huh? Don't start bringin' ya ghetto drama where I live girl. I ain't playin' either."

"How I get up in there? Well Bible Boy, that's for me to know and for you to find out, or not. I WANT TO SEE MY SON BARKER." She storms off clinching her teeth.

She reaches the end of the walkway. She sits perched at the top of the staircase. Starring into space broken into pieces by the heated exchange, her cell phone rings. "Wrecking Ball" by Miley Cyrus blares from the lone speaker. She had chosen that as her ring tone. She momentarily looks down to I.D the caller. As she recognizes it's her son Gregory, as much she misses him, as hard as she battles Barker to spend time with him, she is frozen in time and she just can't pick up. Not now. "Imma call you back tomorrow." she whispers to the screen. Stacey has checked out of reality temporarily. As the ring tone continues to loop, a tear falls from the corner of her bloodshot eyes, she's exhausted and thinking of the last time she was able to see G. She had noticed that as he ages he is resembling his dad more and more inside and out. She can't help but to think that she is losing him in every way. Everything about it is tearing her apart. She is just as resentful towards the father of her only child as she is in love with him. He affects her deeply. Like no other. She found it easy to have meaningless sexual encounters with countless men because for her, everything outside of what she had experienced with Barker was just business. Resolving to never give herself over to love again, Stacey was 'bout her business. She pulls out a Newport from her pocket as the song continues to loop. She lights up, she blows out the initial smoke, singing in a lull, "...I will always want you. I came in just like a wrecking baaaallll!! All you ever did was wreck-eh-eh-eck me... Yeah you wreck-eh-eh-ecked me".

Barker speeds off to his destination now more frustrated than ever. Mumbling, "Oh God, what did I do to my life? I used to love that woman. But back then, she was a girl. And even after all of that drama, the boy in me always will. She still gets under my skin like nobody else. Ladies and gentlemen, the incomparable Ms. Stacey James." He turns on the radio. "Wrecking Ball" is blasting through the speakers. He's driving down the NJ Turnpike in a haze. "Shake it off kid." he tells himself.

WE   BELONG

TOGETHER

A full-figured, 5' 10" statuesque, honey-coated, Hershey's chocolate covered amazon steps out of the shower. Patting her soft, toned, youthful skin dry, "Dang that felt good. Lord thank you for showers and hot water. The little things we take for granted. Yes Lawd!"

She, emerges from the bathroom. Liza was the splitting image of Connie as Connie was the splitting image of Rose and Rose, Hyacinth. Each one, strikingly beautiful, highly sought after and forces to be reckoned with in their own right.

Traveling down the hall to her bedroom, she stops and opens the door on the right side of the corridor. Softly she says, "Oh my goodness. They are gone for the summer. I am going to miss my babies. But that don't mean I won't enjoy this break. Thank God for responsible fathers."

Jay is her ex-husband. Married at 18, fresh out of high school, the union was doomed to fail. In efforts to secure against her daughter being anything like those that had come before, Connie had done all that she could to groom Liza towards a better mindset. She had talked to her endlessly about the realities, pros, cons and the effects and consequences of having casual sex or following in her footsteps. She couldn't bear the thought of her beloved only child inheriting the rights to the family business. There was no legacy to be left there. Whatever generational curses were, Connie was doing all that she had the power to do to deter them. Connie wanted more for Liza. So much more so that she brought the family business to a screeching halt when Liza grew old enough to ask questions that she could not avoid answering. Plus with the rumors buzzing through the neighborhood about the Debrils, Connie did not want to embarrass Liza any further than she and the legacy of the "Honey Pot" and Rose had done already. Connie was a living legend and Rose, the Queen, was an urban one as far as the local underground sex industry was concerned.

Jay and Liza didn't have a fighting chance as both Liza and Connie were determined not to allow ANYTHING to ever come in between. Jay had moved into the Debril home following high school. After he and Liza had eloped on a trip with mutual friends to Las Vegas. They were young, bursting with passion and in love. They had dated all throughout high school. Later on, tensions began to develop between Jay and Connie, as Connie tended to be overly protective of Liza. Not to mention that the Debrils were notoriously independent and prideful women, a man had never ruled the roost. Rose had manipulated Connie into believing that every man had nothing more than the intent to manipulate, manhandle and pimp women; Men were unnecessary unless they were on the paying end by trade. Happiness could never be derived from the union between man and a woman. Not even a lawful one.

 Everything was business for the Debrils and nothing more. Or so it had seemed on the surface. Secretly though, Liza had big plans to fall in love again one day but she dared not discuss that prospect with her mother. Connie was her world and her word was gospel. Liza's marriage lasted just long enough for her to bare her husband three beautiful daughters. Connie's constant balking had driven an emotional wedge between the two newlyweds. Sooner than later, Liza had filed for divorce at her mother's urging, breaking her husband's heart.

At the age of 22, Jason had chosen to pursue a college degree to provide a better life for the girls; maybe move Liza away from Connie so that they could have a fighting chance. Yet, all attempts at reconciliation had failed over time due to continued interruptions at the hands of Connie. Nagging Liza to forget her husband and move forward, Liza began dating to please her mother and to ease her deep loneliness. Despite periodic socializing, a void still needed to be filled. A void Connie Debril would never be able to fill for Liza Rose and vice versa.

Jason eventually decided to let go. He began to visit with less frequency. He had to contain what was left of his pride. His mother-in-law was in his way and only his ex-wife could change that. Jay was powerless. He called the girls every other day. They visited with him at his home on holidays and during summer vacation months. Eventually he got on with his life and started dating casually. He was still in love with his ex-wife. He was never really ready to give up on the hope of reconciliation.

For him, it was also a fear factor that held him at bay. Jay did not want to face the heartache of permanently separating the family. He loved his children. He couldn't imagine his life without them. His daughters could not imagine their lives without him. He and Liza had grown to regret ever allowing someone to come in between them and now they had to live with the reality of living without one another. Even though they were no longer together, they still, for whatever it was worth, secretly had deep affection for one another.

They were just teens, but they were one another's firsts in every way. They would forever be linked. Times they would see one another or even speak briefly on the phone, they spoke softly and kindly to one another because, even though they had both moved forward on the outside, the possibility remained that between Liza and Jay, there would always be something there that could reconnect them. Even in their embraces when Jay came to pick up the girls told a story of love lost and regret. In the embrace, each time he would squeeze her waist tightly with his strong masculine hands and whisper softly in her ears, "Liza, you know you can call me for anything. I will always be here for you. You know I'll do anything for you."

Liza never pulled away from him even though he would whisper the same words every time they had an intimate embrace. As he held her close, he'd feel the warm tears that dropped from her dark brown eyes on to his loving shoulder. He'd pull her closer with such an irresistible tenderness, "Don't cry. I got us here. I should've been a stronger man. Baby I'm sorry." he'd say kissing her tears away.

Liza would yelp into his shoulder as if not to let the girls hear her, "I will stop crying when you stop being sorry. It's not your fault. Maybe I should've stood up to my mother Jay. Maybe I should have. But I never have...not sure I even know how to."

Caressing her small chin, he would reassure her, "You can do it. And one day you will. Your strength will kick in someday. You're gonna be fine. And when it does, I will be right here as always. I will always be right here. Not just because of the kids, because of you. You are a beautiful woman Liza, inside and out. You're strong. Don't you forget that! Now what you have to learn how to do is assert that inner-strength and not be afraid to let go. Aight? SAY NO. When you're ready. Promise me you gonna work on that?"

"I promise you." she replies.

He kissed her neck softly three times, "Miss you ma. Imma always miss you. Still so pretty, so soft, so sexy. Damn Liza! We damn sure ain't kids no more, but you still as delicious as you was in high school. Aw man... Let me get goin'. Y'all ready?"

"Yes daddy! Mommy and daddy yaaaaaaaaaayyyyy!!!!" their daughters cheer from the back seat of his SUV.

She was powerless when it came to him and she knew it. He was tall, soft spoken, athletic; He lived for basketball. A die hard Lakers fan, book worm and a noble gentleman despite his dysfunctional upbringing.

Jason Rodriguez was from the North Ward of Newark. He was a dark Puerto Rican and if you didn't know him personally you would think he was a young African American man from Los Angeles. He dreamed of the West Coast laid-back lifestyle and emulated it at every turn, down to the dialect. That annoyed Liza yet, other females ate it up. It was altogether different for their region. His whole demeanor was attractive. He loved movies like Boyz in Da Hood and Baby Boy. He just wanted to distance himself from everything that had anything to do with his life as it was. Everything that is, except for Liza and his daughters. He could never totally leave his family.

Golden brown. Overflowing with rugged masculinity and rugged boyish looks to match. Tatted down, sweet and smooth as tres leches cake; Respectful. Only confrontational when confronted. Jay Rodriguez was very well a feast for the female eye. Jason was every homeboy's homeboy. Jay was a man's man by all means. His father made sure of that. Yet around women he was extremely protective and gentile, which only enhanced his attractive factor. Jay had yet to encounter a woman he could not easily have his way with, but he was a gentle soul, he couldn't bear the thought of playing on anyone's emotions and breaking women's fragile hearts. Jay was extremely close to his mother and through her learned to value everything about women. Even when he found them to be less than reasonable and lady like, he didn't put up arguments against them. He was not forceful. And that among other things had kept a rip in the relationship between him and his father.

His father was aggressive and had abusive tendencies. Those things, those negative attributes, Jason had promised himself he would never mimic in his own life. He did admire his father's work ethic and the way he handled his responsibilities to family. Raul was faithful to Jay's mother and an upstanding church leader plus, a local volunteer. Jay admonished how his father was adored by others outside of the house in the neighborhood; A father to the fatherless. He did whatever he could for anyone he could if and when he could. Yet it was the common belief amongst the neighbors that for Jay's dad, family was always first. "What a quaint little hallmark card of a family." was the general consensus. But everything that glitter ain't gold. Depending on where you get it from, it could be a gold-plated knock off that will eventually turn your neck green. Jason and his brother knew that first hand.

As a teenager growing up, he would often pray that he would not turn out like his father. To ensure that, he spent as much time with his mother as possible, mostly while his father was at work. Jay picked up her kind, peaceful spirit. As did his brother. But much more so as John, his older, brother was homosexual. Jay had always known but he didn't agree with it because he knew what the Bible taught about it. Yet, he dared not judge what he could not figure out or understand. He chose to pray and continue to love his big brother...his lifestyle didn't matter to him. He was young but mature enough to know that he didn't have to understand him to love him.

John would tell Jay when he would question him about it, "Look bro, I can't explain it ok...I didn't even choose this thing man...Things happened to me when I was little and you were just a baby. There was no one to tell...and well, just know I never wanted it to happen to you bro, so we'll talk about it later, when you're older and I think you can handle it. Until then, Imma protect you from that kinda stuff. O.K.? We still homies right? J&J for life buddy?"

"J&J for life buddy!" Jay agreed.

When Raul found out, he threw John out of the house and disowned him. John got bullied at school. Nevertheless, Jay being the standup guy he was, although he was the younger brother, he was the larger brother; He always stood up for John. Disagree with the lifestyle or not, Jay was still his brother. And you just didn't mess with the Rodriguez brothers if they didn't mess with you first; they never messed with anybody. And while he was young and powerless over his father's decision to totally cut his brother off, he knew outside of that house and away from his father, he stood as tall as the mighty Sequoia in the western slopes of the Sierra Nevada California Mountains and well, what his father said did not matter. He knew the bible talked about love and though it was not being shown at home, he was determined to get to know God for himself and spread the love starting with his brother John. While loving his brother John and not denying the truth in the Bible, Jay was still very young and understandably, his heart was hardening towards his father and that was something else he had felt powerless to stop. Jay would never deny his brother and would defend him to the end against bullies, even if it meant they both walked away battered and bruised. The Rodriguez boys would always live to fight another day by the grace of God.

Raul had forbid his wife Marisol from seeing their son ever again. Jay somehow though, would always find a way for the two to meet unbeknownst to Raul. Marisol, Jay and John would meet up every chance they got for years until one day the meetings just stopped. John had stopped calling Jay. There was no communication from him for an entire year. One day a friend of John's had run into Jay. He told him that John had been murdered as the result of a biased attack outside of a night club over in New York where he had been living for the past two years. He remembered seeing a brief news report on his way out to school that morning a year ago.

He brushed it off, with the belief that it could never be his brother, "Nah man, can't be John. John can scrap! Plus he too smart to let anybody ever run down on him like that. After all we been through together over here...That ain't John. He too smart. He woulda saw it comin'." He was sure it could not be his big brother John. "Not no Rodriguez....Hell no!" he thought to himself. But sadly, it was his brother. The friend had presented Jay with a letter he had found, "I always said I would give this to you if I ever saw you again."

"What is this?" Jay asked.

"It's from your brother. He had started coming to church with me and my family a few weeks before he passed away. He said he wanted to re-discover God. He wanted to get saved."

Jay opened the letter, and as he read the letter, it was as if he could hear John speaking to him clearly:

"Hey bro. I hope y'all good over there. Sorry I haven't been to visit, been busy. Tryin' to get me together. I'm writing this letter because I miss y'all and I don't know when I will be available to see you guys again in the near future. So this, lil' bro is just an update. In a nutshell, I got some things to change. I been goin' to church bro. I can change. I now know what happened to me was not my fault, and well, my lifestyle...I mean that lifestyle, that was chosen for me. I don't want to choose IT no more Jay. I just don't. I want to be saved. It ain't for me.

I never told you how I got intro'd to 'The Life'. In my circle I done heard a lot of stuff about why every individual may be in "The Life". Some say they were born that way; they don't need to explain. They comfy in they skin. I hear religious people say it got somethin' to do with demonic activity and this thing called, generational curses. Some say it's the company you keep. Some say they chose it. Some like me, it was chosen for them. Me...I say, watch who you allow to watch your kids. Anyway people don't always have the answers bro. People can't always figure out why they are the way they are ya know? I try not to judge what I don't totally understand. Maybe everything ain't for us to figure out right?

Jay, you don't know what it is to be sittin' around with a group of people, everybody tellin' they story; everybody got the same issue; how they all got to that issue and how they all respond to it ain't the same. Some use and abuse drugs, alcohol, sex other people crazy day in, day out to cope with the lifestyle and the judgment. Some like me, we dance. We party our lives away and pray that God don't hate us as much as people say He do. Still, others cut themselves and have unprotected sex with strangers because they have been brainwashed into believing they life ain't worth a damn; Rejected by friends, family. I know how they feel. Guess I'm a little bit stronger. I was raised in church, (for whatever good that did or didn't do us, whatever that means), so I guess I know better in a way. I know Jesus loves me. I know Jesus just don't throw people away. I always heard older people say He hate the sin not the sinner. I believe that.

Jay, people just be layin' on the floor ballin' bro...talkin' 'bout committing suicide. I can't go out like that Jay. Not me. I mean...It crossed my mind a gang of times. But I think about you and Marisol and I wake up from that. Man, I miss her flan. Mami make the best flan.

So, I have my struggles, struggles I ain't ask for, but bro, please believe, I'm still a man. All man! I ain't goin' out like that. I seen it too many times out here. It's so serious. The pain so deep. I been on the edge. I just never went over the cliff. I know God is with me somehow just because of that. People don't know man...rejection is a slow killer like cancer. It eats away at you from the inside out. Man, I seen so much out here Jay. Pray for the hurting and rejected bro. Not just me. It's a lot of us out here and everybody rejected and hurting ain't gay. Everybody that's suicidal ain't gay. Everybody gay ain't suicidal or hurting. Everybody in "The Life" don't feel like they confused. That's what other people on the outside lookin' in judgin' don't understand. I don't want you to be confused though. I want to help you to understand other people. People like me. I want you to pray for everybody. I still pray for y'all. Even Papi.

I been in they shoes. I just figured... I deserve to live and grow like everybody else. Everybody deserve a chance. You kill yourself...they won...the devil wins. That's what I tell 'em kid. I'm from the Brix, we fight 'til we can't fight no more. Anyway, hate hurts. It hurts everybody. I hate HATE. I love LOVE. I wanna love the way Jesus did. Why is it people can remember Leviticus 18:22 and pull that rabbit outta they hat when it's convenient and they high off the fumes of they own self-righteousness, but, them same people can't remember John 13:34-35? I don't get it man.

 Anyway baby boy, this is my story. I promised to tell you how. Well, here goes baby boy. Remember we used to get dropped off at the babysitter's when mom and dad wanted to go out? That lady Marissa (she was so pretty right? I thought I was gonna marry her some day and move out of the Brix...Funny right?). Remember her boyfriend Jose? The one with the big muscles always in and out of jail? Scary dude? He used to touch me a lot when he would make you go outside to play or off to the store with Marissa. He used to make me do things to him and call me his 'girlfriend'. I was scared Jason. I didn't know what to do. I was a kid. He threatened to hurt you so I just let him because I needed to protect you. I couldn't let that happen to you. I couldn't tell mom because I didn't want to upset her. Mami always see the good in people even when ain't no good to be seen. I think she just be sweepin' a lot of stuff under the rug so she don't gotta deal with it. I really wanna talk to her about that next time we get together. That's unhealthy. See, it ain't all bad. Me bein' over here in The City. I'm learnin stuff Jason.

Remember we ain't like to see her cry? Raul always made Mami cry man. I wanted to make her happy. I ain't wanna bring no more pain to her life. I just didn't. I never told the old man because I knew he wouldn't believe me and you see what happened when I did get up the nerve to try, he blamed me, called me a faggot and a liar and threw my ass out. But I don't know why he's like that. I know he got problems he probably don't even know he got. But, hey man...who don't?

Remember we used to always say: WHO AM I TO JUDGE? He's crazy man. But he's still Papi and even if he never change, I still love him. DON'T TELL HIM THAT! You know Papi. You know that joker gon' blow his stack if you even mention my name and I don't want him takin' it out on Mami.

Moving forward, I forgive Jose... Papi too. Who am I not to? I know I'm ready to change, cause I don't hold on to resentment or bitterness. I ain't angry no more. I don't wanna be like Papi. I live to forgive. I live to love; I want to love the way God loves me. I'm ready Jay...want to make y'all and God proud. For the first time in my life, I am proud of myself. Never stop praying bro. It's just talkin' to Jesus and waitin for him to answer you back. Don't be afraid to open up Jay. Let it out! He listens. I used to hear older Black ladies say prayer change things. Well bro, they was right.

Anyways, it's Thursday night and Imma go out wit' my peoples one mo' time before I give myself to Jesus 100% and call it a wrap. I really am ready to do this Jason. I used to think about doin' this 'gettin' saved' for Papi. You know, make him happy. Make him proud. Make him love me. I thought about doin' a lot of things, like being a garbage man or some extra masculine job like mechanic or somethin' to prove to him I can be the son he wanted me to be...I can be that MAN Jason. But I had a talk with myself and I realized that a job don't make you more or less of a man any more than having a deep voice, muscles and a moustache like Aaron Rodgers makes you any less gay. Jay, I just realized, I gotta get saved for me. This is what I want, my choice.

I used to choose my desires over God's, now I'm tryin' to choose his over mine. Sad that I spent my short life in church and never knew what salvation was until I met up with Anthony. He's a good guy. A pastor, a brother, a friend. He the real deal Jay. He know what it's like out here in these streets. His church is small, but believe when I tell you, this cat keep a packed house! Jokers come from all over to get the word from him. Maybe one day you come over here to a service with me? These good people man. They don't make you feel like an outcast. Oh yeah and Anthony is Italian. Remember we used think they only ate pasta and sauce? Well it's not true! They eat other stuff. He like soul food bro. Can you believe it? New York is so cool. So many different people. So many different things. The city is full of surprises. So pretty at night. I can't wait to show y'all.

So that's my truth baby boy. I hope you not disappointed in me. I know my choices caused you mad pain and confusion bro. I'm sorry. Really sorry. I really love y'all. I promise you bro, next time you see ya boy, Imma be a new man. All man like I already am, but new and improved. I promise. Kiss Marisol for me. See y'all soon.

P.S- Thank you for keepin' my secret and for defending me. You the best brother ever. I never told you this but, you my best friend Jay. I love you the most. Can't wait for you and Liza to get married. Man! Papi would flip if he knew you was chillin' wit' a Black girl. I know it's killin' Mami to keep your secret bro. But I know she's excited! I'm excited! Give

Liza my love. You picked good bro. I'm proud to call her my sister-in-law (hopefully one day. I'm praying. Y'all good together. She's so pretty. I might just snatch her up when I get myself together). Proud to call you my brother. I hope you are just as proud to call me yours. I know you are. You always was. I will always love you for that.

Truly yours,

J&J 4Lyf

Jason wept bitterly as he crumbled the hand written letter in his fists. He fell to the ground. Jason wailed at the feet of John's friend. Inconsolable, overwhelmed by grief he lay on the cold, wet autumn ground pleading, "God no......No please.....God why? Why him....Why God why? He ain't never hurt nobody! He was tryin' man...."

   John's friend went on as he bended down to help Jay to his feet, "He was supposed to get saved that upcoming Sunday. I tried to tell him he could receive Jesus right where he stood, he didn't have to wait until church service on Sunday to do it. But, for some reason, he wanted to do things traditional. Guess that's how y'all was raised. I don't know...Thursday night he went out with his friends to party one more time...they left the club...they were attacked...he died at the hospital man. Son, I'm so very sorry. They gave us his belongings because the hospital staff had no way of contacting you guys, those punks robbed his phone. I found the letter in his pocket. I am so very sorry man. He was talkin' about meeting a nice girl and maybe getting married last time I saw him alive. He really wanted to get saved and change. He was hyped. That's all he used to talk about. So many people think they got time to wait to get it right with God and change. But for so many, tomorrow don't ever come. He paused, "Forgive me, I know this may not be appropriate, but time waits for no man and I'm willing to risk the beheading that may follow. But I gotta ask, you saved man? You know Jesus Christ as your personal Lord and Savior?"

Jason wiping his tears, "Yeah man. Yeah aight. I'm saved. I believe. I'm good. But what good is that gonna do me now? Where was God when John was being attacked, huh? Why he let him get shot if He love like the Bible say He is? That ain't right man! He didn't even get a chance bro. He was trying. If Jesus saves, why he ain't save my brother, huh? Where was God when John was dyin' yo?!"

"I'm so sorry. I wish I could answer that question for you man...But, I can't. Look, I am not Jesus. I can't tell you whether John ever really accepted Jesus in His heart as his Lord and Savior or not. I'm not here to judge his personal relationship with God in private nor am I here to judge his choices or lifestyle. Like I said, I'm not The Lord. I'm nobody if you want to know the truth. Judgment is reserved for God Almighty alone. Not me. I got my own stuff to answer for. Livin' right and making the right choices consistently, day to day, is a battle for all of us, no matter the lifestyle. I do know The Lord gave His life for all of us. Maybe that is all I'm supposed to know in this situation. Again, God I am not.

 I will tell you this though, sometimes we make choices that ain't exactly wise and God don't always interfere when He ain't asked to. We have free will. He did not create us to be puppets on a string, you know? Maybe you don't understand at this very moment, but someday, you'll get it. Some things we just will not get the answers to this side of Heaven. If we really think, we have to know that if God told us everything we think we really wanted to know, it wouldn't make the pain go away, ease the grief process or make life any easier. It would probably stress us out all the more." He placed his hand on the young man's shoulder, "There was this King named Solomon son. He was the wisest, richest King that ever lived. He said he tried to know everything. He found it only makes you sad. He said all is vanity. The older you get, the more you find that to be true.

Nothing means anything at the end of the day or the end of our lives. Not even having our deepest questions answered.

I don't know how God's mind works. I wish I did, but, I don't. Believe, I have questions too. I get angry with God; I get confused too; I get hurt too. I've lost loved ones to senseless crimes over the years. People I believed to be good people. I still don't understand why. I still question God. Don't be afraid to. He can handle it all. It is so ok son. It's normal.

I am extremely sorry for your loss. Know that my family and I grieve with you and yours. You are not alone. I wish I could answer your questions but, I can't. Only God can. And even He won't answer everything the way we want to hear it or in our timing. Sometimes, He just remains silent and we don't know why. Can't figure him out Jason. If we could, He wouldn't be God, we would. Best not to even try. All we can do is pray and trust Him. We do a lot of waitin' this side of life. But while you're waiting, please whatever you do, don't give up. Hold on even when God is silent, you don't understand and it's a long wait for an answer or solution.

If I could bring John back, I would. But son, I'm sorry, I can't. The crazy thing about people wantin' to make a positive change in their lives and do right is while they're thinkin' on it and takin' their own sweet time to get to the mercy seat of the Lord, we gotta pray. We must be aware they need that prayer. We hope that God get to 'em before the devil do is all. That's all we can do. The choice is ultimately theirs. Get what I'm sayin' son? Know God loves you no matter what. O.K.? And He did love John. No matter how it looks. Here, take my number. Call me if you guys need anything, day or night. You will be ok....hear me son?"

Jay walked away broken, clutching the letter, he takes the man's phone number, "I don't know." Jay was in his senior year of high school, it was the best and the worst year of his life. He held on to Liza. He never wanted to let her go. He wanted the family he wished his family could've been. A dream he would never let go of.

Jay had remembered how he and Marisol would go to visit John whenever he couldn't make it over to see them. Central Park in the spring. Jay's heart was broken. John's untimely death caused the tension between him and his father to increase dramatically. After high school, Jay had decided not to ever step foot back into that house of horrors. He wanted Marisol to leave too, "Mami, what is it gonna take for you to leave this man! Huh? How much more can you take from this mother..."

Marisol interrupted yelling in a thick Spanish accent, "HEY! HEY! YOU WATCH THAT MOUTH OK! THAT IS STILL YOUR FATHER, MY HUSBAND AND THE MAN OF THIS HOUSE. CALLATE LA BOCA! YO NO QUIERO OIRLO DE NUEVO COMPRE ME ENTIENDES?!"

"Yeah aight." he replies. Jay didn't visit his mother much after he graduated high school. Marisol felt as if she had lost both of her sons. She never completely healed from learning of John's death. She mourned him until the day she died. Jay believed she died of a broken heart. He carried around unresolved guilt for neglecting her for so many years after he moved out. All of which he secretly blamed his father for. Issues he had not even discussed with Liza, his best friend. When he felt his relationship with Liza beginning to break, he had begun to have meaningless sex with endless women to ease the hurt. Everything he loved was all but gone it seemed. It was so hard for him to move forward. Liza and the girls were literally all he had. He and Liza had paid homage to Marisol, naming their girls Marisol, Maria and Marianna. His mother's first, middle and the name of her favorite sister; he and John's favorite aunt. Marisol had loved that. She loved even more that it was Liza's idea. She knew how much Jason loved Marisol. He loved Liza even more because of this. He was in love with Liza and his daughters. They all shared a tattoo on his chest titled: DEDICATED TO MY FAVORITE GIRLS. An old school R. Kelly song he used to dance to with Marisol every year on her birthday and his.

Liza had been celibate since their parting, though she had dated several men, Jay was her first and only and she was not willing to serve herself up like dessert after a decadent Sunday meal, as easily as other young women. She had been taught better. She had more self-respect than that. That was part of the reason Jay still loved her, he knew that. Their attraction was strong and she secretly invited his passionate kisses and warm breath in her ear every chance it was allowed. They came just shy of kissing each time they parted. Each time her ex-husband would faithfully watch her walk up the front steps to the door. Watching her hips sway, he swooned over her curves often calling her back for tight hugs and open mouth, corner-of-the-mouth kisses. He never went too far and in her mind too far would not be far enough when it came to him. He was the only man to ever touch her thus, her only point of reference. Liza was special to Jay as Jay would forever be special to Liza. She seemed to be a good girl by anyone's standards but, that did not mean she wasn't thirsty for more. Celibacy was all but driving her to the brink of insanity! She was well versed in scripture, but after a while, scriptures, cold showers and prayers weren't helping her much anymore. The routine of single motherhood, being the 'Good Girl' and lack of much else were drying her up quickly in all but one place.

After Jay and the kids pulled off, she'd close the door and slide down to the floor on the other side, out of breath and heated up she confessed, "Lord, oh Lord, I need something. Something more than what it is right now. Thankful for right now Lord, but I'm being honest about tomorrow...if it ever comes. Whew! He still does it for me. I'm sure he does it for me on purpose...Jesus!"

Liza was a catch in every way and so different from any other female Jason had ever met. It was often unbelievable to him as to how such a soft spoken, demure, seemingly pure creature could come from such a pill of a woman. That was a shrew he was sure no man could ever tame. A shrew he dared not tangled with at the urging of and out of the high respect he held for Liza. Connie had taken up most of the space in Liza's heart. The very space Jay had longed to be for years. He was willing to be #3 in her life, only to God and their daughters but, never for the likes of Connie Debril. Not this side of life. He believed the hold Connie had over Liza was nothing short of pure witchcraft. He would not be wrong. Jay knew more than a few things about the Bible and he knew very well that trying to control anybody or the outcome of anything by force or manipulation was outright witchcraft. And though God is in control of everything, God himself, is not one to force or impose His will on anyone without being invited. Maybe Connie was just doing what it was she knew. Either way, it wasn't right and lives were being deeply affected by it.

Driving away, peeking in the rear view every time, wishing she would run out of the door and call him back to the house and kiss his lips, he would savor the taste of the corner of her mouth all the way home. He saw her face in the faces of their children. They personified her beauty and mannerisms. He enjoyed being with them in part because it was like being with her and laughing all day like they did in high school. Jay was still smitten. He felt powerless to stop it when he was in her presence and with their daughters. A constant reminder of what once was. Remnants of what was not. He would lie awake all night looking at the moon, fantasizing about Liza; Wondering if she was doing the same. Just like a school boy.

She makes it to her bedroom finally. She shuts the door and locks it. As she sheds her plush cotton robe that surrounded her curvaceous body, she pours a luscious, fragrant, imported, expensive body cream Jay had purchased for her that past Christmas into the palm of her hand. As she passes it over her ample, ebony frame all she can think about is her ex-husband. "He used to do this for me every night." she thought. Passing over every curve insuring she didn't miss a single spot, as he would, she thought only of him. A knock on the door to bring her back to reality, "You on your way out?"

"Yeah ma. Don't wait up."

"Oh I won't. You go enjoy. Al comin' by tonight."

"Oh O.K. Tell him hi for me please. He's coming on a Friday? Not Sunday? That's different..." as she slides into her under satin garments.

"Yeah I know. Crazy huh?!" Connie squealed at a school girl's pitch.

"Yep!"

"Well, be careful love."

"You got it!" promises Liza as Connie retreats to her bedroom on the lower level of their home.

Liza paints on a strapless, lace, fuchsia mini-dress, accentuating every crevice and curve; Tweaking her Bordeaux butt-sweeper; Clicking her turquoise red bottoms, clutching her turquoise and gold leopard print, clutch purse, Liza is locked and loaded. "So tensed up man. Hmm! somebody might get it tonight. And that ain't even my style. I need somethin'. Lord help me to be on my A and make sober-minded decisions tonight. In Jesus' name, amen. Lord knows the spirit is willing but, the flesh is weak....Have mercy."

BABY I'M A STAR

She pulls up to the spot bumpin' 23, singing: "High off purp wit' some shades on...Ayyyyyeeeee".   She puts her Range Rover in park. She applies a thick layer of nude, shimmery gloss to complete her look. Bobbing her head to the music, she leaves her clutch beneath the passenger seat for safe keeping.

"...run up in here and get my stacks and bounce. Keesha better be ready and they better not ask me to stay! I ain't even playin.", she thinks to herself as she does a final fly check in the rear view. Gliding her tongue across her teeth, she steps out working her hips with attitude on her way to the entrance; serving up some Naomi Campbell. She was giving the passengers in the passing cars life. She flings the door open, on cue, a Kanye West verse blares from the speakers surrounding the DJ booth on the upper level as if Yeezus himself were paying homage to her curvaceous form live, up front and in person: SHE GOT A ASS THAT'LL SWALLOW UP A G-STRING. AND UP TOP, UNNHH...TWO BEE STINGS....

"Oooooo Weeee!" The DJ screams "The badest shorty in the Garden State just graced us with her presence y'all!" "Hey Wax!" she screams at the top of her lungs.

"Sup sexy."

"Watch that mouth Wax."

"Watch it go anywhere on your body you want me to, any time you like, day or night, whenever you ready!"

She shakes her head and rolls her eyes as she continues to walk to the back office.   She swings her hair as she sways her robust hips. Beyoncé commands, "Bow Down" in the background as every head turns. The other women burn with envy.

"J.R, where my stacks?"

"Ma, you know I always gotchu, you don't gotta role up on me in my place of business like that playin' gangsta. Don't play me."

"Yeah aight! I know YOU bruh! DON"T PLAY YASELF! I know how you get down man. You ain't nothin' but the second comin' of Stevie J. So miss me wit' dat slickery."

"Aye yo whateva man. Aye yo! I need a favor...."

Before he could finish she turns her back, "HELL NO! HELL NO! I AIN'T DOIN' IT! NO J.R...JUST NO ALRIGHT?! IT'S MY NIGHT OFF, ME AND KEESHA GOT PLANS. SO NO!"

"Awwww come on man. I need you Jazz. Please babe? It's a slow night for it to be a Friday. You my best and you know..."

"I know what?!"

"You know..." looking over his sun glasses.   "You know that ass bring the most cash. I can't even front bae. You the poppinest thing in this piece Jazzy. I need you tonight ma. Please? You gon' make a brother beg? Huh?"

"Alright man. Alright! But I want double my usual and the rest of the weekend off! No callin' me in! No more beggin' man."

"Yeah on the weekend. No on the beggin'. And the double, I'll think about it. Best I can do shorty."

"Oh you can do better. And you will."

"Is that a promise?"

"Oh it's a promise. You best believe!"

"I love me a confident woman. You got dat ma. Imma have ya paper when you done. I gotchu."

"Alright now."

I KNEW YOU WERE TROUBLE WHEN YOU WALKED IN

The lights go dim in the club as the DJ introduces the next act, "As I told y'all before, as if I needed further introduction, I'm DJ Wax, I'm what the game is missin' and I got a surprise fo' y'all tonight man. Yeah man! Makin' a rare Friday night appearance here at the Hole in One, also what the game is missin; For all of the chocoholics out there, hope you brought ya sweet tooth and ya appetite. Fellas is y'all ready? Never mind, man. Y'all ain't ready. Imma just shut it down." The crowd boos. "Aight y'all sure y'all ready?

"Ay yo! Didn't nobody come here to hear you talk dawg! Man just bring the bitches out damn! We wanna see some hoes!" a customer shouts.

"Then let's go! The one, the only, ain't no fun 'cause I ain't never gon' get none...Y'all heard of Juicy J? Well I got somethin' juicer for y'all... Juicy Jazz brothuz!"

She steps out on to the stage fixing her eyes on a target; "Oh wow! He's not a regular. Show time." she thinks to herself. The audience goes wild. Salivating, they search their pockets.

A shadowy figure emerges from the corner slowly. The new comer sits up. He takes particular interest. All that had come before had bored him. This was the final performance he was willing to sit through. "Why am I even here? I ain't got no business being here." he thought.

She begins to slowly undress. Her thong is the exact same color of her of her dusky flesh creating the illusion of full-frontal nudity. The sexual tension in the air is as thick as the African brush. Men claw and paw their way to the front of the stage. Her bare breasts gently bounce as she pops and winds, teasing the men with every move. She sends the crowd into a testosterone driven, primitive frenzy. "Pour It Out" is playing. Her long hair softly caresses her buttocks. It clings to her damp brown skin as she climbs the pole barely escaping the clutches of the thirsty, flesh hungry souls just yearning for a touch of her sweat. They swipe at her dewy, melanoid skin. She drives the crowd and the DJ wild with her acrobatics. She slides down the pole upside down continuing to lock eyes with her target. Reaching the floor, she rides the hardwood as if she was riding his. He is the most attractive man in the room. Her guest is undeniable. The magnet of attraction becomes stronger than her drive to perform for the masses. As they continue to delight in their sexual ocular tryst, Rihanna sings, "Still got my money." Inspired, she walks over to the mysterious male in the corner with two fists full of money. The other men showered her with cash like she was a Greek Goddess. She in turn, showers him with that money, nothing less than $50 dollar bills. The regs, were only used to seeing her on her usual working nights; they knew she wouldn't stand for less. Jazz was worth every penny of their children's child support money; Juicy Jazz made it rain all over her mystery man as he sat and played aloof allowing single ringlets of blunt smoke to cascade from his lips. They were both in rare form.

He presented himself as if unamused, vowing to keep his composure and play down his angst as she drew even closer. But secretly he was as aroused as a teenage boy watching a rated R sex scene in a movie without parental supervision for the first time. And just the same, he was taken aback by her boldness and her beauty.

As their eyes remained locked and their hearts raced, she approached in with a sensual gentility. "Hot Sugar" played in the background. Jazzy gave him a decadent, lavish lap dance in front of all of the other suitors of the evening. Making them pant with envy, their pride and jealousy had forced them to shower her with even more of their hard earned dividends in efforts to gain her attention. But, it was all to no avail. For, she was just as intent on securing his company for the remainder of the night as he was hers.

They were locked and loaded. She thrusted hard and convincingly as if to get him to see how desperate she was to have his company that night; something she had never done before. She was out of control. This wasn't even her thing. But, she liked it. She liked knowing he liked it. He liked knowing how much he knew she liked it; it was a physically binding, non-verbal agreement between to ships that should have only passed in the night. But, this woman, this man, these two were all in. They were in so deep, it was as if no one else was there with them.

He held her waist. The stranger had begun to control her pelvic thrusts to the tempo of his choice. Onlookers became bored and moved on the next act as she continued her sleazy lap dance to his egotistical delight. As his eyes burned through to her soul, she remained visually entranced by the dark stranger. He positioned himself accordingly as she gripped the crisp collar of his Gucci shirt. They both began to escalate to the height of ecstasy. Without warning, removes her from his lap.   She whispers in his ear, "What's wrong?"

He kisses her on the cheek, "I prefer not to indulge in my fantasies in plain view of a live audience. Do you watch porn in front of people?"

Appalled she replies, covering her bare breasts, "I don't watch pornography at all I'll have you know. Didn't anyone ever teach you not to judge a book by its cover? Huh?! How rude."

He teased, "...Can't tell by the way you ride. You got skills. You learned that from somewhere."

"Excuse me?" she chimes alarmed at his arrogance.

"I'm just playin witchu ma. I ain't here to judge. Psshhh...Ma, I'm here right witchu. How Imma judge you? I was joking. Apology?"

She was confused, emotional and aroused, "Yes. I do...I mean I WILL accept your apology. Sorry. I'm cautious of the phrase "I DO". But yes. I accept."   She knew right then, something was different about this mysterious stranger. But she put it to the back of her mind. Tonight her reasoning and curiosity would take a back seat to the flesh in the driver's seat.

"So what's ya real name? I can't bear to even repeat that stage name. Girl...that is so wack." It was as downright amateur and corny as could be. He knew something was off about her even being there if she couldn't even choose a better name than she had. Nonetheless, he found her sexy and irresistible. He was turned on. High, just from the fumes of the lust in the room. Her name didn't matter much, her skills did. He continued, "And please don't say 'Jazzy', because I know and you know, that's hot garbage. So come on wit' it."

"Alright. O.K., you got me...You want my name? Here it is...It's Jazz! Ha! Ha! Gotchu! I don't give out my name that easy baby boy. Whatchu a Jake?!"

"No. I ain't no Jake. And I see you got jokes. Corny ones, but you got 'em...I hear you ma. But guess what?"

"What?"

"Just because I ain't one of the boys, don't mean you can't put ya hands up like you under arrest and all dat..."

The beauty releases her breasts and puts her hands up. He looks at her, "Let's go get you up outta them wet clothes." Referring to her soaked thong.

She runs back up on stage to cheers. Wax plays: "APPLAUSE" while she collects her clothing, her money and heads backstage. The man of the hour walks out of the door.

"Ladies and gents, we interrupt this regularly scheduled program to bring you this brief P.S.A: My future wife has now left the building! The most beautiful woman in the world to me. What she doin' up in this funk box? I don't know. But she make my day every time I see her smile. We now return you to your regularly scheduled programing already in progress." She runs up to the booth and gives him a kiss on the cheek.

Concerned he says, "You know you better than this don't you? I will never understand for the life of me, why somebody like you is up in a place like this. Don't get it man... why is it the most beautiful girls have the lowest self-esteem? That is crazy! And what is goin' on with you tonight girl? What was that all on the homey just now? That ain't you ma. Things good at the house? You aight? Somethin you need to talk about"

"Yeah, I'm goin' thru a lil' somethin', but I can't talk now. Gotta get my money from J.R slick ass. Imma get back to you though. Love you Wax! And thank you k? Oh, and if you see Keesha tell her somethin' came up and Imma call her. You're a great guy. Like the big brother I never had."

"Love you too!" he yells "And Imma hold you to that talk!". He mumbles, "Yeah somethin' came up alright… Been tryin' to get at you for the longest. But this black ass joker come up in here one night for a couple of hours and you just walk over there and ride him like the Path Train. It's all good though. Big brother my ass. Hoes."

He sits on the edge of her Queen-sized bed rubbing his eyes for it is now the wee hours of the morning yet the dawn has not approached. She returns to the bedroom draped in a satin robe that is clinging to the shower mist still dripping from her body. She removes the robe, her back turned to him. He can see the very outline of her statuesque frame. Once again, he is revived. She proceeds to remove the butt-sweeper from her head only to reveal a lush mane of natural, jet black, loose coils.

"Man. Is that your natural hair?" He asks.

 "Yes it is. Is that ok with you?"

"Yes it is.", He's watching her every move. "It's black and beautiful just like you. I don't understand why more of you beautiful black women don't rock your natural hair. Confidence and natural beauty is so sexy man. Y'all don't know."

 "Is that the truth?"

 "Woman it's the gospel! Listen, any man that can look at a sister and not accept her, flaws and all in her natural state has a problem with himself. Y'all allow men to put too much of the pressure on y'all. It's all game man. Pssshh man...These jokers been fooled by the media and the beauty industry, just like you women, into thinking processed anything is everything. I know its all choice, but at the same time, gotta admit.... its all garbage and big business. Your self-worth gets lower, so your hair gets longer and straighter and their pockets get fatter. They know this. I don't get it. Man, I just don't get it."

"Preach!"

"Yeah man! Think about it. We are not of European decent, yet we use European standards as the gauge on which we measure how beautiful we are. Men and women. It's tragic. Nothing against Euro, but Afro, needs to get it together. We can keep more money in our own community if we just think and begin to do the small things differently. Black women are so beautiful man. But when they gon' just sit up and take notice themselves? I mean really. Before the days of hot combs and lye-based relaxers, wigs and weaves that eat away at your hairline, y'all was rockin' fros and braids right? I mean think about it..."

"True story."

"Black men wasn't bothered by that because it was natural and we were just as natural and just as kinky, coily and nappy. So what I wanna know is why on Earth did y'all change? Who put the pressure on that made y'all start destroying y'all hair with chemicals and heat? I just wish y'all ain't spend so much money covering it up and manipulating it. Y'all know eventually y'all gonna have to get naked in front of some man, be it a doctor, ya husband or ya stylist or beautician...so why y'all carry on so wit dat mess? Don't y'all know we know most of the time that those eye lashes ain't really that luscious or that that hair ain't yours? Those claws y'all call nails ain't real? Y'all look good but at what cost? Lay down with Janet Jackson, wake up with Freddie Jackson. Ever heard that? Or something like that... Jeeez man! I have been through that so many times ma. Girl, you don't even know."

"Ummm....you done Pastor? Is this the part where the church says amen? Benediction maybe? Oh I got it...here it go...Doors of the church are now open."

"Pastor?! Mad jokes huh?"

She plays with her curly locks, admiring her own reflection in the mirror. He examines her body, inch by inch. Noticing the outer curve of her breasts by moonlight. The dew on her body shimmered."

She glances back at him and smiles. She turns her head to gaze at herself once again in the mirror, she knows she's beautiful, he knows that she knows she is and it turns him on.

A bead of moisture glides down the deep arch of her mahogany back. It reaches the end of her spine. He's tracking it's every move with his eyes. He stops it with his thumb. She pauses at his touch. Her body freezes and she exhales. He kisses her softly on the small of her back drinking in the moisture that rushed down her back like a water fall in the Amazon; all of the way up to the tender nape of her neck. She digs her fingers into her thick afro, pulling gently as the heat from his breath sends chills through her body.

"Do you like what I'm doin' to you?"

In a feminine sigh of burgeoning hedonism, she whispers, "Yes."

He towers over her. He opens his eyes to look at her reflection in the mirror, cupping her breasts as he massages her nipples with his huge, masculine forefingers, he whispers to her, "Open your eyes for me." She watched him touch her softly. He spoke such unspeakable things into her ear. Things that made the walls sweat. Things that made the moon blush. Words that made the covers want to pull other covers over themselves. Even the air conditioner needed to be cooled off.

"Please stop." she begged.

"Oh you want me to stop? Really? If you want me to stop...Stop me."

Overwhelmed by his own bravado and overtaken by his libido, given in to his ego, he spins her around forcefully and lifts her atop of the bureau as he gently bites her bottom lip. Slowly, he makes his way down to the cul-de-sac between her thighs. She leans back against the mirror and he pulls her thighs forward as she parts them like the Red Sea. The flood gates open as he teases her inner thighs with his lips. His host is panting like a dog in heat, "Oh God..."

He pauses for a moment to remove his shirt. He's about to go to work the way grown men do. He wasn't planning on stopping until the job had been completed, as grown men don't. He prided himself with a certain amount of integrity. He had planned to earn his keep. He ran his hand smoothly, yet firmly up her thigh; His grip is strong. She welcomed the intertwining of the masculine and feminine energy in the room as the moonlight continued to spy on them. This was grown folk business and these grown folks were about to get busy.

Touching her skin made his manhood throb uncontrollably. He ached with desire to feel the warmth and the great wealth of fluidity and stickiness that await on the inside of her. He could not wait to devour her.

He reaches his destination. As he proceeds to untie the lace bow of her pure white panties on the side of her round hip, he commands her to look at him, "Watch me!"

She opens her eyes and looks down. He kisses the crease in between her inner-upper thigh and her vagina and he can feel the heat and the moisture that is the result of his tasting and teasing. She watches as he licks his lips and looks into her eyes, her heart is beating rapidly, her breasts are heaving. He pushes her knees back and peels back the crotch of her panties to reveal the prize. Firm, juicy and ready to be taken as a summer fresh summer fruit on a tree ripe for the plucking.

Excited, his upper body muscles tense up as the muscles in her lower extremities relax. He pauses right before he goes in for the first bite of the tree ripened fruit, "You are so beautiful and you smell so good. Oh my goodness...you are my fantasy." Breathing deeply, excited he opens his mouth. He approaches the threshold, like a lion going in for the kill. His cell phone rings, playing: "Someone Watchin' Over You".

"Damn it! Excuse me, I gotta take this." Her legs collapse. He falls to the edge of the bed. Exasperated from the passion of the night, he answers angrily, "HELLO!"

On the other end, "Whatchu doin'?"

In that moment, reality sets in. The fantasy is over. Frustrated but relieved, she lowers herself from the dresser top and makes her way back to the bathroom to shower. In her mind, she knows she has just dodged a bullet. That is not even who she is. He too, relieved yet, frustrated at the interruption ends his conversation and falls back on to the bed, "Thank you Jesus. I think I've lost my mind. God help me. Women man...Lawd Ha' Mercy!"

Jazz returns from the bathroom smelling like Raspberry Cream Sensations and strawberry body mist. Sunlight begins to intrude on their morning. He's lying on his back at the head of the bed with his fitted over his eyes. She disrobes as the sun's rays make every curve on her body come to life. He briefly lifts his cap as the scent of her body catches his attention. Crawling over towards him slowly with an innocent smile she asks, "Wanna oil me up?" The sexual tension is still so very thick.   He sits up as she lies down on her stomach and proceeds to massage her body with baby oil. She's flawless, dark; her skin is rich like devil's food cake and he's still hungry but he denies himself.

     "Turn over and move up.", he commands. She rolls over seductively and they both breathe deeply as he begins to massage the front of her body.

     "Let's stop...Let's just stop before it gets realer than it's supposed to get up in here. Damn ma I haven't been with a woman in a long time. I'm being honest when I tell you that I'm tired of pretending it ain't killin' me. I need some so bad but I made a vow I gotta keep. It's killin' me man...I'm so backed up. Feel like I'm doin' a life sentence in Trenton man...Damn. You probably don't know what I mean. You got cats grabbin' at you all night and when you go out in the day time, I just know you ain't at least halfway down the block, ridin' or walkin' wit' out jokers trippin' over themselves to get at you. Y'all chicks got it so easy. All the work is on us. Especially natural beauties like you. Look at you man. Jesus! God must be some kinda wonderful if He created women in his own image. Lawd girl!"

"You celibate?"

"You shocked?"

"Hell yeah I'm shocked! Look at me?!" she licks her lips and kisses him on the chest softly.   "Sexy look at you! C'mon, I know you got ya choice of who's who anywhere you be at so don't play me! What you think got me over there to you back at the spot in the first place? Boy! I don't just be wildin' like that on everybody......On nobody basically truth be told. Talkin' bout backed up. Jack, I ain't been with a man in years. Not since my split. I may dance like a pro. But a pro I'm not. Don't get it twisted soldier. I don't pay these jokers out here or in there no mind. I'm savin' myself for marriage and real love."

"Yeah," he says. "Spirit is willin' but the flesh is weak."

"Exactly. What you saw me do on stage, I don't even need to do. I'm not even sure why I do it. All I know is that when I'm doin' it, I feel like I'm the one in control. Its fantasy for me and it makes me feel free. I feel alive. I feel open. No pretense. No pressure. Sometimes real life can add so much pressure to the stress you got just existin'. People see me as the 'Good Girl'... But that I ain't. I'm human and I have flaws and desires like everybody else. So much pressure. Just trying to live in a pretend bubble of perfection so I don't let nobody down. She looks over at him, "I'm babblin' now. Pardon me. It just feels good to let it out and get a release."

"It's cool. Talkin bout some pressure? I know about pressure, break down, fear of let down and being as flawed as the next guy. People refusing to let you just be human, just a man and mess up from time to time. Believe when I say I know EXACTLY what you talkin' bout. Sometimes you think you the only one goin' thru. Then I run into somebody as beautiful as yourself, and I mean inside and out, and we're going through the same thing. That's crazy. God works in mysterious ways, I guess. Maybe I shouldn't put God in this." he laughs.

"By the way… like you never gave me your name and what exactly is it that you do?"

"People closest to me call me Boom and I'm a lawyer." he says confidently.

"They call you...they call you?" she laughs. "Shorty I ain't ask you what they call you...I said SHAWTY WHAT YO NAME IS?!" They both laugh hysterically.

"I'll give you my name JAZZY, when you give me yours. Aight SHAWTY?!"

"Aight SHORTY!"

"But seriously though, why do they call you Boom? Boom…" The name sounded familiar. "And where you from BOOM?"

"I'm from around O.K. Miss? And why they call me Boom?", laughing he continues as he eases back down to the bed and pulls her close. She lays her head on his chest, "That's somethin' you was about to find out before I got that phone call...Trust! Dat ass got saved by the bell."

"Whatever man... Oh my goodness!" she whispers then sings, "He got a big ego...such a huge ego...but I love his big ego. It's too much..."

"I talk like this 'cause I can back it up! Ahhhhhhhhhh....Like that don't you?!" He kisses her softly, "Now, let's get some sleep babe. Thank God it's Saturday."

"Yessir! Boom...what kinda lawyer allows himself to be called Boom?"

"Oh my goodness! Lay off the name lady please! You fine but you sure can talk! Jesus! Can we get some sleep woman?" he says, fitted over his eyes.

She whispers, "Maybe I should cover up?"

"No. You shouldn't. I need you right here. Right now, just like this. I'm a man. Don't move. Just breathe and relax. Last thing on my mind is disrespecting you. I wouldn't dare."

Resting on his chest, listening to him breath while he falls asleep was something she was missing. His hard muscular body felt like she had fallen softly on to a brick wall. It was nice. He was the Man of Steel. It felt so good, she shed a tear. She kissed his dark brown chest as they lay. She loved how his skin tone matched hers perfectly. As if God had used the same batter to bake up two chocolate cakes.

As he drifted off to another place, he gently caressed her waist. She lie locked in his embrace naked, feminine, soft and secure. In that moment, it was all so pure. It was all so necessary. It was all they wanted. It was all they needed. Cell phones vibrated throughout the morning but nobody moved to answer a call. For between the two, all was right with the world. They were in heaven so it seemed. They dreamed of what might had been if the phone had never rang. In between dreams; they kissed deep and passionately. She rubbed his bare chest and concrete abs as he rubbed her bare hips and buttocks. They fell in and out of sleep all day until the wee hours of the next night. They were strangers. But, in their dreams, they were the only two people on Earth. In their dreams, they were in love and nothing mattered. No pressure; Flaws and all. For what is was worth. They were living out their fantasies. But reality was surely about to set in.

SWEET DREAM OR A BEAUTIFUL NIGHTMARE

The summer between the two young lovers would be sexless but, sensual nonetheless.

The nights she danced on stage, they would lock eyes as if she was dancing to his personal delight as the daughter of the wife of Herod. In the same fashion, he would deny her nothing for she was pleasing his senses. She was an untouchable fantasy. Many nights, like Samson, he would spend his time falling asleep in her lap to the sound of her soothing feminine voice; to the touch her soft, small hands; to the smell of her perfumed body.

The affair was private, which made it all the more exciting; there was no pressure; all pleasure. It was between the two of them. They were all that mattered. It was what they both needed. The break in the monotony of life they had been seeking.

One sticky summer night as he was preparing to leave, Jazzy had emerged from the shower, ready to be moisturized. He shook his head as he routinely watched her from the edge of the bed, "Girl, do you know how fine you are? Let me get that for you..."

Laughing she replies, "Yeah...please...get that for me. Oh my goodness babe...Who's gonna do this for me when summer ends? It's almost time babe. It's already August."

"Who said it had to end?" he kisses her.

"Ok. Ok. You gotta go. You know how we get." she pushes him away gently. They walk to the bedroom door. At the threshold, he kisses her again, passionately.

"I don't wanna go. Can I stay here and just hold you?

"Boy stop playin", she begs him.

"I'm not playin' ma....Please?"

"You are crazy. You know that?"

Just then, a dime bag falls from his pocket.

"What's that?"

"It's nothin'. Bad habit I been ridin' around with all summer on the just in case..."

"Just in case what?"

"Nothing to concern yourself with beautiful. Old habit. I just get tempted sometimes when I'm stressed that's all. It's just somethin' familiar from an easier time in my life. I apologize. I hope it doesn't make you look at me any differently."

"Why would I? I know plenty of professionals that get down with harder stuff. I just prefer it not to be in my house or around me. Ok?"

"You got it ma. See...that's why I..." he bends down to pick up the weed. Her eyes and her heart lit up like the Christmas tree in Rockefeller Center.

"That's why you what?"

At the bottom of the staircase, two voices burst into laughter. "I...I gotta go. Get some rest. I will call you later." he kisses her on the cheek.

"Oh...ok." She didn't know what to think.

As they walk down the stairs, "I know that voice", he thinks to himself.   They approach the bottom of the staircase, he kisses her softly, as he stares into her eyes, "I lo..."   Before he can finish his declaration, they're interrupted by another couple walking, giggling and holding hands like school children coming down the hall.

She's distracted by the noise. She reluctantly looks past him. Swiftly she closes her robe, "Mother?!"

He turns around, "What do you mean mother? What the....Dad?!!!!!! What are you doing...Dad?"

"Barker?" his father.

"Liza?!" her mother.

"Ms. Nene?!" yells Barker.

"Mr. Al?!" cries Liza.

Barker and Liza face one another, "Your name is..."

"Your father is..."

"This is your mother? The sweet, loving mother you've been talking about all of this time? Really?! Dad, how could you? You're a Pastor! You're my mother's husband. You're my father! HOW COULD YOU?! WHAT THE HELL ARE YOU DOING HERE?!"

"I could ask the same of you PASTOR! Whatchu doin' here with this sweet child at this ungodly hour? Liza, you alright?" he puts his arm around her shoulder.

"GET YOUR HANDS OFF OF ME! A PASTOR?! A DAMN PASTOR?! YOU A DAMN PASTOR?! WHO GON' BUST HELL WIDE OPEN MORE, ME OR YOU?! A FRIGGIN' PASTOR?! GREAT! YOU.....YOU....Y'ALL ALL A BUNCH OF HYPOCRITES AND LIARS! BARKER?! FROM WEEQUAHIC HIGH SCHOOL? NOW I REMEMBER YOU! BARKER GOLDEN, MR. QB. GOLDEN BOY. OH MY GOODNESS. WHAT KIND OF PEOPLE ARE YOU? NOBODY WOULD BEIEVE THIS MESS! HELL, I CAN'T EVEN BELIEVE THIS HERE. BARKER YOU MEAN TO TELL ME..."

In the midst of Liza's fury, Connie urges her to calm down.

"YOU SHUT UP!" yells Liza. Connie is stunned to even hear her child speak in such a rude tone. "You been creepin' around with this cat for years! YEARS! And this bastard is a Pastor!!!! YOU JUST SHUT THE HELL UP! YOU...YOU PROMISED ME NO SECRETS. NO LIES. YOU COULDN'T EVEN KEEP YOUR WORD! WHO ARE YOU ANYWAY? ARE YOU EVEN WHO YOU SAY YOU ARE? JUST WHO THE HELL ARE ANY OF YOU?"

"Brava. Brava. And the Academy Award goes to...Oh, yeah, yeah, that's good Miss 'Juicy Jazz' from the Hole in One...that's rich. Where you even concoct that stupid name from anyway? Whack!"
He continued, "Got a brother all wrapped up. Your mother is a whore! You live in a brothel! Yeah, and now I remember you from Weequahic. The sweet, little innocent, good girl; Untouched, stuck up, wouldn't give it up. All pure and shit. My, how things have changed. Talkin' about livin' a double life. You're a double agent yourself, so who you judgin' stripper?"

"You know why I do what I do....so SHUT UP!"

"Barker, baby, don't be so hard on her ok? Be nice to her now. She don't mean..." Connie begs.

Barker beat his chest angrily, "IS THIS DIRTY WHORE TALKING TO ME?! YOU DON'T HAVE THE RIGHT TO EVEN SPEAK MY NAME!"

Liza slaps him, whispering softly as she points in his face with tears in her eyes, "Whatever she is or she IS NOT, is none of your affair for one. For two, this is not a whore house and you gonna find yourself in THIS house right NOW. For three, who do you think you are? Where is the L-O-V-E, PASTOR? And finally, counselor, my mother has all the rights in the world to talk to you especially while you are standing in HER HOUSE! The house she paid for. No matter how it got paid for, it's hers. Welcome to the American way. She hustled to get everything she has. No welfare. No begging. No 9 to 5. She ran her own business. She made her own business hours. And yeah, now I remember yo ass too! And from what I hear, she ain't the only one well versed in the world's oldest profession."

"What you mean girl?" He turned to Al, "What she is she talking about?"

"Furthermore, for whatever she WAS. And whatever she DOESN'T HAVE, the one thing she ain't lacking' is your father you ass! Peep game partner...She got him wrapped around her little whorish finger and ain't a thing you can do about it. Once again, from what I remember, this ain't first time around the block." She turned to Al, Ain't that right PASTOR? Back down memory lane is it?"

Al and Barker stared at one another while Connie covered her mouth.

"Damn Church folk. So judgmental and self-righteous. Fake no moral havin' asses. At least everybody else out here ridin' hard with sin in hand, not in pocket like the likes of y'all. Y'all don't care about nobody. Everything, all y'all sin, sick secrets kept nice and safe behind those church doors. Y'all got people out here thinkin' y'all got up leg up on righteousness. But that ain't it. Nah, what it is, y'all got other people's legs up." They stared at her in amazement.

"Y'all need to come out the closet. Come from behind those church doors and be real. Tell the truth about how imperfect y'all are. Maybe then people would wanna get down with Jesus. Y'all turn people off! Y'all make Jesus look unattainable. Y'all make church look like a hustle. No different than the people who give away stuff to the poor and needy for all eyes to see at fancy events for the tax right off they think we don't know about. What's the difference between the Pastor, Pimp, Priest, Pusher and the Politician? Huh?"

"Liza, I know you're angry. It's all gonna be ok. Let's just all calm down, take a deep breath, regroup…"

She blasted, "They all into outreach. The difference is the hustle. They all got the gift of gab. Just a different hustle. Five degrees of separation jack."

"Liza. They just men baby. They human. These are men of God. Don't disrespect…" Connie pleaded.

"Hmm. Outreach." She laughed, "When it comes to what's really goin' on out here with the people y'all supposed to be reaching out to, y'all always hidin' behind them church doors. The last to know everything and when you find out, it's too late and y'all can't help nobody because ya so scared to come out here with the real folk like Jesus did. You just stay behind ya iron curtain and judge the world, the music, the people with misinformation and little compassion. I really don't believe Jesus was like that. So old school and religious. Y'all so slow on the draw and always the last to know everything. So sanctified. So righteous. So Holy. So full of crap. Like y'all so different. Out here doin' the most. Same stuff you preach against, you indulge in. Yep! That's Jesus way alright. In God we wanna trust. It's hard when we're out here trying to figure out how God trust y'all with His word and the hearts of the people so much. Especially when He know y'all ain't shi…"

"Lyza!" Connie yells.

"Let her have her say Connie. It's ok. Let has the right to air her grievances. It's cool."

"Why y'all keep them doors closed anyway? So we can't get in? Or so y'all religious folk can't get out? Which one Pastor? My mother, may have been the neighborhood whore but your 'Holier than thou' father been runnin' over here to her for as long as I can remember "RIGHT AFTER SERVICE! So where's his judgment? Huh, Pastor? Where's yours for livin' at the strip club stalkin' me all Summer long, huh? Remember, this is the whore house that you was just beggin' me to let you stay in with my strippin' ass? Ain't that some bull…. Lord have mercy. Well, doors of the church are now open. Y'all get the hell out my momma house."

"Liza, I'm sorry I…"

"Did you not hear me? Get the hell out!"

Connie grabbed her daughter's hand, "Thank you for standing up for me."

"Don't thank me. I didn't do a damn thing for you. I did it for me. For the first time in my life, I stood up for me. You mother, you can go straight to hell."

"Liza. Liza! How can you talk to me that way? The Bible says honor your mother and father that thy days may be long..."

"Mother please, ok. Don't try to manipulate me with the word. Was you quotin' scriptures while you was in the backroom makin' it happen with 'The Pastor'? Miss me with that bull..."

"Now wait just a damn minute here!" Connie slaps Liza's face and grabs her chin,   "You don't know what you are talking about child and you will NOT disrespect me!"

Liza slaps Connie, "Get your filthy hands off of me! Don't you ever touch me like that again! Do you understand ME? If you do, believe me like you believe in Christ himself, you will live to regret it. And as far as respect goes, it's a little too late for that, don't ya think? I know if God can forgive the lot of you people, surely he will forgive me. Now like I said, MOTHER, go straight to hell and good night!" She slams her bedroom door at the top of the staircase. Connie falls to her knees. She holds her face in her hands. She cries, "Oh God...what have I done?"

Al Golden and his son, leave with their tails tucked in between they're legs.   "Son. I know I haven't been as honest as I should've been."

"Dad."

"Yes son?"

   "I wish you were not my father. If God don't make mistakes, then why is my mother dead and you still here? How can you do what you do and sleep at night? What kind of God do we serve? Who are you anymore?"

FOOLISH

He uses the spare key she usually leaves under the plant on the side of the house. He walks back to the kitchen. There's music playing from the second floor. He opens the refrigerator out of breath, exhausted. He's hungry and thirsty but there's nothing there that will satisfy him. "Where are you?" he yells through house. She's upstairs in her bedroom, lying across her bed sobbing as she rifles through old photos and reminisces over what once was. She can't help herself. She's aware of his presence. She could feel him from the time he entered the house. She never heard him call out to her. She could just smell his natural scent in the air. His bravado excited her. She lie across the bed in shambles and refused to look back at him, when he asked, "What are you in here doing?" It was the Midnight Magic hour on the local station. Keyshia Cole sang, "I Remember." Love songs for the next six hours.

He scanned her carcass. She was topless. He mourned, secretly reflecting on how plump and satisfying she used to be. A red bone with lengthy, light brown hair, grey eyes. She used to be so beautiful. So irresistible. She was every guy's fantasy in high school. She, had taken his virginity and many others but, he got caught up. He fell in love with her. She gave him a child. She would always be special to him but, at that point he wasn't about to tell her that. That would only add to her brokenness, he knew that.

As the song comes to an end she wipes her eyes. She turns over and leans back on her elbows, "What are you doing here man? Haven't you made my life miserable enough?" He hears her yet, he's not even listening to her. He pulls his t-shirt over his head revealing the brick wall. As he walks on the side of the bed towards her, she can see his nature rising through his jeans. He ogles her small breasts. He begins to softly caress her breasts as she breathes deeply with tears flowing from her eyes. "What do you want?" she asks.

"I want you."

The blood courses through him. He inspects her body. Dominant and authoritative, he gently pulls her hair back. She parts her legs to invite him inside. Her panties, grey, worn, ragged with a small, jagged hole in the front. Unphased, he forges ahead. He licks his fingers, true to form like a quarterback in the pocket on Sunday afternoon. He slowly forces them through the hole, past her hairs as deeply as he can, into her body. She squeals and moans as she lies down on the bed. She is ready to receive him. She's flowing like a stream. Adam's ale is refreshing. He's ready to dive in. He pulls his fingers out and caresses her southern region to ensure she is prepared for the launch of his missile. Firmly assured, locked, loaded and ready, He rips her ratty, old panties off aggressively, to her delight as she parts her knees even further. She sits up. He pulls a condom from his pocket. She holds it as she looks into his eyes and he slips into it like he had into her so many times before when they were younger. He maintains eye contact as she strokes his ego and his manhood. He pushes her back down to the bed, she arches her back as she holds tightly to his. He dives deep into her and swims for his life.

He's stroking in and out, sweating with each heartbeat. He moves to a rhythm like she had never experienced before. He holds her waist as his face sinks down deep into the pillow beneath her head. His thrusts become more and more intense as he exhales. She opens her eyes. She knows from the way he is moving, from his less than passionate embrace and disposition, he is not even present in the moment. He is making love to another woman. She can't help but moan as he pushes himself even deeper inside of her. It feels so good to her but it feels so wrong all at once. She whispers as he works, "Do you love me?"

He whispers, "Yeah."

"Tell me."

"I love you."

She bursts into tears quietly. Holding him tightly, she knew at the point, she had really lost him. Devastated. After all of these years, it was finally over. He moans with severe masculinity and kisses her neck as he thinks of the woman he really wants to be with. "I'm in love with you." he whispers to her. Thinking of her with every stroke.

Concurrently, his fantasy lie in bed, on the other side of the city. Nude, wanton. On the phone with the her ex, talking slick in her ear; fantasizing about him. They explode in passion like fire hydrants at the height of summer at a block party. Leaving the other parties to wonder why they are not calling out their names and of whom were they thinking.

They both reach ecstasy separately but with equal intensity. Their partners baffled and grief stricken. An ex-husband with broken pride. An ex-girlfriend with a broken heart. Liza and Barker eject from their fantasy, fulfilled yet, more empty than before both with broken dreams and spirits.

"This sneaky, disrespectful son-of-a...", Stacey is cooking breakfast as Boom arrives in the kitchen the next morning.

"Mornin'.", he mumbles. "How'd you sleep?"

"How did I sleep? How did I sleep? You barely looked at me. You didn't even kiss me! Like I'm some common street booty you tryin' to patronize....DON'T PATRONIZE ME BOOM! WHO IS SHE?" she yells.

"Why are you yelling woman and who is who? C'mon man...Jesus Christ! It's too early for this." he leaves the kitchen and walks back up stairs.

She followed him brandishing a spatula, "The chick you were making love to last night? Because you sure wasn't makin' love to me! You used me Boom." She cried, "You used me and I let you. I never thought you would do me like everybody else. This is my worst nightmare. I set you apart from other guys in my mind. But, you...Boom, you just like them. You just like everybody else. If you so in love with this girl Boom, why you come here to me, huh? Huh?! Why you come over here and get me in my feelins? Why you got me caught up in ya mess man?"

She lit a cigarette, "I saw you with that uppity chick Boom. I saw y'all. Uh huh. Mr. Lover. I saw y'all together plenty of times. I know her too. Her name is Liza. I remember her from school. She was 'Miss Goody Two Shoes'. Wouldn't give nobody the time of day. Wouldn't give nobody nothin'. How you gon' be that stuck up with a hooker as a mother? Both of y'all! She ain't no better than anybody else Barker! And neither are you!"

"Both of us?! Both of us?! Stacey! See that's what I mean. That mouth! See you talkin' about my mother again! What man on Earth is gonna put up with that mouth?! And what did I tell you about disrespectin' my mother? What do you have against my mother?! Keep her out of your mouth!!!!" He punched the wall in frustration.

"Both of y'all? What is that supposed to mean anyway? Girl are you crazy? My mother was a saint! You go too far Stacey. Do you even know when to stop?! That's enough now! Goodness girl! She ain't no better than nobody else...How about she ain't tryin' to be! She doin' her. Hate is bad for your health girl. You really need to see somebody about that. I feel so sorry for you. Stop knockin' the next woman down. She ain't the same person and you don't know a thing about her, so please. Just get off her."

"Oh so I see, that wasn't just the heat of passion last night. You caught up. You in love with this Liza girl huh? So why you cheatin' on her with me? Why you here playin' pool in my panties?"

"Do you hear yourself? Don't you ever want to pretend to be a lady at some point? Ratchet mouth."

"WELL, DO YOU LOVE HER FOR REAL? AND I'MMA ASK YOU ONE MO' TIME: WHY YOU HERE?!"

"I DON'T KNOW ALRIGHT! AND I'M NOT CHEATIN' OK! WISHFUL THINKIN ON YOUR PART! WE ARE NOT A COUPLE. NOT YET IF YOU MUST KNOW!!!! I'M LOOKIN' FOR ANSWERS. THINGS ARE CRAZY RIGHT NOW. I GOT TOO MUCH GOIN' ON. IT'S COMPLICATED. OK!"

She mumbled to herself, "He done changed. He's really one of those guys. He used me."

"Who you talkin' to over there? Jesus! Look Stace, I'm sorry for last night. I was wrong. I can't say no more than that right now. We'll talk later. I'm sorry. You wouldn't even begin to understand."   As he looks around her shattered and torn bedroom, he pulls her up from the floor and holds her, "Why you keep it so dark in here? Man, we both need to get it together. This ain't right. G can't have two messed up parents." She sobbed heavily.

"Let's make a deal, you go somewhere and get clean, I'll fund it. I'll go deal with my mess. Later we get together when we're both level headed and have clear minds and talk it out. Deal?"

"Ok. But you really in love with her?"

"I don't know what I am right now to tell you the truth Stacey. When I figure it out. We'll talk. I promise."

"Barker I wish I wasn't, but I'm still in love with you."

"Stacey, I know you think you are right now, and you'll figure out what I'm talking about when you go get the help you need. But do me a favor, while you're there, try being in love with yourself. Right now, nothing else matters. And your son needs you. Every boy needs his mother. Call me when you're ready to go."

He walked down the stairs. He turned back to look at her, "Nothing I do is ever to hurt you. You gon' be alright. I promise. Everything gon' be alright."

"How you know? I'm not so sure Boom." She leaned on the post of the door broken and betrayed.

"Babe, you gotta get sure. You'll get sure when you get help. Believe me." He slammed the car door, "I gotta go. I never meant to hurt you. I I care about you Stacey, believe it or not. I am so sorry I hurt you."

Speeding to the light, guilt ridden and confused, he says to himself, "What kind of idiot are you? Now you have broken your vow to God and hurt that girl in the process. Now what?! And you need to get tested. Stupid. Stupid. Stupid! Can't buy her forgiveness with a trip to a rehab. Stupid!"

Stacey stands at the door crying uncontrollably. Speaking to herself she whimpers, "Yeah Boom, you say that but, you keep doin' it."

The next door neighbor lifts her window to offer some

wisdom and encouragement. "Stop letting him. I know

you're confused. But see, God ain't the author of confusion

child. He is the author of peace. If somebody come around

you and you notice every time they show up, the confusion

starts...Let 'em go! Sometimes us women, being so

emotional and things, cause our own confusion. Ain't

nobody else to blame. Sometimes it just takes for us to look

inside of ourselves for the answers. They're always right

there. We're just scared to look because honey, the truth is

ugly. Medusa ugly! Girl, men say what they mean, even if

we ain't listenin'. They do play games and things too! But

we got just know when its game time and either play or get

off the playing field. Women hear what they want, not see

what men mean. I mean look at the way they treat us. We

all go through it. But we can't just keep blaming them. They

do what we allow. Now, Stacey, you have allowed too

much to be done. But baby, it is gonna be ok. You hear me

girl. Wipe your eyes Mama Linda! You will be ok.

God will always take away from us what we don't need in our lives when we ain't wise enough or strong enough to do it on our own. That's if that's what we want. Even when it ain't, believe God knows what He is doin'. That boy been God to you for far too long honey; from high school. God is a jealous God. Can't put nobody before him. He'll take 'em away. Even a child. Now go on, clean yourself up. Come on over here and get yourself some Arroz Con Pollo while it's hot, ok?"

"Yes ma'am."

Come meet at the gate. She wraps her arms around Stacey's neck. "Mmmmm… Big hug for my girl." Stacey broke down. She hadn't been hugged like that I years.

"Girl, I've been praying for you every day. You been through. Still goin' through. But you gotta believe God is on your side and you will get through it. You don't need nobody but The Lord. People will fail you honey. Gotta expect it. We just people.

God knows you're hurting. But, the same God knows that ex of yours is too! Hurting people hurt other people. Even and especially those they love. Because they know most of the time the people they love will tolerated it. But there comes a time in everybody's life when they gotta flip the script, as you young folks say. You gotta look out for you. You ain't no good for nobody if you ain't no good for yourself girl. Bible says: Love your neighbor as you love yourself. Means ya gotta love you first then give it away. Before you even do that though, you gotta receive the love of God...Can't love without it. Now I know you know him...thing to do now is trust him. Go on get your life together baby."

"Yes ma'am."

She wiped Stacey's tears, " I know you hurt, but you ain't by yourself and you gotta stop havin' such a pity party. Your parents, they made big mistakes, but we all got a past and a story. All parents mess up. You're not a perfect parent right?"

"No ma'am. But I wanna get it together and do better. I do my best considerin...'"

"Well then ok!" The old woman smiled, "and they did the best they knew how. Forgive as you begin to heal. Let it go. You also need God's forgiveness and the forgiveness of others. Ain't no high horse for any of us to sit on and be comfortable child. Your son's father is a product of his upbringing. He's spoiled, arrogant and ignorant. He's still young. Too much has been given to him. He hasn't suffered much adversity. He's prideful. But pride goes before destruction the Bible says. Ain't all his fault though. There's more to his story than even he knows.

See I been around a long time girl. Lotta secrets that's been buried soon gon' rise from the grave. Watch what I tell you. In the meantime, forgive that young man, forgive yourself, pray for him. He gon' need it. Pray for your son. He gon' need it too! When he comes back to you, you ain't gotta take him back. But you do have to forgive baby. You are stronger than you know. He gonna need you baby. He just don't know it. Now, go get cleaned up, we can finish talkin' when you come over. I love you Stacey. I love all of y'all out here. I watched all y'all grow up. Y'all like my own children and grandchildren."

Stacey smiled. Love you too. Imma be over there in 20 minutes. I promise. And Mrs. Amora, thank you."

"Anytime angel. Anytime."

PLANTANOS AND COLLARD GREENS

Mrs. Amora Esperanza Santiago-James. An old Spanish relic transport from Puerto Rico that loved her own Latin heritage and culture. But she was also an Afrophile. Though she was a proud Puerto Rican, she was enamored with everything Afro-centric especially, Afro-American men. She was a devout Christian that had converted from Catholicism and had been married to her husband Richard James, a true Latinophile, to the dismay of her family, all of her life from the age of 21. Richard was the great love of her life.

A proud Black man, hardworking, full of integrity and kindness. Richard James had been a migrant from the segregated south and a true southern gentleman. He was fascinated with all things Latin, especially the food and the women. They both loved the Lord. They were a great match made in heaven. They respected one another's cultural differences, embraced them and even in the face of racism from both sides, their love stood ever strong and their union only strengthened over time.

They prayed together regularly, attended church when they could, traveled the world as often as possible and forgave one another a lot. That's how they had managed to last for so long. Temptation, financial ruin, lack of family support and lack of the thing they desired most, to be parents, would come over the years to test their faithfulness to God and one another. They passed every test. Not without accruing copious amounts of tears and pain, but they survived it all. They lived a rich, full life of ups and downs until the day Richard died. It was the saddest day of her life, but, they were mature enough to talk about it and prepare themselves for the inevitable as nothing this side of heaven is forever. One day, somebody was going to have go first.

For better and for worse, for richer and for poorer; in sickness and in health, 'til death did them part. He had passed away 10 years earlier.

Having never been able to have children, they had become the honorary matriarch and patriarch of the neighborhood. Elderly and full of wisdom, everybody came to them for advice, love, comfort, food and even protection from time to time. Amora and Richard were head of the block association and neighborhood watch; ran all of the block parties and neighborhood celebrations. They knew everybody's birthday; Richard always bought a gift and Amora always baked a cake. They were wisdom-wealthy and they only passed on what God told them too...nothing more, nothing less. Full of the Holy Spirit. They were assets everywhere they went. Mrs. Amora had seen so much in her lifetime in that neighborhood. She was a necessary fixture. You could stop over to her house to get a good meal, a laugh and some good advice. Everybody loved her Spanish food. But she loved soul food and would only cook it upon request or when her husband was away on business.
He fancied Spanish cuisine, she did all that she could to make him happy and him. They loved, respected and treasured one another.

Mrs. Amora her was a treasure. Everybody loved knew and loved her. She had been forgiven much in her lifetime, so she gave away much forgiveness. She knew God was a merciful God. A loving God. She had prayed all of her life to be just like Jesus, so she suffered much and loved much, just like Jesus. She would be unforgettable and a force to reckon with, like no other, just like Jesus.

Through suffering she learned obedience just like Jesus did. Mrs. Amora from Puerto Rico, was fit for the Master's use. God was using Mrs. Amora all of the time. She kept herself prayed up, positioned and available. She was a woman small in stature, but powerful nonetheless. She knew before her husband went home to be with the Lord, that her story, journey and ministry would not end just because that part of her assignment did. Mrs. Amora, widowed, elderly, childless and living alone, still had a lot of life inside of her, much love to give and much more wisdom to pour out. God was not through with her yet. She was still on assignment. She had purpose even if on the outside, it didn't appear that way. Society has a tendency to devalue the elderly. Fiery Mrs. Amora, refused to be thrown away like yesterday's newspaper. There was still work to be done.

She invited Stacey inside, "Come on honey."

"Man, Mrs. A. I ain't been in here since Mr. Richie passed on. You still keep this house so immaculate. Like you waitin' on him to come back home or something. You waitin' on ya man even though he long gone Mrs. A?

"No. That part of my assignment has long passed. I keep it clean for me. Plus you never know who stoppin' thru. I do things for me now honey. Me and Jesus. I suggest you do the same. Amora don't wait for nobody but Jesus. Life goes on after your spouse dies or a relationship ends baby. Ain't nothin' forever this side of Heaven. The Bible teaches us to remain joined to Christ, not things, places and people. That's temporal. Everything we see is temporary. The things of God that we cannot see are the eternal things. We're on assignment here. Life ain't about us and every moment lived is not about our comfort or enjoyment. We all have a purpose. Born with one. Purpose is something God had in mind for us to do when he created us and commissioned us to be that is bigger than us. That's why we have to make wise and purposeful decisions in our choices and connections. Even our relationships must have a purpose. Can't just be about lovin' on each other because people change, things change and love evolves. Richie and I had a purpose in getting together that far surpassed us. We had goals. We were careful and prayerful from day one. It wasn't always easy but it helped to remember why we were together when things got tough, temptation came and passion was dying. No relationship is exempt from trial, wear and tear. Gotta do maintenance and remember what brought us together. Yeah, it was bigger than us and life does go on. Not easily but it has too. Purpose ain't got time to waste or wait. I know I will see my Richie again. Mmm...God knows I loved me some him mama. I loved Ritchie so much but, I love Jesus more. Now, HE'S THE ONLY ONE I can't live without. Speaking of which..." she eludes in a thick Spanish accent, "When you gonna get on with your life my love? Ay que linda...get off the garbage Mama and live. Si?

"Yeah you right Mrs. A. But you was in love with Mr. Ritchie right? All of those years. I mean...you know what it's like when you in love with somebody. It's hard to let go. Y'all was together for so long. Man...I wish that was me and Boom! You don't even know Mrs. A. I wish he felt the same as I do. But he don't. I know, I know..." she sniffles, "I'm a fool for bawlin' over a man who rejects me every time he gets a chance. What's wrong with me Mrs. A? Why is love so hard?"

"Baby, it's sometimes hard because that's how we make it. Especially when we don't love ourselves or put God first and do things His way. His way is always best Stacey."

"I guess you're right."

"Oh baby girl, I am right. I've been there. I learned the hard way. I know what it's like to think you're in love with someone who ain't got them feelins' for you. Somebody you hold on to so tight because you feel like you ain't got nobody else. I also know how it feels to have a man take advantage of that side of you." She explained.

"You have? Really? When Mrs. A?"

"Girl please. Yes. With my Richie.
 I guess you thought Rich was pure as the driven snow? Not really. Not always. See we all got flaws and we're most Was flawed out of the public eye and behind closed doors. Richie was a good man overall. But we were young at the time and full of baggage and issues from our families. Ain't no guarantees in marriage girl. Marriage takes work. People and their needs change as time passes. We was a couple but not a perfect one. Takes a lot of forgiveness, patience and understanding to be in a relationship with the same person for a long time. Ain't nothin' to rush in to and I'm sure if he was here, he'd agree.

We loved one another so much. But were we head-over heels in love every single minute of every day? No. And Stacey, we were ok with that. We grew to find out love is not based on how you feel. Love is a choice. Something you do even when you don't feel like it. It's a decision. A conscious decision.

We, like everyone else had our highs and lows. Especially in the beginning, well...throughout. I remember a time Rich wasn't in love with me. I was so crazy for that man. I gave him all of me. Girl, I gave Richie everything ok? But the more I gave, the less he appreciated it, the less I had for me. It had gotten to the point where I became...how you say...empty. Nothing more to give."

"Wow. That's deep Mrs. A. You just never know what other people go through I their personal lives. Can't tell by looking in from the outside. That's somethin'. I wouldn't have ever thought you and Mr. Ritchie had problems or that he hurt you."

"Well, it is true. There are no perfect relationships. I remember when I let go and let God; I stopped chasing Richie and started chasing Jesus, things began to change. Nothing in the Bible tells us to chase what we think we want. The Bible says seek God's kingdom first...all of its righteousness...then, and only then, will these things be added unto us. Who's to say what those 'things' are to each individual. Acknowledge HIM in all of our ways, and HE will direct our paths. Honey, when I let go of Rich, I held on to Jesus. Then slowly, Rich, began chasing and holdin' on to Jesus as well. Then me. Things changed after that. I had to stop being so desperate and value myself. It was turning him off.

God is a God of order and putting any 'thing' or any 'body' above Him, is out of order. Even if it is a love He ordained. Oh Richie." she sighed.

"Oh! Oh my. I'm sorry Mrs. A. Did I make you cry?"

"No baby." She wept. "I made myself cry. Thinking about my Richie. It's been ten long years. It's just some days, like today, it seems like just yesterday I lost him."

"Is that why you cooked the Spanish food? Is it because you miss your husband? I usually smell greens and ham and stuff comin' from over this way. I bet you really miss Mr. Richie, huh?"

"Oh yes my dear. Yes. He was my best friend. He was very handsome too. Moreno Guapo I called him."

"Yeah. For an older dude, Mr. Richie was handsome. No disrespect." said Stacey.

The old woman winked, "None taken sweetie. Some days I just wake up with him on my mind and he stays there all day. My Richie. Good man. Not perfect but, good." She wept a little more.

"I know what it's like to lose everybody you love one by one Stacey. I know your parents wasn't saints, but mi amor, neither were mine. My parents got word back in Puerto Rico about how I was gonna marry Richie. They disowned me. I wasn't even allowed to attend their funerals. I don't even know where they buried.

My whole family deserted me because I chose to love a black man. A black man who shared my love and respect for my culture as I shared and embraced his love for his. What outside of the love of God could be more beautiful than looking past skin color and everything obvious, deeper into the soul of another person and loving that? A man and a woman just loving each other. The Bible says, God ain't like man. We look at the outside appearance. We go by what we see. God is so loving and smart, He knows the real deal baby. God looks at the heart. I wish we could love like He loves and see how He sees. He's so awesome!"

"Yeah. God is awesome. But wait...how did Mr. Richie's family take it?"

"His family couldn't accept it either. Ignorantly we wed, never minding the harsh repercussions of the times. But I promise you, I would not take back a single second of our lives together. Good, bad or ugly.. We loved hard. We held on. We refused to give up. We didn't give into pressure. That's what you saaaaayyyyy.....ummmmmm...Yes! Old school. Old school love. Even when we felt like we didn't have the strength to go on together, we knew we didn't want to be apart. So we fought hard for what we wanted.

We had purpose. Purpose was bigger than us. Richie and I wanted to change the way people thought about love and race. At the end of it all. I could only pray we made our mark.

Now my dear, the moral of the story is this: If you and that young man were meant to be. Let go and let God. And if, that's IF God has put you together, believe it will not be easy staying together. The enemy despises agreement. There will be resistance. There will be trials, temptations and testing and see, I know the boy from when he was born; y'all both good lookin', so be careful. People gonna try you. Devil is always lurking' around looking for a weak spot to expose. Be strong girl! Y'all gotta be strong. Arm yourself with the word of God; the sword of the spirit. As matter of fact, put on the whole armor of God the Bible says. Be ready for the fight. In the meantime, you let him figure him out. You go figure you out. You both need to heal and grow. Give it time and pray for the will of God no matter what you want. Sometimes we only want what we can't have, then when we finally get it, it's not what we imagined it would be. Then, we don't want it no more; Time wasted. You get girl?"

"Yes ma'am."

Mrs. Amora wipes Stacey's eyes as Stacey wipes hers, "It's all gonna be ok. You'll see. Now, eat up girl. I'm gonna play some Motown. You mind?"

"No I don't mind. This food is bangin'.", Stacey smiles.

"Good! So that means you get the left overs. There's plenty." She danced from the kitchen to the living space. She pauses the music, "Girl,"

"Yes Mrs. A?"

"You have a son. You two had better pay attention to that boy. Children are a blessing. Don't forget it. Don't leave him out Stacey. He needs you both. Life goes by so fast girl." She looked at the wrinkles on her face in a mirror. Then a photo of her dancing as a young girl. "Believe when I tell you."

BLOOD, SWEAT, TEARS, JUICE & GIN

Its six months later. Barker finally decides to go and mend things with his father. He turns the key in the back door and walks up to the front of the house. Al is sitting in the living room listening to jazz, enjoying a glass of gin, smoking a cigar.

"Why you smokin' old man. You're supposed to be a Pastor and you indulge in this mess?" He notices a bottle of gin on the coffee table. "And you're sipping?" He eases down on the chez lounge across from the couch where Al is sitting. "Not even a glass of wine...HARD LIQUOR! Man what has gotten into you?"

"Afternoon officer. Or should I say judge? Jesus. Is it ever ok for me to be a normal person in my own house? When did you become such a nag anyway?"

"Oh so now, encouraging people to do the right thing is nagging? Really?"

"Well it was when you was just a peasy-headed teenager who had the world figured out and I was trying to encourage you to do the right thing. My how the tables do turn. So to answer your question: Yes. I guess depending upon how the message is conveyed and received, encouragement can be considered nagging son. Oh and by the way," he shakes the ice in his glass. "I'm not sipping. I don't sip. I drink. I'm drinking boy. For the record, women sip. Men drink. And your honor, just in case my appearance didn't alert you to the fact, here's a hint: I am a man. Full of faults, flaws, failures, temptations on every side, weaknesses, short comings. With a calling, might I add. Just like you. Whew boy....Ain't that funny. Thank you Lord for grace."

"God's grace doesn't give us license to sin. You know that. So knock it off."

"Well Pastor, if you gonna throw them stones, you very well might wanna rebuild your house first. Said the kettle to the pot."

"Man what?"

Al walked over to the dining room to help himself to another glass. "I didn't go looking for this... this ministry thing son. Ministry, came looking for me. And once it caught my heart, just like ya mother did, I tell you son....on both accounts, I never looked back; they both were my passions and in my mind, they were both mistresses that could oppose one another at any given time. Somehow, because of a patient, gracious, loving God and a patient, faithful, understanding wife, things worked out.

Barker as a Minister, dedicate to ministry and family, I burned the candle at both ends for years. It nearly tore me apart. I loved my family and my ministry. They both had my heart. Does that mean I was perfect the entire time? No. Of course not. I'm human. I'm susceptible to everything every other man is. I'm in this flesh. Everyday there's a battle somewhere. Every day, a conflict erupts. I messed up in both areas so many times. I let everybody down from time to time. I was trying to be everything to everyone. I was nothing to myself.

I thank God for your mother. She was a kind, patient woman who loved hard and always knew when I needed a quiet house. She was great. I couldn't have done it for so long: Minister, business owner, father, husband, counselor, etc. Couldn't have worn all of them hats without my wife taking a backseat sometimes. She was perfect for me Barker. She rarely complained. And when she did raise sand over my lack of attention to her and you guys, I never barked back. I have to admit she was always right. Right about everything. My ego wouldn't let me admit that while she was here. She probably needed to hear that every so often. I was too distracted. Too busy.

 I regret that I didn't have enough balance in my life. Ignorantly, I didn't give her the time she deserved. I was selfish. She was serving me while I served everyone else. She deserved better. I was young. I didn't know then what I know now. Marriage and family are a ministry too! Ministry almost tore me and my wife apart. I didn't know how to set boundaries Barker.

Back at that time, nobody talked about the 'Burn Out' Pastors suffer from. Nobody talked about how your work, your passion, your calling, your anointing, can slowly pull you and the ones you love the most apart. They didn't warn us about the "Busy Burnout". Busy being everybody's superhero and neglecting your wife. People admire what they see. They only gettin' a glimpse of the image...it is more than that. There's a behind the scenes to everything. Just because you smilin' and singin' hymns and shoutin' hallelujah down the hallway, don't mean you got it all together; don't mean you ain't cryin' on the inside. Pastor's cry silently in ways other people never notice or care to even see. But, ya learn to accept ya walk and well son, you just keep walkin'. Yep! You keep walkin' even when it hurts and nobody notices. Nobody ever stops to think about how much taking on everyone else's issues may be taking a toll on you. A labor of love. A labor indeed."   Barker knew all too well what Al was talking about. But he refused to acknowledge his father's pain. He still had questions. He wanted answers. All else, would have to wait.

 Al shook the ice in his glass, "Was I ever unfaithful to God? Only with your mother. Was I ever unfaithful to your mother? Only with God. Was your mother ever unfaithful to me? I wouldn't blame her if she was. I wouldn't like it if I found out. But, hey, she was human too. Hmm. I guess it had never crossed my mind until now because again, my ego wouldn't allow it. Men, we got a lot of nerve. We forget women get tempted too when their needs go neglected or they're dissatisfied. We always believe our own hype. Thinking we have all of the bases covered in our relationships as long as the sex is good for us and the bills is paid on time. Ego mess ya up boy. You age, you slow down, you reflect. You learn the error of your ways. And after years of selfishness and chest beating, when you finally settle down in to the truth, your love is gone. Life has passed you by on a one way ticket to Regret Ville and it is too late to stop it." Barker shakes his head watching his father pour another glass of gin.

"The two great loves of my life. My motive for getting into marriage and into ministry, though I believe I was called to do both, on the surface, weren't exactly pure. I was young. I was troubled. I was lookin' for a way in...lookin' for a way out. I'm a man son. Just a man. I never asked to be put on a pedestal, idolized, exalted, reverenced or even looked at as more than that. I never wanted the title 'PASTOR'.

Your mother introduced me to the word of God. Both she and Jesus saved my life. She healed my heart Barker. You both did. Jesus healed my hurt. He saved my soul and so much more...still saving me from myself."

"Will you stop shaking that ice?" Barker grumbled.

"But that being all well and good, I am still just a man. Just like you. You get that son? I need you to get that? Very few people in my life ever got that. When people refuse to get that, it leaves you isolated; sometimes puffed up; disillusioned. People feed the natural pride every man has and you begin to believe your own hype. In that pulpit...everybody's lifeline and their indirect connection to Jesus. Man, Ministry and so many expectations and responsibility can wear you out. Folks don't understand boy. They treat you like a rock star. Especially women. Hear me boy? Sometimes you wonder if they there for you or for the Word. Especially in a church as big as ours. People can lose touch. I mean all of us."

Al puffed on his cigar, "People treat you like you the only one can get a prayer through or like just because you give a message once, twice a week...that you got God personal direct number and they not privy to it. IT'S CALLED PRAYER! Why on Earth don't they just try it? I can't answer every question, visit all of the sickly, be every youth's surrogate father, role model, and mentor. I don't always feel like officiating every wedding and funeral. I'm tired of pretending like I don't need a break or long vacation. I don't know man...Sometimes as a leader your pride get so big, you think you can do it all alone. You don't delegate. Sometimes as a Pastor, your burn out is your own fault. The bigger the calling… well, the bigger the calling; the more the responsibility. Just need a break sometimes.

Father to son. Pastor to Pastor. No! Man to man. What's wrong with wanting to be touched by a sweet, beautiful, sexy woman? Even hold one on my way to sleep at night? Can you even fix your mind to imagine what I go through being without your mother for so long? I'm not dead! I'm a middle aged MAN, I still have a libido. I'm no angel. But I damn sure am not the devil. I know I ain't God. When will these people get that and just let me be a man? Serve them as a MAN of GOD, not perfect, and let me be? I don't wanna put on airs and wear no more masks son. I'm tired. That's why I miss your mother. Carla Marie Golden. The love of my life. She knew me, flaws and all. And just like Jesus, she accepted me anyway. Loved me past my faults. Yes she did."

"We don't live for ourselves man." Barker lectures.

"Oh so I guess you gonna try to preach to the Preacher now? How YOU, of all people gonna tell ME ANYTHING? YOU?! Boy please. You don't know what you foolin' wit. All you see me as is one dimensional. A one trick pony past his prime and ready to be put out to pasture. You don't even respect me as your father...as a man right now. I can see it all on you. Comin' in here all riled up; puffed up. You too prideful boy! Need to be broken and saddled. And its gon' end bad for ya if you don't humble yaself.

Yeah you appear humble on the outside. Psssh man...what happened to you? You used to be humble! You're so smart man. How can you be so one-sided and uncompassionate? You really don't know me do you boy?"

Barker sucks his teeth. "You just see me as your Pastor, ya father and a grandfather. Boy, I'm more than that. We all multi-dimensional Boom and seasons change. Nobody stays the same. And if you don't know that, then what you got to say to me when you ain't lived my life? Let the Lord deal with me. He the one know me. Live for ourselves...please! I been living for other people my whole life. I'm entitled to be tired. I'm human Barker. Subject to wear, tear and weariness. Just like you."

 "Like me? Like me? I can't even believe I came out of you right now! Like me? You ain't nothin' like me."

"How dare you? You think you better than me? You think you can disrespect me because you saw one harmless act that you didn't understand? You didn't even ask me any questions or give me time to explain. As if I needed too! Man, I love you, but life ain't just black and white. I don't owe you nothin' son. Nothin' but love. And I pay my debt in full regularly. So don't you dare preach to me until you done preached to ya own choir.

Talk to me after you done repented, suffered and walk my thousand miles. Oh and wait, in my shoes. That's if, and only if you can fill 'em. Go and sin no more. Then come back when you've fallen off ya high horse. Maybe, just maybe then you'll have somethin' to teach me. Need some reality checks and a few more bumps and bruises humpty dumpty. Til' then, keep listenin, hear?"

Al's words were prophetic and sharp. Barker refused to admit that he knew most of what his father was going through. He was stricken with pride. At home in his bitterness and resentfulness. Thinking he was justified in his anger, he remained silent awaiting the opportunity to arise.

Al picks up a picture of Carla from the coffee table, "You don't understand son. She was the love of my life. My best friend. You don't know that kind of love from a good woman boy. Kinda love that even in the face of the strongest of temptation, when things in the house and in the bed ain't on the up and up...kinda love that no matter what, no matter who...make you wanna come home to be with her in that crazy house, in that cold bed, just to be with her every night anyway. She had the kinda spirit, humble spirit, sweet spirit; made you remember: This too shall pass. Carla was a prayin' woman. Had to be to put up with me and all the stuff that comes with Pastorin'. Carla was strong. There will never be another Carla Marie Golden. Cold how The Lord took her from me." Al shook the ice in his glass once more, "It is well with my soul. It is well son."

Barker was boiling mad. Rocking back and forth, he stared at his father with a murderous look in his eyes. He watched silently as his father drained the remnants of truth serum from the bottom of his glass. His breathing was so heavy. So intense. All of the blood that flowed through him seemed to rush to his head. His adrenaline was high. He was amped and the more he had tried to calm down, the less it had seemed to work. Al, calm and relaxed passes his son as he walks back over to the dining area to refresh his drink. He puts on an Al Green CD. "Love and Happiness" begins to play. Finally Barker closes his eyes as he leans back on the chez lounge chair, covering his eyes with his fitted cap, he breathes deeply as he takes in the lyrics of the song. A calmness appears to wash over him.

Abruptly, Barker sits up, twists his brim to the back; irritated. He jumps to his feet and claps his hands as the song nears its ending, "So let's get to it man. Why was you over there with that whore cheatin' on my mother? I mean you keep talkin' all this "Love and Happiness" nonsense...spillin' yo guts outta complete guilt. Layin' it on thick with the song playin! And the Oscar for best leading actor in a short film goes to... I mean come on man!"

Al's son paced back and forth, "Alright. Alright. I guess I hear you. I'm a man too! I was there too. I'm not here to judge you man. Who am I? I know what you mean. I know what it's like to have needs and for your desires to get the best of you sometimes. I get everything you sayin'. You haven't been with a woman in a real longtime. I'm there with you bruh. I get it. I feel you man. Even King David was a man after God's own heart and he had major flaws and weaknesses. God forgave him and their relationship was great. I ain't knockin' you dad. I'm upset but I ain't here to knock another man for being a man. Feel me? But what was it though for you? You just needed to get a lil' taste? Get near it? Be around it? Stand next to it? I mean what man? Why her? You can be with a better grade of woman. I mean look at you? Don't you know who you are and what you bring to the table? You could probably pull somebody like Kenya Moore, Tina Knowles, Vivica Foxx types. You know some ol' hot vintage pieces. I just don't understand your reasoning. Just tell me and let's be done with this." Barker meant every word of disrespect just as he had said it.

"First off..." Al blowing smoke in the air.   "Watch your mouth about callin' that WOMAN, my woman, a whore boy! Ain't about to be too much more of that there. I promise you that. How you young folks say it: 'FORGET WHAT YOU HEARD'.... Huh? Ain't that how it go? Second of all I'm going to marry that WOMAN so prepare yourself. Respect that and get over it. Carla Marie Golden is dead and gone and been so for a long time now. Let's be clear, I'm not going to be alone not one more second than I have to! You hear me boy?! I won't! Now, like I was trying to say months ago before you got high, mighty and self-righteous...I'm sorry I didn't tell you and your brothers sooner. I didn't know how. I guess I never found the right time. Don't blame Connie. Connie is a fine woman. Ain't her fault. Put it all on me. Oh yeah, fourth and final, I'm in love with her. I want all of us to be a family."

 Barker was fuming. He walked around the coffee table in circles clutching his fist, reluctantly soaking in his father's proclamation. "I'm just gonna forget everything you said, everything I saw and Connie gon' forget it too! We forgive y'all. Y'all young people. You all get angry and say destructive things. Things we never even thought about sayin' to folk you s'possed to respect when we was younger. Now you and Liza can't be together. That ain't proper...won't look good in front of the church or around family. Yeah," he laughed "we all gon' be one big happy family. I can't wait to tell ya brothers. How you think they gon'..."

Barker snapped! He threw his cap down to the floor and smacked the cigar out of his father's hand; He grabs his father by the collar and punches him in the mouth. Yelling, "YOU ARROGANT JERK! JUST LISTEN TO YOURSELF. YOU'RE A PASTOR FOR GOD'S SAKE! SHE IS A WHORE! A WHOOOOORRRRREEE!!!! AND YOU....YOU....YOU...I DON'T

EVEN KNOW WHAT TO SAY ABOUT YOU!   He drops Al onto the floor,   "YOU VOWED TO BE FAITHFUL TO MY MOTHER! YOU ARE A PASTOR! OR HAVE YOU FORGOTTEN!?"   "I CAN'T EVEN LOOK AT YOU! YOU DISGUST ME!"

Al was out of breath, coughing, wheezing loudly, "Baby boy, Carla is gone...you gotta get past it. It's been a long time son. You gotta let go."

"I AIN'T GOTTA LET GO OF A DAMN THING! THAT'S THE PROBLEM. THAT'S IT. ALL Y'ALL LET GO! THAT WAS MY MOTHER!" Barker kicks the coffee table, breaking the glass. Tearing up and tossing pillows he continues while Al lay there trying to catch his breath, "WHY? WHY? COULDN'T IT BE YOU THAT DIED? SHE WAS SO BEAUTIFUL, PURE AND SWEET! WHERE IS THE JUSTICE IN THAT? WHERE IS GOD? HOW COULD HE LET SOMEONE LIKE THAT WHORE LIVE AND LET MY MOTHER DIE?"   Crying aloud he falls to his knees in the shattered glass, "HUH? HUH? YOU HEAR ME GOD? WHAT KIND OF GOD ARE YOU? HOW COULD YOU LET HER DIE LIKE THAT? ALL OF THESE NASTY, VILE PEOPLE OUT HERE THAT DON'T EVEN CARE ABOUT YOU. THEY DON'T CALL YOU UNTIL THEY NEAR DEATH OR THEY NEED YOUR HELP DOING SOMETHING THEY CAN'T DO FOR THEMSELVES. AND THE WOMAN THAT DEVOTED HER LIFE TO YOU AND HER FAMILY, HER YOU LET DIE?! HOW AM I SUPPOSED TO KEEP BELIEVIN' IN A GOD THAT COULD BE SO COLD? WHY DID YOU DO IT LORD? WHERE IS MY MOTHER? SHE WAS PERFECT MAN...SO PERFECT GOD. WHY'D YOU DO THAT?"

He pounded the marble floor with his fists until they bled while Al watched helplessly. He had once again become that broken young man that he had been reduced to on the day of Carla's burial; revisited. That's what Al saw. And just like then, now the father was powerless over helping his son; Deep down he felt useless as father and as a man.

Al cried as he wiped his blood-soaked mouth crawling through the glass to comfort Barker. He looked down and moaned from the pain of the broken shards of glass ripping through his flesh pieces at a time. He couldn't help but to think of how the blood spill and the broken glass were a reflection of his relationship with the boy. These were conversations and confrontations that had long been overdue. What the boy didn't know was that Al could've raised himself up from the floor anytime he had wished but he lay there broken, just as he had been many a day and night since Carla's passing. They were both grieving heavily even still. Neither of them coping well.

After the funeral, the Golden men did what men traditionally do, they drowned themselves in work and women; they had never even considered confronting, processing or talking out their feelings. They were alpha males and emotions were a feminine specialty. In house full of males, without the any female energy, motherly nurturing and healthy emotional outlet to create some type of balance, their home became just a house full of luxurious items and memories. It had become soulless and unappealing. The house that Carla, the matriarch and confidant had made a home had been reduced to nothing more than a five star locker room and boys club where feelings where put aside and emotions were buried. Where there was a false sense of strength and talk was minimal, archaic and harsh. Everybody missed Carla. Everything about her. All of the Golden boys, when they had reached age, sought to wed a woman in the spiritual and emotional likeness of Carla Marie Golden. There were hefty tests to pass and unbeknownst to the young women, big shoes to fill. All of the Golden boys found love in mini Carlas. All except Barker. None of them had ever really grieved properly. Each male carried a level of dysfunction the women in their lives couldn't reach. The wives never knew just quite why. Carla was the love of their very lives they would never quite get over. But Barker, Barker Golden, the eldest, the one who spent the most time with her... He had it bad. As perfect as Carla came across to the outside world, she had had a favorite child, and Barker was that child. She never let on to the other children, but he knew it. Al knew it. Barker couldn't figure out why. But Al knew why. Secrets were about to spill like the blood from Al's mouth and seemingly perfect lives would be forever shattered like so much broken glass on that flawless marble floor.

Al finally reaches out his hand to Barker at an arm's length, broken and pitiful. Barker slaps it away.   "Get away from me.", he whispers gritting his teeth. "I wish you weren't my father. You....you should be dead." he glares angrily at Al through bloodshot eyes.

   "Son, I know you're angry. I know you don't mean it. Let's just calm down..."

   "YOU CALM DOWN! DON'T YOU TELL ME WHAT I MEAN OLD MAN! DON'T YOU DARE TELL ME ANYTHING! YOU ARE NOT MY FATHER! YOU ARE NOT MY FATHER! DO YOU HEAR MEEEEEEE!!!?" Barker screamed at the top of his lungs still kneeling in the broken glass.

   "YOU KNOW WHAT? YOU KNOW WHAT?" Al rises quickly like a phoenix from the ashes.   "YOU ARE RIGHT! EXACTLY RIGHT! YOU ARE NOT MY SON! THERE I SAID IT. OK! NOW THE ELEHANT CAN LEAVE THE ROOM! BE CAREFUL WHAT YOU WISH FOR COUNSELOR. YA JUST MIGHT GET IT! OUT OF ALL OF THE BOYS, YOU ARE THE OLDEST, THE MOST SPOILED, THE MOST SELFISH, THE MOST JUDGEMENTAL AND THE LEAST LOVING. THERE IT IS! PROOF IS IN THE PUDDIN'! YOU ARE NOT MY SON!"   Barker couldn't believe what he was hearing. But his pride wouldn't let him show it. Al picks up a photo encased in a platinum frame of Carla, himself and Connie.   "LOOK AT THIS..."   Barker turns away. Al grabs Barker by the shirt collar, "BOY YOU STARTED THIS... NOW IMMA FINISH IT.

LOOK AT THE DAMN PICTURE! THIS IS US! THIS IS ME, CARLA AND THE WOMAN YOU CALL A WHORE! THAT IS CONNIE DEBRIL. WE WERE ALL TEENAGERS AND ALL GOIN' THRU MESS AND ALL A VICTIM OF SOME GARBAGE WE AIN'T ASK TO BE BORN INTO. OK!"

Al takes the photograph and sits down on the chez lounge chair, pulling Barker down with him, he weeps, "We all grew up south side of Newark man. Connie was still in high school when we all started hangin' out together on Hawthorne Avenue. Me and ya mama was drop outs. We had to make our own way to live. We ain't had no choice.

Connie and Carla was good friends. Connie was raised in a brothel and the first time she had sex wasn't pretty. She was raped and nobody saw fit to do nothin' about it. She ain't ask for that title or lifestyle Barker, her mother, Mama Rose, kinda reared her into it. Sometimes when you're young you go with the flow 'cause you feel like you ain't got a choice or a snowball's chance in hell out there on the streets alone. Sometimes people find themselves doin' things they don't wanna do outta obligation and loyalty to others. We all do what we do and what it is we know; whatever is familiar, until we know better. Sometimes its stuff we been taught. other times it's stuff that's in us from birth that we ain't even ask for, didn't see coming and don't know where it came from exactly. You know I taught you about generational curses. Sometimes it's ya up bringin'. Sometimes it's ya culture. Sometimes it's ya mindset. Boy, sometimes it's just your environment; its conditioning. There's a whole lot of stuff to consider when you judgin' people son. That's why it's God's job to do the judgin', not ours...The Almighty knows why we do what we do. Even when we don't even understand ourselves; the Creator knows His creation.

Now, me and Carla was always out there on the streets, day and night. We had no choice man....we both came from families where people couldn't take care of us. We was both abandoned by drug addict mothers man. Whew boy! Folks was doin' smack left and right like they doin' crack right now. We was young. It was the early seventies. It was a different time. We both fell in with the wrong people 'bout the same time man. We was just doin' what we knew how to do in order to survive. I hustled for a pimp. We called him Ease on the street. He wasn't just a pimp and king pin, he was a dirty cop with his hand in everybody pockets and the law in his. A dirty man; No morals. No integrity. No heart. That joker had his hands in everything man. Runnin' numbers, pimp game, dope game...I mean everything. Me and Carla was always together on the same strip down Frelinghuysen Avenue when we wasn't 'round Hawthorne or hangin' with Connie tryin' to soak up what she was learnin' in school or just in her hallway tryin' to stay warm in the Winter and cool in the Summer. Man I tell ya...we had some laughs in that hallway. We laughed until Mama Rose would run me and Carla outta there and make Connie get to work. It was sad. But we all tried to make the best of it. Wasn't nothin' we could do. We never really talked about it.

One day I just stopped seeing Carla around. Some years had gon' by....I mean a bunch o' time had passed. It was months later when I caught up with her again. I was still out there hustlin' dope but, this time for myself. I had done paid that cat his money I owed him and came up on my own in no time at all. I had made my own connections and money just wouldn't stop coming in. Man, being honest, it got so good at times, I didn't even have to go outside. I got some young cats to work for me when I needed them to. I laid back and collected and counted. Ain't nothin' new under the sun out here son, nothin' new. It was sweet for a season...a long season. So anyway, one night, me and my boys smoked some bush man, and we wanted to get laid so we went over to The Honey Pot. That's where Connie lived. It was her mother's place. Boy, Mama Rose wasn't no joke. We got there, we paid up, the girls came out, lined up, and as we was makin' our selections. I look down the line, I see Carla."

Barker stands up, "No! Stop. Just stop right now."

Al continued to reminisce looking down at the photo, "She sure was beautiful. More beautiful than before. I always thought she was the most beautiful creature I had ever seen...just never got the nerve to tell her before then.

Guys. We have all this bravado. Pride. Ego. And can you believe it? A beautiful woman can come along and make us shake in our boots like little boys just by doin' nothin' but being her beautiful self. That's all she was doin' son, she was being her naturally beautiful self. Young, sweet, fresh-faced, soft-spoken, sometimes shy Carla Marie. She was something. I was jealous. I had to have her. Boy, I ain't want the guys that was with me seein' her half-dressed and all; Woman had a power over me like no other. Now I ain't never been shy or scared of nothin' or nobody. Can't be if you gonna do what I was doin'. If you scared, you ain't gonna survive long. But see, Carla...even after all of that time, she had the power to humble me son. She was the boss even if she didn't know it. I was afraid of her. Men, we don't like to admit that. But when we're young and insecure, still growing, unsure about just who we are...something like staring down the barrel of a gun or facing jail time might not even be a terrifying as talkin' to a pretty girl who you know is way out of your league. She was too good for me. Even in her line of work, she was an angel to me. I dared not judge her. I understood. We were both from the same side of the tracks. I didn't like what she did but, I still respected her. I didn't wanna own her. I didn't like the thought of other people thinkin' they owned her. Too much like slavery to me. Just evil. I wanted to set that angel free. That night, I chose her. We went to her room..."

Barker yells, "GET TO THE POINT MAN! DON'T NOBODY WANNA HEAR THIS! DON'T FORGET YOU TALKIN' ABOUT MY MOTHER!"

Al never looks up. "We sit down on the bed to talk. She grabs my hand. I'm nervous and so is she. She feels my hands as she helps me out of my coat. She rubs my hands to warm them. She stared into my eyes the whole time. She pulls them close to her mouth and breathes hot air into them to warm them up some more, all of the while we stare at one another. It's like we're having a conversation without saying a word. There would be special times when we would communicate intimately like that for years to come. Even across a crowded room wall to wall with people, we were so in sync and in love, we would just find one another like God built us with GPS systems custom made to match....We would just stare at one another and carry on a conversation without saying a word. We were like that until the day my angel went back to heaven. God only made one Carla Marie. I will NEVER love another like I did that woman. I still do. I always will. Forever.

Finally my hands are warm. She kisses them softly, not bothered by the weed smell; She was so sweet and humble, she never judged me. I know I wanna kiss her. I leaned in and somebody starts banging on the door, 'Everything cool in there? Kinda quiet! Give him his money's worth. I don't want no complaints or you outta her girl!'. It was Mama Rose, always comin' through like the Tasmanian devil caught up in a hurricane in the south pacific. I lean in for the kiss again. Now, instead rude banging, from the bottom of the closet I hear a baby cryin'. She jumped up and ran over to the closet, I follow her. When I look down, what do I see...A baby boy. I see you son. I saw you. Ya mama was ashamed and embarrassed; afraid she would lose her spot there, I comforted her as she cried. That night I paid all of the money I had in my pocket just to spend the night with her as she tried to rock you to sleep. She comforted you as I comforted her. That night we stayed up talkin' and gettin' to know one another. Believe it or not, .long story short, I fell in love with her and her son. I respected her and I never touched her until we got married. I wanted to take y'all away from there. We both had longed for a real family for so long son. We finally had one with one another. We wanted a normal life. We had plans to get that normal life. Whatever normal was.

Over time she taught me about the Lord, we read the Bible best we could for dropouts. I guess somehow, God wanted us to understand it, because over time and by a lot of prayer, we did. Connie taught Carla stuff about God and the Bible. In turn, ya mama taught me. We all just knew a little bit at the time. Carla and I started going to church and The Lord increased our knowledge. We were young and thirsty for that living water. Hungry for the bread of life son. See none of us was perfect but, God had a plan. He'll use anybody in any situation son to get His will done. That's why we shouldn't be so quick to judge people. God is Lord over all. We don't know what He got planned. We eventually got saved. We gave ourselves to Christ in the raggedy kitchen of our first home with you between the both of us. There was no turning back son, I adopted you as my own after I took care of all of my legal issues. God has been better to me than I deserve. I know I don't deserve this life. I didn't deserve ya mama son.

The Apostle Paul called himself the Chief of Sinners...Well, I know I can give him a run for his money. You're right son, your mother should still be here. God should've let me die".

Barker kneels down to meet Al eye to eye and he whispers, "Old man you are one nasty drunk. You are such a liar and I can't wait for God to deal with you. What did she ever see in you? You're a fraud. It's all gonna come out one day. I hate you. You know that? I hate this house. I hate that church. I hate God. Do you hear me? I HATE YOU AND ALL

YOU STAND FOR!" Her slaps the photo out of Al's hand and spits on the floor.

Al jumps up, "NOW I DONE HAD 'BOUT ENOUGH OF YOU AND YOUR ATTITUDE AND YOUR MOUTH. I'VE BEEEN HUMBLE UP UNTIL THIS POINT! NOW...NOW...NOW, YOU HAVE FORCED MY HAND BARKER! I'M DRUNK. I'M A LIAR. RIGHT! DRUNK MIND SPEAKS FROM A HONEST HEART AND A SOBER MOUTH SON. DON'T YOU FORGET IT! WHY YOU MAD AT ME? HUH? BECAUSE YA PERFECT LIFE AIN'T SO PERFECT? WHY? BECAUSE YOU GOT WHAT YOU WISHED FOR. I AIN'T YO DADDY? WHY HUH? TRUTH HURTS! WHY? BECAUSE I'M IN LOVE WITH CONNIE AND YOU JUDGIN' HER WHEN CARLA WASN'T NO DIFFERENT?

YOU LOVE TO JUDGE PEOPLE BUT YOU CAN'T DO THE MATH ON WHO YOUR FATHER IS CAN YOU? CAN YOU MR. LAWYER? DO THE MATH MR. COLLEGE GRAD! HOW CAN SOMEBODY SO SMART BE SO STUPID?! YOUR FATHER COULD BE ANY DAMN BODY! I BOUGHT YOUR MOTHER FROM HER PIMP! I HAD TO PAY THAT HORRIBLE MAN TO GET HIM OUT OF HER LIFE! HE ACTED LIKE HE OWNED HER. I AIN'T WANT HER FEEL ENSLAVED BY NOBODY...SO I PAID HIM SO SHE COULD FEEL FREE. SO CARLA COULD BE FREE TO BE HERSELF AND LIVE A GOOD LIFE! I GAVE HIM ALL OF THE MONEY AND DRUGS I HAD AND WALKED AWAY WITH NOTING BUT YOU AND HER TO LIVE FOR...Y'ALL WAS ENOUGH FOR ME. I LOVED HER ENOUGH TO GIVE UP ALL I HAD...MY LIFESTYLE, MY FREEDOM FOR HER! FOR YOU BARKER! I LAID IT ALL DOWN. LIKE JESUS DID FOR THE CHURCH! I GAVE IT ALL AWAY. I NEVER REGRETTED IT. CARLA WAS MY WAY OUT AND MY WAY IN. A DRUG DEALER FELL IN LOVE WITH A PROSTITUTE SON. THAT"S REALITY! YOU, OH MY BOY. YOU HAVE BEEN LIVING A FANTASY!

THE REALITY IS, SHE WAS SELLIN' HER BODY BOOM. THAT'S WHAT SHE WAS DOIN' WHEN WE MET AND ME AND CONNIE IS HOW SHE GOT OUTTA THE GAME. OK? YOU GOT THAT?! YOU KEEP CALLIN' CONNIE A WHORE BUT CONNIE AND THAT BROTHEL WAS A SAFE HAVEN FOR YOUR MOTHER WHEN SHE GOT PREGNANT WITH YOU AND RAN AWAY FROM THE PIMP THAT WAS BEATIN' ON HER. YA HEAR?! YOUR MOTHER WAS NO DIFFERENT THAN CONNIE DEBRIL BOY. LIKE IT OR NOT! BUT SHE WAS THE BEST THING OUTSIDE OF JESUS THAT EVER HAPPENED TO ME! YOU HEAR ME! WE ALL CUT FROM THE SAME CLOTH. WE ALL GOT A PAST. AIN'T NO ONE PERSON NO BETTER THAN THE OTHER. NOW IF GOD CAN FORGIVE ALL THREE OF US AND USE US WHEN WE DIDN'T EVEN SEE IT COMIN', DIDN'T FEEL GOOD ENOUGH AND DIDN'T ASK FOR IT, WHY CAN'T YOU FORGIVE, LET GO AND GET OVER IT AND YOURSELF?! YOU A MAN RIGHT? WE JUST MEN REMEMBER? DON'T MATTER WHERE YOU START IT'S HOW YOU FINISH. GOD IS THE QUALIFIER SON. IF THE LORD QUALIFIES YOU, BOY...YOU QUALIFIED AND AIN'T NOTHIN' A MAN ON EARTH OR DEVIL IN HELL CAN DO ABOUT IT. You gotta get over yourself man."

Barker was more agitated than ever now. He drew back to punch Al in the face.   Al catches Barkers fist with his open hand and squeezes it, "Boy, if you EVER raise your hand again to strike me... Imma show you just how old of a man I'm not and Imma WHOOP YO YOUNG, POMPOUS, IGNORANT, PRETTY BOY ASS OLD SCHOOL STYLE LIKE OLD MEN DO. Try me! Now, just like you tell my grandson, YOU GOT YOUR NAME, GAME AND FAME FROM ME. DON'T LET THE TITLE 'PASTOR' FOOL YOU YOUNG MAN. I MAY BE SAVED, I MAY BE A MAN OF GOD. I MAY EVEN BE OLDER BUT, I AM STILL A MAN. YOU KNOW WHERE I'M FROM AND NOW YOU KNOW WHAT I USED TO BE ABOUT. BUT YOU DON'T KNOW ME LIKE THAT...SON, NOR DO I WANT YOU TO. I PROMISE YOU LITTLE BOY, YOU DON'T WANT IT. KEEP BRINGIN' UP THE FACT THAT I'M A PASTOR. WELL, YEAH...OK! AND SO WHAT. SO ARE YOU! AND LOOK AT YOU. YOU ANY BETTER?"

Barker chimes in flexing his chest, "You damn right I'm better...better than you, any day with your old recycled 'COME TO JESUS MEETIN', sermons you been spittin' for as long as I can remember. Yeah old school... I'm a whole lot better than you. I can preach circles around you! I'm twice as good as you and you know it."

"I got ya old school right here frat boy!" says Al as he spits on the floor. "Now you put your hands on me for the first and last time boy. I let that ride because I know you just gettin' ya feelin' out. But what you will not do is challenge me in my own house. EVER AGAIN! I'm the king up in this piece! You stay in a child's place little boy and daddy won't have to spank you, here?" Al lights another cigar, "Pastor. Hmm...Oh so now after you done did everything but denounce God you a Pastor?"

He blows out the smoke as he laughs. Throwing his head back, "And....and...Wait a minute now....YOU ACTUALLY HAVE THE MARBLES TO SAY YOU A BETTER PASTOR THAN ME?! That right there...now that's rich! Boy you missed ya callin' as a comedian. You know that? Mama probably rollin' in her grave right now. Better than me..."

He walks over to Barker cigar in hand, blowing the smoke in his face he whispers, "You ain't suffered enough, nor are you experienced enough, to even be half as good as I AM. And even when you think you done suffered enough and been seasoned enough through your experiences, believe when I tell you, you still will have a long way to go to catch up to me and my 'Come to Jesus meeting' sermons young buck. What kind of Pastor has hissy fits in the middle of the floor and shout that he hate God just because his life ain't what he want it to be? Boy! You a baby. You ain't no man. You ain't even man enough to fill my shoes boy. And I say that with ALL the love of Jesus. Doors of the church are now open."

The air is thick with testosterone, tension and pride. Blood, sweat, tears, spit. The ammoniated stench of tainted bark from the constant stream of concentrated urine. Confrontation in the school yard. A wrestling match fast food parking lot. The roles of father and son that had been secure up until that point had become questionable. No one was sure what the future held. On the surface, nobody cared. Pride and ego had ruled the day. At present, they were merely men at war.   Al puts Barkers cap back on his head then pats him on the top of his head and walks across the room to play some more music. Barker walks back through the house the way he came throwing the keys on the floor. Before he shuts the door he yells, "LONG LIVE THE KING!"

Al replied, cigar clichéd between his teeth, "GOD WILLING. YOU KNOW IT!" Barker pulls down the lengthy drive way visibly shaken. His ego battered, heart bruised. Al leans back on the couch, gin in hand. Al Green sings, "I'm so tired of being alone". He grabs the nearest Bible and tries to find a comforting scripture. Yet, it had seemed the Lord was more interested in chastising him than comforting him at that point; He had no interest in being chastised. He had been battered and bruised enough for one day. Oh how the mighty have fallen.

That night Barker drove all over until he had just about run out of gas. At one point, he stops at a light in Newark and sees a young white girl, prostituting on a corner. He can only see her from the back through the windshield of his car. As the light turns green, he passes her as she turns around to get his attention, she's pregnant. He's in complete shock! He can't believe it. He circles the block just to make sure he saw what he thought he saw only to arrive at the same spot to see a pimp slapping her down to the ground. He pulls past her as the pimp gets into his car and drives away. He gets out of the car, "Hey....Hey...ma you ok?"

"I'm good. That's just my daddy. I made him a little upset. He gets like that, but he loves me. I know it. He the only one I got. He takes care of me. He said we gonna get married. I'm having his baby. See?" she smiles.

"My goodness! Your neck is red and blue! You need to get to a hospital. What are you doing out here girl? I know you ain't from down here? Where's your family?" he asks.

She lifts up her head only to see him drive by slowly, "Look man, you got a lot of questions. Just tell me what you want so I can lay down the price. If you ain't wit it don't waste my time. So you want some o' this sugar or what sexy?"   Barker pats his pockets and invites her to the car. They drive off.

"$50 for..." he stops her.

"What ma? Oh no babe....you got the wrong one! I don't want nothin' you got! And I mean that exactly in the way you received it. Oh no!" He grabs his hand sanitizer. "Here. Jesus."

She yells, "Then what the hell am I doin' here?! Oh you ain't about to kidnap me!" She pulls out her cell phone and he grabs it and throws it out of the window.

"Girl, I'm not tryin' to kidnap you. I am trying to help you. Ok? What's ya name first of all?"

"Look man, you can't help me alright. He gonna kill me if I ever try to leave. And besides even if you could help me...How you gonna do that and how do I know I can trust you? You probably a pimp too! As a matter of fact... LET ME UP OUTTA HERE!" she yells with the car door open as he speeds down the street.

"HEY MAN SHUT THE DOOR GIRL! YOU CRAZY! I AIN'T NOBODY NO PIMP AIIGHT! I just saw you and you remind of someone I used to know and love. Someone dear to my heart." he says with tears in his eyes. "I just want to help. I just heard some terrible things about the mother of a friend... just wanna help that's all. Aww man, why am I tellin' you this. I don't even know you." Barker fought back his tears.

"...probably because I understand and you know that. Maybe I remind you of her or somethin' like that, but I ain't her. I'm sorry. Super saver, you gon' have to find another ho to save tonight."

"Super what? What did you just say?"

She looked around. "Look, I don't know what kinda bath salts they got down this way. I didn't even know black guys were big on bath salts. But Imma just let you down easy...I can't be saved ok. I'm not into that kinky religious altar boy crap alright."

"Wait what?"

"Damn. You're hallucinating. Alright so, before you start foaming at the mouth and gnawing at my flesh...ummm...I better be goin'. I been away too long and I ain't got my phone. Boy oh boy, he probably gonna kick my ass man! See what you done man! Psssshh man...just pay me for my time and let me out!" she screams.

"I'm not letting you out. I'm taking you somewhere." he says.

"I knew it! HELP HE'S A MURDERER, RAPIST, KIDNAPPER, CRAZY ZOMBIE BLACK GUY!!!! I'M WHITE... HELP ME PLEASE!" she yells out of the window.

Barker looks at her and pulls over. In a soft voice, "First of all, you know where you at? You in my hood ok? You down here surrounded by black people gettin' pimped by a white man, yellin' for black people to help ya crazy, butt-sellin', doped up white ass?! And you playin' the race card? How convenient! How do those brothers in the NFL do it? Keep tippin' over there to white girl heaven...psshhhh man, seem like all kinds of black man hell to me if you think you can scream like that and get a brother cased up so easily. Ain't that some...

"What are you even talking about?"

"You can just play the race card like that and expect the good ole Calvary to come to your rescue just because you're Caucasian? Not down this way Cinderella. Wow man. Yo! Let me let you out before you sick the boys on me. OUT! OUT NOW! I know my limits. Get out of my ride and have a nice night. Be safe ma. I tried. Lord have mercy. From now on I guess I'll let Jesus do the savin'."

She opens the car door to get out and then she shuts it, "Ok, Ok! I'm so sorry. Nobody ever tried to help me before. It ain't got nothin' to do with race..."

"Coulda fooled me. Look ma, I had a crazy day, better yet, a crazy year. I better quit while I'm ahead. Especially messin' wit a case like you! Imma let you go. I don't need no trouble. Here...Take my card and here...here's some money for a new phone and a horrible time. You actually need to be payin' me! Call me when you want that help. I'll be sure to send somebody white to pick you up. Somebody from Bergen County. Aight?"

She reads the card, "You're a lawyer?"

"See, that's what I'm talkin' about. Wait let me guess? You trust me now right?"

"Huh? I never said…"

"Oh you've said plenty Miley Cyrus. Let me guess, now you want my help? Right. Let me ask you this…how is a white girl in a predominantly Black and Latino city gonna be a racist?"

"What? Hey I'm not a…I never meant to…"

"Whatever Justine Bieber. It's called selective racism. Look it up! Unbelievable. What because I'm African-American, I drive a hot ride, I just gave you a wad of cash just of the rip… you think I'm out here hustlin'? Typical! Well, just know if I was hustlin' baby girl, I wouldn't have to be out here playln' let's make a deal for some dirty, knocked up box!"

"Golden. Golden. That name sounds familiar. Hey…I know, you related to this Pastor from…?"

"No habla ingles?" He speeds off.

Walking down the street. She tries to remember where she knows the name from exactly, "Golden. Golden. Barker Golden. I know that name from somewhere. Hmmmm..."

SHARE MY WORLD

"Man, its brick out here. Where could she be? Wait, is that her?" A curvaceous figure approaches from the pathway. Sitting on the park bench in the frigid cold, he barely feels the touch of Jack Frost as Liza continues to glide towards him, her hips each taking their turn moving up and down like a seesaw. Left to right, up and down. His face lights up like a child unwrapping a gift on Christmas Day. A brown sugar vision in a vanilla, form-fitting, cashmere mini dress accented with a plush, faux-fur, Caramel scarf and Cream thigh-high boots. Her natural coils being tossed about by the blustery winds that flow through every strand. She steps up. He warms his hands with the hot breath from his mouth. He is excited to see her. He is more excited to touch her. It's been a very long time. He rises to greet her. She walks straight into his open arms. He smells her hair, he kisses her neck softly. As he embraces her curves and caresses the fabric surrounding her hips. He leans in to kiss her soft, honey-coated, nude, shimmery gloss. Liza suddenly pulls back.

"I can't have a kiss?" he asks.

She resists. He relentlessly continues to link their lips. When it seems he's ready to give up, she moves in. She kisses his lips softly; with a cool, lingering sympathy.

"The woman of my dreams. You feel soooooooooooooo good girl. You smell like peaches. You still taste just like you look...like hot chocolate. I miss you."

"That's the problem. I'm your dream; your fantasy. I don't want to be anybody's fantasy. I want to be somebody's reality. Dreams pass. You wake up from dreams. Fantasies bring temporary satisfaction; they fade. Reality, now reality that sets in. Reality is what we live with. That's what I want to be to somebody."

He sits down on the park bench. He pulls his hoodie over his head, "And dreams come true. Come here ma." He pats his lap, "Sit down. Let me warm you up a little bit. Where on Earth are you getting this nonsense from? Huh? I know we haven't seen one another in a minute. I know a lot of things were said. I didn't mean you any harm. I was buggin. I apologize. That being established, previous events and current knowledge have no bearing on the way I see you and how I feel about you. I think you're beautiful inside and out. That has not nor will it EVER change. You hear me? You are my reality Liza. Believe it or not."

He tries to wipe her tears away as they trickle down her face. "Don't cry. I hate to see women cry. Especially at my expense. I'm so sorry for the hurt and pain I caused you. I'm sorry for the way I disrespected your mother. I was angry and after talking to my...THAT MAN, I can't say I'm any less angry, but baby, I promise you this, it has nothing to do with you. I want to see you smile not cry. I don't wanna be the one who breaks your heart. Ever. Can we start over? Allow me to reintroduce myself...?"

She laughs, "What was that? Hi. My name is Charles. Boy! Don't even try it. Float on my brotha."

"See...that's what I'm talking about. That's what I love to see...that pretty smile. And you still think you got jokes? How extravagant."

"If you say so. Bourgeois." she giggled.

"Actually I've surpassed that."

"Arrogant."

"If you say so. Anyway. I know we have things to discuss but, I wanted to tell you this before all the drama kicked off at your house last time."

"What's that?"

He gently strokes her cheek with his thumb. Gazing deep into her eyes he proclaims, "I...I...I..."

Frustrated, she interrupts, "You...You...You... you can't say it Stuttering John, because you don't mean it. You don't love me so why put yourself thru this? Huh? Why front?"

"Put myself thru what man? I don't see or hear from you in months and soon as we hook up again, instead of pickin' up where we left off...WE PICKIN" UP WHERE WE LEFT OFF! You're making it difficult right now girl. Besides that little hiccough at the end of our last date, I thought things were perfect between us."

"You right. We are pickin' up RIGHT where we left off. We're back at the charade Boom. We're going thru the motions again. Playing charades. Ain't you tired of livin' a lie? Don't you want somethin' real?"

"C'mon girl." He was grew more impatient, "Is this what we came here for? This is not why I called you. Liza I don't wanna fight. I have enough stress. Believe me baby, I just want us. I want us the way we were. A charade? Pssshhh man...What are you talkin' about? I mean, what is this Liza? What am I not getting?"

She calmly explains, "I know what it is. I'm your escape. I'm a coping mechanism or tool so to speak. I'm just the drug that masks the pain that in the end adds to the problems that already existed before you starting getting high on me. I am not your reality like I said. I am the buffer in between what is real and what is not in your life. That's it and that's all."

"Girl what the… Yo. What are you talking about?"

"Oh you know exactly what I'm talking about. You met me in a strip club at a confusing, miserable, mundane point in your life and vice versa…we connected physically and we have been getting high off of one another ever since. We were having a borderline illicit affair. You know it. You're just runnin' from you problems. Like me."

"Wait. Now you're confusing me. So you were using me the whole time?"

"I guess so if we're gonna tell the naked truth and keep it one. I mean this is reality Boom. It is time we get back to it."

"Woman…"

"Just listen alright."

"Alright man. Go ahead.

"Now you're a pastor right?"

"Can we not get into that right now? You're starting to me off."

"I can live with that. You know the way we hooked up ain't even God's order and you know that. Since when is God into strip club hook ups?"

"Since Hosea and Gomer. Since Adam and Eve messed everything up. He's everywhere and can use anything; any situation to get His glory. In Psalm 139, supposedly, David wrote: Even if I make my bed in hell, you are there. Don't play with me about those scriptures woman."

"Don't try to manipulate me with those scriptures man."

"I'm not…"

"Knock it off. You people ain't the only people who know and can quote scripture. It was wrong from the rip Boom. You just runnin'. You just ran into the arms of your fantasy on that run that's all. You met me when I was naked, we dry-humped in a dark corner of the club. We was both high off the lust. I was tipsy and we was searchin' for stuff we probably ain't have no business looking for. On the other hand maybe life just happened to us both. I mean, you are a man and I am a woman, we both are human, we have needs. Maybe those factors are what brought us together. Maybe on our separate journey's to find self, we just collided. I don't know. But I do know God ain't in this. I do know this ain't love. We both just runnin."

"I'm sayin God can use anything Liza. I'm just nervous. I'm sayin'…I do…"

Liza speaks up sternly, "You came home with me that night. And though we've come close to it, time and time again...We ain't never make it happen. We wanted to, but, we didn't. You get it? I'm something for you to hold on and aspire to capture. The only woman you dated that you never smashed. I'm your escape from the everyday. I'm your summer fling, your video girl. I'm your wet dream. I'm not stupid. That's what I represent. On that stage, in that club, I'm whatever your girl or wife ain't; can't be, won't be or used to be. That's it and that's all. We just took the game too far. We was living a fantasy. If God was in this, we things wouldn't have ended the way they did."

"Ended? What do you mean ended? No ended. I lo..."

"Oh my goodness Negro! Would you shut the hell up! You sure you saved? You sure do lie like a bad rug to be claiming salvation." He looked ashamed and appalled. "Now I know behind all them looks, education and influence you're just a man. I mean if don't nobody else know, I do." She kissed him on the cheek then whispered in his ear, "All man. I haven't forgotten." He starred into her eyes yet again. She mumbled, "But, you don't love me. You love what you think I represent. I'm actually insulted that you would try to play me like that. I'm not as innocent of a girl as I used to be. No longer, that naïve little house mouse. I ain't stupid. "

"Obviously.", he grumbled.

"Can I be honest with you?'

"Now you want permission to stomp on my heart. Why quit while you're ahead? Just say it."

"I know you're disappointed. Don't be. In all honesty Boom...you're my fantasy too! I know that. You wanna know how I know? Because my reality would've at least tried to talk me out of what I was doin'. I mean damn... At least try to get my ass not to go back. Talk me down off the pole or somethin'. Motivate, elevate; show some real interest and concern. You know, protect me. That's the reality I want. Don't encourage my nonsense. Show me you care. Show me you want me. Show me you want to try to build with me if you really want it to go down.

My reality is the one that's gonna come and get my ass of the stage. My reality is gonna cover me in every way. My reality ain't gonna wanna share me with the world Boom. You used to come to the club and watch me dance in front of a room full of other men. You never once came to talk me down off the stage. See, its fantasy. On another note, we both have too many issues to resolve in our family lives. And I know you still have feelings for the mother of your child."

"NO I DON'T! Where is all of this coming from Liza?! Huh?! I messed up. I know. I get it...I get it! You don't want me! I can live with that. I'm a big boy. But don't put her in this! I know exactly what it is...You still wrapped up in your ex and you tryin' to turn this thing over on me to ease your guilt. THAT"S IT AND THAT"S ALL.".

Liza stands up. She laughs, "There you go. Well I knew it. I knew I was right. I done struck a nerve, huh? Why is it that the mere mention of your ex can get you all stank like that, huh? Boom just admit it man...she still gets under your skin. You don't like it. You can't control her. You wish things was different sometimes when you see her..."

"What you sauced up? Or you in some remedial community college courses as a Psych major and you think you get to analyze the world because you got accepted to some mediocre program? You proud of yourself? Huh?"

"Hold up Breezy. I'm not Tamar or that Adrienne girl so slow up aight. It ain't that serious. I was just making an observation and stating the obvious. And by the way, I don't do guilt...remember PASTOR, YOU AIN"T MY MAN! So ain't no guilt! Don't you forget that bruh!"

"While you bringin' up my boy Chris. Remember he's human and his girl was right when she told those chicks if they can't take it, they shouldn't dish it. He said it best though: Sometimes you're the fly. Sometimes you're the windshield. You should take notes and catch up." He mumbles, "Breezy...yeah whatever. Everybody need to get of his back and mind they're own business and leave somebody else's alone. I feel him. Breezy. Yeah you right. I'm a flawed man. I'm human just like he is. Sue me."

She turns to walk away. "You can be so cruel when you wanna be. You're like a frosted mini wheat. Sweet side, crunchy side. And Pastor...you need to fix that. Even I know that ain't the love of God and I was raised by a whore. Or did you forget? FOR THE RECORD. SHE WAS THE BEST MOTHER EVER. I DIDN'T WANT FOR ANYTHING. WE WENT EVERYWHERE TOGETHER. I HAD A NICE CHILDHOOD THANK YOU VERY MUCH. I KNOW PLENTY OF KIDS WHO GREW UP WITH TWO PARENTS. TWO MESSED UP ASS PARENTS THAT TURNED OUT TO BE TURNED OUT AND THEY PARENTS WAS TO BUSY DOIN' THEM TO NOTICE IT. I HAD A GOOD LIFE JACK ASS! YOU KNOW WHAT THEY SAY ABOUT JUDGING BOOKS DON'T YOU? BETTER YET ASSUMING." She whimpered like a broken little girl.

"Why you gotta bring that up? I said I was sorry Liza. Aww man. Come on now."

"Just stop it. Please just stop it."

He wrapped his arms around her. "I'm a jerk. I know how very special mothers are. Please forgive me."

"It's ok. I guess I had to get that out. Forgive me for lashing out at you. I had no right to speak to you that way. I was raised better than that. I hope I didn't hurt you."

"No apology necessary beautiful. I deserve much more. I had it coming. You have every right to defend her honor. I'm just going through so much in my mind, heart and spirit. I'm conflicted."

"I understand that. You know I do."

"Come on. Let's walk. It's cold out here."

She smiled, "Ok."

He appreciated that she knew how to speak to a man without being harsh and abrasive unless provoked. Connie had taught Liza what men needed to a certain extent. After all, it was her business to know. The way Liza spoke to Barker calmed him, soothed him. She had all of his attention whenever they were together. He sensed that within her it wasn't an act. He had spent enough time with her over the summer months to know whether or not she was manipulative. She didn't put on the charm to ask him for things. She didn't use sexuality nor feminine wiles to brainwash him into catering to her every little whim.

An independent thinker, Liza had her own opinions and ideals. He found that attractive. She didn't agree with everything he said just to appease his ego; He found that refreshing. She knew how to talk to him, when to talk to him. What tones to use. It just seemed to come naturally to her. He had never met anyone as layered; complex; as sensual as Liza ever before.

She wasn't educated. She spoke broken English, but that didn't bother him. So did he; they were from the same neighborhood. He dare not judge. He knew so many things about Liza that dazzled his mind. She could be as articulate as Oprah Winfrey if she had so chosen. She was a social chameleon of sorts. She had the ability to move amongst diverse demographics and social circles with ease. Not that they had been everywhere together. Nevertheless, Barker being intuitive and bright, he knew what she would never have to articulate. Where he had found other women beguiling he had found her honest; honorable.

Knowledgeable about many subjects, Barker was intrigued by her mind. She made him question what he thought he knew about God, life and people so often. She was cool and laid back. Every bit of that, all without losing her femininity. At his hardest, she stayed soft. When his ego inflated, she often moved over and made room for it. But she spoke up and lived her own truth when she deemed it necessary; she knew how to pick her battles. As a woman, she knew the best way to win the war sometimes was just to be silent, even when a man is being reckless and foolish. She knew to let go and let God, for soon the storm would pass.

Still young she wasn't sure of just how wrong or right that was. Whether it made her weak or strong. It had been woven into the fabric of who she was as a woman. For all of the things she did wrong, there were many things Connie had taught her daughter that were right. It was as if she knew she would need certain qualities. As much as she had hard wired her against fully submitting to male authority and leadership for fear she would be reduced, devalued and abused, she knew deep down inside that eventually Liza would break away and want to carve her own niche in life with the man of her dreams.

Connie had lived a hard, all too realistic, hurt-filled life. She was trying to teach Liza many different levels of strength and independence without getting the wires crossed. How successful could she be when no one had laid a secure foundation for her? She became overbearing, manipulative and controlling; nothing she had planned. The last person Connie Debril wanted to turn into was Rose Debril. Later she would realize that sometimes we could be running so fast, far; so deep away from something that, we're looking backwards while running forward without even knowing it. Then BAM! We run right smack into the very thing we were running from, so hard that we become a part of it or it becomes a part of us. Mother was just doing what she knew. Loving the best way she knew how.

She tried to protect Liza based on her experiences. She wanted better for her daughter. As confusing as her methods and messages were, she had only given her precious child the mother wit she had formulated based on what she had known. Connie did her best even if her daughter, in the moment, didn't realize it. Hindsight is 20/20 they say. People can only pass the baton to you from the person they received It from during the race. She was only giving her daughter what her mother gave her with more love added, peppered with desperation laced with memories. Generational curses.

He wraps his arms around her to keep her warm. He nestles his face in her neck and whispers like a shattered little boy, "I'm going thru a lot right now Liza. I have been for some time. Probably since my mom passed. I honestly don't know what it is I feel for the mother of my child or for anyone else besides my son at this point. I am lonely. I am tired. I am weak. I am bored. I am as confused as ever. Hell, I am human. Man… even if I wanted her back, after the way things have been over the years between us, it would surely be a long road back. We aren't the same people. Too much has taken place. We aren't the same hormonal fame whores we were at Weequahic High School Liza. We both got big things to sort out. Man! I don't know what I feel! But basically, you probably right. I guess you think I'm a fool."

"If you a fool Boom, so am I. And I ain't no fool. The Bible says, the fool has said in his heart, there is no God. I don't believe you've said that. I don't believe you want to live like you believe that. People go through things. Don't you know God understands that? We're weak…just dust. He's aware. We shouldn't use the liberty Jesus gives us to sin, but that why grace abounds much more than the law does, because who can keep the law? God is merciful. The Bible says His grace is unlimited. You're not a fool. We may do foolish things, but fools we are not. We still young and what look grown on the outside ain't always grown on the inside you know?"

Everything happens for a reason. My eyes are open now Boom. I'm definitely not the same. I can't ever go back after this summer. I finally got the courage to stand up to my mother as a grown woman. I've moved out. Now I'm working on me. I'm trying to grow up on my own. It's a challenge, but it's a welcome one. I'm discovering me. I don't regret a thing. If I'm supposed to, I'm sure The Lord will deal with me about it sooner or later. And Boom, I know you a man. I see that, I recognize that, I respect that. I love it…all that machismo, ego and masculine energy…I'm so into that. But I need to let you know, for all of the man you are and all of the imperfections, ego and pride, I do believe in you as a Pastor. I believe you can get back and be better than ever because of everything that done happened. All things work together for good to them that love the Lord right? Even the screw ups. The ones who are called; the predestined...the justified... the glorified."

Shrouded in brokenness he replies, "Yeah, but I'm not sure I love Him anymore. Look at all I've done. Look at the mess my life is right now. Girl, you don't know the half...my whole world is crashing down. Everything I thought I knew to be true in my life is now a lie. Liza, I don't even know who I am anymore. I don't even know who I'm becoming. For the first time in my life, I'm afraid. I'm not sure I can do it again. I'm not sure of anything, I'm empty and fruitless. I feel powerless. I don't understand God. I need time to sort things out. But thank you for believing in me. Whoever this ex is, he is a very lucky dude. He has a great reality."

"And so do you Boom once you get it all sorted out. You can do it. All things thru Christ remember? You're gonna be a great Pastor. You already are. I can see what you can't. I know its hard now, but just believe. I really do believe in you. You are more than a man Barker Golden. So much more. More than a conqueror the Bible says!"

"Oh boy. Here we go." he groans.

Yeah, I know you don't wanna hear that, but we're gettin' back to reality right? So let's be real. That's what you are. That is your calling beyond just being a man. You are more than that. Barker, you are a man of God. I know it's in there. I still feel kinda dirty about what it was between us, but I understand it. I do...you're a guy that needed a break. You had it babe, now go back. Ok?"

"I don't know Liza."

"Oh come on. The Lord is still with you. He is still in you. Plus you're already on the right track! You doin' what Jesus did. Hangin' with society's rejects. People that ain't readily accepted, but who are readily judged. People like me. You gotta go back. We need people just like you."

"Girl, you far from a reject, I don't care what anybody says or thinks about you. Can't nobody judge you. I told you that before. Ministry wise, well... I hear you. But it ain't that simple. It's just not that simple. The pressure is a lot and people just have this fantasy about leaders being flawless and pure and holy every second of the day. Honestly, you are one of the very few that know and understand. I have a calling and maybe one day I'll go back. Maybe I won't... I don't know what the future holds. I don't think that far ahead. I'm just so sad inside. So much goin' on girl. You don't know.

I'm tired of trying to be and look perfect. They got me trapped in a bubble Lyza. I've been on a balancing beam Liza; Father; son; lawyer; Pastor; mentor...on and on. I just can't be everything for everybody no more. Why is it none of the other Pastors talk about this? Huh? I mean the ups and downs, temptations, when you get tired; Burn out, sex, love, frustration, baby mama drama...you know? All of that. Nobody's talking about the reality. Oh my goodness."

"Now what?"

"I sound just like my...like him."

"Who your father? Like Al?"

"Let's not go there. I'm not ready."

"Yeah. Neither am I."

"See what I mean. Reality can be too real. I'm spinnin' like a top and they don't see it and if I let them see me fall, they gonna judge me and crucify me and judge my ass some more. I'm a man...not perfect. A man, not Superman. I'm not always as strong as I appear. It's crazy how society got it so a man can't even display his weakness, cry or say he needs help with his issues without looking weak or feeling like he let the whole world down. We carry the world on our shoulders but ain't a soul out there thinking about how heavy the weight of the world gets sometimes. It's just 'CARRY IT! DON'T CRY EITHER! LIFT IT HIGHER! BE A MAN!' That's what you hear from a little boy. They don't even give you a chance to get your strength up to be able to life the world to your waste before they start screaming at you to lift it all above your head without letting it fall and letting everybody down. Especially when you're doing it all by yourself and man code plainly states that you grin and bear it. Your woman don't understand. Can't explain it all to her without looking weak. Mom has went on to glory. Then what? What's the answer? Go to another woman. NOW YOU GOT MORE TROUBLE.

Go to ya boys to unload on them. What's the solution? Fight your feelings, drink, smoke, cheat and lie. But DON'T YOU DARE! TELL YOUR WOMAN OR CRY IN FRONT OF ANOTHER MAN ABOUT THE WORLD AND ALL THAT COMES WITH IT IS GETTING TOO HEAVY FOR YOU TO HOLD." He shakes his head.

"Pray! Oh always. But what if even in the arms of God you find no relief because you just don't know how to anymore? It has gone that far. Misery is eating away at you like a cancer. And guess what? You're Man, a leader everywhere you go and you're supposed to never show how you really feel. Mo' responsibility, mo' required. Mo' required, mo' problems. Sometimes people lean on me and depend on me too much instead going directly to the source. It gets heavy Liza. Pssshhhh man...Even Superman had weaknesses." He squeezed Liza as he fought back tears, voice cracking, he buries his face in her breasts. She continues to comfort him.

"It's ok. It's so ok. Let it out. I get it. I really do. I'm so, so sorry. Hey! Hey! Can't nobody judge you. Now I'm the one telling you."

"Thank you for coming to meet me. Thank you for listening. Thank you for just being a real woman. I wish there were more women out here like you. You're something Ms. Liza. I guess we're friends? After all of this?" He looks into her eyes kissing her gently.

Hugging tightly she answers, "Friends don't kiss Boom. You know that. Jesus! It's freezing. I stayed longer than I expected too. Can we go now? Please?"

They hold on to one another for dear life in the freezing cold. They kiss passionately.

"Mm mm...You are so sweet! And you still have the sweetest kiss in Jersey! Hershey's kisses baby. Laaaawwwwdddd you fine. That joker better behave and he better be thankful for what he got! Have mercy Jesus. Let me walk you to your car. Come on."

"So I got the sweetest kiss in Jersey? That means you kissed how many women in the great Garden State?"

"Well, I AIN'T YA MAN and you AIN'T MY REALITY so I guess I don't have to keep it real. This was all just a Mid Summer's Night Dream remember beautiful. Never happened..." he laughs.

"Wait! Just one more thing. Why didn't you just come out and tell me you were a pastor the night we met?"

"You see the way you reacted when you found out I was a pastor? That's why. I haven't dated in a very long time because I decided, at one point, to give myself totally over to the Lord's work and His will. I couldn't find quality women to fit my criteria and the fact that I am was a pastor didn't make the search for 'Mrs. Right' any easier. It's hard to even approach women outside of the church for even a cup of coffee and a conversation sometimes because all they see is what you do. They don't see the man behind the robe. Even as a lawyer, they don't see past the title and the suit; that's all they see. They see acquisition; I see it in them. Who says I really want to spend the rest of my life in and out of court rooms? What if I wanted I to quit litigating because something else is pulling me? What if the season for that is over in my life and I did decide to go into ministry full time where there may not always be consistent pay and the work hours were awkward? Who can deal with that? Who is going to just let me be a man when I'm at home and the game is on and I haven't shaved or showered and it is one in the afternoon?"

"Yikes Boom. TMI." She snickers, "Just joking."

"And that is exactly what I mean. I can't really just be me...you know, the way I can be with you. I know you're kidding. But every woman ain't as chill as you. That scares me. I want the right one Liza. I need to be able to be Boom and not Barker. Barker has an image to protect. Boom. Well hey, Boom just don't give a …."

He thought to himself, while explaining to her "Stacey. She never gave a ….I was always able to chill with her. She's not easily impressed. She never cared about any of that. Titles and status never meant a thing to her. With her, I'm just Boom. And she always just tell it like it is man. No shorts. Nah...But she too wide open. She's on a nut farm right now. Man, I don't where I'm at right now with nothing no more. Get out of your head man."

"...even the women in the church...they bow down and go out of their way to impress and put on because they think they have to cater to an image or their perception of just who I really am. I need to be able to have fun, kick back, laugh and have regular moments and regular conversations. When I'm wrong I may not want to acknowledge it...I have pride like every other man, but, be my woman, be my best friend...tell me the truth; Give me the real, tell me I'm wrong; And please don't expect me to know EVERYTHING or be right all of the time. I only know what I have learned and what the Holy Spirit tells me. And since we're ever evolving and I see life as a class room, there's so much I will always need to re-think, undo and learn. Just because you have received education in an area or field, doesn't mean you're an expert. You can still be taught. Experience is the best teacher. Since life is a series of experiences, no one can claim expertise I every area. Somebody can always one up you on something. I guess I'm waiting on the woman that can one up me in some fashion. I'm lonely."

"Not only are you lonely. You are long winded. Boy…"

"Pardon me. It just comes naturally."

"The whole sermon thing right?"

He laughed, "Yeah. I guess."

"Remind me to never come to your service." she teased

"Ha! Very funny pretty lady. But one more thing…won't be before you long. I'm about to let you go."

"Here we go." she thought. "This is another reason people don't come to church…"

He laughed, "Alright. Alright I coming."

"What he said." she teased.

"Ok. Let's keep it clean. Be a lady now. Don't turn on me Liza."

"Great. Now all of a sudden you want me to be a lady."

"That's always been love."

"Hypocrite.", she coughed.

"What?"

"Huh?" she laughed.

"Whatever. Anyway, I love sports. I like challenges. I don't want a woman that's so religious she feels the need to dress up in smocks and prairie skirts to fit an image that she thinks fits me. I mean be classy, be sophisticated, be comfortable, be casual; Yes be saved, sanctified, Holy Spirit filled, fired baptized. You gotta be anointed. With me...you gotta be patient; I'm a work in progress like everybody else. Be a real woman of God. But be my woman, be my wife. Make me want you. Keep me guessing'. Make me chase you. Be sexy sometimes. I'm a visual, physical, red-blooded, young American male. I like sex. I want it. Be feminine. Be sexual behind closed doors, be open, be my fantasy and my reality. Be creative. Be able to adjust. Be my private dancer, be my lover. Imma be your man. Just do me a favor...be my woman. You get that Liza? I hope I'm not laying too much on you, but who else I got to confide in? Ain't nobody else I can let go with. I'm sorry if it was too much. But I'm bringing you the real, rap raw right now. Feel me?"

"Whew!" She laughed, "I get it. You crave understanding. You're a man beyond the titles, status, standings, expectations and responsibilities. But Boom you sure got a lotta 'be's and me's. Your list is too long and you are too long winded. And I thought women could bring it. Lord man."

Liza was well versed in the requirements on Barker's list. He was preaching to the choir. Everything he desired, she could be. Yet, she knew she wasn't the one. She knew why men cheated. She knew what they expected. How they liked it. How they liked to be rewarded and that reward, most often was sex. They liked to win and to be acknowledged. They like being spontaneous. Role play, adventure, games, hunting and exciting new things. Keep their secrets. Hold their hands when their unsure. Tell them when they're wrong in loving ways in respectful tones, but only at the right time. Liza was groomed to be mindful of the right time. Most importantly, be feminine and only submit to a man who is submitted to God and remember the male ego is fragile. She knew what he needed. She had it. Yet, he wouldn't be the one to receive it. Right thing. Wrong motives. Wrong place Wrong time. Wrong person.

"Maybe next lifetime. But not today." she giggled as she pondered the possibilities.

"Well see, you can't put every man in the same box. Some men like to talk. Especially when if the conversation is meaningful. I need you to understand, I don't get to have many meaningful conversations with women. I'm not sure I've ever had one this meaningful in my life honestly. If I know I have your confidence, I will talk to you. I know I have your confidence Liza. I don't run across many women like you. Sometimes I just want to beat-down you know? Enjoy a fulfilling exchange without an ulterior motive. Every time two people of the opposite sex get together, I don't believe it has to be about sex; not even if there's history or mutual attraction. Sometimes a brother just want a connection Liza. That's real. Gotta grow up sometimes you know? I really appreciate this talk. You're understanding and easy to talk to. You're a good listener and an awesome friend. Thank you for not judging Me.", He kisses her on the cheek.

"You know I'm the last to judge. I must say though, in keeping with the honesty theme, I'm having a hard time moving past that list. I understand it. But I have to ask if you're asking for too much?"

"Too much?"

"Think about it Boom. Is it realistic? You ran down your list of 'be's' like you was creating a Fantasy Football team. I'm not sure if you're going to get all of that in one woman Boom.

 Seems like you're still dealing in fantasy. Perfection is a job even Eve and Wonder Woman couldn't handle. I'm not quite sure of exactly how fair that is."

"Wow Liza. I guess I never thought of that. Do you think I'm selfish?"

"Now you're an educated man. You know how it goes. If you have to ask the question, it means you probably already have the answer. My question for you is this though: While you're itemizing your list of 'Do's and Don'ts', have you ever thought of what this woman may require of you? I mean, besides the obvious, what do you bring to the table? Will you able to meet her standards? Can you handle her confident woman with your same personality type who is a born leader and not feel intimidated because she is as or possibly even more successful than you? What if she makes more money than you do? What if she requires a lot of your attention? Ever thought about sacrificing what you want to make someone else happy? Are you willing to be uncomfortable to make her feel at home in a home you've been a bachelor in all of your life? What if the woman of your dreams doesn't really need you? Could you handle that? If she's not tidy, organized and domestic, could you handle that? How would you deal with a career-driven counterpart that doesn't really make time for sex because her mind is on her money? What if you meet the one and she starts off solely dependent on you. But she has her own dreams and goals. She's working on herself, times goes by, her hard work is paying off; she's a success. Seasons begin to change and she can no longer cater to your every whim...How do you handle that? What if she's more sexual than you? What if you can't keep up? You say you want all of these things. Sounds to me like you want a custom Stepford wife, limited edition, mail order blow-up doll with a battery pack and a kill switch."

"Whoa. Whoa. You just went in. You're going too far girl. What's good?"

"Hey. I'm just sayin'. We all have lists. If you can dish it, you gotta be able to take it. Don't you think your ideas are a little chauvinistic? I mean seriously. What are you willing to do for this woman? What is your contribution? What is your sacrifice? What do you have that's so good that she would want to cater to you so much? What are you willing to 'BE' for her? I guarantee you, I don't know many grown, level headed woman that want to be owned. And nobody wants to be made to feel less than unless she doesn't know how to value herself. Sounded like you wanted a mail order sex slave.

"What?! No."

She grinned, "I'm just sayin."

"Good point. I'll take a good look at that." He stares off into space. "Ever thought about being a prosecutor?"

"Never."

"You'd be a good one. I have yet to meet a woman that wouldn't be a good one."

"Funny." He continued to stare into nothingness. "Something more?"

"Thinking about a lot. I don't know. Sometimes as Christians we can just be so religious. We forget it is not about religion. It is about relationship. Do people ever think to wonder if the man or woman for that matter, behind the message is doing ok in their walk with God? We can be anointed to do a thing and be good at it and wrestle with fears, issues and struggles on the other end. Why don't people get that and just check in on the pastor sometimes Liza? Pray for them. Shepherds walk a lonely, rough road. A road that can get as cold and as dark as it is going to get tonight.

As pastor and a lawyer, you spend so much of your time counseling, consoling, praying for people; You hold the bereaved and grieving after the funeral, you reassure, fight for and support people in mediation, at the bargaining table, during power lunches, on conference calls and in courtrooms; even on the golf course and the basketball court it's networking and consultation when you just want some recreation. You hear more than your fair share of woes, excuses, tawdry details and horror stories. You weep with those that weep. Laugh with those that are celebrating. Emotions go up and down and black is sometimes white and vice versa.

In both genres of professionalism, you're the confidant, the shoulder to cry on. We're the keepers of secrets, oaths and promises without compromise. But whose shoulder do we cry on when the world is laying their heads on ours and we're supposed to remain solid and stoic? King Solomon said himself that knowing too much can make you sad. We pray. But when that ain't enough, and we need to be held; the lion needs to trade places with the lamb...Where do we go? Especially when you can't even find a mate who understands. I don't know everything. It's a myth that pastors and lawyers have all of the answers. It's a myth that lawyers don't have integrity. I do! And it is hard to keep it sometimes I must admit, but it is possible. Life is tough Liza. Nobody knows what it's like to be me. They just assume its grits and gravy from outside appearances. But if they look inside they will see my heart, mind and spirit are just as fragile as my ego. I'm not a man of steel. I'm just a man. A man that doesn't know what to do."

He had a lot bottled up inside. Barker knew had a lot of issues and many more questions that weren't going to be resolved in one night. All of his biblical knowledge, education and physical fortitude was doing him no good. It was as if he was losing everything he had thought he knew. Like he needed to be back in Sunday school. It was frightening and refreshing all at once for Barker to be that bare to anyone. He hadn't been so transparent and real since before his mother passed. Until then, he had kept everything locked away. He was slowly coming undone. It was time. To everything there is a season. A time and purpose for everything under heaven. Spring was approaching. It was time shed the heavy layers in his life.

"Well you know I ain't got the answers. I ain't God either. I still have a laundry list of questions myself for Jesus. See, that's another reason we ain't meant to be. We're both still broken. God don't put two broken pieces together to make one another whole. We're supposed to be whole alone with him before we sync up. And when two people that God put together sync up, ain't no brokenness involved. The Bible says the blessings of the Lord make us wealthy and to them blessings He adds no sorrow. Something more to consider. We was just feeding one another's dysfunction. That's all. But brother...Brother you done said a mouthful. Child, you done preached! YOU BETTER PREACH PASTOR!" she screams.

He looked around as the passers-by looked on. "Girl don't you start that mess. So anyway, you don't have to preach to me ok? I'm well versed in scripture. And sense you up in the pulpit giving the good word, I got a question for you PASTOR: When you comin' down off the pole? I told you girl, you better than that. People kill me man. You know so much, you in the word, but when you gonna apply it? Don't just be a hearer. Be a doer homey."

"Oh my goodness. Iyanla fix your life before you attempt to fix mine aight?"

"My sentiments exactly baby girl. Let's go home." They stroll to the park's exit. Liza was stone silent for a minute. She knew he was right. He knew what she had said was right. They were both too prideful to admit it.

She roared, "Gettin' at me. How you gon' come for me?"

"Say what now?"

"I see you. You call yourself droppin' jewels on the kid?! Boy, don't YOU start that mess. Everything in God's timing. King Solomon said there's a season for everything right?" she replies.

"Oh no! You not one of them are you?" he charged annoyed.

"One of who?" she remarked sharply.

"One of those people that manipulate scripture to suit their situation. Just tallying up excuses to keep in their mess."

"No I am not! And how dare you with your broken wing, use the one half o' good one you got left to try to smack me in the face with it! How dare you Barker Golden. Judge not lest ye be judged."

"Whoa! Hold up! Shots fired! Aight ma, put ya gun away. I don't want no trouble. My bad. You even prettier when you get angry. I like that."

"Shut up. And for a lawyer, you sure got the Ebonics down packed."

"There you go with your stereotypes and puttin' people in boxes. Whatever Stripper Barbie. I'm a Brick City baby just like you. Don't sleep."

When they get to her car she invites him in to warm up a bit. Keyshia Cole can be heard singing, "I Choose You" in the background. Liza's daydreaming about Jason.

"I know this may come across as phony, but I'm being earnest when I tell you right now, there really is a part of me that does and will probably always care for you. The man within, the real me, the flawed me cares for you Liza. I'll always be here for you. You've been there for me. I appreciate that."

"Aww. That's a sweet thing to say. I appreciate you not judging me and allowing me to spread my wings and fly in whatever direction I feel is right for me at the time. I haven't found that anywhere else. Imma be there for you too, when you need Me.", she promises.

He stares longingly into her eyes, "I really do mean it Liza. I appreciate you. Whoever your ex is, he is so blessed to have you in his life."

In that moment, they were not confusing lust with love. It was the purest, most innocent, most intimate moment they had ever had. A moment in time that would forever be frozen. A moment they would move on from, but never forget. A rare moment in life that they would take to the grave. It was deeply personal. In that moment, at that final private meeting, they had become the gust of wind beneath one another's wings. They had slowly escorted one another to the threshold of the door of their realities. Whomever they were about to become, whatever the future held, the people in those futures would inadvertently owe a debt of gratitude to these star crossed lovers for the what they were about to inherit. With God, nothing is ever wasted. All things really do work together for good to them that love the Lord and are called according His purpose. The predestined...the justified...the glorified.

She drives him over to where his car is parked as they part ways, the mood is somber and with the cruel wind whipping into their cars. As one door closes and the other opens, reality creeps in and they both drive off to their separate lives. "Ok girl, yep! He's hot. But you had your fun. Get it together. We movin' forward." Liza whispers to herself.

"Now that is a woman boy. Yo! Damn! Aight man, shake that off B! Let's get it! Whatever's next...you got dis.", Barker tells himself.   He tunes his iPod to his "Oldies" playlist and Sam Cooke tells a story, "I was born by the river. In a little tent. Oh and just like that river, I've been runnin' ever since. It's been a long, a long time comin' but I know...a change gonna come. Oh yes it will. It's been too hard living but I'm afraid to die. 'Cause I don't know what's up there, beyond the sky. It's been a long, a long time comin' but I know a change gonna come, oh yes it will." He's in a daze driving home with the song on repeat all of the way.

AGAINST ALL ODDS

"Doors of the church are now open. If you don't know Jesus as your Lord and Savior, it is not too late. It is never too late until God stops breathing life into you. The problem with that is, only He knows when that will be exactly. With that being said, time waits for no man, tomorrow isn't promised. Tomorrow may never come. This may be your last opportunity to get right with Jesus. I promise you this, I was just like you... still have my days, my struggles, my battles.

Temptation is a fact of life and marriage, being a member of the clergy, being held to a higher standard; living your life in the public eye under a microscope and being a parent are factors that clearly do not make one exempt. A lot of pressure comes with each one of those callings and responsibilities. Actually, all that comes with those pressures might be what makes temptation all the more difficult to resist, naturally. Amen Church? I know it's not just me. I know firsthand, it ain't just men who experience the throws of temptation. Pressure is pressure. Don't put your leaders on a pedestal folks. Nothing in the Word encourages us to exalt ourselves or others. Be mindful of puffing people up; especially men. We have greedy, hungry egos that like to be fed. Don't O.D on the stroking ladies. People are people. Men and women leaders alike. We will let you down someday. It is human nature to falter y'all. And leaders, household or otherwise, the Bible warns us against exalting ourselves more highly than we ought. After pride comes the fall people. I'm speaking to you and myself at the same time. Gotta check yourself be for you..." The parishioners give him a standing ovation.

"Please you all have a seat. It's just family talkin'. Y'all know the rest of the hook. I see some of you all in here looking to be around my age. Hip-hop generation. I'm still a fan. I won't lie to you. I'm human. Got a teenager in my house. I listen to some Jay, some Kanye; some Chris Brown. Some Frank Sinatra; Chaka Kahn and all that good stuff. A lil this a lil that."

The young people leap to their feet. "Yeah Pastor. That's why we love you man. Yeah."

He looks over the top of his glasses. "I know y'all older people in here ain't gonna confess to knowing how to do the 'Nay-Nay'. You won't tell these young people that they didn't invent tight jeans and the 'Dougie'. Aw, y'all ain't gon' tell 'em that Chris Brown ain't the first Chris Brown. I guess y'all forgot about Bobby Brown?" The young people cheer. "Tell the truth Pastor!"

"Y'all know I'm not ashamed of the truth, whatever it may be for whomever it may be for. I was young. I messed up a lot. I was angry, misunderstood, violated some laws and a few people. I can listen to a brother like Chris because I used to listen to a brother named Bobby. I ain't ashamed of it. I understand some of it... the issues. I know what it is to be a young man and be making the wrong choices. I think Chris Brown is a tremendous talent. I listened to his freestyles. I looked at some of his art. I sing his songs to my wife. I try to dance to his music with my daughter. See, he's not an evil supervillain. People are giving him too much power. He's a kid. Forgive him for as many mistakes as he makes. Pray for him. He deserves as many chances as he asks for. Look at how many chances God gives us. How much do we mess up real big in secret places, behind closed doors where no one can see but God and the Devil himself? The boy is growing. Do we ever stop to think that in his frustration, he keeps responding the way we expect him too? Maybe it's conditioning? I don't have all of these answers. All I know is we should, as Christians, show the same love, mercy and grace to all of the Browns. The same Browns that entertain us. The same love, mercy and grace God shows us each and every day. Make room for forgiveness in your heart. And let's start being honest with our youth because ain't nothin' new under the sun." The congregation claps. Some reluctantly.

"I know some of you are thinking to yourself, 'How can he support that boy after what he's done. Doesn't he remember what he did to that girl?' ...and well, you're well within your rights to think it. For the record, I do remember. But because I'm not perfect, I have a checkered past, I have a father I love with all of my heart that I grew up watching smash my mother's face in whenever he got tanked...I learned to forgive him over time.

Now to clear things up a bit, I don't support domestic violence against anyone. I do though, support kindness and forgiveness. God is a god of many chances. I have received much forgiveness, grace and mercy…so I now give it away. To whom much is given…"

 The congregation responds harmoniously, "Much is required."

 "That is all I'm saying. These are our children. Our future. Doesn't matter if it's a Brown, Bieber, Cyrus, Kardashian or anyone else. Take your pick. But do me favor, pick your children too! There are supposed to be different. Many times though, they are not. Saved or not. Young people gonna mess up… A LOT! Give 'em room to grow. Most of us here grew up sans social media and hyper-opinionated talk show hosts. I remember when talk shows were informative and discussed topics that provoked thought and change. It ain't so no more. Nothing's the same. But back to my point. All music ain't bad music. I just try to be careful of what it is I consume and just how much of it I consume. Young people, I'm not here to judge you. I do however, suggest you do the same. You feed your body healthy things to keep it in proper condition; do the same for your spirit. You won't be sorry. I promise you. Keep in mind that what we feed will always grow and dominate. Amen?"

"Amen.", agrees the congregation.

"Ok.", he looks at his watch. "Like I was saying… and I'm about to wrap this up. We are no different than you are. We're just people who are supposed to know and do better. We're still human. We have issues, short comings; areas to work on and grow in like everyone else at the end of the day. Don't be disappointed when your leaders fall.

Don't be shocked and disgusted when scandal comes to rock your church, your city, your country, your household. Your chosen leaders, more specifically, your pastors, are just people who know Jesus with a calling to deliver unto whom The Lord wills, a timely message. We are ministers.

Christians you're all ministers. Ministers of reconciliation and hope. Perfection does not qualify you for ministry. Know this, God searches the reins of the heart. That's what He did when sent the prophet Samuel to go choose the successor to King Saul. He chose the dirty shepherd boy, the least of all of his father's sons David. Never mind what He knew David what do. We forget that our God, Lord Jehovah is omniscient; all knowing. He knows it all. Beginning to end and back again. We never take in to account that God chose David to be the next King of Israel as a child. He anointed a man He knew was as flawed as they came with real masculine urges, tendencies, issues and weaknesses."

A woman cried out, "Hallelujah!"

The pastor whisper ever so gently into the microphone, "God called him, chose Him. Anointed him anyway... Yes. He calls us, all of us anyway." The church erupts. Tears and cheers.

"Glory be to God. Come Holy Ghost come. We welcome you into this place. Have your way. All is yours Lord. Oh blessed be God. All is yours Lord Jesus. Have your way Father. Hallelujah. Thank you Lord. We want you to have your way Lord God. Yesss Jesus.", the First Lady of the church prays. Shouting and praising can be heard from a block away. The doors of the church are open.

"Yes! Yes! Have your way Lord Jesus! Yes! See that's what you do. That is how you do it. Praise Him! He deserves the highest praise." The Pastor begins to speak in tongues. Others soon follow. Thirsty souls cry out for refreshment and rest.

He motions for the musicians to stop the music. "Most of you in this room know my testimony. You know how Jesus came into my heart, changed my very life; saved my soul. Not just one time did He save me; over and over again...every day the Savior comes to my rescue. We all need a hero. I need a hero. I'm man enough to admit and submit to it. Guys, I need a hero. Every day I need another chance to get it right."

"Yes Lord. We all do. Amen Pastor." his wife yells.

Men! I want you to pay attention to this message in particular. Ladies, you all listen up too! Many of you are raising little men; that's how you have to see your sons. As little boys we are groomed to believe all strength lies within us; we're invincible...the providers, the protectors. All the pressure is on us; we are groomed to be society's heroes. We were never taught that it's ok to say we need one sometimes; a hero that is. It's a tragedy. It's a falsehood. We are taught to bear the weight of everybody else's fear and pain and to grin as we do it all. Hmmmmm....do it all. We think we can do it all until we break and crumble like cookies on a floor. Suppress the fear, the anxiety the pain. Hide the flaws beneath the work load and bravado. Never show the chinks in the armor. Be an Incognito not a Martin. Well...," he paused to clear his throat.

He continues after a drink of water and a deep breath, "Hold back the tears. Show no weakness. DON'T BE A PUNK! TAKE CONTROL! FIGHT BACK! BE A MAN! MAN UP!

Can't even cry to your woman. Wow! ...And you wonder why we have problems showing emotion and being intimate with our spouses? Why there's such a disconnection?

Where in the Bible does it say men can't be emotional, sensitive when necessary and intimate with the women in our lives; supportive? God has emotions beyond jealousy and anger you know? Jesus was masculine, authoritative, confident, assertive, strong and loving, caring, sensitive and intimate all together. He was whatever he was being called to be at the time in which it was necessary. He was confident in God and his manhood and no one questioned his masculinity. David cried; a king, a warrior...he was even weak and afraid at times and he wasn't afraid to show it. David needed to be saved and covered...he needed reassurance, comfort, provision, protection... King David; David the man, needed God. He needed a hero. That hero was God. Read the Psalms!

Jesus wept! It's a reality we men face as we cry alone in the dark or run to the open arms and legs of another woman we have no business even associating with because inside, we are broken, fragile; just little men who need a lap to climb into sometimes like we used to do our moms. We need someone to tell us it's gonna be alright when we're not sure. I can hear some of the younger ladies saying right now, 'Pastor you mean my daddy, my uncle, my big brother doesn't know everything'. No! We don't know it all. Now I know I sound weak to you all, but, I'm confident in my manhood. So I'm not bothered. God made me the man I am. I am because of who He is. He is the great I AM.

We want to hide behind someone sometimes too, like we used to our fathers, some of us. Well, today, I'm here to tell you, God is still that lap you can crawl up into. He is still the strong figure you can hide behind; the shoulder to cry on, the listening ear, the relief from burden and stress lies within His arms.

Fathers, mothers, ladies, gentlemen, brothers, sisters...Jesus is our hero. No one can get through this life and its hardships alone; we were not meant too. I assure you. And yes ladies, like I said before, this message is for you too! You don't have to be super woman. Don't let no MAN, woman or child hold that to your charge. Do what you can, when you can and when you can't, say so. Never be ashamed to say you need help or that you're tired. Don't allow a man to hold you to a standard his mother couldn't even keep without her mother helping her or going out for a night on the town with the girls or sleeping with the milk man while you were safely tucked away in your bed. People tend to judge single mothers too harshly especially. The pressure is too much. It's not easy juggling everything. Don't judge them when they need a babysitter because they want to go out and do something for them once in a while...they need a break! My wife taught me about that stuff. She was a single mother before we got married. It is hard. Everybody ain't good at balancing and juggling everything. Everybody needs help sometimes. Let's just lay the truth out there. Amen?"

All of the young mothers in the church and a few of the older woman stood up and praised God.

"Now fellas. I'm looking at some of you. You don't seem too happy about that last statement. That's fine. Ministry is not about keeping everybody comfortable. In fact it is quite the adverse. Ministry is about motivating, undeniable truths. Truth is supposed to cause you not only to think; truth is supposed to move you to act.

Truth is, as men we forget how heavy your load is ladies, sisters. Mothers, daughters, aunts, nieces, etc... Because traditionally we don't carry it. When it is too hard to bear, take it to the Lord in prayer. Husbands, share your wives loads. They need help too! And a break sometimes. They're stronger than we are in many ways. They can be our heroes sometimes, nothing wrong with a strong woman. Those of you that come from single-parent homes know this more than I do. Where does it say a woman can't be a man's hero?" A few of the younger men began to clap and embrace some of the older woman at the service.

"We must love and respect them as they love and respect us. We can't do everything they can do. They bring us balance guys. Lest we forget. They make our lives easier. A good wife/woman does anyway. Ladies...men are not perfect. Don't apply unjust pressure and expectations to human beings with limitations. No man is perfect. Where the man in your life falls short, and we all do, know God won't, He can't! Make Jesus your hero ladies. Put Him first. Realize men are just people doing their best. Good men are anyway. Don't take the men in your life for granted. Be they sons, fathers, husbands, uncles, brother, etc. Tell them how important and necessary they are to you. Show them appreciation and kindness; reward them. We like rewards. Encourage them. Don't laugh when they fall; help them up if you can. Not so much that you emasculate him; Men need responsibility, structure, discipline and accountability. Give them the space they need to be the men they are. Hold 'em. Respect them. And finally, if they are your heroes, let them know. We need to know. If there is no man in your life...no woman in your life; someone dependable, loving, and strong ...even if there is, you can still call on the mighty name of Jesus. He will answer. For no one can be your all. That is The Lord's job and distinct pleasure." There wasn't a dry eye in the house.

"In the beginning, God, the Father looked at Adam and said 'IT IS NOT GOOD FOR MAN TO BE ALONE.' Created Eve to be by his side; a helpmeet. Now is the time for you to let Jesus be your helpmeet so to speak. All of you. We can do all things...but through Christ alone; not ALONE. Brothers and sisters I say all of this to say, Jesus changed my life when I asked him to come into my life and be my hero. He is my hero. Christ is who I rely on. The Lord is who I trust. I'm no different than you...only difference is the Christ within. Will you allow Him to be your hero and make the difference in you today? Right now? Today, before it is too late? He stands at the door and knocks. Will you allow Him inside of you TODAY brethren, I promise you he will change your life. Will there be one TODAY?"

A man crawls up to the base of the pulpit on his knees. Broken he wails, "JESUS HELP ME! PLEASE SOMEBODY SAVE ME! I NEED HELP! LORD I CAN'T DO THIS ANYMORE!" The Holy Spirit had filled the chapel. All of a sudden, people from every corner were slowly making their up to the feet of the Pastor, thirsty to be filled by the Living Water. Surely a drink from His cup and they would thirst no more. Voices cried out in repentance. Every voice that cried out longed to be fed. They were hungered for the Bread of Life. They would hunger no more as that day, they would be filled with Jesus Christ, the risen Savior. The Pastor fell to his knees in tears, "Thank you for this bountiful harvest Jesus. Thank you for all of these thirsty souls. Be lifted Lord...oh how we need you tonight in this place."

Cries, prayers and praise bellowed out from beyond the stained-glass windows in the sanctuary for about an hour continuously in that place. The anointing was powerful and heavy. The draw was strong and undeniable as the Holy Ghost did His work; God's Spirit had His way. Many were delivered that night from various demons and addictions.

"Know right now brothers and sisters, there is a party being thrown in heaven for you all right now. To every backslider, God is saying I am your friend. Welcome home. I love you. Be made whole. Go and sin no more." The Pastors shouted while jumping from one row of pews to the other, anointing every head he could find. People began shouting, some began to speak in tongues as the Holy Spirit fell on each.

"IT AIN'T ABOUT PERFECTION, IT IS ABOUT BEING BLAMELESS. IT IS NOT A LIMITATION. SEE SALVATION AS A

LIFESTYLE. HE LOVES YOU! HE LOVES YOU!" he points to the choir director. The choir begins to "Calling My Name".

"YEEEEEESSSSSSSSSSSSSSSSS! SHOUT HALLELUJAH! YEEEEEESSSSSS!!!!! BACKSLIDER... HE AIN'T DONE WITH YOU! HE LOVES YOU! JESUS LOVES YOU! DOESN'T MATTER WHAT YOU'VE DONE! HE IS HERE TODAY. YESTERDAY DOESN'T MATTER! YESTERDAY IS DEAD! YOUR PAST IS OVER! YOUR PAST HAS NO POWER OVER YOU! HE'S SO HAPPY YOU SHOWED UP TODAY! BACKSLIDER... OH BACKSLIDER... OH BACKSLIDER. HE LOVES YOU! JESUS LOVES YOU!

HEAR THE FATHER SAY: I AM! I AM! I AM! I AM GOD! NO OTHER! THE SAME YESTERDAY, TODAY, FOREVER MORE... I AM! BACKSLIDER, I AM THE GREAT I AM! I LOVE YOU! I LOVE YOU! BACKSLIDER... I LOVE YOU! IT DOESN'T MATTER WHO DOES NOT... I AM GOD ALONE! I LOVE YOU! COME HOME BACKSLIDER! I LOVE YOU!" he yells at the top of his lungs from the pulpit. The choir continues to sing, all of them, now in tears. Hands raised. The chapel erupts into shouts of praise and worship to Almighty God.

A slow hush passes over the congregation. Everyone worshiping. "Will there be another?" he whispers into the microphone. "The door is still open I hear the Father saying. It's not too late. Will there be another? Pretend it's the last call for alcohol on Saturday night." He took a deep breath, "JESUS SAID COME GET IT!"

Just then a thin, frail shape presses through the crowd on her hands and knees at the exact moment the Pastor turns to walk back to the pulpit. She grabs hold of the cuff of his robe. The choir sings with authority, "YOU'RE CALLING MY NAME..." He looks down only to see a broken, pregnant woman. He bends down and lifts her up, "Child, what are you doing down there? What is your name?"

"My name is Stacey. Stacey James pastor." He grabs her malnourished body and the women of the church come to hold her up. He anoints her head and prays for her with tears in his eyes. The choir still singing, "OH LORD I'VE SINNED BUT YOU'RE STILL CALLING MY NAME…". They lower her down to the chapel floor, draping her in a brand new white sheet. Stacey has passed out. She has no idea that God is in that moment, giving her new life. Another chance. The church gathers all around her, prayers rose up to the heavens that night. All for the deliverance and healing of one Stacey James.

MAKE ME OVER

"You aight?" The pastor hands Stacey a cup of cold water.

She's trying to revive herself, unaware of all that has taken place while in her subconscious state, she shakes her head, "Ummm….yeah I guess. What…What happened?"

"Holy Spirit took over Stacey."

Still shaken she remarked, "Pastor, I've been saved from childhood, grew up in a small church. My father was a pastor. I just never had an experience that deep before. I don't understand. What is God doin'?".

"Makin' you over again sis. He is the God of not just second chances, but the God of many opportunities. His mercy is renewed every morning. I hear the Spirit saying restored. You have been made whole. The Lord of Hosts has chosen you; before the universe had been even spoken into existence; before you were formed in your mother's womb, you already existed; God knew you. He planned your course. All of your days were written. Today, by His grace be made whole." He kneels down as tears fall from her puffy eyes in to her lap, "Believe God has always had his eyes on you. Watching you, pursuing you, protecting you and loving you. Following you when you did not want Him to. Guarding you when you didn't even care to acknowledge his presence and sovereignty. He never leaves us nor will He ever forsake us. God is faithful. He keeps His promises even when we break ours to Him. He does not change."

"A plan? For me? How can He use me? I'm so messed up in the game. You don't even know. And I know me. I just know I'm gonna mess up again and again! How on earth can God really love me and accept me? He's too good for me...I know that man. Ain't nobody gonna tell me no different! I'm no good. I'm used up. Dirty, stupid; I'm not good enough for Him or anybody else. What could he possibly want with me? What on earth does He see?"

A feminine voice chimes in from just beyond the door of the Pastor's office, "He's not through with you yet honey. He sees us through His eyes. Not our own or those of others. Man's view is limited. He sees you as a finished product. Not even a work in progress. Not a factory reject. You're special to the Lord. We all are. Handcrafted, each one, created to be different. Every born-again believer bears His seal and stamp of approval. He sees you the way He created you to be. Not your mistakes."

"Who are you?" Stacey responds, "How you know?"

The woman walks over to Stacey and as she takes a seat next to her, she cups Stacey's hands and says, "I used to be where you are. Maybe I was you."

The pastor raises up from his knees, "Keesha can you handle this?"

"Yeah Pastor, I got It."

"So you his aide/assistant? Here to handle his light work?"

"Well, you can say that. I don't consider being a servant to you light work though. We're all equally as important here and God is no respecter of persons. I serve everybody I see, in and out of these walls. That is the calling of every blood-washed believer. We are called to serve. There is no such thing as a menial task or a low or high position. We are all equal. The Lord equips with different gifts and talents to do various works in the body. We're connected. All equal."

"All equal? I don't think so. Hey. To be in the position you in, you must be good at what you do. Perfect probably. I mean you the pastor's right hand ain't you? You can't be he close to somebody that important and have his back and not be flawless." Stacey scoffed. She looked the woman up and down, "Look at you. You even look flawless. Uh huh...he probably all into you."

She laughed, "Girl looks ain't everything. Let me be the first to tell you. We all get old and gravity does not discriminate. I'm just doing my part."

"Whatever. You can be as humble as you want to. But I remember when I looked perfect and hot. Just like you. And I wasn't as humble though. I don't think you have to be when you flawless." She starred at the woman. "You look like you do everything right. Like you never miss a beat."

Again, the woman chuckles, "Don't be fooled now. I'm not perfect in any area. I'm a mess like everyone else. I Mess up every day, even and especially when no one else sees what I did or knows my inner-most thoughts. God does though and yet, He forgives me as I confess, I receive His new mercy every new day He allows me to live. I'm thankful for it and I just live this life the best way I know how...like everybody else, saved or unsaved. I take things as they come and try to be better than I was yesterday. Girl, every day is a day to get it right. Every day is a day full of new opportunity and every day is a day where yesterday don't even matter."

"Miss...That's all well and good. But see, I'm not like you. I'm pregnant with my second child out of wedlock and THIS TIME I don't know WHO the father is. I used to get high like clockwork until I found out I was pregnant. I lost custody of my oldest boy a long time ago and I don't know how to face him. I know he gon' have hard questions I ain't ready to answer man...Look lady, I turned my back on Jesus long time ago. But today, somehow, for the first time, I believe He ain't turn His back on me. I just still ain't sure what He can do with me. I mean today...today, I want something different. For the first time in my life. But how is change gonna come to somebody like me?"

"Oh baby," Keesha held Stacey in her arms. She rocked her like a child who has lost its mother, "You have low expectations of the Master. He can do ANYTHING. Nothing is wasted where God and purpose are concerned. You are so valuable to The Lord girl. Jesus loves you. He is gonna use you and all of your experiences, flaws and failures to speak to his people, people others cannot reach; all in His timing for; all for his glory. You and your family have purpose. God wants to restore your broken relationship and heal your broken places as you continue to cling to Him. In the book of Romans we are charged to not be conformed to this world but to be transformed by the renewing of our minds. Baby, you gotta get in the word and begin to see yourself the way he sees you. He who has begun a good work in you will not fail to complete it until the day of Christ Jesus. His word will do what He sends it forth to do and it will not return to Him void. HALLELUJAH!!!!!! BE MADE WHOLE IN CHRIST!!!! HALLELUJAH JESUS! BE MADE WHOLE! She pulled Stacey up to her feet.

"It is already done....already done...already done...the doors are open...God is saying you can walk on through. The way is made....go on through child. Go and sin no more. Go and sin no more."

"I hear the Spirit saying, your past is gone, it's over Stacey. Although you've been saved a long time, you had not known the real Jesus. Everything before this was a religious experience. Now you will meet the real Jesus and have a righteous experience. I make you knew. Now is the season. Now is the time to surrender your life to me. The baby on the inside of you is a girl. This baby symbolizes a new beginning. Stacey, you get a fresh start. New beginnings. Expect blessings and prosperity. I have favored you this day."

"This baby was conceived out of wedlock though. How can God ..."

"Nothing is impossible with God. Nothing is ever wasted. You have conceived a miracle. Behold this day, a sign of things to come. We are called conceived in sin and shaped in iniquity. It is a great equalizer. Child, behold your open door. The Lord is not held to human rules nor is he held to traditions and boundaries that confine creativity and give birth to human reasoning. He has chosen the weak things of this world to confound the wise. Watch what he does. She is your second chance. Only just trust and believe. Take care of this child, a prophet to the nations. Pray for your son. He needs you too you know?"

"Baby you ready?" The pastor asks.

"Baby? Baby? Y'all foolin' around up in here? I knew it. You too hot." Stacey quipped.

"Yeah baby. I'm ready. I'm hungry too!" Keesha kissed him and giggled.

Stacey squeaked, "WHAT ON EARTH IS Y'ALL DOIN'? I THOUGHT YOU WAS HIS ASSISTANT. WHATCHU DOIN?"

They look at one another, watching her blood boil, they burst into laughter.

"What's so funny? I done seen enough of this in my lifetime. Church scandal. Hypocrites! I'm outta here! You know church folk the biggest hypocrites! Phony people man...YOU CALLED THE MAN PASTOR!!!"

As she storms off Keesha calls her back, "Stacey..."

"WHAT? WHAT NEXT? WHATCHU GON' TELL ME NOW, HUH?" she replies in a huff.

"Shhh..." Keesha replies, "Girl, this is still a sanctuary...".

"Sanctuary? Oh now you wanna keep it holy? YOU JUST KISSED THE PASTOR RIGHT IN FRONT OF ME! Seriously lady? Oh my goodness."

Keesha smiled, "Stacey, this is my husband. We are very married. And yes, I called Him Pastor because he is my pastor as well. He was my pastor before he was my husband girl."

"MARRIED? But he...he's white! I mean blue eyes, blonde hair, Anglo-Saxon action white boy white. And you're...girl you...Hershey chocolate brown...how y'all?"

The pastor shook his head. He whispered to his wife, "This 2014 babe. Can you believe this? And they say white people are ignorant and prejudiced."

"Relax honey. You should be used to this."

"No. It's 2014. Our mayor is married to a black woman. They have bi-racial children Keesha."

"I know babe. Just chill. It's okay."

"...President is bi-racial for goodness sake!"

"You're sounding a bit crazy now Tony. I can't right now."

"I can't ever. Unbelievable." he grinned.

His wife daintily beamed, "Welcome to 2014. Welcome to New York baby. Welcome to the melting pot."

"Oh my goodness, forgive me for assuming. I'm so sorry. I..." More embarrassed than she would like to admit, Stacey covers her mouth. "I always did have a problem with my mouth. Lord ha' mercy..."

"My name is Anthony Cappiola. I'm not Anglo, I am Italian American. And yep, we come in different shades, shapes, sizes and colors like Black folk. I'm from Brooklyn, my weaknesses are cigars and hip-hop. Oh yeah, and my beautiful wife."

"Pastor, you don't have to explain. I..."

"Tony stop. Don't..." Keesha laughs

"I speak broken English. I'm from the streets. I've been to prison. I used to hustle and get high. I grew up in the

Catholic Church and converted while in prison. I am not perfect but, I am a pastor. I am just like everyone else, only differences is Jesus and the choices I make now that He is the head of my life. I am still a work in progress. So be forewarned my sister. You may see me screw up. I am a substance abuse counselor and an English teacher by trade. God is able." He reached out to shake Stacey's hand.

Keesha walks up, "Hi! I'm Keesha Cappiola. I know I look Afro-American, but I'm of Dominican decent. From Brooklyn, raised in a predominantly Black and Latino community. I was a single parent of two boys before I met my husband. I have made plenty of mistakes in my life. I was married to a beautiful African-American man before he was shot and killed right around the corner from the house we were raising our young children in. he didn't do anything wrong; He was just coming home from work. Routine evening. He was carrying a bouquet of my favorite flowers in his hand when he was shot. To cope I began to party and drink. I had to give up custody of my boys to my late husband's family for a few years. It was a fight getting my boys back; getting myself together; gaining their trust as they became teens. But God is faithful. God is able. God did it."

A teen-aged girl with curly brown hair, in the exact likeness of Keesha, runs up past the pews to the entrance at the back of the church and grabs Keesha's waist, "Ma, I'm hungry. I wanna go. Daddy I want fries."

"Oh yeah, this is my daughter Kayla, she was conceived while I was out runnin' around in the streets. I wouldn't know her biological father if he was standing right next to me on the Path girl." Kayla's danced to the loud music blaring from the overheads glued to her young ears.

"Oh my goodness y'all. I…" Stacey was overcome with embarrassment.

Keesha embraced her. "See I told you, I used to be you. And I'm here today to tell you, all things work together for good to them that love the Lord and are called according to His purpose. ALL THINGS, NOT SOMETHINGS. Before I got to know the real Jesus, I felt I had nothing more to live for. I blamed God for taking everything I had loved away from me. My identity was so wrapped up in my husband, I lost myself when he died. He was all I had known my whole life. I had never gotten to know myself before him because he was always there. I did anything to please him. I followed him everywhere. In a sense, I worshipped him and not The Lord. I was raised non-traditional, in a Baptist Church and like you I wasn't fazed by it. But I knew His word was true and that He was real. I forgot all about Him though. I was doin' me. I had taken the one who died to save my soul for granted. I forgot about the one true God who is the giver and sustainer of all life."

"Hun, we'll be in the car, don't be too long.", Pastor Anthony explained to his wife.

"Ok baby, I won't."

"So wait… I know God is a jealous God, so you sayin' God allowed your husband to be killed?"

"Well, no, I wouldn't say that. He is a jealous God, Understand though, He is also a loving God. God don't kill people. People kill people. So I resolved years ago, after Kayla was born to let that go. Every question this side of heaven ain't gonna be answered in a time and fashion we would like it to be. Heck, even if God gave me an answer, would that have been enough to sooth my pain at the end of it all? Stacey, answers to our most pulsating, burning, earnest, justifiable questions just may not bring us peace at the end of the day. King Solomon in all of his wisdom said in Ecclesiastes, said that knowing too much only makes you sad; that all in life in meaningless; It is all vanity.

While it is true that God is a jealous God, I had look at myself and understand why I had such a hard time recovering from my husband's death. The Lord was not to blame."

"Well a crime was committed. You lost your husband. A life was taken right? So somebody got get the blame right? I don't know how you just don't blame nobody for stuff like that. How you just let that mess go like that? Jesus!"

"Stacey, we ain't meant to hold on to nobody tighter than we hold on to Jesus. We can't worry our whole lives over things we can't control. I may never know why. But honey, it won't do me any good obsessing over it. I know my husband wouldn't have wanted that for me. He liked to see me happy. I wasn't happy all of those years I held on to my mourning. One it just had to come to an end. I take responsibility for my own life. No one to blame. Blame doesn't get anybody anywhere. I could have shared a seat on the train or a meal with his murderer at any time over the years; maybe even slept with the cat... I'd still never know. I just had to realize where I went wrong for the sake of my own sanity and healing. For the sake of my relationship with God and my children. That look in the mirror; that cold slap in the face called reality ain't pleasant. Yet, they're both very necessary for healing and moving forward. We are not meant to walk around in circles while getting nowhere honey. Wake up call. It is our job to learn and then to know when to let go even if we're afraid we don't know how. God is there. God is able."

Keesha was exhausted. It had been a very long time since she had shared her testimony in depth. It had been too painful of a walk for her in the past.

"So, long story short, I went through the painful process of healing, looking at myself and restoring fellowship with God and getting my family back. Little by little and God favored me as I was faithful to Him and trusted Him. He restored unto me the fullness of joy. I believe God used my daughter. He used Kayla to keep me hanging on. She was my miracle. And as much as I love all of my children and my husband, I have learned from past mistakes not to ever put another living sole over the Lord. For even in my sin and rebellion; my disobedience and confusion; when I was in darkness and despair, even when I didn't want Him there and I had blamed Him and others for all I had lost instead of looking at myself and taking responsibility for my own choices, He remained steadfast, loving, and faithful. God wasn't afraid of my anger, concerns, doubt, blame, disbelief or questions. He ain't ever scared! No matter what we throw at Him Stacey, He can handle it. He knows we are human. He knows we are hurting. He knows we are weak. He knows how to handle us, heal us and hold us. He is everything I never had. Everything I've always wanted and needed. Jesus is the only one I cannot live without. He knows how to help us to see ourselves, pick up the broken pieces of our lives, forgive ourselves and others and move forward. Stacey, He can do the same for you. And He will. It's your season."

"Wow. Thank you for sharing your testimony."

Keesha's reassures Stacey, "Girl, you gon' be aight. And you are welcome. Girl let me get out here to this man. No matter the color child, men are men and I've learned not to play around with hungry bears."

"Wait. I mean please...one more thing. So I've been thinking about movin' over here to Brooklyn. I love this church and I love this neighborhood. I want a fresh start. Something new."

"You sure Brooklyn is the place for you? I mean, it can be pretty rough... I don't know. Maybe you need to pray about it before you..."

"You're right. But I don't hurt to have a look around just in case God says yes."

"Well. I guess. You really should talk to my husband though. He knows these Brooklyn streets way better than I do. Maybe over dinner? You down?"

"Always for food."

"Great! I hope you like soul food? You must!" The pastor's wife covers her mouth in complete embarrassment, "My mouth! Lord forgive me. I'm sorry sister, I hope that didn't come out wrong. I mean because you're... I mean, I don't assume that just because..." she laughs.

"Because I'm Black? Girl please. Nah you good. Thanks for askin' and for your sensitivity." Stacey smiled, "I like soul food. So ok. Y'all better get Kayla her fries or she gonna be upset."

"Girl, she ain't gettin' no fries. She had fries yesterday. One and done. I keep telling Kayla she is not going to keep that beautiful figure shoving fries down her throat every chance she gets. ".

"I hear you Keesha. Oh man, I'm sorry, I keep calling you Keesha. I don't mean no disrespect. You are the First Lady of the Church. I respect that." Stacey says.

"Girl, I if you don't cut that out! I'm human and here to serve just like you. I know who I am and that's all that I am. Titles don't float my boat. I'm your spiritual sister above all else. I do thank you for respecting me. But I'm cool. Just a person with a calling to fulfill, just like you. We have more in common than you think Stacey." They embraced one another.

Stacey pulls back. She stares at her in admiration, "You are so blessed and anointed. Just look at you."

Keesha then pulls back, "You are equally as anointed. Equally as blessed. Sista...just look at you! Blessed and highly favored. Oh Hallelujah. Look at what God has done. God ain't through workin' on you girl. Hold on and watch Him work. There is nothing too hard for Him. What He has done for me HE WILL DO FOR YOU and rest assured, greater things than these will ye do in the name of Jesus and all for His glory. Amen?"

Stacey whispers, "Amen First Lady. Lord, I can't believe you got me chillin with the pastor and his wife. I know I'm not worthy."

She hears a small voice say, "Yes you are. They are honored to have you."

They leave the church hand-in-hand as pastor Anthony lays on the car horn. "Let's go Keesha! Christ! We're meltin' away out here like butter in a fryin' pan!"

Kayla screeched, "Ma come on! I need fries please!"

"Girl, you want Brooklyn? Well there you have it! My Brooklyn born and bred husband and child. They get antsy after church. They're like sharks in the Hudson and what not. I'M COMIN'!!!! Girl come on...We're gonna go park the car at the house. Then, we goin' to Harlem." Keesha teased, "Girl, I gotta get these people over to Red Rooster before I get whacked."

Stacey takes a deep breath at the bottom of the church staircase, "Feels like home."

On the train ride to Harlem, she swallows the sights and inhales the sounds, both aromatic and odiferous. Living in the Brick City, taking a daytrip to New York was nothing short of commonplace for the residents of Newark, especially Stacey. It was the norm and no big deal as it had been in her childhood years when anything outside of Essex County was a treat. As she aged, Stacey found the experience to be mundane and routine. She knew the routes to each of the five of Burrows like she knew the God-designed lines in the palm of her hands.

A ride on the Path to into the City was like going to your cousin's house where they had bigger, better toys in a bigger, better house; always something new. You could eat what you wanted, stay out as late as you liked, no rules, no rest, and no retribution. The City was a free-for-all for people from the Bricks. It was very much your favorite Aunt and Uncles place to visit. There were more people, places, opportunities; this was the place. This is where life begins. This is where life starts. And it wouldn't be as it was in times past that were not so long ago. Even though yesterday wasn't very far away.

She savored each moment. Every stop. The draw and allure of it; The City was sensory overload. The profanity and the carnality that she had become accustomed to had even been rebirthed as total nuances to her.

Gone were the days of jumping on the Path Train early in the morning. Silently scoffing at all of the white and blue collar workers scrambling anxiously to meet unforgiving deadlines and fill stressful quotas; trying to please the powers that be; make a living; Most trying to find the space where they could try to force ends to meet. If not they could pray about it or work harder. A never ending story. Wet. Lather. Rinse. Repeat. They, like Stacey were like zombies in a daze following the order of the day. The order of everyday with no real break from the routine they called their lives. They weren't living at all. Slaves to the rhythm.

Like so many that had come and gone before, though they indeed had the courage and strength to physically move, so many did not harvest and cultivate the tenacity it would take to live better than life had previously afforded. Much like the slaves of old that had refused to leave the plantation. Their bodies moved, but their minds and hearts were frozen. Everyone was free, but so many failed to recognize just how free they really were.

 Jesus died to make us free. Life, love and liberty were not meant to be labor intensive. She concluded, "Maybe the slaves couldn't see the can in the air around them rather, a big menacing cloud of can't blocked can in every which way. They couldn't see the can carrying their dreams on the wings of freedom moreover their dreams had flown away behind the cloud. Maybe it hadn't been about seeing the can. Maybe it was about not being able to hear the can over the thunder of the 'can't' they were accustomed to. The chant of the 'can't' was possibly too loud." It had been that way in her life, the 'can't' had been to menacing, to present, to loud. "There's gotta be a way to shut down the 'can't' so we can hear the can."

She thought, "Maybe doing something different takes too much effort? I don't know. Why is it I've never tried?" She looked at all of the faces around her, "Dang though, if you didn't even know Jesus, how in the world could you trust Him enough to set you free? I wonder how many of us out here will never really know what free really is? How many us think we're free and we're really locked the hell up?"

She mused, "Hmmm...I guess I don't know Jesus as well as I thought. Man, I ain't no different than these people. What was all of that churchin' for all those years? I know I missed something." She had forgotten how to reach out to God. He had been just a prayer away all of that time. He hadn't moved. Nor had he changed. It had all been on her. The Lord had been right where she left Him. She had lost faith a long time ago. Nobody ever taught her that prayer wasn't some religious ritual. Prayer was but a conversation between the Father and His children. She was afraid The Lord would be harsh because of her rebellion and backsliding. Stacey was wrong. Jesus was ready, willing, able and waiting to love her. All of those years in church, week in, week out and she had never known the love of God. She had only heard about it. She never really experienced the real Jesus. Nevertheless, God had a plan. He always has a plan. He never gives up on His children no matter how far away we stray. Stacey knew it was time for change in heart; even if her mind, body and surroundings were not ready. Her first step, "I need to get away from mess." Her misstep, not remembering that you can't outrun trouble, for it could follow you everywhere. She didn't think that she her demons would ever catch up to her if she moved away. But trouble and temptation lay in wait for every man at every station in life. Her issues had legs and her nightmares had feet. Her demons wore Nikes. She not only needed a change. She needed deliverance. She needed a chance. A gift she would have to give herself if change was going to be ongoing.

She was would learn sooner than later that changing your location doesn't necessarily mean your location would change you.

Everything but God, and His infallible word, in this life is subject to change. In life, we learn that many of those things only change if we do the changing. Life is an endless series of choices. In her recollection, every broken face that screamed for release, that seemed to not have the courage to reach for it for fear of change and failure, she saw a mirror image. She tried so hard not to judge. Even in doing so, she knew that she was only judging herself. To ease the guilt of what she knew deep down inside was her personal judgments, she justified her thoughts by labeling them deductive reasoning and astute observations.

At first glance, her gaudy appearance presented her one dimensional and macabre. Stacey James for all of her misdoings, was not your average addict. Insightful, analytical, deep. She processed everything. Everything besides her subcutaneous disfigurements. It was a side of her no one knew she had. A part of herself, maybe the only part she kept in reserve; something to keep her sane and afloat whilst all else seem to be disintegrating in her universe.

A reasoner. A thinker. A rationalizer. Deducting all possible outcomes and weighing all options. She was into variables, facets, seasons, levels, processes of elimination. Indisposed, she held the annoying gift of mental processing as did no other. She had a way of evaluating and diagnosing the populace. However, she hadn't raised a clue on just how to evaluate and diagnose herself. The ones that seem to have all of the answers never seem too able to provide those same answers to the curiosities that plague them so. Stacey had a wisdom that deep inside of her that she in anywise manner could not reach. A very conflicted, complex being. Isolated within.

She balled up uncomfortably in a corner seat, observing the hustle and bustle from beneath the brim of her hoodie. "So sick of this. Wet. Lather. Rinse. Repeat." she thought.

 Bloodshot, runny eyes stare through the darkness. Disgusted and focused as they dance atop of insulates, encased in darkened circles that mirror smeared coffee dregs at the bottom of those same coffee cups that are causing anti-fashion suicide right in front of her very eyes. In the morning light they shown like the remnants of a stolen car joy ride; skid marks on the asphalt on a dead end street from the night before. Sin is only enjoyable for a season. No matter. She was on a mission to get out of the gate. How could such a small amount of fine powder unleash so much hell and havoc and usher in so much of the release, relief and temporary happiness her body had grown dependent upon? Her third hit was her last tango in Paris. A seductive dance with an abusive lover. She needed her medicine. What was making her sick also had the power to make her well. And if you had never taken the ride on that train you couldn't tell her anything about why she got on it, where it had taken her, or what stop to get off on and for how long.

Puppet on the Devil's string. The people on the train had their own schedules and agendas. Goals to meet, places to be and people to see. Stacey had hers as well. Like a trapped race horse, she just needed to get out of the gate to be able to move a little faster, for she would be running all day, every day. Chasing and wasting away. Speeding up just to slow down. Being on E, at that time, in that place, was not the place to be.

 She reminisced of days gone by when she exited in the undercurrent of the living dead. Secretly, she envied the people she tried not to judge because even though they had issues and struggles; their lives were a mess; on paper, they were all teaming successes with real lives and normal human problems compared to hers. Problems she would almost kill to have on any given day. Or were they all addicted to something, grappling with their own particular vices in less than obvious ways? Whatever their issues were, on the surface, theirs had seemed so much less volatile and damaging than hers could ever be.

Nevertheless, they had their lives and their work and well, she had hers. Everybody had a hustle and a problem they wish they could eradicate with the click of a button, snap of a finger or at the opening of an app. No one in plain view wanted the life they had chosen. They all wanted what they thought they were entitled to. No one had taken responsibility for their own choices. They all wanted someone else's life. A do over. Life didn't come with an exchange policy attached. Not unless you were Born-again. Then you could exchange your life for His as He did for yours. For most of the people, non believers and backsliders alike, just the same as the ones Stacey encountered on her daily chase, life wasn't ever going to be that simple. Not for anybody, not ever. They lacked the same coping skills that she did on varying scales. Everyone just went on, masking their pain, day by day with simple, damaging fixes that weren't fixes at all. Each one had their routine and chosen coping mechanism or lack thereof; everybody had some form of sin to answer for that neither addiction, education, status nor fantasy could erase. Everybody, great and small had their dope. They all needed Jesus, even if they didn't know it. Stacey knew it. She was all too familiar with her own short comings. Stacey James was well versed in chaos and dysfunction. She tried so hard not to judge. Last thing anybody needed was judgment. Everyone wanted to be understood. Not misjudged by outside appearance. Especially Stacey.

What they all knew, was that life and the choices we all make are often complicated and not as black and white, cut and dry as they come across in person, on paper and online. Everyone seemed to have craved understanding on some level, even if that level was subconscious. Those that had moved past the season of desiring understanding had either hardened over time or had grown so confident in who they were, what they knew, or in who Christ was that they no longer gave way to apology or human reasoning. There was no longer a need to explain or shy away from their own truth. They had aged. Life was too short. They had resolved to enjoy the rest of the ride they had left. All else had become insignificant in their sight. Right or wrong, this lot had resolved to live their lives on their own terms.

Stacey observed and recorded. She processed in complete silence. They came and went, day in day out. She thought as often as day gave way to night and night gracefully bowed to day and the intellectual hierarchy of God's creation remained the same, "We all want to be loved in spite of. The way God loves us. In spite of."

A subtle breeze blew into the subway car. Passengers feverishly entered and exited. In a hurry to everywhere, anywhere, somewhere and nowhere.

The faint odor of urine offensively emanating from a homeless man mixed with Victoria's Secret body spray that the teen mom seated across from her must have spilled on her shirt; it's overkill. It is beautiful. Old things had passed away. "Lord forgive me for judgin' people. Who am I? Jesus, I was in a fog and full of nothin'. A jealous junkie dying' slow. And yet you loved me anyway. I don't deserve your love. Forgive me?" Stacey murmurs apologetically under her breath.

"You are forgiven. I understand. I love you."

Stacey felt a warm rush of love. It was a feeling like no other. It was the kind of warmth that years of shooting up dope couldn't give her. There was no beat down, no judgment, no harsh rebuke, no caning, whipping or flogging; No condemnation for her. Jesus had handled it all at Calvary, on the cross.

 In that moment, she wept silently as like never before, she realized that what she had heard, read and struggled to believe and adhere to all of her life, was concrete and real. She saw a new side of Jesus. One of love, mercy, faithfulness and grace. She had been taught all of her life that God was angry and condemning; A God of punishment, wrath and hell fire. Waiting to strike down every unrepentant sinner and unfaithful backslider. In that moment, all of that fear and anxiety that she had built up over time was dissipating.

The revelation within Stacey was strong and all confirming, as it was comforting, as it was with Jesus about Lazarus as others stood around and believed what they saw when they had wrapped his body. They had believed all hope was lost. But, Jesus, her Lord and Savior knew better. He had the drop on everything! Jesus was God in the flesh. He already knew what no one else held a clue about: His friend, Lazarus, would rise again.

In her mind she heard His voice call from afar, "Lazarus! Lazarus! Come forth!"

Lazarus was resurrected from the dead, in all of the trappings of the rags; confining cloth they had buried him in. But that held no restrictions to the saving and resurrecting power of Jesus the Christ.

All hope was not lost. And so, just as Jesus had done for His friend, whom He loved, He had also done for His friend, whom He loves, Stacey James. She, in that moment, began to view Jesus for who He really was. The same Jesus who cried for Lazarus when he died, cried for her when she died. That same Jesus had brought her back to life; calling her to come forth from amongst the dead, just as He had Lazarus.

"Let the dead bury the dead. God is the God of the living. Let the redeemed of the Lord say so. Can these dry bones live again? Dry bones, the Lord and King says LIVE!" Wiping her tears thankfully,   she felt a covered. It was as if the wings of a mighty angel were surrounding her. All of that, all in that moment. The voice of the Lord had returned to whisper in her ear, "It is finished." This was one of the moments she had been taught could only occur inside of a church. Yet, there she was, on a filthy subway car, having a priceless experience with her Lord and Savior.

Behold, all things were being made new. Her eyes were opened. She was alive. It is a new day. At that very moment, as her senses were being overloaded by the monotonous, uneventful events, she felt her belly jolt. Stacey looked down at her belly. She placed her hand near her navel and there it is again...A sharp, aggressive thump! She moves her hand to a new area on her protruding belly, again!

She tapped Keesha, "It's kicking! My baby is kicking!"

"That's awesome mama! So yo! Boy or girl?" asked the teen mom.

Keesha prayed silently while Stacey rubbed her tummy, "It's a girl. She's special. Prophesy. She is my blessing."

"Congrats!" screams an old Jewish man sitting next to the teenaged girl, "All children are a blessing from Yahweh! Mazel young lady! Mazeltov!"

She looks at Keesha, "God really is the God of second...MANY chances. I'm more blessed than I deserve. Can't wait to tell my son. Girl, I just wanna see my son. Can you believe it? I get to be a mother again, and do it right this time."

"So what's the baby's name ma?" the teenager interrupted.

The car quiets down as it nears the next stop. "Beckham. Yep. That's it Beckham."

"Like David? Oh he's hot!" Kayla asked. Pastor Anthony is not amused. Before he can respond and scold his daughter, she grabs his arm and kisses his cheek, "Joking pop. Relax. I'm still daddy's little girl." She winks at the teenaged mom and smirks.

Stacey grinned from ear to ear, "Yep ma. Like David. And I think I'll call her Becks. I pray she gets to live a posh life too"

The Jewish man, "Hey young lady, that guy is a legend! Odd name for a girl. Must be some special kinda baby girl you got there."

"She is a special baby sir. Very special." Stacey is elated. Bowing to speak into her stomach she whispers, "Beckham. You kick like a champ... bend it girl."

Keesha puts her arm around Stacey, "What a name for a girl Stacey. Why'd you chose that name pray tell?"

Stacey raises her eye brow. She looks Keesha up and down, "No offense Madame First Lady, but I could ask you the same question: Where'd Keesha come from. Girl, ain't nothin' Latina about no Keesha."

She laughs, "I didn't mean to offend you Stacey. I'm just curious is. But, ok. I have an answer for you. My Birth Name is Giselle Daiana Rosario. When I met my now deceased husband, we were young kids and he used to see me around the way a lot. He would tease me about my name. He had told me that I didn't look like a Giselle. He said I looked more Black than Spanish, like my name should be Keesha. He started callin' me Keesha. I always liked the name. I always liked him. I fell in love with him and the name over time and from childhood, through much drama and many ups and downs, they both stuck. We were never much for traditions he and I. Guess you can tell by my mixed family and our ministry. So there you have it. Ain't nothing wrong with breaking tradition in some areas."

"I dig it.", Stacey says, "That's so awesome. Non-traditional. Outside the box. I guess that's what Beckham is for me Keesha. Outside the box. Non-traditional you know? Just time for somethin' different."

"Plus he fine girl. Ain't nothin' wrong with a little cream in the coffee. Well you know that better than Me.", Stacey clowned.

Pastor Anthony blushed. He hung his head in disbelief. Keesha leaned in to whisper in his ear, "Patience Pastor. You know it's a journey and a process. God is a slow cooker. He who began a good work..."

He responded impatiently, "I know. I know."

"You know that better than I do right baby?"

"I know that better than most. Thank God that He is patient with His children. Lord, may you find us being equally as patient with one another." Pastor Anthony says prayerfully.

"Amen." The First Lady agrees.

"Yeah, it's me. I've been trying to reach you since yesterday. We need to talk. I need to know what's really good with you. You ain't actin' like yourself. You not givin' me no updates. That ain't us. Hit me back." Sitting in his truck he can't helped but be stressed and worried about his ex. She had been growing more and more distant from him. Internally, he felt as if he was losing control. He was losing patience with her. She was not the girl he had left her as.

A wise man once said, if you keep refusing to accept/download regular updates to your computer, software, devices; that heightens the risk for viral infection. Often as we age we don't want the update. We ignore the warnings; we don't want things as we know it to change. Inherently, it is human nature to reject change. But without change, we the computer, the software, the devices; the mindset; the relationship tends to suffer the risks, gain momentum causing lack in varying areas. Somehow, someway, somewhere, someday, things have to change in order to keep things moving forward and functioning in a positive manner to which they were designed to function.

Throughout life, we are receiving continuous updates all around; within us. It is up to us to download the necessary updates to keep up with life, God's plan and purpose; those we love. The end of one season equals the genesis of another. Revelation. Nothing this side of heaven is forever. To everything there is a season. A time and a purpose to everything under heaven.

"Like I said man, you gon' get up in there, you gon' chill, you gon' see some huns, you gonna rest your mind and enjoy. Aight?"

"Yeah man...but my wife man she got a brother mind spinnin' like a top son. I can't keep up wit' her man. That ain't us. That ain't her."

His friend punches him in the chest, "MAN UP YO! She not ya wife no more kid...she's your EX with a capital X! Grow up. Let go. Enjoy the ambiance. And afterwards we can go chase some gazelles aight? You know this is what we do. Boys will be boys, huh?"

"Yeah aight Ty man. I guess. Let's just get this over with." he sighs.

"Aw man c'mon bruh. Don't tell me you still beat for this chick yo. What's ya issue man damn! I mean, you've been practicing like a licensed gynecologist for a minute now. I mean it's been years. Why you still so stuck like that? That's some old female, emotional, irrational, need closure bullsh.."

"Man what?"

"Aw you heard me! You think you need to talk to somebody?"

"What?!"

"I'm just sayin.'"

"Sayin' what?"

"I mean, you getting' a lil' soft on me. You a G. Man up! I'm beginning to get a hint of smell Bath and Body Works and estrogen the more I'm around you."

"Funny loser. Real funny. I ain't afraid to admit I still love her. In my mind, she's gonna always be my wife. Outside of my girls and her, my life don't mean much. And those other chicks is just that. OTHER CHICKS. Just bodies and forgettable face with no names that make noise. I don't mean that in a disrespectful way." he points up to the sky and bows his head. "She raised a brother better than that."

"Hey man. I feel you."

"Nah son, you don't feel me. You can't. You're not in my shoes. I'm raising a gang of beautiful, ethnic, bi-racial princesses right now. They got they own mind, they have their dreams and opinions... already. I love that yo. They keep me goin'. I just want to be around them all of the time. Those girls are my world Ty man. You don't get that because you ain't there yet. But when you find the love of your life, start slowin' down and you begin to see that there really is more to life than partyin' and chasin', you'll understand where I'm comin' from. Feel me?"

"Yeah man. I get it. But you to into they mother dawg. Y'all not even together no more. Why you so caught up like that?"

 "I'm in love with her alright? I can't be emotionally connected to no other women than the ones I'm connected to already son. They got my heart, so yeah man, for the record, I am caught up. Imma always love that woman. She gave me my daughters. She's been making my days in hell feel like heaven since childhood.

She reminds me of my mom. Sweet; always happy and positive. Never out of pocket. That's just her. No drama, no mouth and no attitude. She only turned up when she felt the situation called for it. That was my baby man. She reminds me of Marisol man."

"Damn dawg. I didn't know it could get that deep."

"Yeah man it can. You never think you gon' get caught out there like that. A man, you supposed to always be in control. But you meet that one and man… game over. She give you three lil' mini me's and… game over. She rock ya world and change the game and… game over. What you have with her is better than all the sex in the world; it's deeper than that… game over G. Word up."

"Wow dawg. Game over. She gotchu like that for real?"

"Facts my G. I can be with a million huns but, ain't no other love for me but hers. Now, if that makes me look like a weak punk, so be it. If I'm wrong, Lord forgive me. If I'm right, Lord bless me, keep me and thank you. If it all boils down to I'm stuck on stupid and she done moved on...hey...call me the village idiot. At least at the end of the day, I know I loved who I wanted to with no regrets not really givin' a damn what people think. I can live and die with that. "

"Jeez Shakespeare. I hear you man. But you know what?"

"What man? Get it out ya system brother."

"For one, you are not a bother by far. So stop sayin' it, ok? You be wearin' it out. Looking like us don't make you one of us aight?" He laughed, "All the time with this kid man."

Jason, grinned, "Man please! This is the hood. Black and brown out here together son. It's a Victor Cruz era B. Let me live kid."

"You know what? Imma give you that son... you right. But you wrong at the same time?'

"Wrong? How?"

"Joker! You bandwagon as hell. You know you don't even like Vic man. Knock it off!"

Jason exited the car. "I ain't gotta support them sorry ass Giants to use him as a point of reference aight? Bandwagon? Me? Whatever yo? Let's go. I'm tired of talkin' to ya simple ass."

"Why you get so heated all the time at small stuff man. Oh yeah, number two, you really do need therapy. Plus..."

"You really gettin' on my nerves man!"

Ty opens the door to the Hole in 1, "Welcome your first session. Thank me later."

Jason entered the club. Unimpressed. Unsure he was even supposed to be in there he stood at the door for ten minutes before he actually walked over to the bar to join Ty. Jason wasn't an avid prayer. He believed in God and was saved but life had gotten in the way of his relationship with God. After seeing his father live a hypocritical life as a Christian leader, anything remotely resembling religion in any fashion was on its way to becoming a turn off to him.

His mother, died brokenhearted and caged in by his father. That, coupled with the unexpected, tragic death of his brother, had up until tonight been the icing on the cake everything that had happened in his life made him question if God actually cared about his family. The violence and poverty he beheld in the inner-city growing up made him calloused towards God in small ways beneath the surface. Liza was the only thing that had him holding on to God while they were together. Although distance made his heart grow fonder for Liza, he grew ever increasingly distant from the Lord. The one thing he did want is for his three princesses to be raised in the fear and admonition of the Lord. He and Liza had been failing in that area. He taught them what he could and all he knew but, in the end, even he knew, try as he might sparingly, more had to be done. But all was not lost. As he made his way over to the bar to accompany his company, he began to feel convicted. He had never been a strip club before. Let alone a dive like Hole in 1.

"What did I let this joker talk me in to? Jesus man! I'm too grown for this. I have a family, a degree, a business and a life. This is gotta be the bottom of the barrel. This is your reward for all of your hard work? You know you can pull better than this just sitting at your desk." he said to himself.

He imagined, "This is what hell must look like without the fire and brimstone. Whatchu you doin' in here J? What if Liza found out? What about the girls?"

He reaches down into his pocket to grab his phone. Scrolling through the missed calls, he notices he missed a call from Liza. Ecstatic, he makes an about-face. He runs to the door, just as he reaches the threshold of the exit, a soft hand grabs his shoulder. He doesn't even turn to face the woman, "No. No. I'm sorry. Please don't touch me. I'm good."

He walks out, returns her call. She doesn't answer. "Games Liza? Really? C'mon pick up. This is crazy!" he tries to reach her again with no success. Angry and confused he breathes deep, "Girl, don't do this now."

Liza is within reach of her cell but she chooses to ignore every call. She sucks her teeth as she bruits, "Jason. Oh my goodness. Why do you keep calling me at the wrong time? Boy you ain't about to mess up my groove tonight. Later for you. You'll be there. You always there."

Now he's passed concerned. He's worried. But on his way back inside, he had determined that if she wasn't gonna stop what she was doing to answer his call at least once, he would return the favor by not calling her again until she made time to talk to him...not even if it was about their girls. Jason was pissed. "Tired of chasin' you." he grunted.

He had made his decision. Tonight another run of the mill, nameless body with a forgettable face that made noise would have the pleasure of his company. As usual they could have his body for the night, but that would be all. They couldn't even have his ear. He was too distracted for anything more than a sensual tryst. And so Jason was back in the game. Up to stalk his prey like a lion lying in wait in the bush of the Sahara Desert. He approached Ty at the bar, "Time to chase some gazelle's boy."

Ty was ecstatic. "You in boy"

"Boy, I'm so in."

"See now, that's what I'm talkin' about. Get this grown man a drink over here baby. He's back! Owwwwwwwww!" Ty charges in a celebratory tone.

"Nah Hun nah! Cancel that. You know I don't drink son. Clean livin' man. You know me!" they huddle together and laugh like jackals as they feast on the sights and sounds of the night.

"It's about to go down." he whispered to Ty in anticipation of his next move. "Let's see who bout to get it tonight..."

He surveys the room. So many flavors, shapes, sizes, types, colors, ethnicities. His head was spinning. Just then, a lofty, sweeping figure appeared on the stage. The lights dimmed, a hush came over the room.

DJ Wax provides the intro, "Now boys and girls, your favorite stripper's favorite stripper. Y'all regs know she don't need no intro. She's the HBIC! The moniest maker in the Bricks and she work hard for it. Y'all get ready...," he plays the intro to "Drunk in Love".   "Here she go..."

The spotlight outlines her alpine frame. Disrobing slowly, she wears a mask and a full curly wig. Jason looks up. He tilts his head to the side, "Liza? Yo is that my..."

He rushes the stage. He snatches off her mask. "What the hell? Liza?"

"What the hell is right! And if you wasn't sure, then what you doin' up here? Boy, what you doin' in here anyway? Since when you..."

The crowd is astonished. Jason promptly covers the mother of his children. He picks her up and carries her out. Men are reaching out to touch her. She kicks and screams all of the way as he swings from his invisible vine past the tigers, crocodiles and anacondas. DJ Wax assures the crowd that the scene was all part of an act planned for the night. Outside of the club, cheers can be heard through the door.

"Yes yes y'all! She turnt it didn't she? This is all a part of Fantasy Fridays here in the Hole y'all. Tell a friend. Drink up fellas...pssshhh man. WE JUST GETTIN' THANGS POPPIN IN THE PIECE. TURN UP YO!"

"GET OFF OF ME JASON! WHAT IS YOUR PROBLEM AND WHAT ARE YOU DOIN' HERE?"

"DON'T QUESTION ME! LYZA WHAT ARE YOU DOIN' UP IN THERE? HOIN' YOURSELF OUT LIKE THAT?! WHAT ABOUT OUR KIDS? HUH?! GIRL, YOU KNOW YOU GONNA HAVE ME OUT HERE LOOKIN' CRAZY IN THESE STREETS AND WHERE MY DAUGHTERS AT ANYWAY?!"

"AIN'T ABOUT YOU JASON AND MY DAUGHTERS ARE WELL TAKEN CARE OF OK! GET IT? NOW GO AWAY! JUST GO AWAY! JUST LEAVE JASON!"

"YOU LOST YA MIND GIRL! I BEEN BY YA MOTHER'S A MILLION TIMES SINCE YOU STARTED BUGGIN' AND SHE TOLD ME Y'ALL DON'T SPEAK!? YOU MOVED OUT?! YOU BEEN SEEING SOME FAKE ASS PASTOR FROM THE SOUTHWARD? WHAT THE HELL GIRL? ARE YOU ON DRUGS? HUH? COME ON. LET'S GO. NOW LYZA! AND WHEN I CATCH THAT PRETTY BOY PASTOR I'MMA...."

"NOOOOOOOOOOOOOOOOOOOOOOOOOOOOOOOOOOOOO OO!" she screams. "No!"

I ain't goin nowhere Jason. Please just let me go. You do not own me. I'm not your property. LEAVE ME ALONE!"

He releases her slowly. Gently, he cups her face, "Look at me. Just look at me."

He notices her eyes are bloodshot. He smelled her mouth, "So you drink now? Huh ma? Ohhhhh no no no! This ain't you. We gotta go. Come on."

She grit her teeth in a smug, low, resentful tone. She snatched away from him and fell to the ground. "How do you know what's me Jason? You ever think to ask instead of assuming? Huh? I'm not some mindless ragdoll you take off the shelf and play with and put me back expecting for me to stay put and be there when you ready to come back for me again which will be God knows when. THIS AIN'T TOY STORY JASON! I'm not the girl you met when we was teenagers and I ain't the dummy you divorced when we was livin' with Connie playin' house...babies raisin' babies. That girl is dead Jason. Let go. She don't live here no more. And you ain't the same no more either if you can just come up in here wranglin' me like I'm some baby calf on a ranch that done strayed from the herd and all that. I'M NOT YOUR PROPERTY JASON!" She lifts up the back of the shirt, "I ain't been branded since I stopped wearin' my ring....I mean your ring...you know what I mean Jason. Damn. And if you're implying that I'm drunk, you're mistaken. I don't drink. I SIP! I'm a lady okay? I'm good. Just taking the edge off."

Jason had fell down to his knees in utter disbelief. He wasn't used to the way she cussed and fussed. He wasn't used to her resistance. Yet, he found her defiance as refreshing as he did puzzling. She was different. He couldn't figure her out. It was scary. She sounded possessed. He was confused and for the first time in his life, afraid. He was broken. His world was falling apart and he had no control over the chipping and the cracking. With each harsh exchange between the pair, he could here cracks forming in the foundation. His last link to God and love was crumbling before his very eyes. He held on to her. He hadn't been that close to the cold, harsh ground since John had died. He refused to let her go as much as she fought.

Finally he wiped his eyes and raised to his feet. He looked around. He grabbed the sleeve of his shirt while she was still wearing it. He wiped his eyes and blew his nose. Jason cleared his throat. He couldn't believe what he what about to come out of his mouth next.

He thought, "Look at yaself. Sucker for love. Ty tried to tell me. Livin' a dream that done turned into a complete nightmare. She ain't the same. Let her go J. You a man. Get ya ish together yo. Just let her go."

He composed himself as much as he could. "So yeah...aight. I see nothin' ain't the same. You and me just ain't meant to rock I guess." he spat on the ground. He wiped his nose on the shirt again, "You want to be 'bout dat life Liza Rose? Then go ahead and wear yaself out. You wanna ho out?! Ho the hell out then! I'm done. Just tell me one thing?"

"YOU WATCH HOW YOU TALK TO ME JASON! AND HERE! TAKE THIS NASTY SHIRT! HOW DARE YOU TREAT ME LIKE TRASH? I AM THE MOTHER OF YOUR CHILDREN. I AM YOUR WIFE! Since when you start speakin' that way?" she barked rolling her eyes.

He forced her look him in the eye. "You ain't nobody wife yo. I'm done. Now I know you don't have no love for me. Damn. You ain't even got no respect for yourself." He looks at her up and down, "Look at you man..."

"What?" she looked away. Her heart knew she still loved Jason. But in her mind she needed to maintain control so she refused to answer directly, "I don't want nobody controlin' me no more. You don't get it. I want to be free. This is me. I wanna be free Jason."

Although he wanted to give up, something within kept him holding on. "Listen to yourself silly. You talkin crazy like the rock monster gotchu. I know you in there somewhere...so...so..." he choked up, "You sayin' you don't even wanna be my friend Liza? You wanna be that free?"

"What? What are you saying?"

"You know what I'm sayin. Come on ma. You and them girls is all I got." She turned her back to him, "You are my best friend." He embraced her, "Please don't do this. I know this ain't you. Maybe this ain't me... I'm not sure. Just...just...please...please come with me so we can talk. I need you." his voice cracked as if he were in the dawn of pubescence.

She wiped her eyes. She wrapped her arms around his waist, "I lo... "

Before she could finish, Wax comes running out of the door, "You good? Who is this clown?"

"Who is this fool Liza? Better yet, who you callin' a clown fool?"

"I'm good Wax. It's nothing. Please, just let me..."

 "Fix this Liza before you have to bring my daughters to visit me in Trenton." Jason warns.

"J.R. kinda pissed. Y'all females always bringin' y'all personal issues past the doorway. You know he ain't havin' that. You better come on before he come out here."

"Wax please alright. Just go back inside. Thanks for checking on me. But ain't nobody scared of J.R. You might be. Maybe you should be. But I'm not." she touts.

"GO GET HIM! AS A MATTER OF FACT. TELL HIM TO COME GET HER SO HE CAN GET DEALT WITH. THIS IS MY WIFE!"

Wax mumbled, "Nigga you ain't ready."

He grabs her by the arm, "So who is J.R. Liza? He ya pimp now? Oh so whatchu gonna tell me huh? You gonna blame it on the alcohol or generational curses?"

Liza pushes Jason back, "Now you can go Richard Sherman. Just go! Get out of my life. How dare you! You don't love me. Loser! Step off. Clown.".

Wax walks up and pulls Liza back, "Come on bae. Inside.".

"What's with all of the man handlin' tonight? Wax stop it! You don't own me either. Now you're over stepping your bounds and I don't appreciate it. I can handle myself. This my personal business. Let me go."

That was the icing on the cake for Jay. He pushes Liza to the side and punches Wax in the jaw. "Now! Touch her again. Did you...you just let this joker grab you?"

She screams rushing to Wax's side, "YOU BROKE HIS JAW YOU MANIAC! JASON...THIS IS NOT YOU! WHAT HAS GOTTEN INTO YOU?!"

"Maybe the same thing that's gotten into to you. Maybe we both crazy. And two wrongs don't make a right. So guess what? I'm done with you Liza. All I want is too see my girls and after tonight. And if you're thinking about court, let me tell you girl, that's the last thing you ever want to do. We don't have to ever speak again unless it's about them. As a matter of fact, don't ever call me. I'll have my lawyer draw up an agreement for visitation. Sign and send it back. Oh yeah, and tell ya lil' bodyguard to get his weight up. Can't believe this man.

He walks to the entrance, stepping over Wax and Liza, "Hey yo Ty...Lets bounce man! Bring shorty wit da pink thong. I need that for somethin."

She walks behind him as he crosses the street. "Jay wait. Where you goin'? Come back."

"Oh now you wanna get sweet like Betty Crocker on my ass 'cause I'm about to go make it happen with one of your co-workers? Jealous much? Bit too late for that shorty."

She grabs the back pocket of his Dickees, "Jason wait."

He snatches away from her, "I hate you. Don't you ever put your filthy fingers on me again... thought you was different. I'm disgusted. Just look at you."

She'd never seen him like this. Conflicted, she found it refreshing. She had only known him as a boy. She hadn't had the chance to see him evolve into a man. A man with pride and ego. Although she found his tone jarring, she found it sexy to see him stand up for once and speak his mind. She had seen other men do it. Liza wasn't quite sure of where the lines between control and protection were drawn or where they blurred.

"You know what Jason? You don't talk to me like that. Like you Gandhi."

"Girl what?"

"You heard me. If you so perfect, WHATCHU DOIN UP IN HERE JASON!? Y'all jokers kill me. Up in there on the hunt, on the low. But when the lights come up, the show over and you done had your fill, everybody back to bein' a ho. Pssshh man... Miss me with that garbage! I know better! No thanks to you. You ain't no better than me. GROW UP JASON! JUST GROW UP!"

He continued to rant, "I give you whatever you want and everything y'all need because I love you that much. Didn't matter if we were together or not. I always kept my family my priority. I would've done anything for you Liza. Anything."

No longer his mother's little boy. He had evolved into his father's son. What he had been trying to fight was winning the war. He was convinced that he was being a man. A man always had to be in control of everything.

Jason was getting nastier and angrier by the minute. Out walks Ty and two females.

Jason snatches the keys away from Ty, "Gimmee yo! You toasted. You ain't killin me tonight. Y'all get in."

"Man, why yo so angry all the time?"

"Shut up and mind ya business bruh."

Liza's stood across the street in front of the club consoling the DJ. He walked over to her, "Liza, I ain't no thug by no means. You know that. But I ain't takin' no disrespect off of nobody else."

She kneeled down to apologize to Wax. Then she walked to her car in tears. Jason followed her. She turned around, "Just go. I'm done. I can handle myself."

"Girl you know I'm not about to leave you out here alone. You know I'm not about to let you drive home tipsy either. Let me take you home Liza. Get in."

"Hold on. This is my car. You don't tell me..." she stumbled on the gravel.

"Whatever man. Just come on." Her ex-husband carried her to the car.

They pull out of the parking lot. She notices no one had come to help the DJ. "Wait!" she begs. "Stop! Look at Wax. We can't just leave him here like this." She jumped out of the car. "Let's drop him off Jason. It's the right thing to do."

"Drop him off? Drop him off where? Girl I ain't about to..."

"At Beth. Please Jay? Come on."

A little of the young Liza Rose crept through and seeped into his heart just a bit. He could never resist when she was that endearing, innocent and sweet. She always had an effect on him.

"Aight man, only because you asked. I still ain't got no love for this joker. You know this is Newark. If you ain't bleeding out or a gun ain't involved, you ain't got no real emergency. You get in. I got Mighty Mouse. Straight to Beth Israel Liza. That's it! He better tuck and roll and I ain't playin'." He shoves Wax in the backseat.

Halfway down the block he slammed on the brakes. "What are you doin'?", she asks.

"He is getting out." Jason pulls him out of the backseat.

"Why? I thought we agreed..."

"Girl just let me handle this. Somebody'll find him. Or he can hobble back down the street. His jaw might be broken, but he ain't crippled. He can walk."

"JASON!" Liza yells from the passenger seat.

"Let me handle this. Ok? I know what I'm doin'."

"You really have changed."

"You talkin' girl?"

He drove off. She asked, "What about your friends"

"Girl, stop playin'. You know that was a fake out just to make you jealous. My man can handle them. Hopefully they won't rob him." he laughs.

"See that's not nice. We should pray for him."

"I have other things to think about. He's gonna be fine. I promise. He's in his zone. And besides, same God look out for us, lookin' out for him. He's good. If all else fails, he can talk his way out of whatever. That's all he does is talk."

They drove around all the wee hours of morn enjoying the warm air. He wanted to milk every second he could with her hoping each one would be longer than the one previous. Never knowing which one would be their last.

When in conclusion, they had arrived at their destination, she invited him inside for breakfast as a peace offering. He leaned back on her couch, "Nice place!" he shouted. "I'm proud of you!" His mind raced with anxiety wondering if she had ever entertained a male companion. Yet, he refrained from delving into harsh waters that were too deep to swim in. "Do I really want to know?" he pondered. "What man really wants to know?" Yet, he felt he had a right to know if he was funding the entertainment and the up keep. Jason wasn't sure if it was his money or the money she made at the club that kept her living lavishly so he decided to let sleeping dogs lie.

"Make yourself at home!" she echoed.

Liza showered with the bathroom door open when the girls were away. Jason laid back on the sofa. Moments later, Liza skipped down the stairs from the shower unveiled.

"Whoa! Whoa! What are doing? Where are your clothes?" He was delighted and alarmed. His eyes danced with excitement. In his mind, confusion abound. "I wonder how often she does this?" he judged.

"Whatchu mean Jay? I'm goin' to the kitchen to make breakfast. I always walk around this way when I'm at home alone. You've seen me before. What's the problem?"

"That ain't the point girl. You shouldn't do that. That's not a good look for a house full of females and no male presence. People be watchin' Liza. Now, I want you....I mean can you cover up?" he pleads facing the plush flooring. "And this carpet feels like a cloud. Am I paying for this? Man....I don't even have this at my house. No wonder the girls are always complaining my floors are too hard. They're floors! This! This is a magic carpet ride from Aladdin. I gotta step my game up."

She steps closer to him at a gradual pace. "So you're not attracted to me anymore?"

He cases her figure. Recalling within seconds, every nook, every curve, and every crevice he had explored before their lengthy hiatus. He began to sweat. Weak, he caressed her hips and kissed around her navel as he breathed deeply. "What's that you smell like? Coconut?"

Immediately, disgrace set in. "Go get dressed girl before I die of a massive coronary in here."

"Why you actin' up? It's just me Jason."

"For the love of God please go ahead Liza." he sighed.

He watched her walk away. He fell to his knees, "What was that?" He ran to the nearest window and stuck out his head to get some fresh air. "Man that was torture. Straight torture. Is she trying to kill a brother?"

At that very moment, Ty's voice rang in his ear, clear as a bell, "For one, you are not a bother by far. So stop sayin' it, ok? Looking like us don't make you one of us. All of the time with this kid man." He laughed to himself. "He gon' hate me when he wakes up." It worked as a welcome distraction for the moment.

Liza emerges, this time dawning a lavender goddess gown. She looked elegant. She was vibrant. She captivated him. For her it was like prom night all over again.

Jason couldn't believe his eyes. "Liza Rose, you look so beautiful. He guides her down the last few steps. She takes the final step right in to his arms, "So beautiful girl." He stroked her hair as they embraced tenderly. "You cut it!" he gasped.

"Yep! Something new. Pixie cut."

"....so proud of you Liza Rose."

"Thank you Mr. Rodriguez. Time for a change. Change can be hard. But it is definitely necessary."

"Anytime Mrs. Rodriguez".

He escorted her into the kitchen. He grabbed a seat directly behind her. He couldn't help but stare.

"What do you want to eat?" she asked.

"Whatever you make is fine Liza Rose. I won't complain." he continued to ogle her like a pubescent teenaged boy. He imagined all kinds of things.

She turned around to look at him. He turned away like a shy young boy. "You good Mr. Rodriguez?" she giggled shyly.

Blushing he remarked, "What she said. You know it."

Flushed, she gathered ingredients from the refrigerator. He crept up behind her and stroked the small of her back with his thumb, "Anything I can help you with?"

"I'm good."

"I believe you." He kissed her on the neck.

She nears him to toss egg shells into the trash. He takes her by the arm and pulls her onto his lap. "I love you Liza Rose." They kiss devotedly.

Suddenly she jumps up, "EGGS!"

They burst into laughter.

"Cereal?"

"Lucky Charms?"

"Now you know Marianna love herself some Lucky Charms."

"Just tell her daddy had some. She won't mind."

"So that's another thing..."

"What other thing? I don't know if I can take another thing."

So, "what do we or do we not tell the girls at this point?"

"I'm not sure." Jason mumbles eating his cereal. "We'll figure it out. I guess we can pray about it. We can pray about everything I mean. Can't hurt nothin' that ain't already hurt."

They held hands across the kitchen table. He looks at Liza, "You can start. I'll finish." He was too ashamed to admit he hadn't sought the Lord in such a long time. His faith had weakened over the years. He barely had any left. His pride wouldn't allow him to show that to Liza. He had shown too much emotion previously. As much as he loved Liza Rose, he wasn't about to give up every bit of himself. He had to reserve something. Liza had become unpredictable to him. Although he welcomed it; it was refreshing to think how he'd probably never get bored with her, especially after being with so many different women over the years. Knowing how apprehensive, bare and vulnerable her versatility made him feel, he became secretly mummified at the thought that he wouldn't be in control at any given time. He had to guard his heart. Especially after last night.

She ended her portion of prayer. "Baby steps babe." she whispers.

He was aghast. She saw right through him. He knew deep inside that his walls meant nothing to Liza. She had a simple power over Jason that nobody else had. Not even Marisol.

He closed his eyes and began to pray. The words seemed to flow from not just his lips; they flowed from his heart. He was soft spoken. Jason appeared harmless and childlike. Now she stared in astonishment, tears flowing from her eyes dripping onto the table top. There was a deep difference in Jason. Together, they had something. Together they had power. He prayed hard and deep like he was praying for the life of his child to be loosed from the grip of death itself. Just as softly as he had begun, Jason closed his prayer. His eyes met her tears. Her lover kissed her hands. As he gently wiped her tears away he said, "Thank you."

"What for Jay?"

"Loving me anyway."

"Same here. Thank you."

"So where do we begin?" he questioned.

"Here. Now. We just did with prayer. That's how we keep it. We take it slow. Baby steps."

"Well alright. But…"

"But what Jason. Here we go."

"Relax. I got stuff I wanna get out and on the table before we proceed. I don't need last night regurgitating itself ever again, ok? I want to start off on the right foot. Okay?"

"Alright. I'm ready. I guess."

"No babe. I need you real ready. I mean, real ready. So think about it... You ready?"

"Yes Jason. I'm ready."

"Where the knives at Liza?" he teases.

"Jason. Please already."

"Aight...ummmm..." he clears his throat. She pats her feet impatiently. "I been with a lot of women since our divorce. I can't put it no simpler than that. I just have to be as organic as you allow me to be in the moment. I didn't plan it. It didn't start out that way. I couldn't be with you so, I did what I had to do. I needed an outlet for my energy and my frustration. I could go to the gym and box to let out my aggression; Ball or run. But that wasn't helping me in other areas so..... So little by little, I did more and more until it just started to become natural to me; you know like it is for most guys to just be with multitudes of women. I don't know man...You were my first. At the time, my plan was for you to be my only. But, life happened. People and things got between us and now here we are.

The more women I sexed, the more my desire grew and the more I needed to keep me from dealing with us or not dealing with us, depending on how you look at it. It was like a drug addiction. Needing more and more to get that old feeling back; that first high back. Our first time back. Me and you back. Or to avoid thinking about that stuff, again, depending on how you look at it."

"What? I don't even understand why you're telling me this."

"Clean slate. I want a clean slate. I was out here being sloppy. So if something ever gets back to you."

"Oh boy…"

"Let me finish. I'm trying to give you the respect of the heads up because I love you. I really don't have to explain anything to you. We were not committed. We are divorced. I want something real with you though. Something grown-up this time. I'm trying to be a man about this stuff. What I'm saying is, men cope differently than women do. Not makin' excuse or sayin' its right. I'm just sayin' for some, not for all, it just is what it is."

She stared in to her cereal bowl tossing the milk. She was disappointed. Her lover had moved far ahead of her and was now trying to convince her that it was all a mere coping mechanism.

He nervously awaited for what he perceived to be her judgment. Surely he was to be crucified by judge, jury and executioner today. He put on a poker face and dove into the soggy bowl of sugary goodness before him. Pretending to enjoy the remnants, his heartbeat like an 808.

She dropped her spoon on to the table and retreated to the living space without so much as turning in his direction or blinking an eye.

He thought, "I guess that's my cue to leave. Stupid me! What man spills his guts like that to any woman? You breakin' the code boy!" A small voice spoke to him, "Yeah. But she's not just any woman." He was frightened. He thought he was hearing things. "Let me just get out of here. I messed up. That's it. I mean who does that?" Abruptly, before he could leave his seat, that same still, small voice confirms, "A man in love. A man trying to change. A man that wants to right the wrongs. A man who is ready for a new start. A man with integrity. Be patient. Love is a process." The voice was all too familiar. So familiar it was scary. A voice he hadn't heard since he was a teen. A voice he had stopped listening to. He refused to believe it was God.

The voice returned, "You just spoke to me Jason in your prayer. You didn't think that I'd listen did you? I was waiting for that. I miss our conversations. I am still real. I am still here. I answer. I am going to help you all if you have faith and hold on. I want to restore your broken years and fill them with joy. But you must believe me and hold on." Jason was frozen stiff.

Jason full of pride, combated the craving to fall to his knees and praise The Lord like he used in his bedroom. Back when he had felt the presence of God more strongly. As a child, nothing could persuade him against the love of God. But time and experiences; life and people had hardened his perspective. God was patient as usual. He knew Jason. The Lord knew a man so hardened by his hurts wouldn't be so open to receiving Jesus again as the head of his life so readily. It would take some convincing. Jason wasn't that young boy anymore but, God was still the same God. Yesterday, today and forevermore. God the creator of time, had time. For all time is in His hands. The book of Ecclesiastes touts that God is in control of the timing of every event and He plans the way things turn out. There is a season for everything.

Jason remained in his seat with his head on the table top like a little child bent over by the shame of his wrongful deeds. He really didn't want to face Liza or God. Nevertheless, he was a man and as a man, he knew he had to run into the fire sometimes to save what he valued most. He valued his family above all else. So Liza was the shortest straw in his hand. He chose to face her instead of God or both. He wasn't yet ready for the Lord. He was still embattled with bitterness and unforgiveness. Resentment towards reality. Jason still struggled with anger management and didn't know what the root was. He had questions for God that he didn't think God could handle. But God sat back. He wasn't worried. He had His appointed time. He gathered the courage to walk into the living space. Yet, as he neared where Liza was sitting, he had lost the nerve to confront her on her verdict. So, he marched towards the door.

Before he could turn the door handle, she hisses, "Come here Jason. I don't want you to leave. Please?"

There's that sweetness he can't resist again. "God, I love this girl."

He eases by her side gently. "What's up? Whatchu thinkin?"

"I'm thankful that you told me but it might have been a bit too much for me to digest all at once."

"Yeah I know I just started spillin on you. I love you though. I just wanted to bet it out and over with. I just wanna be back with my family. I love y'all Liza."

"We love you too. But we still have a long way to go. Jason, I don't wanna do this without God. I can't no more. It's gonna take some faith. Remember we used to just read the Bible when we was younger? We just believed what it said?"

"Yeah I remember that."

"We used to believe Jesus for the best no matter what we was going thru." She smiled, "Remember?"

"Yeah...I do."

"Remember when we said I do?"

He beams, "I do." Staring into her eyes memories come rushing in like an autumn wind.

"I get it Liza Rose. Still, before we go further. I need to know if you have anything you need to lay on the table that could damage us in the process."

"Meaning...." she replies sharply.

"Meaning, tag, you're it."

A red alert went off inside of Liza's brain. It flashed as it read: WARNING, CONTENTS COULD BE DANGEROUS. PROCEED WITH CAUTION. REPEAT. EXERCISE STRICT CAUTION IN YOUR DIALOGUE. THE MALE EGO IS EXTREMELY FRAGILE. THIS HAS BEEN A TEST OF THE EMERGENCY BROADCAST SYSTEM. IF THIS HAD BEEN A REAL EMERGENCY...YOU WOULD KNOW IT. THIS IS ONLY A TEST.

He prodded her. "Well?"

"I saw somebody over the summer. It was nothing Jason."

"And..."

"And what? Whatchu fishin' for? Like what do you want me to say, huh? WE WASN'T TOGETHER! REMEMBER?"

"Where did you meet this character? Church?"

"No. At the club."

He jumps up, "He met you there! THERE LYZA! HE SAW YOU NAKED?"

"We were not together Jason. Just stop it."

"HE SAW MY WIFE NAKED?!" he howled pacing back and forth.

"Boy sit down before you wear a groove in my carpeting."

"NAKED!" He slams the front door.

She sits there for ten minutes. She thinks to herself, "Childish. Double standard nonsense."

She calls his phone. She hears ringing outside of the door. She looks out of the window. He is sitting there with his head in hand cursing the day he was born.

"That's unnecessary she Jason." She opens the front door. "It was a summer fling. I was trying to find myself. And JUST LIKE YOU...I was longing for something. We... "

"No we Liza. There is no we. So, oh Lord... So...did you? Oh my goodness man. Girl did you...?"

"No Jay. I'm still the same old' G. I mean not the same but the same. You know?" she joked.

"STOP CLOWNIN MAN! THIS IS BIG BUSINESS! DID HE EVER TOUCH YOU?" he demanded towering over her.

"Jason don't take it personal. You're coming off way too sensitive right now. It's killing your sexy."

"That's a yes. I knew it. I knew it. Look at you man. Who wouldn't... I... Man oh man...I'M PISSED LIZA."

Liza was calm, "Well be that. But be nice."

He was fuming but he kept his composure. "It was that sneaky pastor dude right?"

"Does it matter?"

"Yes or no Liza?"

She's refused to answer.

"Oh so you protectin' this punk?"

"Calm down Puerto Rico, I ain't protectin' nobody and I don't belong to nobody aight?"

"Now I'm goin' back inside. You can either rock wit me or you can roll out." She shuts the front door. "Big baby!"

He followed her into the kitchen. "Alright. Alright. You right. We wasn't together. I appreciate the honesty. But the thought of another man seeing and touching you is always gonna have me seeing red Liza. I am a man. I'm in love with one woman. That woman just happens to be you. How am I supposed to feel girl? Be for real!"

"Ok so you're IN LOVE with one woman. But that didn't stop you from being with OTHER WOMEN in the meantime. Right? Same difference. You know, just to let you know and please tell a friend, we women can sure do without that double standard nonsense. Its 2014 just in case y'all slept through the calendar flip. LET HE WHO IS WITHOUT SIN..."

"Cast the first stone. I know. I know. I'm sorry. But men have ego, pride and are very territorial. You ain't gonna ever get that Liza. You women don't get it. It's serious. Brothers get cased up over stuff like that. Some lose their lives man. It's that serious! And don't let a joker be in love and his feelin' get wrapped up in it. That's a whole 'nother beast Liza."

"I am not your property JASON."

"I wasn't implying that LIZA."

"Well, that's the way it sounded to me so…"

"Typical woman with that selective hearing."

She balked, "Typical man, peeing on a tree, locking horns and sword fighting as usual. And how you know what I know about men Jason?"

"Let's not go there Liza."

"Oh don't get cute. How do you know I just didn't get it Jason? Give me some credit. It's real out here. We're having adult issues. We've both made bad choices and wrong turns. We either gonna get past this and move forward or the buck stops here. Seriously."

"No I feel you ma. You're right. You sound like a mother and a grown woman. I like that. You're definitely not the girl from yester year." he claims.

"Yester year? Who says that Jason? I mean really? Who you be wit?" she laughs.

"You." He kisses her, "So seriously, we workin' on us?"

She kisses him, "We workin' on us. The past don't matter. What happened in Vegas stays in Vegas like The Hangover."

"Get off of me Liza! You mad corny."

She runs behind him and wrestles him down to the floor.

"Question, what made you leave the GOOD REVEREND alone?"

"He wasn't my reality."

"SEE I KNEW HE WAS FUGAZE! Ain't no real Pastor gonna be up in no strip club watchin' shorties throw box like stock clerks at Stop N' Shop in the middle of the night. Ain't no way man!"

"Let me just say something, I need you to be patient and mature."

"Wait let me guess, You're gonna defend this rascal? Liza don't be so naïve."

"I am not naïve and I'm not defending him. Listen, every man regardless of title, position, calling or responsibility is susceptible to temptation, hardship, confusion and failure; No matter how great or small the man or how perfectly put together they present themselves in public or folks perceive them to be on the outside. That goes for women as well. Pressure comes for all of us Jay. Don't judge too harshly. We all got stuff to answer for. Nobody's perfect. We're both grown enough to know that obviously."

He sat up, "Look at that."

"Look at what?"

"Look at Liza Rose droppin' jewels." he laughs.

"I just believe in grace and mercy Jay. Lord knows we need it. We all got issues." she smiles.

"Still don't like him. Amen."

"Thank you for the ride Mrs. A. I'll let you know when I'm on my way out."

"Let me help you in with the bags..."

"Not at all. I've got it. You've done more than enough."

"But honey, you should let me help. You're..."

"Pregnant. Not handicapped. It's a temporary condition. It's ok." Robust and struggling to get through the gateway of her house, she toddles through the entrance. "Dang. These bags are heavy."

She hears a moan. It's the dark of night. She grumbles, "Men...always in your face when you ain't beat. Never around when a lady needs assistance."

A full-toned voice rattles her from beyond the darkness, "Is that so?"

Stacey drops the bags. "Boy! What are you doing lurking around in the dark like that?! Like some random mall weirdo in a trench coat from a low budget 80's movie. ARE YOU DOING? TRYING TO KILL ME?"

Mrs. Amora emerges from her driveway, "Stacey? You ok baby?"

"It's just me Mrs. A! It's Barker! No need to be alarmed."

"Call the boys Mrs. A!" Stacey chimes. "We got a stalker."

Mrs. Amora snickers, "Oh Stacey. Play nice. Hello young man. You two behave now. Stacey I'm here if you need me. Good night kids. ".

"Night Mrs. A!"

"We'll see!" Stacey yells.

"Let me help you with these bags Stace."

"No. I'm good. I had enough of your help last time. Remember?"

Progressive moans impede the conversation.

"Shh!"

"Shh what girl? And why are we whispering?"

"You hear that Boom?"

"What? Are you insane? Girl, give me these bags. Let me help you in...."

"Uh huh! Told you! You hear it now don't you?"

"Yeah. What is that? Better yet who is that? Stacey please don't tell me you owe somebody money. I can't be out here acting like a thug. I got a lot to lose."

"Will you be quiet Boom? Sounds like it's coming from over here." Stacey walks in the wet grass and peeks just beyond the rose bush. "Aaaahhhhhhh!"

"WHAT?! WHAT IS IT?" Barker trots over towards the rose bush unamused. He parts the hedges, "YO! IT'S A BODY! WHAT THE... AND IT'S A WHITE FEMALE BODY! JESUS!"

Stacey peeks inside again. "GIRL GET UP FROM THERE! WHATCHU DOIN' DOWN THERE IN THE DARK AND RAIN IN THE MIDDLE OF THE NIGHT? YOU BETTER NOT BE TRICKIN OVER HERE. NOT AT MY HOUSE! THIS AIN'T THAT KINDA BLOCK! AND WHOEVER YOU DOWN THERE SERVIN' BETTER COME OUT NOW OR THEY GETTIN' BLASTED!"

"Really Stacey? For real? You a G now Stacey? Unbelievable!" he shook his head.

"Mind ya business pretty boy! I got more stain than you out here in these streets. I'm a hustla. Ask about me.", she charges. "But never mind you right now. I ain't got time. GIRL, GIRL, GIRL...IF YOU DON'T COME UP OUTTA MY BUSHES!"

The young lady crawls from beneath the bushes. She's black and blue. "Stacey.", she attempts to get up. She collapses. "I can't go no further. I'm sorry."

"Oh my goodness Maya. Maya baby. It's gonna be ok. I'm here. It's gonna be alright. Hear me? It's ok. Pick her up Boom."

"Stacey, now listen, I just went through some ghetto drama you wouldn't believe, with this crazy little white girl that had no business down here and she..."

"Boom, I know you bourgeois. I'm used to it. But brother, this is not about you right now ok? The Bible says He makes the rain to fall on the just as well as the unjust. THE LATTER MEANS YOU! You just the only one don't notice it. Now please, pick the girl up and bring her inside. I know what I'm doin'. Thank you."

"Jeez man. Look at my shoes. Oh boy! B what have you gotten yourself into? You know she always got a hot cup of drama waitin' for you, freshly brewed, whenever you show up.", he thought as he picked up Maya's lifeless, body and entered the house. "Where you want her?"

"Lay her on the couch. And stop looking at her like she a leper. Where is the love and compassion PASTOR?"

He approached the dilapidated love seat. When her long, blonde hair fell away from her face, he dropped her.

 "WHY DID YOU DO THAT? SHE'S IN PAIN! CAN'T YOU SEE THAT?! WHAT ARE YOU AN ANIMAL?!"

"Why are you taking in strays Stacey? If it's about money... "

"Money, money, money. Why is it when people have money that's all they think about? Life is about more than your stupid money. And everybody don't want your stupid money, let me tell you. I didn't understand Todd at first. But now I feel him. All y'all worry about is money. Lord have mercy on these poor rich people."

"Wait Stacey. I wasn't trying to…"

"Save it man. Just save the Superman/Sugar Daddy routine."

"Girl what? And who is this Todd? Oh you got a man now? Don't you think you need to?"

"Boy what? Mind your business. And for the record, Todd is Kandi's…"

"Who?!" he snarls. "Girl, I don't know none of ya lil' cracky friends."

"First of all, it wasn't crack. It was diesel Golden Boy. And Kandi asked Todd to sign a pre-nup and he…"

He rolled his eyes, "TV right? You know those reality shows ain't nothin' but another form of junk food don't you?"

"Now after you done threw the girl on the sofa you wanna play pastor and preach to me about what I watch? You got a lot of nerve. I was trying to make a point."

"And your point was?" Barker tapped his feet.

"You missed while you were off vacationing on your arrogant island again. Forget it."

"Fine."

She grew more annoyed by the second. "As a matter of fact, if you don't mind, I need you to leave. Thank you." Stacey dabbed a cold washcloth over the girl's face as she squirmed on the sofa.

"Stacey I think she's going to convulsions. She's having a seizure. Imma call 911."

Barker was from the inner-city. He knew a lot. There was probably nothing he hadn't heard, seen or done. Things his parents didn't even know of. Teenaged boy excursions and secret activities filled with debauchery had escorted most of the boys he had grown up with into another zone. He had acted just like them in many ways outside of his parents' sight; away from prying eyes of church folk. He had just determined not to get too wrapped up. Barker Golden was determined to be the exception to the hood rules. His parents hadn't raised him to be a statistic. God was on his side. Not that God wasn't on everyone else's. Barker had a distinct calling on his life. He had known that early on.

Still, his parents leaving the inner-city to provide a better quality of life for he and his siblings couldn't decrease his curiosity and taste for devious deeds from time to time. He left the hood but, it had never fully left him. He didn't want to be that disconnected from his roots; the things, places and people that challenged him; helped make him strong. Something he got from his parents that stayed with him.

With all that he experienced, said and done, Barker had never had seen anyone kick a heroin habit before. Not before tonight anyway.

"Boom what you scared for? Hang up the phone. She don't need no ambulance. She don't need no doctor. Nothing they can do for her right now. She needs her medicine."

"Well where is it? Where's her purse?" He ran out to the bushes to search for a purse. He belts back inside, "I searched all through the grass and the bushes. I can't find it." With tears in his eyes he whimpers, "I can't find it. Is she gonna die? Stacey we can't let her die!

She looks up from Maya to the ceiling, "Lord, I don't know what I did to deserve this. But I thought we was ok now. I'm trying to get myself together. All I wanted to do was stock the fridge and go back home. I don't get it."

"You should be praying for her not you Stacey. Where's her medicine? Well..." he stares at Stacey.

"WHAT?!" she screams.

"CHECK HER POCKETS STACEY HURRY UP!"

"Not here. Nope not there either." you satisfied?

"What kind of medicine is she taking? Maybe I can go buy some?" he pleads.

"Nah you good. Everything over this way is garbage last I checked. The best stuff over the Hudson and that's too long of a drive. She's good. Chill out." she laughs.

"Oh! So you know what she needs? Good! Just tell me where to go and get it, I know people over in the City. I can make it happen in no time. Please?" Filled with anxiety, he paced back and forth.

Stacey encouraged him to relax. "Please just sit down. You are really actin' like a teenaged girl right about now and you're workin' my nerves. You know, I been goin' to church and prayin' and stuff? This gotta be the devil. Or a real bad joke. I CAN'T BELIEVE YOU'RE REALLY THAT NAIVE AT YOUR AGE BEING FROM HERE. I mean really! I can't. You really should leave Boom."

"Okay. I'll leave. Just tell me what she needs so I can pick it up. Stop playin'."

"DOPE BOOM! OK! YOU GET IT! DOPE! NOW IF YOU MAN ENOUGH TO GO AND GET A BAG...BE MY GUEST! BUT TAKE HER WITH YOU 'CAUSE IT AIN'T HAPPENIN' IN MY HOUSE. NO MORE! GET IT! I DON'T EVEN WANT TO BE NEAR IT! SO THERE YOU HAVE IT! SHE'S TRYING TO KICK BOOM! SHE'S DOPE SICK. SHE'S AN ADDICT. LIKE ME OK!" Exhausted, she walks into the kitchen.

He stood in the doorway, "Ummmm.....I, didn't know. I had no idea. I'm sorry."

"I know her Boom. I've been trying to help her. She was hiding from her pimp. I was supposed to meet her here a while ago. I got caught. I feel like I let her down. I failed. I tried to help, but I failed. And look, he beat the hell out of her. Probably beat the baby out of her too! Last time I saw her, she was pregnant."

She wiped her tears, "Boom. I tried to do the right thing. I'm trying to make amends and pull people out of the lion's mouth. Maybe this just ain't my thing." She takes off her over-sized jacket on her way back into the living room. Barker gets a glimpse of her pregnant belly but he doesn't say a word.

They stood over Maya. "Don't be so hard on yourself Stacey. You're doing what you can. That's good enough. No one can be everything to everybody all of the time. God is with her."

"How do you know that? Look at her Boom."

I know He is because she is here with us right now. It could've been worse. She's safe. I know he's here right with all of us. I'm proud of you. She's going to be ok." He puts his arm around her.

She walks away, "Imma get a blanket. She's shivering."

"How can I help?" He asks.

"Well, if you gonna be here, ONE: DON'T FREAK OUT! It's gonna get uglier the closer she gets to kickin'. And it will take a few days... 'Bout a week on average. TWO: You gonna think you're watching the exorcist if you stay through the process, especially tonight and tomorrow. But DON'T FREAK! Just keep it quiet. Give her space and rest. THREE:"

"I know. I know. DON'T FREAK! Ok, I get it."

"No! And take notes. We're gonna take her to the room upstairs and lock her in there. Things are gonna get intense and nasty. You're gonna hear some devilish words and get called some names. But you should be used to that by now."

"Yeah right. Only when I come here." he whispers.

"What's that?" she scorns.

"Nothing. I'm listening."

"So, as I was saying, she gonna try to break the door down with what little strength she has. Pay that no mind. I've already had the window boarded up and nailed shut. I got it covered. And she's probably gonna cry out loud a lot, beg to be released and claim she's gonna die. But that's ok. It's normal. If you let her out for a second, be forewarned, she may try to kill you if she has to just to out of here and cop. And the dope spot ain't that far off, so take heed and try not to be so sensitive. Finally...." she takes a sip of water and exhales. "Look me in the eye black man. You ready? This is some sound doctrine right here Pastor."

"Yeah. What?"

"You better be prayin' like a nun that got locked in a broom closet with a shirtless Channing Tatum. And by all means, DON'T FREAK!"

 Trying to download it all, he murmurs, "Aight.".

"Now that she's simmered down for about a half o' minute, let me stock the cabinets, get some pots jumping' and run her some bath water. She's gonna need it. Pastor, it's gonna be a long night. If you ain't here to stay, now is your chance to exit stage left. Brother, it's about to get real."

She flips her hair and waddles to the kitchen. "Okay Stacey James, what we are going to do first girl?"

He injects, "Boil some water and get some fresh towels? Put your legs in an upright position and push on three?"

"What?!" she shrieks.

"When were you going to tell me? Huh? At the baby shower? At the hospital? At the Christening? The birthday party or the graduation? Oh hold up...I know! The child support hearing right?"

"Well I might have told you after the first pre-natal visit if you was the daddy."

He shook his head in disbelief.

"Look Barker. I'm trying so hard not to be who I used to be. So that means no more arguing with you. So don't pull me out of pocket. Especially if you gonna be here."

He walked over to touch her belly, "Can I?"

She grabbed a butcher knife from the cutlery drawer, "I will KILL YOU! You won't take another child from my arms. I will end your life tonight Barker. I mean it."

"Stacey please. I'm not trying to..."

"Don't matter! Just keep a safe distance. Don't ever touch my baby. Nobody's taking my daughter away. Nobody! Hear me!?", as she laments in torturous momentum, a pain strikes her abdomen. She falls to the floor doubling over.

"Stacey!" he screams.

"I need to lie down." she whispers.

He carried her to the sectional in the living room. He carries Maya upstairs to the master bedroom and locks her inside after he runs her bath. He covers Stacey with a blanket and plays her soft music.

"Whatchu doin' Boom?"

"I remember this use to relax you when you as carrying G.". He puts a pillow under her head. "Just trying to help. I'll get you some tea and some crackers."

He remembered as a child his father would get tea and crackers for his mother when she wasn't feeling well times he was at home and not off somewhere deep in his ministerial duties. Searching through the pantry he couldn't help but feel awful for the way he had left things previously. He wanted her forgiveness yet, he wasn't sure how to ask for it. Inside he felt a battle was waging within her. A battle he had started that he wasn't ready to finish. He was no longer ready for war. He wasn't sure he was ready for love. He was though, concrete in knowing he was ready for peace talks to begin.

The water danced in the tea kettle on the stove top. He waited patiently. He turned the fire down low so he could steal a few extra moments to look at her lying there helpless on the couch. He stood in the frame of the door post and watched as she adjusted herself to get comfortable. He wanted to serve her. He wanted to elevate her feet and make her comfortable. He was willing to do anything to make her time with him in that house more pleasant; to begin to make amends for his bad behavior. He knew he had stabbed her in the heart too many times to be recollected. Staring at her, he recognized her as person, a human, a woman; someone with value and worth. More importantly, Stacey was a mother. She rubbed her belly with her eyes closed. She looked peaceful and content. Even as a teen mom, Stacey hadn't looked so serene. It was endearing. "Sweet.", he thought to himself. Stacey was radiant. She glowed like candlelight in the dusky space.

How dare he keep her away from her only son? The only thing she had to hold on to after her parents had passed away. "Who could be that cruel?" he pondered. At a turn and a glance, suddenly, he caught a reflection of himself in the mirror. When Carla was alive she made every effort to keep Stacey abreast on Gregory's progress. When she didn't hear from her, she went looking for her. She found her. She brought Al and Gregory along, when she could. They shared a meal, said a prayer, refrained from judgment; they ministered to her. They were kind and gentle with everyone. Especially a difficult one; a fragile soul, Stacey James. She was almost like the daughter they had never had. The Goldens weren't perfect by far. But, they knew how to give away and show mercy and grace. They had been given so much of it themselves. It just flowed out of them naturally. Anywise, Barker, their oldest child had missed the mark on many occasions.

He wondered what Carla would say if she knew how he and Stacey were treating each other. Let alone how he was treating her. He had never seen Al mistreat Carla in anyway. For much of his life, he had remained shielded from their adult, personal issues. The Goldens kept their problems to themselves. All disagreements would be settled away from the delicate emotions of the children. They tried not to utter a word of discontent before Barker and his siblings. Life, most of the time, in and outside of the Golden house, appeared perfect. "They did right." he mumbled under his breath. "What is wrong with me?" He knelt down in a corner of the kitchen to pray. "Father what have I done? I'm not sure of who I am anymore. I'm miserable. I've hurt people. I've left everything I know. Now I'm empty inside. Nothing I searched for had any meaning. I don't know where I am. Why do I mistreat this woman?"

A still voice spoke to him in gentleness, "They spoiled you. They did what they thought was best. But it was a disservice. They coddled you too long. They didn't give you all of the truth. They were just being parents. Everything was handed to you. You walk with too much pride. A spirit of entitlement."

He recognized it was the voice of the Lord. One he was all too familiar with. He bent lower to place his face on the floor, "Lord, I think I've lost my mind. I'm so sorry."

"Barker where have you been? Why did you leave me?"

"Lord I was tired. I guess I was impatient and I lost control. I sinned against you. I turned away...so much I'm not proud of. I guess I was afraid to come to you."

"You thought I would treat you the way you treated others. With judgment and rejection? That's not who I am. I am God. I know why you do what you do. I am not like man. My grace is unlimited. My mercy is new every morning. You know you can talk to me. I'm always here. I will always love you. It hurts me to see you turn away from me. It hurts me to have to turn away from you because of your sin. Come back to your rightful place son. I love you."

"Come back? Father, I'm not sure I can come back. I have so much going on. I want to change but I don't know how. Look at what I have done to that woman in there. I have been so cold and distant. I want her forgiveness. But I'm afraid to ask her for it. I'm sure she doesn't want me in her life. I don't blame her for the way I treated her. I'm so sorry. I don't know how..." he lays on the kitchen floor. "I can't make it right. I don't deserve your love or forgiveness. How can you ever use me again?"

"Son, how can you be a shepherd over my sheep and not believe? How can you lead my people if you lack confidence? I am with you. Be accepted. Be loved. Repent. Be forgiven. Be made whole. All is well. Endure the process. I am with you. Love her like I love you. Love even when you don't receive it in return. Love doesn't require much yet, it gives everything. It gives and gives until it hurts and beyond. Let her live and love that woman. Go and peace. I love you. Welcome home."

"Lord, thank you."

"I am here. Pursue me. Learn of me. Learn who I am. Learn what true love is. Then you can give it away as you receive it. Delight in me and I will give you the desires of your heart. Grace and mercy forever in all you do. When it gets hard. Hold on to me. I promise I will be holding on to you."

The Father had seen the son afar. He ran to His son to greet him. He held his son in his arms. The father walked all the way back up the road to the house with the son. When they got back home. The father announced the return of his prodigal son. Heaven threw a party that night. A lost sheep had been found.

In that short time in prayer, he had already begun to learn about love, mercy, forgiveness and grace. It was like he was seeing God and everything else for the first time. Right then, he believed love was an endless cycle of giving and receiving; often more giving than receiving. He was just beginning. Inside things were bursting. A metamorphosis on the horizon. He was excited.

Mrs. Amora was in the alley between the two houses taking out the trash. The window in Stacey's kitchen was always ajar. She could hear the goings on from time to time when she ventured out into the alley. She heard Barker's prayer. She felt for him. She felt for them both. Knowing them from birth, before they had known one another or themselves, she had watched them grow. She was still watching them grow. She felt like she was a part of their lives. She had known many things about them both. Things they didn't even know about one another. Mrs. Amora was very observant; very protect of children. Especially the ones she knew, babysat, corrected and often helped rear. She knew Barker had been fighting his feelings for Stacey. She even knew why. Mrs. Amora just watched and prayed. She knew a long time ago Barker's feet would get tired from all of the running. The only thing left for him to do was to fall out before the throne of God and bare his soul as his knees gave way. He always loved that girl.

Mrs. A knew he was excited and afraid of rejection. She said to herself, "Can't hurry love. Like the song says...you just have to wait. He wants her love and forgiveness now. Ha! Ha! That won't happen. Not tonight. Time baby. Everything that will ever be worth anything takes time and preparation."

She liked to read before she went to sleep. Before she retired to her bedroom that night, after her prayer time with the Lord, she picked up an old book with no cover. Curiously she thumbed through it. The binding was loose. A page fell out. When she bent down to pick up the page, she saw a portion of a paragraph was highlighted. It read:

The book Song of Songs encouraged one lover not to wake up love to soon; not to be so in a rush for what isn't in a rush for you. Evolution. Preparation. Time. Details. The Lord had all of the details and if genesis was to be birthed out of revelation, the Lord knew it would take time. All time is in his hands. We must learn that even where there may be purpose and promise, we have to have patience for there is, there always will be process. Process to allow progress. Everything takes time. Maturity is all about process, patience, preparation, time and progression. It was as if The Lord was confirming what she already knew. "Oh Holy Ghost!" she whispered. "What looks grown is not always grown. It's springtime. Thank you Lord."

The tea kettle whistled. Barker raised up to gather himself. He collects his faculties, clears his throat. He tip toes over to where she is resting.

He kneelt beside her, "Lord be with her. Take good care of her." He prayed like a child. He tip-toed over to turn the music down. Brian Courtney Wilson sang in a sweet lull, "YOU'RE ALREADY HERE. HALLELUJAH. YOU'RE ALREADY HERE". God was already there. God was speaking to Barker's heart. He was already there just as Barker had prophesied to Stacey just moments before. He still had it despite his shortcomings and rebellion. He was still anointed. He still had a calling to respond to. This time, God's way, ego free. It was time to serve in humility. He grabbed a Bible from the coffee table. The same Bible Stacey walked around with as a teen that had been untouched. He remembered he used to ask her, "Why do you carry it around if you you're not going to read it? What? You wanna look saved?"

Her response would always be, "Nope. I do it because my parents tell me too. This keeps them off my back. They always buggin. Tellin' me it's not right for the pastor's child to be seen without the word. Tellin' me how to dress and talk when I'm around people. But when we in the house, I don't listen to them. They do whatever they want. So I do whatever I want."

Everything seemed a joke to her at the time. It was like she was just attending church to keep up appearances at the urging of her parents. They were the heads of the church. Things had to look orderly. In hindsight, he couldn't blame her for how loose she had in school; for a lot of things she had done. He knew outside of church, everything associated with church was a lie to Stacey. His parents weren't the only ones that served up a hearty bowl of disservice. He began to see her differently. He hadn't paid attention before. She was riddled with issues and pain. Outside of the church, Stacey couldn't keep her parent's attention. His eyes were ever widening. He opened the Bible. As he thumbed through it, he was floored by the ground Stacey had covered. He felt silly. Even if everyone else had counted Stacey out, God didn't. Jesus, the author and finisher of our faith knows our end and our beginning.

That night, he laundered her clothes. Her son's father had cleaned her kitchen and arranged her pantry. Just the way he had seen his mother do it as a child. When he was done he sat on the floor and listened to Maya's attempt to cope with the pangs of withdrawal. He lit scented candles and snacked on dried fruit. He watched Stacey all night long, periodically listening at the door of the master bedroom to make sure Maya was safe when things got too quiet. Whenever he heard a thump or a growl, he knew she was ok. He was starting over. Everyone was starting over. Everyone would have their withdrawal symptoms to bear. But in the end all would be better for it. It was the dawning of a season of transition.

As the daylight is summoned by the darkness of night to, Barker retreats to the kitchen. After a morning cup of coffee, prayer and meditation. Stacey finally ascends the staircase dawning bathrobe and slippers. Her belly more evident. "Oh no. No. And so what is this pray-tell?" she says.

"A healthy start to an uncertain day. Oatmeal to warm you up. I know you love green tea. Orange juice for folic acid. Egg whites for protein and..."

"Boy! Where's my yolk? I need the yolk. It's the best part."

He dumps two teaspoons of sugar into her cup of tea. "Stacey y'all don't need the cholesterol. Man, y'all really don't need that sugar. But Imma let you live because life ain't perfect, so why should breakfast be. Can't be religious about everything. Too much trying to walk a straight line and playing the "perfect role" can make you overdose on things that should only be enjoyed in moderation."

"What Boom? We speak English up in here alright?"

"I'm just sayin'... Diets don't work ma."

She leaned up against the wall and stared. He wondered stood across from her, wondering what was on her mind. She wondered just what on Earth he was talking about. Barker was talking about himself. Thinking out loud. Remembering how his need for balance had lended to his bad choices. Still unsure of exactly how God would use him, even after hearing all the Spirit of the Lord had revealed unto him over the past hours, he still questioned Jesus' authority like the chief priests, elders and scribes did Jesus when He walked into the temple in the Bible. He didn't see how The Lord could ever use him. He had forgotten how deep the mercy, forgiveness and grace of God runs. It ran deeper than his sin ever would. He, as a Pastor, still had yet to receive the full love of God...fully. He had equated the love of God to that of human beings. He saw the Lord through a limited scope. In his subconscious, he thought, "I heard what you said Lord but I'm having a difficult time grasping the reality that you can still use me."

Just then the Spirit of Lord spoke up, "...and all of your shortcomings. Nothing is ever wasted. Stay humble son. Only just believe."

Without warning, Stacey spoke up as she took a seat at the breakfast table, "Boy, ain't nothin' ever wasted around here. I use it all. Everything can be used for somethin' my Grandmother always said. Even the things that don't seem good for you have a purpose if God is in control. God knows how to make it all fit. You know Boom? So it all evens out in the end. Ain't nothin' ever wasted. Good, bad or ugly. Get it? Now fry me up them yolks. How you gon' deny me? I'm with child! Give 'em up partner. Don't waste 'em."

What a confirmation. He turns away from the stove to see Stacey wolfing down her food like an abandoned child. She looks up, "Oh, I'm sorry. Guess that's not lady-like. I am eating for two though you know. Plus the doctor says I could stand to gain a few. Don't mind me please."

"Nah, I don't mind. Do you. I'm just glad to see you eating."

"That's what's up Boom. Now where my yellows?" she grumbles with a mouth full of food.

"Whatever pleases the lady." he smiles.

With her face almost buried in her bowl of oatmeal she remarks, "Brother, you cook like a pro. Where you get them skills from Ms. Carla?"

"Not really." he replied, "From her husband.". He rolled his eyes.

"Who knew Mr. Al could chef up like that? Who knew you could?"

"Well I had a lot of practice as a single father raising a young boy that eats like five linebackers. Grown man and a young boy at home alone, nobody to give them portion control. No woman there. No mother. No wife to shut it down. If I didn't work out I would probably be about…" he turns to give her the fried yolks.

She interrupts, "Thanks but no thanks. I'm full now. Sorry for the trouble."

He takes a seat across from her, "No trouble at all. If you need anything from me, I'm there. Even if it's an egg yolk you're just not gonna eat after I just cooked it." He always knew when Stacey was lying or trying to cover up something. He thought, "Uh huh, she's changing. But she still got that issue. Guess some things stay with us. But I gotta give her credit. She's trying her best to be kind."

As much as he desired to be a part of her evolution, he was wise enough to know to keep his distance. If he still had some ways about him, she was entitled to have some ways about her as well. And if he knew anything about Stacey, he knew that no matter how well she behaved, how calm her demeanor, how tranquil her speech, if you pushed her, the Brick City in her could erupt like Mt. Vesuvius in a New York minute. He walked on eggshells in efforts to stay in her presence as long as she would tolerate him. He wouldn't admit it, but he was chasing. In a moment of weakness he reaches out to touch her hand. She grabs her pregnant belly, "Don't you dare. This one is mine."

"Stace, I would never hurt you or the baby."

"Boy, ain't nobody worried about that. You got the message the first time."

The Lord was working on her but he was right. Stacey James still had some ways about her. Barker had no idea of the disservice he had done himself and the mother of his son by bringing up the fact that he had been a single parent. Not just any single parent, the father of the son she had lost custody of. His words brought back sour memories. In her mind, she was led back to a place within herself that would never be too far away. She began to think back to the lost years. Swiftly she reconciled within, that he was her enemy. She had been trying to let go of the pain of the past. Today, the progress she was making wouldn't matter much to her.

He threw his hands up, "You got it! You got it ma! I don't want no trouble. Guess I'll clear the table. You gonna finish your tea?"

She grabbed the coffee mug full of hot tea. Hate filled her eyes. She pulled it back as if to aim it at his face. As she began to speak, as still small voice whispered to her, "Don't do it. You've come so far. He didn't come to hurt you. You can't be angry with people for what they're unaware of. He's not aware of your pain Stacey. He's in his own pain. Forgive him. He needs a friend. We talked about forgiveness. Remember? I know it can be hard sometimes. But do all you can to walk in love. I will be with you. Love is never about us my child. Forgiveness is never about the other person."

She cleared her throat, "So I noticed when I brought up the cooking bit you called your father, your mother's husband, not dad, old man or even pop. You might as well call him THAT MAN. What's going on Boom?"

"Nothing I would like to discuss right now if you don't mind. Imma take out this trash."

She shakes her head, "That ain't the only trash you need to take out."

"Girl what?"

"You heard me. Stop runnin' Boom. Deal with your life. If I have to cope without dope, you have to do the same thing."

"Girl, I ain't on no drugs. You know better! What's wrong with you?

"A lot and not much. Just like everybody else. But unlike most, I'm learning to own up to the garbage in my life. I don't just mean the drugs and the sex...that's just the surface...the secret hurts and pains from yesterday that I was medicating with the dope and the sex. I was runnin' Boom. We be runnin'. Just like you're doing now. Who was that God told to get up outta the cave and stop acting like a punk? Oh yeah, Elijah right? It's time Boom. Man on up dog. You ain't the only one with issues that run deep. If God can help me with mine, I know he can help you with yours. Psshhhh man please...I guarantee you that small nonsense pales in comparison to mine."

He drops the trash bag. "Pales in comparison? What the... Since when you start talking like that?"

"For all you THINK you know about me, there is truly so much more that you do not know. I may have run these streets. And you can bet your bank account that I know Brick City like the back of my hands. But you can also bet the house that there's more to me than what you and everybody else chooses to see. Boom, word from the wise to the wise, just because a person has been down, does not mean that they're out. God don't see us like that. Jesus had to be crucified in order to be resurrected. How soon we forget. I'm not as stupid as I may have acted in the past. Don't judge a book by its cover brother."

"Alright Stacey. Alright. I see you, I get it. Touché and all of dat. But I promise you, you don't know what you're talking about concerning me and him so I humbly beg your pardon."

Stacey taps her fingers on the table. Reaching for a piece of bacon she laughs, "Boy, I don't know why you made bacon if you gonna fight me on egg yolks."

"That bacon was for me and the white girl thank you. I am allowed a cheat day. I work hard to maintain my health and physique. Rewards are just that. We talked about the OD factor remember? And hold up...don't change the subject. Don't get involved in my family affairs! Especially when you have no idea of what the truth is."

"Well ain't no fun if the homies can't have none. So, with that being said..." she closes her eyes as she chews, "You sure Ms. Carla ain't teach you how to cook? Your father seems just too busy with ministry to be chefin' up and stuff. Figured one of the ladies at the church might be trying to wiggle her way into the fold by now by cookin up some downhome, backwoods goodness and bringing it by in a clingy Friday night mini instead of a long Sunday go to meeting uniform. Hey! Go figure. I just can't believe all the time your mother been gone Mr. Al ain't moved forward. I mean shoot, he's a nice looking older man. I know meeting ladies ain't never been hard. Your father was always easy on the eyes child. Guess that's where you and your brothers get y'all..."

"That's it.", he states. "I'm out. Still so very crass I see. Some things never change." he whispers. Just then he hears the Lord say to him, "And you can judge her? On what day? That wasn't nice. Love."

"Pride rearing its ugly head huh? She teases.

"Girl why don't you leave my business alone? You don't even know the half."

"You're right! I know it all. Guess what, we can talk about it. It's gonna be ok. My people weren't perfect either. When the fairy tales and pipe dreams of what once was or what we once believed to be are shattered, we're left the remnants to deal with. And boy Boom, is picking up the broken shards a labor intensive chore. Getting sliced up and bleeding the whole time. Left licking our wounds. Suffering from seemingly irreversible damage. Lying awake at night amidst the whole of the wreckage floating on those shards from those broken dreams that cut so very deeply. Floating on a sea of tears in the middle of nowhere. Somewhere between yesterday and tomorrow. Running from the one, in no hurry to get to the other. Hmm! Say what you wanna say about me. I'm not like you."

"And it starts. Here we go. That means what Stacey?"

She licked her fingers, "I'm honest about mine. I mean, sometimes I like to stew in my own juices. Feels good to be in your feelins and your flesh sometimes. It's wrong but it's real. It's a shame people won't be more upfront about that." He was astonished. Barker couldn't believe how articulate she was.

"Uh huh, we don't even ask God for help to get off of that shard barge because we're addicted to the pain and the pity the barge represents. But at the same time we runnin. Ball of confusion man. Just a ball of confusion. Frustrated at the world for something they ain't got nothin to do with. Everyone around us suffers because we subliminally disconnect. All the while, The Lord is watching his child suffer in silence. Calling to our hearts, 'COME AND SIT WITH ME. TALK TO ME. I CAN HELP YOU. I WILL TAKE THE PAIN AWAY.' Yet we refuse.

The cycle continues. We end where we are. Running fast and getting nowhere on a hamster wheel. Seeing the tomorrow God has for us off on the horizon in the distance, knowing it's going to take self-evaluation, painful consideration, spiritual observation; faith, forgiveness, prayer; diligence and dedication to get us there…Wait for it…Wait for it…". She takes a sip of orange juice and a deep breath, "Child that was a journey! Whew! But do we really want to do the work? More often than not, the answer is no. So we hold on to bitterness, sadness, depression, confusion and anxiety.

Floating on that bloody barge in that salty sea. Singing WOE IS ME. We never get what God has for us in tomorrow because we refuse to be helped today. We like the burn of hurt. The pity party seems like the poppinest party to be at. We invite other people to it, but when they don't come…Houston we have a problem. Yeah, that's right and that problem is us."

Barker thought to himself, "Since when this chick start makin' sense?"

She went on, "You think I don't know the backstory of Carla and Al? Huh?"

"Please don't do this girl." he begs.

"Do what Barker? Tell the truth? Huh Golden boy?"

"Stacey why we gotta go back instead of movin forward huh? Don't call me that!"

"The Goldens. Ironic the name, huh? I mean with that rusty past and all. But who can judge? I know I can't. I ain't here for that. I'm here to get you to man up and move forward. It ain't gonna be easy Boom, but it's time."

"Alright, now you're being disrespectful and I don't have to sit here and take it. I asked you to leave it alone."

She looked him in the eyes, "IT IS TIME BARKER." He tried to leave, but his body wouldn't move. He didn't want hear what she had to say but he knew he needed to listen.

Angrily he snaps, "What you think you know?"

"I know Carla and Ms. Nene was as thick as thieves out there back in the day. I know what they was about. I know Mr. Al used to hustle. I know he's not your biological father Boom. That's what I know."

Barker lay his head on the table. He tapped his feet. He pounded is fist.

"You might wondering how I know. Boom, you know me, I been in theses streets for years doing my thing. Its people older than us still out here getting high. You know it ain't many secrets in this city. It was what it was. My point being, when you roamin' wit da Romans, the Romans talk. I'm not here to tear you down. I'm here to help you. I got people helping me. So I'm just paying it forward. God has been good. I'm doin' what I can to change. But I had to start that process with the truth. Boom can't nothing be done until the truth is told. You ain't gotta feel embarrassed or ashamed. They past made them what they became. Your parents helped the community best they could. They came from the mud and reached back trying to pull other people like me out. They drew people to them in love and kindness; just like God drew them to him. Just like Ms. Carla, Ms. Nene and Mr. Al was drawn together out here in the streets. In love and kindness. Friends to the end. Shoot man, your father getting up there in years, but he still hustlin.'

He lifts his head, "What you mean he hustlin?"

"For the Lord. He still drawin' people in. I told you earlier, nothing is ever wasted. I thank God for your family. I ain't like how it all went down with my son and all, but even then, they continued to pursue me, invite me into his life and show concern for my wellbeing as a person. They didn't judge me Boom. They past don't matter. They real Christians. From the heart. Not just from the mouth. And I dare anybody to say otherwise.

"Whatever man. Al ain't my father."

"You're right. Mr. Al is your dad. Where in the Bible does it say that your parents had to be your biologicals to be your parents? Huh? Joseph wasn't Jesus bio but he raised the boy up, took care of him and his momma and he didn't care what people said. Joe covered her, married her, obeyed the Spirit of The Lord. Jesus was even disciplined by Joseph; subject to him in every way. Joe was his daddy. Anybody can be your father B. It takes a dedicated, loving man to be your daddy."

"Subject?!" Stacey when did you start talking like that? I see change. I even welcome it. But girl, you startin' to scare me. Lord have mercy. Am I in the twilight zone?"

"Boy no and hush!" she chuckles. "Just listen, give the man the same respect you would want if the shoe was on other foot. Just because your biological standings are fresh out the box to you, don't mean they brand new to him. Obviously not. Obviously he loved you anyway. He still does."

"Wait a minute. Now I KNOW for a fact nobody would know that situation but me and him. How you…"

"You so hard headed. I just love me some bacon, mmm!"

"Girl stop eating that bacon and get to it. Your feet are gonna be swollen."

"Oh sorry. Cravings." she smiles. "I told you they was the real deal Holyfield Christians. Al and I still talk. They never treated me like I was invisible. Even when I wasn't kind to them, they continued to be kind to me. They helped me pay off this house Boom. My parents left me with debt. But that's another story for another time. I ain't got the energy right now. You done ran my nerves. I wanna go lay down."

He walked over to help her up out of the chair. She clutched her belly. "No. I'm good. Pregnancy is a temporary condition. Ain't no handicap. Get away from my baby."

"I don't care what you say Stacey. I'm going to help you. Look how swollen your feet are."

"All that sittin' and schoolin' you youngin'. Don't worry about it. It's my circulation." she whimpers.

"Nah, it's all that bacon man. No more. I'm taking the rest upstairs to the girl."

"No leave it. I'll take it in a few. You might freak her out."

"Tell me about it. Did I tell you...?" He wanted to tell Stacey all about his encounter last winter but he knew it wasn't the time. Everybody had a lot on their plate. That issue seemed trivial in the moment.

Stacey rested comfortably on the couch rubbing her baby bump. One eye open, one eye closed. Watching the father of her son.

"Hey man, why you playing me close like that? Huh? You over there actin' like Imma induce your labor when you go to sleep and kidnap your daughter and sell her on the black market. I'm insulted man. Why don't you knock it off already? Jesus!" he walked to the door.

"Leaving?" she asks.

"And you care because?"

"Oh don't get it twisted bruh. I really don't."

"You asked, so somewhere in there, you really do. I'm going for a walk."

She joked, "Kevin Hart says it means you're happy when you go for a walk."

"Well I've seen his stand up and I know for a fact that he was taking a walk or two thousand, because some crazy women was getting on his nerves. Trust me. This is what men do. He only told y'all half of the story ma."

"Whatever bruh. And wait, how you know I'm having a girl? Who told you?"

"You did! Remember the knife gate? Nut job."

"Whatever. Have a good walk."

"Whatever.", he mumbles. "Oh yeah I'll do that. But while I'm out, do yourself a favor."

"What Boom? I'm tired."

"Take a look at yourself and get off that bloody barge. It's slicing your back up. It's not a good look. Don't nobody wanna hurt you or take your baby. Get over yourself. Now there's some truth for YOU Stacey James."

"Whatever!" she yells.

"Swim for shore. Don't drown in your sea of tears. Ain't nobody got time for that!" he belts as he shuts the door.

He stood on the other side of the door. She turns over. They both take a deep breath and say to themselves, "Childish."

Mrs. Amora peeks out of her window. She smiles, "Children.".

ALL IN LOVE IS FAIR

"Hey! Hey! What are you doing up on your feet? You're supposed to be resting. I go off for a walk, come back, and you're doing chores."

"I'm up cleaning up the mess you made this morning."

He looked down the hall into the living room. "You missed a spot." He maundered.

"Last thing anyone in recovery needs to do is to be idol...mind starts wonderin'. Especially in a neighborhood like this one. You don't know how hard it is...me being here. It's like I'm being forced to revisit my past every time I look out of the window. Shucks man, just being here period. Just let me... let me just work."

 She stopped to catch her breath. She stuck her head out of the window to breathe in some fresh air. Immediately she began to take in all of the familiarities. Attempting to redirect her thoughts, she found there would be no such escape. It was the dawn of the strenuous task of coping without mechanism. It hadn't been easy; being newly saved, clean and pregnant. This had been the first time in her life that there would be nowhere to hide from pain and the responsibility of responsibility. She had been naïve about the process; Giving her life to Christ. "Things are going to be so different. All things made new. This is going to be good." She could hear Barker talking in the background as he had taken over cleaning. She was irritated by his voice.

Life had been especially hard on her; on everyone she knew. Everyone except Barker. Seemed he had a free ride his entire life. Whatever the issues were he had been whimpering about earlier, they were nothing compared to hers. She wished her issues were so small. Secretly, although God was doing a mighty work within her, she was embattled with resentment and bitterness. His name seemed to describe everything about his life for so long. Deep inside, when Stacey had discovered the dirty, little Golden family secrets, she had felt a sense of relief. At present, his confusion, brokenness and almost obvious refusal to forgive his father struck a chord within her. Rendering her prideful. She truly believed it was a reversal of fortune; somehow vengeance was on the horizon. It was his time to hurt like she had for so long. She in her ignorance, believed God had it in for Barker instead of her. "'Tis the season." she spoke aloud as she closed the curtains.

"Pardon?" Barker asked. "What season? I asked you if you wanted a refill. Folic acid..."

"I'm good Boom. So tell me why you and Mr. Al got beef? I know his side of the story." she pried.

"Girl, I've been up all night, I'm wiped and I'm not in the mood. I didn't come here to lay on the couch and spill my guts and you're not my therapist. Let it go. Don't you have more pressing matters to attend to other than those that surely don't concern you? I know the Bible says something about meddling."

"Now where is this comin' from? Why you mad, huh? I just asked a..."

"You're in recovery. You're the caretaker of another young addict which I'm not so sure is the right thing no matter how noble the deed; timing is everything. You have a child on the way, not to mention a son you haven't seen in ages. Looks to me as if thine cup runneth over. So do me a favor, don't worry about me aight?" He walked into the living room. "And if you ain't gonna rest, then let me."

His comments infuriated her. She heard the Lord speaking to her, the proverbial tap on the shoulder, "Walk in love. I know you hurt. I know it's hard. But..."

She ignored the voice. "Ain't he tippin'?"

"What?"

"Wit' Ms. Nene? Is that why you have a problem with him?" Stacey was having a 'Lord I'll be back' moment. Her mother used to say that when she got upset with people and she wanted to read them. She had inherited her mother's sharp tongue along with her father's addictive personality. She knew she was wrong but, in that instant, the disdain she had for Barker felt so right. This was her moment, pure vindication. "Love is not easily provoked." she heard the still small voice on the inside of her say. "He is still my son. Touch not mine anointed. Do my prophet no harm." the voice warned. "Justified anger is the worst kind Stacey. Be still and know that I am God alone. Judge not lest ye be judged. And who said anything about your anger being justified?"

She held her head down, then she looked to the sky, "You're right Lord. I am sorry. I am trying. I guess not hard enough." She continued to whisper, "I'm just... Ooo I'm just angry! How could you allow this? He's so blessed and I suffer so much. How is he any better than me? I know you love me Lord, but do you love him more? His family never suffers. Don't want for nothin'! They have everything. I am angry. I can't help it! I know of your favor, at least I've heard of it...God, when will it be my turn to prosper? And when is he ever gonna suffer for the way he treated me? This ain't right."

The Spirit of the Lord comforted her. "I know you're hurt. I know you are angry. Believe when I say, it will all be ok. For everybody. Trust me."

"Trust you? I've been trying to trust you all of my life and things hardly ever change. Why should this time be any different? It's hard to trust you Lord. I've been through too much. You let him get away with everything. It's not fair." she lamented.

A warm breeze caressed her cheek. The warmth of the sun dried her tears. It was as if God himself, was drying her eyes. "Stacey, you are my child, and I love you very much. But I am God. Work out your own salvation with fear and trembling. Don't worry about the next person. What has anything I allow in heaven or on earth, have to do with you concerning them? I am God. Be still and know. All the things will work together for the good to them that love me. Vengeance is mine child. But what if I choose to show him favor and he never suffers? What has that to do with you? You do know all of the laws and the prophets hang on the two commands my son gave?"

"Yes Father, I do.", she whimpered.

"They are based in love. Love for me. Love for yourself. Love for your neighbor. I am love. You can't hate him and say you love me. You just can't. Now I love you. I don't stack up your wrongs. Stacey don't do that to people ok? That is not what love is about. Love suffers long my child. Long suffering is a fruit of the Spirit. You know that don't you?"

"Yes Lord I do."

"So if you're going to life a love. If you're going to live out this salvation thing and be an imitator of God. If you're ever going to be a doer and not just a hearer; be like Jesus, long suffering is part of the deal sweetheart. Look how long Jesus suffers for mankind. Look at how hard and intensely he loves humanity; all of creation with little return on his investment. Oh child, get in to the word and look at how much your savior suffered. All for you. Everything else Stacey, is light and momentary affliction."

"Ok Lord. I guess I get It. Please forgive me."

"There's no condemnation to them that are in Christ my daughter. That isn't just for you. It is also for him." Again, she wept.

"Live a life of love and be an imitator of God. My love, people don't always know why they do what they do. I am Lord over all. The creator of the universe...every creature great and small. Even when people don't know why or aren't even present enough to be concerned about their behavior, I know why. That's all that matters. You don't have to. Love and forgiveness doesn't always require understanding. Love and forgiveness always require action. I know you hurt. But who says he doesn't? You're not here to become a part of his hurt. You're here to become a part of his healing."

"I don't understand. That seems backwards. It doesn't make sense to me. How can I help him when I need help myself? This can't be you Lord. I must be going crazy."

"It is me Stacey. And love doesn't have to make sense. But it has to be sacrificial. Love doesn't seek its own. Despite damage, pain, hurt and abuse, love remains faithful and firm. In the face of great suffering, love remains silent. Love believes the best even when the worst is apparent. Love walks by faith, not by sight. Love always suffers long. It is selfishness and unforgiveness that is impatient. Those things take exhaustingly. Love gives."

"Huh?"

"Love is always the giver Stacey. That's all love knows how to do. Sacrifice is in loves DNA. Love is so sacrificial it is willing to die, give up everything, even justified anger so that someone else may live. Love gives until it hurts and beyond, expecting nothing in return. Remember Jesus? Remember his walk? Remember the cross? Remember the cost? In the scripture you are promised trial and tribulation. The scripture also promises that you will overcome. Didn't say when, where, how. Just promised. Be of good cheer daughter. Jesus the Christ as overcome the world. I will help you."

She wiped her tears. Barker sat watching the mother of his son. He thought, "My goodness, she's gone mad. Thank God I'm not a woman. Lord I couldn't handle that pregnancy stuff. I mean they're emotional by nature anyway. But man, if the physical changes cause those types of ups and downs and they can go from 0 to 60 and back again… they can have that." Stacey looked up at the sun and giggled. A butterfly had landed on the tip of her nose. She hadn't noticed him.

Barker continued to pray, "Yeesh! She wasn't even this emotional the last time. This is a different woman Lord. I don't know what to do with this creature. This is a whole different beast."

"Let it go. Be there when she allows you to. Give her space as she needs it. Love her apparently, consistently yet, subtly and silently. Allow her to just be. She is in pain. Just like you. Respect her pain. Respect her process. Serve, even if you get rejected. Serve 'til it hurts and beyond. That is what love does Pastor."

"I'll try. This is scary."

"I will be there always. Just hold on."

"Alright. Here we go." he shrugs his shoulders. He offers her a tissue, "We good? I meant, you good? Aw Jesus."

He was noticeable nervous. He hadn't been that tender to her even in high school. Pleasantly surprised, she looks at him and smiles, "Nah, you good. What you doin' wipin' my nose? I ain't no baby Boom."

"I know. I see that." He moved closer to her. She stood still. "You're a woman. I know. And you have feelings. I… "

Before he could reach down deep enough into his soul to search for enough and guts to spill,   she backed away from him. He shook his head and said, "Jesus! What the…"

"Patience and love." he heard the still small voice say to him.

"Girl, why you keep running from me? Is it really that bad?"

"Let's not go there Boom. Not now. Please. You ain't ready and neither am I."

"Stacey I…"

"Save it. Let's get back to the matters at hand. Now why…"

He interrupted with a desperate look on his face, "Stacey what about forgiveness. When you gonna forgive me?"

She barked sharply, "Rome wasn't built in a day man. That's as far as I can go with you on that brother."

"Okay. I understand."

"Speaking of forgiveness,"

"Not again."

"When you gon' stop crucifying the man for being a man? You a man right? Hell, my father was a Pastor, but I swear fo' cheese that seemed to be a part-time gig. He was as flawed as any man can be. I still think about the sights and sounds of him and my mother up in here. They played a lot of different roles in front people. I never knew who they were gonna be from minute to minute. A child can't wrap they mind around all of that hypocrisy and be expected to reason it out and sleep well at night and perform well during the day. Wow. I'm grown now. At least that's how I feel today. Some days, I ain't sure though. I try not to hold on to my past. But being here don't make it easy to let go. So I..."

He glared at her, "Uh huh, keep talkin'."

"Now no! Nah uh! This is not about me. You almost had me."

"No way! You totally had me. I thought this was a psych office and we were in session for a minute. Man, I was about to charge you." he joked. They laughed. Immediately Stacey turned her head and put on her poker face. Her teeth had yellowed and some had even begun decaying form the years of neglect and abuse. She wasn't feeling attractive. Nevertheless, he was still attracted to her. This time it went beyond physical.

No other woman had made him feel so alive. She made him think. He secretly admired how she could juggle so much inside and out. He wanted to get to this female, this woman, who was keeping him interested, at bay and questioning who he thought he was and what he thought he knew.

 Stacey brought new perspective. She was still very challenging although, on another level. She was physically present but mentally and emotionally elusive. She seemed to be spiritually confident in her own right; on her own level. He was fascinated at the peeks of vulnerability she allowed him. She made him breathe and think deeply. She wasn't afraid to confront him; she had never been. Before he had felt so strong, tall and powerful as opposed to Stacey. For all intended purposes, on the outside, he had always possessed what she had needed. Total opposites. He was the one in control.

Now, in the blink of an eye, things were beginning to change. She didn't have anything. On paper she was ghetto statistic doomed to fail. But he saw excess where there once was deficit. He saw a well beneath the surface. It's like now, he was looking through the very eyes of God himself into the soul and spirit of one Stacey James. He liked what he saw.

The mind and heart would be not be as easy to penetrate, try as he might. In those areas, she had become very reserved where she once had been so lavishly reckless. She was coming into her own. God was on her side. She was evolving into an erect, unstoppable spiritual force. Barker knew that. He wanted to be a soldier in her army. She was game for resisting. And he was now awake and up for the chase as a lion, head of the pride, dominant male; young and strong, in the thick of the brush. Shoot him down as she might, he was apt to dodge every bullet or at the very least, endure the pain of every blast. He would never give up.

Their adversary the devil is always lurking about, roaming in the shadows. In search of whomever he may devour. The enemy always has his next meal lined up. He is well versed in scripture and he knew exactly what God's plans were for each of them, so wherever they were going, he would not make it easy. Too much power between the two. He would have to do something. Something they could never even dream of.

Everything can't be prayed away. The enemy is always looking for opportunity. They would not reach the goals God had given them easily. They had been assigned to work together from the beginning of time. Before He formed the worlds He knew them. But they would have to get to know

Him. And on their way down that road, they would have to get to know the enemy. For how can you fight what you don't know? How can you kill what you cannot see? Faith is how. They would   need plenty of it.

"I wanna get back to business Boom!" she demanded. She had his undivided attention.

"Yes ma'am. Whatever pleases the lady?"

The comment made her blush. It was something he would always say to her in high school when he said something stupid or had mistakenly regarded another in her presence. Whenever he wanted a makeup kiss. Whenever he was setting her up for sex later in the day. Even when he knew he and his boys were going out later that night to get into some things he knew he should have no part in. He had never cheated on her but as a male, in a house full of other boys, him being the oldest; the start athlete; the man in his hood, it was his job to show every other guy around him that he was not henpecked. Allowing anybody to see even a hint of weakness in him in public view would lessen his standing in the Southward of Newark. He couldn't have that.

In public, Stacey would let him beat his chest a bit while she rolled her eyes and chuckled. She knew the real deal, behind closed doors, she was the boss. She had the goods. He wanted the goods and he would have to behave accordingly to get them. He learned quickly, thus getting the goods at his own discretion, thus Gregory. She had the real power. She was in control. She would even check him in public if his ego got too out of control. There was nothing shy about Stacey James. She was what all of the boys wanted. What some of them had conquered. Still, no less than a treasure to Barker. She was Kim Kardashian before Kim Kardashian was. Stacey reminisced while he stared.

Clearing her throat, "Knock it off! This ain't throw back Thursday! Can you just answer me?"

Irate he responds, "I DON'T WANT TO! Jesus, that's what I get for trying to be nice. I should've stayed down and went to sleep. Man!"

"You know what?"

"WHAT NOW?"

"Have your rest...but we are gonna talk. He's my son's Grandfather and YOU ARE HIS SON! Don't matter what the name is on the birth certificate. Luke, he is your father. Now go on to sleep. And on your way there, get on over yourself."

He rests his head on the arm rest of the sofa, "Girl, will you ever learn how to talk to a man? I mean Lord have mercy on that mouth. And that attitude." He yelled, "You can't keep a man like that!"

Stacey peeked out from the kitchen doorway. Resisting the urge to fire back, she knew he was right. "And who tryin' to keep you? You can go 'head on." she muttered. She had been struggling on her own so long, been used up by men and being manipulated by Barker didn't make her negative attitude towards men overall any better. "Shoot...talkin' bout my attitude. Ever stop to think that maybe you the biggest part of the problem? Tired of this mess! Jokers always complainin' bout the attitude on a black woman but don't see how they disrespectful ways add to it. You gotta be kidding me already. I mean really. The very man she come from, the man that's supposed to love and understand her the most don't even see they the ones causin' some of the problem. My attitude. I know my attitude need some adjustin'. I know I need to change, I just don't know how. Been down so long. Sister can't catch a break. "How about you adjust your tone and watch how you talk to me?"

Stacey went back to the window for air. She heard a neighbor on the phone, "Yeah man. I need to do somethin'. I have to go work every day for people that I KNOW don't even respect my black ass."

"Oh that's Sean. He must be talkin' to that hot Puerto Rican. Lord he fine. Sean, who you talkin' to?" He waves to her and motions for her to be quiet.

"If that's who I think it is, tell him I said HI." He turns his back to her.

"Tired as hell. Can't take a day off, they got somethin' to say. Can't scream on 'em and stand up for myself. Then, I lose my job. I don't have a criminal background. I went to college and I don't have kids out of wedlock. I pay my taxes. I provide for my family. I vote. I don't beg, steal or borrow and you know what dawg? I still don't get no respect. That's some real bullshit."

Stacey prays, "Poor Sean. Lord bless that black man."

Yeah man. She's a real good girl man. I'm blessed. But she don't get the pressure I'm under every day, just to make sure they aight. Too much fussin' dawg. Word up. Soon as I get in the door man. Damn. I know she got stress too. But damn! She be wantin' me in here locked up with her and the kids all of the time. I need a break. She don't get it. Only break I get is when she's out of town visiting her family. Damn! I get tired of listening to complainin' and babies cryin' every night. Then when we do talk, it's about her day at work. Not mine. I get so tired of... What? Oh yeah. Yeah aight man. I'll see you about ten. I gotta find a way to get out of here without the bullshit. If you don't see me, you know she won. Again. What? Man I know you aint my therapist joker! Stop actin' like I never listened to you man. What? Ain't nobody over here cryin! Shut up!" He laughed, "Pray for me man. One."

His wife creeps up behind him, "Hey babe. Who was that?"

""Who was who?"

"You were talking to? I heard you talking to somebody just now."

"Oh. Oh yeah. That was the crack head girl from over there. We was just talking about somethin' that happened yesterday on the Ave."

"Oh ok. It's crazy what she let those drugs do to her. She used to be so pretty."

"Yeah, that was way back at Weequahic. That was a loooonnnggg time ago. She was so hot back then."

"Oh really Sean?"

"What did I say? I was just supporting your statement."

"Really?"

"Oh come on babe. Now we beefin' over a coke fiend? Seriously? I got bigger issues to deal with. Ain't nobody thinkin' about that girl man." His wife stormed off. He looked over at Stacey. She had tears in her eyes. She stared at him in amazement.

"For real Sean? I never did anything to you. I thought we were cool."

"I'm sorry. I didn't mean that Stacey. You don't know. I can't win with this woman. I..."

"Save it. I'm used to it. And by the way, it was dope. I was a heroin addict. Not a coke fiend. Not a dope head. An addict. A person with a disease; often chronic; extremely fatal. If you're going to implicate me in your lie, at least know the facts."

"Aw man. Stacey, you misunderstood what I was trying to..."

"Sure I didn't. God bless you Sean. Both of you. And thank you." She shut the window quietly. She opened the back door, holding back her tears. She swept out the dust from the floor, "It's all good. Treat me like yesterday's news and today's trash. It don't matter. Everybody out here strugglin' with an addiction they didn't ask for is just invisible to y'all anyway. We don't matter. We don't have feelings like everybody else." Clouds hovered over her house. With the crackling of the thunder, the rains came down. She stopped sweeping when she saw how the water began to wash the dirt away. She sat on the edge of the stairs sobbing. "It's ok if nobody ever loves me. I don't care." She's soaked from head to toe.

She balled up in the corner of the porch. He gently whispers, "Don't cry. I love you. I see you. All of you. You matter to me. You are not your past. You are not your mistakes. You're not who they say you are. You are who I say you are." Swiftly, the raindrops whisk away. Cavalierly, a refreshing spring breeze comes in and strokes her face.

"Hey! Child of God!" A voice cries.

Beaten and somber, Stacey gripes, "Hey."

"Listen, I got some flan and pernil! Come have lunch. Let's feed that baby girl. You want her big and strong. Come on… meet ya out front."

"Alright. Let me get changed first." No matter what mood Stacey found herself in, these days, and the last thing she was going to do is turn down a home cooked meal.

She dashed inside to change. Before she could get out of the door, she thought to herself, "What if I see Sean and his wife? I'm gonna be so embarrassed. I never knew they felt that way about me. They were always so nice to me. I feel like a fool. Aw man! I'm so pissed at them. Phonies. Bet he didn't tell her we shared our first bag among other things. Bet he didn't tell her that! Think she so much better than me. I'll deal with Sean though. He got selective memory now that he cleaned up and educated. Make me sick."

"Forgive them. They know not what they do. Now, hold your head up high. You are mine. Don't you let the enemy steal your joy." She smiled. "Thank you Jesus."

"Dang Mrs. A. You sure put a whoopin' on some pork! So friggin' good. Thinkin' bout ya husband today huh?"

Mrs. Amora smiled, "He's on my mind quite a bit today. I miss him so. I wish everybody to love the way we did. What a love it was girl." She noticed how quickly Stacey had scarfed down the meal. "Mama, you sure were hungry. You been eating properly?"

"Oh yes ma'am I have. See..." Stacey lifts up her shirt to reveal her hips. "I'm gaining. Doctor said I need to gain a few. Ummm, may I have some more please? Flan on the side this time? I like salty and sweet together. OH! That's it!"

"What's it baby?" asked Mrs. Amora.

"Yeah can you put it on my meat please? Starving. That's gon' be good Mrs. A."

"Honey what? Let me get this right, you want flan on top of pernil, yes?"

"Yes please." Stacey licked her lips and sucked every bit of Kool aid from her cup. "And more cherry Kool aid too. If you don't mind. Mmmm..." She smacked her lips. "Just sweet enough. How you learn how to make Kool aid like black people Mrs. A? I mean just right. I mean just to the point of bringing people to the borderline of diabetes. Ghetto style. I mean mayonnaise, syrup sandwich, water in the cereal watchin' Saturday cartoons, back in the day good!" She starts singing, "All that I got is you...". She reminisced on the lyrics that old Ghostface Killa song she remembered from back in the day. The lyrics alone brought tears to her eyes.

Stacey thought about her parents. She contemplated as the music played in her head, watching Mrs. Amora fix her plate; she prepared every spoonful with care and concern, as if she was presenting it before the Queen of England or Oprah, Gail, Tyler Perry, Barak and Michelle were all stopping by for a chat and a bite. Her mind ran. Imaginative, Stacey day dreamed quite often with vivacious grandiosity.

She loved old musicals, stage plays. Costumes; old Hollywood glam. Make up, 70's drag and the like. On her way back around from her panoramic cornucopia of interludes to her first consideration, she reasoned, "They probably did all they could. Maybe they just did what they knew. Lord why this woman so sweet? She so nurturing. She ain't got nary a child. How is that?"

Smiling, Mrs. Amora walked the few steps to get back to where Stacey was seated. The Lord answered, "She is the way she is because she has been barren. She is compassionate and tender. Kind and loving. She is sensitive to the needs of others and to the promptings of the Holy Spirit. She is the way she is because people like you need people like her. She may be barren but, childless she is not. She is a mother to every child in the neighborhood for a reason. Every one of you has different needs.

Sometimes people on the outside can see what the parents on the inside cannot. On the stage of life, everybody plays their part. She is a mother in the non-traditional sense. Remember what you told Barker: Your name doesn't have to be on the birth certificate for them to be yours. Remember Jesus and Joseph. Parenthood is a matter of heart and soul. Physically giving birth doesn't automatically make you a parent. Motherly instinct and intuition are a matter of spirit. Some women give birth and have a lifetime detachment; no motherly instinct at all. And that's not for them to be judged by man. For who can know the mind of God? I have chosen the weak things of this world to confound the wise. Every mother is not a mama. This is why I created people like her. They are filled with the Spirit of Adoption. Matters of the heart and soul."

Mrs. A finally reached Stacey. Each time Stacey visited with her over the years it seemed she was moving more slowly. It was perfect timing for Mrs. A. As long as she could walk a distance without falling at her age, all timing, no matter how long was perfect timing. Mrs. A presented the plate, flan atop of pernil just as she had requested. Mrs. A, looked disgusted, "I've never seen such a mess in all of my life. I'm embarrassed to give this to you..."

Stacey held her hand as she lowered the plate, "Don't be embarrassed. This is perfect...Just how I wanted it. You're very kind. Thank you." Stacey smiled.

Mrs. A threw her hands up, "How can you eat like that child? Ay dios mio! My mother must be spinning in her grave as they say!"

"Mrs. A," Stacey said licking flan and scraps of roast pork from her fork, "Now, you see me. I'm eating for two. Why you getting mad? Huh? You like bustin' my chops. You know how it is when you..."

Mrs. A gave her a look and walked over to the sink to wash the dishes. Stacey's mouth had done it again. She had spoken without thinking and just that fast, had insulted her most benevolent host.

"Aww man Mrs. A, I'm sorry. I'm not thinking. My mind be goin a million miles a minute. I didn't..."

"Hush child. It's ok. I'm old enough to be able to walk in the truth. You didn't mean it. I know you're a sweetheart. I can understand your mind moves fast. Seems it hasn't caught up with that mouth yet though love." It was a subtle jab. A jab in the fashion of any mother to a child. Stacey then returned the same look to Mrs. Amora. Yet, she wasn't bothered by it. She knew what she said, she also knew why she said it. She was going somewhere. Hoping Stacey would come along for the ride. Stacey was insulted. Still, she knew Mrs. A was right so she remained silent.

"Well baby, I know you're probably pissed with me right now. But, I can't help that. I'm taking chances today." Mrs. Amora spoke with confidence.

Stacey sat up straight. Straighter than she had ever done for her own mother. She respected Mrs. A. Everybody did. Stacey was excited. Attention! The attention she had never gotten from her own parents. The straight talk, the sweetness, the protection, the concern. All she had been missing. If this was chastisement, if it meant she was gonna get some positive attention for a change, though she was a grown woman, the little girl within, the one with pig tails, a baby doll dress and shiny patent leather shoes. The raunchy, vamp of a teenager, getting caught smoking in the bathroom, sitting in the main office, awaiting her parents' arrival; the parents that never showed up. The parents with the smidge of influence in the community because they were pastors of that small church and were cool with the Golden family, had some juice, pulled a string, made a call, got her off the hook. The very parents that never showed up, never disciplined her. The ones that had never shown her that they cared. She had done so many things because she wanted somebody to care. Watching her grow up, seeing how she used to so easily give her body away, Ms. Amora had known that.

All of her life that was part of the glue that had her stuck to Barker for so long. Many nights, the Goldens and their son had been the only ones who cared. "Everybody just needs somebody to care. People love to sit in judgment of what others do cause they lookin' in from the outside; they can't see the whole picture. They don't know you only get the real story, the real view, if you step inside. It's like looking at a house that's decorated beautifully on the outside. Then you get in there and it's Louisiana right after the hurricane. Just debris and dead bodies floating all around. But they be too scared to come up in there. So they stand outside the gate and judge. They never care enough to ask why we do what we do. Or at least care enough to say 'Hey! Now you know that ain't right! What's your problem? Come here...let's talk about it. I want to help you.' Nah, people too busy just being concerned with them and they own family. Even people in the church walk past you like a water fountain nobody want to drink from. They ask you if you alright as they smile and put they hand on your shoulder and keep movin'. Ain't really concerned at all. Just wanna ease they conscience for the week I suppose. Goin' through the motions. Only God knows." Chronicling, she churned. "I'm do somethin for the young people. The ones out here crying out. People see 'em actin out and cuttin' up. Call 'em a waste of life and go on 'bout they own. But nah...I ain't gonna do it. I know what that's about and Imma help. People just need help. In the streets, in the church, everywhere. Somebody gotta care." she thought.

Stacey perused down the avenue of the panoramic view of the process in her mind. Mrs. A, is giving her an old school tongue lashing. On the outside, she appeared attentive and receptive as did the little girl within; the teenager in rebellion, she was glad for the attention, but her pride wasn't beat so she heard what she wanted to hear.

"And why do you speak to him that way? That's no way to speak to a man sweetheart." Mrs. Amora was firm yet tender like well cooked pasta or asparagus. Stacey finally came back from her trip a drift.

"Mrs. A., no disrespect but, I talk to him in a way that he's accustomed to. Okay maybe that came out wrong. I don't know... I'm trying to be different. I really am. But, he gets under my skin like no other! Dang! Just talkin about him gets me upset. I'm sorry. He run my nerves Mrs. A! He really do! That's just how we do I guess. I give respect where it's due. He just…Lord my pressure up. That negro…"

"Let's move to the couch where you can relax a bit. Put your feet up."

"I didn't mean to upset you Stacey."

"No. No, it's not you. It's my circulation."

"I'm thinking if it's not me, maybe it's all of the pernil. You know pork has a lot of salt."

"See, see now you sound like him."

"Well if we sound alike, must mean we have the same goal, lookin out for you. He cares." Mrs. A laughed, "Great minds think alike. Sweet boy. Baby I know he's not perfect, but he's sweet. He's trying to change. Like you."

"Ya think so. Hmm! I can't tell."

"Oh believe me. You see, sometimes we've been waiting all of our lives for someone to show up and care. When they do, and it is not our way, our timing or the person we thought it should be, we don't appreciate it. Just something to think about. The care you've been wanting has finally resurfaced. What you gonna do mama? You have to be nice to the man. Respect the man. He is a man Stacey. Men thrive on recognition, reward and respect. You can't talk to him like he's a worthless dog. By the way, even dogs, no matter how wild they act or how mangy and wayward they appear, have worth. Every living creature has worth child. Even if we don't understand what they do, why they do, how they function; even if what they do hurts us, they are God's creation. Everything has a purpose and worth. Even dogs. Even poop."

Stacey sat up and yelled, "Poop!"

"Lord, let me take you to school. Even poop! Yes I said poop. Poop is waste but poop rids us of unnecessary things. Poop gives people jobs. People had to come up with creative ways to handle, use and clean poop. Animal poop even helps fertilize things we eat and plant. Even trash has value. Recycling, compost. Think baby."

"Poop? For real ma?" Stacey giggles kicking her feet like a little girl.

"Si mama! So the next time you run into Mr. Wrong, or you think about all of the Mr. Wrongs that you've let go of, think about poop. Everything serves its purpose under heaven. Gotta get rid of the old to make room for the new. Poop stinks, it's messy and nobody wants it around but used properly the nastiest things can be recycled to bring something beautiful to life. With God nothing is ever wasted. No experience."

"Wow. My grandma used to say the same thing. That's crazy."

"I knew your grandmother. She was as wise as she was beautiful. When you read the Bible you see what The Lord can do with left over scraps that people would otherwise through a way. He breaks, he blesses, he recycles; makes it useful. Everything has purpose. Give it up for poop! There's always something to be thankful for. Even when you get constipated or impacted at my age and ya can't go...when you can go, you thank God for poop. It's necessary. The things we feel we can do without in our lives are often the very things God uses to bring us relief and restoration. Ok baby?"

Stacey looks at Mrs. A again, "Poop! Are you calling Barker poop?! They both let out a hearty laugh.

"No I am not! I would never do that! I love that boy. I would never disrespect him. Respect with every man, goes a long way. Just like love with any woman goes a long a way. Genuine respect and real sacrificial love. You can always tell how much a woman respects a man by the way she talks to him, especially around other people. Even if he gets out of line, she will remain in pocket, she knows his pride and ego are everything to him; so is respect, especially in the presence of other men.

Now she may chew him up when they get home in private. He may not mind, especially if he knows he deserves it. But even then, she must be careful of her words; tone and delivery are everything. Men pick that up like sonar baby. That's just how they are. We are very different. Keeps our relationships interesting and challenging.

A man will leave the most beautiful woman in the world for a frumpy maid any day of the week if he feels as if he is not being respected, appreciated or needed. Gotta make him feel necessary or else why is it necessary for him to be there with you?"

"Why is that?"

"Gives him purpose girl. Women make the mistake of thinking that keeping a man is all in cooking, cleaning, sex and maintenance. I know many young men who have said to me that they can care less about that superficial stuff in the long run when they think about who they want to grow old with. They want a trust worthy partner, lover, friend and confidant. A woman who knows how to treat him, keep his secrets, talk to him. Yes! Of course be creative and unpredictable in bed; keep his interests. He's a man, physical, visually stimulated and driven. But at all costs, when all else fails and fades because there are seasons for everything so the Bible says and it is true. For he will not always require an acrobat in bed or a submissive elsewhere. I can tell you from more experience than you have years, that I don't know a man whom I have ever met that does not require respect. Passive, aggressive, hard, soft, accountant, nurse, teacher. Stockbroker or athlete...a man is a man mama."

"Wait! So why you puttin the responsibility on us? Woman got enough loads to carry and burdens to shoulder Mrs. A. Especially black woman. You sound like you on team guy code. I don't know."

"All of the responsibility?" Stacey shakes her head yes.

"It is not on women. It is not a blame game baby. My point is, you are a woman, I am a woman. We know what we want yes?" Stacey agrees.

"Are we the only ones here?" Mrs. Amora looks over the rim of her glasses.

"Umm yeah. I don't get it though. What's your point?"

Crossing her legs at the ankles, she advanced, "Let me finish now. My point is that we don't need to discuss what we need as women or as individuals. We don't need to talk about how we want to be treated or how our minds work. We know. Now..." she fixes her skirt and takes off her glasses. "If we were in the company of men, then we would have a lesson to teach on women, right now yes?" She arches her back confidently folding her hands like a proper lady.

"I guess you're right." Stacey whimpers.

"I am not only a woman, I am a lady and I pride myself on being just that. I am always how you say pro-woman, but I am also pro-life, I am not pro-choice. The Bible says everything that is lawful is not profitable. I believe that. But that is not the point now. Right now, I am just rambling. I just need to talk sometimes. Now that. That is something men need to understand."

"Oh the talking thing?" Stacey sits up. She lights up like a puppy ready to go out in the yard and play.

"Yes baby. The talking thing. Now and again we just need to talk. We don't always need a response, just an ear, a shoulder. You know? They don't always need to ride in on a white horse and save the day. They don't always need to chime in with their logic we don't always get. On occasion we just need to be heard."

Stacey laughs, "Yeah, and those times seem to come when they don't feel like listening. I wonder why God created the sexes so different. Ever ask Him Mrs. A?"

"No love, I've never asked Him. But if I had a guess, I would guess balance and challenge. Just my logic."

They both laugh and say in unison, "Logic."

Stacey asks, "Why does it seem that things always have to fit perfectly in place for men mentally Mrs. A? Like everything has its own box. It's compartmentalizing I hear. Prioritizing...organizing...jazzercising...somethin' like that."

Mrs. A laughs heartily, "Girl, now I guess you'd have to ask a man. You know he will give you the answer...exact and to the point."

"Guess I'll have to do that then."

"They look at one another, "Logic!". They scream with laughter. They had always enjoyed a good time together since Stacey had been clean.

"Men. Can't live wit' 'em. Can't get peace of mind when they around." Stacey scratched her head lying back on the couch.

"Oh now baby, can't be that bad having him there. Has to be some fun. He has to be useful in some way. I mean now you have conversation, a balance of opinion, someone to check things out when they go bump in the night. I know he's taking care of you. I know he cares."

"He aight. On my nerves real bad. He's being too nice. I don't know how to take that. I ain't been wit a man in so long, I don't know how to sit back and let him handle. Man, come to think of it, I haven't been with a man EVER! He was last and only real relationship I had. Shoot man, we was kids way back then. Just when we was on the cusp of becoming, things got real. They got real, real quick. I got pregnant with G and before you knew it...Golden boy was off to college. Off to his life. I guess I just got lost after that and we changed into to different people. He forgot about me and we drifted apart. Friends became frienemies. We ain't been the same since. "

"I understand." Mrs. Amora comforts her as she nestles down beneath the plush throw pillows on the couch. "I get it. But you know you can't go back. You can only move forward. You have healing to do. You both have healing to do. You two also need to talk. I'm sure there's tension."

"Yeah. We got issues. But I don't know how to address them and, it seems like he's ignoring them. I have resentment. Maybe that's why I talk to him the way I do. Maybe I don't respect him. Maybe I'm trying. I'm praying and I'm trying but I don't know how still to let go." Stacey weeps. "Being around him hurts. It hurts bad. I want him to burn with hurt too sometimes. And I know that ain't right Mrs. A, I know. God on me about it all the time. I keep hearing him say love, forgive. And I'm tryin'. I promise I am." She holds Mrs. Amora's waist mewling bitterly into her lap, "I don't wanna hate my son's father. I promise I don't. I wanna love him and forgive him but I'm scared he's gonna hurt me again. I'm trying to stay clean and help other people and stay in the will of God and just do right...trying to change the way I walk and talk and everything. But it ain't easy. I'm tryin. I promise....I'm tryin. You don't know how bad I wish I could be perfect. I wish I didn't have a past. I'm not as strong as I act. I want my mother and I wish my father was here to protect me." With empathetic tenderness, the elder clinched the younger. "Let it out." She advised.

"They wasn't perfect, but they was here. You know? They was alive. I'm tired of being tired, being strong, trying to make it on my own and faking like I can handle everything." She screams, "I CAN'T! DAMN IT I CAN'T! GOD HELP ME. I CAN'T HANDLE MY LIFE ANYMORE! HELP ME PLEASE! I

CAN'T DO THIS BY MYSELF. I'M BREAKING INSIDE. LORD I JUST NEED YOU TO SEND SOMEBODY TO HELP ME."

In that very hour, Stacey found herself in the throw of the frustration that is the midst of becoming. She was in the depths of healing, navigating the salty sea of tears, fighting the waves she rode so highly. She tussled and fought in the season of transition. Toiling and boiling beneath the surface. There would be no more pretense for the sack, the uterus had been ruptured. In more ways than one she was in labor. Her next step would be to push on God's count.

Mrs. Amora hadn't had her experiences. Knowing full well that Stacey's wailing meant her silence and support, she cradled Stacey like baby. It was just what the doctor had ordered. The Holy Physician had a plan all along that included Mrs. Amora. Instrumental in the healing of Stacey's wounded soul, she was the old stick found floating nearby in the sea of salty tears, by the barge of broken, bloody glass that Stacey would need to get her ashore to heal her wounds. The wounds in her soul, on her back, gaping holes dripping with fresh blood, crusted with dried blood, oozing with puss. Infected wounds that had voices that cried out like ghosts of yesterday. Demonic forces that really didn't exist. A spiritual mirage of sorts. They were a complete figment of her fractured psyche sent from the enemy to impede her process and her progress. He knew where she was going, and if she got there all hell would certainly break loose. Fortified, Stacey had a powerful anointing. The Holy Spirit abode with and within her. It hadn't mattered to the Lord of Hosts what Stacey James past had looked like. That was a matter of no consequence. He was with her.

Seeds of righteousness flailed on the bed of her soul as she hurried to reach the shore in her subconscious. She fought, she cried out, "Mommy. I want my mommy. Lord I just want my mommy." She squeezed Mrs. Amora so tightly that her brown skin meager, copper skin bruised. She held

her belly and screamed, "MOMMY IT HURTS! IT HURTS!"
Mrs. Amora bore the pain as her nails dug into her acutely.
She could feel the blood seeping through her clothes. She
dare not let go. She prayed silently, "Lord what am I to do?
She aches. I ache with her."

The Lord replied, "That is what you do. Do what a mother
does. Ache for and with your child. Mary weep at the foot
of the cross for your child. Rejoice at the resurrection, for it
soon come. Weeping may endure for a night, but, joy
comes in the morning. Not just the morning when the sun
rises; the mourning when the Son rises. Purging can be
painful. Let the blood and water flow like a river deep. As
deep as the issues run, as deep as the hurt; that is depth of
healing. Now rock your child. Sing o' barren woman. Sing
for the healing of your children."

She sang "Take Me to the King". She sang and cried until
her throat ran coarse. Their tears mingled in a sorrowful
cocktail that pooled in her lap. She thanked God in heart for
all of the children he had given her. For the opportunity to
be a surrogate mother to those in need. That moment had
allowed Mrs. Amora to come full circle in her wondering
about why she could never conceive physically. She knew
that The Lord wasn't into tradition. He was unconventional.
He had blessed her to conceive spiritually. A mother to the
motherless. For over the years there had been many who
had mothers who there but not there. Alive but dead. The
walking dead. They just didn't care. They had given birth
yet, the spirit of motherhood had not befallen them. It was
past post-partum. It was sheer neglect. Mrs. Amora never
judged, nor did she criticize. She became God's eyes, ears
and arms to so many. She and her husband. She truly was a
mother of many nations. Though none had been birthed by
her womb, she nursed them spiritually and shot them out
like arrows into the air. She never thought she had a right
to call herself a mother. She had secretly for so long envied
those who could physically conceive and carry a child to
term.

She began to think to herself as she held the rattled woman-child, "My body has never known seed, nor borne fruit of my flesh. Yet I am. I am because He has made me so. I am because he who causes all things to be had shut up my womb only to open the vessels of my mind, ears, eyes and heart. I am because of what He has done. His ways and thoughts are higher than mine. Who can even know His mind? His wonderful mind. The pain these women had to endure to bring forth fruit. Yet I...I the old barren woman, have reaped where I have not sewn and gathered where I have not planted. I have plucked the fruit of the wombs of others and have nourished the many that have nourished me. The Lord has blessed. Now my eyes have seen. I can truly say thank you Lord Jehovah. Jehovah Jireh...My Provider you have provided food for my soul. My womb overflows. Gracias Jesus." She kissed Stacey on the forehead tenderly. Stacey slept like a baby.

After Mrs. Amora eased from beneath Stacey, she ascended the staircase singing, "I love the Lord. He heard my cry. And pitied every groan." She fell back into a nap as she sat in her husband's old leather recliner in the bedroom. "Oh, if he were here to see this." she whispered to herself. This was one of the many rich and rewarding life experiences that she wished she could share with her husband Ritchie. "But he's gone. Aye dios mio! Senor Jesus, que dia!"

Family Matters

"Mrs. A?" Stacey had awakened revived but puzzled. Unaware of what exactly had just happened, she had reasoned within herself to move forward, recognizing that something was different. She searched within for the voice of The Lord to clue her in on what had taken place. He was still. There was a different type of peace abiding within her that she had never known before. The peace that surpassed all understanding. From the bottom of the staircase she yowled for Mrs. Amora, "I'm leaving Mrs. A. Can you come down and lock up? If not, I'll just turn the lock on the knob. Ain't all that safe though. You know these fools out here is crazy. They'll try you! Mrs. Amora!? You good up there?"

Mrs. Amora finally emerged from her bedroom, looking a disheveled wreck. Her wig was twisted. Her blouse blood stained. Her skirt soaked. It had been a spiritually strenuous day for all. "Now, Mrs. A, you know at your age, you don't need to be climbing all them steps. Come on, let me help you down."

She snatches her hand away, "Don't mind if I refuse your offer baby. I'm aging, not handicapped. Let me remind you, I am the one who takes you to the grocery shopping yes."

"Okay. Alright. I ain't got the strength to fight right now mama. I'm done. Have it your way. Just be careful please. For God's sake! If anything ever happened to you I don't know..."

Mrs. Amora grabbed Stacey's hand once she had reached the last step, "You care for me child? Did you call me mama?" Her heart was full. "You care what happens to an old lady like me? I mean something to you Stacey?"

"Well...duh...umm...yeah. You're like my mother. I mean hello! You know me from way back. You know I'm rockin wit' da Lord now but, I still got some ways about me. You're the only one that knows me the way you do. The real me. You don't judge. You take me as I am. I will always love you for that. I didn't come from you but I will always come to you. You're everything to me. Lady you don't even know."

She puts her arm around Mrs. Amora, rocking her back and forth, she looks her square in the eye, and "I love you."

"Mrs. Amora rests her head on Stacey's breast as a child would their mother. Role reversal, now she comforts Mrs. Amora. Her tears seep through Stacey's top and drip on to her pregnant belly. "What you tryin' do huh? You tryin' baptize my baby? Can she get here first?"

Mrs. Amora spanks her on the bottom, "Don't get cute." They both laugh.

"You mean it? When you say you love me?" says the surrogate mother.

"Every bit."

"Ay, dios mios! Nena, nunca decir esto antes de hoy!"

"What did you just say?"

"Aye! Forgive me mi Amor. I'm just excited and confused. I said you never say this to me before today?! Why not?"

Stacey kisses her on the forehead, "Maybe because before today I didn't realize a lot. I mean maybe I see clearly now. Mama, I was young and stupid. I thought I was hot. It was all about me. That's how it is when you're young. I ain't know no better. Thought it was all about me and Boom. I don't know. Then I started getting' on and..."

"Getting it on?"

Stacey rubs her back, "Mrs. A, you so cute. But nah, I said GETTING ON. I mean getting high. Sorry I just say things how they come to me."

Mrs. Amora grinned, "Like your mother."

"I guess. Anyway, I walk in my truth no matter how raw it reveals itself. I wasn't scared to be out there sellin' my stuff to get what I needed. So why be scared to say what it is. Right?"

"Mrs. Amora interrupts, "I forgot to record Law and Order. Don't you just love Law and Order?"

"Cops and courtrooms? Me? No. Plus Ice-T as a detective is a smooth turn off for me. I'm good. Nobody born in Newark got no business playin' no cop."

"Oh, but you haven't seen the episode when…"

"I'll pass thank you."

"You might change your mind if you see him in this episode when…"

Stacey smiles, "Mrs. A?"

"Yes?"

"I'm losin' you now. Come on back. Stay wit' me. I'm goin'

somewhere. I'm about to wrap this up.", she looked up the

clock on the wall.

"Aye! You sound like a pastor!"

"Yeah, you forgot my father was one." Stacey shakes her head, "You get distracted easily don't you?"

"Oh no! I'm sorry baby. Come to the kitchen with me. Continue please?"

"Like I was saying, I thought it was all about me and then I started getting high. I know I treated you mean an ignored you a lot when you was just trying to be friendly. But, when you're getting' high, especially when you're young, you're not yourself. I remember you always being so nice to everybody. Man, even when they wasn't nice to you. I remember when Neef and 'em broke in here and stole some of ya stuff. They got locked up, you wrote 'em. They never responded. They came out and started back getting high, you saw 'em, you fed 'em, you ministered to 'em. And I know you was praying for 'em. They tried it again after Mr. Ritchie died; you still showed 'em love. I used to think you was crazy. But now I see you ain't crazy. You just know what real love is.

Shoot man, I was so mean to you sometimes. I cussed you and yelled at you...can't believe I'm here with you. I ain't got no business here. I remember I would tell you to mind your business when you just was lookin' out for me. Girls comin' to jump me over some joker that ain't belong to either one of us. While we fightin like animals over scraps, he laid up wit' da next chick. We was silly."

"You all were young. No crime in being young and ignorant. Who hasn't been there?"

"Yeah. Look at you though. You're so relaxed and wise. How do I get there?"

"Child, it takes time. Every wrinkle I have is earned from a lesson learned. Wisdom takes time and openness. Wisdom comes with reflection, trial and error. Insight begins with having no sight. It develops from there over time. Just like wisdom comes from ignorance. Remember with The Lord, nothing is ever wasted. Every lesson learned is a treasure to hold on to. Don't you forget that. And don't feel bad about what you didn't know. You will know when it's time. Like they say. By and by. Wisdom is the crockpot of knowledge."

"Listen to you woman. So deep."

"Well all glory is God's so I won't be taking credit for a thing. You just thank the Lord if you feel I've done you some good. I'm just a vessel."

"Oh come on now. Look at you all modest and stuff." she laughed. "I don't think the Lord would mind one bit if I showed you some love. You deserve that and more Mrs. A. I remember that time you came out with a broom and swept them girls off my porch like they was sunflower seed shells in the summertime. I appreciated it. I was locked out my house that day. I didn't have my key. I ain't have no help. That day and many more, I appreciated your nosiness." The old woman clutched the collar of her blouse. "No disrespect. You been a mother to everybody in the neighborhood. A grandmother, a counselor, a shelter, a soup kitchen, a clothing drive, a mentor, a neighborhood watchperson; a teacher, a preacher, a friend. Always kind and humble. You and Mr. Richie. I just wanna say now what I didn't have the frame of mind to say before... I thank you. I love you. I am sorry. I speak for me and everybody else who either forgot or who ain't live long enough to come back and say it to you. You are special. We love you. We really needed you. You always been our Mama. We still need you. Grown ain't always grown. Some of us still need a mama."

Mrs. Amora remained reserved. You could hear a pin drop. Stacey starred at her and listened as the squirrels raced around the trees. She listened to Mrs. Amora's tears drop one by one on to the aluminum foil she used to cover the care packages she made for Stacey to take next door. Not a word was said between the two. The point was still and serene. What went unspoken was heard loud and clear. They held hands as they walked quietly to the front door packages in hand. "Thank you." They expressed on one accord. With the touch of a hand Mrs. Amora concluded, "Go. You have given me peace. Now go and offer that same peace to him. Remember respect. The same love and kindness you've been shown despite your past actions. Remember the past is as sterile as silence. What goes unsaid speaks volumes to the sober-minded and the wise. Be at peace. Exalt others higher than yourself. He has pain too baby. Be his peace. It's never about us."

Stacey received the food and went on her way. She watched Stacey waddle back to her house. "Thank you Lord".

The Lord replied, "Thank you Amora."

"I have done nothing Father. I have only received your grace."

He replied, "You have done more than enough. You have been faithful child. I love you. The rest of the evening is yours. Rest."

Stacey discovered Barker waiting on the front porch when she entered the gate. Concerned she asked, "You aight? Why you out here? I hope you wasn't lookin' for me. I'm a big girl in case you haven't noticed." she smiled.

"I was hoping I didn't wreck your nerves too bad and run you off. Hoping you wouldn't relapse because of me. But you're strong. You've always been strong. In the back of mind I knew you wouldn't do that. You're one I never really had to worry about." he explained.

She thought to herself, "That's the problem. Here we go with those assumptions. Just like my parents. Thinkin' I don't need the attention; I'm strong enough. I'm good. I don't need no help. Lord help me to handle this with love and like a lady. Please! He really do pluck my nerve Lord."

She went on to remind him, "Everybody need a lil' lookin' after sometimes Boom. No man, or woman for that matter, is an island. In the beginning God saw Adam by himself and God said it ain't good for man to be alone. Again, man or woman. Shucks! Even God ain't up there alone. He got company all of the time."

Barker threw his hands up in the air, "My bad Stace. I was trying to compliment you on your strength. That's all. Why we always gotta battle? Huh? I mean talking to women sometimes, I mean trying to enjoy even the simplest conversation or show the slightest bit of concern can be a chore. Man y'all make it hard. Pshhh, and y'all wonder why brothers don't talk much. Can't get a word in? Can I live?"

"Exactly!" Stacey yells. At that point, she happens to look over at Mrs. Amora window only to find her peeking out shaking her head. She closes her curtains. Stacey was about to let Barker have it. "You gotta be kidding me.", she said handing him the plates Mrs. Amora had made. "Let y'all talk! Let Y'ALL talk…." Suddenly she hears Aretha Franklin's song "Respect" blaring from Mrs. Amora house. She looks back over, the curtains are once again pulled back but, Mrs. A is nowhere to be found. Stacey got the message.

Barker looked at her with a raised eye brow. She knew that look. She had seen her father look at her mother that same way plenty of times while they argued in the car on their way to church. He had to mentally prepare to go before the people and give the word of God. She wouldn't give him a break. She recalled her father's words, "Where's the respect? Huh? I mean you do see I'm a man right here don't you? Huh? Where my respect woman? I mean do you even know when to shut up?! And women comin' to me after service in tears wonderin' why they husband won't come home. And when he there, he just wanna eat, sleep, play wit da kids for a lil' while and that's it. One day I'm just gon' leave the Bible home and get up there and spill it! I'm tell all them cryin' gals to hush up! Ya man ain't comin' home 'cause you don't respect him and he ain't got no peace! The way they tell it, half y'all keep a nasty attitude, mouth and house. Keep ya mouth shut, stay off the phone and stop gossipin', for God's sake clean up and don't use his kids as an excuse to why food ain't done and house ain't clean. My momma did it! You can do it. Daddy came home every night. Why? Because my momma made him want to! Not 'cause he had to….naw! He wanted to! Now don't come to me cryin' bout how wrong ya man is no more! I don't wanna hear it! You want him home? Huh? Get it together. And if he still don't wanna come home and get right after you done all you could, then hell wit' it! You tried. But sometimes tryin' ain't enough! When frustration and the other woman wit' no kids and a clean quiet house done got under his skin, y'all done already lost the war. I can see 'em now. Suckin' they teeth and fast tailin' it out da church. Go ahead then! You wanted my advice, y'all want the truth. There it go! Yeah, Imma tell it one day. And Ann, you ain't got nobody but yaself to blame. Know why?"

She heard her mother say in her head clearly, "No Nathan, I don't know. But just as sure as I sit here, I know you gon' tell me. So preach pastor." Young Stacey James grinned as she covered her mouth trying to stop herself from giggling out loud.

Stacey thought about how her father would go rambling on all the way to church and her mother would stare at him shaking her head. Periodically, she would look in the backseat at her and roll her eyes and stick out her tongue. She had to stop herself from laughing out loud all of the time.

"Look at you Ann!"

"Honey. Look at me. That's what I say." Her mother played with her long, wavy, sandy strands and pushed up her breasts. She unbuttoned the top button of her blouse and reapplied her dahlia maquillage.

"You can't ever give me no respect. We in front of this girl. How she gon' respect me and you don't? Huh? How is anybody supposed to respect me if you don't? Why you marry me Ann? Huh? If you don't respect me, I know you don't love me....so why you do it Ann? What? What? Was it because of her Ann? Huh? Because of the baby?"

"Just drive Nate ok?! And stop talkin' like that around her.

She's right here for God's sake."

Stacey wiped the smile off of her face. She quickly tried to change her thoughts before the bad memories began to resurface. "Wow! They never called me their daughter. Not once. Most of the time it was like I wasn't even there. Even when they argued about me. Crazy! People envied me because I had a lot of things being an only child. Oh but, they don't know I was a lonely child. Bought and sold to the highest bidder. I've always felt alone. It really is not good for man or woman...not even child to be alone." She looked over at Mrs. Amora's window once more before she stepped inside of the house. Mrs. A was in the window again, this time playing Yolanda Adams, "Just A Prayer Away." She blew Stacey a kiss. Automatically, as if she could read Stacey's mind she whispered as she pointed to the sky, "You're never alone." She waved goodbye and shut the window. Just like a mom, Mrs. A, knew the right words to say at the right time. For the first time in a while, even though the thoughts hadn't been pleasant, she was filled with hope for a better tomorrow. Somehow, she understood how she couldn't allow the past or how she felt in the moment to dictate the outcome of her day or for that matter, her life. She was waking up from the inside out. She was going to take her life back.

A few moments later she arrived in the kitchen to see Barker eating two plates at once. He was eating like he hadn't had food in a week or so. "I tried waiting for you." he spake shoveling tablespoons of food in his mouth. He was so hungry he swallowed without chewing mostly.

"Boy why you so hungry? My goodness that don't make no sense! Slow down before you choke." She handed him some napkins and a cold drink.

Once again he raised his eyebrow, He glared at her. Wiping the corners of his mouth he touted, "I'm a man. Please stop calling me a boy. Thank you." He shook his head, "Damn!" He dropped his fork, "I'm tryin man Why ya mouth gotta be so ratchet?! I haven't eaten all day and now here you come. Can you try being a lady?" She turned her head.

"And I respect the fact that this is not my house. But mind you, I'm here voluntarily; here to help you. I'm trying at least. Can I get some acknowledgement? Some credit? I mean come on ma! I used to see Mrs. Ann treat ya dad like a king. What happened? You wasn't takin' notes?"

She mumbled under her breath, "More like a dog. You better be glad I wasn't taking notes."

"Say somethin?" he barked. "No thank you being here no nothin."

She reconciled within herself that he would always be a prideful man. More like Mr. Al then he'd ever want to admit. She thought back on days she would visit her son over at his parent's home. His mother had always made it a point not to talk too much or lay down a list of complaints or criticisms when he was tired or hungry. His attitude always reflected how his day had gone. Carla studied her husband. She knew him very well. Though he was a kind, loving man; an honest, selfless clergyman who worked hard for his family and his community; the same man who lacked balance, she appreciated her husband. His wife knew he had many flaws. Just a man, she accepted him. She respected her husband.

 Sometimes when the going got too tough, and she found living with a man so dedicated to his calling unbearable, Stacey would pop by unannounced. She would just unleash all of her frustration in buckets of tears on to Stacey. She was the first lady of the church, mild-mannered and sweet. Wise, kind, patient. Yet, behind closed doors where no one else but God could see, there were times she wanted to walk away. Carla often longed for a normal life. She confided in Stacey that ministry seemed to be her husband's mistress. Since the affair was much deeper than physical, she felt resentful at times. She said to God a few times that she was thankful Al had been called. Ministry, salvation and the preaching of the gospel had given him a new life; purpose; fulfillment, meaning; drive. It also had taken her place. She believed in her loneliness that his calling had called him away from her all too often.

Carla had expressed her guilt over her true feelings quite often; unbeknownst to her husband. Carla said to Stacey in one of their final conversations, her weakening eyes filled with tears, "How can this man have so much discernment yet, be so ignorant of the fact that I am lonely. I feel neglected. I didn't sign up for this Stacey. I did not always want to be in ministry. This here, I did not ask for. I prayed that the Lord take over my husband. I did not want the Lord to take my husband from me. Forgive me honey, I know I sound selfish. Maybe I am. Maybe I'm entitled after all of these years of smiling on the outside and crying within.

Waiting my turn; waiting in line to touch my husband. I just need to vent. I'm human.

Girl you don't know the other side of this thing. It can get

real ugly. You gotta have thick skin and a lot of poise to be a

pastor's wife."

"Really? My mother doesn't discuss that with me. You make it look like a cake walk Mrs. Carla."

"Looks can be deceiving child. Can you imagine having to

turn a blind eye to vultures in the church? Praying for the

women that don't give a care about me and mine."

"I thought they respected you?"

"Girl, I just said looks can be deceiving. People think because you're uneducated, you're a stupid. Or that because they are educated, they can take your man. Ha! Women is women everywhere you go girl...don't be fooled and don't forget it either! They just be waitin to take your spot. What's a First Lady to do? More importantly, what on earth is a women to do? It can be a very lonely road. No one to talk to or confide in. Be his backbone when he ain't strong. You don't want to go to him with your complaints. You know? They seem so small compared to the stuff he gotta deal with every day. Last thing you wanna do as his wife is burden him further."

"I don't know Mrs. Carla. I'd have to holla at him about that. That's too much for one person. Somebody would have to get popped like a pimple. I'm sayin…"

"Honey, you wanna be his peace. You have to be his peace; even when you're falling to pieces. I have always wondered if being the First Lady of the White House was like that. Or if any of the women married to these larger than life, powerful personalities ever feel the pressure or the vacancy. I wish I could ask somebody else what happens when the dream y'all had together becomes a nightmare for one of you and you can't tell the other party because their married to that dream. You know? There's a lot of pressure to not look like you're under pressure. There's also a lot of pressure to not put pressure on him.

What do you do? Play your position. Wave to the people. Smile when you don't feel like it. Hug the woman who just slipped your husband her number. Don't cause a scene. Try not to come off as jealous, even in private, no matter how normal jealousy is in relationships."

"Yeah. I heard even God gets jealous."

"He does. You're right. But you almost become a robot as the spouse of leader. It's all very Stepford. Schmooze with the other first ladies and pretend like you always feel holy…that life is perfect. Hold your husband and everybody else up. Never let 'em see you sweat. Don't fuss. Don't be sexy. Don't ever cuss or yell. Don't drink. Don't smoke. Look perfect. Be perfect. Be his wife. Be a pillar of strength. Lose your identity. Lose your husband to his work. It's so funny. A hundred nights he cried in my lap telling me ministry was taking so much out of him. What he failed to realize is how much ministry was taking out of me. He never took the time to realize."

That was Carla's truth. A truth Stacey wasn't sure Al had ever known. She held Carla's hand as she cried. She had a lit cigarette burning in her free hand. Carla didn't smoke. She didn't do anything. It was her one act of rebellion. She believed God laughed every time she would retreat into the backyard and light a cigarette that would never touch her lips. She kept it far away from her face as not to inhale the second hand smoke. She thought God got a kick out of it. She was quirky in her thinking. The Lord accepted her for who she was. He never scolded her for lighting the cigarette. He understood why she did it, even on the days she wasn't so sure He was laughing. God knew how she felt and why she felt that way. He knew why she did what she did. It was not a sin as sure as it was not a laughing matter. Carla had hidden issues. Some secrets she would carry to the grave. The only one who would ever be able to get all the way in with Carla was Jesus. He was her best friend. He never condemned her. Even in times of conviction, His Holy Spirit comforted her. God doesn't keep His anger long. Not with His children. She knew He was loving God though she had been confused about what her husband's calling meant for their lives. She was frustrated. Life wasn't at all what she wanted it to be. And still, to Al and her children, she rarely complained.

So with the lit cigarette, Barker's mother laughed and looked up. Once she heard The Lord say, "What are you doing? Carla, why do you do that?" She knew that The Lord never asked a question he didn't already know the answer to. He just wanted her to be aware. "I'm chillin' Lord. That's all. Just chillin'. I ain't gonna smoke it. It's just like me. Just here burning out. I don't know what else to do. I don't always know how to handle life. I wish things were different. I miss my husband. I don't know, maybe I was expecting too much. But I know, it's not about me. This is service. Service is sacrifice. I guess sometimes I just wish I lived another life. If I seem ungrateful, forgive me. I try not to be. I need your help while I take this life day by day until my days are up."

The Lord spoke to her, "That's all you can do. I am here with you. I love you. You can do this. You are strong. I am always with you." So, Carla went on in between those bouts. She went on day by day until her days were up and her Lord called her home.

Stacey learned quite a few things from Carla. In her own way, she missed her more than she missed her own mother. For as perfect as Carla Golden looked on the outside, she let people perceive what they would...she knew she wasn't perfect. That's what Stacey loved about her. She never pretended to be perfect. Not around Stacey. Neither did Al. She knew that everything that glittered wasn't Golden. Yet even with their hidden flaws, they were a whole lot better than her family had been. At least they had one another. They loved and accepted one another. The parents tried to give the children what they needed but, too much of what they wanted. They paid attention. She envied that. She always would.

She listened to Barker grumble, just like Mr. Al. She felt bad. She knew she was wrong. He was his father's son. She knew how grumpy he used to get when he was a young boy after playing in the game all day, long ride home on a noisy, smelly bus, especially after a hard loss to a long standing rival or a lesser team. He wasn't that young boy anymore, but she knew that when he was hungry and aggravated, the tactics to keep off of his radar couldn't be that different. She thought being kind and apologetic would help. She replied to him as gently as she could, "Well, I'm not your mother. You ain't a lil' boy. And I'm tryin too Boom. You go on enjoy your food. Imma be in the other room."

"Don't leave me at the table by myself Stacey. I don't mind the company." It worked. She was kind, gentle. She oozed humility and femininity. He liked that. He used to respond to it long ago. Some things would never change. She sat across from him. She watched him eat. He looked up briefly, "What's wrong? You good?" She continued to stare,

"I'm good." He was still confused as to why she was watching him inhale the food. He thought, "Man, she's pregnant. What about her?" He came to the end of himself, "My bad. One of these plates was yours right?" She laughed.

"What's so funny?" She laughed harder. "Oh I know, you don't want it because I ate out of it. My fault. I'm not thinking. I can go get you some more. I'll be right back..."

"Come on Boom. Sit down. You good. Imma be alright. I just went food shopping remember? Helloooooo.....You organized my pantry."

"Aww yeah. But this was already done. Come on ma. Let's go over to Mount Prospect and get you some more.

He pulls out her chair. He picks her up to carry her to the threshold of the doorway. She taps him on the shoulder. "Put me down Boom. I don't want to go anywhere."

"Alright. So what you want? Mc Donald's, Chinese, Subway, Buffet, you wanna order in, go someplace fancy? What ma? Where you wanna go? What you wanna do? I'll do whatever you want me to. Just let me do something. Please?" he spoke softly as he looked deep into her eyes. Still holding her in his arms, he knew something was different. He was touching her and she wasn't guarding her pregnant belly. He didn't want to alarm her so he kept his eyes locked on hers, savoring the moment, "What is it? You don't want to be seen with me? I've had these clothes on too long. I know. Just let me..." She just stared at him with her arms around his neck. He was playing the caretaker; the hero. Moments she had longed dreamed of. Moments, she too would savor. "What's good ma? You ain't sayin' nothin."

"I'm lettin' the man talk. Are you done?"

His heart melted. "Not until you let a man help you? Let me get you somethin to eat please? Last thing I wanna do is take food from a woman or a child. Too many females puttin' up with that. If you're a woman with mouths to feed, if a man is not bringing anything in, then he doesn't need to be taking anything out. My father raised me and my brothers better than that. You see her, you want her; want her time and attention...you gon' be taking some of that from her kids? You had better be willing to give something back. But anyway, enough preachin'. Girl you gon' let me help you?"

"Did you hear yourself?" she asked.

"What? Hear what? Me beggin like Keith Sweat? Yeah I heard it!" He puts her down, "And my ego just got wind of it and he don't like it so get it while the getting is good."

"You called Mr. Al ya father."

"Oh my goodness. Can we go now so I can shower?" he pleads.

"Alright. Alright. Let's go. But just know, you called him your father and you gave him props. No disrespect...I'm just sayin. Oh and by the way, I am a woman, not a girl. Please refrain using that word when referring to me. Thank you Sir."

"Oh word?! You got jokes? Father, props, refrain, refer and Sir Boom? Really?" he laughs.

"Word up son. In that exact order. Aight...let's go Boom before my feet swell again. And you promised me I can stay as long as I want and see my son's room so don't get funny when I get there."

"So you gon' change right?"

"What you mean change? I'm good. I'm comfortable. I'm pregnant Boom. You gotta be kidding me right now! Oh I forgot. You the Oswald Boateng of the tri-state." she rolled her eyes.

"Woman what would you know about Oswald Boateng?"

"I'm full of surprises brother."

He whispers under his breath, "That's what I love most about you."

"Now I know you got a few of his suits in your walk-in closet."

"Yessir!" he boasts.

"So come on." she grabs his hand and pulls him out of the house. "Take me there. I just want to feel the fabric. That brother is DOPE! You seen A Man's Story?"

"You know I did. Knock it off."

Just as they take a step to go down the stairs, they hear a thump come from upstairs. Stacey pauses, "Wait Boom. What was that?"

"I don't know. This is your house. Maybe it was the resident evil you got locked away upstairs."

"OH MY GOODNESS!" she yells. I forgot all about her. Boom, we can't go."

"What you mean?"

"You go on ahead. I can't leave her like that. It aint right. I'm supposed to be caring for her. Oh my goodness. I gotta get up there." She races up to the second floor to find the young girl has passed out in a small pool of drying emesis.

"Oh my goodness! Jesus help me! Maya baby. It's me Stacey. Wake up baby. C'mon...we have to get up now. I'm here. It's gonna be ok. Oh my goodness! Boom you gotta help me." Stacey panics as she tries to revive the young girl. "Get up baby. C'mon Hun. Stay with me."

"I think we should get her to the hospital."

"We ain't goin' to no hospital Boom. What they gon' do? Judge her? Not today. I've been there. Get me some cold water now please!" she yells.

He rushes back in from the bathroom with the water, "Ok. Ok. I got it. Imma call 911 and...."

"Boy please aight! This the streets aight. We take care of our own, that's why she's here with me. 911 is a joke! P.E said it and I know it's true. This is the hood and if you ain't almost dead from a gunshot wound, ain't nobody comin' 'til tomorrow. It's a shame too! Like all 250,000 people in this city marooned on a desert island or somethin! Gimme a break already! This is the biggest city in New Jersey. The third wealthiest state and we can't even get ambulances to the door unless we got one foot in the grave. And that she ain't got so since you came up with a blue collar plan, Imma have to ask you to step aside. Please and thank you."

"I'm sure I can get to the hospital in two Stace. It's right down the way. Let's..."

"Ok. Ok. Ok. Shh...Ok. Calm down Barker. You hear me Hun, relax. Shhhhh...breathe. That's it. Breathe. That's good. She's breathing see," she puts a make-up mirror under Maya's nose. She's ok. You just gotta trust me. K?" She speaks to him in a calm baby voice. He begins to wind down. "See. That's it. Big, deep breaths. Just sit right there for me. If I need you I'll call for you ok?" He shakes his head yes as he takes deep breaths. He says to himself, "You're a lawyer. Man what are you even doing here? You've surpassed your obligation. This is enough. You know if she die, you wearin' dat right?" He stood up. He begins to walk around in circles, "Alright. Call me soft. Call me whack. Say I'm a punk. I'm booty...whatever. Don't even matter. It just got too real for me. I got a lot on my mind. I'm about to be out."

Stacey stepped out of the bathroom where she had been running a cool bath for Maya. She stated calmly, "Hey bruh, this ain't ya thing. Not for everybody. You out of your element. But me, I'm in this….this is my zone. These are my people. It takes much more than some shallow breathing and vomit to run me off. I have watched people O.D so many times Barker. I don't even smoke, but just runnin' with people and getting into stuff, hustlin', sellin my body…I been up in so many crack houses from here to upstate New York ok. So I'm pretty much a pro. I got this. You can bounce. I won't judge you. The court room is your arena, the streets is mine. It is what it is. Just one thing before you leave…"

"What's that?"

"Help me get her in the tub. I need to cool her off and wake her up. She gotta be withdrawing from more than diesel. She's too gone."

"Stacey I can help you, but I'm not takin anybody's clothes off"

"Oh now you so sanctified? Great!"

"I didn't mean it like that. I just meant…"

"Did I ask you to undress anybody scared straight? Huh? No I did not! Just pick her up. Dang! I know you worried about your career and your rep and ya lil' change and all dat but, this ain't Law and Order Boo-Boo and I ain't tryin' to make it the First 48 either. We tryin to keep her on the bubble until she gets over the hump. That's all. Now, put her in the bath and you can go. I'm good."

He scoops her up off the floor and gently places her in the chilled caldron. Stacey splashes water in her face and shakes her face. Maya! Maya! Come on now! Boom, just hit the cold water for me. She wakin' up right now. I ain't playin' either!" He turns the cold water on full blast. Stacey lets it run and begins to dash it in her face again. Maya begins coming to, vomiting.

Boom backs out of the bathroom, "Oh my God! Yo! What the…? I'm out!"

"How is a man as big as you are, scared of some little ole sickly white girl? We're from the same hood Boom. This here, this all day. What you scared for?" Stacey heckles.

"Hey ma, I'll do anything for you. You should know that by now. But this…THIS HERE! I can't handle. Later."

Stacey simpered, "Aight Boom. All you know to do is abandon people. Lord! Just go ahead. I can take it from here. Thanks for everything. Get some rest. Imma hold you to that food though. I be hungry. Bye." he slowly walks down the stairs. He glances back to catch Stacey wiping her brow and shaking her head. "Maya, it's just us now so you gon' have to help me." The girl groaned. She attempted to lift herself to no avail. "Girl I can't lift you up. I know you in pain, but I'm pregnant. We gotta help one another now. Ain't nobody else ok?" He notices Stacey struggling to get off of her knees as Maya struggles to get out of the vessel.

"What you doin man? Go help them. What is wrong with you? You know better!" He runs back up the steps, "Aight so let me get you up Stace and then Imma get her up outta there. He looked as if he wanted to vomit just being around all of the mess and breathing in the foul stench. But he held on. He went out of his way for her again. He wasn't trying to impress her but, Stacey was impressed. He was impressed by the sacrifice. Rubbing his hands together he asks, "What's next? What do I need to do?"

Stacey looked over her shoulder at him, "You can go home and shower and relax now. Then after you do that, you can pray. Thank you."

"I can stay here and help just let me..."

"No really it's ok. Go. I got it from here. Besides I'm gonna be up here for a while cleaning up and helping change her and all. It's cool. I will call you if anything."

"Promise me.", he commands.

"I promise." she says.

"Alright then. Whatever pleases the lady."

Stacey blushes.

Barker reached home exhausted from the day. He drinks down a quart of water. He heads for the shower dropping his clothing along the way. As the hot water cascades over his chiseled body he closes his eyes. "Virtuous thoughts, praise worthy and true things, whatever is honest...think on those things man. Lovely things. Come on." he said to himself. It wasn't working. His mind was stuck on Stacey. He grinned, "She is lovely though. Man, what is wrong with me? I mean its natural right? She had my baby; we have history. Maybe I just feel guilty about all of my nonsense? I could just feel sorry for her. I mean I gotta care about her, it is the Christian thing to do. She doesn't have anyone else. She needs help. I mean, I gotta care about her right? Listen to me man! In my head. Look at yourself dawg...she got you in ya own head! Havin' a conversation with yourself! Why Is this woman always able distract me and knock me off of my bike? He retreats to his room and flops down on the bed, towel around his waist, "Well bed, it's been a minute since I've seen you. Mmm... You feel so good. Good to be home." He yawns, "Home need to be cleaned up. I'll call the service in the morning; hopefully they can shoot somebody over here. I'm wiped."

Two hours later he wakes up in a cold sweat panicked. "Stacey!" He had gotten dressed. He raced back over to Stacey's house. He reaches her door ringing the bell constantly. Finally she answers, "Now what on earth is the problem Boom? Why you back here all bugged-eyed and on ten like you out here on a mission? People sleepin' Boom!"

"I know. I apologize. I just needed to make sure you and the baby good." He embraced her. "Y'all alright in here? Any problems?"

 She pulls back sucking her teeth, "Look bruh, no disrespect, but we good. You don't have be runnin' over here like that. You could have shot me a text Boom. Psshhh...could've been sleep. I'm tired."

"I feel bad now. Just considering the situation I just thought…"

She gives him a hard look, "You thought what at this hour of the night Boom? Huh? I mean who on earth but hustlers, hoes, thieves and the jokers runnin the strip clubs in the back room countin' money is up thinking at this time of the night? Why am I on your mind for anyway?"

"Alright. Ok. You doin that ratchet mouth thing again. I guess I made a mistake. I came because I care. I thought of you because I care. I thought you may need my help. I want to help you because maybe I love you. Ok?! Why you gotta be so difficult? That routine is getting old Stacey."

"Be out then."

"Oh I'm out alright. It won't happen again. I promise." He stood at the front door, "Jesus! Why is it the man always making a complete fool of himself for a stubborn, ingrate of a woman? She's a shrew Lord! A straight shrew." He slammed it. Sitting on the front porch gathering his thoughts he breathed deeply, "What more do I have to do?"

"Mrs. Amora gazed at him from her bedroom window. She coughed, "Who is that?!" Barker, taking a defensive stance, blustered, "Try me. I promise you I'm in the mood."

Mrs. Amora laughed, "You wouldn't hit an old lady with glasses would you? My heart couldn't stand it son."

He looked up. "Oh my bad Mrs. A, I thought you were somebody else. I'm in a bad mood right now. Pardon me. I wasn't aiming my anger at you. I would never disrespect you."

"Oh Niño, I understand. I do. I had a husband. He could be sweet. But when he got angry...Aye dios mio Niño!"

"Aw yeah Mr. Richie. I remember him. That was my man. Good guy. Everybody loved Mr. Ritchie. We loved you to Mrs. A. Still do."

"And you all must know I love you too! Speaking of love. Be patient with her. She's pregnant and in recovery from that junk. She is dealing with many, many things my son, give her time to heal. I know you love her. I know you have things too. Love is not always easy but it is worth it. Even when we can't see the results of the love seeds we plant. From whatever seeds we plant, good or bad...eventually, something got to grow and bloom. You just keep watering those love seeds Niño. Let God do the rest. Love her. Be still and know. Let Him do it if that is His will. His way is perfect."

"I hear you Mrs. A, but what if I don't want to love her. I don't want to feel like this. I don't want to love her if it hurts this bad and I keep getting rejected. I have feelings too." he sobs.

"Aye Poppo, I understand but, remember how she felt when the shoe was on the other foot. She didn't want to love you either. But she felt helpless over what she thought was love. Was it really love? Especially if she didn't have it for herself? How can she give away what she didn't even have? Think about it child. And anytime you feel neglected, abused, unappreciated and hurt for sacrificing for someone else and not getting that back in return, you just think about her. No wait, think about Jesus on that cross and all that He did for us. He loved sacrificed for people who he knew wouldn't appreciate it or love him back. Just look at how we reject, neglect and abuse Him daily, yet....still He is faithful, still He pursues us. Still the savior loves. He longs for us. He loves us although we don't deserve it. He died that we may live. He is the greatest example of love Pastor. He is love. You already know this. Keep your mind on Him. Keep loving. Be still and know. People say love does not hurt. Sure it does. Christ, our risen savior, is a witness."

"Man you just preached Mrs. A. You're so right. You got that wisdom Mrs. A. Thank you. I'm selfish. I know. I was raised in the church. I know the Bible like the back of my hand. I should be ashamed of myself. I been runnin around doin everything wrong and having tantrums like a child. I'm not worthy of being a pastor. I wish people would just let it go. I'm not good enough."

Before he knew it Mrs. Amora was walking up Stacey's stairs holding her arms out to him. "There, there baby. It's gonna be ok. You are too hard on yourself. You are young and still growing. The Bible says train a child in the way they shall go and when they are old they won't depart from it. Get it Niño...O-L-D. You my dear...you...you both have a long way to go to get old. So there is so much more learning and growing to do. Youth is for folly. It did not say everybody except for the young pastor, still trying to find his way. That scripture includes everybody. Even you. We all make mistakes. Don't beat yourself up! Yes? It's ok." He held her tightly. He closed his eyes. He felt Carla Golden for few minutes.

 "Son, it's going to be ok. Give yourself some time. You kids...your generation. The one after you; you all want things now. Right now. But strength is power over time. It takes time. Slow, home cooked meals will always be better than microwaved garbage any day. Why? Because low and slow often means better ingredients; healthier; there's love in the food. The flavors marry. Everything in the pot has a job. You get it Niño? All things work together for good to them that love the Lord. And baby, no matter what you've done or will do, God knows you love Him. I do too. "

"Yes I do.", he whimpered.

"Yes you do son. Now knowing the word and living it are two different things. You can go to church all of your life and never grow and still be on your way to hell because you don't have a real relationship with God. So many of my children I see just going through the motions. Now youth is for folly, and there is a season for everything but, that means seasons must change. And it's not that they don't...sometimes baby, we just don't get the memo and we are not keeping up with God, so we can't hear the voice of the Lord when He says it is time to move on...change of the seasons Niño."

"Yes ma'am."

"There is a scripture that encourages us to flee youthful lusts. Another sign that seasons are changing or they have changed. We must keep up with the Lord and learn to adjust. It all comes with time. Like gray hair, aches and pains. I'm a witness....just look at me. I haven't always been this perfect." Rubbing his back gently, as a nursing mother burping her newborn, she laughed.

"Huh?" he says. He lifts his head from her shoulder. They look one another in the eye and snicker.

"Young man. Accept your calling. You will do wonderful things for Christ. I see it. You just have to believe it. Pastor doesn't mean perfect. Give yourself a break and get a real understanding of just who the true and living really God is;

the religious idea. Not a painting or a statue or how someone else describes him to you. Find out just who He is and what He means to and in your life. We're all His children. He created all of us. He has no favorites. He loves us all equally but separately and just like children and parents, we all see him through different eyes. Our Father nurtures us like a loving mother and chastens us like a caring father. All custom-tailored to fit our needs. He is everything. In Christ, there is no separation. No male, no female. Christ is in all. Whole. Total and complete. Get a different view son. Renew that magnificent mind. We can know everything and nothing all at once. I say with due respect. A degree in something does not make you a master at everything. Aye counselor?"

He smirked, "I guess. I never saw it quite the way you just laid it down. That's something."

"I wouldn't lie to you. And if you won't take my word for it, believe in grace son. I know you know about grace."

"Yes ma'am I do."

"Great! Then you know the truth and that means you're already free! Hallelujah baby! He's not a slaver driver nor does He condemn the brethren. The enemy is the accuser of the brethren. The Spirit of The Lord convicts. He doesn't hold His anger long. Forgive yourself for being a human with a calling and a lot of flaws like everybody else. He don't call perfect people like me baby. He calls available people He can use. Make yourself available. He wants to use you. Humble yourself. Let Him. And be patient with Stacey Niño. She is my baby. She is a gift. So is her child. A profit to the nations. Love her mother."

"I've been trying. That's the issue."

"Try when she lets and when you see resistance, back away. Remember she's coming off being addicted to poison. She needs you even if she doesn't realize it. God made it so. God will bless you. I heard Joyce Meyer say on her program today, your history has nothing to do with your destiny. She's anointed; Powerful lady. I know that word was for you today. I love you Niño."

Barker kisses her on the cheek, "You made me feel better. You sound like my mother. She would've said some stuff like that."

"Ahhh Carla Golden. God broke the mold when He created her. She was special. But sometimes we have to let go and move on yes? Everything this side of Heaven is temporary and every meaningful, profitable relationship is an investment and an assignment. He time was up. She did what The Lord had sent her to do. You have to believe that. When begin to see that in a more positive, less selfish light, knowing we're all here on assignment and God is in control, then you will heal and find peace. Everything you go through, every hurt, all of the celebrations and mourning in this life; the ups and downs. T.D Jakes calls them the vicissitudes of life, are all for those who are coming after you that you will have to help grieve, heal, mourn and even celebrate in healthy ways. Nothing with God… " she winks her eye as she closes the gate and shuffles back over to her porch.

"Is ever wasted." he crowed.

"Exactly."

He mumbled to himself, "How you just gonna play Yoda then switch to Jeopardy at the end? Women! Should've asked for some more food. Dang! I know she kept Mr. Richie happy. Good woman."

She could hear him complain. She giggled as she locked the door. "It's gonna be ok son. Soon you will know. The Holy Spirit will show you everything." she said.

Stacey cracked the door just before he arrived at the bottom of the stairs. "Hey. Boom..." He pauses but never looks back. "I heard y'all. Don't nobody got respect for the weary no more? Jesus! I'm right here. I can hear everything!"

"Stacey it's late. I'm sorry alright. Please don't yell. Neither of us needs the added stress, let alone the baby. Good night. Good morning. Good day. Whatever. I'm out. If you need me call..."

"That's just it Barker. When I really needed you, you wasn't there. So what makes you think I need you now?"

He hung his head. He grit is teeth, "I said I'm sorry now get past it. Grow up and be a woman. Wait I thought you forgave me? What the...? Know what? Who has time? Take care Ms. James. I'm around if and when."

"I do forgive you but you keep getting on my nerves trying to play hero all of a sudden."

"All of a sudden! All of a sudden!" he whispers angrily. "I've done my best to be there for you when I could. Now, I love you, I care. I will forever. And we both got issues so Imma leave that alone. I didn't cause every problem in your life and I refuse to allow you to keep spewing nastiness my way." He turned to her, "You don't have to love me back, just let me be there. I need to help." Pleaded from the gate, he did all that he could to harness his emotion.

She saw the pain in his eyes. It shifted her mood instantly. "Look Boom, I'm obviously expecting. I'm moody, I'm tired. I'm busy. I'm fighting. I resting in the Lord and always hungry all at once. Hungry for a lot of stuff. You have no idea."

He interrupts abruptly, "What do you mean? Drugs? I know that can't be it. You're doing well. You're so strong. I am so proud of you baby mama."

She smiles, "I'm trying to be serious here man."

"And I'm trying to make you smile here lady."

She covers her mouth to disguise her laughter. "No but seriously, sometimes I want to get high. I ain't that far from yesterday. I'm human. Saved don't mean perfect. Devil ride you harder when you give your life to Christ seem like. Strong..." She takes a seat at the top of the staircase, "Christ keeps me strong. Just Him. I can do all things...more than a conqueror....all that...is all Him. I'm weak Boom. Alone I am weak. Especially with so much on my plate. I want to get high almost every day. Especially when I'm not doing anything positive. Too much me time ain't good."

"But you got the baby Stacey."

"Man ain't no baby stoppin nobody from getting on aight?! Jeez! With all of those smarts, there is still so much you don't know. People kill me! Education obviously ain't everything. You go somewhere, get educated real good and lose touch with people 'cause you so filled up with facts and stats. Want some truth baby daddy? This baby don't stop nothin. It is The Lord. I pray hard every day. If a baby was that compelling, there would be no more babies born addicted. Shoot man, I'm no better than that young girl upstairs. We're one and the same. Difference is, I know Jesus. I also know how to fight. Now the baby gave me a little more purpose and a few more goals; more responsibility. The baby also giving me more physical pain and stress. I have a son I didn't even raise. In my early thirties and I don't know how to be a mother. I haven't done a thing with my life."

He walked up the stairs. Barker sits below her. He rubs her feet. "I don't want her to be like me. I so don't want to bring another Stacey James here. I wasn't thinkin' man. Just high and crazy as hell. I don't know who her father is. I have support but where is her daddy Boom? Girls need they daddy. Trust me they do. I don't know how to be her mother. What can I offer her besides a statistical life and a rough start? See, you can't love my mess away. You can't help me with everything. You don't have the answers Sway. You've never been a mother. How Imma be her momma? How am I gonna keep her from feeling invisible?"

He reached up to stroke her hand while she caressed her belly. She cradled her stomach as tightly as a wide receiver running towards the end zone in the fourth quarter down my five. He knew what he was doing. It worked.

"You see that? That right there. You protect. That's what you do. See how you eat the way you do? You nourish her every time you feed yourself. Nourish her in every way. She won't be invisible to you. Keep watching her, pay close attention, the way you do now. You provide. That's what you do. It's not only a man's deal to protect and provide. Mothers do it from the day they know that child is coming."

"Yeah. That's true."

"That concern about stepping ya game up...you don't want another you? Keep that in mind when you feel like giving up and getting high. Look at yourself. You carry her precious little life inside of you. You are responsible for her life. Now continue that. Remember she is a precious life, she didn't ask to be here and she is your responsibility. I promise you gon' be the BEST mommy out here. You already off to a good start. You gon' rock it. I know it. Now let your past go. Forgive yourself. Don't worry about being perfect or getting it all right all of the time. You're going to miss the mark plenty. Everybody does. It's ok to mess up. Learn from it. Correct it. Forgive yourself and move on. That's what decent parents do. Gregory is still your son and

I know he loves his mother. Can't nobody make a son stop loving his mother if he does not want to. Not even her mistakes can get in the way. I know though, life happens. Life is not perfect. Things happen and people don't always love one another the way they should. Not even parents and children."

"Tell me about it."

"Sons always need their mothers. Mothers teach them how to love. Mothers are important. His first relationship with any female will be with his mother and every other relationship with a female after that will be an extension of that relationship. Just the same with fathers and daughters. That is a very special bond. He teaches her. He her value and worth. How she is to be respected; protected, provided for; treated like a princess until some worthy man comes along and makes her his queen. He's supposed to treat her with complete respect at all times whether she is present or not. Don't always work out that way. It should though. Ain't nothin worse than a broken woman that don't know how beautiful, precious and worthy she is because her father failed her and she has yet to heal.

Nothing worse than a man that hates his mother. There is nothing like the good love from mother to son. It's a crime when man has a relatlonshlp wlth hls mother that Is so fractured, it is beyond repair. Believe when I tell you that wound cuts deep into the very fabric of a man. It alters his views and perception of the opposite sex. A hurt and angry man is a dangerous one. Tragedy is too often these people, these broken people, end up together. Abusive relationships, old wounds that haven't healed. Hurting people hurt people." He shook his head. "See it all of the time. Counseled so many broken people trying to disguise their brokenness with things. That don't work. Looking for other broken people to fill a void and fix what's broken. Don't work. Too broken pieces don't fit. Don't work." He knew in that breath, as he had known so many times from the pulpit, as he delivered his sermon to Stacey thus, the people in the pews. He was very well, speaking to himself; surveying his own situation. He would have to love Stacey from a distance. They were both broken in different ways. Reality had just bitten him. He tried to sooth her, "I know you don't know who baby girl daddy is. I just wanna tell you I can be that if you need that. Whenever you need that. I'm not trying to push. I'm just sayin, I'm here Stacey. You don't have to walk this thing out all by yourself."

"You're sweet Boom. And you right. You're right about everything. But at this time, I'm thinking you should save all that love, all that concern for your own father. He's still your father. Go deal with that. Give all of that to him. I don't need it. I don't love you. Maybe I never have. I can't think about that right now." In a flash she was up and back in the house.

His pride was hurt. As he walked over to his car he remarked, "Whatever pleases the lady." In the back of his mind the only relief he harvested came from knowing God was on his side. He was settled because he knew whatever he felt for her; the things he did; all he wanted to do, stemmed from genuine concern. He was relieved to not have heard the words "I hate you. Get out of my life." Barker was grasping at threads with his huge masculine hands. "Lord what am I doing?" he questioned. "Holding on to hope son. Walk by faith not by sight. Seek me."

Back at Stacey's house Maya was stirring about the house like a restless spirit in the black of the night. She climbed down the staircase only to find Stacey bundled up at the base of the front door. "You know what Maya, I care about you and all. I even know what you goin through...been there too many times. I know how it is when the voice of the devil is way louder than the voice of God. So if you relapse, I ain't here to judge you honey. I get it. It's not easy. People just think it is because they not walkin' in ya shoes. I still ill from the withdrawal. So yeah ma...I get it. You wanna get outta here right?" Maya rocked back in forth looking as if she wanted to kill Stacey. She remained silent. She moaned. She stamped her feet. "That's what you want right?" Maya offered no response. She headed for the kitchen. "The knives are in the drawer farthest to the left. If you goin for one, pick a good old big one. Better yet! A rusty meat cleaver! Make it quick huh? I'm tired."

Maya cried and ran to get the meat cleaver. She ran back to Stacey. She kneeled over her, "I will end you tonight." Clinching her teeth, foaming at the mouth, she put the dull blade up against Stacey's throat. Stacey lay there with her eyes closed, "Girl, man up. You can't be down here in the hood and be all soft. Will you just go for yours already?" Maya pushed the blade deep beneath Stacey's jaw bone. Her musty, sticky sweat dripping on top of her forehead. "You bitch! I'm getting out of here. Move right now or..."

Stacey sat up. She rolled her eyes. She snatched the tool from the grip ravenous child. "Ma you want out? Girl that's all you had to say." She pushed Maya back, "Girl move. That's all I was waitin' for. I mean I usually score my own bags but you can go get a bunch for us. Or wait! We can go together. Yeah...that's it. I'm pregnant and I need the support. Girl, I swear, if I lean too low this time, I might not make it back up. Feel me? That lean be good to you don't it? Be floatin' and stuff. Somebody told me I got so low one time, that the tip of my nose just about scraped the concrete. But, just before it did, I rose like Jesus from the grave." She rubbed her belly and laughed, "Yeah man. Those were the days. So high girl. I don't even remember that. Can you believe it? That must have been that boss right there."

Maya walked over to her placing the blade directly at Stacey's navel. Just then the baby kicked! Stacey looked down. Without warning, she slaps Maya down to the floor. She kicks Maya in the stomach. She grabs the meat cleaver, "See! See that feelin' that's how I feel when you disrespect me like you just did. Now you done turned fool! If you EVER come that close to my body or my baby again, Imma cut you down to the white meat! Hear? Then I'm gonna grind ya little fragile white body up and make me some good old chili. I love white chili and yes I AM JUST THAT STUPID!" Maya groaned uncontrollably the pain was so great.

"Girl let me school you…You already off the radar. Just invisible. Aint nobody gonna miss you. Maya you just a whisper walking around until a strong wind come in and blow you away like a dirty, used up paper bag in the subway. That's this life! That's these streets. When you out there like that, you worthless to people. Live or die nobody cares. They just don't. So if I chop ya little boney frame up and make you into a stew and share with friends, who you gon' tell? Who gon' notice? Huh?" Maya lay balled up on the floor.

"Real talk, try me again if you wanna. I'm saved and all but I stay under construction; he still workin' on me. I'm not good on that turn the other cheek stuff. Now be clear, you ain't the only one in here Jonsin'. You ain't the only one in here wit issues. We both goin thru it. Now they say crazy people strong. And they right. We both crazy, streets do it to you if the drugs don't. So, if you leavin', go head. If you copin', bring me a bag. I'm just that gone right now. I ain't gon' stop you Maya." She falls down to her knees to whisper in Maya's ear, "Let's get high ok? I wanna get high."

Stacey opens the front door pushing Maya out. She throws money in her face. As a matter of fact keep it. I don't trust no stupid skank like you to come back. And I don't wanna have to beat the brakes of you over my stuff. You don't even know how to get away from a pimp without getting rocked! You ain't 'bout it. Friggin amateur. Go! Go dummy! Fade to black white girl. Who cares anyway? Worthless!" She slams the front door.

Out of breath Stacey snivels, "Lord I'm wrong. I know it. I know that ain't love. But Jesus I am tired. I can't save this child. I ain't got the energy. You gon' have to do it." She wept bitterly lying at the bottom of the front door praying. "I don't know what I'm doin. I can't handle it. I can't. I just wanna get high right now." Her embryo begins to churn within her. She prays earnestly, "Jesus, this child ain't strong enough to stop me tonight. It gotta be somethin more. I need you. Jesus I might not make it tonight. I need somethin. For real. I need to get high." The Lord offers no reply. She touts impatiently, "Oh for real? You just gonna leave me hanging when I'm illin' like this? Great."

Maya walks down the stairs and down the street riddled with pain. Two minutes later Stacey gets a faint knock on the door. "What!" she screams. "Get off my door this time o' night. Ya know better! Don't make me..."

"What?!" a deep voice calls thru the thick wooden door. "Ma! It's me. It's G."

"Who? My son? Oh don't play me. I got somethin for you keep talkin' and not walkin' hear? And Maya if this is you and ya lil nasty pimp, y'all better go on before it get real." She reasoned, "Lord have mercy. The man was trying to protect me and I let him go home. Now look."

The man kept banging on the door. "Aye yo! Come on now ma. I'm tired." He had taken a seat on the porch, "Damn man."

Stacey runs back to the living room window to peek past the curtain. It is pitch black. The young man is wearing all black. She listens as he makes a call from his cell phone. "Aye yo man, I don't know what this nutty buddy in there doin' but, I can't stay out here. Not all night. It's too hot out here; the boys out here actin' up. Psshh man, come back and scoop me. I gotchu when you pull up. I just need a place to chill for the night." She lifts the window slightly to get a better listen as she begins to dial Barker's number, "No I can't. Guess I'll call these jokers. 911...let me go get my last glass of orange juice since I'll probably be mummified by the time they get here."

Just as she reaches up to lock the window the young man says, "Ma! What is wrong with you? Let me in man. I been out here for like 10 years."

Stacey screams bloody murder dropping the meat cleaver barely missing her foot. "G?! My boy?! You scared me." She hurried to unlock the door, "Baby! Oh thank you Jesus! Look at my son."

"I miss you too. Aw ma." He disturbed her bulge, "Another one ma?"

"Yeah man. Don't make me feel bad G. I already feel bad enough."

"I ain't here to make you feel bad, I just wish you would've told me. I feel left out."

"Aw baby. Don't feel left out. I didn't know how to tell you. I know I done let you down enough."

"Hell. Ain't nobody perfect right? Well, except for me."

"Just like your father! Arrogant and rightfully so. Just so handsome."

"Ma you so crazy. But you so honest."

"Boy you a mess. My mess."

"Yes I am. But we can talk about that later. Can you make ya mess something to eat? Please?" he smiles.

Having had never enjoyed the distinct pleasure of having cooked for her son. What was a norm, often frowned upon; what seemed to be a chore to so many mothers who had taken the connection of motherhood and all it encompasses for granted, Stacey had been dying to perform what for what seemed like an eternity. Whatever she didn't get to experience, that had become commonplace, expected and run of the mill for everyone that had experienced what had been missing in her life, she was most grateful for. It was her honor to finally serve her son. She had waited a lifetime it seemed to feel worthy of the title, the responsibility, the privilege. The call of duty: Motherhood.

Her mind was in a frenzy as she raced into the kitchen surveying the pantry to see what she might prepare that would be suitable to set before the prince of her heart. What recently had seemed to be the worst of times was shaping up to be the best of times. In tiny increments she was learning to change her perspective on the current events. She had recollected as she sifted through packaged goods on a quote from her favorite pastor, "Everything thing that look good ain't good and everything that look bad ain't bad." Secretly, Bishop T.D Jakes had become like a surrogate father to her in her mind. He was everything she thought a spiritual leader should be. Everything her father was not. She beamed when his wife Serita would show up on screen with him. Her spirit so confident; so sweet. She echoed motherhood, class. A quiet spirit. She admired their daughter Sarah for her resilience and strength, "Look at what she's been through. Her testimony. Look at her. God has blessed her so. I wonder what He can do for me if He did so much for her. Lord she's winning. Jesus I wanna win. I don't want to be nobody else, I just wanna win in the skin I'm in." She figured if all the recent happenings were what was necessary to be reunited with her son, be they good or bad, then maybe she was winning. Stacey was a champion in her own skin. She cried into the bowl of batter she was stirring, "Lord, I didn't want him to see me like this; under these conditions. He deserves better. I wish I could've done better. But if this is orchestrated by you then this is my moment. I may never have another one like this, I'm thankful. What I prayed for, my heart's desire didn't come in the way I thought it might, but I will take it. She wept like a grieving mother, I will take this. Thank you Lord." Gregory could hear her weeping from the living room, "Hold on yo. Ma, you good?"

"Yeah. I'm alright baby. Tears of joy." she yelled.

"Son, Imma hit you back. I gotta go check on my moms." he ended his call. When he had arrived at the kitchen doorway, he noticed her wiping her eyes with a kitchen towel. "Ma stop now. You gon' make me start if you don't stop. If you're happy, why are you cryin?"

"Boy. Didn't I tell you tears of joy?" she laughed.

"What's that though? Why do women cry so much man? I mean over everything."

"Well, you're never gonna be a woman, so it would be hard for you to understand. So let me just say, we're emotional. Guess God made us this way. Men are logical. Guess the universe needed balance. The Lord always knows what He's doing G."

"Does He really? Messed up as this world is. For real?"

"G! Now even if I don't know better, God knows you do. I don't even have your education and I know that man got his hands and nose in everything. The Lord gave us authority and dominion over His possessions. That showed He had some type of faith in us to do the right thing. But we messed it all up. It an abuse of power. From slavery, racism and police brutality to the poaching of innocent wild animals and mass produced super marketed, super-sized, chemically induced meats and produced we consume in this country that are only making us sicker and more obese; to the destruction of the ozone layer and the ecosystem. It's all due to greed, capitalism and the pure vanity of mankind. Man's selfishness, ignorance and arrogance; our lack of respect for God and life itself has contributed to the demise of the world. Man created social structure of pride and insecurity. God is no respecter of persons...wasn't His doing. Not when Jesus chilled with everyone except for the religious hypocrites. You gotta be careful of those who always want to compartmentalize others. It's not always safety that does it. It's insecurity and a sense of false superiority mostly. When the oppressed wake up, rise up and take steps towards fighting the power or one man, one voice, a beacon of change for an entire generation, begins to plant seeds that begin to stimulate growth and renewal in the minds and spirits of those oppressed people, that person or those persons become a threat; they must then be contained. If they can't be contained, before revolution begins and the oppressors are overthrown, then the person or persons must be exterminated. And that my son, will be done by any means necessary. Recall your African American civil rights leaders. Recall any figure in history with a dream, a voice and a bag of seeds to plant. See them imprisoned like Nelson Mandela. Watch the people who were bold enough to live out their calling murdered like your Kennedy brothers, Abraham Lincoln or Dr. King himself. Not perfect men, just seed planters. When they can't control or contain you, they will come for you when you least expect it."

"Wow mom. You're so smart. You're right. Like Medgar Evers and Malcolm X."

"That's right. Like Jesus the Christ too."

"G, you always have to find yourself getting the proper perspective on things because there is always more than one side to why things are the way they are. It all stems from fear. Fear is paralyzing. Fear makes people paranoid and defensive. Think about the civil rights movement and how blacks were treated post-civil war. How we are still viewed and being compartmentalized; especially black men...young black men. The mass incarceration and high prison sentencings for non-violent crimes. The racial profiling and police brutality. It seems like there's not only an ignorance concerning blacks; not only in America but everywhere; there's also a fear. A fear that if we would ever rise up and stick together instead of turning against one another for once; if we actually began to renew our minds and educate ourselves on our own history and invest in our own communities and children, we would strike a most powerful blow. Altogether."

"Like a fist."

"Just like a fist G. Slavery started in Africa. See, we were tearing one another down even back then. Even though at that time, it was a class thing, it was still very wrong. And no, we didn't invent slavery, but utilizing it, no less was wrong in and of itself. Then you move to the Europeans bringing us to America after the Spanish had us…they flipped the script and it turned into a race thing. They broke down the strength and structure of the family unit. Labeled us, separated us and introduced to us the 'crabs in a barrel' mentality. Still, to this day, we live with that mindset and we still haven't returned to decent family values as a people on a whole. There's still the falsehood in the black community that women don't need men in the home to lead and protect and provide. Then we wonder why our sons don't know how to b men or they receive a false sense of what manhood is by running around with other young black males who have a warped perception of manhood having children with young black females who share a fractured sense of what womanhood is; everybody thinking it all hinges on sexual maturity and nothing more. Never realizing that adulthood has everything to do with perspective and preference and priority. Those young males, terrorizing the neighborhood think that it is ok for men to have women and children spread all over the place and not be responsible for them nor committed to them."

"So you're saying we were brainwashed?"

"Yes I am. Self-included. Brainwashed and as a race, cattle-ranched." She weighed on her conversation with Barker. "Maybe I should've let him help. That pride girl." She mused.

"Yeah, I feel you. Look at how they built the projects and why. They didn't even teach us that in that fancy school pop spent all of that money for me to go there for. I had to learn about this stuff in my African American studies class in college. That's crazy."

"Yeah. It is crazy. And if you ever get the chance to look at Maafa 21, it will change your perspective on the products you buy, where you shop, who you cast your ballot for and the truth behind abortion and the plan to eradicate minorities. Namely blacks."

"Eugenics?"

"Exactly."

"Ma. I didn't know you knew all of this stuff."

"Boy, I may have made a lot of stupid mistakes and some really bad choices but stupid I am not. Just like those brothers in prison that made that one wrong move that altered their lives, I am not my mistakes. I still have value and worth. I'm full of surprises. That's the lesson of today...don't count people out. Don't put people in a box. Don't allow pride, ignorance or fear to stifle your thinking or your love, compassion and respect for God and His creation. Be they human or animal."

"I see. Wow."

"Well, that was just a small lesson on perspective and truth Gregory. Don't forget...Whether it be classism or racism-sexism or ageism. The Bible says there is no Jew nor Gentile, neither slave nor free, nor is there male and female, for you are all one in Christ. Don't blame God for the ills of society boy. Blame society. Lord have mercy! I done cried in this bowl. Jesus! Let me make a new bowl. I know my tears ain't part of the recipe. Food will be done in a few. Go wash your hands and face."

"I'm good." G grumbled.

"Not really. You just came from outside."

"Ma, I'm a grown man."

"Don't gimme dat G. Now you ain't gonna ever be as grown as me while I'm alive. These two boats shall never dock in the same marina. Show some respect."

"Pop never made me wash up before breakfast." he growled.

"Yeah, well, I ain't Barker. I'm Stacey. See, it's that woman thing again that you'll probably never understand. Germs are the enemy. Now go wash please."

"But I ain't no baby. I'm a ..." he puffed.

Stacey slammed the wooden spoon own that had been handed down in her family from generation to generation, "Now you gon' make me break this heirloom. Go on and do what I said G! I'm still your mother. This is my house, what I say goes."

"Ok, ok. Dang! You rough lady. I'm goin ma."

"Good!"

"Hey ma!?" he screamed as he ran up the stairs.

"What?!"

"I love you."

"I love you more boy. Now, go ahead and come on before it get cold hear?"

"Coming."

Gregory zoomed back down the staircase like a little boy starving after a hard day at play. He wolfed down every morsel of food. Seconds and thirds. "Ma! That food was right! You hear me? Jokers always braggin' bout they mama cookin'. And I tasted some good food along the way. But ma! You get it in."

"Boy, you know you goin' too far now. It's just food." she blushed.

"Nah ma, trust me. It's way different. You can BURN. What you put in here?" licking the gravy from his knuckles.

"Boy here. Take a paper towel. You too cute to be a savage. Now ain't nothin' more in this food but some old school love cooked up in some old school pots and pans. Pots and pans older than me and you put together. That's it G.".

"If you say so. Mmm! This food is rockin."

She watched him savor every bite from across the kitchen table. "Hope you don't get a tummy ache. And where's your girlfriend? How many you got? What you studying at school? Tell me?"

"Ma. We gotta talk about this stuff later. We got mad stuff to catch up on and plenty of time to do it in. I just wanna eat and lay down."

"Alright. And you got plenty of time for that. I never see you. You can't spend a few minutes talking to your mother."

"Ma please alright? Can a man eat in peace?"

"Who you talkin' to?" she asked him. Hand on her hip.

"You man! Stop buggin' and pass the salt please. God man."

"You're demanding and arrogant just like your father and your grandfather."

"Yeah. But, I ain't them. So pass the salt."

By his tone, she could tell he wasn't just there on a social call or to play catch up, he was there to collect a debt. Hurting, wounded and confused, they were both entering a comfort zone of dysfunction. Her moments of worthiness would be frequent but short lived. Her sense of guilt would begin to override her faith as his resentment began to bubble to the surface. Stacey believed her son had every right to own his feelings. How she would pay her penance would be to allow him to relieve himself of his the bitterness he held towards her anyway he saw fit. She was still a work in progress. It seemed as though when she decided to give her life to Christ, all of her issues came back to haunt her all at once. Enemies. Filthiness of spirit. Old habits. All working against her. Odds weren't in her favor. She found herself preaching and teaching a good game. On the other hand, she would find the challenge in living it out and believing her own hype. But all of those things were going to work together for her good. "Why is the people who can give a good word, provoke thought and encourage have the worst time living out their own words? Lord why are we all hypocrites?" Stacey would ask time and time again. Each time the Lord revealing, "Human nature."

SUPERWOMAN

"Pass the salt."

Connie slides the salt shaker across the table. "Al, you could be a little nicer. A please and thank you couldn't hurt. It would be a refreshing change from the demand and grunt routine. Must you play the cave man so often?"

Al responded with a mouth full of food, "I am nice. I'm here ain't I? I could be somewhere else. Coffee."

Connie had spun around from the kitchen counter in a huff. "See! See! You doin' it again."

He thundered, "What?!"

"Being a demanding jerk. A greater man would say please and thank you; only a lesser man would say things like you say that make his woman feel as if she should be grateful for his time."

"Only a lesser woman who wasn't confident in who she was…a woman who didn't know her own power and place would complain and grasp at straws for pleasantries where they may not always be warranted. A lesser woman doesn't know how to be peace for her man. A LESSER WOMAN isn't wise enough to choose her battles wisely. A lesser woman is a woman unaware of the bylaws of servitude.

Recognition and respect aren't always givens in service Connie. We serve out of love full of thanksgiving at the opportunity to serve another the way Jesus served people. Jesus never got bent out of shape about a please or a thank you. Son of man didn't come to be served. He came to serve. See now…" he scrapes his plate. "This is why you need to come back to church. Can't get all you need at home. You need to be fed. You can learn how to serve in humility if you served at church. Or anywhere outside of this house for that matter. By the way, it takes a lesser woman to pick up a stick and poke a hungry bear while he's eating. Do yourself a favor, whoever this is this morning…take her back where you got her from. I don't like her. A man need peace when he eat and while he's thinkin. This woman, she don't understand that. Ain't no room for her at this table."

"Pompous. I guess that's a bylaw of service huh Pastor? Arrogance?"

"Yep. Yep. Yep." he eased back from the table, "My cue to exit stage left. Good day my lady. I love you with the love of Jesus." As he rose up from the chair, his wallet fell from his pocket. It flipped open to reveal a picture of Carla.

"There it is right there." Connie shook her head.

"I can't right now. I don't need this. Got a lot on the dome woman. I ain't used to this. Let me be."

"Yes indeed. There it is honey." she took a seat at the kitchen table.

"There what is?"

"There she is."

"Woman what? Who are you talking about?"

She picks up the picture from the floor. Connie shoves it in his face. "Her. Carla. Your precious wife. You keep comparin' me to her Al. It ain't fair. I feel like I'm the third wheel all of the time. I know that lesser woman thing didn't come out of left field Al. You want me to be Carla. I can't be that. Hell, I can't even measure up to her memory let alone fill her shoes."

"Now THERE IT IS!" Al yelled. "There it is. You still competing against her. Always have."

Connie stood up. "What?"

"Yeah. Let's get to it. I know even from the background you wanted what she had. Her anointing. Her gift. Her family. Her life. Her lifestyle. But woman, you should've asked her when you had the chance how she work it. Serving in the home, at the church, everywhere you go in the community. I know it wasn't easy on her. But she did it without begging for applause. She served with dignity, in silence, with a smile on her face. Even raising a house full of boys; having a demanding husband with a demanding calling, Carla never made it about her."

"That you know of."

"I beg your pardon? I rarely heard her demand anything. She knew service wasn't about her. Even when the people she served, even when I wasn't being, so kind and loving, she persevered in service. She never had taken anything negative personally. My wife was a rock. My rock. So many women look on from the outside, wanting to be the wife of a leader without doing the homework. They don't do the math Connie. Those are some difficult shoes to walk in..."

"Even harder shoes to fill." she mumbled.

"People have their fantasies. But, they don't know what it's like. They see power, position and prestige. What they don't see are the problems; the pressure. The strain service can put on a man, a woman, a relationship, a marriage. Takes a strong woman to be at the side of a leader and be a humble leader in her own right. Not just a spiritual leader-any leader. Carla, never complained." he continued.

"How do you know she never complained Al? I seem to remember things differently. Sorry to burst your bubble but, while you was off traveling from city to city like a rock star In hls prime, she had..."

"What do you think you going to tell me? Huh? A lot of lonely nights and mundane days? A lot frustration? She had temptations? Hard time with the boys? Felt like she was living the single life most of the time without the benefits? What are you going to say huh? She missed me? She loved me? She felt ignored? She lit cigarettes when she got frustrated? She was angry with me and God? Ministry was my mistress? She felt cheated out of her marriage? She lived, she served, she loved then she died with nothin to show for it? Was that what you was gonna enlighten me on? Huh? And why? To make me feel worse off than I already do? Huh? Because the way I see it, can't be no other reason than you want to hurt me because I still honor the memory of that woman."

"I'm not trying to hurt you. I just…"

"Yes you are. Sure you are. Why I deserve it don't I? After all of these years, the chickens have come home to roost. It's my just deserts right Connie?"

"Al don't…"

"Don't what? I know it was hard on her being a pastor's wife. Ain't nobody gotta tell me nothin bout my wife. I studied her. I knew her. I knew things about her she didn't think I knew. We were married. It was a partnership. I loved her Connie. Even if I never spoke a mumbling word about some things…things I couldn't change, hurt I couldn't heal; it was my job to know her in every sense of the word. You think I don't feel like she did. Like I failed her? Do you think I don't wish I would have given more time to the ministry God had given me at home?"

"You did a good job. You did the right thing. You answered the call. She didn't blame you for that. You're a great man Al."

"Oh please. Don't lay it on so thick now! I'm not perfect. I was just doing what I could at the time to balance everything to the best of my ability. Connie, Carla didn't complain because I truly believe she was anointed to carry those loads; most women couldn't carry the loads that come with being the spouse of a leader. Flowing in that anointing with grace, in love, patience and understanding; both parties being flawed beneath the surface…keeping those flaws under wraps from the prying eyes and hustling ears of the public. I don't think she knew how much I really needed her. How much I and the boys depended on her to be our strength. She never knew exactly how much I respected and valued her. I never got a chance to really express that stuff to her. It takes a special someone to be the spouse of a leader; to be the backbone. It can't be easy being the one called to bear all of the weight with none of the recognition. You know how many interviews I watch where these politicians and celebrities get all of this sanctimonious glory for doing what they're called to do or some menial charity work; sometimes some humanitarian effort that these tossed a few dollars to or dropped by on site for a publicity stunt be it real or contrived with no mention of family or at the very least, the spouse, the very support that does the real work behind the scenes, that they couldn't have made that far, to be who they are or do what they are able to do without? Even if that spouse contributes nothing more than moral, spiritual and emotional; isn't that enough for someone to say to them; thank you. I appreciate you?"

"But I've always supported you."

"When you've got a calling on your life and a vision The Lord has given you, it's important that the support comes from somebody who get it; gets you. That support has to come from someone who loves you, flaws and all that is there to serve; a person who knows who they are and why they are; why they are there and how they fit in confidentially. Someone not looking for their spot on the world stage or rehearsing their lines for their big debut. A person you can trust to hold your hand when the ship is sinking. A person honest enough to know their limits but, not ridicule or reject you for yours. Many are called, few are chosen."

"I've always been honest with you Al. Even now."

 "Carla knew I was just a man behind the robe. That's why I loved her. Carla allowed me to be human. Even as a first lady by all rights, behind closed doors; when she saw my fragile, broken side. When I was afraid, weak, ill, insecure...she supported me. Did her best to be there. She gave me what I needed. She rolled with the punches. I don't need nobody to make me feel worse off than I already do for being too wrapped up in serving other people than being at home serving my wife Connie." I was young and full of vigor Connie. Excited to be doing something good for a change. I just wanted to give back. God blessed me with a love for people and for Him. I just never wanted to choose."

"I never asked you to choose. She wanted you to choose." Connie sneered.

"Oh, I have no doubt! I know she voiced her concerns to you Connie. I thought I had time to make it right. Time wasn't on my side. In the end, I took my first lady for granted; I put her last. Yet, she never complained." Connie rolled her eyes. "She was my peace. I truly believe she didn't say much because she saw the strain serving had put on me. My wife was a great wife. She was my backbone. My strength. My silent partner. She did her job well. She served in silence." Tears filled his eyes, "I know a lot of times she was broken and wasn't happy. I'm sorry I missed the mark. I am sorry I missed out on hat beautiful woman. I regret that I missed out on fully enjoying my family...my marriage. All of these years I thought The Lord wanted me working hard. Obviously I was wrong. I wish I could go back. But I can't. She's gone. All I can do is move forward...make it right from here on out. I'm sure deep down inside, if we had daughters she would've advised them not to marry pastors or leaders in general. I don't know if I would agree. Where would so many of us be without women like her? It takes a strong woman. It's a calling." He stared at Connie, "When it comes to being the spouse of a leader, if you're not sure you're strong enough; fire too hot...don't step into that kitchen. Your relationship with the Lord had better be rock solid. For as the man, community, parish leans on you, so you must lean on The Lord. Better be strong and confident. Be flexible and willing to share your man if you're gonna be anybody's backbone. Such a role is not for the faint of heart or weak in spirit."

"So what would you advise your son? He's a pastor?"

Al rubs his salt and pepper beard. Starring off into the distance he answers as he reflects on yesterday, preparing a sermon. A creature of habit. With a lump in his throat he verbally captioned, picturing himself hand on shoulder, having a man to man with Barker, "Don't take ALL God has given you for granted. The Lord gives and the Lord takes away. Cherish what you got while you got it. Tomorrow ain't promised. Love your wife as Christ loved the church. Sacrifice for her. Lay down your life. Your marriage and family are not just your assignments, they are your ministries too! She's your backbone. Your wife is your partner. Don't take her granted. She is you; one flesh. Find time for family. Make room for the people you love the most. Pray that God make you able to discern the needs of those around you. Pray that He supply the knowledge and understanding you need to be able discern those needs and utilize the wisdom He has provided as necessary to fit the needs of your loved ones; just like you do when you serve His people in the body. Lastly, even as you put God's business first, which is priority, remember as you're serving The Lord, the body, the community..." Al choked up. Fighting back tears he concluded, "Don't forget to serve those closest to you. The ones you love. The ones who love you, flaws and all. The ones who know that underneath it all, you are just a man."

"Still in love with her. She's still here. A woman who served relentlessly, effortlessly but, resentfully. I knew behind closed doors she wasn't perfect..."

Al barks angrily, "Ok! Alright! So what! Who is?! Why are you comparing yourself to her? Don't you think it's best to just be you and do what you do? I knew you were always jealous of her! Were you ever really her friend? Huh? Who really cares about the flawed Carla? Hell! We all flawed! And if she loved me and I loved her...we loved those boys ...did the best we knew how, then what does any of both of our flawed behavior matter at the end of the day? Why are you grasping at straws? We all sin and come short of God's glory. But who can judge save Him?"

"Whatever. You're just making excuses for her. She was saved right? And a leader herself right?'

"Woman, what's your point? I'm losing patience with you."

"She was a phony. That's my point! Ain't no sanctified, holy woman supposed to be that dissatisfied with the path The Lord chose for her. Who does that? She was an ingrate. Baby, had it had been me…"

"You don't even know what you're talking about Connie. To tell you the truth, I DON"T FEEL LIKE SERVIN' ALL OF THE TIME! Ministry take too much out of you. Make you weary, sad and tired. I mean my goodness! Folk take you to be some kind of spiritual superman when that ain't the case. You just as susceptible to failure and breakdown as they are! I DON"T CARE HOW CLOSE YOU ARE TO GOD OR HOW MUCH SCRIPTURE YOU KNOW, MEMORIZE OR CAN QUOTE IN YOUR SLEEP! We're all human Connie. If you have never been in her shoes, how can you sit and pass judgment?"

"I'm not judging her. I'm just saying…you know how many women would've killed to be in her position Al? Nothing to worry about. Great life. Husband, family. All of that travel and people admiring you; going out of their way for you. Kids had the best of everything. That's all a woman can ask for. She had a lot to be thankful for. And she had the nerve to gripe about it. Even if it was only from time to time…it wasn't right. All I'm sayin'."

"No we ain't supposed to murmur and complain…but JESUS! Who doesn't from time to time! People frustrate you. Life can take a lot out of you and people can ask for more than you really want to give without taking so much as a thought for your family and their needs. Ministry is hard work. Preachin' alone put so much strain on ya heart woman! Even if you were in her shoes, and you found them roomy because God knows you couldn't fill 'em…" Connie covered her mouth in astonishment. "You still wouldn't have enough room to be able to judge her. God knows why we are the way we are and why we do what we do. There's a core to everything. If you don't the core…you only know part of the story. The skin or the outer part; what's immediately visible is not the beginning of the story of anything. The core; the seed; the inside is where it all begins. At our very core, from the inside out, we're all born with stuff and we accumulate more as we move through this life Connie. No one is perfect. What you may perceive as the perfect life looking in from the outside, may very well be hell or at the very least mediocre to the very one assigned to that life. Why do we always want what we were not assigned to? You weren't meant to handle her assignment Connie. You couldn't. Just the same she couldn't handle yours. From the start, you were destined to go down different paths.

"How you gon' tell me what I'm capable of handling? You don't know the mind of God."

"If you could, He would have called you. See, your whole perception of marriage and ministry is off. He never promised us a perfect ride or problem-free matrimony. He promised us challenges and trails. Who said Jesus was a happy camper every day? Especially when it came to making sacrifices for other people? Even he ran to avoid the crowds for alone time. He was in this flesh. On His way to the cross in the Garden of Gethsemane, He even petitioned God the Father for another route on the road redemption; the redemption of His children. He sweat profusely as the droplets were likened to blood. See, it was commitment. Covenant. Ministry and marriage. It was always sacrifice. Sacrifice is hard work. We go through what Christ went through as Christians. Only difference is Jesus was perfect. He's the only one. But God, see God don't call only perfect people to serve. For there would be none to answer the call. He calls willing people to serve. Flaws and all. Carla was willing Connie. She wasn't called because she was perfect. Beyoncé sang that song didn't she? Flaws and All."

Connie smirked, "You shouldn't be askin' me nothin the way you just read me the riot act. So sensitive when it comes to that Carla. What you doin' listenin' to worldly music anyway?"

"You one to judge on worldliness? Didn't I just say something to you about judgin' when you ain't in the person's shoes? Huh? What you don't listen? This ain't a time for jokes Connie. At my age, one thing I don't have time for is religious people alright?"

He reprimanded her while she stood staring at him quietly. His ego was in full flare up. As often as she could, she tried to not take his flare ups personal. She believed men needed to be listened to, not challenged. Connie respected Al. She sometimes felt the need to remind him as often as he reminded her, she was not there to fill Carla's shoes. As much as he barked that she shouldn't compare herself to other woman, namely Carla, he had neglected to realize he wasn't making that any easier for her. He expected her to perform, think, speak, behave; respond to his ways in Carla's fashion. For a prolonged season Connie tried to jump through hoops to keep what seemed to be their happiness regulated. Every trick she performed to keep him happy had went against the flow in the vein of everything staunchly relative to woman's liberation that she had taught Liza. The very same ideals that aided in ending her daughter's marriage. She had been the epitome of hypocrisy. She was willing to do almost anything at this stage in her life, not to be alone. Yet she was selective. Only Al Golden would do. She had to have him specifically. No matter how ill-fitted the glass slipper, she had to be the one brandishing it for all to see when the timing was right.

Her motives for wanting to be with Al seemed genuine on the surface. Al was no fool though. He knew they weren't. Yet, he digressed in confronting the truth. He, himself was also living a lie. If he was going to confront anyone, he would have to take a page from Michel Jackson's book. Al had to start with the man in the mirror. The look would be a long, hard one. He wasn't ready to face the truth. No one was. Everyone, had found contentment within the comfort of the lie.

The couple had not consulted God on His plans. Even when everything within told them this was in ill-fated connection, they had brushed every warning sign off to fit their own selfish desires. They both were deceiving themselves. Thinking they were closer to The Lord than what they were. They weren't walking in His will. Everybody had only been concerned about what they wanted. It had never been about doing what makes them feel good on a whole, they were two human beings, deceived, lost…stumbling through the darkness of their minds…holding on to the past, trying to fill a void. The very least of what they had in common besides both of them being directly connected to Connie. Each trying to get that old thing back.

He stared off into the distance, his voice cracked as he continued to stroll along in his truth, "I don't feel like serving most of the time anymore. I can't believe I'm saying this out loud. But there…at least I got it off my chest." Connie came up behind him and wrapped her arms around his waist. He breathed a deep sigh of relief.

She poured him a glass of gin. "Let it out."

He sipped cautiously as he scratched the scruffy hair on his neck, "Man. That came out of nowhere. Forgive me. I'm being emotional." Al cleared his throat. He released himself from her embrace, "I never even talked to The Lord about how I really feel." He couldn't even remember the last time he had said a sincere prayer. "I don't think I have the fire in me anymore. I think I'm tired. Season seem to be changin'. No passion. My sermons are watered down. Nobody sayin nothin. They all out there hoopin' and hollerin' like I'm the second comin' of Dr. King. Man…" he gulps what's left in the glass. "Sometimes I don't even think I believe anymore…Can't call it. Pour me another one." he demands. Connie places the bottle back atop the refrigerator. She takes a defensive stance. Arms folded.

"What?" he says.

She turned her head.

"Sorry. I've just been this way for so long..."

She charges, "Don't mean you can't change. We can all learn new things. Change old habits. I know old habits die hard. The key word in that sentence is die though Al. They can die. We have the power to change. That's if we want to. Renew that mind...be ye transformed."

"Yeah but when I was with Carla, she didn't mind..."

"I'm not Carla Al. I ain't got that kinda patience. Lord knows I don't know how she put up with you. She loved you. I know you loved her. But what y'all had died with her. I'm not sure why you don't get that."

He thought to himself, "I wish that were true." He grew resentful at her statement. His thoughts then demanded a voice. He quipped sternly, "When you've had a long standing successful marriage, and I don't mean to just any Joe Blow from Idaho, you know...your usual. I mean someone with purpose that adds value to your life. Someone that's going to believe in your dream and share your vision, that's if you even have one... Then, and only then, can you come back and talk to me about what's supposed to die and when. Until then, don't YOU DARE tell me how to feel or when to bury ANYTHING!" Connie stood shocked. He stormed out. He slammed the door. After twenty minutes. He rang the doorbell. "Please forgive me. There's just so much goin' on right now and debating how I feel with me, when you are not me, is not helping. Not at all. But that's no excuse for me to be rude to you. Forgive me Connie."

"I do forgive you Al. I understand you're under a lot of pressure. I'm just trying to help."

"Oh really? It don't seem that way when all you're sitting there doing is judging my dead wife for things you have you will never understand. That ain't fair. I can't allow that. You don't want me to love her...I get that. But at the same time I don't. You women and your insecurities and emotions along with all of this comparison nonsense. It's like unwarranted jealousy or that body bashin' y'all do. You know I'M FAT or DO YOU THINK SHE'S PRETTIER THAN ME? It's nonsense. Thank God I'm a man! Lord have mercy! That mess is so unattractive. I mean win in your skin. Be you. Carla is dead Connie. Now, there is a huge part of me that will always love her. You just have to understand that. She WAS my wife. She WAS my partner. WE HAD a family together. WE shared dreams, visions and goals. Now, obviously, SHE is gone. I AM still here. That part of my life is OVER. It's a new season. IT's ME and YOU. Concentrate on that."

She just stared at him.

"I'm confused. Let me just get that out of the way. Why on God's green earth are you soooooooooo obsessively jealous over such a flawed woman? I mean you sat here and for her to have been your friend for such a very long time, all you did was pick that woman apart. I don't understand you women. What is friendship to you all really? What value do you all place on friendship? I thought Carla was a friend to you Connie. She loved you. You have just changed."

"Alright. Ok. I've been letting you talk. You've been having your say. But, I have the right to speak my mind, just like you. So watch out here it come."

"See that there. That's what I mean. Look how you talk to me. You're different."

"You're right. I am different. I AM PISSED OFF! Damn it Al Golden. You're such a stubborn, prideful man. Times change, people change, seasons change. You're a man of God. It's a shame before him if YOU of all people don't get that or maybe you just don't want to."

"Woman what are you talking about now?"

"YOU! I'm talkin about YOU! You're criticizing my relationship with Carla? How dare you? A good marriage. Ha! How do you know it was good for her Al? The way you are with your antiquated caveman mentality. You have got to be kidding me. You never recognized your wife needed something different. And even if you did, you manipulated her into believing you didn't because things not changing, her serving you….you never serving her….served your needs."

"What?"

"Yeah I said it. What about her needs?"

"All of her needs were met. What are you talking about? As a matter of fact didn't we just go through this? Didn't I say I know I messed up?"

"She had changed Al. Her needs had changed. She didn't want to just be your first lady anymore but you didn't get the memo? Or maybe you did and you balled it up and tossed it to the side like you did her life."

"I did no such thing."

"Yes you did. You were selfish. You're just too stubborn to admit it. She wanted to be your wife. She wanted to share your life. Not just your burdens, stress and responsibilities. She wasn't allowed to be herself in the marriage. She never voiced that to you because maybe inside she knew you wouldn't take the fact that she wasn't where you left her constantly so well. She knew you. She knew you didn't like change. Carla was unhappy most of the time because she was non-confrontational."

"She was non-confrontational because she was selfless." he barked.

"No! No she wasn't! That ain't it. See you still don't get it. She was non-confrontational because she knew you were selfish. Bullheaded, arrogant, prideful. She knew even attempting to have you take a break from ministry to run away for a week or two just to be her husband, notice her, serve her, love her...was a no win situation. Oh yeah, she could've talked to you about her changing, her evolution, but you being the YOU that YOU are, would've have let it go in one ear and out of the other. It was always all about you. Oh she was strong. Just not strong enough. Not for my taste. And why on earth would she have to tell you she was changin? Huh? If you her best friend, lover, partner, husband...you would have watched her more closely. YOU would have recognized the signs of her changing. Even when her health began to fail in the beginning. You kept doin you. And Al, I know you probably closer to God than I will ever be. I know you have all of the insight I'll probably never have. But, truth be told, I have a real problem believing God wouldn't give you a break from all that rippin' and runnin' to be at your wife's side while she was goin' down. You took it too far Al. Now she's gone. I don't want it. I'm not like her. I ain't got it in me. I won't tolerate being single in a marriage. No way! Question my relationship with Carla. How dare you! I was more of her friend to her than you could ever be. I've earned the right to say how I feel. At least she could talk to me. I was there."

"I was doing God's work. You don't know what you're talking about Connie. Shut it down right now."

"I ain't her. Keep up. The season is changing. You still don't recognize it. I'm no longer there. Don't you EVER speak that way to me again Al. I am not your child. I am your woman. I want respect. Just like you do. See, you're so caught up in yesterday, you probably still think you're dealing with Carla. But, I ain't her."

"Don't blame me Carla for your shortcomings. And don't fault me for being who I've been all along. Catch up Connie."

"You know what Al? I am caught up. You're the one with the cave man mentality."

"Meaning?"

"I admit, I may have let this thing ride out a little too long. But it's a new day and change has to come in order for us to move forward from this point. What worked for me at the beginning of this, ain't workin' for me no more."

"I see your lips movin' but, I still don't hear anything."

"I'm telling you, that you staying you only benefits you. A relationship is a two way street. When are you going to start to care about what benefits me? What benefits us? How long am I supposed to go on like this?"

"You talkin like I don't love you."

"Sometimes I wonder." she snaps.

He covered his mouth in frustration, "Ok. Just tell me what you want from me. Whatchu want me to do?"

"Kiss me."

"Kiss you? All of this over a kiss. Woman! I kiss you all of the time. What do you mean?"

"I want you to touch me Al."

"I do..."

"You never kiss me on the lips. All of these years. You've never stared into my eyes; caressed my body. We hardly ever leave this house. I feel like your dirty, little secret."

"Where is all this coming from? Huh? And just how much of that am I supposed to take?"

She walked up beside him. She whispered in his ear. Her tears dropped on his shoulder, "Al, am I your dirty little secret? Am I just a seat filler since Carla's been gone? Are you holding on to her when you're holding me?"

"Oh now you're just making thing up. Here…" he grabs her hand. "Let's have a seat. I'll get you some water. You need some fresh air? I'll open the window, hold on."

"You wait just a minute now. I ain't damn crazy. You the one seein' dead people. Not me. I will have you know I am of complete sound mind. How dare you Al Golden."

"Whoa! Whoa! Honey, you got this whole thing wrong."

"Oh you think so Al?"

"I know so."

She lit up a cigarette. Takes a deep pull and blows the smoke in his face, "Bullshit!"

She began to strip off her clothing, "Look at me."

He turned his head.

"Touch me." She places his hand on her breast. He drew his hand back like he was touching a hot diamond in a back alley in the shadiest part of town at two in the morning.

"Look at me!" she demanded. He obliges her. He could not help but notice how youthful and taught her skin was. His mouth began to water. Connie Debril was completely flawless. He takes a deep breath. He scans her body unaffected. At her age, her body had seen its days. She had been pawed, ravaged and rummaged through like the polyester inspection rejected irregular cut $1 panty bin at the local store. Yet, she was still tight and desirable. Tears flowed from her eyes but, he could only think of Carla. He dared not compare. Nor did he comment. It was apples to oranges.

She had a better body than Carla had even in her younger days. It was as if Connie hadn't aged. Al knew the game, he knew Connie would never have a problem pleasing him. But he respected himself, her and his calling too much to even touch her in a sexual way before then. They had been friends too long. He loved Connie in his own way. The season had passed where Bible study, casual conversation, a quick meal and a stolen flirtation in the shadows in the wee hours of the morning would do. That had ceased to be enough for her. Al, held her hips as she stand before him nude as a playboy centerfold; just as beautiful. He could not bring himself to desire her past being fascinated with how sexy she was. His mind always shifted to Carla.

Connie's form rivaled Liza's. She was a sub fuscous grenade in her own right. Al periodically watched Connie shower. A romantic ritual he would perform frequently with Carla. Though he had watched Connie bathe like Bathsheba on the roof, drooling with anticipation, contemplating possibility, his mind always recalled Carla's form, flawed as it were, she would always appear absolute to him. A greatest attributes remained hidden from the naked eye; within her. A place where only he and The Lord had been allowed to venture. That well of profoundness and attention had meant more to him than the fleeting outer beauty of any woman who had ever caught his eye for even the most trace amount of time. He knew, as it was with Connie, he could very easily lay with them. But living with them would be a whole other situation. "You think you can handle me. But can you?' he imagined, "You can't." They would be a mere tease. A snack, to a man of his magnitude. A man like Al Golden, he had left junk food behind long ago. He, even as a young man, had developed the taste for not only satisfactory nutriment, but furthermore nourishing. He dined with purpose in mind.

 Radiant as they may have been, those tempting trinkets would never be able to sustain his interest with their immediate beauty. Carla captured his heart and mind; she kept him fed and as curious as a new born kitten with her end of rainbow thoughts. He was always curious to know what she was thinking even if he didn't understand how she had arrived at the conclusion of her thoughts. Her mind wasn't average. That made the body attached to that mind even more of a treasure trove. Carla Marie Golden was quite the acquisition. Al had experienced quantity as a young, accomplished, virile hustler. Carla had been the first woman whose body he didn't want to conquer as much as he had her mind. The appeal of the chase beyond physical attraction would be that he would never be able to completely figure her out. She couldn't even figure herself out. She had been an explosion of wealth. She was the gift that kept on giving. His dearly departed complement had enriched his life. She was his quality. Her body didn't have to be perfect. Her mind and spirit were equally close and of higher value. "No more fast food. I'll wait until I get home." He reflected on the endless choice of elite figures he had passed up over the years. Although it hadn't always been easy, it had always been worth it.

After giving birth so many times back to back, he still saw her as a sexual creature, even in her times of insecurity. He admired her body. Even in the pulpit, a glimpse of Carla's thick calves and ample cleavage would cause him to sweat and fantasize to the point of him stuttering his way through several sermons time after time. She would often take the boys, leave church before him, race home to prepare a Sunday meal for her family and a raunchy romp with her husband. The boys never understood why beyond having to get up early for school the next morning, they would have to retire so early. "Mommy and daddy need some play time." Al would say.

"Babe!"

"What?"

"You can't tell them that. They're just children."

"Carla, they don't know what I'm talkin' about. You worry too much. They gonna grow up one day. They'll be men. They'll know what I'm talkin' about. Can't keep 'em babies forever. They're little men." he'd tease. Making her upset made for better lovemaking in his book.

The Goldens were devoted to keeping their private lives interesting. They had counseled many couples who had grown complacent in their marriage; they had driven themselves to boredom. They were unfulfilled. That led to them seeking pleasure in other parties. Mistakenly, they had believed that being Christian and leading a lifestyle of morality and salvation meant their intimate moments had to be pitch and drab. The Golden laughed at such notion. They loved pillow talk and games. Games like hide and go-seek.

She made it a point to be at an undisclosed location. She played games with him. Carla drove her husband crazy with desire and a little jealousy. She wanted his mind to wander. It was game they enjoyed playing. Carla wanted to keep his interest while they were still youthful and had the energy to expend lavishly. She was exciting. Carla was creative. He would always chase Carla Golden. Sometimes it had everything to do with her mind, her spirit. Most of the time, he was a boy, doing what boys do, chasing her body. They had never stopped being hot for one another.

So often on those evenings he would race home, she would be waiting in the shower. He would pull the shower curtain back with the force of a superhero and have his way with her. Her body was his. She knew that every tradition duty she had performed within her marriage and family went against the very fiber of the modern women's movement. She cheered for independent women. She loved to see women educated, competing with men in the workplace, gainfully employed, opinionated and changing the world. Her calling though, was of another sort. Carla was very traditional in her ideas about marriage and family life; gender specific roles in the home. It was want she and Al had always wanted. They wanted the American dream for their family. Family stability and core values were constant priorities in the Golden household. They watched a lot of movies as a young couple. They wanted what the white people on the screen had. Or what it seemed they had. Later they would find that everything they thought it was to be a wholesome American; a white privileged person from a seemingly good home and neighborhood where advantage and opportunity was a fresh and ripe for the plucking as the weeds in the front yard of their home in the ghetto, was just a fantasy. You never know people until you live with them or around them. The very people that everyone in the hood thought had it all, either had the same problems on a different level or they were struggling with issues underprivileged people should very well be glad they know nothing about. They learned quickly that the old adage that all that glitters ain't gold is true to the core. Beyond that, the traditional family dynamic had been the most appealing to the ones that had grown up deprived of the stability and structure of that foundation. In life what we get later, after a prolonged season of longing and lack can be a gift if we know how to handle it; the contention of our nightmares can birth the connection on that is our dream if we view it properly. If we don't take for granted what others who have been spoiled by the soiled do, those spoils become such fruit to be savored. The Goldens were living their dreams. Those dreams, a do all dreams, came with a cost.

The chasing, the longing and often the time spent apart, kept the fire burning in their marriage. They rarely argued but when they did, even that ignited passion within them for one another. They used a lot of the rough times to keep them connected. They used the hard issues to keep them fighting for something when their marriage was in a lull.

Scanning Connie's body, Al continued to reminisce on Carla's imperfect form. Minutes turned into moments. Her slightly sagging breasts were beautiful to him. His wife had nourished all of his children with the milk from her bosom. The stretch marks that graced her waist and thighs that in her most confident of days, she wore like a badge of honor.

She was not only surprisingly intellectual, spiritually deep, attentive, functional and nurturing; she was wise. Carla spent a lot of time with the Lord. She was filled with the Holy Spirit. She was overflowing with compassion and insight. He was largely, attracted to that. His wife was a woman with many layers. She kept him in awe. She was his useful in every way. His helpmeet in every sense of the word.

Over the years, she had developed the ability to console many women who could not conceive whose husbands had impregnated other women. She had an uncanny, instinctive dexterity to weed out truth. She knew that some of the men hadn't forsaken their wives totally out of lack of respect. Nor not out of lack of love for their wives; out of sheer frustration, pain. Their fragile male egos needed that confirmation of manhood, control, dominance, power. They wanted the assurance of a tomorrow through their seed.

She had explained to the wives that it was a basic male instinct to impregnate a female. Didn't always matter who, as long as she could receive, conceive and he had perceived her able to carry his seed to term bringing his vision to fruition. For some, it was as simple as a confirmation of their manhood. It was a statement of arrival beyond going through puberty, having sex, making money, etc. For many men, it was part of being successful. There had been instances where the husband had even abandoned his barren wife in favor of the pregnant mistress. An emotional bond had formed via a physical act by way of frustration and a previous failure to launch. She had seen marriages destroyed for lack of fruit bearing. Wives that blamed husbands. Husbands that blamed wives. Neither to blame. Only the strong survived the breakdowns; temporary break-ups. Only those deeply rooted in the love of Christ knew the secret of success in a physically fruitless marriage was holding on pass the disappointment; the agony of silence, tear filled nights; beyond the jealousy, envy, questions, concerns.

Above individually shaking their fists at one another, collectively shaking their fists at God. Those couples held on to their faith. They had to make the decision to let go of what they could not understand. They pushed pass yesterday, enduring today, they built a bridge of strength in their relationship for tomorrow. What had not killed, scared them, leaving them a memento for the next battle; reminding that they can conquer if they fought together. "Two can chase ten thousand y'all. It gets better if you go through it together. When you got married, you enter a contract of agreement. Don't break the contract. The penalty fee is high." She warned. "There is always power in agreement. Marriage truly is survival of the fittest. It's a jungle out there with so much to overcome. Obstacle, temptations, heartache, interference; setbacks, high expectations and hard let downs. Enemies, snags, traps, difficulties and differences. Hmmm..." she thought. "Who can avoid 'em? No one. Who can overcome them? Anyone. Anyone that is willing to do the hard work and endure the process. The ones who use those challenges to strengthen them. Troubles come to expose our weaknesses. View hard times as opportunities to grow together. Only the strong will survive. Long term love ain't as glamorous as TV and love songs make it seem. We will be tested."

She wished she could post a flashing billboard that could be read all over the world that read:

"WARNING! DON'T LET THE WEDDING DAY/NIGHT FOOL YOU! THAT IGNORANT BLISS LASTS BUT 24 HOURS. THE REAL WORK BEGINS WHEN THE PARTY IS OVER AND EVERYBODY GOES HOME. MARRIAGE TAKES WORK. THE WEDDING IS A FEW FLEETING CELEBRATORY MOMENTS. THE MARRIAGE CAN LAST A LIFETIME IF YOU'RE IN IT FOR THE RIGHT REASONS. IF YOU'RE NOT A FIGHTER, MARRIAGE IS NOT FOR YOU. LOVE IS NOT ABOUT HOW WE FEEL. FEELINGS CHANGE. PEOPLE CHANGE. LOVE IS CONSISTENT

IN THE FACE OF ADVERSITY. LOVE ENDURES, HOPES, BELIEVES ALL THINGS. FEELINGS DON'T. LOVE ONLY CHANGES IN ORDER TO MAKE ROOM FOR GROWTH. IT BLOSSOMS. IT BLOOMS. NOT UNDER THE BEST CONDITIONS. BUT, AGAINST ALL ODDS, FACING THE ELEMENTS, THROUGH UPS, DOWNS. DIFFERENT SEASONS…IT GROWS IN DIRT. THE LOVE SEED IS PLANTED IN DIRT. IF IT IS ROOTED IN GOOD, FERTILE SOIL. IT WILL SURVIVE AND GROW DEEP ROOTS. BUILD YOUR HOUSES ON THE ROCK CHILDREN. IF YOU DO, NO MATTER WHAT, YOUR HOUSE WILL STAND. MARRIAGE, LIKE MINISTRY, IS NOT FOR THE FAINT OF HEART. PROCEED WITH CAUTION. DON'T JUST ENTER IN FOR LOVE…EASE IN FOR PURPOSE. ON PURPOSE. WITH PURPOSE. LET THAT DRIVE YOU CLOSER TOGETHER WHEN THE WORLD COMES TO TRY TO TEAR YOU APART." Carla was very serious about marriage and family. They were her ministry.

People began to speculate as to how she could counsel people so broken when she hadn't had their experiences. Secret was, Carla and Al had lost a few children along the way in between having successful pregnancies. Beyond those setbacks that tested their marriage in the early years, God had blessed her to be fertile. Not just with any man, a man she was in love with. A man that was in love with her.

He thought about how her thighs rubbed together. How it annoyed her. He loved her just the way she was. She had developed a small pouch as she aged. She tried to hide it. Al enjoyed it so. Her body wasn't perfect. Their marriage wasn't perfect. But they seemed satisfied on the surface and beyond that when the seasons allowed. He knew he was part of the reason her body had changed. After all, he was the father of her offspring, he didn't have to grow to love or accept her physical changes; he was the cause of them. He admired women who had given birth. For all of the strength and physical attributes of men, they would never be able to bring a life into this world. He was fascinated with her selflessness. She sacrificed so much to give him a family. She had given so much. He could not be who he was without her being who she was. Sacrificing her time and giving her precious God-given resources was one thing, but sacrificing her body, continuously to provide for him an army; a few good men almost brought a tear to his eye. Her sacrificing her own dreams to ensure he lived his, made question his calling.

Connie wiped her eyes, "When you gon' let her go Al? I can't be her. I can't replace her. I deserve more of you. I've been here the whole time. Somethin gotta give. Or else I gotta let go. We too grown for this. I want a real relationship. I want to be wanted. I've been having sex all of my life. Al I want to make love. I need it. I need a man that can give me that. I'm the reason you even had Carla. I was always there. It's been me Al. It's always been me. Before Carla there was me. We were friends first. You chose her. But I have ALWAYS been there Al." Connie could no longer hide her envy of their relationship. Secretly though she was a close friend of Carla's, Al was right. She had a slow burning jealousy. Along with a long-standing desire for Carla's husband.

Carla was an observant woman. Still she never voiced a concerned though she had exercised much caution concerning any time, be it brief or extended her husband and Connie spent together. She watched with the eye of an eagle gracefully. Internally, she knew Al had never been attracted to Connie. That obvious never stopped a woman like Connie from trying. Carla sometimes referred to Connie as a 'lesser' woman. It wasn't because of who Connie was or what she did. It was because of how she had done things. It was a less than loving charge; Al's beloved wife, did not always feel loving. She was human like everybody else. Like everybody else, sometimes her flesh rose up and got the best of her. Connie figured she was being respectful; careful as she waited in the wings licking her chops. She held some affection for Carla. After all, she had known her most of her life. But, her lifestyle and mindset superseded her reasoning many a time. Carla took mental note. She was no fool. She was aware. She would not be moved. They both knew silence was golden. Carla knew Connie had yet to renew her mind. Knowing Connie had not been transformed, she just kept praying for her. Carla loved Connie past her flaws.

Carla appreciated the realness that came with Connie. She knew many women in ministry but they all seemed to be wrapped up in the pomp and circumstance of title, privilege and religious practice. Carla was content to be without title. Equal to everyone else. She was a servant. Equal or even less than those she served. She thought it important to esteem others higher than herself. To Carla Golden, that is was service was. It was a mere bending down. Washing of the feet. Everyone's feet.

She liked to be with everyday people. People with nothing to risk, hide; nothing to lose in being who they were. Living out their stories. One day at a time. Imperfect, sometimes insecure, flawed people just like her. That is what Connie represented...the realness of the street.

Connie had issues. "Who doesn't?", Carla would reason. Connie was the one she could take off her bra and shoes with. Carla could let down her 4b hair and let it all just hang out when she was with Connie. That's what she valued the most in the twisted friendship. Connie had not grown in leaps and bounds as did Mr. and Mrs. Golden. But, Carla hadn't altogether viewed that as a reason to totally end the relationship. She just didn't believe in abandoning people who didn't have a shoulder to lean on. The Goldens advanced yet, the complex relationship between the two women who had grown up in the world's oldest profession hadn't evolved. Everything in conjunction with the Goldens grew, bore fruit and prospered. All but Connie; She grew at a snail's pace for reasons only The Lord knows.

Carla knew she personally had not reached her full potential spiritually because of her loyalty to Connie. The one thing that held her back. The one thing Carla had left behind although she had not altogether let go of it. The opposition within her also made way for many opportunities. That's what made them such great leaders and servants. The Goldens ventured into neighborhoods and places within hearts and souls of society's rejected that most of the many people who bragged about how they give back to their communities would not dare enter. They understood the people they were serving. The community loved them for it. If God could make a difference in the Goldens lives, then surely there would be hope for them. The Goldens were walking testimonies. What onlookers did not know was that anointing, that elevation, it all came with a price. It required major sacrifice; discipline, self-control. It was a lonely journey. Even being in a fruitful, loving marriage did not exempt the wife of an up and coming Pastor in high demand from lonely nights. For however glamorous it looked from outside the bubble, it had been far from on the inside.

It had annoyed Carla to think of how fascinated other women had become with her life. She knew the truth. Being married to a leader wasn't easy. Ignorant eyes looked on with eager desire. Mounting up ideals. Layering fantasies about how luscious the life of the spouse of a spiritual leader must be. Glassy-eyed, bushy-tailed, green young girls; they refused to let go of their preconceived notions of what that life is all about. They saw reward, not responsibility. They saw accolade not aggravation.

What of the late nights at endless conferences when your children are cranky from lack of proper sleep; your feet hurt; PMS is alive and well? Smile through the hormonal storm, keeping your natural cycle of monthly mood swing under control. The times when you just don't want to be bothered. Sitting through a long, drawn out, boring sermon and trying not to let the congregation and all of your husband's constituents see you go into a nod. Be attentive at all costs! "Wake up girl. Remember you're the First Lady. Represent your husband well. Church etiquette. Their watching you. Up, up, up!" she flouted. "Take notes for the networking sure to take place right after the benediction."

Shaking hands, kissing babies like a politician running for office. The endless luncheons, breaking bread gracefully with people you wouldn't otherwise socialize with outside of that realm. These were guidelines for spouses of leaders; Spiritual and otherwise. Keeping every aspect of life in the public eye polished, politically corrected and compartmentalized. She had become a top notch professional at balancing the acts.

Smiling pass the tears when your husband has a kind and encouraging word for everyone except the people in his own home. Sharing your spouse with the world. Being in the spotlight all of the time. Being super woman when all you want to do sometimes is be human. Dot the I's cross, your T's. You're the Jackie O of your community. Being held to a standard you didn't ask for. Be flexible. Be sweet. Be approachable but just out of reach.

Adjust. Adapt to different mindsets, personalities, surroundings, opinions, ideals, lifestyles. She and Al both learned very quickly that if they would ever see the vision God had given them come to fruition, they would have to roll with the punches. While she was young, she had the energy to serve the community while police growing group of hormonal, rambunctious boys. Over time though, jumping from church to church had begun to wear on her. The hustle and bustle of multi-tasking, once a thrill, she no longer found increasingly rewarding. Even in her weariness, she forged on though. Carla was dedicated to God along with the calling to serve. We are all called to serve just at different capacities. Just like the master in the Bible who delved out the number of talents he felt each servant could handle, so the Lord does with His children. What had been a love for so long began to feel more like labor. What made it worse was that husband that seemed to be so attentive to her to the naked eye, the eyes with limited view; that same husband didn't see how it was all washing her away like a structure being worn away piece by piece by the crashing waves of the relentless seas.

Hurled into a world you know nothing of. Sitting amongst the elite of the spiritual community relying on The Lord for confidence, the Holy Spirit for guidance. She made it a point to pray for God's wisdom daily as she never wanted to say a word The Lord had not licensed her to utter. Especially around such knowledgeable people. Even in advising the masses; namely young women. Sister Carla Golden walked a tight rope as it wasn't always easy to not just say how you really felt. To execute self- control. She had never been a brash woman in the style of Connie Debril. It was wonder to those who had known them from their former days that they had become friends. In many aspects, they were opposing forces. In closer times, even in Carla's final days, they had always nestled cradled in one another's strengths. They tried not to judge each other's weaknesses.

Surrounded by women who grew up in church that were groomed like British royals by the best etiquette coaches (Their mothers who desired to live vicariously through them), to be successors of the spouses of the leaders that sat on the spiritual thrones of the mega churches. "Girl if you don't pull that skirt down and sit up straight Imma...Lord help me. You know that's the pastor's son. He'll be lookin' for a wife in a few years now. Don't you want to be up there? Then get it together. And learn that Bible like you know all that mess you be boppin' round the house to! He won't have you if you don't know the word and you don't keep yourself pretty. That's all you have to do. Now sit yourself up!" She had heard it time and time again. She felt bad for the young men in the churches. "They have no Idea."

Carla wasn't as well versed in scripture as the other young women. She didn't know a salad fork from a desert fork. She was from the street. No stage mother. No manager. No etiquette coach. Not even a eunuch sent by the king to groom her for where she was going. No Ruth to train her.

No one voted her into this office. No one came to prepare her for her station. There had been no morning briefings. There would be no lunchtime updates by assistants and handlers to keep her abreast of church politics and power moves. Unlike so many of the others, she wasn't the daughter of Pastor So and So. She held no religious pedigree. Nevertheless, she was highly favored by God. Though it was a well-documented fact that Carla Golden had not risen up through the traditional church cultural ranks, she was undeniably highly-favored by The Lord. He had chosen her. God had always been on her side. Even amongst the spiritual elite ad educated, her anointing carried her farther than those who had invested so much time, money and effort in what they thought they knew. Self-doubt and downright mean church folk, had allowed her to believe she always stuck out as did a sore thumb for all of the wrong reasons. She wasn't like the more seasoned, trained wives. Lord, what am I doin here? I don't fit in with these people." She'd pray. "Strength training. I am with you." he'd whisper.

Carla had experienced a level of discomfort in the beginning, nevertheless, she used what she saw in those falsely delicate ladies to shape just who she was destined to become. Each moment, bitter and sweet, a teachable one. From the lot the ingénue cultivated courage under fire. Strength under duress. Dignity in the face of tragedy, uncontrollable circumstances, devastating loss. Poise beneath the weight of public pressure. "Chew up the meat. Spit out the bone." She rehearsed in the mirror before every gathering. The strength training had served her well.

 She observed. Where she saw ugliness she reserved judgment and remained humble. Sister Carla Golden learned poise, refinement...what real inner beauty was, where it came from, through admiring those women from afar. Whatever The Lord had placed within her, she grew to believe, that He placed her smack dab in the middle of the people she felt least in tune with, to draw out her what had been there all along. It was exactly what they had. She didn't particularly want it. Not if it was going to cause her to wax calloused, antiquated and religious. If it was going to transform her into a replica of who they were, she wanted out. That was too far out of her zone. Yet, Carla humbled herself even further. She was wise enough to know she needed it to get where God was taking her and Al, the family, the ministry. It was all a stepping stone. "Meat bone. Meat bone."

To complete the mission, she would have to be transformed beginning with her mind. She had to see things differently. Carla knew she had to change the way she saw herself. She, was no less regal than they were. Although she may not have appeared to be much on the outside, from within the light she was as a Christian shone more brightly than any other in the room. She was in a new environment. A new world. So much she wasn't used to. The green novice. Aware that, God cannot fail, the understudy readied herself for the challenge that was stepping far outside of her comfort zone. The challenge of believing that truth be told she did not look or speak the part, she had been born to play born for the part. Hand-picked by the Master for such a time as this. The God of all creation had placed within her everything she needed to get the job done. Every step from start to finish would be a faith walk. Carla's complete confidence was in God alone not her husband, not herself or the opinions of others. "If they're talking about me, the enemy must be mad. I must be a threat. Hmm…" A fresh perspective.

God had allowed the very things that had made her most uncomfortable to shape her into who she was to become. Who she already was in His eyes. Exactly who He had created her to be. All of her life experiences were lining up to guide young Carla into destiny. Just like she watched those women. Soon young women would be watching her. The way she carried herself, the way she dressed. The way she spoke or didn't speak, spoke volumes. She was a leader. She had a plate full of responsibility. As she often felt overwhelmed to the point of giving up/breaking, it would always be in those dark moments that The Lord would send someone in, out of nowhere to encourage her. Someone to remind her of her impact, her purpose. A stranger to thank her for the good work she had been doing.

A budding soul, listening to her testimony after testimony, would come up to her with a tear stained, painted on face, hug her and say, "I just love you. Thank you for not being ashamed of your past. I can't believe you stood up and told your story. You're a living legend out here in these streets. I can't believe where you came from. Don't seem like…"

"Like what sister?"

"I mean like you was out there like that."

Wiping the girl's tears she assured her, "I was. Yes I was. But that was yesterday. Today is a new day. And God got a new day for you too. You ain't come here tonight by mistake. You were led here to receive hope not just for today, for your tomorrow as well. God has great plans for you sister."

"Listen to your words Sister Carla. You're strong and inspiring."

"Honey I'm under constant construction like everybody else. Those are not my words to you. My opinion is worthless. Those little sister, are God's promises to you. He keeps His promises. Speaking of words. Your words have moved me tonight girl. Believe it or not, I need encouragement too. We'll keep one another in payer right?"

"Definitely Sister Carla. I just love you!" the young girl squealed with excitement.

"Would you believe me if I told you I love you more? God loves you most? Ain't no greater love." she smiled.

"I believe you."

"I know you do. Never forget it don't matter what people think. I know they tease you about your past. If they can't get past your past, then leave them where?"

"In my past?"

"Exactly."

"Thank you so much Sister Carla. You're just everything"

"No sister, thank you. And only God is everything."

Humble yet, strong. Unlearned yet knowledgeable. She was a spiritual quiet storm. Carla Golden had become the prized pig at the state fair much to her chagrin. She delighted in The Lord. Not so much in what came with the level of service her family had been called to provide. For all of the new levels there were new devils. She, over time had become wise enough to know: Nobody has it all. And if you even got close enough to think about having it all, the enemy would surely send something your way that threatened to turn your dream into a nightmare. There would always be doubts, naysayers, insecurities and the enemy himself to fight. Sometimes that enemy lied within you. Other times, he'd use the very ones you thought would never betray to try to tear down everything God had used you to build up. Nobody was exempt from life. Not even the leaders at the top of the food chain. "We gain something, we lose another thing. Sacrifice isn't called sacrifice because it is easy." Yes. They wanted to be Carla Golden. She snickered, "They have no idea."
Carla knew that quite often the things we want so desperately aren't always the things God wants for us. "Lord if they only knew." wobbling her head.

 They had no idea of how it felt to be the backbone of the man with the plan, watching other women subtly do subliminal belly dances around the pulpit in efforts to gain his attention while you're sitting right next to him. Knowing he probably isn't paying attention, wondering if he ever may bite in a moment of weakness, when things at home ain't so sweet....after all, he's still a man. They didn't understand how sexy might get his attention temporarily...it wouldn't keep his attention permanently. They had no substance. No girth. Nothing to offer beyond their beauty. It would take something far above the obvious to keep the interest of a spiritual man like Al Golden. They knew not the things that went through her mind. Surely, she was still a woman.

"Girl, if I had a man like that! Mmm...Should've kept that one for myself." Carla on occasion would catch Connie peering from the sidelines. She marveled at the way Al cared for Carla. They cared for one another. She was eager to serve him. He was eager to show his appreciation for her service and dedication in any way he could. Whether it be showering her with gifts or excessive public displays of affection especially where there were flocks of thirsty spiritual groupies lying in wait. His wife, being the dignified woman of God that she was, would not be moved unless movement was called for. The pastor's wife was too big for petty things. She had no time to play with the lesser women that constantly nipped at her heals. Everything the Goldens were about; the marriage, the ministry, was bigger than that. Carla Golden had an air of passivity that surrounded her. At least that was the general consensus. Those closest to her knew though, as much as she seemed to let minor offenses go over her head, she would not be outright disrespected.

Carla was still from the mean streets of Newark, lest anyone forget. Connie knew not to play her to close. When it came to her family, Carla Golden did not sleep nor should anyone sleep on her. Disrespect would not be tolerated. She had a formula for handling everything. She was far removed from resorting to physical violence. She knew how to hand your tail to you on a silver platter with a refreshing cup of 'Don't Get Me Started'. Always traveling the high road, Al Goldens spouse was the epitome of what a lady hood. With a certain level of refinement, she could tell you about yourself without so much as a profane word or a harsh demeaning tone. She did everything within her power to use her words to heal, build people up. She made every conscious effort to choose her words wisely even if she was thinking otherwise. Yet even in that, she failed to be perfect. Which did not bother her at all. Carla was at home in her limitations and humanity. She knew who she was.

"Girl," Carla smiled grabbing Connie's hand squeezing it firmly. "You couldn't handle a man like that. You have no idea. And honey you didn't keep him so let's just move forward shall we? I mean really, only a lesser woman would even allow such sinful words to fall from her lips, let alone enter her mind. More tea friend?"

Almost on cue, unaware, Al had come up behind Carla. He greeted her with depth of passion. "I love how you put this luncheon together. I know I don't always say it. I'm not always there. But I am proud of you. You're quite a woman." He brought tears to her eyes. "I couldn't be the best me without you baby. And it ain't easy on you. But I love you. Thanks babe." He handed her a huge bouquet of yellow, white, pink and red roses. Each color symbolized the different roles she played in his life.

She smiled as they ladies all around her, flushed with envy, rushed forward to get a look. "My dear, sweet husband y'all.", she gushed. "Y'all see y'all pastor got game right?"

"You know you love it!" bellowed an onlooker."

In the act of her flirtation, her husband's cheeks grew rosy. She played with his tie, "Yes I do. All of it." They all gathered around and laughed to Al's embarrassment. "Brothers you all need to be taking notes. Sisters, y'all better get y'all one of these. Just not this one. Oh wait! God only made one. And this ONE is mine." she stared at Connie with a grin.

Al placed his strong, manly hand around her thick, curvaceous waist. He spoke in a blush undertone, "You look beautiful tonight. Clean, crisp, classy."

She looked into his eyes, "Sexy?"

"Well I wouldn't say sexy." he teased.

Carla licked her lips, "What would say you then Pastor?"

"As a pastor, I feel it's my duty to only say what's true. Can you handle the truth young lady?"

"I can handle anything you throw at me Pastor."

"Is that right?" he breathed into her ear heavily.

She whimpered "Yes. You know I can."

Al looked around just as he gently pulled the back of her hair, "Okay then. Here it go. I think you look cheap. You look dirty. You look nasty." She shut her eyes in pleasure. She buried her face in the breast of his tuxedo. "You're filthy. I can tell. You need to get home. You need to strip. You need to take a hot soapy shower."

"Yes pastor. And then?" her heart raced with anticipation.

He bit her neck with force, "Then let then water cascade over your body. Wait there for your husband."

"Dripping wet?" she asked.

"Soaking wet young lady." He bit her neck once more with more intensity than before.

"Please stop. That hurts." she begged.

"It's supposed to. Did you like it?" The couple locked eyes as they become revived to where they were.

"Yes.", she sighed.

"Good. Now go home and do what I said." She rushed out to her car, flowers in hand.

On the drive home she reflected on their first night together. They were finally married. She had prayed to God that he make her feel like a virgin again. Like she had been but like never before. Initially she gave herself away because she felt she had no choice. She had to survive. Her body was her worth and only asset. She was new, for she had discovered Christ. Reading in God's word about how with Him nothing was impossible, she felt bold enough to ask The Lord to make her feel like a virgin to her new husband. She wanted every night, every time they lay and know one another; each time they connected to feel new to the both of them. She had tricks she had learned by way of her profession. Things she had heard Connie and The Queen speak of. Things other men had turned her on to that made their time alone with her more exciting; money well spent. But she wanted to wash all of that away. She wanted to be taught, trained and turned out by her husband. Doing things God's way, she vowed to leave it all behind. She wanted to please Al in a way that pleased him. She was turned on by the thought of being remolded into what fitted his fancy. She wanted to be everything for her new husband.

She thought about how she had casually mentioned to Connie their plans to elope. Connie tried whatever she might to put a damper on the wedding day. "You know you can't wear white don't you girl? You know being who you are and thangs. You know what I mean don't you? Doin' what we do the way we do."

"Listen, I am not my sin. I am not what I USED to do. I am free. I am a new creature. Child, Imma wear what I want cause I can. I really don't care what you or anybody thinks or says. What I ain't is what you still believe you are. I actually feel sorry for you that you're so stuck in yesterday. Now, if you will excuse me, I'm gonna wear a white dress, white panties...a bra is an option I don't have to explore right now so I won't. The girls is good. And just like that bra, I thank The Lord for this moment and where he brought me and Al from, because we don't need your support. When I do, I will come for it. Thank you." Carla politely pushed past Connie, leaving her stunned. She continued shopping as if the conversation had never happened.

"Girl you like this? Something different huh? I'm trying to do a sexy twist on conservative. You think this goes?"

Connie stood speechless.

"So now when I want your opinion cat gotcha tongue? That's great Connie." Carla continued shopping. "Let me get what I can get while I can get it. My man tryin' to get out the game." She looked at the cashier, "We're going to take all of this. We'll be paying in cash thank you. Oh yeah, you can gift wrap the panties."

God had answered her prayers. Even after all of the experiences she had had, she felt like a new woman, a new experience; an unexperienced experience to her new husband. He had known her past but that night and every night after that, it seemed to not even exist. Truly, the Lord had made everything new.

Connie watched with furious envy unseen. He networked until the carnality for his plump wife overcame him. Al hurried off into the night. Connie arrived home on the fumes of covetousness. She avoided Carla's phone calls for a week. Carla knew Connie wasn't a good friend. She felt guilt at times as the Lord had forewarned that she should distance herself from Connie. Their relationship had since, run its course yielding no purpose. Try as she might to distance herself from Connie, she felt an allegiance to her. Connie had no one else. Both would become increasingly lonely over the years. So from time to time, though there remained an unspoken begrudging, they confided in one another as necessary. It hurt too much to be alone.

Before the end of her days, Carla had all but given up on her relationship with God. Feeling as if she had been cheated out of her relationship with Al. A bitter root had sprung up. She attended church as she felt it was necessary to publically show her support of her husband's work in ministry. Behind closed doors, she became resistant to anything affiliated with ministry. She felt as if she had paid her dues; she owed God nothing more. He had taken more than his share. At the very least, The Lord had taken enough. Now, still young in her own right, he was taking her life. She had not the energy to fight. Contentious, from her heart she believed Connie and Al might have deserved one another.

"She can have him now. I'm done. If you think this is what you want. There's nothing more I can do to please him. I spent what little life I had trying to. I just came to realize the man don't love nothing more than he love serving God. He just can't. Nothing wrong with that. Maybe there's something wrong with me. Lord I know I'm selfish for askin...but what about me?" she looked on Al and Connie through fading eyes as she drifted in and out of consciousness. Connie consoled Al. He had neglected to return the favor.

He spent night after night bawling by Carla's bedside, pleading for her forgiveness. She could hear him, even in her subconscious state. She just couldn't respond. She opened her eyes one last time to see his face. Surrounded by her husband and her sons, she looked around at them all, "Look at y'all. Big boys. I'm proud of each and every one of you."

Al asked them for a private moment with the love of his life. "Carla? Baby I love you. I need you. I loved you from the first time I saw you. That never changed. It got stronger. I know I was too busy. But, I never stopped loving you. I just didn't know how to choose. I wish I could get some of that time back." He laid on her breasts, "I am so sorry." He burst into tears.

She sobbed, "That was your life Al. That was your calling. You always were an extremist. God first. God always. I just wished you could've squeezed in a little more time for me. I just didn't know your calling would require so much sacrifice. I can't say I was happy every day. But it was worth it to see all you've done for God's kingdom. Al, just look at all you've done. All that hard work. I'm proud. Al, I love you. I've asked God to forgive my selfish ways. Will you forgive me too?"

"Baby I couldn't have done anything if you had not been there. Another woman couldn't have done it. Another woman wouldn't have been strong enough to put up with my mess. A lesser woman, couldn't have survived sacrificing her husband; her life. You haven't done a thing but support me. You have a right to feel the way you feel. What am I supposed to do baby? Forgive you for being human? I can't…"

Carla grabbed his face with the little strength she had left, she kissed his snotty lips, and "We lay our lives down. Deny ourselves for Christ…just like He did for us. Deny ourselves. Pick up our cross, daily and walk. That's all. I made it about me. Babe it was never meant to be about me. Many are called, few chosen. WE were called and chosen. WE answered. Where in the word did it say serving was gonna be easy? He required obedience, not sacrifice. We did both Al.

  I blamed you for being human. You were just a man doing what God told you to do. You're faithful Al. You always kept your word to everybody. Even in the street. God knew He could trust you with his work. You was dedicated to Satan when you was in sin. You was dedicated to God in righteousness. That's why He called you. You're outstanding in every area. I'm glad I was along for the ride. What a ride it was baby. I just wish we had a lil more time to ride some more. Just you and me." With that, Carla Golden had taken her final breath. It was over.

All kinds of thoughts raced through Connie and Al's heads in the tick of what was taking place. Although, no more concede a thought except to say, "She introduced me to God." Al hummed.

"What?!" Connie pulled away from him in disbelief.

"Imma step into the kitchen. Cover up.", he insisted.

"But..."

"I'm not there anymore Connie. Seasons change. People change, remember."

Connie walked into the kitchen fully clothed yet, sullen. Al drew her close to him. "Now stop Connie. It's time to be a lady. I'm sorry for what I've done. I let things get away from me."

"WHAT KIND OF MAN ARE YOU?!"

"What?"

"You heard me! What kind of straight man can watch a naked woman soap up and not..."

"Don't challenge my manhood woman. Don't you ever in your life..."

"I don't understand how you can watch me shower my body. But you won't touch me. You never think about..."

"No. I mean yeah. I know I'm wrong. I mean, I try not to." He takes a deep breath, "It's complicated.
I want a meaningful relationship. I can get sex from anywhere. I'm trying to keep it respectful. At least I thought I was."

"That's respectful?"

"Don't start that nonsense Connie. You opened the door. I just came on in. I never touched you out of respect. You don't get it."

"Did ya ever stop to think that maybe I don't want your respect all of the time? Damn it Al! I want you to take me! Don't you get that? Your precious Carla did not always want you. Can't you see?"

"I don't believe that for one minute. And even if what you say is true, I don't blame her.", he sobbed.

Connie beat her chest. "Me! Me! I've always wanted you."

"I know Connie. I know. But for the wrong reasons. I don't want what you done gave every other man. It's deeper than that for me. We're too old for that mess Connie. Don't you want something deeper than sex at your age? Jesus!"

"Al I can't help how I feel."

Al shook his head in frustration, "Connie, you are old enough to know you can't believe your feelings. They don't have loyalty. Emotions will lead you astray. Emotions will mess you up.
If you ever gonna be my wife, you have to be more mature."

Debilitated from the back and forth, he sat down. He bowed his head mumbling, "This is so hard. God, I love her but it is so hard."

"Do you really love her?" the Lord asked knowing the answer. "Or is she just a seat filler?" He wasn't sure if he loved Connie for the right reasons. He knew he was not in love with her. She knew it too. They were both tolerating. Afraid to confess it. Scared to let go, neither of the two wanted to be alone.

Connie thought, "Am I in love or in love with the idea of being in love? Why do I want this man? He's still in love with a dead woman. I could never compete with her. She's been dead for a long time and I still can't compete. Maybe she was right. Maybe I really am a lesser woman. Who am I to think I could ever be a pastor's wife? Can I even handle this man? We ain't even cut from the same cloth. I thought

I could love the man past friendship. I thought if I ever got my hands on him…how we would be. Reality ain't nothin' close to my fantasies. He holdin' on to her and I'm holdin' on to him. This can't be real love."

All of their lives she had let her malevolence towards Carla eat away at her like a vicious, slowly progressive cancer. She had been jealous of Carla's anointing. Something she would never have. Something she couldn't handle. Something she never was supposed to. Deny as she may. Try as she might. Connie would never be able to fill Carla's shoes. She didn't have to. However, she could not understand that. She continually withered, holding on to something that was never meant to be her own; Carla's entire life.

"Al I thought about it, and I forgive you for everything. I understand. Will you forgive?"

"That goes without saying. When you've been a certain way so long, it's hard to let that go. Change isn't always easy, especially the older we get. Just because one way is all we know, don't mean we can't know another way. God said He would do a new thing." He beamed. He picked up his glass of vodka to take a sip. He heard the voice of the Lord say, "This is ain't it. Put the glass down. Go home." Al knew he had heard from God. He was shaken. He remained silent.

Connie, overjoyed, ran around the kitchen table singing, "I'm getting married!!!!" He remained frozen.

Concerned about his catatonic state, she pumped him, "Well Al, Imma be ya first lady. You not happy?"

Al picked up his keys. Entranced, he walked to the door. Before he opened it he spoke in a flat tone, "You still don't get it. You don't get me. I don't want a first lady. I want a lady. I want a wife. I need companionship. You got issues Connie. Issues I'm not sure I even qualify to help you with. I don't have the energy. I gotta go. Have a goodnight."

She opens the door, "You got some nerve! And you don't?"

"Oh sure I do. But they don't run as deep as yours do." Al stumbled down the front staircase bewildered.

That night, around the corner from her house, he sat in his car for hours just staring at the moon. All kinds of thoughts running through his mind. He just couldn't bring himself to move. He was spent beyond his limit. He contemplated, "How is it I can counsel the world yet, I can't help myself. Lord have mercy! I can't even encourage myself." He prayed, "Father, I am broken. This time, I think I'm beyond repair. If you don't help me, I'm done. Lord I'm spiraling. I don't have it all figured out. I'm carrying guilt I shouldn't carry. I'm frustrated. I'm angry. I'm lonely. I'm bitter. I'm resentful. I'm beginning to hate ministry. I just realized I been playing games with this woman. I don't even want her."

"I'm here for you son." God said. "I am with you."

"With me? How can you be with me? Huh? I AM ANGRY WITH YOU!"

"And that's okay son."

"Son! I'm glad you're alright with rejection. Of course you are! YOU'RE GOD!" Al rolled down his window. He breathed studying the dark sky, "My son, who I'd give my life for, tonight if I had to, is rejecting me. Lord, I can't take it. I'm so lost. God, you've taken everything from me."

"Son, I've been waiting on you to call on me. I miss our conversations. I miss your honesty. I love you. I miss us. Where have you been?"

"I been frustrated....thinking I'm ok. Trying to handle my life on my own. My flesh. My spirit. The battle. The war. My mind. My heart. Why did you call me anyway?"

"Because I knew what I had placed inside of you. Even before the earth was formed, I knew you."

"What if I don't know me? I can spit scripture to anyone at any time in my sleep and not miss a beat concerning their situations, sometimes without them even uttering a word. And I know it ain't me. I respect that. I get that. Glory is yours. All glory Lord. I don't even want it. It's just...well."

"Go on son."

"Why am I goin' thru this right now? I am a pastor man!"

"You are human. There is a season for everything son. Cast your cares on me. I will take care of you. I love you. Rest."

"But I'm not perfect. I'm all in my flesh these days. All I seem to do is disappoint people and mess up."

"I never said you were perfect. I never told you that you were going to be. I don't call perfect people remember? I call available people Al. This thing is not about perfection pastor. It's all about grace. It is well within you to do just what I've called you to do the way I called you to do it." All of sudden, a warm feeling rushed over Al. Within minutes, he had fallen under a deep sleep. He wasn't in the most savory of neighborhoods but, God kept him all night long. No harm came near his dwelling. Crime had been occurring repeatedly all around him. But his God had kept him. God doesn't repay us according to our iniquities. The Lord is patient. He is slow to get angry.

At twilight, a police cruiser pulled alongside Al's vehicle. A passerby had reported seeing a body in a vehicle not knowing whether the person was dead or alive. A tap on the window, "Hey! Yo! Aye man, you aight?"

Al sat up abruptly, "Oh yeah. Yeah man. Sorry officer. Guess I fell asleep. Long night."

"Yeah well this ain't Florham Park or Livingston or none o' dat so you shouldn't be out here after dark. Especially in a ride like this." the officer warns. He shone his flash light on Al's face, "I know you ain't out here wit' these knuckle heads hustlin'. You been drinkin'?" Al covered his face.

 "Let me see your license and registration."

"Aight. Let me get It.", Al agrees. "Don't panic. See…I got my hands up. Now I am slowly going to reach into my glove compartment…" A bible tumbles out.

"Man ain't nobody gon' shoot you. Just hurry up. And that Bible don't mean nothin'. So don't think that's gonna get you off. Don't nobody care about that."

He looked at his partner, "Jokers kill me ridin' around wit' a Bible." They both laughed. "Especially when they got it on the dashboard. Please! You a man like every other man. Kill me with dat. Whatchu a preacher?" they tease. "Probably out here tryin' get some."

"Excuse me young man? I beg to differ."

"You beg to differ? Man don't play me. This the stroll right here. As a matter of fact, don't that middle aged ho and her fine ass daughter live right here? Yo…you been up in there man?"

"Officer no disrespect but, please watch your language."

"Yo! This guy really playin' the Holy Roller role." the officers laugh. His partner chimes in, "That's funny. Well, we can have some fun while we run your plates. It's almost end of shift. So what should we call you? Bishop, father, minister…oh wait…wait…I got it…rev? Rev is it?" he smirks.

The first officer comes back with his head hangin' low, "Pastor."

"Ah yeah, that's rich. Pastor." his partner teases.

Al shakes his head. "No it's cool. I'm not caught up in titles. It's true but, just call me Brother Al. Better yet, just Al. No need for formalities. You're right, I'm just a man. It's cool."

"Damn right you just a man. And did I ask you to talk?" the officer asks.

"Hey man! Watch your mouth. He's tellin' the truth. How could I be so stupid? I knew he looked familiar. That's Al Golden. Pastor Al. Cut him man."

"Cut him? What you mean?"

"What I said Negro! Let him go!" the first officer warned his partner firmly. "Aw man, Mr. Golden! I mean Pastor...I mean Brother Al...I mean...Man I'm sorry."

Al smiles, "Young buck, don't apologize. Y'all just havin' some fun while y'all doin' your job. Ain't no sin. Gotta be stressful not knowing what you're walking into out here. It's ok. I was young once. Just don't be out here killin' our men. That's all I'm asking."

"We aln't out here trying to hurt nobody pastor. That ain't us. We were raised here. We know what it is. That's those other officers in other places. These are our people. We just out here tryin' to keep order and go home in one piece in the process. It's not easy being an officer. And we're not all killers. I became an officer to help, not to harm."

"Glad to hear it. That's what we need. More of our own patrolling our communities. Not fearful outsiders with biased eyes and information and low tolerance for the ills of the inner-city. We don't need nobody shooting for sport out here. We get enough of that with these ignorant gang bangers. All of this black genocide. We don't need no more senseless killings out here."

"We're aware of that sir. That's why we're here. I grew up being taught about my history at home. I'm trying to build up our community, not tear it down further. I don't just police, I educate the youth off the clock. It's a shame how we got here."

"Yeah. Our people have come so far in positive and negative ways. We need to educate our children. America did a number on us beginning with slavery."

"Yes sir. They still doin' big numbers on us. It's mental abuse. It's mental slavery. It's a cycle that never ends and nobody sees it and everybody's scared to talk about it."

"You know why young man?"

"Why pastor?"

"Because talking about exposes the ugly truths that some people don't want exposed. Talking about it raises the awareness of the oppressed. See it all goes back to education. They don't want us educated. They never wanted us to educate ourselves."

"Knowledge is power. So is agreement. They want us uneducated and separated. Divide and conquer. Old school tactics."

"Yes! And as a people, we still fall for it. It doesn't benefit the haves in America to have not empowered and informed. It's the slavery mentality beat down over and over again."

"Yeah. It's like if we find our identity and strength apart from the lies they've inundated us with for centuries, we rise to power, govern ourselves, maybe even them, and take over and make things right. Right?"

"Right. Our ignorance keeps the oppressor fed, fat and happy. Even mass incarceration is a business now."

The officer rang, "Oh it's a bigger business than the public knows to capture a bunch of black men. As soon as I heard they were gonna privatize, I knew what time it was."

"Yeah. There are people out here that will do anything, to keep blacks and other minorities, not just here, but all around the world, oppressed because it benefits their greed and selfishness. They like to cultivate prejudice amongst their own because it keeps the cycle going. Only hate wants to keep people divided. Love is all embracing. Love wants you educated, elevated, illuminated and free. Love wants your light to shine; it only wants your best even it means you surpass it. Darkness only wants your worst."

"Uh huh. It's like that Civil war. It's a shame that those people really were willing to die just to keep an entire race of people they stole from another land, down and bound. Too lazy to harvest your own crops and keep your own nasty house and bratty kids. Wow! And they say black people are lazy?! Who do they think built this country on their bloody backs and knees for centuries?"

"Yep! And we built the White House twice."

"Yeah. We were good enough to build it but they still didn't want us in it."

"Preach!"

"Oh pastor. I ain't the preacher." The young officer laughed.

"I'm not sure if I am either these days."

"Sure you are. Everybody knows you."

"They don't really know me. But okay."

"I know you. You're a good guy." Al winced.

"Yeah, how about them Giants?"

"The New York Giants? They more like grasshoppers these last few seasons. Talking about renewing a mind. Jeez they're horrible these days. It's sad."

"Couldn't be sadder." Al lamented.

The officer looked around, "You never told us what brought you over this way."

"I was visiting a friend. Fell asleep having a talk with God. That's all."

"Pastor. I mean Mr...."

Al interrupts aggravated, "Al is fine brother. Relax. God is no respecter of persons. By the way, that's what I'm doing' over here. God is everywhere. He's married to the backslider. A friend of sinners. You ever read Matthew chapter nine verses nine thru thirteen?"

"Aw Pastor, I mean Al, I ain't been to church in so long. My wife stay on me about it. My mama always preachin' at me..." he replied nervously.

"Well if that's your answer. I'm hip enough to discern a yay from a nay...either one woulda done. But I feel you brother. Take a look at the passage when you get a chance."

"I don't when I'm going to be at church again."

"Son," Al said. "Listen closely, you don't just study your Bible at church. More importantly, it's what you do when nobody's looking that matters to God. Some people come to church like it's an addiction or they got OCD bout it or something; all they life. Still ain't got no real relationship wit' Him. Still ain't no real growth or change from the inside out. No fruit, no nothin. Don't know Him! They just come out habit or to socialize. Funny thing is, they think they make the pastor happy or get brownie points with God by showing up. Tell ya what boys...ain't so. But guess what?"

"Preach pastor."

"That's all so many people know is routine. You know how many people come because they from another generation or even if they young...because that's what they were taught?"

"Wow.", they answered intrigued.

"People ain't teachin' 'em bout what a real relationship with Jesus about. They're just lacing them with religion. But wanna know the truth?" he asks.

"Yeah.", they said.

"Salvation ain't just a two-step into heaven. It's a tango. A romantic dance. A wooing. A love affair with God. Just like with your wife. It's a marriage. A covenant. A blood contract we sign when we accept Jesus into our hearts as our Lord and savior. It's a relationship with different seasons, ever evolving. And just like any other relationship, it has its ups and downs."

"Just like a real marriage." The first officer spoke.

"Just like a real marriage."

"It takes maintenance and a lot of forgiveness, patience, understanding, sacrifice, dedication, commitment, honesty, focus and work. Minute you start turning ya head and looking elsewhere 'cause you ain't satisfied, you bored... That's when you get into trouble."

"See young man. You got it in you. Preach! Funny thing about it is, a spouse ain't perfect. Only God is. Can't expect people to keep you happy and fulfill every need in your life. Happiness a choice. So is contentment."

"That's somethin'."

"It is. And it is so very real y'all. Just like our walk with God. That relationship is very real. We get out of it what we put into it. How bad do we want it? How much do we love Him? Love takes sacrifice. Love is sacrifice."

"That's real."

"And you won't always find love where you think it should be."

"What does that mean pastor?'

"I mean church folk are just folk. Some of them can be just as nasty and cold as the people on the street."

"Even more so. That's why I don't go."

"Well I can argue that. I know you don't get along with all of the officers in the precinct do you?"

"No."

"Okay then. Rodney King asked that infamous question that took the world by storm: 'Can't we all just get along?' The answer is no! We should as the body of Christ. Reality is though, we won't because we're all different. We can come together on one accord, worship corporately and sing in unison and not all gel. Why because we're human and we all have issues and we will never totally see things the same way. That is just natural. The Bible says: 'How can two walk together unless they agree? We can agree and just not like some things about one another; things that may never change because we're different people. Peter and Paul did not always like one another; they had opposing views; different personality types; different experience but the same agenda. There was friction, but they had the same agenda. Young man, don't let people keep you from fellowshipping. That's a poor excuse. You can come to serve and get what you need to get for your spirit and soul and go home. Just like you do for work or family gatherings. Where in the word did it say we would all just get along? All of the disciples did not just get along and they physically with Jesus daily. There was some jealousy. They were human. Yet, they shared the same agenda and goal. Like your work and family gatherings son. We're better together even if we don't always agree or like things about the other person. Like a marriage son. The body of Christ itself is a working relationship. We put our differences aside for the greater good."

"It's like all of these different denominations right?"

"Something like that. We all have different views about the word of God and we receive it all differently. He speaks to us all differently. He knows we are not the same. He created a diverse body with many functions. We can't all think the same. We're here to serve a diverse humanity. Respect people's right to be people. Let's judge less and move forward. We waste so much time on differences that we may be missing out on golden opportunities to reach and teach and more importantly to love."

"Where's the offering plate? Man!"

"Don't get excited son. We just men out here talkin'. I drove home those points because I believe we put too much emphasis on church and the negative things that come with a group of human beings attending that particular service or who associate themselves with the religious aspect of Christianity. We tend to forget that where people gather, there are sure to be differences. Walking with Christ does not ensure seamlessness. It in fact, guarantees friction. The enemy knows there is power in agreement and he will always make it his business to show up. Let the differences be a learning tool that drives you to a place of compassion and prayer for your fellow man. Not to the judgment seat reserved for Christ. Keep in mind, when many people speak of church, they're speaking in terms of the building and the gathering of a group of people in that setting. Church is more than that. The Church spoken of in the Biblical sense, refers to the Body of Christ. The people and their function in it that body; not the building. Remember the people of God are everywhere, just as God is everywhere; it ain't about just goin to church boys. Church is necessary for fellowship, strengthening, service, growth, edification." But, what happens the other six days when you ain't collected with the people? Huh? Gotta get fed right? So if you don't eat, sooner or later ya die. Now my point is, I don't want you think the only time you eat is on Sunday. Good as a nice, big, slow cooked, homemade meal is...and y'all some big boys so I know you can throw down, that ain't the only nourishment you need. You can't survive on one meal a week for the rest of your lives. God simply did not make us that way. We're human. We are fragile.

My son used play football. My wife and I raised a house full of boys. I know how big boys eat.   So I know one meal on a slow and easy Sunday, ain't gonna sustain you all week. No matter who you are what ya size....ya just gotta eat. Body require a certain amount of nourishment to survive. So does the spirit and the soul. Got it boys?"

"Yes sir." they replied.

"Well..." he said starting his car, "I'm not sure y'all got it. But Imma be prayin' one day y'all get it."
Al puts his car in gear, "Aye you Aretha's boy ain't cha?"
Referring to the first officer.

"Yes sir." he answered.

"Ya mama anointed. Filled with the Holy Ghost. She wise. Listen to her. And don't talk down to ya wife. She's your queen. I met her. Now I know y'all got problems. Going thru some financial issues but, y'all get thru it just fine if you stick it out, unite, pray and have faith the storm will pass. Because it will. Trust me. Boy you ain't gon' find no better woman. She ain't perfect. Ain't no perfect woman. But look at you, you ain't no perfect man. Keep your eyes on the prize and off these other women. Stay faithful. God will bless ya marriage. And stay away from him."

"Me?!" his partner yells.

"Yeah you! You single and lookin'. He already under strain in his marriage. He don't need no added pressure listenin' to talk of ya weekend escapades and trysts. Nothin but temptation he don't need. Devil got a trap set. Married man don't need no single friends. Trouble. Especially at a time like this. He's past that season. Listenin' to you gon' make him wanna dip back. Then he gon dip off. It all begins with a thought. And Marcus..."

"Sir?"

"You was talkin' good to me. Don't mess up boy. You know the right thing to do. I know ya wheels been turnin'. Don't do it! James chapter one, verse fifteen. Find it. Read it. Meditate on it. Don't turn from God's word to the left or the right. He promised to keep us in perfect peace if we keep our mind on Him. God must have sent y'all here at this time. He don't do or allow nothin' without reason. I gotta go boys. Marcus..."

"Sir?"

"Go home to ya wife. Come back to church. Tell your mother hello for me. Choose your friends wisely. Work on your relationships. Pray. And get a new partner. God loves you son. I love you. Think about it huh?"

"Yes sir."

"And you..."

"Sir?" says the partner.

"He loves you too. But if you ain't gon' encourage him right, leave him alone. If you his friend keep your private life to yourself. You welcome to come to church too. Lot of single women there. But don't just come for that. They're like daughters to me so be careful how you treat 'em. If you gon' mess over 'em and you ain't got no good plans for 'em. Leave 'em be. That's all I ask. God bless you young man. And don't be offended by my talk. That's just my way. Mean no harm."

"Sir I understand."

"Gentlemen, it's been real. I understand you all have a job to do but be good to the people while you're out here. Black need to be understood, and educated not assassinated." he pulls off slowly.

"Man I just thought about who that was." says the partner.

"Yeah I told you. Pastor...I mean Brother...I mean....MAN YOU KNOW WHAT I'M TRYIN' TO SAY! Everybody knows him. He good people. His whole family, the Goldens. He was always there for everybody."

"Man I was gonna say that's Boom's pop. Yeah he was always there for everybody. Good guy. It's like them Goldens can't do no wrong man."

"Yeah I know. It's crazy. They got the right name. I know ain't nobody perfect but, they sure close to it."

When Al got home he sat on the couch deep in thought.

"Son, why do you reason?" the Lord asked.

"Father, as far as you have brought me, as much as I know about you. As deep as I have delved into your infallible word, it even amazes me at this point that I still struggle with trust in some areas. My faith is not flawless." He covered his mouth, "If people only knew. I get scared too. Lord, I'm having a hard time trusting you. I am afraid. Never been here before. The in the meantime; in between time is the hardest time of them all. Lord the uncertainty."

"I know son. I know. Remember Jesus in the Garden of Gethsemane. Uncertainty, apprehension even fear is natural. But I'm here. I never promised you a certain season every season. What I did promise you is peace. I promised to be there. I am here. Hold on to me."

"Tryin'", he sighed. He fell into another deep sleep. This one prolonged.

"Oh boy." he moaned. The next morning the sun peeked in as if to sound the alarm. "Ok...I'm up. I'm up."

Today was a day he had been dreading. He had to eulogize the funeral of a beloved friend and church member. His beloved secretary Bonnie. Bonnie had been a trusted friend and confidant to him over the years. She was a treasure. A secret keeper. A surrogate mother. A dedicated, dutiful servant who had been there from the birth of the ministry until the Lord saw fit to call her home. While Al had presided over many home goings, being master of many ceremonies had almost become like second nature to him; this solemn occasion to him would be a labor. Not particularly of love. This time, he had for the first time in many years of ministry, requested another leader step in and perform his usual duties. He wanted to be the one to enlighten people on the one he loved like the mother he never had a real relationship, the one he called friend.

Al arrived at the church. Entering through front doors, he had taken everyone by surprise as he usually entered stage right by way of the Pastor's Quarters. Al was so weary of redundancy that he decided to do something different. Something different indeed! Everyone sat aghast as he bopped down the center aisle sullen. Cloaked in street garb, unshaven, emotional. The Pastor was broken. Disjointed, he arrived at the podium on cue. In amazement he starred out expecting to have a sea of mourners in plain view. Yet there appeared to be fewer than one hundred people in attendance. It was the most disrespectful sight he had beheld in years.

He scanned the room of scattered mourners. "This is it?" he choked. He looked at Deacon Finley as he shrugged his shoulders. "Deacon, how could this be it?" he stammered angrily.

"I don't know Brother Al. I don't understand it myself."

Al cleared his throat, "No matter. People that matter are here. All that matters."

He continued to survey the room scanning each face, nodding at each one in thanks. Tapping his foot he said, "Now this blessed creature gave so much of herself for others. She served everyone she met with equality and love. She wasn't just my secretary. When my wife wasn't available, she was my assistant. She wasn't just my assistant and she didn't only assist me here. Lord, she assisted everyone she came across that needed it, best she could. And this her home goin'? Lord help your children." He continued on, "Sweet Bonnie. The many knew she was going home and the few came to send her off. Well Jesus' boys couldn't even stay awake to watch and pray. Lord woman, you sleep and they didn't have to do anything but show up to pay respect. No watching. No praying. Just celebrating your Home going and they couldn't even do that. Lord bless 'em'."

Pacing the stage, his voice thundered, "Ahhhh but we fail Lord. Yes we do. Without fail we do fail. I stand here thinking about Bonnie. The many times I have failed. The many times she saw me fall, you know, out of from public view. She knew better than most that Al Golden was human. Yet she loved me anyway. I see y'all lookin' at me. And I'm not tryin' to make it about me but I," he stammered. "I couldn't help but hear the whispers when I passed y'all walking down the aisle. Wondering what happened to me? Am I alright? Well yeah..." he paused. "I'm alright. Life happened to me just like it happens to every one of y'all. And if you're young and it ain't happened...well, you just keep on living.

I'm here to celebrate the life of a friend. More than that. A PERSON WHO LOVED!" he screamed into the mic in a fractured accent. "SHE LOVED NOT JUST ME! SHE LOVED EVERYBODY! SHE WAS SINCERE! SHE LOVED LIKE SHE SERVED! ON PURPOSE! WITH PURPOSE AND EMPHASIS!"

Deacon Finley handed him a tissue. "I don't need no tissue man. Water brother."

He sipped from his cup, "I'm taking y'all somewhere. Just hold on. Y'all gon' walk wit' me today?" A few faint amens could be heard from the back of the sanctuary. "No man is an island. God himself said it is not good for man to be alone. Sometimes a brother just need somebody to walk wit' him. Will you share my grief on today church?"

Deacon Finley maundered, "Preach Pastor. I'm witchu."

A woman just below him wailed. "That's sister. Gone let it out. It's good to let it out. A vessel is only meant to contain but so much before it bursts."

The Pastor nodded and continued, "See she, Mrs. Bonnie, Sister B, Sister Alan, whatever moniker you please, she loved people just as they were. No matter what state she found them in, like our Lord and Savior, she looked past the outward appearance. Bonnie chose to see beneath the surface. It had nothing to do with gift. People called that her gift. Naw it wasn't. It was her choice. A choice we make less often than we should whether we'd care to admit it or not.

I came here today dressed to unimpress because this the way she saw me. Bonnie saw pass the title, responsibilities, sermons and things. She saw pass the ego. She chose to see me for who I am. She saw me at my worst behind closed doors when everybody else thought I was at my best. She had an eye to see through it all. Past the mask.

I had a strategy in coming here today dressed down. Y'all I woke up today wanting to do something different. Not particularly wanting to come here, to do this, on this day for the dearly departed, I decided not to wear the mask. I left it in the closet. Along with the cape and the boots and all of the superhero flash and flair. I wanted to come as Clark Kent today church not Superman." He starred down at Bonnie's face in the casket. "This is how she would have wanted to see me. Dressed down and relaxed. She said I didn't relax enough. She told me like it was. She was right as usual. She encouraged me to walk in my freedom and rest in my truth. I neglected her advice so many times over the years. Should've listened but, I didn't and well this is where it has gotten me. I encourage yo males out there to pay attention to the females in your life that you know love you and have your greatest interests at heart. Love don't have nothing to lose in telling you like it is. It takes nothing away from your manhood if you give ear to sound advice no matter who it comes from. Don't ever limit your growth potential by limiting who you learn from. Every living creature is a teacher whether they know it or not."

"Go on preach that thing son!" an elderly woman cried out.

"Wise woman. No pressure ever. When she walked into my office, whatever state she found me in, she didn't judge me. Times that I didn't wanna come out here and preach, she didn't ride my back about my calling, she just let me be. She and my wife was the only people that really knew me, they knew how and when to just let me be. So today in honor of her, the way she loved and served, I just decided to just be."

The worn man stepped down from to the pulpit, grasping the podium along the way. He held on for dear life. He breathed, "Thank you B. Thank you for letting me be weak. You allowed me to be tired. You gave me permission to be fragile. When I had no family out there in the streets before I knew God, he knew me and introduced me to you. Even then, you was a nice lady, you saw me doing things, and you kept quiet. One day you took me by the hand and told me God had a plan for me. You smiled and walked away, still letting me be. I didn't even think God knew who I was the way I grew up. But you assured me that I mattered to Him. He knew me. He saw me and he would change my life. Even after all of the women and the drug dealin'. You was right. He used you to plant the seed. Carla water it and He was faithful to give the increase. Oh what a mighty God we serve. I was a little boy lost when you found me. Who knew a woman like you, older, and wiser than I could ever pray to be, would come to serve a God like that under a wretch like me. I needed you. I just didn't know how much. Glory be to God in heaven. Thank you for just letting me be." He wiped his eyes as he gained his footing, "Let the dead bury the dead. God Is the God of the living. Amen." His voice roared through out the empty sanctuary, "Don't give up on people folks! Especially the children. Everything that look hopeless ain't so. Every living creature has purpose and promise. That's not to say every creature is living. For there are many zombies amongst us, trees that bear no fruit, haunting space. These shadows, these empty vessels merely choose to just exist. They choose not to expose or expound upon their purpose, promise and power. Poverty and perversion are the reward of the sluggard I say. Pour into to the youth I employ you! For the future is there's and time is on their side. Pour into the promise so that they may prosper with power! DON"T GIVE UP ON PEOPLE SP EASILY! PLANT THE SEEDS! PLANT THE SEEDS! YOU DON"T KNOW WHAT CAN

GROW! POUR OUT WHAT THE LORD HAS POURED INTO YOU! POUR IT OUT! EVEN IF YOU DON'T LIVE TO SEE THE FRUIT! PAY IT FORWARD! EVEN IF IT MEANS THEY GO FARTHER THAN YOU! DON"T BE JEALOUS! IT'S THEIR CALLING NOT YOURS! PLANT AND POUR SO THAT OTHERS MAY PLUCK FROM WHAT GOD HAS INCREASED! YOU DON'T KNOW WHAT CAN GROW IF YOU DON'T PLANT A SED BY FAITH!" The few shouted and broke out into tongues. The Holy Spirit came in. He sauntered His way around the room and each person had been filled where they stood. From the outside, it sounded like an army. Al wept over Bonnie's casket. Deacon Finley held on to him.

The small group had gathered at the front of the church while mourned. They had never seen him so emotional; not even when Carla had died. Even then he had put up a strong front. The very man they had looked up to; admired for his strength in the midst of many storms, had fallen prey to humanity. They all watched and prayed silently.

"Yeah Bonnie has moved on. Absent from the body present with the Lord. Go Bonnie. We had been encouraging her to move forward for years. Take a step back. Relax. Sometimes we don't realize taking a step back can be taking a step forward. We must pray to know what season of our lives we're in and move with the Holy Spirit accordingly. That Bonnie, she was stubborn. Lord knew it. He knows all of us. Sometimes when we refuse to move, He do what He gotta do to move us. Often times He'll sit us down when we're doing too much and he can't even get a word in or He wants to prepare us to do something different. People say they'll rest when they die. Foolish words from foolish folk. Gotta watch what we say.

Often our words are our prophecy. Where in the word does it say work until you die? Huh? Didn't God rest from His work? Didn't Jesus run away from the crowds sometimes to be alone and pray? Didn't the disciples find him asleep on the boat when the storm raged? Huh? Don't we just need a break sometimes? It's our egos that get in that way and tell us the project won't survive if we take some time off. The business will crumble if I go on vacation. Somebody gon' steal my man if we take a break? What?! Don't you know what God has for you was yours before the worlds were formed if it really is yours? And if it is not, why you want it so bad anyway? Can't do nothing but bring you pain if you got somebody else's stuff. It's stealing. LET IT GO!" The mourners sang out, "Hallelujah! Tell it Pastor!"

Alive and bustling in his element he loitered, "The ministry won't stand a chance without me. Heeeeeeyyyyyyy! I'm preachin' to the choir! Heeeeeeeyyyyyy!" The group jumped and howled.

He dynamically admonished, "Being terminated on a job when we know He been telling us to leave for a long time. An eviction when we know the Spirit had been ringing the alarm on the inside telling us it's time to go. An ill-fated relationship, doomed from the start, know God ain't in it, we stay anyway, trying to make it work; writing been on the wall and yet we stay in the name of loyalty. What about being loyalty to yourself? What about what God is telling you? All the ways the Holy Spirit tap on our shoulders to get us to wake up and move on. His unction. Why is it we will stay somewhere that ain't serving us no purpose or that has gotten too small for us like an old pair of shoes, and die for the sake of familiar or is it because we're racked with frigidity of fear? Take them shoes off and buy some more! You know they hurt! And yeah, the new pair may be uncomfortable for a minute but so what! Endure the pain and keep walking. New things, the unfamiliar, anything out of our zone is always gonna be uncomfortable. Discomfort comes to challenge our creativity and strengthen us where we are weak. See y'all done got me goin' off on a tangent now… We ain't come here today to have church did we? I…"

"No now, keep on now brother!" said Deacon Finley.

"A job, a home, a relationship. A church." He looked around, "What is it that makes us not want to move? Now I know trusting God can be difficult for the most seasoned Christian. I know. Believe me when I tell you. But what of the adventure of not knowing and just throwing caution to the wind...just going without knowing? Don't new things excite y'all. Challenges and uncertainty make ya head spin and ya heart beat fast. Y'all men know what I mean. Come on now!" The men all shouted, "Amen brother." Some of the wives looked on in anger. Others bowed their heads in embarrassment.

"Aww now, I ain't trying to cause no trouble. I'm just talkin' to y'all. I'm a righteous realist. I hope that's alright wit' y'all today? You know what I mean. Like a young spirit. Just free like the wind. Young people have one thing that can work for and against them."

Deacon Finley asked, "What's that Pastor?"

"I'll tell you what it is Deacon. It's the ability to be uninhibited. They fearless. It's a blessing and a curse. The asset is also the liability. Many are extremists in the vein of King David. Good or bad. In or out. They down for whatever. Goin' hard or goin' home. We tend to, with wisdom or with a lack of faith as we age, to lose that. Call it caution or lack of passion. That too is can be a blessing and a curse." They looked on in amazement for their leader had begun to expound like never before. They wondered where it was all coming from. His message was spicy. He was changing before their very eyes.

"When did we lose our desire to let the Holy Spirit carry us, going along on that fantastic voyage.   That sweet surrender."

One man blurted out, "Amen to that! I ain't had no sweet surrender in a long time. I'm wonderin' what happened too! Thinking 'bout getting' me somethin' young and uninhibited more and more every day. Shoot!"

"Don't do that to your wife man. This ain't the time nor the place. Get your mind right. Respect your lady man." Al shook his head.

"Yeah bruh, marriage counseling on Fridays at eight. Show some respect." touted Deacon Finley amongst a sea of amens.

"Is it okay for me to speak now?"

"Preach Pastor." the old woman bawled.

"Bonnie had ideas y'all. She had places she dreamed of going, people she wanted to meet and things she wanted to do. She never got around to it. She was too grounded here." He looked around once more, "She was stuck here. Her drawback. Bonnie ain't know when to hold 'em or when to fold 'em. Kenny Rogers had it right. Gotta know when to walk away; know when to run." The mourners nodded in agreement.

"Amen.", came a voice from among the crowd.

"Amen is right! She didn't listen to that inner voice. She had the Holy Spirit alive on the inside of her, she just chose to drown out His voice with the sound of hers. Finally she started getting slower and slower. All in a year's time. Boy she slowed down quickly. Can't believe how fast she declined. One minute up and healthy, thinking she was superwoman...she could manage it all. She never took off the cape, the boots, the mask. She never allowed herself to be human. She probably reckoned to herself that would've killed her. Looking back now, she was wrong, it probably would've saved her life." he shook his head.

"Don't get so busy in your assignment that you lose touch with your dreams. Dreams are the goals God placed in your heart. Our minds know before our feet get the memo. Remember the head control the feet. Don't let your feet control your head. That ain't gon' do nothin but have you walking around in circles in them old tore up shoes. If you get the feel for fresh air, go get some. Try something new. Do something different. Don't die full of woulda, shoulda, couldas. Serve yes. Give it your all. But know that there is not just one way to serve God. Everybody ministry ain't within these walls. Most of the people we encounter ain't comin' up in here. Everybody can't receive a word or message from the Lord the in the traditional sense. Work your gifts. Do something different to relate to some different people. Do something unorthodox. GO AGAINST THE GRAIN! Jesus did. Be bold as Lions; gentle as Lambs. Do what God is calling you to do. And listen, if it is to stay, stay...that's fine. What He tellin' me, He may not be tellin' you, but whatever you do, listen to the Spirit of the Lord. He that has an ear, let him hear what the Spirit is saying to the churches. I don't know why I'm saying this. I didn't even plan on staying this long."

"Keep goin' Pastor. That's alright. Must be The Lord. He sayin' somethin'. Y'all better listen up!" a young man yelled.

"Yes sir." shouted Deacon Finley.

"It's a whole world of people out there that are looking for Jesus. Different people that are looking for Him in a different way. We all different. Why we keep feeding people the same food when everybody on different diets is beyond me? Gotta do something different. Everybody don't take in and digest the same way.

We created by the same creator. Every man, woman and child created in His likeness. We all bear the resemblance of a Sovereign God, a God who created a beautiful universe full of diversity. I mean come on y'all. He even graced us all with different gifts and talents based on what He knows He placed within us. We all here on assignment. We all here to bring Him glory by using what He has placed within us to show Him to one another. But where does it say we have to do it the same way every day of our lives? Especially when we as beings and everything in our atmosphere is constantly changing? Our needs are always changing.

Our attention spans are shortening because of technology. We get far too much too soon. Therefore we're less patient, less tolerant and far less connected. We desire more in a shorter time span. To be effective and efficient, our message must stay the same but the avenues in which it is delivered, even the forum has to change in order to keep up with an ever growing, rapidly evolving world. The faster people go, the more of a hurry there is, the more junk people tend to consume. The world ain't gonna slow down. Do we the people, the body, the church have to speed up. The real work is outside of those doors y'all." The congregation remained seated and silent.

"Life is about adventure. Our God is adventurous. If you don't know God is a God of wonder, surprise and adventure after a certain point, and you're saved; I wonder if you've drowned out the sound of His voice by shouting over Him with your own. The Holy Spirit is a gentlemen. He ain't gonna force. He will not shout. We must decrease that He may increase. What is The Lord saying to you? He who has an ear….and the church said…" They responded, "Let him hear."

"Amen." The Pastor drifted out the same way he came leaving everyone breathless and pondering. Al was still a hard act to follow.

"He left the mic smokin' like your favorite rapper's favorite rapper." boasted a young man.

Al Goldens gift was undeniable. For all he had thought he'd lost. He had actually gained. It was as if with each tragedy, he became stronger. The man's eulogy had quickly evolved into a short sermon and teachable moment packed with power, overflowing with truth, it was now time to release his gift in a different setting. It was time for something young and uninhibited.

When he had reached the bottom of the staircase outside of the church, a car had pulled up blasting loud music. It's Newark, it's the largest city in the state of New Jersey; the inner-city. The weather was unseasonably warm. The local hustlers were about spending their purses as fast as and as lavishly as they had filled them. It was the time of year where the windows in the apartment buildings were up. Folks trying to catch a breeze and a break from the winter blues and the smell of deep fried food that saturated the furnishings and drapery. Below those windows, on the street, the windows were down. Hustlers breezin' through trying to catch a honey with no self-esteem, long legs, in a short skirt, with short term memory.

It was the norm in many major cities. Al didn't judge. He remembered what the routine was like. The attitude, the mindset, the goals, the shortcomings; the need to survive. He stopped and chuckled to himself, remembering the pride, the chase. It was all for nothing. But when he was in it the game was everything to him. At a point in time, the streets and everything attached to them were all he had. Deep into it, Al felt empathy for the young men, even the older men who had not detoxed off of the high, the addiction to the game.

He had a great love and compassion for people in the street that would not die. He even had compassion for the naïve young girls and immature older woman who had chosen to play a part of the chess piece that gets passed around on the board of the game. It was a valuable piece that the game wouldn't be the game without. The female was the Queen of Fools that held everything down for every Street King. That piece on the board could always be replaced. The game came with extras. The Street Kings never saw them as valuable pieces with priceless worth. In the game, they just got used and tossed to the side whenever the Street Kings decided they wanted a new piece. He prayed for the ladies most often. For them to know their value and their worth.

It was a part of him that was destined to die with him. It was part of what got him to where he was. It was what initiated his thirst for business; his drive for success. His desire to prosper was birthed out of a lifestyle of lack; Poverty pushed him. Hustling gave him business sense. He desire to win and be the best at everything gave him marketing strategy.

He closed his eyes as he nodded his head to the music. He knew the hustlers mindset, they were Street Kings. They were the gods of their community. There had been no larger than life rapper to emerge from the nasty Newark streets. There was no Mos Def, Talib Kweli; no Kendrick Lamar or Wale. There would be no J Cole, Q-tip, Nas, Kanye or Common Sense to wake the people up. No one for the young women to aspire to emulate. The residents had no well to draw from. No template. No blueprint. Lauryn Hill and the Fugees had come and gone. The very Governor of the state had been born in their city but, he was a staunch republican that had been long removed. There was no hometown hero to connect to. Sarah Vaughn and Amiri Baraka were gone. Ras Baraka, he carried the torch and he was the closest thing they had to a hero. Ras Baraka was the newly elected mayor. His victory had been a long time in the making. But the mayor of Newark wasn't a Christian leader. What of the Christians? "Where the leaders of the new school at?" Al reasoned. The pastors in the city didn't seem to be that connected or concerned for the people. Ras Baraka wasn't a follower of Christ, yet he had proven himself dedicated and faithful thus far. He was the man for the job. He cared for the citizens. Nevertheless, Christians needed a Christian leader. How far would they follow the new mayor? Would the Christians even connect? He adduced, "How can two walk together unless they agree?"

No blueprint for the citizens of Newark, NJ. No black heroes for Brick City; for black America for that matter. Sure there had been plenty of famed faces that had been birthed in the Garden Sate; in Newark alone. The most famous and notable being Whitney Houston. But, she was gone and though the circumstances surrounding her death, were not shocking to the locals, some of which had known her personally. It was the negativity that tarnished her legacy that disappointed many of them. Al reflected on a scripture the Lord have gave him the day before her home going as he prayed with a heavy heart, with the rest of Newark, for Cissy Houston and her family. "Lord, what the heck happened? How could this be? The streets was always talkin' the people that knew her from way back when; the people that she would talk to now and again, they knew it was coming. But Lord, like this? Why like this? Oh Jesus, and that poor young girl. Those people… they partied like it was 1999 with that woman's body still just floors above them n that hotel. Forgive them Father. They knew not what they were doing. They must not know you. Your word said the very hearts of men would wax cold. In her honor?! That's what she would've wanted? Really? Why Lord? I know she made her choices. But why? Man! One of the pastors just told me he had a recent brief conversation with her about some things he wanted to get done in the city; she seemed on board he said. She seemed alright. He said he remembered her being humble, cheerful and sweet. She told him she would be glad to meet him to further discuss doing something positive for Newark." He prayed sorrowfully, what happened?"

The Lord had given the pastor Luke chapter thirteen, verses eleven thru seventeen. That brought Al not only temporary solace, but the answer he sought and understanding in the midst of his bewilderment.

The next day would prove to be a difficult one for the citizens of Newark, NJ. The streets lay quiet for four solid hours as her funeral was broadcast live. Hearts laid heavy inside of most. Many drug dealers stamped the name of their most potent product with hers. It was disrespectful. Nevertheless, it was the street. A host of addicts would be in search of whatever they believed she had. Whatever brought her to death would in their minds, bring them to life as it were with addicts in the Brick City. He would think her life, her death; the cautionary tale it all had become, would bring the addiction that so rapidly plagued the streets of his beloved city to a decline. Not so. Nothing he could do. The Lord had Nippy. The streets had the dealers. The drugs had the addicts. All he could do was keep praying.

"Rest in peace Whitney. No matter what they say about you. We loved you. When you looked good, it made us proud. When you didn't we prayed." Those were his final words at church that Sunday as his sermon hinged on addiction and the monsters that are fame and media. The people who had known Whitney Houston from way back when; those that really knew her brothers and her family history; they knew the image the people that surrounded her had created wasn't who she really was. The citizens had never bought into the fantasy they had seen on TV. Newark was an open book. There weren't too many secrets to be kept. They didn't judge her harshly. She was from where they were from. Some of them even partied with the young Whitney. The Newark Whitney. The tough Whitney. The sweet Whitney. The real Whitney Houston. Her behavior had never been a shock to them. They just hoped it wouldn't take her under. She had been one of the blessed few to get out and do something with herself.

Yet, they knew, doesn't matter how saved you are, we all have weaknesses. Some of them will ride us into our graves if we allow them to. People have a tendency to think Christians should be flawless. They think we're all supposed to die in our sleep, wrapped in the arms of Jesus with angels singing hymns at our departure. Maybe even rays of sunlight surrounding us. They think we glow and fade straightway into heaven. The religious myths. Ha! People forget how bloody and violent Jesus' death was. AND HE WAS PERFECT! They forget." He spoke to Deacon Finley after service.

Newark, NJ hadn't had much to be proud of in a very long time. The divisional deviants were the heroes of the hopeless in the Brick City. Every politician that had governed the city, all that had come and gone had left a stench; a residue of selfishness, corruption and greed that loomed over the people of Newark.

And so the people created their own gods. The hustlers. They believed they were gods and were treated as such in their own hood. They couldn't help the way they ran their lives. You only do what you do until you know better. Al knew even that what was conditional. "You gotta want to know better. Just getting information is not enough. The information has to be received and processed. Then action must be taken. What good is information if it is not utilized?" he mused. Having walked in their shoes, he knew at base, those guys and girls were just trying to survive. The hustlers were no different than the corporate suits that came to cop product from them, everybody was just trying to be successful in life on their level until they found a way to level up. Everyone was just doing what they knew. Just like the corporate heads, on opposite ends of the spectrum, they had ambitions and business sense too! They used people to package, move and market their product. How were they any different? If selling junk food, tobacco, alcohol and fast food were legal and highly profitable and addictive, what was wrong with what they were doing? It's all killing people. It's all supply and demand. It's all a hustle. They suits that bought weight from them were a mirror image with better clothes and cars, and a license to kill sponsored by the US government. The difference was the drug dollars were totally tax free and the woman the suits were taxing were not. The hustlers did have a couple things over the suits. Content in their world. They're the superstars in their community.

Al marveled as he reasoned within himself at how the movers and shakers in corporate America, scoffed at and judged the street hustlers when there was just a hair's fracture of a difference between the two. He counseled many of them. They had the same addiction to money, power and respect as the people they judged. The big wigs were just as shrewd in business. Just as sinful. Equally as lustful and indulgent if not more so. Yet unbelievably, Al found, the hustlers were more honest than the suits. They had less to lose by being straight forward. The game was the same, just different process; different product. He found the corporates to be shady, elusive and dishonest with their consumers. While the local street hustlers were brutally honest at all costs. What they had in common when it came to a lack of integrity in marketing was that neither of them would ever be totally truthful about the ingredients in the products they pushed. Products that killed. The game is addiction and the aim is to gain a lifelong consumer. "'Til death do you part." he thought. The customer may not always be right but, they always knew what they were getting themselves into. They weren't forced. False advertisement was legal and all is fair in hustling. Be street level or corporate level. Legal or illegal they're all dealers of death.

Business is business. Networking is done hand over fist twenty four hours a day seven days a week; Rain or shine. "'Cause you can't knock the hustle." he heard Jay Z claim from the cars blaring speaker. He looked up to discover his grandson staring at him.

Gregory shouted over the music, "Uh, huh. Look at you! What you know 'bout dat man?! You don't nothin 'bout Hov. Knock it off man."

Al responded, "Boy, I know everything about Hov. Don't get it twisted." He raised His bible.

Al walked over to the car, "Boy why you out here? Just smelling like you came out of a room full of up to no good. I done been up to campus for lookin' for you a few times and I can't get nobody to tell me nothin...whatchu up to?"

"Nothin Granddad. Cruising'", he looked away from his Grandfather.

"Yeah...uh huh. I know what cruisin' mean." Take me for a ride boy.

"But Granddad, you got ya own wheels. And they hotter than mine! I got somethin' to do..."

"Well we can do it together. Whatchu don't wanna spend time with me? Much as I love you. I thought we was tighter than that man?"

"Nah. We good Granddad." he smiled.

"Aight. That's what I know. Push it then."

"Yessir."

They drive a few blocks in dead silence. Al looks over at Gregory, "Ain't no need to switch up."

"Whatchu mean Granddad?"

"Let me get some sounds man."

"Ok." He puts in a gospel CD.

"Wait. Wait. Wait. Wait...boy whatchu doin' now?"

"I'm giving you sounds Granddad."

"No joker. Play whatchu was playin when you pulled up. Be yourself. Don't do me like that G. Don't treat me like I'm slow. You know what it is boy."

"...I didn't wanna disrespect you Granddad. That's all. You being a Pastor and all."

"Son, only disrespect is in thinkin' I'm not human. Don't play me G. You know where I'm from. Just like I know what you doin'." he stared at his grandson.

G failed to respond.

"Come on drive now." he patted G on the shoulder. We'll discuss it later. After you treat me to lunch. Aight?"

"Ok."

"Now, look alive boy. We just family. Two men having an exchange. I'm not here to stress you."

"Aight Brother Al.", G chuckled.

"Don't get crazy boy."

"You got it man. I luh you man. Granddad you da realest."

"Can't be no other way son."

"I feel dat. Aye yo!" G pulls over to speak to a group of guys in front of the bodega on the corner.

"These ya people son?"

"Somethin' like that?"

Al knew every young face on that corner. They all used come to youth meeting when they were younger. He raised his fist through the window to greet the crowd.

"Aye yo! Brother Al. What's poppin'?" one young man rang out.

Al quipped, "Jesus joker. All day."

"I hear you Brother Al. Imma be at church on Sunday. Me and my girl."

"Man you say that all the time. When you ready man. Hopefully sooner than later."

"Imma try Pastor."

"Tryin ain't what do it Jasper. Doing is what does it son."

"Oh ya name Jasper son?" Jasper? Why you got people callin' you Rock dawg?" G teased.

Jasper walked over to the driver's side of the car, "Cause I'm hard Negro. Somethin ya lil' spoiled, cushiony soft, monkey ass wouldn't know nothin about Goldie Locks."

"You don't know what I know man. And get ya old greasy, mangy body away from my ride yo. And watch ya mouth man. Respect my Grandfather you common thug."

"Oh Pastor, my bad. Don't listen to him. I ain't no common thug."

"Yeah you right. My bad Jasper. You're a common hustler. Sorry son."

"Got jokes." Jasper waves his hand and heads back to the corner.

"I'm out!" screams G.

"Whatchu doin' yo? When you comin' back man?" Jasper asks.

"In a few. Let me finish drivin' Mr. Daisy around." They all laugh.

"Oh so I'm Mr. Daisy?" Al looks over his glasses.

"Jokin' Granddad. We're just two men talking remember? I ain't here to stress you Granddad."

"Boy drive." Al commands. "And G, I'm not one to judge nobody. But, you my Grandson and I ain't gon' never lie to you. You ain't like the rest of those boys. You saved. Watch the company you keep. Huh?"

"Granddad I be tryin. But you know I inherited my swag from you. Can't help it sometimes." He look at his reflection in the rearview mirror, "Ya boy magnetic. People just be drawn to the kid."

"Boy, you just as foolish as the day is long. And I know you know better. Arrogant like ya father. I tell you what, in all of your SWAG, be careful about who you draw to you and why. Aight man? Everything out here ain't fun and games. More to the game than meets the eye boy. And you do know where the word 'SWAG' originated from don't cha?"

"Huh?"

"And those sagging pants...you do know don't you?"

"Sir?"

"The high fiving?"

"What do you mean Granddad?"

"Do your research boy. Y'all just be out hear following trends and don't the origin. Swag! Lord where our leaders at? Long hair havin', tight pants wearin', two earrings, man purse carryin'... And when men start wearin' so many diamonds and being adorned with jewelry? All this metro sexual, manscapin'. Men supposed be soft and smooth? For real?"

"Whoa Granddad!"

"Shut up boy. I'm entitled to my opinion! Y'all done got feminized. Y'all need to wake up! I swear y'all the most glamorous men I've ever seen. Just soft and pretty. It's disgusting. No wonder women don't respect y'all. Y'all sharin' beauty secrets. You don't walk like a man, you don't dress like a man. Ya gossip and giggle like church wives and teenage girls. You don't work hard. You want everything given to you...like a woman. Just perched. Waitin' on somebody to take care of you. Got too much in common with females. I guess they'll respect men when they start seein' 'em. Don't y'all we come from kings and warriors? Explorers and leaders? Masculine ones. Masculine ones that loved women and those women respected.

Y'all scared to work hard. Everything come easy to y'all. Y'all new people wanna feminize football. Oh, okay. Let's not call names no more. Don't hit too hard. We'll fine them for being men."

"Oh you talkin' about that Jonathan Martin thing right? You do know every male is not an alpha male don't you Granddad? They taught us that at school."

"What else they teachin' y'all these days? Huh? How to bake the perfect casserole in a pretty pink apron and wow your family? Guys these days are too feminine. Too sensitive. Lord have mercy. You don't wanna get off your mother tit! On your parents insurance until you're nearly thirty. Pampered and babied. You can't wait to be eighteen. You want your freedom and respect but you're still under your parents roof being served like a little baby girl. So your father gets tired of seeing you and feeding you because what is that? A grown man feeding another grown ass man. He kick ya out so you can become your own man. Whatcha do? Go find some woman with low self-esteem to live with. She's working. She comes home, services you in every way. She got kids. She takes care of them. She gets up in the morning to take the kids to school and go to work and you still sleep.

Hip-hop artists bringing the whole hood with them wherever they go. More grown men taking care of grown men! Pay 'em to carry your bag and run and get your food. Feminine. My boys. My boys. That's why you all stay boys. You can come back to where you came from and give them the tools they need to get where you worked hard to get; more importantly, where The Lord wants to take them. I don't remember too many men out here when I was growing' up that took handouts or whose dream it was to follow other men around like puppies and eat the scraps given to them like slaves. Men used to dream about owning things. Carving their own niche. Making a way for themselves. Slavery had emasculated black men so much and had broken down the family unit so, that men just wanted to get their rightful place back. At least some men. Others, well, they weren't strong enough to hold on. They began beating their women; objectifying them to make money."

"Pimpin' them you mean?"

"Yeah man. Put them down to make you feel up. If not that. They just lost it and got high. They stole. They robbed. They killed out of frustration. A lot of us though, wrong as it was, we hustled. That's how we survived. We wasn't lookin' for welfare, women, the government or our boys to take care of us. Black men, hard as it was and still is, used to look for ways to be independent. Some of us did anyway. That was before sports, rappin', making temporary clothing lines and being a boy servant became the only way out of the hood.

Men need a plan of their own for themselves. They need be taught how to transition from one season of life to another. Brothers ain't ready when the hand that feeds them draws back and they don't have money saved up. They don't have a plan of action or skill to fall back on. Uneducated. Satisfied with being held down by another man or woman."

"Granddad, those brothers and sisters just tryin' to help they hood. One eat, everybody eat. You know how it goes."

"It doesn't usually go that way for long son. People that have goals and visions are dreamers. Lots of times dreamers don't stop dreaming. There's always another mountain to conquer. When you're on the climb, you can't take dead weight with you. It just drags you down or holds you back. So you get a bigger vision. Not just rapping, acting shopping until your accountant says enough! What about when God is telling you to go the place he chose for you Abraham and you bring Lot with you when God ain't say to do that? What happens then?"

"You preachin'!"

"I know it! Like I was sayin' though. You take everybody with you, and they don't have a renewed mind, then you probably ain't gon' get no higher than the ceiling. White people don't wanna be around that mess. You don't give a man something to aspire to on his own and a hole to climb out of so he appreciates that struggle, then what kind of man will he be? If he ever becomes one. For age does not a man make."

"I heard my dad say that."

"Your dad is a smart man G. So okay! You fire them because a lil' birdie that sees your potential done came and whispered in your ear because they recognize your value and potential; soon enough... your boys are bloggin' about you or somebody 'bout to write a book. Or on a radio station kickin' ya back in. Like what? Like little boys. Men need some struggle and hard work. Not to be carrying your bags like they some male servants. If you gon' help 'em.

Teach ya boys how to fish so they can eat for a lifetime and provide for themselves like men. A man has to create his own vision. If he's given one, he won't be able to see it clearly. We appreciate things we had to work hard to get."

"It's the chase right Granddad?"

"Of course it is. It's natural. It's in your DNA. The hunt. The challenge. The climb. Rejection sometimes makes you want it more. Fall down, get up. Not lay there, call ya boy and ask him to let you gold somethin'."

"We all need help sometimes Granddad."

"Not every time though son. Jesus called out to Father God before He went to the cross in the garden of Gethsemane. God was there. His father did not answer Him. Jesus asked for an easier way out. He asked if there was any other way. Apparently there wasn't one. There was no other way but to suffer through it. And look, we're all better for what Christ faced as a man. Even when God was silent and he may have felt isolated and rejected."

"Right! Jesus didn't even have His boys. He just asked them to watch and pray; have His back. They couldn't even do that. Wow Granddad. That's a different view."

"Grandson, the word of God is layered. We just gotta be open to hear what the Spirit is saying. He's not always saying the same thing. The Spirit of the Lord is mobile. Can't always be depending on other men to have your back. Some ish is just your ish. You gotta deal with it."

"I hear that. But that chasin' stuff…"

"What about it G?"

"I don't know too many guys that like to chase anymore."

"It's 'cause y'all spoiled and lazy."

"Huh?"

"It's true. Women so desperate these days; they don't take time for themselves to find out who they are or their worth, that they just take any man, in any condition that brings nothing to the table. And if she don't bring nothing to the table, then y'all just at the table lookin stupid, wastin' time and starving to death.

These young girls come when you call 'em. Every time. Don't make sense."

"But Granddad, in the Bible…"

"In the Bible, that sort of reverence and favor was reserved for Kings only. Not just any man. Remember YOU said, every male ain't an alpha. Not saying that a man that is not an alpha don't deserve respect; we're all different. My point is women give too much, too soon to the wrong men out of desperation. Then they have nothing left for themselves and their children. Many of them also just stay on the ground or by the pool of Bethesda with they hand out waiting for years… Years they can't get back for a hand out or up when the power to get up and out is within them… had been for a long time."

"Umm! That's real. Jesus didn't even touch that man. He told Him to take up His mat and walk."

"Because for thirty eight years, that's all he ever had to do. He didn't need help getting up. He just needed to be reminded he could. The power was already his. Can't keep letting people walk all over you. You just gotta make the decision to get up. It takes a renewed mind to be able to get up. Jesus asked him if he wanted to get well. A valid question, so many don't. Anybody can come along and help you but, question is, do you want to be helped or do you just want to keep carrying bags or laying there getting stepped on? The answers are often within us. A hand out or up will on serve to keep us down sometimes. Women get babied too much too sometimes. It's always worse for a man though. Women give birth to boys. Boys they hold back from becoming men because they hold on to them too tightly; they baby them and treat them like those boys; them sons are their husbands. Mothers can stunt their sons' growth sometimes by giving them too much. Speaking of which, you need a job Gregory."

Al's grandson complained, "A job. A job? I never worked before."

"That's the problem. Y'all spoiled and soft. Everybody cryin'. Everybody complainin'. All in the salon next to ya woman getting your hair done. Next to her in the nail salon, getting your nails done. Nobody protectin' or providin' for the women and children anymore. Everybody wanna be protected and provided for like women and children. Went from workin' hard by the sweat of your brow to havin' meetings about fashion. Damn babies!"

"Granddad!"

"Boy shut up! Like you don't use profanity. All the music you listen to is a cuss every other word, Even the r & b. You got some nerve! I'm human. We just two men kickin' it."

"Here we go."

"Go! Go! Y'all don't move. Nobody move. Nobody get hurt. That's everybody problem. You either too scared to move or to blind to see where to go or to ignorant about how to get started. No movement. All of this money makin' and no movement. No power. No go! Everybody to content in the dysfunction. That's the problem."

"Yes sir."

"Now as I was sayin', everybody you wit ain't really witchu...get it man? You know everybody that followed Jesus in those crowds wasn't there because they loved and supported Him. Just because of who you are, because your light so shines, there will always be somebody that wanna put ya light out man. Never forget Jesus had a Judas. You got a calling on your life, expect a Judas. Trying to do anything off the cuff and positively life altering…expect a Judas. Go against the grain without compromise; have the slightest bit of influence; be a standout that's destined to stand up and make a difference…you gon' get a Judas. He comes with the package called purpose boy."

"Aww Granddad. Them my boys. We good. They would never…"

"You are not like them. You are called to come out from among them. You were raised different. God blessed you with a privileged life and a great head start. You think they ain't jealous or resentful? I mean are you really that thick after all of that education your father paid for?"

"I hear you. I'm just sayin…"

"Be swift to hear, slow to speak boy. Devil hate you just because. These streets ain't forgiving either. Don't play in the enemy's camp boy, he don't play fair and he play for keeps. Bible says God's people parish for the lack of knowledge. Don't be stupid man. Get back in the word. Leave these streets and all that comes with 'em alone. Get out the enemy's camp Gregory. You come from money. So, I know it ain't the money you after. Whatever you lookin for…stop tryin to find it before it finds you. Clear Justin Bieber? Just be yourself. Trying to be hard can make you're soft brain matter real mushy. I've seen it too many times. Tired of broken mothers calling me in the middle of the night to pray over the body of a dead black boy because another dead black boy killed 'em. Get it son? You've been warned man."

"Yessum.", G says jokingly.

"Pull over boy."

"But Granddad I was just…"

"Boy pull the damn car over I said! Now!"

G pulls over. He turns off the ignition. He places his head on the steering wheel. "Granddad...is this about to turn into a teachable moment? You don't have to...I'm ok. Trust me. I move like you used to. I promise."

Al pulls him by the collar, "Look at me Gregory. LOOK AT ME! There is absolutely nothing cool about street life! You hear me? I'm a living witness. And you can take the living part as serious as you know you better. Ain't no glory in loss, bloodshed, people dying by your hand; Mothers losing their children. Children burying their mothers. Fathers missing out on childhood after childhood; theirs and their children's. Boys become men sooner than they are supposed but, remain little boys just playing with bigger toys all at the same time. Boy you got eyes but can't see. Ears and can't hear. You think this is a game? Huh? Move like me. BOY PLEASE! You can't move like me. YOU AIN'T ME! You don't have the circumstances I had, the mindset or the heart."

G looked at him up and down, "No disrespect man. But you don't know me like that Granddad. I got heart."

"Boy who you frontin' for? Huh? You a snooty, spoiled kid from the sweet suburbs. I know ya story. I can tell you more about you than you can tell me about you. Thing is, obviously, you don't know me! If you did you wouldn't try me."

"I do know you Granddad. You an urban legend out here. These jokers respect you and..."

"Boy please! I don't attach myself to them street fables. Don't you know the young soldiers out here runnin' they mouth about me just goin' on hearsay? Greg, they don't know me. Urban legend. Yeah ok...Well if it's true I hope it's a legacy of faith, family, responsibility and love I'm leavin' behind when Jesus call me home. They can keep that other mess. It's garbage. I knew that when I was in it. There's more to life than getting fresh, knockin' down somebody's daughter every night with no remorse and getting' money. And you...YOU...out of all them jokers on that corner... YOU know better Gregory Golden. Ya know better! People done sacrificed and gave you the life they never had. Blood sweat and tears and ya lil' ungrateful behind can't even see it. Boy, ask any of them brothers you on the corner with if they would trade they life for yours in the time it takes to get a Brick City beat down. Go to the jailhouse and ask one of them brothers...whatcha think they gon' say?" The young man was speechless.

"Yeah I know. Like I said. You know better. Boy you stick out like a sore thumb. Those pants don't fit you son. They just don't. So quit trying to put them on! Don't believe what you see. It's a dead end. Sin is truly only enjoyable for a season. And you know that. So when the season up G, then what? Answer me that." Gregory turned his head away from his Grandfather.

"You don't wanna know young man. I promise you. I stopped hustlin' way back when I was about your age. I didn't do it long. Thank God for your Grandmother. Loving her was like an open door for me. Ya Grandmother and your father was my out man. And we gave our lives to Christ and He blessed us. See God had a plan. He knew somewhere down the pike you was comin. He blessed us with the means to be able to work hard so we can provide a greater life for you. We wanted to leave you a great inheritance. We wanted to leave a greater legacy. See son, those things, me and my wife ain't have. Just know I'm not proud of my past. But at the time, I really didn't see another way at the time. I had nobody. I had nothing. I had to survive. And yeah, I get it if the guys on the corner just tryin' to survive. It's that song all over again...Can't knock the hustle'. Especially when you ain't walked in the hustler's shoes. And guess what son, I HAVE...still don't knock it, because I know what it's all about.

And....and ...since I do and you don't. Believe when I tell you. Life ain't a video or a hip-hop song. You heard ya boy Jay, when he said, 'This ain't no movie dawg'. Well I don't agree with him calling himself Hov, I don't agree with the any man calling any woman out of her name, that reality TV nonsense, but I listen to some rap. And because of where I come from, I feel it. Most of them just tellin' they story. I know that story like the back of my hand G. But you don't. That's not your story. Don't live a lie. Live your truth son. We have by God's grace, provided you with a good life. Why you out here man? What you searchin' for? Ain't nothin out here. Believe me."

"Granddad, I hear you. I get everything you're saying. But it's complicated. I'm just not ready to discuss it. Can we just go and eat now? I promise I'll get back to you on everything."

"Aight boy. Keep ya word now."

"Aight Granddad. Where you wanna go? All this listenin' got me hungry now."

"Take me to Spain's. I like the way they make that garlic shrimp."

On their way to the restaurant Al tells G to make a stop at the liquor store. "Whatchu want some OJ? I can run in there real quick. I got it."

Al jumps out of the passenger seat, "I'll get it myself. I'm good."

Gregory stares out on to the street patiently awaiting his Grandfather's return. He sees a young woman running for the bus just as Al exits the store. They witness her fall on her face alongside the curb. The bus takes off kicking dirt in her direction. She lay there humiliated choking on the thick exhaust fumes.

"Did you see that?"

"Yeah man. That's messed up. Dag."

"Whatchu mean that's messed up? Go help her."

"Look Granddad. She's up. She's good. She'll be aight." They watch her limp through the crosswalk as other onlookers stand by gawking. Not being able to walk very far, her knee gives out. She collapses on a bench at the bus stop on the corner. Al walks over to her.

"Miss you alright?"

"Yeah. I'll be ok. I'll make it. Just a little embarrassed. But it's fine. Thank you asking." she smiles as a tear falls down her cheek washing clear through the dirt caked on her face from the bus.

"I understand that." he speaks softly. "But I really think you need some medical attention. You should let me..."

"You a doctor?" she snapped.

"Not at all. But I know a few. I can get you some assistance. Any hospital you prefer. No charge. No wait. Look at your knee! Let me just..." he pats his pockets searching for his phone. He motions for G to come over.

"Aww man. Why couldn't you just leave well enough alone? You ain't on duty man. We just left church. Stay in ya lane dawg." he mumbles as he pulls up along his Grandfather.

"Where's my phone?"

"I TOLD YOU I'M GOOD! I DON'T NEED YOUR HELP. NOW PLEASE JUST GO. I'LL BE FINE! BESIDES, I'M NOT GETTING IN THE CAR WITH TWO JOKERS I DON'T KNOW. GO HEAD!"

"You ain't gotta know me for me to help you. We're not asking you to jump in the ride."

"Damn right." G mumbles.

Al looked over at G in disbelief.

"Sorry Granddad. I didn't know you heard that." Al shook his head.

G mouths the words, "C'mon please. We gotta go. She got too much attitude. Leave her."
The Pastor says to her starring at his Grandson with a menacing look, "I can't. Pardon me, WE can't leave you like this." He mouths to G, "...wrong witchu? Get here now boy. Help her."

Gregory stomps over to the young lady, "You aight yo right?"

She turns her head, "Yeah. I'm good. I keep tellin' him."

"Aight. That's what it is then. Granddad, WE can be out now. She aight she said."

"Shut up boy. Get down here and tend to her. WE ain't goin nowhere."

"Sorry young lady. Sue me later. Help is on the way." Pastor Al stepped away to make the call.

"Oh my goodness. I got things to do. Can you help me up?"

"Yeah. I would but now that I look at it. That knee looks pretty nasty. You should stay right there yo. Let the people help you."

"Nooooooo. Nooooo." she pounded the bench with her fist. She cried, "Y'all don't get it. I gotta pick up my kids. I needed to go food shopping. I got stuff to do. C'mon! Y'all can't hold me here. I'm call the boys. Nah...this ain't bout to go down."

Ever the charmer, Gregory Golden not only looked like his father, he possessed his finesse. There were very few women he hadn't met a woman yet that he couldn't persuade to let him have his way. At the tender age of eighteen. The young golden boy, was a certified cad. He sat beside her, "May I hold your hand?" She withdrew her hand. She rolled her eyes. "Please may I? Just to ease you up a bit. You've been through enough. You should relax.

Nothin' wrong with receiving help. You're being prideful. Before pride goes destruction. Don't you know that?"

"Boy! If you don't get away from me. And quit quoting the Bible to me. I know the word. I don't need no slick ass joker like you spittin' me no quotes. I'm good. Joker like you..."

He stood up, "JOKER LIKE ME?!"

"AIN'T THAT WHAT I SAID? JOKER JUST LIKE YOU! THAT'S WHAT GOT ME IN THIS MESS! NOW I GOTTA A HOUSE FULL OF KIDS. DAGGONE STAIRSTEPS! ALL BECAUSE SOME FAKE CHRISTIAN INVITED ME TO CHURCH THEN INTO MY HEAD AND MY HEART AND OFCOURSE HIS BED. I KNOW YOUR KIND."

"MY KIND. MY KIND? OBVIOUSLY YOU DON'T. I AIN'Y YA AVERAGE. DON'T GET IT TWISTED MA. YOU KNOW DON'T ME AIIGHT?!"

"Negro, I ain't got to. You know what...I ain't got time for this! I'm gone." She begins to hop away on one foot.

"See ya!" G shouted laughing aloud. "And yo! Everybody ain't a bum like ya low-life baby daddy. It's still some gentlemen out here! Maybe you just ain't gentlemen quality! Don't blame everyman for your misguided choices. Point ya anger the other way yo! You the one fell for the okee doke. Guess you don't know the word as well as you thought you did dumb dumb!"

She stuck her middle finger in the air as he hopped down the street. Al retuned to the bench, "Yeah so ok. A few more minutes and...Umm, where she go man?"

"I tried to tell you PASTOR she got too much attitude. Let her hop on to her kids. She probably live in the projects. Rat!" Al punched G in the arm.

"What Granddad? She is a rat. You saw those turned up shoes. That nappy hair. SHE RAGEDY!" He punches him again, this time harder.

"Yo! Ow! What the… What did I do?!"

"You was raised better. Don't treat or speak to or about any lady like that. Now, I know you done picked up some nastiness out here in these streets. But, I advise you to leave it there. We respect women. No matter what. Get it?"

"Yes sir. Jesus! You still got it man dang!"

"And don't you forget it. Now let's go get her." As they were buckling their seatbelts, the ambulance pulled up along with an old friend of Al's. A retired doctor.

"She walked down some. You'll see her hopping along on the side walk." They drove down the street slowly trying to locate her. They found her sitting curbside three blocks away.

"Oh my goodness! Y'all leave me alone! I don't have time." she screamed.

"Al ran over to her. Young lady you need help. Please just let 'em take a look at your knee. It's obviously more serious than it appears on the surface."

"Obviously not I made it this far."

"Obviously so, you keep taking dives like Michael Phelps.

A paramedic walks over. He assesses, "Yeah he's right. Looks like you took an Olympic type spill back up the block. Did you trip or…"

"Yeah, I tripped. I tripped over my own luck."

Al chirped in, "Don't be down on yourself. I know life is hard but it gets better. Believe me."

"Yeah. I hear that all of the time. But when? How long?"

"When we begin believing it will. It takes time. It takes tenacity. It takes strength. It takes God. Young lady it takes faith. Even just a small amount does wonders believe it or not. It's gon' be alright."

"It's that mustard seed thing right?"

"Yes it is. It's now faith, as small as the grain of a mustard seed. You got it."

"Yeah. I guess you're right. Look Mister, I know I came off rude a little while ago up the block. I'm just having a hard time. It's just one of those days. I think I'm havin' too many of those days too often lately. I don't know. It's just a lot for one person. Sometimes I feel like giving up on everything. I'm sorry." She sobbed into her purse.

"Oh no apology needed. Who on God's green earth is perfect? I have my days too. Sometimes I have my weeks. Months. We all have those seasons. Even the most devout Christian is not exempt from life. That class is never dismissed until we go home to glory. It's ok. We're human." he smiled as he comforted her.

"You're a nice guy. You a good encourager. You talk like a Pastor."

"That's because he is one. And where you live that you don't know that? HIs face Is on like a million billboards girl."

"Oh no! No! Not him. Lord have mercy. Why you on me huh? What?! What's good? You beat or what? Because I'm not."

"I'm on you because you on one. Granddad, Imma be in the car. These tricks." he grumbled. "And he ain't got no dough so don't be out here tryna roll him. I'm on you girl."

"You wish future convict of America. Ass!"

"Aww how sweet. So generous. But, nah...I'm Gucci. I get plenty. Speaking of..." His phone rings as he walks away.

"What?!" she attempts to rise to her feet.

The doctor advises, "Young lady, this looks pretty bad. Even your socks are blood stained. Just relax."

"Listen to the doctor honey. Don't worry about my Grandson, I will deal with him. You just focus on you right now."

"Yeah Doc, uh...that's not from my knee. That's just my feet. I walk to work and back every day. I'm on my feet all day at my job. I'm usually not over this way, I just stopped over here to get a few dollars from a friend. Thought I could treat myself to a bus ride today. It's Friday. I got the weekend off. Thought if I got the bus, it would be a great start to a great weekend. Guess I was wrong."

"Good Lord! Young lady, how far away do you live from where you work?" the doctor asks.

"Quite a way. I can't tell you in miles and stuff. I ain't never been good at math. I just know I live over by where Lil' Bricks used to be off Avon and Irvine Turner. My job in North Newark."

"What do you do for a living if you don't mind me asking?" Al inquired.

"I'm a CNA at a Nursing Home."

"Yeah. I think I know where you work. I definitely know how hard you guys work. I commend you on your choice of fields and your skills. Thank you for all you do. You guys truly don't get paid enough for all you do."

"Thank you for your compassion Doctor."

"You're welcome. My mom was a Nursing Assistant long before they started requiring state certification. She worked two jobs, she kept house and raised three kids on her own. She was a soldier. She was my angel. They don't make 'em like that anymore. She's the reason I went to med school. I wanted to help people like she did. I also wanted to make money to take care of her. And I did. I made sure she retired early from those jobs. I took care of my mother. Mothers are so precious. I hope your children know what a treasure they have in you. All of that sacrifice. You're awesome. I guess I stand corrected now that I think about. Your pardon my lady, my manners. I ain't as sharp as I used to be."

"And you workin' on my knee?" She looked at Al, "I do need this thing to walk you know? What he mean he ain't as sharp as he used to be? Lord I spend my day trying to avoid annoying nurses who pay too much attention to detail. Lo and behold ..."

Al snickered behind the Doctor's back. "He's ok. He's a humorist. Good bedside manner. You're in good hands. Have faith."

He continued to examine her knee. "Well, well...The Good Lord still crankin' 'em out. But they are rare. Mothers aren't moms anymore. Too busy trying to be friends. Shame. As wonderful as my wife was, she most definitely was not my mother."

An onlooker touts, "Man, they never are."

The young woman rolls her eyes and says, "They're not supposed to be. Jokers kill me."

"Sam don't tell me you was one of them mama's boys. You had that Oedipus complex thing goin' man? Say it ain't so?" Al, teased.

"Call it what you want. She was a great mother. Dedicated 'til the day she died. Almost to a fault mind you. She was a nosey lot. She was weekend drunk and a hell raiser when she got angry. She wasn't perfect. But she did her job. I salute you young lady. You're one in a million. You're in good company if that brings you any comfort."

"Thank you. God bless you. But one question..."

He winked his eye, "Oh don't worry about your knee. It will heal before you marry. I promise. The knee and the person it's connected to just need some rest is all."

"Ok. But no, not that. Doctor what's an Oedipus complexion?"

"Naïve, sweet girl. Oedipus Complex dear." he growled arrogantly.

"How many children do you have?"

"Three. Three just like your mom did."

"And how many boys?' Al asked.

"They're all boys."

The Doctor and The Pastor looked at one another, "You bound to find out." They laughed.

Doctor Sam concluded, "I wish there was more I could do to help you. But for right now, all I can offer you is a few days in the hospital to recover. Imma put in a call to whoever is on staff at Beth right now. You gonna bypass all the E.R juggling. You'll get a private room with all of the amenities. On me. Give me a minute to make the arrangements. Let me speak to the EMTs."

As he walked back to his car chattering on his cell, she yelled, "No! I can't! My kids!" She whimpered, "I gotta go get my kids. We don't have nobody else. Lord help me." She wept.

"Young lady, did I hear you say you don't have anyone to watch your children?" asked Al.

She pleaded, "Yeah. That's right. If I get admitted. They'll be alone. They can't be alone."

"Alright. I understand. Let me talk to Sam. I'll be back."

Sam walked over, "Young lady, I understand you've got a situation. You don't have a baby sitter while you're on the mend you say?"

"Yeah. It's just us."

"Alright then. What I can do is get you treated, and in and out of the E.R as fast as possible. Then we'll make arrangements for you to go home for respite. I'll even get you an aide for the duration of your convalescence. With your permission of course. I mean you need to be off of your feet for a few weeks at the very least. I'm sure you could use the rest. The joint won't heal properly if there's too much movement."

"I guess. But is there any way they can patch me up and send me home like superfast? I got work, bills..." She tried to stand up. "Man Imma be late getting my kids. They gon call DYFUS on me, plus charge me extra and I ain't got. I need to go shoppin'. Look I appreciate all y'all efforts. I really do but I gotta go." She fell down.

"Ok. Ok. We see how much your family means to you. We see you need help. So here's the thing. You follow the Doctor's orders; we'll take care of everything else. Deal?"

Just then Gregory walked over, "Aww nah! Y'all lettin' her pimp y'all. This was all just a scam? And y'all fell for it?"

Al grabbed him by the collar. He pulled him to the side. "Boy shut up! Aint no scam. What's wrong with you! You was raised better. You know who God is. What is your problem?"

"Ok!" Al yells, "This is the thing, you let the EMT's take you on to the E.R. Get what you need."

Sam chimes in, "We'll have security drop you home when you're done."

Al steps in, "I'll go to the daycare, call you on your cell, you tell them what the issue is, I'll be your witness. I will pay the necessary overages, I'll get a worker to get them home to you safe and sound; everything documented of course for future references."

"Everything works out. How about that?"

"That's sounds wonderful if it can really happen like that. But we still need food. I have my food stamp card. I still need to get to the store. I'm sorry, I have so many issues. Y'all don't know. I be tryin' to do better. I just need help."

"And today is your day to receive it. That's why we're here. Don't worry." Al assured her.

"I can't believe y'all would do that for me. I mean what's the catch? We strangers. Ain't nobody ever been this nice. And y'all a bunch of men. I....I....I ain't got nothin' to offer y'all." She clutched the top of her uniform top. I'm not like that."

"Young lady, we don't want nothin' from you but to see you and your family healthy and whole. See Doc in the business of healing physically but me, I'm in the business of healing spiritually. As the Lord allows. By His grace. He has favored you today. He has favored you always. For despite all of the issues that have plagued you all of your young life, you are surviving. You're not out here selling your body and getting high. You're a responsible mother. You're a tax paying citizen and you manage it all because The Lord is truly with you. You must know this by now. There's no other explanation for it."

"Oh I don't deserve any credit sir. I had three kids out of wedlock. I make a lot of mistakes a as a mom. Sometimes I'm too tired to help them with their homework and I think I discipline 'em too hard. I haven't been to church in so long. God probably mad at me. I try to send tithe money along with my boys when the church van pick 'em up but, I can't all of the time as much as I would like to. I barely have enough for bills and rent most of the time. I ain't no good person. I'm just out here maintainin' and trying to make it like everybody else."

"Beloved, there is no condemnation to those that are in Christ Jesus. God ain't mad at you. He sees your struggle. He knows your pain. Today is the start of your breakthrough. You have an honest heart. He loves you. You're special Him. All things work together for good to those that love Him and are called according to his purpose. Even that spill back there, it's working out for your good. Make no mistake."

"Yes Ma'am.", Doctor Sam grinned. "I've seen people with more money and less problems committed to psych facilities for less. You are blessed and highly favored. The blessing and the favor come in the being able to sustain, maintain and endure. You've been waiting on the Lord a long time. He's here child. Answers to prayers don't always come in pretty packages." Al glanced at G.

She sat astonished, "If you say so. But..."

"But what?" said Al.

"This is too good to be true. Man stuff like this never happens to me."

"Starting today you can retract that statement. This is just the beginning. You have sewn. Hear the Spirit of the Lord say NOW is your time to reap."

"But, I don't deserve it. This just seems impossible. Yo! I'm being punched right? This some MTV special or somethin' right? The ghetto version."

"No. No. You're not being punched. Just trust The Lord. Believe for His goodness. He has favored you. Daughter NOTHING IS TOO HARD FOR GOD. Know today, nothing shall be impossible. I know you have been struggling. I know it's been hard. I know you ain't perfect. I know you've been praying. I know it seem like God done forgot about you. Ain't so. Remember, He may not come when you want Him..."

She finished his statement with tear filled eyes, "But He'll be there right on time. He's an on time God."

"Yes He is. Now! Let's get you on the road to good health and wellness. Let's go get these babies home to their mommy. And oh yeah..."

Al looked at G, "We need you to write down your info. Tomorrow, we'll send some women over from the Women's Ministry to your house. You can give them a list of the things y'all need. Money is not an object. But for tonight," He moves closer to G, "Give me fifty dollars man."

"Huh?"

"Give me fifty. You can spare it. God blesses us so that we can bless others."

"Granddad, why I gotta give you fifty dollars? For what? FOR HER?"

"It's ok Mister Pastor. We'll be fine. I hate being a bother."

"Now you listen. People been makin' you feel like a burden all of your life. You ain't gotta tell me that. Plus you full of pride. Let me tell you young lady, before pride goes destruction/after pride comes the fall, however you need to receive it, just do! Never mind mindless behavior over here. Take the money, feed your family tonight. Let people help you. You too prideful.

You're hurting yourself. You are most assuredly hurting those children. Let go of your pride. Just let go honey and let God." Al had preached.

"Amen!" agreed Sam.

He grabbed the money from G, "Take this. Order some take out for tonight. Early in the morning expect a call from one of the sisters at Breakthrough Ministries."

"Ok. I just don't understand your kindness. How can you be so..."

Al interrupted, "Girl, God been good to me." He looked at G, "To my entire family. To everybody I know even if they too stupid to recognize it and revere Him because of it. Moreover, because He is Almighty God. He is Holy. He is God alone. Creator of all creature great and small; No respecter of persons. All glory is his young lady. Give all glory to God. I am just a vessel."

Sam walked a few feet away. He turned around, "By the way, ma'am, you never gave us your name. I need a name before they take you to the E.R."

"Bendita. My name is Bendita Greenly. And thank you. Thank you all."

"Well Bendita Greenly. The best is yet to come for you. Don't thank us. Thank Almighty God. Like the Pastor said, we're just vessels. We're just paying the love forward that's all. Your name means blessed in Spanish."

"Yes doctor, it does."

"That's what you are. Don't you forget. You've got the right name. See yourself that way from now on. Get into the word. Find out who God says you are. Believe that. Walk in it. And don't worry if you don't get it right straight off...takes time. Take time to renew your mind young lady. You are not your mistakes. Nor are you your past. Shake it off! Yes Lord! God got good plans for you. Today is just the beginning. Even if every day ain't a sunny day. It is a blessing. For it is a gift. It is the present. We tend to let that go over our heads when things aren't going our way. We make our problems bigger than God. We forget He's larger than life. There's not a thing He can't fix in His own timing. We just gotta trust Him."

"Wow. Nobody has ever spoken to me like that before. I hear you. I understand. I'm just a work in progress."

"Girl, you'd be surprised to know how many Christians don't know to speak life into other people. Let alone themselves. God created everything we see just by speaking. The Roman soldier told Jesus if He would just send a word, his servant would be healed. Speaking is live action faith. It is now faith. All it is. And oh yeah, we're all a work in progress until the Father calls us home. Evolution is an ongoing process. You're not alone. We're in this flesh. We fail. We're human. We fall down but we get up, just like the song says. Ain't that right Pastor?" Sam laughed.

"Sho' nuff. Ain't a person alive who ain't got stuff. That's why we need Jesus every day. We born wit' stuff. We die wit' stuff. Nobody is exempt from stuff."

"Oh yeah, you are a Pastor." They load her on to the back of the ambulance. "But wait, if you a Pastor and so nice, how is that mistake your Grandson? Don't add up?"

"Young lady, that right there, is a story ain't nobody out here ready for. Take care. I'll be in touch."

"Wait. What did that mean? I ain't stupid." G questioned.

The Pastor slapped is Grandson on the back playfully, "Prove it by keeping your mouth shut. Girl don't need not one more man beating her down in no kind of way. When you see these women G, whether you like 'em or not; whether they respect themselves or not, treat 'em how you treat ya own mother. Respect from the door. God is no respecter of persons. Meaning treat everybody with love and equality. The cost of discrimination is so high, no one can afford it."

He knew his Grandfather was correct. Bitter, the boy remained silent. That's exactly what he was doing; He treated every women like he had been treating Stacey.

Finally, the two men arrive at Spain's. Just as Gregory pulls in to park, a beautiful, young woman tips across the parking space, working her hips like a Hula Dancer, she has his immediate and full attention.

"Laaawd Jesus.", he says.

Al looks at Gregory, "Boy leave that alone. That's a pretty package full of nothing. That right there son, is a vacant apartment. People keep comin' by to check it out...don't nobody ever sign the lease. Know why?"

"No. But go ahead and preach Pastor." he rolled his eyes.

"False advertising boy. Just park the car." He pops his Grandson upside the head. "And stop staring at her like you wanna eat her. That scares some women off. They don't what you're thinking man. In their minds, for all they know, you could be some type of predator, future stalker or whatever."

"Granddad, trust me, only the wrong type of girl gets freaked by a man staring. Anyway, females be buggin'! They don't know how a man think. How they even know what I'm thinkin' to even try and guess? I could just be staring because she's the most beautiful creature I've seen all day or EVER!" He continued to sneak peeks at the woman as he exited the car. She stood off to the side. She bent over pretending to adjust the strap on her heels. He couldn't help but stare.

Al looked at her. He looked at G. "Or you could be thinking about something totally different. I'm a man. I know what you're thinking. Obviously the women do too. Come on predator. Get ya eyes back in ya head. Let's go eat."

"Granddad?"

"What boy?"

"Tell me you ain't see that? I mean really. Man to man. Me and you. Keep it one wit me."

"Oh I saw it. But I made up my mind to unsee it right after that. Need more than that to keep my attention. My interest reaches beyond that at my age. You'll get there. Hopefully sooner than later. One day pretty packaging and desperation won't be enough to keep your attention either. Right now you goin' for the taste; you just tryin to feel your stomach every time you get hungry. As you mature son, you'll begin to see how your taste buds change. They become more refined. You won't want to just feed your hunger any longer. You my boy, will be Jonsin' for somethin or someone to feed your spirit. You gon' want somethin with substance. And man….if God blesses you with looks, taste, substance; something to fill you up that is of quality….then looks alone aren't even gonna matter that much. You will just be happy to be filled. You'll be thankful that you're able to walk around full when so many other guys out here still lookin'. Still hungry. They load themselves up with junk. Empty calories. It's like Chinese food out here. You full for the moment, then soon after, You will find yourself hungry again. It's all to your disadvantage. Like drinking sugary sodas and stuff; empty calories."

"Aw Granddad. It ain't that serious."

"That's the problem with your entire generation G. It's never THAT serious. Weaker and wiser the Bible say."

"Aight Granddad. I hear you. Don't think I'm not listening to you. I do. Imma think about it."

"That's all I want you to do G. Think about what I tell you. You're young. You're in your rebellious stage of life. Where you are is where you should be, naturally. I understand it. I've been there. The key is not to stay there. Grow. Learn. Evolve. Renew your mind over time. It takes time. No pressure man. I'm just happy to hear you say you're thinking about it. Don't think too long now. Too much thinking leads to less and less doing. There comes a point where you can't be thinkin. You gotta get doin'. Aight man?"

"Facts."

When they were seated Al suggested they pray for the young woman Bendita. "Yes. And amen. That was a fine young woman Gregory. She's gonna make a great wife someday. Gon' make somebody life rich. She's gonna bring favor to some blessed young man one day. Now that's somethin' you can full from son."

Gregory couldn't understand just what his Grandfather was getting at. He asked, "How somebody broke and broke-down gon' make anybody rich or full? She's a no name Granddad. Don't nobody want her. She's too much of a fixer-upper. Plus that mouth. And that attitude."

"Boy what?"

"You know what I'm sayin' Granddad. She a hot mess. Too much of a fixer-upper. Ain't nobody got time…"

"You can't be serious man."

"What? What did I say this time?"

"Aww young buck. You ain't ready for no real woman man."

"Huh?"

She's strong because she has to be. She's a single mother raising boys. She's doing it alone. Maybe her attitude is a defense mechanism. Did you ever consider that?"

"No."

"I know you haven't. But I don't know why when you're a black man with a black mother."

"Huh?"

"Black women get a lot of flak from weak brothers and people outside of the black community for having attitude. So what though? Aren't they entitled? Black women struggle and suffer a lot. They all too often are forced in to being the heads of the households and the bread winners. Started from slavery. The cycle continues. Then, they get devalued by their own men. Weak men who fail to understand their own women but in the same breath, selfishly want those same women to understand and bow down and cater to them. It's crazy."

"Wait. But didn't Grandma cater to you?"

"Yes she did. And I took care of her. We took care of one another. I didn't beat her mind down and take my personal problems out on her. And when she did give me a bit of attitude, I didn't complain about not being able to handle it and run off to other women. She understood me. I understood her. We had common goals. That's what's missing in our communities and homes. The black man has been displaced by slavery and the black woman now has to take up the slack. Always had to!"

"Heavy is the head that wears the crown right Granddad?"

"Yes it is! How is it we don't take the time to understand one another and nurse one another to a healthy place? We just run to other people because it's easier to deal with them rather than face the problem is in my own community. If she's upset. Think about the hand that's been dealt to your black woman down through the generations."

"Same with the black men right? I used hear a lot of white people talk about the angry black man thing at school. I didn't grow up with any angry black men. So that confused me."

"Another stereotype. And even if there is some truth to it, people have to open their eyes to the hand this country dealt black men down through the centuries from generation to generation. From the emasculation of slavery to the emasculation of mass incarceration. We're still trying to find our way back from the slave mentality. When we get that, then we can build from there. The black community is hurting and we hollerin' but don't nobody hear us. Or the do and they choose to ignore our cries. It's devastating man. That's why I don't want you disrespecting these females. They have it hard enough."

"But if she's a fixer-upper, she's a fixer-upper. Truth is truth."

"Boy, don't you know we're all fixer-uppers? That's why we need Jesus. Ain't nobody exempt. You of all people, should know better. You was raised better than that. See boy! It's the company you keep."

"Aww Granddad. Can you please stop playing that card? I make my own choices. Nobody's putting a gun to my head."

"Not yet. God forbid. You think you know so much don't you? Well I tell you what, you better hope...no, better yet, you had better pray The Lord gets you before the devil does."

"I'm good Granddad trust me."

"Pure ignorance. Son, where you been all ya life? Raised in the church. You don't know nothin' by now?"

"Huh?"

"You mean to tell me you've been coming to the table all these years and haven't been eating? Pardon me, you're young yet, I meant drinking. What? You got somethin' against milk? It does the body good you know."

Nah Granddad you mean A BODY."

"Boy, I ain't old enough to be senile. I know what I'm sayin'! Don't correct me. You the one need to catch up. Can't believe....grew up around pastors. Church all the time. What the..."

"Hear yourself Granddad?"

"Question is, do you hear me?"

"No. I mean yeah. I mean yes Sir. I mean, all that growing' up in church don't mean nothin'." He faced the floor, "Sometimes people go to please other people. Sometimes they're forced. Sometimes you're just trying to keep other people happy or quiet. The goal is to not let anybody down because they expect you to be a certain way because you're son of a pastor. Even other people I know from school who got parents with big names and jobs in high places. The kids feel pressure to be somebody they may not really be. Dress like this. Stand this way. Smile, they're watching. Greet him. Meet her. On and on. You know her daughter is going to college to be this or that; get her number. His son plays on the same football team; maybe you guys can hang out sometimes. I mean, you may not even like these people. And then..."

"Uh huh."

"These kids talk about having to say things you don't mean or subscribe to an ideology that you may be against or just not support."

"Are you saying you don't believe son?"

"No way. I believe. In God. I know Jesus died for me. It's just..."

"I'm listening."

"The pressure. Maybe I want to get to take the time to get to know The Lord and other people my way. For myself. On my own. Granddad, no disrespect, but I would like to be my own man. Just because my family is a certain way or is called to do certain things, that doesn't mean that their way is the right way for me. Sometimes people want you to walk in shoes you don't fit."

"Son," Al replied. "Did we force you? Forgive us? We only meant well. We didn't mean to. We was just tryin' to do right by you. Get you started on the right path. It's not God's will that anybody perish."

"Granddad, I'm not talkin' about being saved. I'm talkin' about being a pastor. That ain't my thing. And honestly, I don't know about all this church stuff right now. I'm just out here tryin' to find my way. I mean I know I'm saved. I wanna love God the way I see y'all do. But, I just ain't there right now. I don't know the Bible like the back of my hand like y'all. I don't wanna live in the church like y'all do. I wanna experience God. Just in a different way. I know there's only one way to come to God, its thru Christ I know...I'm there. I believe that. I pray too. All of the time. But I, I just don't want to do things the way y'all always did 'em. I need to find my way to where I need to be. Where I fit you know?"

"I hear you son."

"Granddad, I'm just tryin to find my groove. I don't know if I'm bitter or if it's just my age. I'm just not there right now. Of that I'm sure. Please don't hate me. I'm not like y'all. I just can't do church. And just because a person always in church, don't mean they saved or changed. Don't mean they are learning, growing or being their authentic self. How many people just drag themselves to a church house every Wednesday? Every Friday? Every Sunday? Routine and Religion. Just trying to be what other people say they should. What if I have the desire to worship and serve The Lord another way? What if I wanna break the mold and do something unconventional? I'm willing to risk y'all stoning me. I gotta live my truth though. I can't do tradition right now Granddad. I've been in church all of my life; seen so much stuff. I didn't get anything from it. I'm honest enough to say it man. So there it is."

"Stand up man.", Al grabbed Gregory. He hugged him tightly. He held him as the young man fought back tears.

Gregory cleared his throat, "What's up man? Granddad, why you holdin' on to me like this? I know I disappointed you. I'm sorry."

"Man, I ain't disappointed. I respect your honesty. That's a big step towards manhood you just took. I am proud of you. I ain't here to crucify you. I'm here to love you. That's it. Not stone you. Not judge you. Just hear you and be here for you. I know how you feel. Own your truth. I don't know where The Lord is leading you to. That's up to you to figure that out. Just don't give up on God, family or church. And when I say church, I mean the body. 'Cause Lord knows everybody ain't called to minister or serve in the building. Promise me you'll do whatever it is God is calling you to do with love, determination and purpose."

He hugged Al tightly, "I promise. I won't let you down."

Al pulled back. He looked G, in his eyes, "No pressure son. It's not about letting me down. Don't you let yourself down. Hear?"

"Yes Sir."

"I love you man. Never forget that. Hear me? No matter what you do."

"Yes Sir."

"One more promise man."

"Okay?"

"Promise me you gon' do the right thing."

"But Granddad, I ain't...."

"Boy. I ain't no fool. You don't need to be out here in the streets doin' what you doin'. You have a calling on ya life. Maybe it ain't to pastor. Or if it is maybe not in the traditional sense. I get that. I want you to know people are watching you. You have influence and power. Use them wisely Gregory."

"Aw Granddad. That's what I'm talkin' about. I don't want all that pressure and stuff. I don't wanna live in a fish bowl or in a box. I need to be free. I'm not like y'all. I see things different. I don't know why."

"Listen G, last thing you have to be is like me or your father. You be you. Do you. I encourage that. Believe when I tell you I feel you son. Just acknowledge Him in all of your ways and..."

"He will direct my path."

Al patted him on the back,"Yeah man, yeah. There you go. It's in there. You a teen in transition. Everybody don't know everything about they callin' upfront G. Don't pressure yourself. Let go let God man. You be aight. But while you're letting go and letting God, ease off what you out here tryin' to connect to. Many times when we ready to let go of sin, the sin ain't ready to let go of us. The enemy is crafty. He don't fight fair G. Make up your mind to let go. When you're ready. I'm here. Day or night."

"I appreciate that Granddad. I ain't tryin' to stress you though. That's why I didn't come to you with my issues in the first place. I know you're always busy at church with church business. I was positive you didn't have time. You was too busy with your religion. I just needed a man to talk to."

"Man, I'm sorry. I'm here. That's the past. I'm present now. I am here. Don't worry about church. That part of my life is over."

"Granddad you serious?! That can't be true! They need you there! The community needs you! What is everybody going to do?! ", G shouted.

"Well what they gonna have to do is shake religion off. Get a real relationship with God. Get spiritual. They're going have to let go and let God. It's a new season in my life. Gotta move on. It's over."

"But wait. When did you come to this conclusion Granddad?"

"G, I've been aggravated. Bored with the status quo. Sick of the routine. Annoyed with people not doing anything different. Craving somethin new; scared to move forward from all I always knew. I guess I'm in transition like you. Old way ain't workin for me no more. Time to level up. Just don't know how. Waiting on God. Nervous boy. Don't know what's next."

The youth marveled at his Grandfather's transparency. "But Granddad, how can you speak with so much wisdom, knowledge and confidence and be nervous. You seem like you got it all figured out."

"I'm human Gregory. I'm not superman. If you can have your issues, why can't I? I'm goin' through man. Can't believe I'm tellin' you this right now."

"Yeah me either." Gregory sat there staring at his Grandfather like a little boy amazed at a live magic trick. He was impressed. He was astonished. He was confused. His young mind raced with thoughts of how this could be. "How does this work?" he asked himself.

"Purging, I suppose. I feel refreshed in a way. I'm glad you stopped by the church boy. I needed this. Thank you Jesus."

"Yeah me too. Thank you Jesus." He hurried through his sentiment. "I'm still trying to figure this out though...what's your motivation. What is inspiring you to just jump ship like that?"

"That's just it Gregory. I'm not inspired. I've been longing to move forward for some time. Never knew when the time was ever gonna be right. Waited for opportunity. All the while, I guess opportunity was waiting on me. It don't stick around long. Stick and move is the way opportunity chooses to do things. I guess I grabbed the coattails just before it got away. Mm mm! The hem of the garment. It's time."

"Not inspired Granddad?"

"Yeah man. Nothing moving. Nobody move. Nobody get hurt. Safe in the bubble. Comfortable in the box. Christians love it safe in the confines of the church, tucked away in religion and routine, where they can hide their sin and duck the responsibility of loving a fallen, hurting world. Many called..."

G added, "Few chosen."

"Facts.", Al remarked. They laughed.

"G, you ever watch Fade to Black?"

"That Jay Z movie thing? Uh yeah. It was dope."

"Well I saw it as more of a documentary. But potato, potato…"

"Wait! Now just hold up! Granddad….you watched Fade to Black?"

"Ten years later. But yeah…why not? I hear Nas got somethin' in the oven too. Time Is Illmatic. I can't wait boy."

"Jay Z? Nas? Come on Granddad. You're a pastor. Whatchu doin'?"

"Aww don't gimme dat religious garbage. I was watching T.V, it came on and I watched it. Too much cussin'. But, I learned a few things. The music was good. And wait….boy, how old do you think I am? I mean really?"

"Oh no disrespect Granddad. Yo! You so gangsta! You da realest. I know people who pop that church mess all day long; know they be doin' stuff. You just get doper and doper man."

"Boy, you know I'm a Golden. Like fine wine, I get better with time baby. You see me." They laughed.

"My Granddad watch Jay z concerts. Wow!"

"Hold on son now. I got my head on straight. I watch what I entertain and what entertains me. Believe when I tell you, I do everything with purpose in mind. I try to anyway. I'm still very selective. You can't judge people for being who they are. Especially when you don't know where they're coming from, why they do what they do or who they're going to evolve into. God knows our end and our beginning. Ain't my place to judge. I just gauge what's best for me in

Christ. I do all I can to do what The Lord has instructed me to do. Got it?"

"Yes Sir."

"Good. That being said, he said something when he was in studio with Just Blaze about inspiration and it made me think."

"Ok. I'm listening."

"I can't recall his words verbatim. But he said something to the effect of not being inspired. Like, when he's not inspired, he has to think. If he has to think then, that means he has to force it. If he has to force it, that ain't good. Now the conversation may have begun with him talking about work ethic, focus or something. That all went over my head, but that bit about being inspired or the lack thereof, caught my attention."

"Wow. I can't believe you're referring to Jay Granddad. That's hot."

"Son. You can learn or get inspiration from just about anything if you step outside of your box. Takes wisdom though. Older people used say, chew the meat and spit out the bones. That means take what you need or what you can use, get rid of the rest. Takes time. Gotta be strong spiritually. Can't be led by everybody or listen to too many voices. Need discernment. I believe He can get a word to us through anybody He chooses to, anytime he chooses to. Even through a song. It ain't gotta be gospel. A commercial, a billboard, instructions that come with a package. Nature just doin what it do. People just being people. Nothing is impossible with God Greg."

"Yoooooo! Drop them jewels man!"

"Anyway, that's where I am. It's just time to move on. I don't wanna force nothin' that don't fit unless it's God's will. Sometimes we get in ruts. We go through storms. We just gotta ride the waves and ride the storm out holding on to Jesus; knowing the winds and waves obey Him. This ain't one of those times though. I been prayin. I know it's time to press on. He knows where and why even when I don't. Rough place to be G."

"Facts Granddad. You talked to my father?"

"Not in a great while young man. Have you heard from your father?"

"He hasn't spoken to me."

Mirror on the ceiling. It was the best conversation either of them had had in a very long time. It was time. A purposeful time. Two men having conversation.

END OF THE ROAD

"Oh my goodness babe. I can't believe what an incredible day it's been. I feel so special. Babe thank you."

"You don't have to thank me. You already know what it is. You're special. Very special. Here, got somethin' for you."

"C'mon babe. You've done so much already. I don't need anything else."

"Oh you don't need nothin' else? Sweet. Then I'll take it back or give it somebody else."

"No. No. No. Ok. Ok. Ok."

"Ok what?"

"I need it.", she smiles.

"No. You don't need it.", he teases.

"Do or don't. I WANT IT! Gimme now."

"Aight. Aight." he laughs. "Here. Now, before I hand it to you, just know I love you. You have to know that if I touched that thing. You ready?"

"Boy stop playin'!"

"Woman, don't the Bible say be anxious for nothing? NO THING!"

"Oh my goodness. I'm done. You play too much. I'm out goodnight."

"Oh word? No kiss."

"Boy bye."

"It's like that for real?"

"I can show you better than I can tell you."

He grabs her hand just as she opens the car door. "No kiss for real?"

"For what? You gamin'. Who got time?"

He pulls her close to him. He whispers, "No kiss?"

"No gift?"

"You always get my sucker-for-love ass. Here...take it."

He hands her the gift. She kisses him slowly before she reaches out to receive it. "You ain't no sucker. Don't talk like that. We in this together. I'm just as gone for you. I'm in love with you." His heart melted. He hands her the box.

"Well this is huge! What on earth? NO WAY! JUST NO WAY! Baby..."

"Uh huh?"

"Bae...A Victor Cruz jersey? An OFFICIAL Victor Cruz jersey?"

"Yeah man. You know I'm ready to chew my own hands off just touching that thing."

"You had it framed in a gold frame and everything. Babe!"

"Yeah. I would've had it autographed but I'm a Giant slayer so you know I ain't goin' out my way to find dat fool just to lower myself and beg him to sign that jersey like some weak ass groupie. Gotta stay loyal to San Fran. So if you tell anybody I even looked at a Giants jersey, we through. I ain't even playin'."

"Here we go. We ain't never gon' be through. You the sweetest. I love you. Thank you."

"Whatever man. You owe me. BIG!"

"Whatever man. I love you. Good night." She walked up the stairs. She yelled, "And don't get mad because we bury 49ers bro. Big Blue! CRUUUUUUUUUZZZZZZZZ!"

Unamused he replied, "Big Blue was a big disappointment last year. Oh wait...that's every year. Oh my bad."

She turned around to set him straight. He sped away. Three seconds later she received a text, "Ya team whack but, I still love my baby."

She texts, "Don't kiss up. It ain't sexy. Get home safe. Y'all QB a pretty boy track star. So bite me."

"I would love to. You know I stay ready. Question is, are you ready?"

She blushes, typing by the light of the moon, "Not until you put a ring on it."

"Tonight? Don't play. Vegas just a plane ride away. You ready?"

"Next day. LoL!"

"You soft. LoL. GN."

"So you remember?"

"Tease.", he joked.

She headed up the staircase to her bedroom. She ran herself a warm bubble bath. Sinking down beneath the luxurious foam she thought to herself, "Man that was a nice day. But it's still early. I should've asked him to stay a while longer. The night is still young." She admired her reflection in the mirror, "Girl now what we gon' do?"

Someone is blowing up her phone. "Whoever that is, they gon' have to wait."

Eventually, she disengages from her pleasure. Off for a date with her bathrobe, slippers, a black and white production; A knock on the door. "Who on Earth?" Its pitch black on the first floor of her house. She peeps through the drapes of her bedroom window. Noticing the sensor lights all around the house light up one after another, she thinks, "Probably that stupid fat cat from across the street. I wish they'd keep that cat over there. Scared the day lights out of me."

She creeps into the center of her bed, "Now a sip would be the cherry on top to this awesome night."

On her way down the steps to the kitchen, a hard rap on the door. Shaken, she loses balance, falling down the stairs to the bottom of the door. Managing to claw her way up to the peep hole with a swollen ankle, she doesn't see anyone.

She hops over to the nearest couch in agony. Again, someone is at the door. This time, she hears a tap, be it ever so faint. "Get the hell outta here before I heat up this toaster and catch a case. Don't get the game messed up!" she pleads. Afraid and alone, she grabs the Louisville Slugger planted strategically behind the potted plant near the door. There's an eerie silence that incites a riotous gaggle of oddities and alarms within. It is the equivalent to the greenish-grey bubbles of a witch's brew in a crusty caldron from a dank, dingy cave near the very core of hell that reaches all the way to the very core of her core. Painfully, she hastens to the master bathroom to grab her cell. She reached out to grab the phone from the edge of the sink, it fell into the toilet. The toilet she had forgotten to flush. "Damn It!" A pounding on the door.

She hops over to the balcony atop the winding staircase, "Look! The boys on they way so keep it up! As a matter of fact, you know what?" Frightened, she looks up, "God help me. It's just me and you. Please." She puts up the bravest front she can muster as she slides down the stairs on her behind, one step at a time, baseball bat in tow. One last deep breath before she unlocks the door, opening it at chain's length. "Bring it!" she touts from behind the door.

A familiar voice sings, "Ayyeeeeee! I need a Gangsta Bit..."

Caught off guard she hindered him, "What the ...You?"

He laughed, "Get the...Who?"

"Oh my goodness boy! You almost caught one!"

"Yeah aight Scary Spice. Whatever. What's good? I came to chill witchu tonight ma."

"Chill wit' who kid?"

"You kid! I can't come in for a convo at least? Ya man don't allow you to have friends? He run it I guess."

"What?!"

"I guess since you a kept woman, he call it huh?"

"Boy bye! Get off my stoop. My life, who run it and whoever call whatever ain't ya concern. Bye Lance!" She tried to slam the door shut with all of her might to no avail.

He pushes the door open knocking her back down to the floor. "Now look at you." he sneers. "Being rude may feel good but, everything feel good ain't good for you." He pulls her up by her cropped hair, "Getcho ass up!" She screams. He grabs her by the back of her neck like an animal. He bites her gently on the nose, breathing his liquor-laden breath into her nostrils, "Who here?"

"Just me.", she squeaks.

"Aight. What's upstairs?"

"Bedrooms and bathrooms. No! I don't wanna..."

"Shut up.", he kisses her neck aggressively. "You got spirits in here?"

"Wine.", she whined.

"Where?"

"I don't want to..."

"Bitch where I said! This ain't no request."

"In the kitchen." she whimpered.

"Let's go then. Let's have a splash. After all. It is a very special day." he grinned.

"I don't wanna..."

He pushed her back down to floor. She hit her mouth against the edge of the accent table in the foyer. Blood poured out of her mouth like a fountain.

"Sure you wanna. And you gonna. Go shawty! It's ya birthday. We gon' party like it's ya birthday."

She lay in her own blood crying. He kicked her in the butt, "Get up! I'm thirsty. Now that I think of it. I'm hungry too! He grabbed her by her injured foot, "Bring yo ass ma. Think I'm playin?"

She screamed bloody murder. Dragging her past the bay window in the dining room, he noticed the next door neighbors lights come on. A shadowy figure peeked through the window.

"Gal, you alright over there?" the voice of an elderly woman rang out in the quiet of the night.

He squeezed her ankle with force, "You know what to do."

She stuttered, "I...I...I'm alright Mrs. Cambridge. I just tripped over somethin'. I'm ok. I'll be over for coffee first thing in the morning. Goodnight."

"Child, let me know if you need some assistance. I got my life alert necklace on. They be here in a jiffy."

She didn't respond. The old woman thought that unusual. She always got a response from her next door neighbor. "Well alright then. I'll leave you to yourself. Call me if you need me. Better yet, I will call you later...make sure you alright."

"What she mean she gon' call you? Where ya phone at?"

"It's not working."

He squeezed her foot even tighter. "Now, we can do this all night if you want to."

In agony she screams out, "No! No please!"

"Mmmmmmm...damn that sexy. Never thought I'd hear ya bougie ass beggin'. Sounds sexy. Like dat." He squeezed her foot again, "Louder. I like dat. Beg bitch."

"Owwwwwww!!!!!!!!! Please don't! What have I ever done to you?"

"Look at you. So beautiful. So desperate. So broken." He bent down to kiss her bloody mouth. "Now this, this is sexy. Girl you don't know the wood you givin' me right now. Damn! You bitches are such teases." He pulled down her pajama bottoms, "Ooooohhhh! And Lawd ha' mercy. No panties. A gift from the gods."

She spit in his face, "'Cho nasty hands off me Negro. It's only one God and He ain't got nothin' to do with this. And when He through witchu..."

"Mmmmmm....talk dirty to me baby." he teased. "Ma whoever this God is, I guarantee you, He don't care about no hoes. Kiss me..."

"You a sick fu...".

"Now. Now. Now. Blessing and cursing out da same mouth. Oh boy baby." he laughed with a dark chortle as he shook his head.

She had always heard the Devil knew the Word too. She had never taken it to heart before. She never fathomed coming face to face with the Devil. He didn't have horns and a tail. He wasn't blood red. He didn't stand on hooved hind's feet and he most definitely didn't smell like fire and brimstone. He smelled like Usher and his pitch fork wasn't in his hands like she had envisioned it from childhood; it was in his pants. Everything she had ever heard about the enemy had all been a myth. Even if she was the one wrong about his appearance, it didn't matter. Tonight, she would learn if Satan's dance card was full over in the Middle East, he'd use any available host to do his work other places. Unlike God, Satan is limited. The enemy can't be everywhere at once. He isn't omnipresent like God. On the other hand though, like God, he wasn't looking for anyone with overwhelming ability or superpower, just someone who would answer the call and do the work. A willing participant is all it takes to accomplish either evil or good. The power truly is in agreement whether for good or for evil.

Tonight she was looking the enemy straight in the eye. It was the scariest experience she had ever had in her life. How could she be doing her best; Going to church, studying her Bible, praying with her children; making room and time for The Lord in her life; she had been walking in integrity. With all of that going on, how could the enemy still be able to disrupt her life?

She had just given her life to Christ that Sunday. All of her life she had known of God. Now, she would get to know God thru His son, Christ Jesus. She had made a definite decision. The ultimate decision to follow Christ. Believing her life would be problem free. Nobody had told her the enemy plays for keeps. He was enraged. He would not give up that easily. The devil hated her. He hated her family. He knew she had made the best decision she could ever make. He wanted to destroy her. He wanted to dismantle her righteousness; make her break her promise. He wanted to make her believe God had broken his promise to her. The enemy wanted her back. In his ignorance, he would try to take her by force using any available agent. A familiar face.

"You know what? Forget the sauce. Let's go upstairs and play dress up." He pulled her pants up. "Yeah, I done seen you just about naked. Had you a million different ways in my head. I wanna see you dressed up. I ain't used my imagination in a long time. Thanks to you hoes."

She snatched away from him, "I ain't no ho!"

He pulled her close slowly by the crotch of her pants, "You whatever I say you is HO!"

He picked her up. He threw her over his shoulder making his way up the winding staircase. "Damn! What was that joker payin' y'all hoes? You livin' right ma! I don't even got it like this. Oh wait! Yeah. Ya punk ass man gotchu. I forgot. You a kept woman. Lil' brown ghetto Barbie." He threw her to the floor. He kicked in the bedroom door. "Oooweee. This must be the master suite. It's fancy. Let's see what y'all workin' wit'." He kicked the closet doors open. "Diva huh?" She lay on her back on the plush gold carpet in tears. "Walk in closet. More clothes than a lil' bit. Fashionista." He walked over to her, ripped her pajama top open. She covered her breasts. "Get up in the closet. I want to watch you play dress up Barbie." He dragged her over to the closet by her hair. "Let's go. Choose well. Imma take a leak. When I come back, I want you snatched or Imma snatch yo ass. Got it?" She turned her head. She could hear him singing Trading Places from the master bathroom.

She prayed, "Jesus. Why is this happening to me?"

It was as if the Satan himself intercepted her prayer. Before she knew it, her unwelcomed guest was towering over her, "Ma, He can't hear you. Put on the gold gown. No bra. For a baby=making factory, ya tits sit up real good. You got good body girl. You got daughters right? Mmm... If they look anything like they momma..." She spat all of the blood she could gather in her mouth on to his feet.

"Feisty creature. Like dat too." He lit up a Swisha Sweet. "Mmm, now that taste's good. You probably taste better though." He laughed, "Just a matter of time before I find out. Ain't that right chocolate?"

She coughed, "My kids. You...you can't smoke in here."

"Girl, them ain't my kids. They ain't here anyway. By the way, that oldest one, she hot, she look like she gon' give good body like her mother. Damn, baby girl got curves like a racetrack."

She found the strength to stand up. She shuffled over to him. She spat blood black blood in his face as she spoke, "You gon' have to kill me first bastard. DON"T YOU EVER! EVER! COME FOR MY KIDS! I WILL KILL YOU. YOU HEAR ME! KILL YOU!"

He wiped the blood off of his face. He licked the blood off of his hand. "Bitch." He pulled on his cigar. "I ain't scared of you or nothin' else. You see me. If you wanna play games, we can play. Wanna play guess who kills who first?"

She fell back on her behind scurrying back towards the broken door. He got on his knees. He scrambled over to her. He blew the smoke from his blunt directly into her nostrils. He had forced her nose into his mouth. His teeth stained with her blood. It smelled like hot death in a cold grave.

She pushed back, "Get out of here. Your breath stink. Smell like hell."

"Don't worry 'bout dat. It's all good. 'Cause it's 'bout to smell like you in a minute. Come here." He pushed her down to the floor. His fist firmly planted in her chest. He forced her leg back with the other.

She screamed, "I HATE YOOOOOOUUUUUUU!!!!! NOOOOOOOO!!!!! WHAT HAPPENED TO YOU!? WHAT DID I DO TO YOUUUUUU???!!! NOOOOOOOOOOOO! DOOOOOOONNNN'T!!!" She pounded him. She fought. Ripping flesh from his face. He became more aggressive with each strike.

His hot breath arrested her ear, "What happened to me? What happened to me? You happened to me. Always thinking you too good for me. Got me chasin' you all the time. This random walk in the club and you just throw that nigga the pussy. And me? What I get after all of that being nice to yo ass? Huh? TALK BITCH!" He in her ear. Her body seized up.

"All I get is rejection. Right? RIGHT?! You don't think I saw you that night," He grabbed her face, "Damn near naked. Ridin' that man like damn rodeo clown. All in front of everybody. You was the star of the show. Brick City Barbie. Homegrown porn star. Kimmy Cakes, Jocelyn and Mimi old put together ain't got nothin on you." He kisses her, "You the star of the show. Don't you wanna be a star baby? Gon' let me make you a star?"

"Stop. No!"

"Oh bitch please!" he hovered over her. "You know you a ho just like yo ho ass mama!" She looked puzzled.

"Oh don't gimme dat Liza. Oh what? You think I don't know you? Under that wig." he touched her breast. "Under everything. I know you Liza." She shook violently.

"I been watchin' you since you was in high school. Pure ass virgin. You and that pickle-headed Puerto Rican boyfriend I used to see you wit' in da hood. Bitch-ass! I always said I was gonna have you. I couldn't believe when I saw you again after all of them years up in the spot."

"No don't..." she begged.

"No don't what? Huh? What? Don't take it? Don't do to you what y'all hoes done to me? All y'all hoes?!"

He ripped the bodice of the gold dress down the middle. "Gotta take ya shit 'cause ya highfalutin ass don't wanna give it up. And what y'all leave me wit? Disease and death. That's what I deserve? WELL IS IT?!"

She screamed, "PLEASE!!!"

"Just tryin to lay down wit y'all stuck-up asses and dis my payback? Stinkin' ass hos!" He kissed her on the neck, "Why not spread the love? Right?"

She breathed in deeply. She belted, "OH GOD HELP ME!"

A car pulls up in the driveway. "Wait, that door looks open. Y'all wait in here. Aye Liza! Liza baby!"

Liza's youngest daughter races into the house. Her father shouted, "Hey! Didn't I say wait?"

"I wanna see my mommy."

"No! Hold up…" Jason chases their youngest daughter inside. The eldest daughters follow.

Jason notices trail of blood leading up the staircase. "Liza?!"

In the middle of the staircase he can hear his daughter yell, "MOMMY!!!"

Jason pushes past the little girl. He grabs the intruder from on top of Liza. The man grabs Liza, "Oh I remember him. This ya man right? Left me for dead in the street remember?"

"Negro what? Oh you about to die!"

Jason lunged at the assailant. The children ran down the stairs in horror. They scuffle on the floor. Somehow Wax makes his way over to Liza. "Nah, her first. He bites Liza on the face drawing blood. She wailed.

Police sirens can be heard off in the distance. Jason crawled over to his fiancée', "Baby?"

He gets up to attack the intruder. Liza's attacker pulls out a .45. He points it at his head, "Aint payback a big fat bitch? World Star." He shoots himself in the head.

HONESTY

"Is everybody alright? I said is everybody alright?" The crowd goes wild. The scene is alive with sound of children's laughter. Women gossiping. Men lying. The basketball court is thick with ego and testosterone. Beautiful black and brown foreheads of every hue glisten in the catch of the sun's rays. The workout is brisk. It's an end of Summer Tournament. Young men playing for pride and boasting rights. Everyone believing it was their time. Each one with their eyes on the prize.

Flirty girls cheer from the sidelines, elevating the male ego; driving the need to champion the game. Winner take all tonight. It is the Rucker of the Bricks. The city was watching. The Southside of Newark was on fire. Aspiring politicians in attendance. Local hustlers, a fleet of flunkies. City cops and employees. The mayor. All had shown up to celebrate not only the end of summer, the youth, the South Ward; everyone had come out to say goodbye to the Newark's favorite son, Al Golden. Homage to the man who was born and raised in the gutter. The miracle that rose up from the muck and mire. The man who birthed the ministry. "Everybody give it up for Brother Al y'all. C'mon give it up for the man of the hour y'all. Ain't a person out here he ain't touched with his kindness. Him and his family. Y'all better act like y'all know and show that man some love." Al rose from a picnic table in a sea of young people waving like he was prom king.

"Brother Al..." A little girl tugged on his shirt, "Brother Al?"

She climbed on top of the picnic table. All of five years old. He couldn't hear for the roar of the crowd.

She took the napkin from neck of her shirt. She tapped him on the arm as hard as she could. He bent down, "Little lady. Now how you get up here?" He picked her up. "Where Needah? I know this gotta be Needah child. Ain't nobody else that bold." he laughed. "Good to see everybody. Y'all far too kind. Glory be to God. Y'all gon' enjoy yourselves."

"You got mustard on your mouth. My mommy said we supposed wipe our face after we take big bites. Here," she hands him the napkin. "You gotta wipe your face."

Al chuckled in Santa Claus fashion, like he hadn't had a care in the world. He enjoyed interacting with the youth. He loved their transparency. He found their lack of filtration refreshing. He looked around, "Needah! Needah! Come get this baby." He hands her off to a young eighteen year old woman who received her with a grimace. "Aww now. Be nice Needah. Y'all young mothers have to be more patient. She was only trying to be helpful. She's a blessing Needah. Put a smile on ya face." The young woman smiled, "Thank you Brother Al. Come on Jada. Say bye to Pastor."

"Bye Brother Al.", she waved wiping her face with the same napkin. It was the highlight of his day. He thought to himself, "That's what I miss. The simple things. The people. Lord, what's next for me? Something is missing Lord."

"Can we get some words of wisdom from the Pastor?" the D.J called him out.

Though the crowd cheered him on, he was reluctant to step on to the makeshift stage. "Y'all enjoy the music and the food. Ain't about me. This here. This all for y'all."

The D.J replied, "If you decree a thing..."

A young man cried out across the recreation center from the basketball court, "Man stop tryin' to preach! We ain't come here for the dat. Play some sounds dawg!"

Al bowed his head and smiled, "My people." He looked around. It had been a great while since he had sat down in the community amongst the people. Usually, he was just passing through, spreading love. Always giving a word of encouragement or a listening ear when he had a few minutes in between speaking engagements and ministerial duties. He took a deep breath. As he inhaled, he savored the aroma of cheap Islamic oils, watered down body mists, cigar smoke; even Piff. It was the environment he was from. The very people that criticized the church; often in justification. Surrounded by a bundle of rabble, speckled with baby mamas, reformed ex-convicts, hardworking grandparents, lawmakers and lawbreakers. He felt balmy in the element. At ease in the hotbed of tension that is the hood. A place where folk that had risen to his stature had dared not return to, distinctive, Al with all of the trappings of this world, the affluence, the influence; everything but the education, found gratification in the cul-de-sac of chaos. Over the years, he had learned he could find peace anywhere. There he found it in the disfigurement. Al recovered a breath of fresh air in between the harsh layers of tension.

Who is it that could relax in the quiet calm of confusion and unrest? Just like Jesus asleep on a boat full of men being tossed around by wind and waves, as they were in panic, he was at peace. He was still in the midst of the storm that was the Southside of Newark. Something always a brew, Al could hear the gurgling beneath the surface. Hustlers quibbling over money. Young gang members angling for space. Teenaged mothers popping their necks, spewing threats at the fathers of their children. Each one still a high school student. Quite a many had dropped out of the youth ministry at Breakthrough. He shook his head, "Lord if I hear 'WHERE MY CHILD SUPPORT; I HATE YO STUPID SELF; WE DON'T NEED YOU ANYWAY; MY BABY 'BOUT TO HAVE ANOTHER DADDY ANYWAY. One more time..."

He glanced over the multitude with concern. He noticed two police officers walking through the sort. They went unnoticed as they were dressed in plain clothes. He found them to be unusually congenial yet, authoritative. When they had reached his table, he remembered that they used to attend Breakthrough's youth camp each year. He asked them how they remained at ease in such a tight crowd where anything could happen.

One officer remarked, "Well Pastor, as partners who grew up in this community, had the same obstacles to overcome, the same barriers; surrounded by the same negative influences, breathed in the same weed smoke..."

The other officer obstructed, "Even smoked it. Pastor we ain't perfect. You know us. You had to come get me from the precinct a time or two..."

"Yeah. I remember. Y'all was just kids. Bored, no guidance, mama workin' two jobs. Granma working two jobs. No daddy in the house. Uncles, cousins, brothers in and out of jail. Each of y'all had a baby mama a piece before ya graduated Shabazz."

"We did." they laughed.

"But look at y'all now. Look at God."

"Yessir. Amen."

The first officer continued, "See we know what they don't know that we try to explain to them."

"And that is?" Al asked.

"We really ain't no different from them Pastor Al. We just decided to make different choices before it was too late. We saw we were becoming part of the problem instead of part of the solution. Can't stay being the question. Sometimes you gotta do an A.I on 'em Pastor and become the answer. We can walk through the crowd and greet people where they are while standing in our authority because we know who we are, we know why we here. We're not afraid. These are our people. These are God's people. We were called to do this, in our own community.

We know these people. We were these people. I got a family full of these people. Any one of us could take their place at any given time."

"Yeah Pastor. There are good cops and bad cops. We're people too with flaws and bad habits."

"Obviously poor judgment. Man I see cops fall off all the time. But they human. You know?"

"With all the killing going on, sometimes I wonder." The Pastor teased. "No disrespect boys."

"None taken. It's a fair shot. I'm an officer. But I'm also a black man. I get it."

 "It's a dangerous job though. But I found, here, where I grew up, where I know people, they just wanna be heard. Everybody wanna be understood. We all wanna be valldated. Everybody deserves respect. That's where I guess some jokers miss the mark. This is a community full of lives that matter. Contrary to popular belief and how the media portrays us, this is not a zoo."

His partner agreed, "Yeah. We have a job to do. Without compromise. Everybody knows that. But we're not all the way the news profiles us. And we're not blind to the crime and the corruption. We're not here to cover that up. We know things need to be fixed. With that being said, we know why these people do what they do. We're out here. We live here. We don't show up to wrangle people we have no connection too and go home. We care. We have insight."

"Yeah man. And empathy. Just like God, knows why we do what we do. The law is the law. Like sin is sin. But as you grow, you begin to see how life ain't so black and white. There is room for grey. That's where grace comes in. We treat people the way we want to be treated. With respect. We give away that same renewed mercy every day that The Lord gives us. And we pray. We protect, we serve and we pray. No matter the load they drop on us in the briefing at the beginning of shift…"

"We choose to chew up the meat…"

"Spit out the bone." Chimed Al.

"Uh huh, my grandmother used to say that a lot, God rest her soul. She kept us on our knees. Now I see why. We needed it. We all need it."

Al smirked, "Amen brother."

"Man Pastor, we see so much nonsense and trash goin' on out here, we don't know how even God can stand to look at it. Why he let it go on. We go home with a lot to be thankful for. But, we go home with a lot of unbearable pain sometimes too. Especially when you see kids that ain't ask to be here, out here roamin' the streets because they parents getting' high or the parents are trying to be friends with them."

"Preach son."

"It's true. What about when parents ain't but thirteen years older than the child. Still feelin' like the world owe them somethin' because they had a child way too soon; because of their choices. You don't get a reward for raisin' kids. It's your duty. They didn't ask to be here. Your reward is getting to raise them. You know how many women can't give birth? Jeez! Kids be just runnin' the streets with no guidance. Then when we gotta come and put them bracelets on 'em, the parents wanna cry foul. It's a shame man. Just raise ya kids! Reward yourself!"

"Yeah man you say that," said the other officer. "But how are you gonna raise kids when you ain't even raised yourself? My mother used to say, everything look grown ain't hardly grown."

"I guess you right man."

"Man, you'd be surprised at how many people don't view raising their children as a reward. They see it as a punishment or a chore."

"Yo, that's so sad."

"Facts my dude. That may not ever change. I love mine. I'm glad for my reward."

"Amen bruh. And what a reward it is."

"Part of that reward is in seeing all the work you done put in to them becoming the best they can be, come to fruition. But let's remember that some people are out here struggling, doing the best they can and that alone, living from paycheck to paycheck and all the hell that comes with being uneducated and feeling hopeless, there's not much reward to see in that. We have to put ourselves in other people's shoes. It's no fun raising kids when you're barely getting by. Doing it alone. Single parenthood comes with a lot of judgment form outsiders and a lot of brokenness. People judging you because you can't afford to by Christmas gifts and birthday presents. It's either get the XBOX and the Jordans or have the utilities disconnected and look good living on the street. Some people, whether they're single parents or married just have a hard time. Stress is stress. It's not fair to judge what we don't fully understand. We should educate and help more so that these occurrences are less and less. We need to teach our people to prioritize, capitalize and maximize. Self-control or indulgence. Investment over materialism." Al remarks.

"Now you preachin' Pastor."

"Nah. I'm just talkin'. It's just a thought."

"True enough. I tell my partner all of the time, I got sisters that are single parents. It's not easy. Thank God they had a great example to pattern themselves after. She wasn't perfect. And I'm not glorifying the irresponsibility of birthing broken children from a broken place…"

"Yeah man. 'Cause ain't nothin' cute or responsible about having kids out of wedlock and continuing that cycle of ignorance and brokenness. That ain't God's will at all."

"I agree with you son. But see. While we don't want to encourage the ignorance and irresponsibility, we must remember that nothing is ever wasted with God. And while yes, we must take accountability and educate our children about priorities, standards, God's will and plan and advocate self-control and discipline, we must also remember all life is precious. If you get here, you're meant to be here. People aren't mistakes. Even if rebellion and ignorance were the mistakes that got 'em here. They're here on purpose. Every life, whether it is recognized, valued and treasured or not; I believe, that at the moment of conception, life begins. While the purpose for that life was written out before the worlds were formed. Now, what we do with that, is a whole different thing. Man and our ignorance. We always want to cover our mistakes and erase what we deem invaluable. But is that The will of God?"

"I guess I never considered that."

Al charged, "Well young man, it's something to consider. There's always something to consider. Abortion, is a hate crime."

"That's a strong statement Brother Al."

"I agree Chance, but, it just baffles me how the same people that somebody else gave a fighting chance to, can kill a life on the inside of them that also deserves a fighting chance, at the very least. Your mistake is your mistake. Don't take it out on a God-given life with purpose! I mean really! The cure to cancer and Aids could be in that child. The healing of a nation or a people may be within your womb. How will you ever know what The Lord has in store if you don't wait to find out? Maybe so many of the answers to the problems we have today have come and gone in the form of a disguarded life, tossed aside like an inanimate object with no worth. No soul. No heart man."

"Jeez Brother. You sound like a pro-life activist."

"I am an all life activist. You can't be pro-life and not be pro-all life. From animals hunted for senseless and selfish reasons to the lives of the unborn and the death penalty. I may be ignorant about a lot of things. But I'm there. That's that. I mean shoot! If it's not a case of the mother' life being threatened by an ill-fated pregnancy or maybe the unspeakable crime of a brutal rape...jury's still out on that one for me...then why take a life if someone had the heart to give you a chance? I mean, you're still here. Jesus man! Fires me up! America just loves the easy way out of everything! Bloodshed. Killing. More and more violence and less repentance leads to more repercussion. From the black genocide of gang violence and police homicides to the wars they send these babies to go and fight that have nothing to do with anything but oil, money, greed, control, power and trade. Peace where? Boys I tell you, we gon' reap what we sew and it's gonna be bad. I hope I don't live to see it."

"I hear you. Man, Pastor. You've given me so much to think about."

"Son, that's the problem. Here, there, everywhere. We don't think enough. Not about how precious all life is. Anyway, God bless the single mothers."

"The single father's too now. Lest we forget. Ya got two right here Pastor. And Boom is one too so..."

"Amen son. God bless the single fathers too. Too many of them too. Ain't good for a man to be alone. We can get selfish and stuck in our ways." Al preached. "Ask me how I know? Ain't nothin' better than a good woman now… And if she's a lady, not just a woman, but, a lady that handles business…"

"She ain't gotta be perfect either.", agreed Chance's partner.

"Man ain't no such thing as perfect. There's just right. Lord, just let her be right. She ain't gotta look like a mannequin either."

Chance shouted, "Lord no! Don't nobody want no mannequin!"

"Had too many of those. They're just hollow."

"Amen to that. Good looking on the outside and full of nothingness. Lifeless. Dead in the eyes."

"I see you brothers are at the point in life where you're hungry. Y'all want substance. You wanna be full and rich."

"I do. Can't speak for this joker."

"Hey. I love the ladies man. And they love me back. Why should I deny them any of this goodness God made for 'em to enjoy? Sharing is caring." They laughed.

"Yous a lie man! Get yourself together brother and stop playin' with these women. You ain't doin' nothin' but makin' matters worse and driving they're self-esteem down further. That ain't godly. That is not the will of God."

"Nah Pastor. No disrespect. But I beg to differ. The way they view themselves is what drives they're self-esteem down. I'm just the benefactor of the remnants."

"Man you're a piece of crap!" Chance yelled.

"Relax dawg. I'm just a man. No need for the name callin' partner."

"Aight. True. But if your age and experiences don't make you a man. It's your state of heart, spirit and mind bruh."

"Being responsible and having integrity, those are stamps of manhood son. And none of us are ever gonna be perfect. We love and admire women. The shape, the mannerisms, the touch, the walk, the talk, the smell, the sassiness, the elusiveness…"

"The variety!" Chances partner laughed. "I love 'em all."

"You're so immature." said Chance. "How did you get this job? Aren't you supposed walk with integrity and uphold the law?" joked his partner.

"My private life is mine Officer Killjoy."

"Man. Just start showin' these women more respect."

"I do. Whatchu mean? I wear a condom." He looked at Al. "Forgive me pastor. God will forgive me right? I mean I'm just being a man. I'm only human."

Al looked away and took a deep breath, "Boy, I'm not here to judge. I was young once. I didn't know the Lord even though you think you do."

"I do."

"Not as well as you think you do son."

"Pastor hold on now. Samson stopped to have sex with a prostitute somewhere along the way after he killed that lion and before he got to Delilah. I know that much. He was the strongest man in the world. I'm sure built himself up a quite an appetite after all of that slayin' and killin'. How are you going to fault that man or any man for that reason, for doing what's completely natural? Huh? Didn't God give us sexual desire? How is that wrong? David, Solomon. His son Amnon?"

"Amnon? Amnon?"

"Hold up Chance. Don't be too hard on 'em. I see your point young man. But you're grossly misinformed. You're also misconstruing the lesson you could glean from those three men."

"What? What lesson? I'm just going by what the Bible says.", said the young policeman.

"And that's my point. You can't just read the word without proper guidance and prayer and draw your own conclusion. We have a tendency to manipulate the word to fit our fancy when we want an excuse to swim deep in our sin."

"What does that even mean?"

"I'll tell you, but I'll give you the crib notes. Basically the lessons center on weakness, disobedience and lack of self-control. They all center on lust in one way or another. And all of those men and they're choices led them down wrong paths. That's what disobedience and lack of self-control gets you. The wages of sin my man. They are quite hefty. And sometimes it is others that pay when we play. I urge you, read up on King David and his faults; his sons and the sins of the father. Read how it all connects. Look at Samson's choices. He had brute strength but he was mentally weak. Consider his choices in women. All of that led him up to his dooms day with Delilah. See even in that, if you're gonna say Samson was just being a man. Is it then true that Delilah was just being a woman and suing what she had to get what she wanted as women often do? It's a tale as old as time itself. Men are weak. And yes sexual desire is natural and God given. But, self-control and obedience keeps it in context and therein lies the reward son. There is a reward stored up for those that endure to the end. I hope you get that."

"I never thought of it like that. I guess nobody ever taught me that."

"That's why you need to assemble yourself together with other believers in the body. Don't feel bad. You're not the only one. Ain't no condemnation to them in Christ. I guess I'm here; we're here for such a time as this. I believe this day, that the Lord is calling you to renew your mind. I hear him saying no more excuses. You're a good man making bad choices. You just need to educated. You gon' make it son. I believe in you and I am a witness to what God can do. You're only responsible for what you know. Once you find out, you can't say you don't now. You've just been charged with the responsibility of being a man. Part of it is looking out for the welfare of some of his most beautiful creatures, his precious daughters. Women and girls. Each and every one."

That's a lot of responsibility."

"I know it is. It's hard. But it can be done. Look! You're an officer of the law. You took an oath and vowed to protect and serve. See man, it's already in you. You're already doing it. Just get up around more righteous brothers like Chance and walk in it."

Chance nudged him, "Yeah bruh, he tellin' you right man. I'm here for you and I been where you are. It ain't gonna be easy to stop. It wasn't for me. I mean, what man don't enjoy sex and being in the company of beautiful women especially beautiful women with low self-esteem and no standards? And the way they out here runnin' around with nothing on don't make it no easier. Sometimes it's even hard to respect them the way they carry themselves. It's just too easy to knock 'em down out here."

"Uh huh. Like bowlin' pins. I remember those days." reminisced the Pastor

"Exactly. You gotta challenge yourself though. It takes a made up mind. Think about how you want the women in your family to be treated. That's what it took for me. Watching my sisters become statistics, thinking about my mother and everything she went through. It just ain't right to keep plowin' through these chicks like that and breakin' 'em down even further."

"Man, sometimes I don't think they even care." A young girl walks by him and glances back at him longingly as she licked her lips. "Damn yo! Oh sorry Brother Al. But y'all seen that!?"

"E, come on man. You not even tryin'. You know that's somebody's daughter man. And she's too young. Man, she spilled Similac always from her house to here. She probably wearin' some Huggies. How you luh' dat bruh?"

"Man please aight. No more preachin'. They all somebody daughter. And she damn sure ain't wearin' no Huggies. Chance man, she ain't have on no panties dawg! You seen her lookin' man."

"You need help R. Kelly. I'm so serious."

"What?"

"You sad yo."

"First of all there's a pastor right here and..."

"Let's just pray for him Chance." interjected the preacher. "Sometimes that's all you can do for people. Lord have mercy on you son. But I tell you this much, if I see you lookin' at these teenaged girls or talking to any of them about anything more or less than the law, I will personally report you to your superiors myself. And ya know I know 'em all."

"Pastor I wouldn't…"

"YOU BETTER NOT!" Al commanded.

"E man, what's wrong witchu bruh?"

"Man just leave it alone."

"I can't. Just holla at me if need to talk or you're having a moment of weakness. Ain't nothing wrong with being human and having weaknesses dawg. The wrong comes in allowing weaknesses to have you. Don't let how you feel control you."

"Aight man. Y'all right. Maybe I do have some stuff to talk about. Just not right now. Aight?"

"And I'm here if you need me. You know that son. No judgment. But the law is the law you know that right?"

"Yeah man I know. I know."

"And, God is a God of grace. Full of forgiveness and mercy. You just have to have a made up mind."

"I get it man."

"You need deliverance." warned Chance.

"He also needs love and prayer. He needs a community of men who have been in his shoes to walk with him on his road to recovery. People kill me shouting deliverance like it's always instantaneous. That ain't true. He wasn't born that way. He didn't develop that mindset overnight. And it may take some time before he is fully restored to righteousness. Everybody don't lay down they sin overnight if they honest in which most Christians are not. And yeah, he is still a child of God.

He just got deep, dark mess and stress that needs to be assessed and addressed. He's not the only man out here with those issues. People forget about Elvis and Priscilla. Prince and Mayte. Countless other men great and small that slithered around young girls under age and green that couldn't wait to pounce when they had come of age. Relationships domed from the start because the emphasis may have never been on love but, lust. Men with manhood issues. Men who were probably misinformed by other men who were misinformed by other men or no men at all. We can't beat 'em down for everything. That don't make 'em wanna stop. That just adds fuel to the fire sometimes. If all you ever expect is for a man to be wrong, maybe in his mind, that's all he ever think he can ever be. He may not reach any higher. He done been beat down to the ground. There, ain't nothin' to reach for. No responsibility. No need to deliver on the promise when you don't have the courage to make one. As much as it is damaging to be down and shackled by the fear of the responsibility that comes with even the thought of attempting to rise; the audacity of hope Barak Obama called it. There still is a level freedom dysfunction that comes with just staying down. No expectations. No giving birth. No preparation. No work. No criticism. No responsibility. And Eric…"

"Yeah pastor."

"I know Chance and I are talking about you like you're not even present. I apologize man. That's disrespectful."

"Yeah it is. A bit."

"Yet, I noticed you took a seat and kept your head down. You never step up like a man and commanded respect."

"Yeah I know."

"How come son?"

"I don't know. I grew up in a household full of women who did all of the talking. Me and my brothers were always told to shut up when older people were talking. That's the way I was taught to give respect."

"Your mother and your grandmother were strong women weren't they son?"

"Very strong."

"Have you ever dated, wait let me rephrase that... messed with any women your own age or older?"

"No I haven't."

"Why not Eric?"

"I don't know." They gathered together and embraced him.

"It's gonna be alright man. We gotchu. We're not here to judge. We're here to help." Al began to pray for the young police officer.

He patted him on the back, "I want you to remember everything I just said. Remember everything you just said. I also want you to remember this, the women, or dare I say girls you sleep with, they feel down some of them have made they're bed there on the ground right beside you Eric. Think about their self-esteem and the call to the responsibility of womanhood they are not answering because nobody taught them how to get up off the ground and answer the phone because nobody taught the females that came before her. And the cycle continues son. Y'all just layin' on the ground like animals. Don't y'all know that most animals are only expected to do only what they know by instinct? Sometimes some are trained to do what people expect of them because people think that's all they're good for. Such is life in the inner-city or anywhere there is seething, copious, bio hazardous amounts of hopelessness."

"Endless cycle of dysfunction." touts his partner.

"Yes Sir. Very good sir. We've become accustomed to just performing at minimum level. We're comfortable lying on the ground. We get comfortable because comfort makes no room for responsibility and responsibility takes concerted effort and work. It's the welfare syndrome. It's all I know. All they require. It's all that's expected of me. My basic need are met. Even if it means these nosey, self-righteous case workers gotta be all up in my business and they the government who just sees me as a number and a statistic or a problem they need to solve or erase from the paper gets to dictate my life and the quality of it for however long. Even it means I pass this poison that is irresponsibility and comfort onto my children and the cycle of dysfunction continues in my family and/or community insuring that nothing ever changes, and we stay slave to the confines of the man and of his view of us, that's ok. I'm comfortable down here on the ground where I just get stepped on and over. At least there's no work to do. Nobody will ever expect anything higher of me. Why would they, when nobody taught me and nobody ever came to help me. People look at you and think just because you walk erectly and because you are gainfully employed that you are alive and with it. Son, you have yet to live. You have merely been existing along with the company you keep. You have a responsibility to bear fruit now that the seed has been planted and watered here, now in the self-same day. No more excuses son. You are called to more. Nothing less." Al preached exhorted with authoritative animation.

"And E, Tamar was raped by Amnon. He was her half-brother. He was a predator so to speak with no self-control. The kind of person we are supposed to be protecting these girls from. We can be wolves in sheep's clothing. That's part of the reason the hood don't trust and respect law enforcement and government now. We've become the big, bad, blue wolves they're afraid of. Oh yeah and E,"

"Yeah man."

"Tamar's other brother Absalom, he deaded Amnon because he violated. That's a crime of treason."

Al spat on the ground, "Treachery."

"Leave these young things alone man. I would hate for anything to happen to you MY BROTHER."

Al picked up his water bottle, "Let the church say amen." He gave Eric a cold stare. "Here's to getting up and getting on. Here's to healing from yesterday's pain today so tomorrow can be pain free. Here's to being over achievers. Here's answering the call to be shepherds and not wolves. And on a lighter note, cheers is to mothers and grandmothers out here doin' the best they can to raise boys up into men...they doin' it wrong. Who can blame 'em for tryin' Lord? One more for the love and support of a good woman y'all. I wish y'all both the love and support of a good godly woman."

Eric stood up to render his portion of the toast, "Here's to a made up mind and seeing the value in every woman."

"Amen young man. Here's to seeing the value in yourself man of God. You gon' make it. Jadakiss said so!" They shared a hearty chuckle.

"Yeah, yeah! Can't fault the women who raised for doin' their best."

"Amen to that. Shoot man, at least they had the courage to stay."

"Some. Man or not, some days you just laughed to keep from crying. Women have no idea." griped Al. The conversation had taken a serious turn.

"I know right? They think we don't have feelings. They think we're actually made of steel. I had this one girl say that to me one day. You believe that? We don't have feelings."

"Operative word is girl Eric."

"Yeah. You're right Brother Al."

Eric's partner Chance was off somewhere in cobwebs of the corners of his mind. "I ain't had the best momma growin' up. I mean, she did her best, but she was young when she started havin' kids because she was molested by one family member; raped by another. There's pain behind people's choices man.

I remember my mother sitting me down one day. I was about fifteen. Thought I knew everything. She had boyfriend after boyfriend. Just men all of the time. In and out. Seem like they stayed with her long enough to get all they could out of her physically and financially then they moved on. It's like she was the gift that kept on giving in our neighborhood. I hated it.

She was so pretty. When I was little, I thought my mother was the prettiest lady in the world. You hugged her, she was warm, soft and strong...kind of like a Grandmother hug, but not so tight. She ran our house like a drill sergeant when she was at home. She was loving, generous and kind. She gave us the world. We was spoiled. Just lonely most of the time.

She demanded respect from her kids. When it came to men though, she just wasn't strong. I began to resent her for that. Man, one day, I went h.a.m on her! I went nuts! I started hating her for how weak she was. I mean, how could she boss up at us for small stuff, but when it came to those men, they got to do whatever they wanted. Why she didn't she know she was too good for that? My mother taught never to disrespect and use women. In my mind she was a hypocrite in my mind so I just let the respect slip. So anyway she let me go off. Get my feelings out and everything. I punched a hole in her favorite mirror, thinking that would evoke some type of response. She sat there quiet. In tears.

I went out for a walk to cool off. I was gone until the sun went down. When I got back in the house, she was still sitting there in the same spot. Mascara running down her face. Snot pouring from her nostrils. She was in the dark. I came in, turned the light on. Instantly, I knew I caused that. I made my mother cry. I promised myself I would never do that. That was my mom. The queen of my world. My rock. I hurt her."

She said, "Sit down Chance Morris Avery."

Y'all already know what the full name roll call means.

I was afraid to sit by her because I thought she was gonna pound a hole in my chest. She was like the hulk when she got riled up. I knew I had gone too far. I sat a few feet down from her."

She said, "Boy get yourself here!"

I refused. She got up. Put out her cigarette. She walked over to me. Man, I balled up like baby in a snowstorm. I just knew she was gonna house me. To my surprise, she got down on her knees. She placed her head in my lap. She wept like Mary at the foot of the cross. She wept silently, she wept hard. Her tears ran down into my socks. I didn't say a word. I rarely saw her cry. But when she did, it always tore me apart. To this day, I hate to see a woman cry. It always takes me back to that day. Anyway, she wrapped her little arms around my legs. She looked up at me after about ten whole minutes of tears."

She said, "How you know how strong I am? How you know I know I can do better? This all I know Avery. This all I ever felt like I was worth. Ain't nobody never told me no different. They always called me pretty. But they ain't treat me that way. People don't know being pretty ain't enough, especially when that's all people teach you to see in yourself. You know I used to think my first name was pretty. My middle name was stupid. My last name was ass-bitch. That's what they called me Avery. That's all I know. I'm sorry."

"For the first time, it made me see my mother as a woman. A real woman with real issues. Not just as my mom. She was person with issues before I came. The same issues she had held on to all of her life. The same issues she took to the grave. Good woman nonetheless. Sheila Avery, was my mother. She was my heart." The two men stared at him. Chance looked up to the sky, fighting his tear all of the while.

"So now you know why I do what I do Pastor. This why I feel the way I feel E. So many of these young pretty, troubled girls remind me of my young pretty, troubled mother. So many of these guys out here remind me of those young, troubled men that came in and out of my house. Who you blame? Who side you take when everybody got issues? I just know two wrongs don't make a right. So I try to counsel and console instead of judge and belittle. So many things we don't read in between the lines of people's lives. People out here hurting while they laying on the ground man."

He looked over at a beautiful woman he had gone to high school with. She was serving cold drinks to the children. "Guess that's why I never got married. It's a part of me that's afraid somebody might read in between my lines and see my issues and not want to stay. I'm out here playin' Superman. When women see that, the last thing they ever want is to see Superman be vulnerable. They don't realize Superman was a Super boy first. He had to grow up. It's a process. Super boy had to go through stuff to discover his strength, how to manage it, control it; use it for good. Super boy still in there."

"He had weaknesses too. Kryptonite and Lois Lane." Al replied.

Eric looked at him, "The lady that can see past the 'S' on ya chest and the badge outside the armor on your vest. Somethin' real. We just men beneath it all A. Nobody is made of steel. Not even the police. I would love to meet a woman that saw me and was alright with me just being a man."

Chance said, clearing his throat, "Facts. Not to get all personal and stuff."

His partner patted him on the back. Chance bowed his head like a bashful little boy. Al took the liberty of embracing him as the beautiful woman looked on. He held him like the father he had never known, "Son. Your mother would be proud of you. She did a wonderful job raising you and your sisters. You gon' make some good woman, a good husband one day. Hey man. I gotcha back dawg. If nobody ever told you, I'm proud of you."

Chance patted Al on the back. "Thanks Brother Al. Appreciate you man." He looked over at the beautiful woman, she was smiling. She clapped quietly staring at him. "Thumbs up." She mouthed.

Chance and his partner continued their walk through the crowed rec center. "Chance.", the beautiful woman called out as he passed the drink stand. Startled and caught off guard, he turned to face her. Speechless, he froze in his tracks. A deer caught in the headlights.

"You thirsty?" She handed him a beverage. She smiled, "We need more like you out here. I mean that. Have a blessed day." She turned away from him.

He remained stern in his facial expression. Within, his heart melted like the ice on the outside of the bottle being instantly heated by his warm touch.

"Hope!" Al yelled to him from afar.

She turned to him, "You call me?"

"Excuse me?"

"Yeah…" she said with joy. "It sounded like somebody called my name. And well, I don't see anyone but you. I know God speaks to us. But I don't think that loud."

"Whatchu know 'bout some God girl?", he teased.

"What?! What don't I know?! That's my man 50 grand. He ain't just SOME God. He's the ONE TRUE GOD."

"There is no other." Avery grinned.

"Speak!" she shouted.

Avery walked away slowly, "Let me find out."

"Yes I am…and sanctified." she laughed.

"I knew it. It's all over you."

She blushed. She thought to herself, "If he can see you all over me Lord, if he ain't runnin' that ole Brick City game, I truly thank you. You have done a mighty work."

"I love you Hope." she heard the voice of the Lord say.

A solitary tear fell from the corner of her eye as she harkened on beforetime. She had a tawdry past. One like that of Chance's mother. The Lord had brought her a very long way. She never thought she could change. All of her life she wondered if anyone could ever love her for who she was, in spite of her past. A great chameleon, she had learned to adapt in varying surroundings. She could be anybody people needed her be or whatever she thought people expected her to show up as at any given moment.

She had put up walls for so long. Impenetrable boundaries. She had gotten to the point in her life, where being beautiful wasn't enough. If this was the spark she had dreamed of, would she be able to allow herself to be vulnerable enough to embrace a confident man like Avery? A Master's Degree in Psychology. A Family counselor. A mentor to so many young girls. She helped countless girls to tear down nightmares and build up dreams despite their pasts. "Who is going to help me?" she often thought. "I don't have my mother. No big mama. No mentor. No role model. No template."

"Uh huh Ms. Preston. We seen you over here choppin' it up wit' Robo Cop. What's on ya mind girl? Better yet, who is that?" A group of young girls teased. "You know we be watchin' you." they laughed. "So what's up? You gon' let him cuff you?"

"Pardon me?"

"Now don't be shy Ms. Preston. You know it's been a minute."

"Yeah. It's the end of the summer. And you know this is Jersey. You know it's about to get brick too! You need you a boo thang. A hot totty to keep you toasty honey."

One young lady asked, "So wait Ms. P, his name is Todd?"

"No Megamind. Where ya head at? You know that's A. What's wrong with...?" echoed another.

"Alright! Alright. That's enough. Are you all getting something cold to drink? If not, keep it pushin'."

"Girl, she got attitude. You done rocked a nerve China."

"Huh? You mad at me Ms. P?"

"I'm not angry with anyone. I just don't have time for this right now. Okay? Beverage anyone?"

"But Ms. P, we just love talking to you. We ain't see you all summer. We miss kickin' it with you. We didn't mean to..."

"That's fine. But by all rights, I don't have to acknowledge any of you outside of the program. I have friends who operate like that. I chose not to because I care. Nobody asked me to mentor you all. I do it because I love it. I love Newark. I believe in the youth and I care. I want you all to win. But don't get it twisted now! I do have boundaries. And they are set firmly in place to keep everything regulated. We don't cross personal lines. K ladies?"

"Well alright Ms. P. But you know what?"

"What girl?" Hope shook her head and laughed. "China you always got somethin' to say. Speak ya mind girl then y'all go head now. I'm trying to wrap things up here."

"Aight real quick." she smacked her lips.

"Tamartian much?" Hope smirked.

"Ooohhh. I just love me some good ole Tay Tay but nope." She smacked her lips again, "Salt n' Vinegar chips boo. Did she do it? She did. What she do? She won!"

"Alright I'm done." Hope said losing patience by the minute.

"Ok. Ok. Ok. For real though... How you get so blessed?

"What do you mean China?"

"Look at you. You got everything. You killin' 'em in every area. I mean you can't lose. And you're just so beautiful Ms. P. I wanna be just like you."

"Yeah Ms. P. Like Beyoncé'. All the boys be on you."

Hope yelled, "Okay SWV! Stop it! Y'all can be so unmaneagble." She caught the attention of a few passersby. She regained her composure, "Y'all come over here. Every last one of you! Now, I'm not perfect. Neither is Beyoncé. Alright? And why is Beyoncé' the only black woman y'all can reference these days? You got Michelle Obama, Gayle King. Hell, Gayle Jenkins, Loretta Lynch, Susan Taylor, Condy Rice, Mildred Crump and many more. Show other people some love sometimes. Why is it y'all don't refer to educated black women? Why, because of image? Because they don't 'look' the part?"

"Ms. P we don't…"

"I don't even wanna hear it! I don't care how it looks from the outside! We all out here doin' what we know how to do the best way we know how to do it until we learn a better way to get it done y'all hear me? Don't put people on pedestals they don't deserve to be on. We're human. Everybody has flaws. One day you'll be women. Learn to focus on what matters. If you're going to admire someone, admire them for their tangible qualities. Forget intangible things that are temporal."

"What does that even mean Ms. P?" asked China.

"IT MEANS OUTER APPEARANCE AND MATERIAL POSSESSIONS DON"T MEAN ANYTHING! OKAY?!"

The teens looked frightened. Nevertheless, they continued to be attentive. A smaller group of younger girls gathered near. Chance drew closer as did Al. No never-mind to Hope. She was mentoring in the rawness of her calling. She was in her zone. Even the D.J became intrigued. He lowered the music and joined the gathering. His daughter was one of the teens Hope mentored. Now, he would get to see the person responsible for his daughter's slow but steady evolution into womanhood, empowerment and responsibility.

"Look girls. What you see…things and make up and push-up bras; lighting, positioning, Instagram filters and trinkets. All of the photo shopping and the glam squads. The hot cars and the seamless relationships. It's not real. No solid, long-standing relationship can survive without there being conflict and disagreement. Don't believe the hype y'all!

The well put together woman in heels and a tailored Chanel suit. She may be going to a fabulous house in a great community driving her Benz but, what does it take for her to maintain it all? What did she have to endure to get there? You have no idea. And her there may be everywhere to you, but it could be absolutely nowhere to her. Maybe she wants to be anywhere but there.

We think money, fame, status and things are all we need to be happy when we grow up without them. Honestly though, when you get big enough to and are able to earn enough to obtain those things, or eve when they're given to you, you grow to realize that things and popularity don't make you happy. Often, they make you feel more isolated and empty.

Girls, if you're going to aspire to anything, let it be something meaningful. Admire people who serve with purpose and lead purpose driven lives. Look for the people in your community that serve. Dig deep and search within for your power. Use it for good and not evil. Women are very powerful creatures. From our frame to the way we think and nurture. God has used us to shape humanity. We influence and encourage great the great men and women who lead the world. We have always had influence and power. Don't limit it to sex and looks. There are so many women out here that aren't famous nor are they educated or popular that go unsung, that are making a bigger and better difference in the world we live in. Women with wisdom and courage. The survivors. The endurers. The backbones of society. They are where you out to gain your strength girls. Entertainers get paid to entertain you. Actors sell us fantasy. Models get compensated to promote a product. It's not real. Even me, myself... don't believe what you see. I am a work in progress. We all are until the day The Lord calls us home. Remember your power. And don't devalue people because they don't look the part. Keep in mind that the people that look the part just look the part. Even educators and lawmakers. We all look the part. Nobody has it all together if you ever follow them home.

Oh to be a fly on the wall of those that look the part. Eye lashes, hair, nails and clothes have to come off! Badges, guns and vests have to come off! I have yet to meet an educator that knows it all. They are inundating you with information yet, you'd be surprised to know how many of them can't figure out the simplest things in life. Common sense just is not that common. People who surrender to elitism; they believe their own hype-they're some of the most insecure. Money fame are their gods. Some people don't have identities away from the spotlight. You'd be surprised. How many women can't leave home without make-up? We've become so insecure. Image has become a global obsession in place of love, truth and service. We've lost focus on what really matters. Don't lose focus. The inside counts. The outside is not going to have as much value as you age if you're wise. It shouldn't. It's dying. The inner man, if we have a solid relationship with The Lord, is being renewed day by day. Focus ladies." Everyone within earshot marveled at her speech.

Hope had a calling. She knew it from childhood. She had gone to church all of her life. That's where she had received a lot knowledge about God. That is also where she had received her sexual education as well. Mauled over, pawed on by men and boys who were supposed to protect and care for her. Church, is where she received the bulk of her pain. Church is where, as a child, she lost most of her trust. It had been a long walk back to Jesus. Hope was still yet, learning how to trust after having her trust smashed into tiny little shards of broken glass that stabbed her in the heart with every unwelcomed touch from men and boys who claimed to be saved. She had issues. Just like everyone else. Issues that fueled her passion to mentor young girls. Hope had been through hell. She had heard an old school pastor say before, 'Tell hell I ain't comin'. That became the mantra of her mentoring camp. She was tough, hands on and brutally honest. Hope Preston was everything the young ladies on the Southside of Newark needed. They knew it. She sensed it. Staying humble, she thrived in her calling. The hurt she had experienced had been too deep, too painful. "No one should ever have to swallow this bitter gall." she thought to herself.

"Now don't me EVER let me hear ANY of you say you idolize ANYBODY but Jesus Christ himself! EVER A DAGGONE GAIN!" She rambled as she broke down her booth, "Got it all together. Nobody has it all together. We're all a work in progress. Don't put me on a pedestal. All I can guarantee you is a bunch of big let downs, some hurt feelings, a million mistakes and a whole heap of forgive ME's along the way. I try to get it right every day. Like everyone else. I depend on The Lord for everything. I don't boast about anything. Because it doesn't mean anything. Easy come. Easy go. It all belongs to Him girls. It all belongs to The Lord. He is God alone. Don't you EVER want somebody else's life. All that glitters ain't gold and you don't what it takes to be them. You're not supposed to. That's why you're you. Carve your own niche. Use your power and influence to serve something greater than yourselves. There's nothing wrong with admiring qualities and strengths in people or taking a page from their book if it helps you to get to be who you're called to be. Just don't go out trying to be a carbon copy. You just be your best you. Seek ye first the kingdom of God and all of His righteousness. Then and only then will..."

"All of these things shall be added unto you." Chance said softly.

"We're here to serve a purpose. And if he blesses you with things you can enjoy, good. But don't forget to share them. Blessed to be a blessing. When your cup begins to run over, give the excess to those in needy. Whether it's wisdom or clothing. Knowledge or food. Love or understanding. Understood ladies?"

"Yes ma'am.", they chimed.

"Good. Now I love y'all. Y'all know that. We'll talk some more. And China..."

"Yes Ms. P?"

"Next time I see you, I want to see clothes from neck to knees. I know y'all growing' up and y'all wanna look sexy. You're finding yourselves and exploring. But don't give away so much. You're giving away too much too soon. Why would anybody work are to get something that walks around with a sign on it saying: FREE FOR ALL?"

"Free for all? Sign? Huh?" the young lady looked puzzled.

"Uh huh. That's how baby girls turn into to baby mamas. Mark my words. That's my second time with you China. You have greater value than that. People hide priceless, precious things."

"What?"

"One day you'll get it girl." She whispered, "Lord have mercy."

The D.J made his way through the crowd to greet her, "You strong. But you effective. That's what they need. I'm China's father Darrell."

"Nice to finally meet you Darrell. Despite the circumstances."

"Yeah. I know. China hard headed as they come. I be tryin to tell her how to dress like a lady. But she don't listen, she don't like the clothes I buy her. So I let her go shopping with her friends. Next day, she walkin' outside lookin' like Rihanna at the West Indian Day Parade. I can't take it Ms. Hope."

"It's gonna be ok. I understand China's mother is out in the street. On drugs."

"Yeah. And before she came to live with me a few years ago, she had China runnin' wit her. From pillar to post. Just leaving my daughter with anybody." he paused for a minute. He pulled Hope to the side, "She been touched on." he covered his mouth. "I don't even want to talk about it. She need to discuss it. She won't. She's promiscuous and disrespectful."

"Okay. Okay. Here's the thing. I'm gonna prayerfully do what I can to spend a little more one on one time with China. She's hurt. She's crying out. She feels that's her lot in life and her worth. It's all around her. Look at where she is Darrell. No fault of yours. I'm a single mother myself. I commend you. You are doing your best. But, a woman needs to reach deep down to the core of where she hurts. Even in that, I can only go so far. Jesus is the only one who reach the deepest, blackest parts of our aching hearts. If you know The Lord, and you pray, keep praying for her. I'm a mother so I know your pain and frustration as a parent. I'm also a woman with a past, like everyone else. I see things from both angles. Speak life Darrell. Do something different. Call those things that are not as though they were. We can command things to be Darrell. We can speak things into existence just like God and Jesus did. Have faith. It may take some time. But a change is gonna come. God bless you Darrell. China is gonna soar with wings of Eagles. You just have to claim it. God sees past what we look like."

"Because the outside doesn't matter."

"Not to God Darrell. No it doesn't. He searches the heart. He's not like us. Thank God."

"Aw man Hope. You should speak at my church." a neighbor called out.

Hope flipped her long, brown dreadlocks. She grabbed her Gucci hobo and slipped back into her Red Bottoms. She adjusted her dress. She complained as she strutted towards the exit, "Not even if they paid me Diddy dollars. Good night."

Chance and Al stood side by side. Both admiring her from equal distance for different reasons. Both seeing potential and power walk away into the night. One knew there was something there. The other knew there was something there. Exhausted from the day. Hope sashayed to her vehicle. She lay her head on the steering wheel before pulling off. She prayed, "Father I love what I do. But sometimes I find myself doing it too much. Why is that, a time of enjoyment for me seems to always turn into an impromptu counseling session? I'm exhausted. I don't have all of the answers Lord. I need balance. Jesus!" She moaned, "And tonight the kids come back from being with their fathers. Lord when do I get a break for me? I can't save the world. Sometimes I think I have too much responsibility. Always the leader. When do I get to take a break and be led? That would be a welcome change. Lord knows I get tired of doing everything and being bothered with people." She drove away. Her admirer looked on. Chance longed to get to see Hope again.

Driving home, overflowing with exhausting thoughts; distracted, she neglects to come to a full stop at an intersection. A blow from another driver headed in the opposite direction awakens her from her daze. She stops just shy of hitting a young couple in the crosswalk. She looks up. Its China wrapped in the arms and charm of one of the neighborhood drug dealers.

"Look at this naïve child and this no good nickel bagger. China! China!" She can barely be heard screaming at the top of her lungs through the thick windshield glass. Hope pounds on the horn in the fat of the cacophony of horns surrounding her as she holds up traffic in the intersection. She is less than patient. She refuses to move without China. She puts her car in park. She dashes across the cross walk under a hail of sharp obscenities. No matter. A future hangs in the balance. Reaching China, she grabs her arm angrily, "What are you doing?!"

"Oh. Ms. Hope. I..."

"Oh what up ma? This ya mom yo? Ma'am I'm just walkin' ya beautiful daughter home."

"Boy shut up. Ain't nobody talkin' to you. Let's go missy."

"But..."

"NOW! Got me holdin' up traffic. Come on. I'm aggravated."

"Well don't take it out on me! And let go! You don't need to be grabbin' on me like dat. You ain't my mother!"

Hope stops cold in her tracks, "You should be so lucky truth be told. Look at you. Lookin' like five dollars in pennies. Get in the car. And y'all pipe down. I'm goin'. I'm goin'."

"Now. Seatbelt on. Start talkin'."

"I don't know whatchu want me to say."

"Tell me somethin."

"Like what?" China attempted to pull her skirt down.

"Tell me why….you know what? I already know why." Hope pulls over. "I'm sorry China. I'm tired. I may be just a bit over zealous. I got a lot goin' on in my head. It's all goin' a million miles a minute. It's like that Hell Hole ride they used have years ago the amusement park. Things are just spinning faster and faster, taking me along for the ride. I wanna get off the ride. But at the same time, I like it. Oh Jesus! I'm purging to a child. Why am I tellin' you this girl? Now, I know I'm losin' it. Just forget everything I just said. Let me take you home." She whispers to herself, "You know that's unethical."

"Ms. P, you good. It's breezy. I feel you. That's how I feel about sex and partying in a way. It's a Hell Hole. I feel like I wanna get off. I want to get out. But somethin' keep pullin' me in. It's like a gang I don't wanna be affiliated wit' no more. I don't how to stop. I wanna get out. But at the same time, I like it. I love it when it's on. It's the rush. It's the feelin' wanted. I feel wanted when I'm doin the things I really don't wanna do. I be on fire for that life. But when it's over. I feel dead inside. I be tired. I feel like da joker I just gave it up to a loser that just sucked all of the life outta me. And I'm the dummy because I just keep goin' back. I know it's twisted."

"I'm not here to judge you China."

"Thank you. That don't make me feel no better though. Most of the girls I know don't even know they father. I gotta father. I know he love me. I know he want me around. He take care of me. But I need more than him barking orders at me and givin' me money. He love me strange Ms. P. He be mad. He never sorry. I can't talk to him. Sometimes I feel invisible. Sometimes he smother me. Sometimes I think he buying time away from me so he don't have to deal wit' me. You know, like guilt money or somethin'. He try to talk to me sometimes, but he yell...like you do. Only you don't do it all the time. You ain't mad all the time. Not like him. I know you yell at us because you love us right Ms. P? They say love don't hurt, but if y'all love me like y'all do, then I guess it do sometimes. It have to sometimes right Ms. P? I mean for you to feel it? To feel anything is better than feeling nothing right?"

Hope couldn't look her in the eye. She took China's hand, "Forgive me. You didn't deserve that."

"For what? You love me right? It's all good. I understand. I guess that's what loving hard means. It's that passion thing right? Make people act out sometimes."

"I yell because I'm passionate. You're right. I care. Maybe too much. I just want you girls to win. And no. Love ain't supposed to hurt. Not like that China. Love ain't supposed to beat you or break you down, even if it is with words. Power of life and death are in the tongue. Bible says it's sharper than a two-edged sword and can't be tamed by man."

"A man?' China asked.

"No honey. I mean man. Whenever you read the Bible and you see man a lot of times it means us, people; humans."

"Yeah. I get confused about a lot of stuff in the Bible. I try to read. I try."

"China why didn't you tell me you had a Bible?"

"I don't know. I guess it's my little secret. It's not cool. Kids my age don't really rock wit dat stuff. If I tell them I pray to God every night and I be tryin to understand the Bible and all of those crazy words, they gon' think I'm a Jesus freak. Or they gon' laugh at me, call me a hypocrite and Imma have to beat the breaks off somebody child AGAIN because I'm out here doin' da most like da rest of these hoes. Uh huh, they ain't gon' ever let me live it down. So I just keep that kinda stuff to myself."

"You're not a ho China."

"The hood and the rappers say different. But thanks Ms. P. It is what it is. All I can do is try to change. I just pray and try to read."

"Oh yeah? And what of the boys that sleep with you? So what are they? You know I get so tired of this double-standard, misogynistic world we live in. Those boys ain't no better than you honey. Don't let them weigh you down with that garbage. They just do it to make themselves feel better. They got mothers and grandmothers with multiple babies out of wedlock. They need to think about that while their perpetuating the cycle of dysfunction."

"You're on fire Ms. P!" China quacked. "And you mad funny."

"No. I'm serious. What do they think about their mothers and sisters and themselves? Where does it say the label 'whore' is gender specific? Don't let them put unjust labels on you girl. They better look in the mirror and take the speck out of their own eye first. Child Please."

"Wow."

"Wow what?"

"That right there. I just love talking with you. That fire. Your passion. That support. Ain't nobody out here like you. I admire that. If that's okay?"

"China. There's nobody out here like you. Don't forget it. That makes you special. God created you special. The enemy knows that. So he'll use anybody he can to lower your self-worth, so you'll never know exactly who you are. And if you don't know it, you'll never walk in the power of it. He'll do whatever and use whomever to keep you feeling less than and average."

"Like words like ho. Right?"

"Exactly. Don't you fall for that baby. We all got stuff. But we ain't our issues or mistakes."

"Oh man. I never knew that." China gawked. "I just love your words. I love politicking with you. Oh my goodness."

Hope chuckled, "Politicking'. Those aren't my words. Those are God's words, specifically for you. You're special to him."

"You really think so Ms. P?"

"Oh I know so. And China?"

"Yes?"

"You can talk to me about anything. I gotcha back. I read the Bible too. I got friends too. Maybe not the best company, just like you. I can't talk to them about the Bible either. Not because I'm afraid of what they think; they know where I stand, it's because where and how they choose to stand."

"How'd you get strong enough to be yourself in front of other people Ms. P?"

"I guess I just got tired of being what people called me. I got tired of doing what was expected of me because of my past and where I came from. I got tired of the labels. Labels ain't nothin' but beat downs girl. It was wearing me out believing what people said about me instead of believing what God said about me. It took too much energy to be somebody I was not."

"How long did it take you to just be you?"

"Took me a long time to be able to take a stand. It was a process."

"You mean not carin' about what everybody thought of you right?"

"Yes. It's not easy when you're young. Peer pressure is a heavy weight. But the day finally came when I got tired of carrying that heavy load and I just woke up one day after crying all night and decided to put it down. I would just have to face my critics. It wasn't easy. I had to ignore a lot of loud voices and resist the urge to argue my case."

"Probably resist the urge to catch a case too huh Ms. P?"

"Sure I did. Sometimes I even failed. But hey, welcome to the Bricks. It's hard for a pimp out here girl." They chuckled. "I might be saved. But, I'm a Brick City baby, certified and qualified. You WILL NOT, roll up or run down on me baby."

"Amen.", laughed China.

"So yeah. I been where you are China. It's a process. You'll get bolder in your faith. If that's what you want. God is able to give you anything. Nothing is impossible to God. I know it's lonely. But, now you know I know what you goin' through...call me. Talk to me. I will answer any question I can. Prayerfully. Whatever answer I don't have, we can pray to God about it together." A woman in a car parked at the adjacent corner, in front of a small church, played "At your feet." Hope looked at China, "You hear that?"

"Yes."

"That's what you do when you pray. Lay it all at his feet girl. Tell 'em Coko."

Hope was dying to offer her a couple of nights a week for Bible study. She knew deep down inside that she would be spreading herself too thin. She was already at her breaking point. Hope knew she needed to get a handle on her own life. She needed time for herself in order to be any good for anyone else.

Hope couldn't help but feel a sense of guilt. She pushed herself at every turn. She didn't like letting people down. Issues she carried over from childhood. Everyone had to see her as almost seamless. That is, that is how it had been up until that day. That day was eye opening for Hope. She realized she had seams. Beneath the pressure of the weight of added responsibility, in the name of pride. Her slip; her seams had begun to show. Humanity was beginning to rear its ugly head.

"Pray. Can you believe I pray? I mean look at me Ms. P. Look at what I do. Who I be wit. How I act and stuff. Sometimes I think I be wastin' my time. Nothin' don't ever change in my life. I heard everything you said. But, the way things goin', I ain't so sure I'm that special."

"What?"

"God probably don't like me. All I do is mess up. I want Him to like me. But I'm a mess. It just feel like I'm a big disappointment to Him. Like I am to everybody else. Especially my father. That's how he make me feel sometimes. So I just keep doin' what I'm doin'. Why change? What's gonna happen? I can't change him. He can't change me. Nothin' don't ever change. Won't make my mom come back." She burst in to tears, "I hate myself! Sometimes I just wish somebody would kill me. I wish God would answer my prayers and let me just die. He don't hear me though. I can't be so special."

Hope held her in her arms, "Shhhhh, don't you say that now. You don't mean that."

"I do! Yes I do! Nobody cares. I feel invisible. Don't nobody see me. They don't see me Ms. P. Not my mother. Not my father. Not nobody."

"I see you. More importantly, God sees you. I know it don't feel like it or look like it China, but He does. Ain't no mistake we right here right now. We here right now, because He sees you."

Hope held on to her as her tears flowed like the rain drops running down her windshield. Hope looked out to see it raining on one part of the street. The side they were on. The other side was completely dry. She looked over China's shoulder. She noticed a bed of beautiful flowers just beyond a fence that had been dried out by the Sun. They were thirsty for rain. Neglected, wilted, withering away. They had grown just outside of the fence. As if they were begging to be noticed. Like they were crying out. As if they couldn't go without water another day. Hope wondered how people could pass such beauty by. She realized for the second time in her life, how beauty was not enough. People could still pass you by; you could still feel worthless. You could be beautiful and dying.

She thought about her life. She remembered that you could be beautiful and people still take your value for granted; not notice your cry for help. People think beauty is enough. They stop to smell the roses but, not to water them. They never bend low enough to hear the roses cry for help. That evening, just before dusk, just before the flowers were doomed to take their last breath, the rains came. They had grown past the breach of the fence, peeking out from beyond their border, dry, thirsty, taken for granted, wanton, lonely...invisible. God saw them that evening. He came in the rush of the down pour. In the right place, at the right time. He had not only heard them, He saw them. He not only saw them, He nourished them. He knew that they had given so much yet, no one had poured into them.

"Pretty really does hurt. Yonce' was right. It hurts in more ways than one. Nobody gets it. China He sees you. He loves you."

Hope drove away after a while. The pair sat in silence, conversing spiritually, from heart to heart. Hope ever concerned, thought on her ways. How she had yelled at the girls, chastising them openly. She knew she had left the gate open for others to belittle and embarrass them. They deserved respect. There was a better way to respond; react. She felt ashamed at her behavior. For even if others had sang her praises, she knew in her spirit she was wrong. Hope was exhausted. Exhaustion plus passion were a recipe for overkill. Something had to be done. She cared too much for her girls to keep the status quo. It was their normal. All they got at home. No understanding. No grey area. No compassion. No patience. The last thing she want to do was drive them into more chaos and bad choices by condemning them. She knew the wheres, whats, whos, hows and whys of it all. Hope had lived their lives twice. Nobody had to tell her anything about her girls. She was their surrogate parent. A substitute caregiver. True to form, just like custodial parents, when times get tough, they get tired...sometimes they get nasty. She didn't like that side of herself. She was becoming preachy. Something she didn't need when she was in their shoes. Hope had to figure out a new way to minister to her girls.

 "Teens.", she thought. "Lord help me. I'm losing it. I need a fresh anointing. I can't keep doing the same old. This is getting stale. I can't take myself right now. There has to be another way. I can't keep comin' at these girls like a narc kickin' in the door at the weed spot. Jesus, I am tired. I can't even tell anybody else how tired I am. How will they look at me? I usually have it all under control. If they ain't got me Lord, who they got? I can't afford to lose them. And lose them to what? What's the alternative?" She prayed within as she drove.

Hope had passing thoughts of Chance. She was curious beneath the surface. She was determined to keep that a secret. "Ooohhh Lord. It's been a minute since I've even been attracted to a man. Oh God, but he is fine! Man, you did so good with that one. Mmmm! But just forget it Hope. You know you don't have time for no man. Your plate is too full girl." Having a private conversation with herself in her head, she continued, "Yeah, but it's been five years. Five long, long, long, dry, lonely years. Don't front. You know you want somebody to touch your body. You don't play that Mariah joint in heavy rotation, driving home BY YOURSELF on Friday nights for nothin'. Who you kiddin'? Hell, you even play it on Sunday night. You need some lovin'. You know it."

"No. I'm good. I'm saved. I go to bed with Jesus every night."

"Uh huh. How's that workin' for you?"

Hope had frowned on religious people all of her life. She never thought she would ever be one of them. "Saved folk don't think that way. Lord forgive me."

Her inner-voice screamed, "GIRL STOP! All these pregnant daggone Christians and you really believe that garbage! Honey, yous a hypocrite. You saved alright. But you have feelings. You have needs. You have desires. You know you want somebody to touch it."

"Touch what?!" she argued within.

"You! Where in the Bible does it say you wouldn't have thoughts? Where does it say physical attraction is wrong? A kiss? The thought of. The prospect of. So saved women don't have desires? Needs?"

"Its wrong." she thought.

"It's human." she said to herself. "Who you foolin'? That's probably why Christians mess up so much; commit so many sexual sins. People got rooms upon rooms full of elephants. Y'all keep trippin' over 'em backwards trying to hide and avoid the truth. Sometimes you want some. You wanna get married. You wanna kiss. You get excited. You have longings. It's all in how you handle that stuff Hope. Now say it wit me...Sometimes, I feel like I need some..."

"What?"

"Say it. Free yourself. Tell the truth. Shame the devil. Stop frontin'. You ain't foolin' The Lord. He already know. Free yourself. Say it Hope."

"No. It's wrong."

"Aww. Yo ass so snooty and religious. JUST SAY IT!"

She came to a full stop at a green light. She roared just as the car jerked forward, "SOMETIMES I FEEL LIKE I NEED SOME..."

Again she had stopped traffic. A homeless man walked over to her car. He prepared to wash her window, "Oooohhhh boy. Had a screamer like you once. Pretty, just like you. Now what would you do for a Klondike Bar?" He joked.

"I beg your pardon?"

"Yep. She hadn't been touched by a man in a while. I respected her boundaries; Contrary to popular belief. But baby girl, I tell you, when I finally put my hands on that woman... Keep in mind, she was a Christian. It was our wedding night. She was a stingy sun of a gun. She made me wait like dog tied up in the backyard in the sun panting for just a drop o' water. Girl, when I put my hands on that woman, she went to convulsing and howlin' and thangs. Man, she got so loose, I couldn't keep up with her. Can you believe she divorced me? Me?"

"Why?" China asked.

"Little Lady, I probably shouldn't be tellin' you this. But you dressed like anything I say you probably already know."

"Man what?"

"Well he's right? What do you girls expect a man to say to you when you throwin' it all at him for free? You're doing too much."

"But I thought you said…"

No judgment. Only observation and cold, hard facts."

"Huh?"

"Just sayin' China." Hope winked.

"She left me because I wasn't givin' her enough." China laughed. "I just plain couldn't keep up with her. Yep. Left me for my father. Yes she did. Her loss. They had about 50/11 kids."

"You lyin'", China giggled.

"I swear on my shoes." he teased.

"Back up. Let me see ya shoes real quick yo."

"Aight.", he took five steps back.

"Man! Ya shoes 'bout as holey as your story. Ga head yo."

"I ain't lyin' sweetheart. Swear on my…"

"What next? Huh? Ya shirt. Don't say it. Dats holier than Jesus too. Don't even play yourself."

"True story. Young thang."

"Whatever.", she laughs.

"Aight don't believe me. But believe this, this lady right here... Oh she gon' hurt somethin' before somethin' hurt her. I pity the fool..." he laughed.

Hope raised her head from the steering wheel, "Please tell me you're done."

"Sho is pretty lady." he winks his eye at China.

"How much so I can go?"

"$2 Miss."

"Here's two fifties. You know what, here, take three. Get a room for the night. Get a shower, a shave and tomorrow, go downtown and get an outfit."

"And some deodorant... some Ax.", China mumbles.

"Don't do that." Hope warns. "Don't ever do that. How you know he can help his situation?"

"I... I..."

"Exactly.", Hope grunts. "Sir, thanks for the laugh. That was quite a tale. Enjoy your evening. God bless you. I wish I could do more."

Tears filled his eyes. He was so grateful. "Nobody been this good to me since my mother passed two years ago. She was all I had. I took care of her until the day she died. She had sugar. Mama was hard-headed. She never listened to the doctor. Ate what she wanted. We fought everyday about her bad habits. She was a shark. A good woman, but a feisty spit fire."

"Can we go now Ms. P? I can't take another lie from this joker. Plus he stink."

"Mind your manners girl."

"But..."

"China hush. Show hum some respect. We all want to be heard."

"Yeah but…"

"But nothing. Look at him."

"Do I have to?"

"Cut it out girl. Can you imagine how invisible he must feel out here in these streets? People everywhere. And he gets passed by all of the time just like his life don't matter. Nobody to talk to. No one to understand him. Who sees him? Who hears him? Get it?"

China hung her head shamefully. "Yes. I get it."

"Sad how the same things we want, we refuse to give away to other people. Giving is how you get China. I believe The Lord just filled you up. He filled you up as opposed to others feeling you up. There's a difference. One leaved you full to the overflowing. The gift that keep on giving. The other is all consuming."

"Sucks the life right out of you. I get it Ms. P. Man, you stay preachin'"

"I'm not preaching China. We're just having a conversation. The same thing God gave you is the thing He wants you to give away. Re-gift it baby. We all need somebody."

The man continued to wax nostalgic, "She had sugar all of her adult life. She was managing pretty well until my father left. She took to bad then, as she would say. Never talked about him again from the time he left unto the day she died. Guess she just ate her feelings. I always tell people, it's important to get ya feelings out in a healthy way. I used to tell her to kill how she feel. Talk about it. Let it out. Free yourself. Keeping things all bottled up inside like you don't feel anything. Just putting on. Ain't never good. Me, I make it a point to vent. Even if it ain't to other people. Wherever I lay my head at night, I take all my ills to the Lord in prayer. I keep it real wit Him. 'Cause I can. Y'all don't pretend you ain't human and you don't feel. You ain't gotta give in to every feeling or let your emotions control you. But, don't hurt to air out your frustrations from time to time. Tell the Lord. Tell a friend. Just get it out. When we don't let stuff out. Stuff go wrong on the inside."

"Amen. Like laying it all own at God's feet."

"That's correct young lady. People crazy. What's wrong with talkin? Especially if the conversation got purpose? Huh? Now y'all pull out the street a lil' more. Stolen cars like bullets...ain't got nobody name on 'em."

China whispered to Hope, "Yo! I didn't know homeless people had it like that. He really got it. Oh snap."

"Don't ever prejudge or underestimate people. Show compassion. Always expect the unexpected. They are people too. God's creation. We all equal in His sight China."

China sat marveling, "That's ill. Yoooooo."

Hope stepped out of the car to talk to the homeless man. China followed in curiosity. "So where are you staying tonight?"

"Right here. At the Riv.", he said.

"Here? I can have you placed somewhere more suitable. More comfortable. I know a few people I can call in the city."

"Yeah.", China looked around. "Somewhere safe. You know where you at? You know you can get it out here don't you?"

"Ladies, I am a man. Not an old man. A man though. I'm good. I would rather stay here where I know everybody. This is my groove, ladies. Thank you. I appreciate your concern. But, I can handle myself."

"Well at least let us walk you in…"

"See there you go. Y'all new women. Taking a emasculating the black man bit by bit. Guess y'all here to pick up where slavery and prison left off huh?"

"No sir. Not at all. We're just…"

"Don't do that. Never to no man."

"Do what?"

"Take charge. Run the show. Try to cover him. Protect him. Let him handle himself best way he can. You don't walk no man in nowhere unless you taking him to a room to show him a good time or you a C.O and you taking him to his cell. I mean that. Don't emasculate the men ladies. Y'all gotta watch that. Men like to feel powerful, useful, needed, in control of something. The money was generous enough. That, I am humble enough to thank you for. A man should never be so prideful that he refuses to be compensated."

China gave him the stank eye. She contemplated, "Uh huh. Yous about a bullshitter if I ever saw one. You ain't have no problem takin' THAT help though did you? Can't believe she just let this sucker roll her like that!"

"Oh I'm sorry. I was just trying to support…"

"You letting me beat down wit y'all is support enough. I don't get to have that much intelligent conversation out here. Let me tell you, when I heard you shout sometimes I feel like I need…., I was shouting inside too. Sometimes I just need an intelligent conversation. I need my ego stroked. I need to be needed. I need to be wanted. I'm still a man. I have needs. A lot of needs. People never stop to ask me what I need. They too busy lookin' down they nose at me, giving me what they think I want. So I keep a lot inside. I give my frustrations to the Lord. I can't let go nowhere else. Why people think because I'm out here in these streets and I'm a man, I don't feel or have needs, I just don't understand. All of this opportunity and education out here and none of these geniuses can figure it out. People need more than just bread, water and shelter to survive. People need other people to survive. The people that have people, take for granted that they have people or that one day, they could be like me and not have people. They ignore people. They compartmentalize people. Jesus didn't do that. No Jew, no Greek, no slave, no free. No male, no female. He specialized in people. He loved people. When did people stop lovin' people? How many scriptures say that Jesus looked at the people or the crowd and He had deep concern for them?" Hope stared at him. "What? Oh I know. You stuck on the word compartmentalize. I know. You don't expect someone like to me to be able to use such a big word." He shook his head.

"No. No."

"Yeah. Yeah. It's all good. I'm used to it. People don't know my story so they assume. I tend to let them."

"So tell me your story."

"Long story short. I have a degree in Psychology. I was lead counselor In Essex County for a number of years."

"What happened?" China asked rolling her eyes.

"Hey! Be nice. Don't pry." said Hope.

"Oh let the child ask what she wishes. WE keep too many secrets from young people in the name of pride and preservation. Secrets turn into lies sometimes when left unspoken too long. Lies that we live out. Lies they carry on. Lies that fester. Generational curses that turn into truths. We need to stop pretending so much. Stop whispering in the dark. Shout it out in the light. Ain't good to hold in so much trying to look perfect. Christians have that down to a science."

The young women stood silent. Absorbing every morsel. School was in session.

"I spent some time in Seminary. I loved the word. I love to learn. More than I love to teach. How could somebody with my education and background end up out here on the street? Things happen. People happen. Life happens. People that spend their lives helping people solve their problems and heal their wounds, have problems and wounds too. The more you take on other people's mess. The thicker your mess gets." he paused. "And mess on top of mess just leaves mess."

Hope squawked, "You better tell 'em."

"Girl, you hear me preachin'?" He grabbed a bottle of gin from his back pocket. "Y'all done drained me."

"Knew he was livin' in a bottle."

She looked China up and down, "Girl would you knock it off? Don't judge. We all got a vice. For some it's get right juice. For some it's sex." China adjusted her short skirt once again.

"After my mom checked out. I guess I checked out. Just like she did when my father left to do him. I hate to think about it. On paper it don't add up. But to me and God, it makes perfect sense. All that matters. I guess I just lost my faith."

"In God?" China said humbly.

"In everything young lady."

"As easy for it is to believe in the air we breathe. We have faith that it is there though we cannot see it. We're just so naturally convinced that it is there and readily available, that we inhale and exhale every God-given day without so much as a thought about it. We're comfortable in breathing that we neglect to thank God for the air he provides or for the life he breathes into us. Air. We never see it. We just believe it's there. Shame it ain't that easy to keep believing in God. People can really do a number on you... mess that up for you. Especially church folk."

China inquired, "Is your father still alive?"

"Pastor at a small church on Bergen. My ex-wife. The first lady. She took my mother's place. What she wanted with an old man, is beyond me. I guess I just wasn't man enough for her.

Y'all have a good night ladies. Thank you for meeting my needs tonight. I know God used y'all. Keep me in your prayers. And next time y'all get to talkin' about homeless people to ya little friends, tell them we're human too. We have feelings. We have more needs than the obvious. Most of us don't bite." He smiled. He walked away.

Hope and China started down the road. "Ms. P, you think he gon' do right wit dat money?"

"I try not to make that stuff my business China. It's our job to bless people as God blesses us. After that, what they do with that blessing is totally between them and God. He knows everybody's why. That's enough. We all have issues. We all have why's that precede those issues."

"Like cause and effect?"

"Yep China. Like cause and effect."

"One more question Ms. P. That was quite some outburst you had back there. Sometimes you feel like you need some what?" China chuckled.

"Mind out of the gutter young lady. Don't over extend. It's not what you think. But for the record, not that I owe you an explanation, but, since you're here...I'm human, just like you. With that being said, I lost control. My flesh rose up. It was just my flesh pressuring me again."

"Whatchu mean flesh? As in skin? Yeah, I see that word in the Bible sometimes. Its skin right? How ya skin...?"

"Well yes it is but it goes deeper than that. I can't have Bible study with you right now. I'm too tired. We can talk about that another time?" She smiled at the inquisitive young girl, "Alright?"

"Aight Ms. P. Don't forget now. Don't let me down. I can't keep tryin to read it if I don't understand all of those fancy Medieval Times words. All them thus's and thous. Thy this. Thou that. I be like huh?"

Hope laughed, "I hear you. I'm gonna see if I can get you a simpler version of the Bible. A children's version."

China charged, "I ain't no child Ms. P."

"Then whose skirt is that because it's child size?"

"Ms. P, don't..."

"Girl I'm just joking. Not!" China rolled her eyes. She unfolded a napkin. She laid it across her lap.

"I know you're of a certain age China and all you want to do is be respected as such. Know this though, just because you out here doin' grown things, don't make you grown. You can have grandchildren and still be a child."

"Oh immature right? That's whatchu sayin'?"

"Yes. Try not to get offended. My point is maturity is a choice and a process. Don't get ahead of yourself. You can be built like a brick house and have the mentality of a mud hut out in the sticks somewhere in a third world country. You can dress up fancy as you please on the outside; like a pent house in Manhattan, all of the amenities, bells and whistles. But, still carry a project mentality. A mindset that will keep you stuck, behavior that will limit you. A backwoods behavior. No sense of entitlement. No drive to do better or want more."

"I see what you mean. Like that looking the part thing from earlier."

"Yes ma'am. Sometimes we can even play the part for a season. But what happens when we get caught with our pants down? We can't deliver the goods when the time comes? Immaturity and all that comes with starts to rear its ugly head."

"You preach a lot. You have a lot to say Ms. P."

"Well, I don't like to think of it as preaching. I'm just passionate. And yes. Sometimes I do have a lot to say. You're right. Sorry if I'm beating you down too much."

"Nah. Don't be sorry Ms. P. You good. I'm just not use to it I guess. I'm into it though."

"What?" Hope asked.

"You talking to me. Most of the time grown-ups just talk at me. Make me not wanna listen. Guess I'm hard-headed."

"You're just a teen. Don't be so hard on yourself."

"Okay. But only if you relax a bit and not work so hard to try to change people. You wearin' yaself out Ms. P. It's for nothin'."

"What does that mean China? What are we talking about? And whatchu know about me?"

"Only what you tell me. Only what I can see that maybe you can't. Ms. P, some of those girls we group wit ain't beat. They just comin' to please somebody else. They tryin' to fill a quota somebody gave 'em or just have somethin' to do. I think they a waste of ya time. A waste of everybody time. I mean, I know girls out here that need guidance real bad.

Feindin' for it. They slippin' through the cracks. They need somebody like you. And here these birds is takin' up space. Ain't nobody got time...?"

"Hush.", Hope demanded.

"What I say?" China said confused.

"Don't let me hear you tear down another female ever again. I don't care what they do or don't do. Too much of that goin' around. All of those reality shows y'all watch. Just empty. No purpose. No positivity. All of those housewives. Middle-aged women with children that get on television to air their business out and belittle other women; Actin' a damn fool! Basketball wives that aren't even married to the players. They don't know how foolish they look."

"I think the shows are good Ms. P."

"It's probably because you don't know any better. They make Black and Latino women look desperate, ill-mannered, ignorant and stupid. All they do is perpetuate stereotypes."

"You think so Ms. P?"

"Girl, I know so. Angry black woman. Hot and spicy Latin female with an even hotter temper. They don't like it on a black woman...too strong they say. Too much attitude. But Lord! Let a Latin woman throw something across the room or an Italian woman flip a table... Then it's hot, entertaining and acceptable. Let a Latin woman be promiscuous or a white woman be loose, then, it's attractive. They're liberated and sexually adventurous; makes them more attractive to black men."

"I get that Ms. P. I see it all of the time in the hood. These boys talk about how easy other girls are that ain't black, but they steady trippin' on 'em. Let a black girl get loose, just because they man asked them to try something different or because even though she don't do that; she ain't wit it 'cause her momma raised her with more self-respect, they get labeled a whore and they get the boot and a bad rep. But them other nastier than thou chicks, oh what they gon' get?"

"The ring and everything. Even if they don't want him or it, just because they can, they'll take it all."

"I know right?! And these jokers be all up in ya face and in ya pants all through high school. They go to college and lose they mind round them white girls. Get on my nerves!"

"Uh huh. You are so right. They go away to school or get drafted. Soon enough, black becomes whack and they off on the Blonde Ambition tour like Madonna."

"It's crazy Ms. P."

"Tell me about it. What's even crazier is those Love and Hip-Hop people. Girl bye! I make my daughters turn from that mess every chance I get. What they gon' make me do is get the cable turned off and take 'em to the library like I used to when I had time. Can't take the garbage. Sorority Sisters this. Bad Girls club that. Please already. Perpetuating stereotypes. Nobody growing. Nobody changin'. Nobody reinforcing positivity or attempting in the very least to guide these young girls. The very demographic they cater to! Mess ain't no better than the cigarette companies targeting youth. Kardashians...Keepin' Up wit who? For what? So now cussin' ya mama on T.V is good profit and showin' ya butt on the internet is what's hot in the street? Disrespect and bad behavior among women draws big ratings? Kanye shoulda added that in there when he made New Slaves."

"Oooooohhhhhhhh!!!!!! Yaaaaasssss! You on one Ms. P! Get yours."

"I'm just being honest. Somebody gotta keep it one. On one or not, I said it. I'm not trying to come for nobody. But, truth is truth. I said it. Yes I did." she cut her eye at China. "You're gonna go home and watch that mess anyway ain't you girl?"

China giggled, "Yeah. I like Joseline. She's pretty. She's funny. I used to like Chrissy and Tahiry too. Sorry Ms. P."

"Girl, you a mess. It's nothing but mess."

"Oh my goodness. You on ten. Can we get back to what I was sayin' before you blasted off?"

"What China? About the girls in group? Oh child please. Don't judge them. Maybe if they keep coming, they'll learn something. Something might click. Like when some people start goin to church when they're young. They may just be coming because their parents insist or force them too. But over time, with patience, by the grace of God, they start paying attention...maybe not until their older, but just from them showing up, over and over, a seed may have been planted China. People pray. Prayer changes things. Their minds get renewed. They get transformed. New creatures. Not all but some. So my point is, you can't throw the baby out with the bath water. You'll kill the baby."

"Oh yeah, Jay Z talked about that in Holy Grail. Like take the good with the bad right?"

"Right.", Hope says. "So let them keep coming. It's not my business what they do with what they're being given. My job is to give it to them."

"Like giving to the homeless right? Like back there."

"Yeah China. Some places in people and in life only The Lord can get too because they are so far down deep inside. We all have those places. Bible says one plants, one waters, God gives the increase. I do my part in a certain season. They may meet another person down the road on a mission from God doing something completely different than me, in another season of their lives. Further on down the line that may gel with the seed God entrusted me to plant. Then years later, in another season, God causes that seed to grow. On the other hand, you all are very young. Under a lot of peer-pressure. They could be listening but, pretend not to be to stay down with people outside the group or other girls in the group. We all want to be associated with something or somebody. A lot of the girls aren't strong enough to stand alone in their conviction. We don't know everything that they are going through inside. Acting out is often a cry out to get out. Like you, those girls want to be seen and heard China by any means necessary.

Maybe those women on those shows have grown up physically or sexually, just not mentally, spiritually or emotionally. Maybe they just want to be seen. Like you, like me, like the girls in the group, they may have felt invisible all of their lives. The attention and the checks make them feel validated. Now they are being viewed. Still not yet seen. There is a difference. A vast difference China.

Again, I'm not trying to preach. I don't like to judge and I know I can be hard sometimes. I'm very passionate about certain things. I get frustrated with the dysfunction I see on TV just like you do with the girls in the group."

"Yeah Ms. P, and the boys in the hood that go off on that tour like you said. How they know them girls don't just want them for their status or potential earnings from those contracts? They need to be lookin' for goal builders not gold diggers."

"Go China! Alright now. I hear you preachin' to me. But all of those girls can't be gold diggers because most of those boys in the hood aren't going to get a contract in the league. I've been to college with some of those people and I must tell you this, some of these guys are just curious about the white girls. They just gotta have one. Some of those white girls just gotta try a black guy. It goes both ways. Sometimes people just want something different. And believe it or not, it really can be love sometimes. Maybe some people that date outside of their race, are just searching for themselves."

"I guess so. Ms. P, you do know though, some people just can't stand to be associated with their own race? You do know that don't you? They just hate themselves. Some people don't want to be black. They want mixed babies because they feel they'll look less black, have better hair and more of a chance to live up in America. Maybe they won't be labeled. Maybe they'll never get harassed by the cops. Maybe white people will accept them and they'll have a chance at more opportunity. I don't know. Some guys feel like they upgrade when they seen wit' a girl that ain't black. Like it will make them less black and more valuable. You know how many times I've seen boys these boys in the hood put on Twitter and Instagram that they like Spanish mommies because they got hair, body and face? It hurts. Now that Jennifer Lopez, Iggy and Kim got they asses out, when black women been having big, beautiful behinds for like EVER, now it's sexy and hot. Before, back in the day, a black woman's body was consider unnatural and unacceptable. As soon as anybody that ain't black do something or get something we been on for like EVER, it becomes fashionable. It's so sad they way they devalue us."

"It's true China. I live in another community and I talk to people all of the time that are fascinated with my body and my hair. They wanna touch all over you like you're some science project. I know girl."

"I don't even wanna be black all of the time."

"China know. Don't ever say that. You're a beautiful black butterfly. Your dark skin is flawless girl. People out here payin' to get brown like you. They get injections and implants to get your natural curves. Your hair is just as strong and as rich as your heritage. God made you the way you are. He doesn't make mistakes. You're fearfully and wonderfully made. Girl, you are so beautiful."

"I don't know Ms. P."

"Girl, you better find out! Like yesterday."

"Whatchu supposed to do when the boys in your own hood and all of the movies and the videos make you feel like the ugly duckling because don't none of the pretty girls look like you? Not even on commercials. Every guy I know is into exotic looking chicks. Your own people make you feel like it's a crime to be dark-skinned. Or like you're some sexual novelty or something among your own people. If I do what you want, everything you want me too, the way you like it, I'm nasty. I'm the whore. But let anybody that ain't black do things you never even thought of doing, first night, you wifin' dat! Even if she been with your best friend and everybody done had and seen her goodies on the internet or on the street. You want her because her hair not nappy and her skin is light. She'll get you places I can't. With her, you get a pass you can't get with me. I'm too black. Too strong."

"Oh China. Don't allow these silly, immature boys upset you. It's their loss. You're amazing."

"You're just trying to be make me feel better. Thanks, but no thanks this time. I've been feeling like this all of my life. Did you know the Spanish boys that live across the street from my Grandma's house used call me Night Rider? The black boys, they used to call me tar baby."

"I've been through all of that China. Their just dumb kids. They probably liked you. Boys are stupid. You know that."

"Yeah, I know, but it doesn't make me feel any better about the way God made me. It's hard to get past all of those words. They really, really hurt." She grieved, "People in your family can tell you all they want, that you're a pretty black girl. All that's ever gonna stick with you from that statement is the word black. I get tired of hearing I'm pretty to be dark. Or you're a beautiful black girl. They don't say that to girls who aren't dark. It's another label.

Growin' up, it is so hard not to hate what you see in the mirror. You wonder why God made you so dark and your hair so hard. Why? Then you get a weave and they make fun of you for that. When all you tryin' to do is make your own attracted to you because you know that's what they want."

"Preach child. You're right. They want the fantasy. Not the reality. I know. It's sad. Don't cry China."

"Why is it black men don't value the women that have they back? The ones that brought them here. They run back to their black momma's when the other women break them down and break their hearts. They run to the black church when they get caught up in a scandal and the media is having them for lunch. Even the singers and stuff... Black people go out of they way to support what they do and they go and give their all, I mean everything to other people. Why?"

"I don't know China. But you can't make it a money thing. Everything ain't a race thing either. Every woman that ain't black ain't a gold digger or scheming on the brothers. Other women go through the same hell we go through with men too. Race don't matter all of the time. Men are men baby. Let me be the first to tell you. I know a gang of white and Spanish women that would love to give some of those brothers back to us."

"I'm not just talking about money Ms. P. I'm talking about their hearts. That's what I mean when I say everything. You know how hard it is to get a brother to love you out here?" China sobbed.

"Ask me how I know China? I know better than most. I wish I had insight on that one myself. Sometimes you just want to dig a hole in their heads and hearts so you can know what's goin' on in there. You wanna understand them. They just shut down. The thing is, like I said, I know firsthand, that men are just men. I also know firsthand, that you'll never find what you're looking for in them. They won't find it in other women. Everything begins within. Love and hate for yourself, your race, other people, it all begins within you. It comes from experiences, environment and seeds planted by other people. You have to love you. You must accept yourself China. Before you do that though. You have to begin to know and accept the fact that God loves and accepts you. He created you. Purpose in mind, no mistakes. I know rejection is hard, Especially, when it comes from your own. People hate you because they think you're a reflection of them. They hate themselves. People think men don't struggle with self-esteem issues. That's a myth. I think they might spend more time focused on figuring out who they are and where they fit then we do sometimes. Especially black men. They've been emasculated and beaten down from slavery 'til now. They're devalued as well. Black women have a way of beating their men down because of what? Self-=reflection and comparison to other men they make go to school with or work with outside of their community. Women try to live out fantasies too! Black women share the same issues, thinking that if they get in another tax bracket and relocate to another zip code, date outside of their race and birth mixed children, that it somehow erases the stigma attached to being black. It's not just boys in the hood that try to wash the blackness off China. They brought us over here from Africa. Where our ancestors were already enslaving their own. It wasn't about race then. More of a class thing I guess. I don't know why, but from the door, our people have always had an issue with unity. The Euros just capitalized on that. They did us wrong. But, as usual, we did ourselves even worse. Colorism is a far deeper hatred than racism in my book. Genocide, is one of the worst hate crimes known to man. Sometimes I wonder if we've ever really loved ourselves? And if so, how did we get so lost? Maybe it's hard for us to love ourselves because at our core, we never really found out what real love is. We'll never be able to unite while we have so much division. A house divided cannot stand. Other races have always banked on that. We foolishly and lavishly keep filling their pockets. I don't know. It's like white slave owners used to brutally rape black women. We were like forbidden fruit they couldn't resist. It's a disgusting thought. And later there was the Emmit Till thing. And it was like white women were the forbidden fruit for black men. Then slowly people became ore rebellious and that passed. Jokers ain't stop pickin the fruit off those trees ever since. It's like it's something your mother told you not to touch but, you just gotta have it. Maybe it's like that for white women too. You know? Like them telling you what you can't have makes you want it more or something."

"That's a lot to think about."

"It is China. I could be over-thinking it all. It could be just simple attraction. I think I just went a little Malcom X for minute." Hope laughed.

"Maybe it is just a simple as the whole cause and effect thing. Right Ms. P?"

"Yeah, maybe it is. Only God knows. What causes lead to those effects."

 "Just like with people on those shows." nodded China.

"Epiphany. Thank you girl. Sex tapes, cat fights, exploitation and all. I can't afford to cast people out of the group because of their bad behavior. God doesn't do that to us. He's not like that. He doesn't repay us according to or wrongs. Who am I? We all got ish. Even if we ain't displaying it for all to see on TV. It may not be the same stuff. But we all got stuff. As women though, black, white, Harlem to Hollywood, I wish... I just wish we would learn to resolve our issues in a healthier manner. I so wish."

"Damn! Ooooppsss. I mean dang Ms. P. You mad smart."

"So are you Ms. China. Give yourself some credit. You made me think today. Caused me to look at what I was saying to you and change my perspective a bit. I try not to limit where I learn from. Thank you for the lesson young lady. And I saw Joseline and Tahiry, even Jennifer from Basketball Wives...they are beautiful. You are correct. I just wish the format was more positive. I wish they behaved as beautifully as they looked. There's so much more to them than selling out or allowing yourself to be pimped until the wheels fall off and the fifteen minutes are up. It's all pimp game. It's a shame that our very own people and TV stations are behind the nonsense. It is really not that different than the blacks in Africa that forced and traded other Africans into European/American slavery. They really messed us up with the mindset they laid on us. Long lasting ignorance. Lord when will black people wake up?! Girl, I'll be glad when every reality is eradicated! I mean it! I wish it would just all go away. All of the drama, the fighting, the name calling, the debt, the lies, the excess. The vanity. The waste. It's voluntary slavery child. Lord I just want them to wake up!"

"I hear you. I do too sometimes. But when you young, I guess you just love the drama. It's so juicy. It's exciting. It's addictive. Like high school." China laughs.

"Yeah. That's the sad part. They have power and influence. There is a responsibility that comes with being famous. People don't like to acknowledge that so they deny it. They think that cancels the responsibility. It doesn't. But again, who am I?"

China stared at her with admiration, "You're something special. We need you Ms. P. A lot of us ain't getting' this at home."

"I need you young ladies too. Believe it or not. You are all very special to me. China you are going to be a bright and shining star in someone's life. You are the answer to somebody's question and someone's prayer. You have worth and value. I see it. I hope you do."

"I want to." Her eyes welled up with tears.

"You will. You are a treasure. Precious. Young ladies like you are why I push. Y'all why I do what I do."

That night, China went home with Hope.

"Who is that mommy?"

"A stray." Hope's eldest daughter mumbles.

"Mommy. Heather called her a stray."

"Well she is. Just look at her." Heather mumbles, "I don't know her. Neither do you."

China belts loud and clear, "China. My name China. Y'all good now?"

"Alright. Alright. Everybody stop. Everybody, this is China. China, this is everybody. Now everybody play nice."

"Whatever.", Heather says.

"She said whatever mommy."

"Ok. Ok. God help me. It's getting late. It's been a long day. Let's talk tomorrow. I'll get up and..."

"Yeah. We know. MAKE US BREAKFAST." The children said harmoniously.

"Same ole bull.", Heather grumbled.

"You got somethin' in ya throat girl?"

"No ma'am. I don't."

"I figured as much. Little ones, let's go. Bed time. Come on. Let me get you guys cleaned up. A story. Then we gon' count some sheep. Heather you be nice to our guest. Imma take it down like Chris Brown. Be hospitable."

China moaned, "Oh she gon' be nice. Or Imma take her down like Chris Brown and she gonna end up in the hospitable."

"Good night ladies. Emphasis on good and ladies."

Heather walked past China heading into the living room, "You ain't talkin' to me. No you not."

"Tell ya story walkin ma. Stray... I gotcha stray right here. Keep poppin' off."

China sat in the kitchen staring out of the window. "Don't know what she brought me up here for if she was gon' just fade to black on me like dat. Got me sittin' here in this chichi ass place. Damn half-breed givin' me attitude like she hard. ...aint brick comin' from up here. She know she don't want it."

Heather waltzed back into the kitchen, "Ahhhhhhhhh! I gotchu heated. Yooooooooo! She over there smokin' like a Pookie in New Jack City. Beam me up Scotty."

"Look white girl, go 'head. You know what. I don't have to stay here. I ain't leave the hood to just to come up here and catch fever from no Mariah Carey wanna be. I'm out." She yells up the stairs, "Ms. P, it's been real. Deuces."

Heather laughed, running after China as she headed out of the front door, "Girl! Get back in here. You gon' have a swat team up here. You gon' scare these white people to death. They ain't used to no ghetto nonsense. C'mon."

"Nah Casper. I'm good. I know my way back down the hill. Y'all ha' dat."

China walks down the street, "Now I know I saw Springfield Ave. on the way up here. Where's the bus stop dag?"

After walking several blocks. Exhausted, she finally finds a bus stop. She takes her shoes off. Heather pulls up, "Girl. You got ya shoes off?"

"Mind ya business before I beat dat ass. I'm sick of you now. Take ya pasty-face home."

"Ya man like it."

"For all I know, EVERY man like it. Ho! Get on!"

Heather giggled, "Maybe. Maybe not. Don't matter either way. You should just let me take you home."

"That sound like a pick up line and you sound gay as hell. I ain't beat. Girl, go 'head."

"Gay? Me? Maybe. Maybe not. Another thing that's neither here nor there. Why does that matter? I ain't tryna holla at you witcha Ashy Larry havin' ass feet. How a girl so black feet so white? Oh how the weak things of this world do confound the wise."

"DON'T TWIST THE SCRIPTURE!" China warned.

"THEN DON'T GET IT TWISTED!" Heather rebuked. "I'm trying to be nice."

"Get outta here you old wanna be down ass clown. When you try hard. You die hard."

"Ayyyyyeee!!! That's my ish." Heather gets out of the car. She starts dancing.

"That ain't how you do no Nay Nay. Girl bye." Heather kept dancing. China tittered, "You stupid. Aight man. I'm 'bout sick of you. Take me home. I'm too tired to go back and forth."

"Why you tired youngin'? The night is ours." Heather ragged.

China yawned, "Between your mouth and ya momma preachin' at me half the day, y'all got me beat."

"Oh. So she talks to you?"

"All the time why? She don't talk to you?"

"I don't wanna talk about that. Imma take you home. But, first I wanna go home and change my clothes. I'm tryna get into to somethin tonight."

"Girl! Stop the car! Ms. P ain't no joke! You better keep ya ass in the house. You don't even have to drop me off. If it's gonna save y'all some drama, I'll stay the night. Just leave me alone and we good."

"See, that's where you wrong. She is a joke. It's all fun and games. You think you know her?"

"Maybe."

Well charity case, you don't! Besides, what she don't know, won't hurt her."

"And what don't she know mutt?" China quizzed.

"A lot. So she stay safe. She know enough to keep up her face in public. Her mask on tight. She good."

"Can't be true. She's such a good mentor."

"Yeah. A good mentor don't equal up to a good mother."

"But..."

"Just kill it. I'm about to burn down. I don't need you blowin' my high."

"Trees?" China asked surprised.

"All day." Heather smiled. "Here. Champ dis blunt real quick."

"Girl I am not about to..."

"Please, don't try to tell me you don't know how? Not dressed like that. I know you 'bout dat life China. Don't front."

"Girl. Aight, I'll champ dis. I'll even roll up. But I don't smoke aight?"

"Uh huh. So when you stop? Yesterday?"

China cackled, "Nah son. The day before yesterday."

"Foolish. Well guess what?"

China let her seat back, "What yo dag?! You aggie son."

"Imma getchu high today Craig. Real high."

Heather turned the music up. They laughed as Heather drove home.

They pulled up in the driveway. Heather sat staring at the bushes.

"Well?" China sassed.

"Well what NAACP?"

"Whatchu waitin' on? Ain't we goin' inside?"

Heather turned towards China. She looked her up and down.

China raised her seat to an upright position, "What man?"

Heather continued to stare at her.

"Aww hell naw now. I know what that is. I get it all the time from jokers. I ain't down Raven-Symone. I'm into sticks not mitts. Go 'head ma. I don't like chicks son." She got out of the car. "Knew you was being too nice. Shoulda stayed my black ass right at that bus stop. Girl bye."

Heather shook her head. She rolled down the window, "Girl if you don't get back up in here and champ this blunt! Don't nobody want you. Getcha mind right." China got back inside of the car.

"Yeah. Now break dat down and light up."

China began to champ the blunt. She stopped suddenly. "You know what? Even if you don't respect your moms. I do. I love Ms. P. She been too good to me for me to ever disrespect. Nah son. Here. You handle dat. I don't even wanna smoke. I'm good."

"Guess everything in the Bricks ain't so hard. Well…more for me.", Heather said cheerfully.

China watched her prep the cigar. She watched her light up. She took a pull. "Sure you don't wanna hit dis? It's bubblegum."

The smell was so aromatic to China. Down in the hood, the smell of weed was everywhere. Smoking blunts was just as common as smoking Newports, if not more so. Weed was a favorite pastime of almost everyone she knew; young and old alike. Even her father indulged. It's where she picked up the habit. He was unaware that she would go behind him and pick up the remnants in the ash tray behind his DJ equipment in the garage. He had always warned her to stay away from his DJ equipment, "Don't go near it China. I'm not playin' with you. That's my lively hood. Its how I keep you dipped. If I catch you over there, its gon' be somethin." As it were with teenagers, a warning was nothing more than another line to cross. Just a dare. A challenge to be met, not even a threat. She mused, "Him and his forbidden fruit. He had to be kidding me."

He had no idea of all that China had been exposed to by being in the streets with her mother for so long. She knew about drugs, alcohol. She had learned about sex pretty early on. Being left alone in various strangers' houses at a very young age while her mother was out tricking to get her next high and a corner store sandwich for China, she had been pawed by all sorts of men. Molested by family friends. She had seen her mother and other women naked far too often. She had been touched by a female family member, over and over again at so many sleepovers, she had lost count. For a very long time, China had blocked it out of her mind. She knew something just didn't sit right in her spirit when she was in the presence of that particular cousin. She had pushed the violations so far down inside of herself that even trying to figure out why she felt awkward around the woman became a strain. So she did all she could to let it go. "Who gonna care?" she thought. "Ain't nobody gon' do a damn thing in this family. They sweep everything under the rug."

One night, she was out at a family barbecue, she had gotten a hold of some liquor in a leftover cup at the end of the night. China was about ten. Her mother, nowhere to be found. Smashed, she stumbled over to a table where the elders of the family were having a lively round of spades. No one even noticed how inebriated she was. No one cared. A concerned neighbor had attempted to comment on her appearance, only to be cut off by an uncle, the same uncle that would sit behind her and stare at her butt while she washed dishes at her Grandmother's house whenever her mother would leave her there.

"Don't do it.", he remarked. "That's Alicia child. Leave that alone Margie. You know how that go. You know how she gon' end up."

China took a seat at the table where she appeared to go unnoticed. As a drunk mouth speaks a sober mind, she volunteered her truth. She spewed honest accusations about the many that had trespassed against her, body, mind and spirit. Her watery confession fell upon death ears. They all peeked up from their hands, continuing their game, as she bemoaned.

Her Grandmother finally broke, "You been drinkin' China?"

China remained silent. Not as befuddled as she appeared she wiped her eyes in anger. Young China crossed her arms in protest. She let her head hang down.

"How many books you got Spank? China? China? Child its gon' be alright. You hear me? Now go get washed up for bed. Come gimme kiss first." Her Grandmother hugged her,

"Don't talk about that stuff ok? Don't worry about that mess. I don't know where you got that from but leave it there. Go on sleep it off. You have such an imagination. God gonna use that baby. And don't drink no more. Drinkin' ain't no good for you."

"Yeah! We don't need no mo' round here like yo momma." her Uncle growled.

"Spank! Don't do that!" her Grandmother demanded.

"Don't do that nothin'. She done had this child...know she don't want her!"

Her grandmother covered her ears, "Spank! What I just tell you!"

"Ma please. Alicia owe me money. Hell, she owe everybody. She ain't what the dogs put out. It's her mother. Who know better than her?" He stomped his feet. China jumped in fear. He howled, "Where Alicia at anyway?" She tucked beneath her Grandmother's beefy arm.

"Arthur Matthias Brinks. Now I done warned you. Leave her alone. She still my daughter. This still my Grandbaby. Alicia could be somewhere gettin' herself together for all you know. I refuse to give up on my child. Ain't that right China? We ain't givin' up on mommy right?"

"Now you know that girl momma out there hookin' Mama. Why you playin' dumb?" her uncle said.

"Spank, don't talk like that around that baby. She a baby. She don't know nothin' 'bout what Alicia do. You know that ain't right. You don't know what my child out there doin'."

"Probably dead long as she been gone. Somebody probably caught up with her shifty ass 'bout they money."

China ran up the stairs crying. She locked herself in the bathroom up on the third floor. Her Grandmother had come to check up on her. But, she refused to open the door. It was an unusually breezy summer night. She washed her face. She cracked the window. That night China slept in the cold, porcelain bathtub with the door locked. On her way to sleep she could hear her family arguing about her mother's whereabouts. Her choices. China, used to the confusion, let the discord and dysfunction rock her to sleep. She figured that was the way family was supposed to be. Nothing could be done. Nothing would ever change. Peace and harmony could only be found at rich, white people's houses on TV. China obviously wasn't rich, white, and she wasn't on TV. These were the cards she had been dealt. "Maybe God love some people more than He do others. I mean maybe He's mad at me. Maybe he hate me. I don't what I did to make Him hate me so much."

She looked up, "God, I'm sorry for whatever I did to make you hate me. Those rich, white people on TV always happy. They have everything. They even got dogs. I want a dog. They have perfect teeth. They always smilin' and stuff. They ain't got no problems. They all sit down at the dinner table together and talk proper and polite. They like each other. They got green grass and stuff. We here in the hood, we ain't got nothin like what they got. We sorry God. I'm sorry. Please help us. We wanna be happy like the people on TV."

"Um, hello? Earth to China. Have some? Take ya mind off ya troubles."

"Smell's good." China smiled. "I always liked the smell of weed. I know I'm wrong, I guess I'm just used to it. In your neighborhood y'all probably used to the smell of fresh cut grass. Where I'm from, we used to the smell of grass aight, just ain't fresh cut and if you smokin' wit somebody you don't know, you better HOPE it ain't cut wit nothin'. Especially if you a dime. Jokers be out here thirsty as hell."

Heather responded as she choked on the smoke, "Facts son."

"Speaking of facts, you was just playin' about dat maybe…maybe not liking chicks thing right?"

"Why? You prejudice against gays and lez's or somethin'?"

"No. Not at all. I just don't understand..."

"Obviously you don't. But Imma shed a little light for you. I like who I like when I feel like liking them and that's that. It's 2014, catch up."

"See that's what me and my friends be talkin' about. That right there."

"What right where?"

"That ole 'it's fashionable to be in the life garbage'. It's stupid. You're either gay or you're not. Not here today, gone tomorrow. God ain't the author of confusion girl."

Heather looked China up and down, "I know YOU ain't standing in the pulpit, on a soap box, comin at me when you sittin' in my car, on my property, in front of my house with that cheap ho-ish collab on, lookin' like you got two Band-Aids over your nipples and a bandana tied around ya booty."

"Whoa! Whoa! Where is all the hate comin' from?"

"You tell me?"

"I'm Just sayin..." China explained.

"Don't JUST SAY anything. Especially when you don't know what you're talking about."

"Oh! I know what I'm talkin' about. But it's whatever. I'm just sayin', people out here dying for this. I mean straight getting trucked. Just for being and you out here frontin' for a cause you know nothin' about. Y'all kids need to understand, a lifestyle, a choice, whatever you wanna call it, ain't no label...it ain't no brand. It's not fashion ma. You gotta understand, I know people that still can't walk the halls at school without being up in arms because they in fear of gettin' they ass beat for being something they feel they didn't ask to be or have no control over. It's like the same thing wit da fiends in the street. They be out here getting trucked on the random just because they get high. Again, they ain't pray to God at night when they was kids to grow up and be addicts. Maybe some of 'em chose it, maybe it's in their DNA, or how they be sayin at church sometimes...a ...a...you know...one of those generational curse things people get. I don't know. I ain't God. I just know it's real out here.

You all up here in these cushy ass bushes, in the burbs. Ma, you don't what's real out here. You watch it on TV, you think that's what's up and you copy it, not knowin' what you doin'. You come from a good home. You got it all. I don't get it son. Why y'all suburban brats be such cases? I mean, y'all don't just have fun and tweak a lil' bit on the weekend to take the edge off like regular folk, y'all get white boy wasted. Because y'all listen to urban music, watch too much YouTube, take everything way too seriously, not knowin' these rappers are pushing a product; they just entertainers. They hustlin'. Tryin' to get away from the lifestyle they pushin' in the booth. We live that ish son. We see it day in day out. It's not a game. None of it. Y'all privileged kids be up here o.d'n. It's not a joke Heather. I know a grip of kids that would trade places with you any day. You don't even appreciate what you have. You have so much."

"Girl, do you even know what you're talking about? Are you me? Is this your life? You live up in here? You just goin' by what you see. And that's the problem between the haves and the have nots. The view. It's all perspective girl. You got it all wrong."

"Whatever."

Heather laughed. She blew the blunt smoke in China's face. "I'll say it again, you dressed like you auditioning for 'For the Love of Ray J' and you comin' at me about my choices and about what YOU THINK it is up here? Like somethin' sweet? Ain't nothin' ma. I'll pass. Let's go get somethin' to eat. I'm starvin'."

"Whatchu is, is ignorant."

Heather gnawed, "Oh I'm is?"

"Don't play. I can articulate at will. Don't sleep. I'm trying to get somewhere in life. I turn it on and off as I see fit. Just like everybody else."

"Oh your parents taught you to speak as well as white people when you answer the phone right? I mean, in case there's potential employer or a bill collector on the other end of the phone right? I can hear your mother now, 'Tell them I'm not home.' Right girl? That's the ghetto script right?"

"Yous an ignorant ass monster."

Heather runs to the mirror in the hall, "But I'm hot as balls though and you're mad."

"Oh please! You're a future meth addict whose gonna have a boyfriend named Tab Boxlightner. You'll live on the outskirts of Anywhere Ville, South Jersey. And your uterus will be so infected with HPV virus that it will rot from the inside out and you'll walk around smelling like hot garbage. And that's after you give him five kids with irregular hairlines. That box gon' be so open girl... Ya gynecologist gon' start callin' you Nate Robinson."

"Nate Robinson?"

"You know it."

"You're so wack! Like what does that even mean China?"

"Three pointers all day. All net. No rim. From across the court. They gon' be able to see that crater from Google Earth ma. Daaaammmnnnn!"

"Ha.Ha.Ha! This, from a lunch lady in the making?"

"Excuse?"

"Not today Bitch. You already shaped like one. You just need the polyester white uniform, the $8 wig. No! The $6 Dominican Doobie and turned over nursing shoes. With your ten illegitimate kids and twelve baby daddies. All of whom are no strangers to the penile system might I add. You'll come to work with an attitude because they cut your food stamps and you'll compensate by stealing the mystery meat and milks and putting them in your bag, which will not be Gucci, because you... Oh you're an over achiever. Your everyday purse will be a diaper bag from the discount store because that's how you roll. Hide the fish sticks kids! Here comes Ms. Thick ankles!'"

"Cute Goldie Locks. You know what. I'll accept that challenge. Because I'll be going to school at night."

"Oh what? To get a G.E.D? Good for you! I had no idea they were allowing slaves to read these days. John Boehner and the boys in Congress have been so generous to you people."

China chortled, "That's not funny. I heard they found out he was the devil."

"Girl no! You're misinformed. I don't think Boehner's that bad. He's just a republican. He can't help it. It's Bill O' Reilly and Rush Limbaugh. They actually take turns. I heard the devil can't be in more than one place at a time."

"Facts ma." They sniggled. "

"Uh-huh. But back to you."

"What girl?"

"Tell me, how many kids gon' graduate from your high school next year with you? Nine?" Heather prodded.

"Nah twelve. And ain't nothin' wrong with a G.E.D. It's a step in the right direction."

"Aww. What a reach. Twelve you say? So that includes the entire city of Newark then? How cute. You guys are moving up in the world instead of killing one another. Sweet. But I know you guys don't wanna learn. So you'll getting your G.E.D yes?"

"No. It will be a degree in Psychology. I'll need to be able to explain to your children why their mother loser and a fire crotch."

"Girl bye."

Yeah, they'll need me to breakdown why their mother is such a waste of a good nu…"

Hope yells from upstairs, "Girls, y'all good down there? Kinda quiet."

They holler in harmony, "Yes ma'am."

"What are you guys doin'?"

"Watching Housewives." Sings China.

"Love and Hip Hop." Heather bellows.

"Now y'all know how I feel about that garbage. I wish y'all would shut that mess off. You'll be acting like them soon. And who wants that. You girls need to know what you feed will dominate. Please turn it off. You'll turn into mean girls just like them." She mumbled on her way back into her bedroom, "Grown behind women acting like high school girls. You lower your standards and forsake your morals to feed your family? Or is it your vanity? Lord help us."

"Okay!" they scream.

"Moose."

"Low down monkey wit' a wig on."

"Hold up. Why are you calling me the moose? That was Nene. I don't look like her."

"Because you're tall and a nuisance."

"Girl bye."

"Plus you chew like one."

"Whatever."

"So why'd you call me the monkey in the wig? That was Kim. I ain't white."

"Yeah but you're wig is had and you look like a silver back."

"Ya mama. And it's a weave hater."

"That's what they told you at the Korean spot? Damn shame. Where you get hooked up at? Somebody name Haneefa's kitchen? She was sewin' you in while the chicken was fryin'?" badgered Heather.

"If that's the same place you got your weave done. Then yes."

"What? This ain't no..."

"My ass. It's a weave. Pricy. Good Remy. But it's a weave nonetheless. I know white girls get down too."

"I ain't white."

"You ain't black either."

"That's not fair or funny. I was brought here. I didn't ask for this. This is me. I was just born. I had no choice in the matter. I didn't know I had to apologize for being human and bi-racial. Forgive me."

"No forgive me. That was a low blow. Sorry Heather."

"I'm used to it. Save it."

"It was funny when Nene called Kim that low down monkey with a wig though." China laughed.

"It was mean China. But yeah…" Heather snickered. "It was funny at the time."

"Yo! Why you say Love and Hip Hop after I said Housewives?"

"Don't matter. She wasn't paying any real attention. She never does. I know her routine. That was a drowsy bathroom break. She won't remember anything in the morning. Trust me. She didn't really care. It's just because you're here. Plus I love that show."

China teased, "Stebie why you gotta treat me like that. You know I don't got nothin'. You take everything from me."

"I'll send ya ass back to the strip club Joseline." said Heather. The school girls giggled. "You better keep Mimi the Maid away from me Stebie or its gon' be suntin'. I don't like the way you treat me Stebie." Heather moaned in a low tone. "Why you actin' like that Joseline? I'm the good guy. Mimi already got off the bus. Whatchu want me to do?"

"Goodness! I can't stand Stevie J." China sat down at the kitchen table, "Real talk though, why you so opposed to your mother Heather? You have a good life." Heather was muted rummaging through the pantry snickering. "I wish you knew how good you have it. I wish I knew where my mom was."

"What's wong wit da baby? You can't find your mommy? Call her silly!" Heather smirked.

China played with her hair, "I can't."

"Why not? Wait, you hear that? Is that my mom? Pass me that bag. Hurry up. I need Visine, Altoids and some of that Khloe and Lamar quick. Oh my goodness girl." she chuckled.

"So stupid." China whispered.

"I just realized this perfume says 'Unbreakable'. That's ironic because you remember Lamar and the whole crack thing? Get it? Unbreakable? Crack? Lamar? Khloe?" Heather fell on the floor laughing uncontrollably.

"Yeah. Um...that's wasn't funny. A lot of people got hurt. We don't know what's true and what's not. We should pray for people with drug problems and for the people that love them. They be goin' through it too. Tough love is hard. It's hard to just let go and let God. It's hard to throw in the towel on a relationship where so much has been invested. We're just looking in from the outside. Spectators assuming. They're celebrities Heather. They choose a public life so to speak. But, they have feelings too. Everybody do. So let's not..."

Heather sits up on the floor, "You here that?"

"No. What is it?"

"It's the sound of my high dying. YOU'RE KILLING IT!" Heather screams.

China walks into the living room, "You're the worst. I hope ya mother come down here and catch you munchin' out. She ain't stupid. I'm goin to sleep. I hope she come down here and bust yo ass. Ignorant."

"Okay. Okay. I'm sorry. I'm all ears my sista. What about your mom?"

"I can't find her. I can't call her. I haven't seen her in a couple of years. She's a heroin addict. She do what she gotta do to get what she need. I really miss her. At least you have your mom here with you every day. You're lucky. You should cut her some slack."

"Girl, first let me swallow these chips. Mmm! So good. Hold up, swig of Hawaiian Punch."

"You swallow like a pro."

"Jealous because I'm a threat?"

"You ain't no threat. You just nasty. You're an ironing board with boobs. Where ya ass at?" Heather rolled her eyes. China teased. "You gon' have to come a lil' better than face and hair to compete with me hun. Girl, did you just mix Doritos and chunks of Hot Pockets in Butter Pecan Ice Cream."

"Yeah. It's to die for. Wants some?"

"Girl bye. Anyway..."

"Oh right. Yeah, so I feel you. But you gotta understand, just because a person has a mom on deck, doesn't mean she is always present. See how she walked in here WITH YOU, didn't ask me and my sister and brother no questions? No how is everything? No did y'all eat? I love y'all. I miss y'all...nothin. See you ain't catch that. But, we don't miss it. We here livin' it China. She's always like that. Out there flying around with that S on her chest saving the world, fixing everybody else's life. Meanwhile, back at the ranch, we got problems here and she don't see it. Thank God all of us have good fathers. Besides her buying us everything and keeping the bills paid; we have a nice house, it's full of stuff. But girl, it's really empty in here. She's never here. When she is here, she's tired or working on a case for another broken soul. Phone never stop ringin'. Or she's playing with the two little kids. She really don't have no time for me. Like I'm invisible. I don't matter. Girl, even when she take me to the mall, she's on the phone counseling somebody else's daughter. I'm tired of it China. It hurts. So in that regard, I guess we both want a life we know nothing about.

You ain't 'bout this life China. Believe when I tell you, you couldn't handle this. At least you're not expecting your mother to show up. Every day I expect my mother to show up and she never does. I know wherever your mom is, drugs or not, you have her in spirit. She carries you with her. And you do the same. I have my mother physically, but in every other aspect, she is dead to me. This is a haunted house girl. She's just a ghost passing through. That's it."

China reaches out to hug Heather, "I'm sorry. I didn't know."

Heather draws back, "its cool. I'm not good with that kind of touch China. We don't do that kind of stuff around here."

China sat back in amazement. She thought, "But she held me in the car. I don't understand." She shook it off. "Umm, so you and ya mom not cool. Is that why you like females?"

"Who you? Dr. Phil now?" Heather barked.

"No. I'm just..."

"Didn't we talk about this just sayin' thing? Jesus Christ! I don't know why alright. I haven't figured it out yet. I don't have anyone to talk to. I don't have any friends okay?"

"I find that hard to believe. Heather look at you. You're so pretty. Look at your hair."

"I know. I know. My hair. Blah. Blah. News flash! I'm mixed China."

"And? What's the problem Heather? Whatchu got light-skinned problems? Some real b.s.", China harassed.

"Light-skinned problems? Well I guess I do China. Black girls are always fascinated by my hair. It's just hair. And before you say anything, yes! It gives me problems; tangles up like yours. Its different textures in different places...like y'alls. Dark-skinned girls be givin' me mad attitude. I always feel like I need to apologize because my skin is light and my hair is longer and lighter. Black guys always fascinated by my looks when I'm more than that. White boys curious and scary. White girls stay touching on my skin like I'm a wax figure at Madame Tussauds. Spanish people think I'm one of them until I shut 'em down. Everybody knows my dad is this big time white business man in New York so they bug me for stuff. I give in because I don't fit in. I be tryin' to. I don't know where I fit in. I get tired of tryin'.

I'm alone China. Everybody wants something from me. If it's not what I can do for them, male or female, it's sex. I don't know anything anymore. Where do I fit in? At least you are one race. With a clear definition of who you are and where you come from." she wiped her tears.

"Ummm yeah. We're almost the same age so just like you, I'm trying to figure myself out, fit in and find out just who I am. As for the race thing, I don't know too many blacks that can say they truly know where they come from. We're in a land that our ancestors we're forced into coming to and treated like animals. They say we're free nut, they still hate us. They can't use to harvest they're crops anymore, so they hate us some more. We hate ourselves it seems. I talked to a lot of kids that don't know where they come from and they feel as if they have no real identity. You know African- Americans are the only ones with no flag? We're not exactly here. Not fully there. And because we are considered Americans, a lot Africans don't even want to claim us. Their ancestors weren't enslaved. People think slaves were brought over from every part of Africa...not truc. So as far as identity goes, I feel like I'm on the outside just like you. We weren't the first, the last or the only people to be taken as slaves, but I feel like we were the only ones left without dignity, pride, a connection and our own identity. We were stripped of our power it seems. Identity theft. Neither here nor there. I feel bad for your pain though. I had no idea. You goin' thru it. You have a pretty life."

"I'm tryna tell you ma. Pretty nice mom. Pretty problem-free girl. Pretty big house. Pretty little town. Pretty sweet life. Everything just perfect and pretty from the outside. Not so much China. Tell a friend. Damn! Tell somebody.

Maybe they'll come talk to my ass. Hopefully they won't want nothin' from me."

"I'm sorry Heather."

"Don't be sorry. Such is life. We all got ish I guess. I'll be aight. I just try to keep my mind occupied by doing fun stuff."

"Oh yeah? Fun stuff like what?"

"Well like getting blazed for one. But since you have blown my high, the punishment shall equal the crime."

"What? Girl, I don't like when white people start talkin' about punishment. Don't play."

Heather races up the stairs, "Shut up silly. I'm not white."

"You're a close second. I don't know if I can trust you."

"That's not funny China."

"It wasn't meant to be Heather."

"Stop it! Come on."

"Where are you taking me?"

"You gonna help me go through my closet. We goin' out. You owe me."

"You can't..."

"Can't what? Please. She out like a light. I'm off like a dirty shirt. Who gon stop da kid?" she laughs.

China opens the door to Heather's room. It's saturated in Victoria's Secret pink horizontal striping trimmed in black. Just beyond a gold statement wall, a walk-in closet the size of a studio apartment in New York City. On the wall, read the lyrics to the song 'Outside'. A song written and sung by The Elusive Chanteuse, Mariah Carey.

Beyond the door stood two life-sized cut outs. One of Mariah Carey. The other, Colin Kaepernick. Beautiful black and white monarchs made of blown glass and Swarovski crystals adorned the space.

"Butterflies and everything huh? You into Mariah that heavy?"

"Oh very much so. I know you probably a bee in the Bey-hive. That's cool. Who ain't these days? Bey is dope. But I loooovvvvveeee me some Mimi! I'm such a lamb. Mariah will always be my girl. She's my idol."

"I don't girl. I like Ariana."

"She aight. She ain't no Mariah though. Mariah is special. She's an icon, like Whitney Houston. I love me some Mimi child. I wish she was my mother sometimes. I just know life would be so fabulous with her as my mom. I know she'd understand me. She'd talk to me while we shopped 'til we dropped. Everywhere we'd go, butterflies with appear and harps would play. We'd leave a trail of fairy dust and flowers all over the place."

"Sounds nauseating and messy. If I had to pick somebody old school that was still hot and relevant. Girl! My girl for the ages is Mary J. honey. People be tryna say Keisha Cole the new Mary, but she can have several seats. Only one Mary boo. That's the 411 Hun."

"Aye yo you got it goin' on Hun?" Heather sings.

China adds, "Aye yo I got it goin' on Hun!"

"Yooooo. Mary was that chick back in the day. Hood as ever."

China smiles, "I know right. She kept it one and she mad fly all the time. Never catch her slippin' yo. That's why she's my idol. Now I love my mother. I don't care what she do. But if I could pick substitute mom, it would definitely be Mary J. My mom put me on Mary. Man, my mom is so cool."

"You really miss her huh?"

"More than I miss anything. I don't even know what to compare that feeling to Heather. I have access to everything else. Stuff I want and much more that I don't. All that's missing is Alicia."

"Oh that's your mom's name?"

"Yeah. But let's hop off that. I don't wanna talk about that no more. It makes me sad. I just wanna be happy."

"Like Mary?"

China smiles, "Like Mary girl. Sho nuff."

"Tell me what he doin' up in there though?"

"Who Colin Kaepernick? Oh he my dream lover. Waiting on him to come rescue me. Take me up. Girl take me down!"

"Alright. TMI. Moving on..."

"Don't hate."

"Girl bye. Kap ain't nothin' to hate on. Not when I got Victor Cruz to look at all winter long. Can't wait for September." China rolled around the floor.

"Oh Lord! You're a Giants fan?"

"'Til death do us part. Girl I live on Wainwright. My father got a shrine built in his office to Big Blue. This Jersey ma. Whatchu thinkin'? They play here. They live here."

"Yeah and they sorry as hell. 0 and 6 starting. Bye Felicia."

"And? What Crabtree do, spray his hands with Pam before that last game with Seattle?"

"I plead the fifth."

"....and end scene."

They both lay on the floor giggling.

China was in heaven. Awestruck, she marveled at all of the wares. The gold, royal décor and old English accent furnishings made her eyes dance.

"Son, I feel like I'm in a celebrity closet. You have so much stuff."

"Oh girl, it's just stuff. Purchased with hush money. Guess she thinks things make me happy."

"Well they make me happy." China cheered.

Heather stood over China while she sat fixated on the shoes on the closet floor, "You only think they make you happy because you don't have them in abundance."

"I see you lookin' down on me Heather. I may not have your fancy trinkets and education but I know some stuff. You're being condescending and smug. I don't like it. That is not called for. And contrary to YOUR belief, I get whatever I want!"

"If you say so. I'm just sayin'..." she laughed lighting a cigarette.

"Oh. You the devil's child. I'm gone. Keep ya pretty miserable life." China starts out of the door.

"Okay. Okay. Wait. I'm sorry. My bad. That's just the way we speak to each other up this way. Everyone is sarcastic. It's the norm."

"Well, where I'm from, talkin' slick like that will have you pickin' pieces of brick out of your teeth after too long. So tread lightly."

"Whatever girl. It ain't never that serious. Why people from down the way always so angry?"

"Honey the hood is a pressure cooker. You gotta be there to understand. I ain't got time to explain."

"Facts.", Heather agreed.

China pulled out some dresses to try on, "So why we in here? You lured me up here to show off?"

"Nope. I said we goin out. Pick whatever you want. Take some home with you. As sure as I'll live to see daylight tomorrow, they'll be more to come."

"Hey, let me ask you somethin'...I heard everything you said about your mom and all, but, I know for a fact she knows a lot about God. So she can't be all bad. She ever talk to y'all about Jesus?"

"Girl who?"

"You saved is what I'm askin'?"

"Saved from what?"

"You know hell and stuff like that."

"Oh that mess. She be tryin to talk to me about that church stuff sometimes but I ain't beat. I don't believe it. I think hell and heaven right here on Earth. We livin' it you know. At least that's what my father always says. He's a smart business man. I love him. He never lied to me. So my father must be right. He always tell me life is what we make it. Heaven or hell you know? I figure we just do our best. Be good to the people that are good to us, love those who love us. Pray when we need something and God will grant our wishes. We get to heaven when we die. I just think people get too deep with that God stuff. The Bible just a book of old stories. I see my mother reading that book all of the time. She even used to have Bible study with us. She's too busy now I guess. She be praying all over the house some nights. Putting oil on us, on the doors too! She's a fanatic China. She gets carried away. I just don't think people should can't get carried away with that historical stuff. It's the past. You know?"

"Historical stuff? You don't think it's real? You don't think God is real? Not even Jesus?"

"I guess. But I don't wanna talk about that right now. Let's get dressed."

"I think it's real. I think He's real. Jesus I mean. I'm not perfect. I'm not sure if He hears my prayers all of the time. I wish He talked to me. People say they hear from Him, they must have a gift or He must like them a whole lot. Maybe they better than me. Maybe they don't do nothin' wrong. I don't know. Maybe I'm not listening well enough. Somehow though, I still believe. I know I sound crazy. I just think if you talked to Him….pray…maybe you might believe just a little bit too."

"Me?! Talk to somebody that don't talk back. Child please, I get enough of that with these guys out here. Even my father gets quiet on me sometimes. I ain't trying to add no insults to the injuries honey. No thank you. Besides, what good is believing in a God you can't see doing you?"

"I don't know. I can't really…well yes I can. Even though I still haven't seen my mother, my life ain't perfect, He gotta hear me or something. Maybe He even talkin' back. Just thinking about it, I been in so many situations where I know I should be dead, in a wheel chair or in jail, but, I escaped with my life and my freedom. I'm still here. Stuff my father don't even know about. I'm still here girl." She smiled, "Right now, as I think about it. Maybe He has been talking to me. He been protectin' me Heather. I don't why. I'm not a good person. It's like that Kanye verse 'I BEEN TALKIN' TO GOD FOR SO LONG AND IF YOU LOOK AT MY LIFE I GUESS

HE TALKIN' BACK.' Yeah! That's it! I pray for protection for me and my dad every day. Every day we good." She looked up to the ceiling, "Thank you Jesus."

China felt a warm sensation in her heart. Heather was on her way into the bathroom when China heard a voice say, "You're welcome China. I see you. I love. I want you to get know me. You are very special to me. I see you trying. I am here. I am with you."

"Heather!" she yelled.

"What?! And don't wake my mother up. I ain't in the mood for no inquisition. I'm tryna bounce."

"You hear that?"

"What?"

"I think. No! I know it was Him. Finally Him."

"Who?!"

"God! It was Him. I heard Him. He spoke to me. I knew it was ok to believe! You should get saved Heather."

"Lord have mercy, this girl caught a contact."

"What? Ain't nobody high! You should get saved Heather."

"I can't do that."

"Why not?"

"Girl, it's too many do's and don'ts. All of those rules?"

"Well look at me. I'm not perfect obviously. I cuss and kick up dust all day, all night. But I believe. I don't know about no rules. I think the Ten Commandments was just for old people back in the day. I don't see too many people following no rules though. I know a bunch of people that go to church... They worse than me!"

"Girl say word. Those church girls right?"

"Girl yes! The guys too. They be tryna holla the most. Just left church and stay tryna get some. Go home and take off them pointy ass shoes first, then come back. Change ya clothes dawg. Lookin like you sell insurance for a livin'."

Heather laughs, "Word. They be the thirstiest."

"Some of 'em be fine though. Especially the Pastors sons."

"Facts. I can't be wit no square though China. No ma'am."

"Well honestly, they not all square. Trust me. My first was a church boy. That was years ago. They know some things. Oh he taught me quite a few of those things."

"I'll bet he did. Heeeyyy!"

"But I don't know, I think deep inside I like squares. Nerds is the biz right now girl. They done stepped they game up. They ain't the average no more. I might be lookin' in to getting' wit me a lil' Poindexter one day. I'm tryna get away from thugs."

"Whaaaatttt? No thugs? How you lo' dat girl?"

"I can learn to love it. I'm going to! Sick of that mindset. Don't go nowhere. Don't do nothin'. Can't walk down this block. Girls everywhere. First date is me coming to ya house, start off watching a movie on your couch, end up face down, ass up in ya bed. Girl, my body can't take it no more. If I can't have what Jay and Bey got... I don't ever want to fall in love wit' no joker from the street."

"Hypocrite."

"In what way?" China asks.

"You preachin' to me about this God stuff and not being perfect..."

"And so? What's ya point?"

"Jesus don't love thugs China? Who wanna join a team like that? Where everybody ain't included? I know I don't."

"I ain't say dat! Don't get it twisted. I just pointed out the fact that I want to exercise my right to make better choices for my future. Girl, if don't, when I do meet the man of my dreams, ain't gon' be nothin left of me. They gon' be done wore my body down. My mind and my spirit too. I wanna have somethin' to give Heather. I can't give everything away. That's all I'm sayin'. Not to somebody that ain't worth it. I know these older women be lookin' at me when I'm out in the street like I'm brainless. But I'm not. I make dumb decisions, I know. But I'm tryna figure me out. I'm only seventeen. It takes time. I be wantin' to say: 'NOW LET'S ROLL BACK THE TAPE TO WHEN YOU WAS MY AGE. I KNOW YOU AIN'T GET THOSE TEN KIDS THRU IMMACULATE CONCEPTION AND DON'T NONE OF 'EM KNOW THEY DADDY. PLEASE! I KNOW MY DAD. SAY WHATCHA WANT ABOUT MY MOMMA. LICIA WASN'T BABY MAKIN" MACHINE FOR TEN DIFFERENT MEN!!'"
A dead silence fell over the room. They lay looking up at the gold starts painted on the ceiling.
"I wish the same women that judge me would just talk to me and be nice. Talk to me like you care. Pretend you think I have some sense. I wish they took time to talk to me like ya mom do."

"Well, I wish my mom would take the time to talk to me like she do you."

China grabbed her hand, "I feel you. I'm sorry. Girls like me need a mom like you got."

Heather withdrew her hand, "That's the problem chick. Girls like me need a mother like I got too. She just don't think so."

China stared at Heather. She watched the tears run into her ears. Heather turned to stare at China. She watched her tears spill across the bridge of her nose. Heather reached out to grab her finger, "I'm sorry. It's not your fault." Heather jumped up, "Enough of this sad talk. What is this a therapy session?"

"Nah. I guess we're just being emotional females. We purgin'."

"Yeah. I'm tired of that now. Sing: All I REALLY WANT IS TO BE HAPPY..."

"Yaaassssss!"

"Let's get dressed then. Let's go."

"Aight. Where we goin?"

"To your hood. I know somethin' gotta be jumpin' off down there."

"Always. But girl, you just gotta be careful of what you jumpin' into."

"Facts."

"Heather I'm serious. And when you get down there, don't be one."

"One what?"

"A J.O."

"Girl! I AIN'T NO JUMP!"

"I hope not. I done enough sinnin' down there for you and me for a life time plus. Don't add to it now. Streets is unforgivin'. It's like Vegas, what happen there, stay there but not in a secret type of way. Get it?"

Heather nonchalantly brushed her hair. "I feel dat."

The two teens talked, laughed and danced. On the way out, China stumbled over a doll in the hallway.

"Omg clumsy the clown. Wake the dead why don't you?!"

"Shut up! I can't help it. I tripped over this damn doll." Heather picked up the doll. China grabbed it, "Oh wow. It's a classic Black Barbie. I love Barbies. She looks like me. In fact she might be the only one I don't have in my collection. Is this yours?"

Heather snatched the doll away from China, "No! I don't play with dolls. I'm almost grown. I hate dolls."

"I love dolls." China smiles. "I collect Black Barbies. Old, new, broken...don't matter. I want them all. Especially the broken ones. I like to restore them. Makes me feel like I'm doing something good for a change. Something positive."

Heather threw the doll down the stairs, "Mmm. Sound like my mother. Always pickin' up somethin broken to fix to make yourself feel good when you probably should be workin' on yourself."

"Well, if you talkin' about me, I am workin' on myself. I try to read my Bible. I pray at night. Yeah, I know I mess up all of the time. But I'm trying. Speaking of...you don't wanna try..."

"What? That saved believing in Jesus stuff again? No China. So stop comin' at my neck. I don't need Jesus to save me. I'm ok."

"Alright then. I will be praying for you."

"That's your choice. But don't pray to your God to save me. If He's real, if any of this stuff is real, and you pray for your mother right? For him to bring her back?"

"Yes I do."

"It's a shame you can't see how fake this stuff is. See how that's working out for you? But I won't rain on your parade if you believe. Next time you praying for Jesus to bring our mom back, pray He bring my mom back too. See if He can save that relationship. If He can do that, that's the only thing that would ever make me believe. 'Til then, it is turn up time. Can't believe you talkin' all this religious stuff at a time like this. Girl you must be crazy to believe God care about people like us." Heather snickered, "You so silly. I don't even go to church. He probably don't even know we alive."

"I used to feel like that. But I never let that stop me from praying. I just kept hoping. And tonight, I believe I heard Him say He loves me. It's like that Kirk Franklin song my father always plays when he feel guilty about some woman he done bagged or about that weed in the garage. He loves me, even when I fall beneath his will. When my broken heart just won't keep still, He loves me."

"Say word? Girl you can't tell me you didn't catch a contact from that Bubblegum. You buggin'. Yes, I'm in the mood for some Loud. You know where I can find some down there right?"

"Yeah but, I don't get down no more I told you. You on ya own. I just wanna chill. I'm not tryna turn up."

"You're such a snooze. Oh my goodness. And look at how you're dressed. Jeans and a tee. You look like my mom." Heather teased.

"Well ya mom dope to me. So I'll take that. Besides I been in heels all day. Nothin' wrong with a pair of J's. That's what we do where I'm from."

"How cute. How ghetto. How boring. You got a Bible in ya purse too don't cha?"

"As a matter of fact I do. I don't leave home without it."

"Damn! Girl, lay off the snooze button why don't you? Ring the alarm! Time to turn up man! You from the hood, you're supposed to be more chill than that."

"Here you go with those stereotypes about how people from the inner-city are supposed to be. Please get a life already and stop believing everything you read and see in hip-hop videos."

"Huh?"

"Let me tell you somethin white girl, I'm a good student. I play volleyball and softball. I'm lining up scholarships as we speak. I NEVER miss a day of school. I am a vegan. My parents were married straight out of high school. Matter of fact, they still are, they just been separated for a real long time. I may come from a broken home but I am not broke by any means. I live in the hood because it's where I go to school. I like it there because my friends are there. My dad and I live in a beautiful home on the quiet part of the block on the South Side of the largest city in New Jersey. It's not a problem for us living there, my dad grew up in that house. He knows everybody; everybody knows him. It's not a perfect life by any means but I love my city. Ratchet as it may be at times. That's my home.

I refuse to sit here and let you reduce the people to stereotypes. They are more than that. WE don't just all day and all night!"

"I didn't mean to…"

"I don't believe that. You're just as ignorant as they come. You probably believe everything they show about Newark on the news don't you?"

"I wasn't trying to…"

"Keep that! Everybody ain't no criminal okay?! Most of the people work hard to provide for their families. Some of them are only there because they can't afford to move out of the city. Some, like me and my dad, we like it there. It is home. We see it different. My dad always said that Newark is changing and there is a lot of potential there. I guess I'm changing too because I see it. Things are changing slowly because all of the citizens don't see it yet. But when ya mind been down for so long and you been livin' in a place that seems hopeless so long, when hope pop up, you either miss it or you overlook it because it ain't ridin' in on a white horse.

My dad says sometimes people in the hood fear change, even if it's for their own good because they only know one way to live. So they resist it, mess it up, break it apart, destroy it and throw it out. Sometimes even burn it down, only to regret it later. People just don't like change.

My dad says that's the ignorance that holds us back as a city, even as a people. We can't get our mind on nothin' different. If it's outside of the box and causes us to have to move over a little bit to have make room for something new, we automatically think it's bad. Why? Because we have to shift our position and leave our comfort zone. Dysfunction gets comfy when you been in it all of your life and that's all you know."

Heather confessed, "I guess I never saw it that way."

"Well you need a new perspective honey. We don't just be in the street turnin' up all day! Heather we ain't a group of savages that just sit around, drink Cîroc, twerk and buy weave and smoke blunts and shoot at each other and make babies all day. There are hardworking, good-natured, spiritual, sweet, loving people there. There are nice neighborhoods and pretty park areas. We have pretty birds that fly in from wherever. And flowers grow there too. People do laugh.

Folks get along. And contrary to popular belief, businesses do well and races come together in the hood. Unlike where you at, everybody welcome down there. Don't matter ya income, you welcome because the one thing everybody got in common is we all just tryna live to see another day. We all just tryna make it. We're all hoping that before our lives are over, or on the other side of the game, there is something more than what we see. And one thing it is hard to be in the hood, is lonely. People everywhere. We ain't got a lot like y'all, but we got each other whether we like it or not."

"So China you sayin' it's like that Jaheim song?"

"Exactly like that. That you can believe. Not sayin the rap songs is wrong. They not. They da truth. That's why we listen to 'em. They tellin' our story/ They be singin' our song. It is entertainment and every rapper ain't from the hood. But we the people, us livin' it, we know the real from the Fu gaze. And since you don't, be careful what you believe. It's a business at the end of the day. Real gansgstas don't talk about what they do in the booth. They just live out they truth. It's still a code out here in these streets and snitches still sleep wit fishes Heather. It ain't cute. People like yourself bump to the top forty hits...commercialized nonsense. Y'all come down to turn up, get high, go back to ya quiet streets and green grass. It's novelty for y'all. Y'all not listenin' to the music thinking, 'I have resources. I feel their pain. I can come down there and try to help with something. Bring something positive to the community. Even if it's something small. Nah...it's all watching Power on Showtime, listenin' to Watch the Throne, think it's all glamorous. But it's not. It's so real."

"Damn China. You went in. You been talkin' the whole ride down the hill. I didn't know it was that deep. I'm sorry if I offended you."

"It's cool. But I was guessin' ya mom would've told you how it go down since she from here. Ain't nothin' change since she left. I mean she's here every day. She should bring y'all down here every once in a while. You say you don't know who you are. Well, you're part of your mom and dad, maybe if you knew more about where they came from, you could start to figure yourself out. You know....why you do what you do the way you do. We ain't gotta be like our parents Heather, but, we carry a piece of them in us until the day we die. Whether we know them, never meet them;

love 'em or hate 'em, they are a part of us and we a part of them. That's probably why you don't like ya mom. Maybe y'all too much alike."

"China please. Alike in what way? I don't even look like her. She looks more like you. Maybe that's why y'all connect like that. She's dark and curvy. Her hair is natural. Y'all even share the same mannerisms. I'm not her complexion. I don't share her mannerisms or her features. We don't have a connection."

"I'm sure you guys do Heather. Y'all just ain't found it yet."

"What's it like?"

"What's what like?"

She glared at China, "You know."

"Not really. Speak up."

"Being dark?"

"What?!"

"Seriously. What's it like to be in your skin China?"

"You wouldn't even begin to understand. You good where you at. So stay there."

"No. I really want to know."

China noticed the distress in Heathers eyes. "I guess its aight. I comes with some b.s like everything else does. I'm not sure how you want me to explain it."

"Just shoot me the real. I just want to know what it's like."

"I can't speak for everybody. But for me and some of the other girls I know, it's hard sometimes. Like… It's like how that woman Sarah Baartman must have felt."

"Who?"

"Jeez! You don't know your history? Of course you don't. They ain't gonna teach you about your ancestry up in that fancy school of yours. Anyway, This European nut job took her around to different places in a cage or something like and put her on display as if she was a wild animal or some space alien. The onlookers, fascinated with her natural thickness, her dark skin and her curves, poked her and made lewd and inhumane comments about her physique. He promised her money that he never paid her. I heard she died broke, in the street somewhere, maybe Paris or something. They scraped her remains off the ground and they went to cutting her up and stuff."

"Girl no!"

"Girl yes! They cut off her vagina and stuff and put some of her body parts on display for years at a museum or something."

"Wait. So why would anyone do that? Just because she was black?"

"Not just that. She was dark and probably shaped something like me. White people was fascinated with how big her boobs and butt were and her vagina. They treated her like and animal. It was other women too. But she's the most noted and memorable."

"Whoa. That's sick!"

"Tell me about it. So yeah, down here, with the boys in the hood, that's how they make me feel. Like I'm a project to be poked and degraded. They grab on me. Men done touched all on me. They say nasty things to you under their breath when you walk by. The lay you down and pull your vagina open and comment on the color of your insides. Like you're a chocolate treat they just gotta have for the night. Like they heard about it, now they gotta taste it. They gotta see it. They gotta have you. Just for that one night. I never heard anybody say I was anything other than pretty, sexy, thick or juicy. My mom and your mom was the only people to tell me I'm smart. Not my dad. Not my teachers. Nobody. All they see when they look at me is body. Like I'm a mannequin or some other empty, disposable vessel.

And then, when you watch videos or TV, there's nobody like you on the screen that you can admire. It's sad. It makes you feel lonely. I don't look like them Heather. We have nothing in common but body and even Beyoncé ain't my size. She slim-thick, not real thick. And I don't know too many black girls with blonde hair and a thigh gap. You know? I don't have anybody to refer to. My mother don't even look like me, she looks more like you. I look my dad. The only dark-skinned lady wearing her natural hair is Viola Davis."

"Oh yeah! That awesome lady from The Help. She gonna be in a TV show this fall I heard. I can't wait. But oh, there's Lupita Nyong'o ya know?"

"Yeah I know. But Lupita would have to take her head and put it on Serena William's body if we ever gon' be able to connect. Like, there's Viola, there's Oprah. And they're amazing. But they're older than me. Whose out there closer to my age that looks like me? Nobody. Even Barbie's body is unlike the girl's I know. All of the young darker-skinned Hollywood girls wear weaves and wigs and they ain't got my body type. And even if they did, if it ain't a Tyler Perry movie or Shonda Rhimes ain't writing and producing, they'll be a formidable lead. Hollywood ain't ready for black girl love girl."

"Wow. You're right. I get it."

"Well you only get part of it. But aight. For me, that's how it feels."

Heather smiled, "Well you have Kelly Rowland. You have Gabrielle Union. There's Chili from TLC. There's Seven Streeter. There's Naomi Campbell. Alek..."

"Yeah. And they are beautiful. But they don't have thick bodies and thick lips and noses and hair. They don't look like me girl. If they got one thing, they missin' the other thing. See you don't get it."

"You just picky. What is it? They not black enough for you?"

"That's not it. They just don't represent what I see every day. I think they're all great! But they're part of the fantasy. Not the reality." You're mixed and these days, you have more to refer too than I do. There's no balance in entertainment. So these boys in the hood look to these entertainers as idols all they see is light skin, long hair. Exotic features and foreign tongues. No happy nappiness, no native tongues and if they are, they're naturally thin, not naturally thick like me and my friends. So we picked over and passed by because we don't meet traditional or acceptable beauty standards. I feel like if I don't try to look like the people I see that don't reflect me, I'll never get a man to accept me. I even go days without eating to keep my waistline right and my thighs down. You don't even know the half."

"So much I don't know."

"Be happy girl. So much you don't wanna know. So there you have it. On a lighter note, no pun intended, you need to get to know who you are. Sometimes you gotta go back in order to move forward I heard somebody say."

"Yeah. But she don't want us down here. We've all been warned and made fully aware."

"Maybe someday she'll change her mind. Right now though, you should listen to her Heather. She ain't perfect but, I know she want the best for y'all that's why she left; she wants better. Ain't nothin' wrong with it. You should cut her some slack. Give her some credit. M.s P is good people."

Heather pretended to ignore China. Only speaking to ask for directions.

"Oh yeah! I just remembered!"

"What? How to get to where we goin'? Because I am sure tired of driving. I need to smoke."

"Ledisi. India Arie. Stacey Barthe. Chrisette Michele…"

"Girl what are you talking about now. Jesus! Can we get off this being black in America stuff please? I feel like you're trying to recruit for the next movement."

"Great idea. Maybe someday I'll do that when I figure out who I am."

"Well we already know one thing… You're black. There's no mistaking that!"

"I know I am but what are you?"

"Cheap shot and weave."

"Your mother." They both cackle. "Seriously though now, I just remembered a few sistas I think are dope. Beyoncé really ain't all we have to refer to. And we don't have to break our legs and pockets trying to be her. There are other people out here that reflect me. I guess I just found out that it's ok to just be me. Thank you Jesus. Now help me to walk in it."

"Yeah like. My mom listens to all of those chicks. I know what they look like. They are dope and I'm happy for you. But Chrisette ain't dark. Sorry to burst your bubble honey.'

"Yeah I know. It's cool though. That's aight. She's natural, she's vegan and she's thick. That's good enough for me."

"Okay. Is the meeting adjourned now? I mean what should I call you?"

"Why whatever do you mean?"

"Angela Davis, Joanne Chesimard or Afeni Shakur?"

"Ahhh… so you do know some of your black history. I'm impressed."

"Don't sleep girl."

"Baby girl. Baby girl… T.J Holmes."

"Girl yes. Who knew Arkansas had it like that? Like, what even happens there?"

China smirked, "Don't you know that's what they say about Jersey? Girl don't sleep."

"Okay Jersey! Preach!"

"I'm all preached out."

"Heather let me ask you somethin'?"

"Shoot."

"Girl don't say that down here." China joked. "Your dad's a republican right?"

Heather smiled, "That's a myth and a sad stereotype. Just because my dad is Caucasian and loaded don't mean he's a republican. He voted for President Obama both times. Black people ain't the only people that got him in there you know."

"Yeah I know. My dad voted for President Obama the second round."

"Not the first time? You guys are minorities. You live in the inner-city. You must be…"

"Nope. Don't stop now. Say it Heather."

"Never mind."

"Democrats right? There's that stereotype. And you people have to stop referring to yourselves as minorities. That's a label on a box designed to keep you thinking you can't be more than what you are. It screams your voice doesn't count. As a consequence, you don't matter."

"Alright. Alright. I see your point."

"No you don't. Let me get it across to you real quick. We're Christians. We don't support gay marriage and we don't do abortion. We're pro-life. We're not republican nor are we democrat. We vote prayerfully. Your vote is your voice. He used his voice how he saw fit. When people fought for our right to vote. I don't think they saw Barack Obama coming down the pike and meant for us to wait for him to get here to cast our ballots. Same goes for women's rights. I can vote because of their efforts. I'm thankful. But they didn't fight just for me to save my voice and scream loud when a woman ran for president. They probably knew that day would be a far off if ever. My vote. My voice. My ballot. My beliefs. My choice. Now if they didn't go against the grain and stand up for what they believed in, where would be? Somebody gotta do it girl. This is America. This is a democracy. Remember the first amendment? Freedom of speech honey. That's what a vote is. It is you exercising your right to speak freely if you think about it."

"Whatever. How y'all not gonna support that black man? Your dad didn't want to be a part of history?"

"Not if it meant he had to go against his personal beliefs."

"I don't think I would've missed that if I was y'all. That was historical. Why did he support him the second time then?"

"Let me break it down. He voted for him the second time because wasn't no body checkin' for Mitch Romney aight."

"You mean MITT Romney don't you?" tittled Heather.

"Whatever. You know what I mean. You just don't get it. President Obama, I respect him as my president and all. I love that he is black or bi-racial, however PC you feel you need to receive that. But, he sucker-punched the black church when he started screaming his support for gay marriage. We didn't see that one coming. Things just went downhill from there."

"Okay. So what? He's has rights remember? Welcome to the American democracy hello? His right to believe the way he wants. His right to exercise his voice for what he believes in."

"Facts. But I ain't gotta support it. Nothing personal against him. I know he can't please everybody, but man. That really was a real sucker-punch. So there. That's how I see it. No apologies. We're entitled to our views."

"I don't know China. I think black people are satisfied with President Obama on a whole. Just because the black church got beef with him, don't mean that's the consensus. People aight wit' him I think. I think there's even been progress made."

"Where?"

"What?"

"Your view is warped girl. The violence didn't stop. So many people forgot about the audacity of hope."

"I don't think so China."

"Right Heather. Like you live in our community. Girl please."

"I think you're wrong."

"Ma, Black people was happy and celebratin' for about four months from November to March. After that. Everybody forgot about Yes I Can. We returned to I'm Not Convinced. I must admit President Obama tried. He said he wanted to leave brothers without excuse. He had a vision. He did his part. Mothers of the brothers believed for a second. They went from telling their sons they can be president one day, back to you're just like your father. Nothing has changed. Brothers still out here gettin' trucked by each other and the pigs and The President's approval rating tanked."

"They all suffer from low approval ratings at some point China."

"Truth. It all happened so fast though. It went from Yes We Can to Awe Damn in zero to sixty. What we supposed to do with that? I'm sayin', moral is down in the black community."

"Black Panther Party or Fox News Commentator? Make up your mind already."

"There you go with labels and boxes. Why is that every time somebody comes with a different view of things, people wanna call the Calvary or brand you like you're a runaway slave?"

"China you're taking things way out of proportion."

"No I'm not. I'm sick of it. At school, on the block. Now you. I'll tell you what! President Obama is not Catcher damn Freeman okay! Get over it! He didn't come to get out black asses outta here! I said it! Y'all better leave me alone... I clap back! Oh my goodness. Y'all ever heard of the Equal Protection Clause in the fourteenth amendment?"

"Sorry but, that doesn't apply here."

"The hell it don't!"

"Okay. I see what you're getting at. But if you're going to go there. I challenge you with felony disenfranchisement."

"How does that even fit here? You know what...?"

"You're a criminal and a Judas. You shouldn't be allowed to vote."

"WHAT?!"

"Breezy was right. These hoes ain't loyal. This is a complete act of treason. You're a graham cracker. That's what Paul Mooney said."

"Graham cracker? And who is this Paul person and why did he go to the moon?"

Heather laughed, "You're silly."

"Ain't nothin' wrong with a lil' comic relief girl. Paul Mooney is the God Father. I know about him from Dave Chappelle. Anyway, I ain't no graham cracker. And back to you! Treason? Are you kidding me? What is this merry old England? I'm loyal to my belief system. If you feel like…"

"China don't…"

"Heather don't you. Let it be known, here and now, I am proud of The First Family. They stand strong and dignified in the face of all of the criticism and adversity. They deserve more respect then they get. I am entitled to my beliefs though, no matter how opposing, non-traditional or mildly, modifiedly conservative. We're all made up of different things. Don't crucify me for that. I'm just being China. I have a brain Heather. Even if nobody notices or appreciates it. My opinion is my own."

"I feel you. My bad. Guess you don't celebrate King Day, huh?"

"I'm numb on that. I think from what he stood for, we've lost it all. Look how his kids actin'. They out here lookin' crazy. Look at how divided America is. We take the day off all over the country and the few acknowledge the dream, the rest of us sleep in.

Same thing with Christmas. It's like Christmas ain't about Christ no more. It's about gifts. It's not even the thought that counts, it's the value of the gift. My dad said we done took things too far and we ain't thinkin'. The gifts the wise men brought to honor Jesus were meaning. All three of those gifts symbolize something. Now, we just but things that ain't worth what you pay for 'em. Gifts, we know these kids ain't gonna pay no mind to but a second. We on some old other stuff. What they did was an act of honor, humility. We've lost something. America is a capitalist society. Ain't no Christ in it no more and we don't trust in God so we need to take that off the money."

Okay black woman. You say that, but I see you rockin' Jordan brand on ya feet."

"And?"

"And, what has he done for black people lately? Or Nike brand for that matter? You spend stupid too! My dad, extraordinary business man that he is, says he doesn't understand why young black people spend so much on brands and labels that spend nothing to help educate them or to build them better communities. You spend all your money on wasteful things for birthdays and Christmases. Be broke and trying to catch up a month later. Then, a month after that, income tax refunds are issued out. You act like it's free money."

"What? How you just gon'…?"

"Quiet China. A grown person is talking. I am eighteen you know. I'm just giving you my dad's perspective. As I was saying, one month later, because you wanted to ball out, you need a bail out because your money is gone! You've eliminated no debt. You have no savings, no investments no nothing. But, them J's look good on ya broke ass feet. PSE&G comin' to cut ya power off because it's warm outside and with that lil' bit o' money, those few thousand dollars, you couldn't clear your three hundred dollar light bill. You can't save it to spend gradually on what is truly important. You gon' look good in the dark though."

"Your father is a know-it-all and he should be careful to mind his. Especially since he ain't black. He don't know why black people do what they do. My dad ain't like that Heather."

"My dad is just making an observation China. He didn't mean all black people. It's his business to know business and trends in marketing and spending in different demographics, he gives the people what they want, went they want it and for the minorities, it's always in the dead of winter or just before spring."

"Well that ain't us. You tried it."

"Let me guess. You and your hyper-opinionated daddy don't celebrate Christmas either?"

"Aww...you're so smart. My dad and I don't celebrate too much no more. Besides, if it's really about the birth of Christ, we can celebrate that anytime like Mother's and Father's Day and Thanksgiving and New Year's. We can celebrate that every day if we want. We don't really know when Jesus was born. We just know that He was born and where. New Year's Day can be celebrated when your personal calendar flips. You ain't gotta go with the masses. Blaze your own trail. Your year may not end or begin until May. Who is to say or judge?"

"What? Not even Fourth of July? C'mon. Summer, summer, summertime. Ayyeeee!! Independence Day? The fireworks China. C'mon now."

"My people wasn't free at that time. Still ain't all the way there. So to that I say, bye Felicia. Y'all need to wake up. Slavery wasn't abolished until December 19, 1865. At least that's what they say. Nobody ever acknowledges that day. We probably need to be celebrating Abe Lincoln along with King."

"Girl. You're like a bag of mixed veggies. Just so many things. You just seem so on the fence to me and all over the place. I'm a bit confused. You're so many things. You have a lot goin' on."

"You, a mixed chick that hasn't decided why she hasn't decided her sexuality, which I still think is crazy, gonna come at me about being on the fence, all over the place and being confused? I have a lot goin' on? I'm so many things? That's funny."

"Don't be offended China. I'm just sayin'?"

"I know. I know. I would expect that you, of all people, would understand being more than one thing. It doesn't make you confused. It makes you human. We're all hypocritical. Who isn't on the fence about some stuff in their lives at a point, especially when you're young?

Why can't I be a little bit of this or that until I decide where I want to fall on either side of the fence? That's if I ever make the decision to fall on either side. I'm not talking about my sexuality."

"Here we go."

"Oh Heather please. You know where I stand on that. I am completely clear. I don't think you're a lesbian. You're missing the connection to your mom. I think you want attention. You know it's wrong. You know I'm right."

"How dare you? You're no therapist! Getcha own life then holla at me aight?!"

"Why you gettin' all testy Heather?"

"Because you have some nerve! That's why. I heard something before that my mother said about not serving two masters. I may not be religious, but I know what that means. You're in the wrong China. Don't judge me. You ain't been in my shoes. I'm trying to figure myself out."

"Then don't judge me Heather! I'm trying to figure me out too! These are my views. Those are my beliefs. Not a republican. Not a democrat. I am a human being with varying perspectives, ever evolving. I see both sides. That doesn't make me any less black or any more anything else. That just makes me China Heather. Broaden you're your horizon. Gain a new perspective.

You being bi-racial and on the fence, should understand. You don't have to be either or. You can be decidedly both. Because that's what you are. I hope that's how you see yourself. Social law may say you're black, I don't mind claiming you. To me you are. But if we doin' away with labels and boxes. Then it is really okay to just be you. You don't owe an apology or explanation to anyone. God made you and He don't make no mistakes ma." She comforted Heather.

"I hope you feel that way about yourself China."

"Maybe I'm beginning to. This was kinda like therapy. You might be more like your moms than you know Heather."

"Maybe. We'll see."

"Yeah. Hey, you ever saw School Daze?"

"What that old movie? Yeah. It was poppin'. Why?"

"Just wonderin' if things is ever gonna change from that? You know between women of color all over the world. That's not just an African-American issue. The colorism thing. People still out here feelin' inferior, bleaching their skin and being color shamed. They still equate darker skin with lesser value and unattractiveness in some places."

"I hope it changes. Death to boxes and labels girl."

"Hell yeah. A swift and brutal one. Make this left. I think if Kim and Nikki stop beefin', there's hope for anything."

"I know right. It's so stupid. They both so amazin'. What is the problem?"

"Girl," China smacked her lips.

"Tamar huh?"

"Girl nah. Sour patch kids. Have some?" The young women howled. "Anyway, Kim feel disrespected, Blah blah. Nikki won't admit to the disrespect. More blah."

"Don't you feel like there would be no Nikki if there wasn't a Lil' Kim though? I mean for real? Kim did all of the colorful wigs and crazy, sexy clothes first."

China agreed, "I know right. Like I listened to some of my dad's music and Kim was definitely the genesis even if Nikki took things to a whole other level. I see similarities and anybody that don't see 'em is crazy. My dad is a Queen Bee fan from back. He think Nikki got skill but Kim his chick."

"Yeah. I like Nikki though."

"I think that beef is dumb. Its young girls out here goin' through real issues. They look up to these females. They imitate them. They hang on their every word. It's so many issues we facing' out here as females and they arguin' over crazy stuff."

"It might be crazy to you China but, it matters to them. It's hip hop. It's a male dominated field. You gotta know some of that rubs off on them. They want they respect. I think Kim deserves it too! Bein' real."

"I know. It's just time wasted that nobody can get back. They fans got bigger issues. And maybe we want to hear about more than clothes and cars we will never be able to afford. Life bigger than that Heather. And still, there is no female rapper that represents me. Feel me?"

"I don't know though. Maybe they ain't never have our issues. I don't see anybody that represents me either Heather."

"I guess we gotta stop lookin' for celebrities to be our examples."

"Yeah. I guess we need to look to our moms to be our example."

"I guess. Where you look if you don't have that though?"

"I don't know. Still tryna figure that out. I just wish we was more united as a people and we cared about each other and stuff that really matters instead things that don't. People out here dyin' and livin' paycheck to paycheck."

Heather passed on, "Yeah, I know."

China closed her eyes as she thought back to Saturday mornings not so long ago. She'd be awakened by the fragrance of grass; freshly cut and smoked; by the sounds of homegrown homegirls like Rah Digga and Queen Latifah. Brick City babies like herself. Lauryn Hill one of Jersey's most undeniable. They were different than today's rappers. They were clothed. They were rough. They were defiant, absolute and feminine without being over-sexual. Her father had always talked to her about a time when rap music and the few female rappers that made it through from the great Garden State, had substance. Maybe everyone else was doing better financially. Obviously, they offered more."

She sank even deeper into thought, "Sex sells my Dad always said. But what happens when the sex is over? The most important parts of a relationship are crafted outside of the bedroom. It's just like having sex with a guy. They get what you got then when it ain't good enough no more and you done showed 'em everything, what's left for them to think about or want? You gotta do stranger and more degrading things to keep their attention. Doesn't stop them from moving on though. Especially when they've made up their mind or you get old. 50 cent said consumers are disloyal so to speak. They will always run to the artist with the best or hottest product. Won't always be you. So then what do you do? Whatchu do when someone younger and ballsier than you come and kick you off of your own block? Young people don't have no respect for the code daddy keep sayin. Used to be codes to the streets, crime, hip-hop. Somebody hotter is always on ya heels out here. Watch the throne is right. Gotta be more to the product you pushin' besides pretty packaging and empty content.

Lord, I guess I'm preachin' to the choir like my dad say. I guess I need to start putting some clothes on if I want to be recognized and remembered for greater things. Its bigger things goin' on out here. Brothers out here dyin'. Somebody gotta care about the greater things. Ain't nothin' wrong with being sexy. It is empowering. And boys be sayin' we the easy ones. So stupid.

But is sex the only thing that makes women feel powerful these days? Especially in an already misogynist industry? The HIV rate out here is still so high. So many girls my age don't know the cutoff point. We out here allowin' them to like it before they put a ring on it.

My dad is so right. He ain't tryin' to get in my business. He's trying to help me. He does know how guys are. He really ain't that old. They get to sample the goods before they make a decision. We runnin' round here like free samples in Pathmark. Umm! Talk about epiphany. Sexy leads to sex which leads to disease, death and destruction if you're uneducated about this stuff.
 Oh! It's like that Self-Destruction song! Oh Brand Nubians... Slow down! Brenda' Got A Baby. Aww Pac. I get it now. Let's Talk About SEX! Omg! Old school Saturdays. There's a message in the music." She sucked her teeth, "My dad think he slick. I love him for that though. He cares. Yoooo! I been so blind. I always think he don't talk to me. Maybe that's his way. Yooooo!"

"Whatchu over there marinatin' on girl?"

"Stuff. My head just be spinnin' sometimes."

"What kinda stuff China?"

"Uh oh. This just in… Even though my dad didn't vote for Obama and I don't support his views, I did get something from that first election."

"What was that?"

"It was good to see our people stick together to achieve something positive. Even in the face of opposition, people came out and forged ahead. Nothing stopped them, twice! And look at what was done. We can do bigger things if we stick together Heather."

"You say that China, but your dad didn't even vote for the man! Y'all ain't stick wit' us."

"Well, I stand by what I said. There are those times though, my dad told me, when you gotta swim upstream and go against the grain for what you believe in. People always tellin' you to just be yourself and stand up for what you believe in. They must mean as long as it's what everyone else believes in. Talking about hypocritical and unfair."

"You're right."

"No. My dad is right. Guess he ain't that bad. We probably just goin' through stuff. I don't know. Go straight then take the next right after the light." China commanded. "Imma show you somethin."

"I know we haven't known each other long China. But I'm guessing from the way you were dressed when I met you, that you haven't always been this deep. No shade. But why now?"

"I can't call it. I guess I'm just waking up. A lot of stuff made me think today. There's this contemporary Christian song that says there's got to be more to life than chasing down every temporary high to satisfy me. I'm not saying I'm all of the way there. I think I'm on my way though."

"You about to be a perfect little Christian I guess."

"I'm sure there's no such thing. I'll never be perfect. I don't think it says in the Bible that you have to be perfect to be saved. Otherwise what's the point? Nobody would ever make it. I just keep prayin'. Right now, that's all I know to do."

"You think that's enough?"

"I hope so Heather. For right now anyway. It gotta get deeper though. My dad says we can't just pray everything away. Some things we gotta go through and deal with. Some things is just life. He said even Jesus experienced life."

"Man China. You really believe like that?"

"Yeah I do. I know Jesus died for me. Messed up as I am, He loved me anyway my Grandma always told me about herself. I believe that's true about me too."

"That's somethin'."

"What?"

"You been cussin' and stuff all night. How you know Jesus love you? How you know…"

"I'm just trusting. Having faith that He does. That He accepts me. That He can clean me up and help me to change if I keep prayin'. My dad says The Lord doesn't see us the way we see ourselves. He sees us through perfect eyes; the way He created us to be. Not the way we are. Like a finished product."

"So then you can do whatever you want and you good."

"No. I didn't say that. We got a part to play. We got do what we can; what we know until we know better."

"How you know when that is?"

"I guess you know when you know. You learn as you go along. It's like practicing what is preached to you I hear. Don't know how true that is. Guess if I keep goin' and do my best, I'll find out for myself. He'll help me. I believe that. I know I don't know everything. But I'm sure I can't do it on my own. I know Imma mess up."

"How you know?'

"Girl I'm China. I been messin' up all night; all of my life. I'm not proud of it. I'm just as full of issues as I am opinion. I'm human. Ain't no gettin' around messin' up. Nobody's exempt from that."

"So then what China?'

"So then, we depend on him. That's all we can do. We can't depend on ourselves. Oh wait. Slow down. Yeah, pull over. We're here."

Heather slammed the car door. "Look at me boo! I'm flawless like Yonce'."

"First of all, we gotta stop callin' each other Boo. My dad says that word is in the vein of the nigger. If we only knew where it came from."

"Stop being so militant China damn! Let's just have some fun! Loosen up!"

"That's our problem. We too loose Heather. By the way, don't mention that 'Flawless' to me ever again."

"Whaaaaaaaaaattttttttttt????????!!!!!!! GIRL! Who ain't feelin' 'Flawless'? Baby girl, that remix wit Nikki."

China yawned, "Boring."

"Hold up now, I know you all on dat old school because of ya dad and everything. It's okay to be team Kim. I got love and respect for Queen Bee. It's due. I'm a loyal Barb and I even understand that. But I don't understand your beef with the song."

"My beef ain't wit Nikki. It's just…"

Heather raced around the car to China. She pulled her to the side, "Girl you bet' not say nothin' 'bout Bey. You don't know if the Bee-Hive out here buzzin' around. They're blood-thirsty girl."

"Tell me about it. It's kinda demonic. I don't understand why there's this certain list of untouchable people floatin' around that you just can't say anything about? How is that? Even Jesus got criticized. We all get criticized. Lord I'm glad I grew up in the hood. Y'all too soft. So sensitive. It's not that serious. It's my opinion."

"China, you ain't serious."

"Oh but I am! I'm also a fan of her music. I appreciate her talent. But those people don't realize, she doesn't even know them. Fans be goin' hard like they under spells for these celebrities that don't lose no sleep over them. You spend all of your time obsessing over them. All of your money supporting them and you out here livin' like a savage. I'm up now Heather. I ain't worried 'bout no Belieber, no Barb or no Bee. What worries me is how throngs of people all over the world can just sleep walk so long. They worshipin' other flawed people girl! Jesus the one died for 'em and He's the one they ignore. Even if they favorite celeb died for them, what would it mean? They ain't Christ on the cross! We out here doin' too much. That mess is cultish! Attacking people on social media for having an opinion about another person. That's cyberbullying ain't it? All of these kids out here getting jumped and beat up because somebody said somethin' about the untouchable girl or boy at school. It's all the same thing! Why nobody don't see that? Why is it that Twitter, Facebook and Instagram still allow this stuff. I mean it's producers out there scared to say a word about certain celebrities because they don't wanna get blacklisted. That's demonic! Anytime one human being is allowed to have that kind of power of anybody. That's so demonic. It's like manipulation. Y'all just fall right under the spell. These celebrities ain't comin' to ya house, payin' your bills. They can't save your life or your soul. They don't have time to write yo ass back personally. They keep security around them all of the time. Why? To keep ya crazy, obsessed ass away from them. They ain't stupid. They don't know ya ass! But still buy their products and break the bank trying to look like them when they have a team that keeps them looking like them."

"Stop preachin'. I get it! You wastin' the last of my high!"

"Who cares Heather? Flawless my ass."

"Don't come for her. People already starring at you while you go on your rant."

"Good! Maybe they'll wake up too! And ain't nobody comin' for her! I just don't like that line about being red-bonded in a song named flawless. That goes back to that colorism stuff me and ya mom was talkin' about earlier. How people just let that go over they head. See! Everybody sleep walkin'! All of her fans don't look like her. Most of them don't. But oh! How they try."

"Brace yourself folks!" Heather yelled, "Church 'bout start. Doors of the church are now open!"

"No I'm serious Heather. Care nothin' bout these people out here! If you cut anybody open, they bones ain't gonna be the color of their skin. Second of all, because you're light-skinned or fair complexioned, that means what? You're of greater value or my skin ain't fair? It's like calling the less agreeable Caucasian people white trash. What in the world does that even mean Heather? Does that mean that everybody that ain't white is considered trash by white folks behind closed doors?"

"Pay her no mind y'all." Heather whispered, "You're going too far."

"Nah ah! Never too much. Never too far. That's what Luther and Mariah said and Imma run wit dat tonight. Obviously somebody need too! We ain't gone far enough as black people that we haven't let what slavery do to us makes us better not worse. It was an insensitive statement Heather. You not walkin' in my shoes."

"You not walkin' in mine either China. I ain't the poster child for other people's ignorance. I'm not here to be the heavy for every light-skinned girl that made you feel inferior. Dark-skinned girls can be just as mean to us. Let's keep it one. I didn't ask to be born on the fence. I sure Bey ain't mean it like that. She can't please everybody. She don't write all of her material."

"I know. But we gotta start watchin' our words. I think it's just time to wake up as a people. Dark-skinned girls all over the world out here bleachin' they skin to try to fit the mold and be accepted. They feel like if they don't look like what music videos portray or what athletes hold on they arm, they ain't acceptable. They ain't good enough. Why does it have to be that way?"

"Stop actin' like lighter people or white folk don't tan China. Grow up."

"I'm growing up Heather. You need to grow up! Tan ain't dark brown. Tan is just darker shade of acceptable. You do know about that paper bag thing from back in the day don't you? Don't y'all know?'

"Let's get off that China. We both have valid points."

A girl their age walked over. "I heard that. I feel you. I'm the darkest girl in my family. Today a cousin that my uncle fathered that we had never met, came over to my Grandmother's house. I was the last one to join everybody in the living room. When I walked in, she didn't even say hi to me. She immediately asked if there was anybody else in the family as dark as I am. My mother lost it! She went off! I thought I was done feeling worthless. I guess not.

I grew up not feeling like I belonged to my family. My Grandmother is very high yellow; it's rumored that her father was a white man. Maybe he raped my Great-Granma. I don't know. But my uncles and aunts are lighter than my mom and the rest of their cousins. They have these pretty eyes and stuff. My Grandma never knew her father. My Great Grandma didn't like my Grandma so much when she was growing up. I'm not sure if he skin was too light; they're from the Deep South; the sticks they say. I don't know if she reminded her off a bad experience or a forbidden interracial relationship that went wrong. Guess I'll never know. What I do know is, I don't look like her or my mother. It wouldn't make a difference if I did. She wouldn't care anyway. She's so wrapped up in her pervy boyfriend. The same nigga that be beatin' her ass. The same nigga watchin' me slow; walkin' around in his boxers while I sleep on the living room couch. Girl I don't even have my own room at her house. My brother do though. So I gotta see that nigga walk around in is drawers in the middle of the night. He even tried to get me to drink. He even tried to kiss me."

"GIRL! Why you ain't tell ya mother?"

"I did."

"What happened?"

"Girl she don't care. He all she care about, Him and my brother. It's like I don't exist to her. Whatever happen to me happen to me. She tell me she love me but, it's hard for me to say it back. I just don't believe her. I'm not sure it's real. I love my brother though. That's my always and forever." she smiled.

"Oh you have a brother? I never knew that." Said China.

"You can't tell by lookin' at us. He's far lighter than I am. He has perfect teeth. Soft curly hair and great skin. I go to sleep crying all of the time asking God why he had to make me look like this. Dark skin. Crooked, off color teeth. I'm short. There's nobody in my family that looks like me.

Growing up, when all of the cousins were around, there would always be somebody around me, namely a light-skinned cousin, that called me bad black names. Always. One would call me ugly every time I answered the phone when she called. They made me feel so ugly." she complained.

"It's because they felt ugly about themselves. I've been there. I don't look like my mother either. I feel like I don't fit in with her family. My dad's side either. Her family is dark and my dad's is white. Me, I'm on the fence. So where do I fit in? Don't matter the complexion. We all go through the same stuff on different ends of the spectrum." They all hugged one another.

A young man walked over to the young women from across the street. "I don't care about none of that b.s y'all talkin'. All of y'all look good. Mmm! All these different flavors. Dark chocolate. Milk Chocolate. White chocolate."

China screamed, "Boy! If you don't get away from here! Show some respect."

"The man said looking at Heather, "Y'all hoes kill me! Dress how you wanna be addressed and I'll think about it."

"Nasty mother..."

"Heather!"

"Come on girls." China grabbed Heather's hand. Heather grabbed the other young woman's hand. They walked away from the small crowd that had gathered. "Let's go."

Heather baited, "Girl, I thought you clap back? You gon' let him get that?"

The other young lady lauded, "Girl ain't nobody beat. He just like that. We go to school with him." She beckoned, "HE KNOW WE WAITIN' ON HIS MOTHER TO ET OFF THE STROLL DOWN FRELINGHUYSEN BEFORE WE CHANGE THE WAY WE DRESS. WE JUST FOLLOWIN' THE LEADER."

He crowed, "YEAH AIGHT!"

China crowed, "Girl welcome to Newark."

AFTER THE DANCE

"Yeah!!! This one right here...this one for the lovers. Now that the kids done gone home and we can be grown and sexy."

"Don't be too grown and sexy now!" Pastor Golden shouted from amongst the crowd.

"I'll try pastor. No promises. Right about now, Imma drop this on y'all. I actually knew this woman. She was just as sweet and humble as she could be. She was too real for TV. The kinda real only people like her, people from the hood could truly appreciate, she was as graceful and live as she was spiritual and beautiful. She a flawed beautiful creature like the rest of us. She had more than one side, like all of us. Y'all come together. Love one another. Show your love for Nippy. This Whitney Houston y'all." The crowd went wild. He played "Saving All My Love for You."

China's father left the booth. He walked over to Al, "Pastor, is that ok? Am I doin' ok? Did I say too much?"

Al laughed, "Young man, I am not God. You don't need my approval to do what you do the way you do it. God's approval is all that is warranted. I'm a vessel. You're a vessel. Is this your passion son?"

"Yes it is. I can't see myself doing anything else."

"Is this your calling, your passion, your talent or your gift?"

"Dee Jayin' a calling? I don't know. All I know is, I fell in love with music, people and the art of scratch all around the same time. I was in high school. I used to dream about it. Now besides my daughter and God, it's all I think about."

"Sounds like passion. What else you passionate about son?"

"The Christ." They chuckled, "I believe Jesus died for me. I know He loves us. The way me and my daughter been kept; can't be nobody but him. It's been a ride man. She been through a lot. I made a lot of mistakes. I wasn't always there. I was young. I was loose and selfish. I was stupid. I wasn't as concerned as I am now. I just pray a lot and hold on to the little bit I do know. I try to teach her things you know. Not sure she always listenin'. I try though."

Al placed his hand on the man's shoulder, "Son, if that's all you know to do, until you learn more, then The Lord is pleased with that. People make salvation too complicated. It's not a religious thing. It's a relationship thing. I truly believe God can and is using you as you are. Ministry is ministry son. It doesn't have to be the way folks think it ought to be. Who is to say what God tryna do through different people? The Master is diverse. Ministry is as diverse. As diverse as the leaves that fall from the trees, rays of sun light, snowflakes and blades of grass that grow. Like fingerprints and seasons are all different. God can use what you do, they way you do it to minister to the hearts of many. Many are called, few chosen. Never forget that. You have a calling. Everybody's calling is not in the pulpit or even the church. We all don't receive the Lord the same way. Believe He'll use your passion, talents and gifts to usher you into your calling. He can use this if He wants to. If you let Him."

"I hear you but what do you mean Pastor?"

"Concerning?"

"Well, everything. Ministry in specific. There's only one way to get to God. One way to receive eternal life. That's through Christ. This I know. You gotta believe from your heart and confess with your mouth that you believe Jesus died on the cross….He gave His life to save you. All of us. You tellin' me different."

Al laughed, "You have fire shut up in your bones. Can't nobody knock you for that. You have a passion to defend the gospel. Believe God is going to use you and your daughter. You have testimonies that can and will change lives. What I'm telling you is that yes, there is one way to receive salvation. Yet, there are many creative avenues in which to introduce Christ, show love, spread love, deliver a testimony and change a heart; a mind; a life; a path. Spinning the wheels of steel may be the route you take. I don't know, maybe it's just the start. That you will have to consult The Lord on."

"I'm not sure I'm clear pastor."

"Son, some traditions were made to be broken. Nothing wrong with doing something old, a new way. Everybody don't get saved in a church at the foot of a pulpit on an alter call. It's a renaissance on the inside. That can happen while you out here hoopin' by yourself at three in the morning just trying to clear your head. One may very well be on a train ride home from a work day, be in a car full of people and at the same time be in a different spiritual and mental space, alone with the Savior receiving sweet, gracious salvation.

God is diverse. He's a triune spirit with different functions. He is the Creator of the universe. We being created by that creator, in His very likeness, not just Christians, mankind on a whole, have that same ingenuity, that same creativity in which we can tap in to. The Father loves to see us using our talents and gifts, the very things he has carefully placed within us to be fruitful, multiply and bring Him glory. We ain't all here to pastor or lead a flock in the traditional sense.

With all The Lord has placed inside of us, and we all have different measures of faith and talents, yet the same amount of grace by which those talents are used, we have a responsibility to use them creatively for the greater good of mankind and God's kingdom. We all have a purpose. Part of the journey is discovering what that means, what that is and what to do with it. We can pray about all of those things. But, somewhere on the road to divine destiny, on the wings of grace, ushered by faith, walking in our purpose, we must use our creativity. He doesn't give us anything just to waste it. Nothing is ever wasted with God. Not even our pain."

"Not even our mistakes?"

"Not even our mistakes young man. God is a God of purpose."

"Purpose, huh?"

"Yes purpose. Now everybody's purpose is different. For some it is very well being a stay at home mother for some child may need that; it may be the best way she can support her husband. That's what my wife did. She stayed at home, I provided. She took care of me. That son, truly made my life easier. I treasured her for that. My boys had a parent home every day. They were raised in a stable environment. That worked for our family for a season. I know a lot of prominent, important women who looked down on my wife because for that season, she felt content in what she had believed the Lord had led her to do. But I defended her to the end. She didn't raise a fuss. I defended her, for who were they to judge her for what the calling on her life was at the time for where God was taking us for His glory? Who are we to judge the path another person chooses? How do we know what The Lord has whispered to them, spoken into their spirit at any given time? How do we know what God has placed within them? What their instincts are? Where His spirit is leading them. In addition why? For..."

Darrell interjected, "Who can know the mind of God?"

"Amen.", Al said. "If that person believes, after much prayerful consideration and wise counsel that is where God has led them to be, even if it is just for a season. We are to just let go and let God.

I don't care if it's hip-hop, producing movies, designing clothes, playing a professional sport or coaching a team. It could be as simple as mopping a floor. No matter what it is son; even being a foster parent… it too is a ministry. A cop, a doctor, a security guard. Whatever. Just whatever what God has for you do to. Work as unto Christ. Do it with purpose. Make it count for something. Be your authentic self. Pay no mind to doubters. Haters will always be. Jesus had 'em."

"Yeah, that the scary part pastor. The way people come for you when you out here doin' what you know in your spirit The Lord is leading you to do. Just because they don't have the courage to do it or because it's out of the box. They wanna condemn you. Even if your views aren't the views of the majority, they wanna come to ya door with pitchforks and torches because well… you're different. I just don't believe because you might share commonalities with people that you have to do what they do or see it the way they see it. If nobody ever steps outside of the box, nothing ever changes. Nothing gets done. People suffer. I think by doing you sometimes, you set other people free to just do them. Somebody has to have the courage to go against the grain."

"So true. That's what Jesus did. Pay no mind to naysayers. Jesus never allowed that stop Him. Stand up and fight for your beliefs. So long as they are in line with God's truth. Do what God is telling you do to keeping in mind your audience. Those who get it are the ones that are supposed to. Those who don't, are not. Even if nobody does, because sometimes you gotta do that Salmon Run alone, don't worry, if The Lord gets you. You good."

"If God be for me…"

"Who can be against you son."

"That's some powerful word. I'll take that. I'll keep doin' my thing."

"The word of God is powerful It's the sword of the spirit. It is a weapon. Sharper than any two-edged sword. Young man, I beseech thee. No matter what, in all thy getting, get understanding. Keep in mind it ain't about you. It's about The Lord and those around you. It's His thing."

"Yes Sir."

"Make His agenda yours and you'll never go wrong."

"That's smart."

"Actually, that's wise. Remember your influence. People always watching. Stay humble and keep glorifying God. Jesus never made it about himself. He was a servant from beginning to end."

"Yes Sir. That's truth."

"Accept what God the capacity in which The Lord choose to use you. Furthermore, don't despise small beginnings. Be a master at your craft in your own arena. No matter how small the audience or the venue. If you give the platform over to the Holy Spirit, none of that will matter. Everybody is not called to the world stage."

"The man gave his servants each a different number of talents. He knew who could handle what. Right?"

"Right. Everybody ain't gonna be famous. Everybody can't handle that responsibility. Fame and all that encompasses it is responsibility no matter how many people try to shun it. A platform is a platform. An audience is an audience."

"Influence is influence."

"Yep! So use it wisely. No matter how great or small the calling, keep in mind your influence. Keep in mind how you are coming across and what message you are conveying. Keep in mind you cannot please everyone. Don't go crazy trying. Even Jesus had critics; He did not always answer them. Let them speak. It is their right. Everybody has an opinion. Let them have it. Be thick skinned son. If you will allow me to speak frankly, ministry takes big plums... man to man."

"Wow!"

"If you're ever gonna be great, if you're ever going to blaze your own trail and do something unconventional; anything non-conformist; anti-establishment you gotta have big plums. Go at it with full force. Be strong in your spot. Rely on the Lord's strength not your own, for the moment you start believing your own hype, understand this now... Life, people or the enemy will come along and remind of just how human you really are. God will allow too! Don't be fooled into thinking He won't. The Lord is a strategist. He knows what's best for us.

He allows falls often to humble us. We are nothing outside of Christ. We all a work in progress no matter how big we get. You never so big that you can't be taken down. Bigger you get, the harder you fall. Stay humble. Keep the faith. You be aight."

"I believe you."

"More importantly, believe God and believe in yourself. Lastly, never limit where you learn from and who can teach you. Be open but guard your heart. Seek godly counsel always. You have my support." Al looked around, "You might be just what the people need. A fresh outlook. Realness. A fresh anointing to meet people where they are. Because God knows everybody ain't comin' to church. Jesus said one day...one day...every knee will bow and every tongue will confess. Thing is, He never said what, when, or how. He doesn't have to say why. I believe the why is because He is unequivocally, irrevocably, Lord."

"Thank you Pastor and amen. For the sermon. And for the vote of confidence. I will try to remember all of that. I got get back. You good people."

"Pardon me if I've kept you too long. Preaching is in my blood son. It's what I do. Glory be to God."

"Teaching too."

"What?" Al asked.

Darrell said running back to the booth, "Teaching man. That's in ya blood too! I learned a lot. God bless you man."

"May God bless you richly son. As well as your gifts and talents. Bless his skill Father. Help him to put the blunt down Father. Give your son the strength to lift you up and hold his family together. In Jesus' mighty name. Amen." The reverend beckons, "Hey man!"

Darrell paused. He called, "Yeah man?!"

"Children do what we do, not always what we say. She's listening to you man. Even if it don't seem that way. She's an investment. We're all investments. That how God sees us. We have great growth potential and increasing value. That's why we're called to be trees that bear good fruit. He has planted seed in us by Christ Jesus; through His word. Also through human connection. We're an expression of His love and creativity. He sees so much he has placed within his creation."

"I gotta run pastor. Why you tellin' me this?"

"Your daughter is your investment. You are God's investment. He has planted seeds within you that you need to plant within her. It is not enough to talk at our children. It is not enough to demand respect. We are to listen, not just speak. We are to respect those investments. Pour into them. Nurture them. Adjust what needs to be adjusted. Seek wise advisors on how to grow those investments. Patiently, waiting for them to grow fat with interest. Maximize the return son. So God can capitalize on the prophet. He is the ultimate shareholder. His investment portfolio can't be beat."

"That's deep."

"That's real. It's a deep as you need to plant those seeds. Plant seeds man. Spend quality time with your investment. See this whole thing is about trust."

"Trust?"

"Yes trust. See, God trusts you with all that He has invested in you. Your gifts, talents, skills, etc. Your daughter. She's his daughter on loan to you for a season. You are charged with protecting and growing that investment. Just as he trusted your parents as His investment, to reproduce and plant seed that would grow with interest and reproduce and also return a profit or a prophet; depends on how you see it. The Master has entrusted you with the same. Our relationship with God is a trust. We are the trustees. Our children; others around us can be considered benefactors. Likewise, we are living trusts."

"That's mad financial talk brother."

"It's all relative brother. Investment requires a certain level of greed. We've been groomed to believe that greed itself is all negative."

"Well it is isn't it?"

"Depends on your perspective. Like violence and rebellion; same as with war or beauty. It's all perspective. I would argue the point that there is a certain greed and entitlement that God comes with."

"God greedy? Violence? War? Pastor that don't sound right."

"I'll keep it simple. Think of earlier in the conversation when we were referring to the man in the Bible who had come home from afar off that had entrusted his servants with the talents."

"Okay…"

"The last servant mentioned was the unproductive one. He buried the one talent he had been entrusted to invest and grow with interest. Yet, he chose to bury it, knowing full well his mater was a shrewd business man that reaped where he had not sewn. You with me man?"

"Preach."

"Okay so. The last portion of that scripture could be attributed to greed. Wanting more; believing, even knowing you deserve more is not wrong. There is a tinge of rapacious desire that comes with investing or sewing and reaping as it were. Take note that the word also expresses that the Kingdom of God suffers violence…"

"And the violent take it by force."

"Amen. God is also a jealous and a known as a god of wrath in the Old Testament. He is a God of vengeance. He was also known to make evil spirits rise. It's in the word. People don't understand that there are many attributes to the very character of the Almighty. Not all of them soft and sweet. After all, who can conduct good business always being soft and sweet? How far would you get? Who would respect you or revere you? What return would you gain on your investment if you're not eager to capitalize by any means necessary?"

"God loves us so much that He is pursuant, patient and even chastises us when necessary."

"Yes! You got it. He loves us so much that even though He has granted us free will, He'll still pursue and punish when His investment is not bearing any fruit. Nobody likes to think of it that way. We forget He is alive. He never sleeps. He loves us. He has a plan. He is our Holy Father."

"As far as violence goes…"

"It is as simple as this son, The Bible says; this is God' word… Without the shedding of blood, there can be NO remission of sin. Sometimes there has to be war. There will always be blood shed somewhere in the world where the oppressed rise up in rebellion against the powers that be.

Jesus gave His very life for mankind in the most violent way. God is gangster man. Not as passive as He is too often painted to be. I think we romanticize The Lord too much. He's a shrewd business man. His word says specifically that every tree that does not bear fruit will be cast down and into the fire. We're supposed to function and multiply His gains.

Think of The Lord as the greatest investment banker, so to speak. His kingdom, an investment bank, facilitating mergers and acquisitions, private equity; placements; corporate restructuring. I'm kinda like an investment broker. Men and women called by God to preach teach and prophesy are merely go-betweens acting on behalf of. Glory be to God."

"Wow! That is some eye opening perspective. What a revelation. Thanks man."

"Uh huh. On another note, be advised young man, Children tend to pick up what we put down. Whether it's sound advice or bad behavior. Especially bad habits. You dig?"

China's father bolted towards the DJ booth. He paused yet again. He turned to Al, "Bruh, how you know I smoke?"

"Boy I ain't stupid. I've been in these streets longer than you've been alive. Don't sleep." Darrell shook his head at Al. He smiled. He returned to work.

"Aight! We gon' keep the lovin' strong out here. One more for the road. And since traditions were made to broken a wise man just told me, here's somethin y'all might not be familiar with... I like this lady. Can't be a good Dee Jay and not listen to all types of music. Excuse me while I put y'all up on somethin'. This is an eye opener for all of the hangers on, Bonnie Raitt ladies and gentlemen. I love y'all South Side. Thanks to Pastor Golden for comin' out and stayin' so long. A lot pastors wouldn't have done that. Thanks for not wearin' a robe and a collar. "

Al smiled, "That uniform don't give us super powers son. If it's in you, it's in you no mater whatchu rockin'."

"You proved that tonight bruh. I got mad respect for you man. We love you Pastor. Whatever you do we gotcha back. Thanks for keepin' it one wit us ... You and your family, for so long. Give it up for the Goldens y'all. Good people. Good night."

"No pedestals y'all. Nobody good but God. Give it up for yourselves and The Lord. He made this possible. You have to know it was Him. Everything went peacefully. Thank you Jesus. This was nice."

Al sits down. His heart filled with joy. To be so well received by the people he has served most of his life. He was respected. He was loved. He was able to be himself. It was official. Out here is where he wanted to be. Unsure of exactly in what capacity. Unsure of what The Lord was going to do next in his life. He basked in the glow of the people, the community he had invested so much in. A community that still needed so much help. A community it seemed the church had shut its eyes too all too often. He sipped lemonade while talked to the drug dealers about court issues and baby mama drama. He enjoyed the energy. Al didn't even mind the ignorance. The profanity and the violent overtones in the music didn't bother him. He knew he wasn't perfect. He enjoyed the same tunes from time to time. "Can't reach if you can't find 'em." He told himself. "You gotta know where they at."

It hadn't been that long ago that he had walked in their shoes. Who was he to give up on them? Even if they had given up on themselves. Al was very supportive. He knew the language they spoke. He understood their mindset and why they had chosen the paths they had been walking down. They needed someone to believe in them. They needed someone that wasn't afraid of them. Someone who could relate to them to come from behind the pulpit. Everybody knew Al and Carla's story. They were trusted figures.

He thanked The Lord for all he had been through. Everything that he had believed all of his life had worked against him; things from his past that he thought would limit his ability to reach people with gospel of Jesus Christ. Those mistakes, the shortcomings, the failures. The hustling and the whore houses had actually made him more qualified to do outreach and evangelize than staying behind the doors of the church; being indoctrinated with religiosity could ever do. He was able to reach God's people. The ones that would probably never come to church. He was wise enough to bring church to them. He left religion behind the church doors. Al brought with him from home; from all of his memories, wisdom, love, patience and compassion. He related to the people in the way he believed Jesus would. The very way Jesus had related himself to him many years ago when he was still in his flesh.

China's dad lowered the music. Bonnie Raitt's powerful, somber voice rang out into a lull. The DJ whispered in to the microphone soothingly, "This is the wakeup call anthem for all the ladies that can't move on. I say this with love: He is just not that into you. Love you ladies. If you feel desperate. If he ain't even trying to give you... what you need. If you longin' for a commitment he done told you a thousand times you ain't gon' get. If you working too hard to keep his attention, remember this: The blessings of the Lord make you wealthy. He don't add no sorrow to 'em neither. You can do better. You deserve more. Standards ladies. Standards. You still have worth even if you're not in a relationship. Don't let a relationship status on Facebook define you. You are more than your relationship status. A queen is still a queen without a king. A man or a king don't make her a queen. He don't give her relevance or status. She owns it ladies. She owns it. Even when the king is dead she still carries herself like a queen because she was queen before the king even gave her a title. You have to walk in it ladies. Standards. Standards. A man does not make you or break you. Know this. Standards ladies. You can't make him love you if he don't."

Al stood up to walk away. He had taken his first step, a hug from behind. He turned around. It was Connie. He hugged her tightly. "I didn't know you were here."

"Been here all day Al, wouldn't miss it. But I miss you. Dance with me."

He held her closely. She buried her face in his chest. A waterfall of woe cascaded down his torso. He buried his face in her hair. He took a deep breath. Her hair always smelled like whatever food she had cooked that day. Tonight it sniffed of peaches. He knew she had baked a cobbler. The only thing she had ever prepared for him that rivaled anything Carla had ever made.

Holding her, he thought on days gone by when he and Connie had been just simple friends in his mind. His heart was full of Carla. Connie was the bridge that had closed that gap. He squeezed her tighter as if to say thank you. As if to say goodbye. The DJ looked on noticing they were off on another plain, so he played the song in rotation for the pair. He sensed what they knew inside, it would be their last waltz. After the third rotation, he played Saving All My Love for You. Connie mourned.

Curious onlookers gossiped from the sideline. Wondering how the People's Pastor could be so caught up with the likes of one such as Connie Debril.

They reasoned within themselves thinking he was just providing a service. Maybe she was grieving. The neighborhood was buzzing with newsfeed from the violent incident that had taken place at Liza's house. They were unaware that her mother had not been informed. They had no idea that there was beef between the two. They supposed the Pastor was just consoling his old friend.

The music began to fade. Couples began to retreat. Al and Connie held on to one another for dear life. It was as if no one else was around. Intent on savoring their finally moments together, they continued to dance slowly.

Without warning, a rabble-rouser cried, "Pastor, you too good for that! Let that ho go!"

Al Golden looked up, "What was that?"

Connie insisted, "Al baby, let it go. They just ignorant kids. They don't know no better. I'm used to it. I just ignore it... tired of fightin'."

Al gently pushed Connie away, "Say what now? Let what go? Woman, you know me better than that."

He walked up to the DJ booth. China's dad handed him the mic and stepped back. He muttered, "Really? On a day like today? A beautiful night like tonight? A family affair. A violence free zone and you think I can allow you to sit here and disrespect this beautiful woman like that? A woman so near and dear to me? A woman who, tell you the truth, I wouldn't be here today without? A woman God used to usher me and my wife into ministry. Don't you know this woman introduced my wife to God? Did you know that? Then, by God's grace, my wife took the little she knew, asked God to bless it, broke that up and fed me and countless others with that over the years. Just as the Lord has used those same fragments of fish and bread to feed many of you and your parents, maybe even you Grandparents over the years? Don't you know how valuable this lady is to me? To God? Just like you? How dare you spew hate at another?!" Connie stood below the DJ booth frozen with fear.

"Naw! She ain't perfect. But I'm not either. Neither are you. Can't a soul in here afford to throw a stone at nobody. Alright! So what! She got a past. Who don't? You gotta respect her though. See, she one the few people I know; ever met in my entire life that never tried to cover hers up. The woman never made excuses for her sin. Just like the woman the men was gonna stone back in Jesus time. She was gonna take her licks without excuses. She didn't opened her mouth once to defend herself. She did nothing to warrant being stoned but make some bad choices she didn't even know was that big of a deal while she was making 'em. She was just doin' what she knew at the time. Until she knew better. She ain't no better until Jesus came to her defense with just a few words to her accusers. He healed her soul. Forgave and restored her. The Lord encouraged her. He did not condemn her for her past. Simply put, Jesus asked her: 'Woman where are you accusers?'

They had all bounced because in essence, Jesus had said to them, that they were just as guilty as she was. They probably was the ones sinnin' wit her, the heat was on and they had to do what men usually do, something to shut the woman up. How you shut her up if you can't pay her off? Shame her to death or stone her death. Condemn her, brand her and beat her down in every way because her walking about freely is a constant reminder of the stain on your sheets that you can't allow anyone else to see.

Wow! Why we do people like that? Huh? What part of this woman… no let me rephrase that… What is it about this woman that makes you believe that she does not deserve kindness, love and respect? Huh? The same stuff all y'all want for yourselves and your loved ones. What is it that she is guilty of besides being human? Huh? Just like you. Just like me. Or is it the same as it was in that Biblical tale, her being out here in the open walking amongst the guilty makes you feel more guilt? Does this beautiful woman represent the stain on your sheets that you don't want other people to see?"

Not a voice rang out. Connie cried. She walked away.

"No you don't Connie. No you don't. You better than that. You much stronger than that. Come back here." He turned to Darrel, "Man go get her." The DJ ran to escort Connie up to the DJ booth.

Al put his arm around her. "I love this woman. I said it. She is my friend. Always has been. If I could be the man she needed I promise you, I would be more than that. She's beautiful, strong, smart; responsible. She deserve love and respect. See I know her past. I was there. I'm a part of it just as she is a part of mine. Don't stop me from lovin' her. Don't stop her from loving me. Where love is concerned, the past don't make no never mind. Yesterday don't matter with love.

God is love people. He don't care about yesterday. God is a spirit. He's always moving forward. Up and onward. On to the next. We got to do the same thing if we ever gonna love right. Leave people alone. Stop holding folk to a standard we can't even keep ourselves like Pharisees and Sadducees. If you read your Bible, you know they were the biggest hypocrites in Jesus' day. They were extremely religious. They held folk to a standard they couldn't themselves keep. That could be looked on as self-hatred. We deflect so much these days. Especially in the black community. What we don't like in us, we trash others for. The way we look. The way we act. Too light. Too dark. Hair texture. The way we speak. How we dress and walk. I only date this type of person because they light skin or dark skin. She's a whore. But its okay for him to be the pimp she hoin' for.

 It's cool for men to be pimps but if a woman sells her body to feed her child or because she doesn't know another way, oh she gotta go. The defining double standard. That's the real blurred line. It's satanic garbage ingrained in us from the beginning of time! We still goin' for the okey doke!

Some of you women secretly wish you had the sexual freedom this woman has enjoyed. That's why you date bad boys. You're really a bad girl on the inside. It's the whole Bobby Brown/Whitney Houston, Chris Brown/Rihanna thing. Ain't nothin' new under the Son? You ain't no different than what you draw to yourself; no different than your choices until you renew your mind and decide to choose differently.

We draw to us what we are on the inside; the way we see ourselves within." The audience stood aghast. "Stop beating these boys up for these women's choices. Especially when they chose to come back to 'em over and over. Whitney and Bobby told the world they had somethin' in common in a song. People turned a deaf ear to the truth. People don't make you who you are just like money doesn't; they enhance or magnify who you are in negative or positive ways. Oh y'all can look at me like y'all crazy if you want to. But I said it. I ain't no advocate for domestic violence either. Boys shouldn't beat up on girls EVER! The case can be made that people do what they know; it is learned behavior; sometimes generational curses. Yet I will say, man to men, that no matter what the case, there is never an excuse. Get some help. Survivor or perp. Ray or Janay Rice, if you stay in or go back to that situation over and over again, what message are you sending to your sons and daughters?

I understand self-esteem issues, financial issues; I get not being strong enough to leave. But plan to do better for yourself. Pray for help and an open door. Tell somebody! It is not the will of God that anyone be abused or mistreated. People say love makes you weak. I disagree. I'm a witness that love makes you strong.

I've never been a woman but, I've been married to one. I know women are naturally emotional. Y'all don't let your emotions keep you in an unhealthy relationship with an unpredictable person in an unstable environment. If you make it too easy on men, they tend not to change. You gotta give 'em some discipline. Suffering does men well. The bible says even Christ learned obedience through suffering. Forgive, yes. Still, there has to be some chastisement. That being said, I stand by my statement.

All too often we hate who we are or what we see in ourselves so we tend to take it out on others. I believe in the strength of women. Y'all take too much off of us sometimes. I will always believe there is a way you are supposed to talk to and treat a man. We're heavy on respect. There is also too, a way in which a man should treat and respond to a woman. I know y'all crave love and affection. You all are heavy on understanding; you need to be heard. We need more togetherness in our community. We need more healing for the brokenness. Please don't even attempt to enter into a relationship with another human being if you're broken. Two broken people together only creates more brokenness. If you need to fill a void, fill that with Jesus. Too often we run into the arms of another broken person expecting healing to come from them. It's like the blind leading the blind. Where we goin'? Nowhere. We all need to change. Lord help us to wake up. The Lord wants us healed and whole. One is whole. One can't be divided. Find wholeness in your aloneness. Be one with yourself. Find everything you need in Christ. The Christ that is alive on the inside of you believers. If you're not a believer, you ca become one today. God, The Father is offering you wholeness. Salvation is yours today if you want it. Jesus can heal your broken heart; all of your hurts. Real love begins with, in and through Him. You will never know real love until you know the real Jesus. Not the blonde haired, blue-eyed Jesus they have tried for centuries to make us believe was the real Jesus. That's an image they want you to bow down to that will keep you bound, thinking that Jesus don't look like you. When in fact, if he lives on the inside of us as believers, he could possibly look like us. God is a spirit. There is no real description of Jesus' looks in the Bible from head to toe until revelations. He was born in a Jewish body. But oh Lord! Lord when he returns I read where it said feet of bronze and wool-like hair. In the Bible it says, in Him there is no specification! No Jew nor Gentile. No slave! Nor free! Nor male or female, for we are all one in Christ! How can he look like just one set of people? How can that be when...HE LOVES US ALL?! HE DIED FOR US ALL?! THAT IMAGE IS FALSE! IT IS OPPRESSIVE! THAT IS MAN-IP-U-LATION! WHERE IS THE LOVE IN THAT?!"

The assembly cheered. "I didn't come here to preach tonight. Y'all done got me started out here."

"WELL THAT'S ALRIGHT!" A woman yipped.

Al asked, "Y'all sure that's alright?"

"IT'S ALRIGHT PASTOR!"

"Well alright then. Y'all gon' have to forgive that last outburst. I just don't like manipulation. Black people been down too long. I just keep hearing The Lord say wake up. It's time for us to wake up. That's the same image that keep people out of church. So…Jesus don't look like me or a Spanish person or an Asian or Indian person. Y'all just gon' present Him as some hippie livin' on Skid Row and I'm supposed to run wit' dat right? And for how long? Lord help me I'm gon' again…" the crowd hailed. "Oh don't encourage me now. Y'all know better. Lord let me get back on topic. They ain't ready." he gleamed. Al cleared his throat, "Bible says we only love because He FIRST loved us. Love is unnatural to us. Sin, hate, disobedience are the natural things. Our flesh, our sinful nature is what causes us to harm other people. Will there be one today? Will there be one to come to Christ to find out what real love is for yourself? Then and only then will you be able to give it away." No one came forward. "Don't let the enemy stop you from receiving salvation and knowing true love. He loves you! Jesus loves you. He's passionate about you! He is for you! He placed us here to love one another! Survivor or perpetrator… you are not your issues. You are not alone! We all have issues. Jesus can help you deal with those issues! I know pastors with those same issues. None of us are exempt from issues. It is all in how we handle those issues. WILL THERE BE ONE?!" Al shouted until the speakers screeched. Ministers in the audience had positioned themselves at the foot of the DJ booth on either side. A few people, male and female came to the ministers for prayer and to receive Christ as their Lord and Savior. Stood behind the crowd of people that stood in silence in tears with lifted hands. "That's right. That's right. Come to the foot of the cross. He's here. He's waiting for you. Grace is available for you. Grace is available for one and all. Forgiveness is yours. Lord Jesus, thank you for your sacrifice. Thank you sweet Savior for your grace. He loves you." The man of God breathed. Darrel played 'He Loves Me", a Kirk Franklin ballad, ever so softly. In all, twelve souls were one for Christ that night.

Al grieved, "I stand before you all imperfect. As imperfect as the next man. I ain't so different from you. Christ is what makes the difference. I have some ways about me too. Some of my ways gon' be with me until Jesus call me home. I am merely a man with a message with issues like every other man. I'm from another generation. Some things just old ways. LORD! WHEN YOU BEEN ONE WAY FOR SO LONG!" He moaned. The men in the crowd clapped. "That's no excuse though. We all can change. As I stand before you, I too, am slowly waking up. We must wake up! Love is not hurting one another. Love is healing one another." Connie looked upon her friend with tenderness. She gave him a thumbs up.

"Preach Pastor.' encouraged Darrell.

"It's all how you feel about you! It's abuse! It's another form of genocide. We be out here killin' one another because we don't love ourselves y'all. It is suicide people! Hate is nothing more than a weapon designed to kill. Think about it. Think about the way you live your life behind closed doors where nobody can see. How are you treating the people that The Lord has commissioned you to love? How are doing on keeping God's gold standard? How are you doing in your daily life on reflecting Jesus in every way or even keeping man made law?

...sit in judgment of this woman. How are you doing on keeping the standards? Can't right? Mess up every day... sometimes all day don't you? Be honest with yourself 'cause God knows. If God really cared enough to punish us for what we did yesterday, we'd all be dead today! Nobody would be alive. I will ask again... which one of y'all can keep the standard?

And see… that's why Jesus had to die…God knew we couldn't keep His standard. So He sent His grace, His mercy, His love down here through a virgin, wrapped in swaddling cloth in a nasty manger…humbled His glorious, most holy self…He came down here, Jesus… God in the flesh to dwell among us. Teach us, keep us; know us. Help us to know Him… He wanted intimacy with us; His creation. Y'all he died for us. He sacrificed, went through hell and high water, all for love. For people like you and me that wouldn't even love Him back. Stiff-necked people like us, people that can't love Him the way that He love us. He know we can't behave 100%. Y'all, He know we can't keep His standard. We ain't faithful. These Christians ain't loyal. Nobody is. Stay with me, I'm goin' somewhere."

"We right here Brother Al! You gon' take ya time! That's all right!" A young woman shouted.

"Thank you young lady. So He gives us mercy and grace. Even though we can't earn it, we don't deserve it, can't do nothin good enough… We refuse it…We mock it… We abuse it. Everyday. Yet every day, His mercy is renewed. Born a fresh. We get another chance. Saved or not. Born-again or hell bound. He still loves us. With equality. He ain't no respecter of persons. You know that movie, 'I Know What You Did Last Summer'? Yeah? Well guess what? God knows more than that! He know what you did last night and what you gon' do tonight.

He knows when you can't help yourself. He even knows when you prayin' to Him lying about it 'cause you just love the sin you in and you ain't ready to stop. He knows people. He created us. Who knows the product better than the manufacturer? Huh?

We ain't getting' away with nothin. Can't hide from God. Even if we make our bed in hell, He's there. He everywhere all at once. Sin is so ugly to God, He can't even bear to even look at it. But He knows when we're in it. He don't miss a beat. He knows why we do it. We all got reasons why. He know when we gonna stop and if we ever will stop. He knows it ALL y'all. Yet, if He see fit to breathe life into us another day, we get up, get another cup of His freshly brewed mercy to carry us on through another day; another chance to right the wrongs and rewrite our song. He's merciful to every living creature. He favors whomever He will. He is God. We are not. He sees us all the same no matter we do. I ain't no better than you. You ain't no better than her. We all the same. Only difference is despite what you may think you know about her, Connie Debril knows The Lord. If you don't know love, obviously you don't.

We need more love out here y'all. We get beat up out here enough. Sometimes you get beat up at work. Beat up at home. Walk to the store, get beat up. Parents beat up children. Children beat up parents. Cops beat you up; kill ya sons, brothers, uncles, lovers; your husbands and fathers. No mercy. But he man who bombed Boston, oh... that joker still got his life. Talk about double standard. They didn't know what they were walking into, yet... He lives. Boy America needs to wake up. BLACK PEOPLE TAKE THE BLINDERS OFF AND WAKE UP!"

"TELL 'EM SON!", begged an elderly man.

"We just bite each other up! Kill, destroy with our words. We wound people with our words. We injure one another every day by how we treat one another. All over this world. It is sad. We all gotta live here together 'til our number is up. We waste so much of the little time we do have hating and bashing one another; Beating our brothers and sisters down, all around the world. And for what? Huh?

Never forget the way we treat others is the reflection of how we treat ourselves or see ourselves. If you gay bash, you a racist, you beat women, you use men, on and on...somethin' wrong inside of you. Jesus didn't charge us with the sole responsibility of judgment. He charged us with the sole responsibility of loving one another. It is our responsibility. We must take it more seriously. Once you heard, you can't act like you don't know. Now you have been charged.

Leave people alone out here! Everybody deserve love and a second chance. Don't be so nosey. Stop making other people's choices your business. Check your selves. Start taking people to the Lord in prayer. If you gon' pray tonight, ask The Lord to teach you how to love your fellow man. Ask Him for His eyes. Go and sin no more." By the end of his sermon, many people had walked away. Others stayed and mumbled criticisms. Few openly supported him. He wasn't moved by either.

Al handed the microphone back to the Darrell. He held Connie's hand. They walked through the crowd.

"Come on Connie. Let me take you home."

Before she got into the car, Connie turned around and walked back to address the onlookers. A vision in white, she stood strong. She pronounced, "I am not my mistakes. I am not my sin. That is not who I am. Last time y'all break me. I done moved on. I suggest you do the same. Thank you."

In turning to face Al, she had noticed an aloof young girl standing near the exit. Connie walked over to the young girl. She was wearing a tee shirt that read: PUSSY IS POWER. Connie read the words. She stared at the girl. The girl asked, "You like my shirt right? Ain't that true though? Niggas out here thirsty huh? Don't we got that shit that bring 'em to their knees?" The young girls that were with her laughed and nodded.

Connie's voice cracked as she answered, "Yeah. I like the shirt. It's the truth. But that ain't the only power we have. If you think it is, then your power is limited. Who wants a man that falls to his knees so easily?"

"Oh I just was sayin'…"

"And. And… If you ain't the only one out here wit' a pussy, that means you ain't the only one that can bring him to his knees young one. What you want is a man strong enough to not let the power of the pussy bring him to his knees. You want a man strong enough to stand up even when that kryptonite is in his face. No matter how weak it makes him, he gotta be strong enough to say no to that drug sister. Y'all got all of these celebrities singin' and rappin' about havin' big booties and pussy puttin' jokers to sleep. But what happens when that big ol' ass start saggin'? What's ya plan when he wakes up from his slumber? How you keep him when there are millions of females all over the planet that got the same power as you? The reality is, we are not super heroes because we have vaginas. If we were... if that was all it took to get and keep a man, we'd all have one. We'd be able to make 'em act right. Then, maybe they wouldn't cheat. Maybe? I'm sure they'd find a way though. Even super powers wear off over time. Its witchcraft and manipulation... a game you really don't want to play with men if you get what I'm saying girls.

We're emotional. They are not. They are visual and physical. Think about them and sports; competition; pride; not wanting to be beat. They paly rough. They hit hard. Why manipulate and play when you can just find out what it is you have to offer that is unbeatable and let that work for you? Why bank on a power that you share with other people. That power doesn't make you valuable. That limited power is what makes them think we're disposable. That is until they meet the right one whose power reaches farther and deeper than between their legs. You can't just give him somethin' he can feel. You gotta give him something to think about.

Entertainment is just that. It is not reality. Don't believe what you hear. Any woman in a successful, long-term relationship knows better. So does her man. He ain't there, night after night, when he knows he can be somewhere else, but he chooses to be there, as does she, just for the sex. He can get that anywhere. Y'all gotta know coochie is coochie to these jokers. Sex is sex. And yeah they weak for it. They'll do whatever it takes to get near it... even if it means they risk losing everything they worked for. Remember Bill Clinton?"

"Who?"

"Jesus Christ! Never mind. He said he didn't have sexual relations with that women, but can't nobody tell me he didn't take a peek at that kitty! I refuse to believe there was just a cigar involved. I know better."

The young girl whispered to her friend, "Who is she talking about?"

A friend responded, "Lewinsky girl. Bey talked about that Monica Lewinsky'd all on her gown thing in Partition. I googled it."

Connie smiled, "Oh young ladies! You foolish Galatians! Who has bewitched you?"

"What nation? Who is Gail? Ms. Nene I don't understand..."

"Girls. Who fooled you all into thinkin' all y'all need is a big booty, some Indian woman hair and some Korean nails that give you fungus to be beautiful and get a male's attention? That's not what makes you beautiful and all of that trickery might get his attention but none of that will keep it. Just ask any of those celebrities y'all worship that can't keep a man or have yet to find true love or have a successful marriage. It is not in sex, being sexy or image.

Pop that coochie all you want, it's yours! Just know there's more to life than what entertainers entertain you with. Believe what I say. You go and pay money to see people who don't care if you live or die because they don't know you, to pop they coochie and clap they ass all night long and what you learnin' from that? Nothin'. Where you goin' with that? Nowhere. Back to the hood to live through them. You invest in garbage and come back with nothing. But you and ya crew..." Connie pointed at the group of girls. "Y'all just bought your American Idol a few more dollars towards a new Birkin bag that is worth more money than you will make on your part-time afterschool job all year or even in two. American Idol." She laughed. "I don't even know why they created that show. America got enough golden calves to dance in front of and worship. Ain't nobody talkin' about abstinence or education?

They cry women's rights and feminism but they all on stage with they booty in the camera. ...thought women suffered back in the day for more than that? Thought misogyny was somethin' we was tryin' to get away from? We feedin' it. Where's the power in that? Like where's the power in exposin' ya crotch on stage in booty shorts and a leotard? Is sexual power the only power we have? That's what we want our girls to know? But people don't get it. They praise celebrity while teachers and mothers get disrespected and stay broke. All of the risk and little to no reward. We wonder why the rate of HIV and AIDS is so high in the black and brown community… What sense does it make to get on TV and talk about it when you're portraying the exact opposite? Why we got so many baby mamas and daddies and not more wives and husbands? Why we have so many child support cases? Pussy is power but, it is not the only power. It's not the greatest power. Before women were fighting for the right to vote; still fighting for equal pay in the work place. Women all over the world getting' raped; women that wear more clothes than we do; women that have less rights and privilege. Welcome to America where we just throw coochie in ya face and call it women's lib. No, what we doin' is messin' these little girls minds up and letting men have their way. That's why they don't complain. We let 'em see everything for free.

The more famous you get, the more naked you get. Wel, l what's left after you done took it all off? What's exclusive for your husband when you done threw it back and busted it open for the world to see? And…if it's all fake… all image…entertainment… that's not really who you are… then why should I follow you or even listen to a word you say when you don't even have the strength to be yourself? That means you're lying to me. That makes you fake. That means something is wrong. That means everything I thought I knew about you as a fan is a lie if that is not your truth at all times. Joke is on you young ladies."

"Man Ms. Nene, that was powerful. I never thought about that."

"This is America honey. Home of the hustler. Land of the liar. Everybody's on the come up at everybody's expense. The Divided States of America, where we worship image and cover the truth. We keep God in our back pocket until there's a terroristic threat or until the National Day of Prayer. Shoot! We need to have a National day of Prayer every day. But what for? We're many nations, divided under many gods with liberty and justice for some. If this country was founded on the grounds of religious freedom, then we've definitely turned away from the God who the founding fathers here; we've all lost our way; every one of us.

Even many of them came, saw conquered, raped and pillaged. They stole everything from the Native Americans and Lord don't let me get started on how they treated black people and Mexicans. We don't have any morals. No limit soldiers. Then we wonder why the world hates Americans. Americans are arrogant and full of crap. We love to police the world; go get in they business; tell them what to do; tell them how to govern themselves; set up structure when our own government is corrupt and biased to the core. Hell, we need structure! Tellin' people to clean up but our own yard is dirty as hell. Even from before slavery! I don't know how we got people fooled into thinkin' rogue Islamists have the market corned on terrorism. America has its own terror tactics to answer for! God is gonna deal with America because we are still a sleeping giant. Money, sex, power, greed, image... All of these American Idols. Lord have mercy. We run to everybody's rescue because of treaties, alliances and agreements. How does that happen when our own children suffer from so much lack? So many child predators? So much ignorance? I know I read before in the Bible where it said: Anyone that does not provide for their relatives, and especially for their own household, has denied the faith and is worse than an unbeliever. Now I'm not sure if that's exclusively for Believers but, I think it can be applied to this country. Especially if the leaders claim to

be followers of Jesus. I know ain't nobody perfect…
somethin' gotta change though."

A wise relic wailed, "Preach girl! Ah huh! I was just reading Jeremiah Chapter two today after I prayed about all of the isms in this country. It's a shame. He showed He gon' deal wit' it. Rich people and those Tea Party people think that money, power and respect is theirs exclusively. They tight on a dollar man. But that's because their money is their God. I don't care what nobody say. Any time you fight that hard to keep the poor people poor and the middle class with their head just above water, that's a damn shame. When will the leaders of this country wake up and realize a house divided cannot stand? And where is the apology to black people, Mexicans and native Americans for the years and in some case centuries of terrorism, racism and all together horrible treatment? Where is the apology to women for the sexism? When does the pedophilia stop? Where is the regulation and stern punishment for rogue police officers with blue privilege? Where is the justice for all of the Sean Bells, Michael Browns and Trayvon Martins? Where is the justice for all of the aborted babies? When are we going to shut down Planned Parenthood? How can we run these bodegas, Chinese restaurants, nail salons, beauty supply stores and liquor stores out of our communities? They rest and nest in the hub of the black community. We ignorantly spend the black dollar lavishly to support their businesses. Because of us, they get to live the American dream and send money back home to those who can't. And we, born and bred here, can't afford to mortgage a home to raise our families in. These small businesses don't pour the black dollar back into the black community. Why do we allow them in? Why do we support them? Why are we the only race that takes their money and out in the hands of other people who come to us because they know we don't know better, they fed off of our ignorance… do we continue to support these businesses. NOBODY IS SUPPORTING US! WAKE UP! We are the only people who take the dollars we've earned and our spending power to people outside of our community as soon as we get those dollars in our hands. Instead of collectively building businesses within our community for ourselves; instead of keeping our dollars within the community and building structure and securing futures for our children, we over spend to over compensate because we believe everybody else's hype; because we're ignorant about fiscal responsibility and immature. THE LORD IS TIRED NOW! WAKE UP BLACK AMERICA AND WAKE UP! We're the only group that pushes our children to date outside of their race. We still believe whiter is righter. It is sad. If God wanted you another way, he would have created you that way! LOVE YOURSELF! FIND THE BEAUTY IN YOUR COMMUNITY! Many of you don't even know your own history, therefore you don't even know yourself. How you gon' run to somebody else and try to get to know them when you don't even know you? Who invented the cell phone? Huh? All of you young people...?" Nobody responded. "It was Henry T. Sampson, Jr.! He's still alive damn it! Look it up! This is what they won't teach you in school. YOU CAN DO BETTER!" One young man said, "Yooooo! That's deep. I thought it was T-Mobile. He smart as hell yo."

"We can do anything black people. The powers that be will do ANYTHING to keep you ignorant and oppressed. Wake up! Black America is the other sleeping giant. Romans chapter thirteen verse eleven says: And do this, understanding the present time: The hour has already come for you to wake up from your slumber, because our salvation is nearer than when we first believed. But see... ain't nobody comin' to save us black people. Nat Turner is gone and it ain't about looting, rioting and marching no more. What is that gonna do? We need a new mind set. We need to get a vision for ourselves. Our civil rights leaders have either been murdered or are living and out of touch with today's youth. We need new leadership. Where are the new leaders? We need order. No one is coming to save us. We have to save ourselves! President Obama done told y'all he ain't the president of black America. He done told y'all Negroes. I laughed like a mad scientist when understood the words that were coming out of his mouth. Ha! Ha! He right though. The man is right. Ha! Ha! He got y'all asses' attention then didn't he? Wake up. Nat Turner ain't comin' back. Martin, Malcom and Medgar ain't either people. Neither is the Brown Hornet! Ha! You better be your own black super hero. Make better choices and use your voices.

Obama's two residencies as POTUS came to show those haters and us blacks that our voices matter; things have to change; we do have power when we stick together. Those historic elections were symbolic of what is possible. Yes We Can is real. How did we forget that? Why we still killin' each other? And Nene is right! Why we applaudin' and worshipin' half naked women on stage all of the time when brothers should be coverin' all of that good good up? Why? Do we really think that what our ancestors got hosed down, lynched, burned and hung for? For our families to be divided still? After slave masters had our ancestors divided against our will for so long…. Oh now we just do it voluntarily? No more commitment. No honoring our women and children. Just put a baby in her and leave. Just lay down and let him because some connection is better than none at all.

Slaves weren't allowed to read and write. We forget they could've gotten killed for even attempting to educate themselves. Now our kids just refuse to learn. We've become too lazy and distracted to take interest in their learning. When did that become okay? School ain't for everybody is a piss poor excuse. All the more if it be true, that is not the case for everyone."

Blacks and women couldn't vote for a long time. Before Obama, blacks still refused to exercise they voice. It was because we didn't have much to choose from, I get it. We didn't feel as if we had a voice. Got that too. Nobody told us we could scream loud and break the mold if we all did it at the same time until Diddy came on MTV with that Vote or Die. I gotta be honest though, just because it there isn't a black man or a woman on the ballot does not mean don't vote! It's your voice! Use it! If you don't then when things go the way they go, who you got to blame but your ignorant self?" They watched in awe while the broken man ministered.

"I'm about to go home. Y'all black people need to wake up! Get on my nerves. Emmit Till got murdered because he was accused of whistlin' at a white woman. Y'all ball players out here... Don't get to college and lose who you are or your mind over them white girls. You got good black women right here in your community. You keep pickin' over 'em and passin' by 'em like they worthless lonely socks in the irregular cut, rejected bin at the discount S&A store. I don't understand it for the life of me.

You laid in a black belly for nine or so months for growth. You came from a black vagina for life. You suckled on a black nipple for nourishment. A black hand fed and wiped your black ass. The same ass you give your black women to kiss when you get on. You leave them for a white girl. Follow the leader. YOU GET GRAND! You lose your identity when you get to them uppity colleges. Black busted they ass to support you all through high school and worked to keep you aight all of your life. Soon as something else come and bat her eyelashes and bake you some cookies and give you they candy...you gone with the wind. Black ain't good enough for you no more. Then your babies runnin' around screamin' no labels please... I'm America's son or daughter. Tell your ancestors that.

What happens when the white cops stop you in your car or another black man gets gunned down and it start to come down heavy on your ass? Huh? You think someone else can relate to what your American son gon' have to go through because label or not he is still BLACK? You think when you fold up like a lawn chair in her lap and she tells you she understands-that she really gets what the struggle is all about, she can really relate? Are you just lookin' for an escape from the world you knew because their world looks better from this side?"

"Man take ya old ass home and stop hatin'! I'mma date whoever I want to date! Don't nobody care about race no more dog!" A young man argued. "That's back in y'all time. We together now. "

"Well, young person, wherever you are out here. I respect your view. Nevertheless, I feel bad that you're so blind and ignorant. I guess you'll have to learn from experience. I've been there. I speak from experience. Y'all keep running over hills, kickin' in doors, diggin' tunnels and scalin' walls to get them white girls and those Spanish women. Do you ever look at the ratio though? How many men from other races breakin' they necks to come get your black women? Huh? Look at the stats. Just look around you! Ain't a lot of them comin' because y'all don't value your own women. Why should anybody else? In turn, that makes it hard for them to value themselves, naturally. All puns intended. They feel like they gotta compete with Becky and Kayla's hair and skin. They ain't got Maria's tropical skin tone or rolling tongue. But they got attitude and that's the one thing y'all sorry Negroes scared of. Y'all partly to blame and y'all got the nerve to wonder why? Black people, when y'all gon' wake up?" He walked over to shake Al's hand, "Bright woman you got here. I see she's awake. That's refreshing."

"We just friends man. She is somethin' though. Surprised me tonight. She wakin' up." Al walked back over to escort his friend to his car. Al looked around at the wanton crowd. He could see they were thirsty for more.

"Yes sir! Doors of the church are now open. Good job Brother! You a good man!" someone shouted. "You too Ms. Nene. We need more of that real talk out here. Everybody don't understand the Bible. Y'all did real good man."

The old man began to walk away. He laughed and shouted, "Ha ha! Y'all go on break up the group now before the boys come through mobbin' like we a bunch of damn wild animals in a zoo. I don't wanna read about no more homicide by bacon here?" The crowd cheered.

The officers already on seen grimaced and shook their heads. Eric laughed, "Crazy old man. Where he come from anyway?"

"I ain't never seen him before." Said Chance. "He's entitled to his view. The way things is goin' out here… you blame him?"

"Nah man. I don't. He makin' sense."

"Yeah y'all gon' back to payin' ya slumlords market rent to live in they cardboard boxes. No! Gingerbread houses! The why them mice and roaches eat through that cheap sheet rock, those houses gotta be made outta nothin'.'"

"Up! He's back on the soap box. Y'all listen up!" begged Eric.

Y'all need to get over to the Iron Bound section a lil' more often and research. Just take the one on through there on a Sunday afternoon before it get too cold out. Daggone Republicans complainin' about immigrants. They can't be all bad. They stick together and build. They make what little they get work until they can do better like Jesus did with the bread and the fish.

They just in search of a better life most of 'em. People keep talkin' about they takin' jobs. Well hell! They takin' jobs y'all lazy Americans won't take 'cause ya too spoiled and entitled. You won't take a job that pay because the pay too low. What's too low when you on welfare or unemployment. It's a start. Why we so scared to work our way up to somethin'? Everything that gets built, anything that becomes great, starts off small. The humility that comes with a small beginning keeps us appreciative when we become great. Humility and small beginnings gives us goals; focus. The small beginning is necessary. Steps are necessary. Small beginnings keep us hungry. It's all opportunity. That's what it is. Where some see opposition, others choose to see opportunity. Everything look bad ain't bad. They stay in one house. They put they money together. They get along. They do what they can to make it work! They come here purpose driven and focused, most of 'em. They come humble and hungry. That is something the American people have lost; hunger and humility. They go hand in hand. We have done one another a disservice with all of this insta-garbage. Instant fame. Instant wealth. Instant food. Instant relationships. Instant everything. We're spoiled and worse off for it. We don't have to work for anything too much anymore. We have bred a generation of bratty ingrates. We have become our own worst enemy. We, as a people, are in our own way in many ways.

 We, born here, take what we have, whatever that is, for granted. Stuff people trying and dying to get in other countries, we throw away. Sittin' up in ya townhouse; in the projects with a seventy inch flat screen, smart TV in every room but no house to put that stuff in. Complain ain't nothin' on cable but paying for it and you barely home to watch it. Mother just went food shopping after working hard all day and y'all kids waste food; complain you ain't got nothin' to eat because you want fast food poison all up in you; ya body crave it now because its conditioned to it. Fast food ain't nothin' but drugs. Same deal. Different pusher. Different package. Legal verses illegal.

Just spoiled! That ain't even based on race. That's all of us. We want it all. We want it now. Hot and fast. The bigger the better. Forget about interest rates and debt. Forget about tax payer's money. Don't stay home on welfare when you can go to a workplace and be productive. Welfare is Temporary Aid to Needy Families people. Men get off of it! If you can work...work by the seat of your brow! God's Word says if a man don't work, he shall not eat. It's temporary aid. Don't stay needy permanently. The Lord wants better for you all. We gotta stop expectin' a hand out because we made poor decisions and did not plan for parenthood. If we do things The Lord's way, he'll cover us. We must wake up! Sisters quit shopping on the very first of the month. Learn to budget your income. Cook pots of meals that last a day or two if you can't afford to cook every night. Nothin' wrong with leftovers. We got these kids too spoiled. People used to bake casseroles and homemade breads from scratch. People used to share recipes and look out for one another when money got tight. We done fell off. Be wise when and where you shop! Bodegas markup individualized items so high when they are not even supposed to be sold individually. Furthermore, seeing as how they know we won't go to the supermarket or cut coupons, just a few extra miles to save a few extra bucks, they keep raising the prices on those items. They gain, we lose who's ready to wake up?"

"Work! Go the extra mile to get more bang for your bulk. Dave your extra change. Clip those coupons. Work smarter, not harder. We need to function together as a people! Brothers, find some work if you can. Wherever you can. Humble your selves and the Lord will lift you up. Bible says don't despise small beginnings. You gotta start somewhere. Seem to me immigrants get here by any means necessary; they hit the ground running. We slow drag and miss the boat. And got the nerve to get mad. I don't see why the KKK... I mean the tea bags... I mean the devils... I mean the Republicans mad anyway." Everybody laughed.

"Ain't like they ain't benefitin' from the cheap labor and under-the-table pay that goes unreported. Everything thing they get is on the backs of the middle class. If the middle class ceased to produce, where would they be? If the upper class ceased to provided jobs, where would we be or the American economy for that matter. One hand washes the other. Everybody needs to wake it on up! Many things they claim that are or were American was built on the backs of the poor and middle class. From the White House to factories. Why they mad? Why so hateful?

The only people in America that are not immigrants or descendants of are Native American. Everybody just need to wake up! You all stop lettin' the welfare system and the gingerbread houses that is public housing and slumlord Ville in Any hood U.S.A be a shackle around your feet. It's a noose around our necks. It tightens every time we make irresponsible choices. Our people need to wake up! Now despite some immigrants taking part in identity theft by stealing our social security numbers and using them to work legally, there is a page we can take from their book."

"You right man!" Shouted a teenaged boy.

"I know I'm right! The Lord ain't gave me all of these years 'cause I'm no fool! I'm out here livin' longer than most of y'all. Sad to say but the truth is, I know about ten of y'all gon' be gone by this time next year. Maybe more, in this neighborhood alone. Guess y'all think ya ancestors died and sacrificed for y'all to kill one another. Oh I'm sure they're throwing a party in heaven for their great greats and their great great greats. I'm sure. They have to be so proud at the progress we've made. Speaking of taking jobs, KKK ain't gotta do nothin' no more. Y'all Negros done took they jobs! But hey, they ain't mad. They just turn on the news and watch the blood bath boil from here to the Motherland! Bravo people. And yes! Of course the Lord blessed us with talent so we can get big. Why not? GET MONEY! You've earned it. Forget that the Bible says the Lord gives us the power to get wealth. Forget it says He favors whomever He will. Sure! He does that so we can ball out! Not give back. Oh please don't give back to your community. Each one, don't come back and reach one to teach some. God is really into blessing people just to bless them. It's not about passing on that blessing to others. Never mind the trickle-down effect. It is really all about you. The Lord really loves you more than He loves everyone else. When are we going to wake up?!" The crowd again stood in awe. "And young brothers, you can admire the talent of the athlete but don't aspire to be them. They are just as human as you are.

Admire their gift and talent for a reason. Don't idolize other people. We're all equally human. We will all fail at some point. Whether publically or privately. Idolize Jesus. I implore you! He is the only one that will never let you down. Don't limit yourself to just being the player on the team if sports is your interest. Aim higher! Jehovah, created you for more. Why not own a team? Be the man or woman for that matter to sign the checks, not just cash them. If you think your favorite athlete is rich, think about the person that signs their check. Talk about trickling down. If the star player is pulling in millions and believe Uncle Sam is taking about half of that, give or take a few for taxes; there's legal people to pay, a family to support; they boys; oh and all of the girls; the lifestyle; the image; the upkeep. That's seems like a lot of money. Without endorsements and investments…maybe not so much if they ain't watchin' what they spend. I know y'all saw that 30 in 30 on ESPN. Take heed. It appears as if the real man, the wealthy one, is the owner. If he and or the organization can afford to pay them millions over time, imagine how much they are raking in on the backs of these men. Most of whom are happy for the opportunity, the perks and the check because many, come from his type of environment. Aim higher. Sign the check. Are you awake over there?"

"I am! I'm trying to be a boss." A young boy grumbled circling the old man with his bicycle.

"Get the coal of your eyes people! The Lord is shaking black America awake with all that is happening! Don't you see! Look at the state of us! White slavers used to rip the clothes off black women and expose their womanhood to shame them. They raped them! Now, y'all just hop on stage from the strip club to the Grammy Awards in ya panties and just open wide and let the world see ya little precious. Show up anywhere see through and naked. You used to fight to keep it. Black men used to fight to defend and cover their women. Daughters, mothers, sisters, friends, aunties, cousins… Used to live with purpose! Hated to hear anybody degrade the black queen. Now, whore and bitch are acceptable vernacular like nigger.

Y'all can't say you're trying to turn everything into a term of endearment and think it ain't gon' backfire on you. It don't always work. Then you have the nerve to get mad and protest when somebody that ain't black say it in reference to or about black people. We made that damn bed! You know blacks have always been trend setters from food to fashion. Anything that becomes exclusive to us, whether it's a music genre, a style, a word or a secret only we share, you know once other people get wind of it, they gon' run wit' because it's trendy. It's hot if it's urban; it's cool. Y'all remember how mainstream massacred the term 'Bling'. I hate to hear it now. It makes me sick!

Everybody wanna take part in black culture when it is convenient or entertaining or profitable or marketable. Nobody wanna take part in it when the struggle is on though. And look at y'all. Y'all just ride wit' it. Oh those slaves that wanted to be respected and free; to be seen as equals would be so proud of us. They would love to see us still divided by shade and class. They would love to see us fightin' on social media when we could stick together. Our kids are dying like animals on a game reserve during hunting season and we will fight for the right to breathe and stand our own ground for five minutes. Then what? We go back to Nigga, bitch, ho on stage, at home; in these streets.

We have the nerve to call out women all day long... Bitch! This bitch. She a bad bitch. Bow down bitches. But see... we feel that free to express ourselves with poetic license, even if it means we degrade one another. Yet we'll jump over people to punch somebody in the face if one of our loved ones is called a bitch or a whore or, if somebody outside of the race uses the word as a derogatory term. It's excusable though when a pop star uses it. Oh, it was just young ignorance. Well in other cases, it was just old ignorance, what's the difference? One is a racist and deserves to lose endorsements. The other gets a slap on the wrist. What kinda backwards foolishness is we on out here? Are we as a society then into promoting ageism? Why has one been taken to task and the other not so much? We just love the words bitch, ho and nigger. How can you plant a seed and not expect something to grow form that? Same men that will defend their mothers, wives and daughters to the death, will run in to the studio or walk down the block and call other women or use the word bitch all day long.

Women fought long and hard for rights equal to their male counterparts. Now, you all have forgotten your essence, your real strength, your beauty, your confidence. The first out of the mouth from woman to woman is BITCH or HO this or that when anger ensues or in a time of celebration.

From Dynasty to digital downloads, it is everywhere and we applaud it. What has happened to us? We need to wake up! Just stop naming your children and lets just start calling everybody nigger, bitch and ho. When ya babies start walkin' around in panties and fishnets and calling one another nasty names because those terms are endearing, don't beat 'em. Don't punish them and don't question it. Apple don't fall far from the tree. Y'all better wake up. Doors is closed now." The old man turned down Leslie Street and disappeared into the night.

The crowd turned to Al and Connie. They clapped and whistled. The gathering showered them with compliments. "Y'all did that."

"Ah huh… y'all planned that?" A woman yelled patting her weave.

"Now THAT… Lord if church was real… just like that, I'd be there every Sunday."

"Ain't nobody done nothin' out here. Glory belongs to Jesus. Not man. Man will fail you. Glory is the Lord's. Good night." Mumbled Connie.

Straight away, an elderly woman walks over to Connie clutching a large bible. "I liked your word young lady. The message was powerful. Just need to clean it up a bit. God is holy."

Connie lit a cigarette. She rolled her eyes, "He's just as real as He is holy. I just gave out the real. That's what I believe He led me to give out the only way I knew how to give it out. I know my mouth is terrible. But it's my mouth. I'm a work in progress. Get off my case. These kids talk like that all day long." The old woman stood there with her mouth open. "You Christians kill me. You'll listen to Beyoncé. Go see anything with Denzel name on it. Profanity in it or not… you praise who you want and put down whomever you feel like but you judge me for tellin' the truth the only way I know how."

"Well I…"

Connie turned her head to blow out the smoke, "They was listenin'. I know what they up to. I get where they at. Can't say the same for you church folk. I ain't out here coverin' up my issues with big hats and high heels. I'm just out here. No filter. Uncovered. These kids need people out here. All of 'em ain't tryna come up in there with y'all self-righteous, stuffy people. Maybe I'm meant to be out here giving them the real the way they can digest it. I ain't scared of the truth. My truth may not be yours. It is mine though. As long as The Lord is alright with me being a work in progress and using me how he see fir in the process then, I don't see what the problem is. Now, you can walk around showboatin' with that bible all you want. Recite it from cover to cover. That don't mean you know what God is doing with me; don't mean you know more than me or what I know."

"Well I never…"

"You right about that! That's why ya husband was always at my mother's house. Because you never! My mother in the meantime, she always…I mean ALWAYS did. And your husband loved every minute of it. I remember ya husband. I remember him sittin' around with my mother laughin' about you walkin' around the house in flannel night gowns and bi-focal lenses with a cap on ya nappy head praisin' Jesus and puttin' oil on top of the door posts. Shit! Should've been puttin' that oil on you."

Al walked over. He grabbed Connie's arm, "What is wrong with you! Why you talkin' to this woman like you crazy?"

The old woman smiled, "Young man. I have been alive long enough to know how not to be easily offended. I knew her mother. I also knew my husband. I did what I did to keep him away from me because I didn't want nothin' he was out there pickin' up from your mother or any other working woman." She winked at Connie. "We all know when you lay down with dogs you get fleas right?" Al threw up his hands and backed away. "Woman stuff. I ain't gettin' in it."

Connie dropped her cigarette. The woman moved in closer, "See, I ain't always been saved. I can give it good as I get it. I'm a work in progress too. He don't stop workin' on us until he call us home. No matter how old we get, we still His children. I didn't come over to you insult you, I came over to encourage you. You have something. The Lord is gonna use you. You just need to smooth out your rough edges. We all got 'em. Some more jagged and more apparent than others. Nevertheless, in the meantime, He can still use that. Nothing with God is ever wasted."

"Yeah well, I'm not a cookie-cutter Christian type."

"What does that mean?"

"I'm not like everybody else. I'm not..."

"Perfect? Baby nobody is perfect. You just right for what The Lord wants you to do. That's all that matter. Ain't nobody Jesus called to follow Him or feed His sheep was perfect. Perfect people don't exist."

"Yeah but my background. And I don't know a bunch of scripture. I wasn't raised in the church and..."

"You just scared. Them just excuses. Jesus ain't know a bunch of scripture. He wasn't raised in a church. His lineage was filled with sordid, sinful people."

"Like King David and King Solomon..."

"Yes young lady. You've got it! Jesus was sinless and pure from start to finish. He was born in a stank, nasty manger under non-traditional circumstances. With a crazy lineage... Who would imagine a king...?"

"I hear you but I'm..."

"Anointed for your appointment. That settles it. Jesus really loves you. He is gonna use you where you stand."

Connie wept, "I'm sorry for the way I attacked you. I just got some old ways about me. I got serious issues. Been this way for so long."

"No need to explain. It's a defense mechanism. You're hurt. And I do forgive you. I need you to forgive me too though." She embraced Connie. She held her.

"Of course I do."

"There, there. Young lady, you gonna be alright. The Lord don't fault you for being hurt. He knows you are hurting. He's ready to heal you so you can heal other people. He is ready to love you, so you can love yourself. Then, and only then can you help heal and love others. You got work to do. He is with you. And if you need an old woman like me to help you smooth out your rough edges, I will be with you too." Connie clung to the woman having known a mother's love. "He'll give you what you need baby. All you have to do is ask. He wants to restore every year stolen from you starting today." Al looked on pleasingly. He was proud of Connie.

Al's friend wiped her eyes, "How you know so much?"

"The Lord pouring in to me. Making mistakes; learning from them. Watching other people. Failing and getting back up like everybody else. Living."

"Listen ma'am, I'm sorry about your husband. I didn't mean too…"

"Oh no. I wouldn't even entertain an apology at this point. Young one, I'm easy like Sunday morning. As a matter of fact, all of the runnin' around he was doin' helped free up to leave him when I finally woke up. It was my blessing. His cheating was my out."

"Whatchu mean ya out?"

"Maybe you've never had to get OUT of anything by virtue of being so deep in it. So deep, so invested, so low… you didn't know how to get out. For some people what's so obvious to one may be like finding a needle in a haystack to others. Chiefly, when the thing you're trying to find is yourself. Largely, we the needle in the haystack.

His indiscretions slowly opened the door to freedom for me. I played my part as the nice little God-fearing church-going wife. Bound to her husband. Born to serve him and not myself as per the word of God... I mean the men of the church."

"Pastor included?"

"Pastor included missy. It was another time. Women weren't as independent as you all are today. This was before we knew we had a real voice. Right to vote or not. Or so it was for the women in the church at the time. The women in the world were free. Free to be themselves or who it is they thought they were supposed to be. Doing things that they believed made them free. Many kept it up until they found out the truth. Many of them, in time, came to the church after finding out freedom ain't always free. Anyway, the women in the world had a leg up on the women in the church. Seem like women in the church; the church period is always the last to know. It's sad."

"But true." Connie admitted.

"Yes. So we were taught to put our husbands first. To relinquish our dreams, goals and thoughts of ever being more to these men. We were in essence treating them as if they were gods. We were to be about family and The Lord's business and nothing more. Women in the world were living and working; socializing, kicking down doors and having fun doing it. Church women, well a lot of us, were at home submitting to the will of man instead of the will of God and getting beat by the go betweens; the mediators; the so-called men of God; the MAN-ip-u-lators. They were no different than the white slavers that had manipulated the African slaves into believing things the Word said that were totally false in order benefit themselves. Later, some of us fund out submit don't mean slave. Submit don't mean sit there and be sorry as hell."

She got a flashback. "Lord let me just say this: I may be wrong for sayin' it but this is just me. I know you will forgive me. Lord, you knew I was gon' say it anyway.

Child, I've been through hell in high water at the hands of people in the church. Still goin' on today in so many places. Lots of secrets girl. Religious leaders do immoral things all of the time. Surrounded by idol worshipers and flunkies that worship them and not God. They cover their indiscretions despite the havoc these men and sometimes women wreak on the other people's lives and nobody takes these people to task or hold them accountable until the media comes to feast on their flesh like blood-thirsty zombies. You don't know how these leaders are idolized. You have no idea of the politics that go on behind the scenes in small and mega churches alike."

"You're right. I had no idea."

"Girl! It's so ugly you don't even want to know. Folks actually are taken in by the charisma of leadership instead of coming to get fed and serve in return and go home. Young girls and sometimes YOUNG BOYS get carried away by the charm of these leaders. Religious, political, business, entertainment, education, parents, police officers...one and the same. They trust in people instead of in Christ. Then they find themselves used and abused and on the cover of tomorrow's news when all they wanted was to be a part of something or connected to someone larger than life. These men and women become gods to them and they take advantage of that. It is sick! I believe The Lord has had enough. That's why so many are being exposed these days. The church used to be able to sweep their dirty laundry under the rug. I hear The Lord saying NEVERMORE! After the storm, people go asking why God let it happen. Well it wasn't God..."

"Parents need to monitor they kids and stop dodging responsibility because they don't want to be bothered. I see 'em, droppin' their kids off at church, don't know them people or what they about behind closed doors. Send them to such and such house because they a leader in the church or good this and that. These people are people and background checks and hallelujahs don't tell you everything you need to know about a person. I talked to so many people out here that have been scared by the church. And nobody from the church ever apologizes or talks about it. These just keep all of those tawdry little secrets behind those closed church doors and inside them pretty stained-glass windows. Lord they treat them men like kings! I can't take it. And the king's kids...so arrogant and rude. I thought the kingdom was The Lord's? What happened?" Connie shook her head.

"That's another reason a lot of people don't go. We in there attempting to out shine God. We've made our agendas priority not His. More in fear of these MEN then we are the God that created them. When did religious leaders become kings and not servants? When did the paradigm shift? A lot of these men still believe that the pulpit is no place for a woman. You could have a word from God or a revelation that will change the atmosphere; they don't wanna hear it because you're not a man. You can have a divine prophecy for them...keep it to yourself. There may be something I can do to reach other women that are suffering that you, a man will never be able to relate to. But, that's not The Lord's will they will tell you."

Connie mocked, "The same men that leave their faithful wives at home and be out there trollin' the streets for that honey."

"Or they got that side piece like the young folks say." The elderly woman Mrs. teased.

"I heard of that. A lot of them not wanting women in the pulpit but they don't mind them in the bed or the kitchen. You can pass the pastor water and a towel for his face; you can wear a nurses uniform and usher, but you better be quiet and look pretty while you're doing it. Sure! You can be the church secretary. You can be the pastor's assistant, just can't give a word. Not even if The Lord say so. That ain't in the bible. Y'all all here to support me. I'm HNIC up in here." The pair snickered.

"Oh Lord! Don't be a woman and ethnic! Oh please don't. There's still a great racial divide in ministry. Sexism is alive in the church! The body and the building. Religion has kept us so antiquated. No wonder the world has our children by the nose. We're still in the Stone Age many of us. We wonder why our churches aren't teaming with new members... We're fighting a losing battle. Religion doesn't want to make room for spirituality or improvement. Sometimes I get happy when these pastors and priests get exposed for what they do."

"Really? I feel bad for them. It's an embarrassment for Christians on a whole."

"Yes really! I lived through the lies, abuse and misogyny. They're men with flaws. We've been groomed to place them on these pedestals and to a fault, hold leadership to a standard that men and women cannot keep. Then when they fall, everybody criticizes because they're disappointed. Don't be disappointed when you the one that put 'em up there! People need to just stop worshiping other flawed people. Nobody is God but God. Nobody is Lord but Jesus the Christ. No celebrity, no political figure, no parent, no official, no public servant, no historical figure, no educator or lawmaker. Keep your title and your statues! Especially here in America. God is the one true god. There is no other. He will have no other god before, above, around, in front, in back, in place of or in reference to HIM. Lord when we gone wake up. I'll bet when 911 hit like a ton of bricks and everybody thought the sky was falling, nobody was calling on man...everybody was scared to death! On their knees crying out to God. Oh wait! That lasted about five minutes. Where were your idols then America?

Lord I wish the women I grew up with were still around. Oh the stories! Yes leadership should maintain a certain level of integrity. But where in the bible does it say they would do that flawlessly? How many great men in the bible failed tremendously? God still loved and used them. That did not make them less great, it was a reality check for them and everybody else. All it did was expose their propensity for failure; it revealed their humanity. Cautionary tales girl.

So when I see the unraveling, I just marvel at it. I come from a different era. Just like people from my generation never thought we'd live to see a black president, some of us church folk that know the reality of the behind the scenes...we never thought we'd ever see the day when the religious kings began to fall. But just like traditions have to be broken. Paradigms must shift. Hear The Lord and King say that is enough!"

"Tell it! They really do hurt people."

"Girl! Sometimes church folk hurt you worse than people in the world. You actually feel safer out her in the world with the devil than you do around church folk. At least in the world, they wear everything on their sleeve without hypocrisy and no apology. It is what it is they say. It's like the burbs verses the inner-city. You may live in a quiet neighborhood with green grass and pretty flower. Yes you have a nice expensive home. Crime may be less. But you don't know if the neighbors next door are serial killers, homegrown terrorists or if their latch-key kid is in the basement making a bomb for show and tell tomorrow. Out here, we see the dysfunction. Ain't nobody got nothin' to hide. We're aware of what's out there. It's ever before us. Streets stay talkin' the kids say. The church atmosphere is weird. It's like Georgia."

"Georgia."

"Yeah. I used to live there. That's another weird outdated atmosphere. It just seems so post-civil war era down there. It's disturbia at its most abnormal. They hit you with this sweet tea talk and stab you in the back at the same time. Now how they sweet talkin' you and gettin' they arm over your shoulder at the same time is a wonder child. Just like church folk...BLESS YO' HEART. It's bunk. It's hurtful."

"You preachin' to the choir. Tell me more about this misogyny thing though."

"Sister, it's like that hip-hop thing these silly kids into. It's misogyny in a male dominated field. I can liken it to the political arena or even the business world. We're in an entirely new century and people still think women have a place and they should stay there. Be seen but not heard. I get it when y'all talk about the girls on stage and in the videos with no clothes on.

 Women suffered and struggled for equal rights and respect and the only power we have is in our femininity? That's so backwards to me. If they only knew! We're promoting misogyny by using overtly sexual imagery to promote our products and showcase our talents. Who knows you have a brain and can use it if all you're showing them is T&A? Are we really winning the war? Young women used to want to go to school and be everything men and society told them they could never be. Now, it's enough to be a model in a video or sit on some sugar daddy's lap. You're awarded for being a socialite. Seems like we goin' in reverse. Instead of working to achieve something no one can take away from you, you would rather it be handed to you even if it means your degradation and a horrible reputation. Sleazy is the new sexy. Mystery used to be sexy. I guess mystery is history."

"You're so smart."

"Glory is God's remember. I'm just an observant servant. I'm not so smart. Just seen and done a lot. I have many a regret."

"I can't believe you were abused. You're so strong."

"I am now. I went through a lot to get here sweetheart. That's where strength was birthed from many women in my time, being stepped on like a bag of dope. When you get up from the ground, you come out swinging. Occasionally from the chandeliers. They don't know the damage they do to people when they force your mouth open and pour gallons of 100 proof undistilled liquor down your throat. They force your hand...into a life of sin it feels like. They ain't doin' nothin' but the Devil's work putting a Jesus label on it. After all of that nonsense you just find yourself looking for balance and yourself by any means necessary. It's that hay stack again. You can get lost in a hay stack."

"Well...!" shouted Connie.

"Anyway, in my mind, I still have not yet apprehended. I'm still runnin' the race. I speak so boldly now as a result of not being able to use my voice in times previous. Suppression and oppression makes you loud when you finally get free honey. What I got to lose by speaking my truth? I've earned the right. I have earned my stripes. Who gon' stop me? I'm a senior. Does The Lord even blame me? I doubt it. He knows why I am the way I am; why I stand in my truth so firmly. Shoot girl... I woke up like this." The women crowed heartily.

"So you were bound."

"Like a Broom Hilda child. Lookin' for freedom. Except wasn't no big trouble maker name Django comin' to rescue me. He beat me like a slave too."

"What?!"

"Yes he did. Wasn't uncommon in those days. Wasn't nobody to fight for us or do nothin' 'bout it. That O.J. Simpson thing changed the rules and the game as far as domestic violence goes. Still some ways to go because people still tolerate it and sweep it under the rug. It's inexcusable. Man to woman and woman to man...some men out here get beat, by women; raped by other men; used, abused and mistreated too! From parent to child. Child to parent. Ab-use is ab-use. Don't matter who the perpetrator or the survivor is. It's wrong. Whether it is straight beating up on gay or gay forcing their agenda on straight... it's wrong. Love me, let me be or leave me alone."

"Um! That's a good word."

"Glory be to God child. So that was my out. After years of abuse and manipulation. One night he stayed gone a little too long, and I took the opportunity and ran off into the night like a runaway slave. Me and my daughter."

"So wait a minute. I heard there are signs before you get with somebody that they may be abusive. You know, before you go in deep cover and lose yourself."

"I have to be honest, there were signs. There are always signs. I just chose to ignore them because he wasn't beating me at the time. It was just his mannerisms. His harsh tone. His quick temper. The way he blamed everybody for the things that went wrong in his life. They were there. I just fooled myself into believing that was just his way. I grew up in Newark just like you. Those types of men were all I saw honestly. Pickins' was slim. I was young, in search of myself, already bruised from a strained relationship with my father. I saw the way my brothers treated they're women; how my mother's men treated her. I thought that was normal. I wanted to be loved. I put up with it. The beatings came later. But, as women often do, I covered for him and made excuses for his behavior to my friends."

"You didn't have to marry the joker because you thought you loved him though."

"That I knew in my heart. I was ready to leave before we got married. But, I found out I was pregnant. My mother found out. She went and told it on the mountain; over the hill and everywhere in that church. I never understood why parents run and tell they kids business all over the church like that. That ain't gon' do nothin' but make 'em fodder for the gossip mill, make them a household name for the wrong reasons and cause 'em no to trust you. Why people think lecturin', praisin' and prayin' gon' stop people from people? When has that ever happened?

Still got a lot of teenage pregnancy out here. People get on these kids like that's something new to the planet. Churches need to catch up and bring saved healthcare professionals in to do counselling. Not just for that, mental illness, divorce, financial, abuse...just so many things that prayer ain't takin' away in our communities that we've turned a deaf ear to because the bible don't specifically talk about that. People in the world are out here hurting with real issues. So are people in Christ. They need to open up them church doors and let that stale religious air out and a breath of fresh spiritual air in. We need a reality check. The church needs something different. In the streets, in the church, in the government, we need a new fresh perspective and a fresh anointing. The regime ain't working no more. We need a changing of the guard. Lord, I don't see how nobody understands the problem with an entire group of people who adhere themselves to a faction labeled the Grand Old Party. The title is antiquated. The Tea Party... please. I believe Obama's two residencies in the White House were as symbolic as that man said earlier. He did is best. It is time for a changing of the guard. He's the only one I seen come along to try to do what is fair for everyone, including the everyday Joe. Not excluding women. Gotta love a man that acknowledges the power, strength and rights of women. Look at all of the women he has appointed to his cabinet. You don't have to agree with his agenda or what all he stands for... I don't. We must be critical thinkers. Especially as women. We must have our own minds. Can't always go with the flow. Notwithstanding, you gotta respect that incredibly capable black man. His walk alone screams hope and confidence. Glory be to God! Say what you will, you cannot accuse that black man of being selfish or self-centered. He's not there protecting his own interests. Tradition is of no effect. I don't know why people hold on to broken things so tightly. Just hoarders with issues these people."

"Because tradition works in their favor. Just like in every other area where the old stuffies don't like change and they get to keep their assigned posts longer than they should. They need a revolving cast like these horrible reality shows. People get tired of the same of mess. People be so scared of change. Jesus was always on the go. How you followin' Christ and standin' still?"

"Whoa young one! Where did that come from?"

"I don't know. Guess I'm just waking up. Good morning." Connie beamed.

"Mornin' glory." Laughed the wise grandmother. "So yes. They pressured us to get married. I didn't want to. He didn't either. We did though, because he was the pastor's son. The same pastor that beat his mother. People that ain't know no better praised these men. The women behind them knew they were just men. So long story short… I never got to thank your mother. She was kind of like my Harriet Tubman in a sense. People think blessings come in pretty packages with red bows on 'em. Not always. That was my reality check. Just one among many. God stay ringing the alarm if we listen close enough. Anyway, I resented my mother for making me marry that horrible man. He resented me. He took it out on me. I did all I could not to take it out on my daughter. I failed so many times out of frustration."

"Jeez, I still feel bad."

"Don't honey. Your momma got paid, your needs got met and I and my daughter got our freedom. It was a win win. I ain't even mad. Actually your mother inspired me."

"So how was your life after that?"

"My life? Adventurous. Sinful."

"Sinful? You grew up…"

"Yeah. That's right. In the church. That doesn't make me any less human than you or anyone else. Sin is a part of everybody's genetic makeup. That's why we shouldn't judge. Who can afford to?"

"So what did you do when y'all left him?"

"I left Jersey for fear he would find me and try to take my daughter. He always threatened he would or he would harm her. He threatened to take my life."

"Oh goodness."

"Uh uh. That's another reason I stayed so long. Plus, I wanted her to have a father. I grew up without mine. I just wanted better. I was willing to sacrifice my happiness for hers. That is until I began to notice the unhappiness in her eyes. How happy could she be seeing her father beat her mother day in day out. I had become an empty vessel with nothing left to give her. He beat it all out of me. So I began wanting something different for her and for myself.

I moved away to another state for a while with some family members. I needed help with my daughter. I needed income. I had never held a job while I was married. He worked, he took care of everything. He gave us everything we wanted. I didn't have to leave the house for anything. We had everything any female could ever want besides love and freedom. Love from one soul to another. Freedom to just be a human. A human that is being, doing, living, breathing, function as The Lord intended. It is every living creature's right to just be able to be free and just be."

"Freedom feels so good. I can't imagine not ever being free. I can't imagine a man lording over me like that. Jesus! Can't believe he beat you like an animal. Animals don't even deserve that! Oh hell no! Talking about bashin' Mister's head in..."

"Girl, he beat me so much, I felt as though he had beaten the soul out of me. What does it profit any man, women or child if you gain the world and lose your soul... the essence of who you are? He made me look into his eyes as he beat me. His eyes were dark and empty. It was like looking in the mirror. Try as I might, I could never locate his soul.

So I get to my destination. So it's she and I. So, we had to survive. Us, alone, in the home my family had lent us. We had to eat. I couldn't keep relying on my family. You know how folk do you… They say they love you. They claim they'll do anything for you, just don't ever ask them to. All of a sudden they ain't got enough. They talkin' 'bout cha. They complainin'. You know, how family do. All I knew was how to be his comfort girl when he wanted me to. So I used that knowledge to further us."

"You…"

"Uh huh. I was a prostitute. When I laid my child down at night, I invited people in to lay me down. When she got up, I got up; they got out. I was a little richer. To boot, she was none the wiser. I got out the game before she got to high school."

"I heard you say people. Not men? People…as in persons? As in men and women?"

"Well yeah. I have nothing to hide. I wanted to be free like the women in the world. I wanted to DO ME as the young folks say. I felt so bound by the church; dogged by religion, that when I busted loose I guess I didn't care about bustin' hell wide open. I was the needle in the haystack girl. Whoever was payin' was stayin'. The only rule I lived by for a long time for pay now, play later. Money is ambiguous as was I at the time. When I was in it, I was in it to win it. When I was done, I was over it. I couldn't look back at Sodom and Gomorrah no more."

"So you just quit? Then what? How'd you make money?"

"Post entrepreneurship era, I returned to Jersey. With a Smith and Wesson no less."

"Whaaaaaattttt???!!! You was stick up? A female?"

"I didn't rob anyone if that's what you're getting at. A woman has to protect herself. I had left The Lord long before that. I didn't believe He would want to protect me. I was unfaithful. Come to think of it, I never had to use that weapon. I guess He protected me anyway. Mmm! He's not like man girl. He's a God of many chances. He's faithful and forgiving."

"Even we're not."

"Amen child. I never did run into my husband. I had an old friend I got reacquainted with. A guy I knew before I had linked up with my husband that would come over and have a drink with me like every other night. He was married. He just always needed to talk. His wife was sickly and dying. I had known her too, for a time. I had always admired her. I had wanted to be her for a long time. She had such a charmed carefree existence. Every time I looked at her, I felt God had cheated me. Why her and not me? Why couldn't I have what she had?

The man was handsome, church-going, successful, educated; faithful. He just needed an ear and sometimes a peek or two. He was a man that just needed the company and comfort of a woman."

"He was married!"

"He was human girlie. Grow up! Shucks, I had already done played Mellie. I was through being the side dish. I wanted to be the main and the dessert. I wanted for once, to be what someone looked forward to. I looked forward to making his mouth water. I was still hurting. Maybe I wanted to make somebody else hurt. I'm human. Not perfect. I was middle-aged woman child. I was dealing with real life. I was in control. Tell like it is, they ain't really have nothin'."

"What are you saying?! Those people were married!"

"Just because you're married don't mean you're married. You hear me? Where there's no connection there's no connection. Girl you can be married and be the bland, lifeless mash potatoes on the plate that everybody tired of. So what you have a ring? If that's all you got? What do you really have if his mind and heart are elsewhere and neither of you is even trying? Marriage is not about the title, it's about the connection and the responsibility; the accountability; the oneness. You ever been married girl?"

"No I haven't. But that doesn't..."

"Oh Samaritan woman. I never said it was right. However, I give you fair warning, it is so very real. Women love fantasy. We just love romancing the hell out of life, love and relationships as if there is no work to do. All play and no work makes Jane wonder where John is. On the flipside, all work and no play made John a dull boy. So, John boy came to play in my sandbox." Connie couldn't believe her ears. "As I was saying. It had been that way in his marriage for a while. Since before his wife had gotten sick. Now she was a beautiful woman, but as they grew, she rested on that; it had ceased to be enough for him. All she did was spend is his money on cosmo. She had always been that way. Resting on pretty. He wanted a trophy, he got one. I don't know why he didn't think about how hallow trophies are inside. He was an athlete in high school. You collect trophies, reminiscent of your accomplishment. They sit on the shelf, look pretty and collect dust. Trophies don't add value nor do they function."

"Man."

"See there! There's more to it than meets the eye."

"I get it. I get it."

"Oh I'm sure you do!"

"What does that mean?"

"Don't you sit there and judge me missy. I got your number already and you ain't told me nothin' about your life." She looked Connie up and down. "Hmm! You ain't even got to!

You know I know you." She glared at Connie angrily. Connie turned her head. "He compensated me for my time. Even paid my way through Nursing School; my daughter's too. He was so generous. Known all over the city as a giver. His wife's health had declined over time. I had always wanted him. I used to imagine it was him making love to me when I was with my husband. That made it feel less like rape and more like pleasure. I don't know why it is men think that just because you get a little excited in the basement that they the ones that got that party started? I guess its ego. If you don't treat me well, how you gon' get me goin'?"

"Ummm... ma'am."

"Oh honey please. Refrain from clutching your pearls and hold on for the ride. I'm human just like you. This ain't no prayer meeting. Secondly, didn't you just say something much blunter in front of a host of others?"

"It's different. I was just schoolin' some young silly girls. Trying to set them straight."

"Touché! As I now find myself doing the same."

"But I..."

"Girl hush. We're just two women enjoying a private conversation. I'm just as real as I am holy. I am created in His image, just like you ya know?" The helpmate spouted.

"You're right."

I know I am. You just keep on livin' child. Everything is not what it seems and ain't nothin' wrong with a little straight talk wireless. Hard to find a genuine woman that you can let your guard down around these days. That cute, young, yellow boy that be havin' the temper tantrums said: These girls out here ain't loyal." She and Connie couldn't contain their laughter. "Well it's true! Shoot....like that cut. Ow!" The lady moved her hips. "Ow! That hurt." She grinned. "Woo! That was fun! Sure hope that boy get himself on straight. Shame to let all of those looks and talent go down the drain. A mind ain't the only terrible thing to waste. I'm prayin' for the young soldier. If he just keep his hands in pockets and his mind on the music he'll be alright. He's young. He just needs to choose his battles and manage his anger. He better not hit nan nother woman! I'll tell you that much...I will find him myself and... Lord my hip..."

"Wow. I haven't had real girl talk since my friend passed away."

"Were you really her friend?" inquired the unfiltered stranger.

"Huh?"

"Oh nothing. Anyway, his wife and I shared many personal exchanges and information in church. I wouldn't have considered us friends by any means. Even when my ears were open to her, my mind was fixated on him. I could never quite grab his attention the way she could. Not even after she passed away. He always had something for her he would never have for anyone else. I suppose what is for you is for you. What is not is for someone else. Can't make it fit it if don't."

"No?"

"No! No matter how you try. Inside I knew he would never want me. I just kept trying anyway. I just had to have my way."

"What happened to y'all? Y'all together today? Never give up right? Fight the good fight of faith!" smiled Connie.

"Well, I'll tell you exactly what happened. After so much resistance and rejection over the years the walls finally came down. He always told me I wasn't ready for what he had. I never did take that seriously. I took it as a challenge. I wanted him more with each push. I actually thought he was trying to turn me on. You know how men talk? I don't know women don't listen when men give 'em straight talk with no chaser. Lord ha' mercy. I ain't ready…" she rolled her eyes.

"Yeah… them and their big egos."

"Always. One day he came to me drunk, grief-stricken, inconsolable. Now, lady that I am, far be it from me to not console a broken man; you know, ease his pain. You know, being the Christian that I am. Brotherly love…greet one another with a kiss. You know how we holy women do."

"Mmm hmm. I know all about that consolation." Connie smirked.

"I eased his pain alright. In like manner, he eased me right out of my panties. We were grown. I had been celibate for a while. I was tired of being alone girl. We were older, I thought the risk would be less. I wasn't gonna let a silly thing like a lack of protection stop me from basking in that triumphant moment. He was finally gonna be with me. Besides, we didn't use prophylactics growing up. Y'all generation the one that ushered in death and destruction in the form of crack and Aids to us."
"Huh?"

"Anyway, before he penetrated me, he asked me if I was sure. I crawled from beneath him. I pushed him down. I got on top of him. I pushed and pushed until he was so deep inside of me, I thought we would get stuck together. It felt like heaven. Over and over again. For hours. I guess he said hell wit' it… we here now. It just felt so good. So right." She reminisced wordlessly, "Lethal weapon."

"TMI."

"Get over yourself. We ain't that different."

"How you…"

"Holy Spirit is just as real as He is Holy."

"He got up when we were done. He cried. He got dressed. He put his hand on my shoulder. He kissed my cheek. Before he left, he looked back at me with a tear stained face and said, "I gave you all I had. I am sorry.""

"At the time, I was too busy reveling in the afterglow to even consider his words. I never saw him again after that."

"So that's it? That's the end of your love story?"

"Were you not listening? That was a cautionary tale. THAT was a lust story."

"Hold on now…"

The declining damsel winced while she obstructed, "Yes indeed. I wanted him. All of him. Everything he had. All his wife had. All that he had inside of him and that's just what he left me with."

"He gave you a baby?"

"No my dear. Something much more generous than that. Something much less rewarding."

"What was it?"

"Ever the giver, he gave me HIV. The gift that keeps on giving, until AIDS blooms from the seed planted; until you die. I've been living with it for thirty years now."

"Oh my God! I am so sorry." Connie mused calmly, "Lethal injection."

She laughed, "What are you sorry for? You ain't do it. I made my choices. I'm okay. I'm back with the Lord. My daughter won't come near me." She explained with tears in her eyes. "But the Lord is always with me." The venerable matron appeared misty-eyed as she disappeared in dematerialized in deliberation. Clearing her regret she fussed, "I guess I came full circle. Went from one extreme to the next and back again. It's so worth it to take time for yourself. Women have been brainwashed into thinking that's a selfish mindset. We've been raised to think all there is men and children. Like a life alone with yourself is an empty life. I tell you girl, I have pleasured myself with everything I could find. Trying to fill voids and holes. Marriage. Women and men. Having a child. A career. None of that filled the void only Jesus and I could fill. He had to fill me up in order for me to be able to have something to give myself. I had to become my own gift. I had to wake up to the gift that is me in the present. I had to wake up.

I felt powerful and in control like Olivia Pope. Men over here. Women over there. I'm in the middle. They all wanted a piece of me. I felt as if they all needed me. The show could not go on with me.

 I was the star. There was no story without me. Everybody wanted me. It fueled my brokenness. Masked my insecurity; it boosted my ego."

"Much like how these young people do for their favorite celebrities."

"Of course. That's the way it is. But what happens when it's all over and they outgrow you; you outgrow them; they don't need you anymore? Where do you go when the latest ingénue arrives as your understudy and they feel you're too old to play the part? What do you do when you are no longer the flavor of the month? They lost their taste for me. The music had died. I then, was left with myself, to rediscover myself."

"Needle in a haystack."

"Yep. Back to that. I was okay for a while until I began to believe the lie that I wasn't enough alone. By myself. I then found the urge to fill the vacuum again. My daughter had grown up. She wanted to live the life she was entitled to live. Admittedly, I selfishly, held on to her with my manipulating ways as long as I could. The way our love affair ended was tragic. In the end, I had to own up to my mess alone. I'm still dealing with the outcome. I held on to another person tighter than I held on to The Lord. Later, as I got back into God's word, not in church, at home alone where I could get to know Him for myself; the REAL Jesus, I learned what I was doing was complete witchcraft. It was idolatry.

My daughter, her name is Angel, was my God. For so long, everything had and everyone had been my God but Jesus who alone is Lord. I went off in the prime of my life thinking I was doing liberating things, trying to be like the world. Thinking the grass was greener on the other side. I was a prodigal. Yet, He met me halfway with open arms when I was ready to come home. Virus or not. He loves me. Everything I ever sought out there in the world, I had already had in Him. I just didn't know it. In the mindset I was in, broken and crazed as I was; as thirsty for love as I was, nobody would've been able to convince me of that back then. I was just so young. I was reeling from hurt. I thought I had all of the answers. I had no family support. All I wanted to do was feel good and want for nothing in the process. I got everything I wanted along with so much more than I did not ask for.

I had all types of money, things; been all over the places with all kinds of people. I thought I was living. I wasn't though. I was just existing. That's what life is outside of Christ. It's empty existence. There is no real love outside of Christ. Not for yourself or anyone else. I started from the bottom as that boy say, now I'm back here. From rock bottom to rock bottom. Been around the world girl… And I, I, I… I never needed those men to take care of me now that I think back. I should've relied on Jesus. The price ain't so high with him. Lord how I have paid. "

"Testify."

"I been out here walkin' these streets for years trying to educate these young girls. I'm old know. I can't go too much longer. Funny how I spent so many years with my husband dying to live. Now, I feel like my days are coming to a close. I'm growing more and more tired. I'm an old sick woman trying to keep it together. I get tired of being out here sometimes. People don't realize how much energy it takes to minister day in and day out. They will suck you dry if you left them. Come knockin' on your door. Ring ya phone all times of night. I try to keep up, but I can't much longer. Time has come for me to rest." She looked deep in to Connie's eyes. "Somebody else gon' have to pick up the slack. Time for some Elisha to receive they double portion."

Al walked up, "Connie, I'm glad to see you're getting along with Mrs. Mary Margaret. She's a wonderful person to have as a mentor. She's steeped in wisdom. She's bold. And guess what?"

"They call me Mary Maggie or just Mrs. Maggie. A select, chosen few call me Mary. I like that though. That's who I am. I'm just Mary. Take me as I am."

"What Al? I don't know if I can take another cliff hanger after that one. Spit it out."

"Lord help that mouth." He shook his head, "She's an evangelist. A street evangelist. She is real, down to earth, relatable, accessible and effective. She's come over to the church a few times gracing her with her truth. I love the real talk."

"God bless you son. If you gon' tell it, tell the truth though."

"What Mrs. Mary?"

"You know I'm in and out like a robbery. I can't stay up behind them doors to long with all those stuffies. I get hives child. I got to be out here breathing in the fresh anointing with the people. The people out here need help. These the people Jesus would've spent His precious time with. You gotta tell her the truth son. She got me all wrong baby."

"Is that so mother?" He looked at Connie, "I just love her feistiness. Don't you just love it?"

Connie thought to herself, "Oh now you like feisty? And they women are indecisive."

"Son, you know me. If I said it, you know it's so! She see me with this bible but she don't see me with the condoms I keep in my purse to give to the prostitutes and the addicts. Some people, no matter how much you preach and pray, just ain't comin' up out they mess. A stronghold is a stronghold. You get help getting loose from it when you ready. Unfortunately, some of us ain't gonna be ready. I just give 'em what I got. God's way. The way I believe He wants me to give it out. I go to church when my health allows me too. Most of the time I'm out here in these streets. You'd be surprised at how many elderly people have the virus out here. Havin' sex with young people that have sex with even younger people. Everybody out here thinkin' go young because they the newest on the scene and the least likely to be infected. They forget young people live reckless; they ain't got no fear. They live in the moment. The heat of passion is their religion most often. So everybody havin' sex with everybody. Ring around the rosy...we all fall down."

"Wait! So you're an advocate for sexual activity out of wedlock?"

The woman chuckled, "No I'm not. I just have been where many of them are. I'm a realist. Better safe than sorry. Everybody ain't gonna believe what the bible say. Ain't my job to force them or to judge them. My job is to love them. If they don't receive the truth. That's on them. I did my part. I don't debate God's word or argue with folks. I just shake the dust off my feet and keep it movin' as the kids say. All I can do is pray."

"I learned a lot today Ms. Mary."

"Oh yeah? Like what?"

"The thing that stands out the most is not to be anxious for things or people. Don't want nothing The Lord don't want for you. Oh yeah... don't lay down with dogs, you get up with fleas."

"That ain't all now. What else?"

"Oh! When you find yourself by yourself, that's the best time to find yourself. You don't need nobody else if God is with you."

"IMMANUEL!"

"God with us."

"Amen. Yes He is. He'll never leave us nor will He forsake us. He has equipped us to do what he has called us to do. He won't bring you to it to do it if He's not gonna help you through it. He is faithful."

"Even when we are not."

"That's it Elisha!"

"What?"

"Oops! I meant Sister Connie. Been out here too long. I'm tired." Mrs. Mary laughed. "Early day tomorrow."

Al hugged her, "Need a ride Elijah… I mean Mrs. Mary?" They winked at one another.

"No. No. Sweet boy." She pinched his cheeks. "My grandson comin' by to get me. We cool. His momma don't know it. Got a temper like his grandfather. I'm workin' on him. You know about them generational curses. Pray for him pastor. Him and that little cute, yellow boy that keep havin' them outbursts and tantrums like he got angry Tourette syndrome."

"Yes ma'am." Al jabbered. "Aight. He kissed her on the cheek. "I love you Mother Mary."

"Son, I love you too. Keep up the good work out here. Carla would be so proud of you." She looked back at Connie. She raised her fist, "Storm the castle baby! Overthrow the kings! Use the Word of God. Carry it with you always. It is your sword. Put on the full armor of God woman! The Kingdom of suffers violence…"

Connie responded, "…the violent take it by force."

"Yes ma'am."

"And the spoils?" Connie gave the mother the people's eye brow.

"The riches? Oh they are to go to the people. The Body of Christ. After all they are the church. Use the resources to further The Lord's causes, not decorate a building that will one day be no more. People need to be educated and assisted. They need help! They doin' home improvements while the people suffer. BREAK THE DOORS DOWN WOMAN! STORM THE CASTLE! THE LORD IS SAYING ENOUGH! NO MORE KINGS. NO MORE QUEENS. ONLY SERVANTS! THE THROWN BELONGS TO THE LORD JESUS CHRIST! NO MORE ROYAL FAMILIES! NO MORE! HIS HOUSE MUST BE A HOUSE WHERE ALL PEOPLE CAN COME, FEEL WELCOME, BE EQUAL, COMMUNE, FELLOWHIP, WORSHIP AND PRAY. JESUS IS LORD. TAKE BACK THE KINGDOM BY FORCE WOMAN!"

"Oh no Connie. You done got this woman playin' Game of Thrones? Why you watch that mess…?"

"Yeah. That's what this is. It's the Game of Thrones." She heard the voice of The Lord say, "Welcome to ministry daughter. Roll up your sleeves. This is dirty work." Connie faced the heavens she whispered, "Oh God, am I the Barbara Walters of ministry?"

"It is not about you. Service is never about one person. It is about everybody else. Jesus never made it about Him. Keep it in perspective."

A man came from behind. He patted Al on the back. Al turned to shake his hand. "Great sermon pastor. You the best pastor in Newark."

The pastor had turned released his hand to turn away. Al kept walked. The compliments were empty where he was concerned. He always tried to remain humble. Knowing his own frailties and how at any given moment a flaw could be exposed. He paid it no mind. "Love you today, hang you out to dry tomorrow." he thought. As a man, he knew there was nothing completely faithful about mankind. It was just a reality. Human nature was to build one up just to tear one down. His skin had thickened over the years. Compliment or complaint, rave or rant, no matter the review, he knew he couldn't take any of it to heart. Everything in life is susceptible to change besides the Word of God. He trusted God's word. Not that of man. He knew what it was like to be just as fickle and unstable as his audience. He didn't judge. It was ok. It was just human nature.

China sat on the bleachers grinning. "Heather this what you don't get in the videos and on the news. This right here, this my community. This is the other side of the hood people don't talk about..."

She looked beside her. Heather was gone. "This thot." she shook her head, "Sorry Jesus. I'm for real though. I know exactly where she at. Damn! Now I gotta walk all the way over to Weequahic Ave to get her. Dummy."

The throng of citizens poured out of the area. Barker could be seen over on the corner talking to Chance and his partner. Stacey, waiting for the crowd to die down, sat at the top of the bleachers by the swimming pool. She could see Barker from there. She recognized his loud laugh. She tried not to look. She couldn't help but peek at him.

"All that bein' loud and talkin' bout nothin. Just wanna be seen."

"I know right girl."

"Uh huh, but back to you, Alicia when you gon' get it together honey? Don't you want your husband back? And where China at?"

"I'm working' on it Stacey. I promise. Dope is a beast. You know that. It's hard to kick man. I don't wanna need it but I do."

"I know it's hard. You know I know."

"You lookin' good though Stace. How you get off?"

"Girl pregnancy and Jesus. Mostly Jesus. God knows being knocked up don't stop nobody from getting high. God knows I want a bag like e'rday. No joke. Stress is high. Back hurting. Feet swollen. G living there. Running' in and out talkin' reckless. Boom sweatin' me, getting on my nerves."

"You know you like it. Don't front.", Alicia mocked.

"Ain't nobody frontin' ma. Don't nobody want that." Stacey glanced over her shoulder at the corner. "Never mind my tea though. What's the tea on you and China? Where she at Alicia? You should know where ya baby at."

"I don't know damn! Stop judging me Stacey. You ain't too long ago came out of bag of diesel yourself. Pump ya brakes with self-righteous bullshit. Ain't like you always knew where G was at. How 'bout I remember you just told me a month ago when I saw you at the store he scared you to death poppin' up on your doorstep. You ain't even know he wasn't in school. So you can't..."

"Great. First you scream on me, then you gon' straight go into a nod. Alicia I'm out. Check on China. Let me know where she at and how she doin. You got my number."

Stacey took her time walking out of the gate. She had seen Barker and Chance walking her way. She walked out in just enough time to bump into them. She had timed it perfectly.

"Stacey. What are you doing out here? You should be home. Off your feet resting."

"I'm chillin'. I needed some air. I heard they was doin' something for ya father so I decided to come out. Thanks for tellin' me. Thanks a lot. Ya father is a good man Boom. You need to talk to him."

"Yo! You beefin' with ya pops man? Ain't y'all pastors at the same church? How...?"

"No and yeah...well maybe...I'm not sure. Man it's complicated. I'll get back to you. And you Stacey... He ain't even tell me. And hold on, you hate me remember? So why would I tell you...?"

"Save it! I got a phone call." she snapped.

Barker looked at Chance, "See how I get treated fam? See how she got me lookin' like a sucker in front these men. Dawg! She don't know how to talk to no man. She needs an etiquette class or somethin'. Home training course of somethin'. She's putting me through it."

Chance laughed, "Better pray pastor. I'm out."

"Aye whatever man. Corny joker. Yo tighten them abs up. They look more like flabs. And get a tune up. Better yet, step ya game up, get some new wheels yo. If you can afford it on your salary. I can let you hold somethin'... You know I got It.", Boom teased.

"Nah I'm good. I got ninety-nine problems but guess who ain't one? Ayeeeeee!!! So I believe I'm doin' better than you. You can have it son."

"That's aight. I'll catch you on the court this weekend. E.O."

"Amen pastor. Leave ya Bible home this time. It's a man's game not a revival kid."

"I gotcha kid right here son." he laughed.

"Boom! Your language!"

"Don't chastise me woman. I'm a man. Not YOUR man. Not your son. Check yaself."

"Still arrogant." she chimed.

"Still nasty." he grimaced.

"Whatever. By the way, speaking of son, you know G is home?"

"Home where? He ain't at my home. He better be at school."

"No. Not at your house. He's where he always should've been. At my house."

"Girl stop gamin'. Whatchu want some attention? Well you more than I was intending to give you. Now I'm gone. I don't have time for your games."

"You know what you always..."

"Yeah ok. I don't wanna argue. God bless you. Stupid man..." he walks back to his car.

Stacey screams, "Boom wait!"

He stops, "I can't no more with you girl. I'll check on G tomorrow. I'll ride up to campus."

"Boy! Didn't I tell you he is here? At my daggone house? Take me there please. Mrs. Amora keep blowin' up my phone sayin' emergency. Hurry up Boom."

They whip through the South Side streets. He pulls into the drive way. There China is pounding on the door yelling, "Bring yo ass out here!" A gang of boys wait at the bottom of the stairs.

"Wait in the car." He says.

"But…"

"No buts Stacey. I said wait here."

"This is my son too. This is my house. I'm gonna…"

"You ain't gonna do nothin'. I said no. Now just stay here. What if something happens to you or the baby?" She wrapped her arms around her belly. He grabbed her chin, "Wait here. I got this. Let me see what's goin' on. I'm not going to let anything happen to my son. Or y'all. Trust me."

She cried, "I'm scared. What if something already happened?"

He wiped her tears, "Stop crying. Nothing happened. They wouldn't be out here if it did aight. Just chill. Let me handle it."

She cried, "Don't get hurt."

He was touched that she cared but he knew he had to put on a poker face to keep her strong, "I'm not. I'm good. And please don't call nobody. Let me do this. Alright?"

"Yeah. Okay."

"Okay Jesus. It's just me and you." he prayed. Reluctant to show it and steadfast, he was nervous walking through the crowd of boys. He figured he more than likely knew them. He also figured they may all be in a gang since gang activity was so high in the area. He spoke with authority, "You. Lay off my door. And y'all what y'all want? As a matter of fact I don't even care. Y'all gotta get off my property now."

"Chill son." one boy said. "We just waitin' for the homey to come down stairs. Who you anyway? I been here plenty of times. I ain't seen you here."

"Don't matter who I am. I said leave."

China yelled, "I ain't goin' nowhere until she come up outta there. You can call whoever you want. I need her to come out." She kicked the door, "Heather! Heather! Girl come on!"

"Young lady if you don't come up off my door."

She threatened, "Whatchu gon' do?"

"Yeah yo. You ain't movin' nothin out here."

"Barker walked down the stairs towards the group of boys. Stacey slammed the car door, "Now damn it that's it! This is my house. I want everybody gone right damn it now! Or I'm calling the cops."

China, still kicking the door, "Girl, ain't nobody goin' nowhere. You might as well give that up ma."

Stacey walked up on the porch, she pulled China back away from the door knocking her down to the floor.

"Stacey no!" Barker screamed.

"No my ass! Get up heifer. Pop off now."

One of the young boys runs up the stairs, "Damn yo. Why you put ya hands on her you big ox? C'mon China man. Leave that ho in there. Whatever happen just happen. I ain't Jesus. I ain't tryna save nobody who don't wanna be saved. Look at ya nose. All bloody. You should sue this bitch. Then who house it's gon be huh? Big ass hog."

"China? Alicia and Darrell's China?"

China cried, "Yeah."

"Oh baby I'm sorry. Come here. I didn't know that was you. What are you doing here? At my house waking up my neighbors with all of this noise.

"I'm tryna get this girl out of there."

"A girl?"

"Yeah. Her name is Heather. She in there with this boy named G we just met tonight. Him and another guy Whip. Oww my nose." Blood seeped throw her fingers.

"See man. I knew that white girl was trouble. Why you even bring her down here?"

"Leave her alone now." says Barker.

"Nigga! We still don't know you. You still can get it. Why you runnin' ya mouth?"

"Boom don't…."

"Mind your business Stacey. I told you to let me handle this."

The thug runs out into the street. He throws his shirt on to the ground, "Handle me then partner. Come on."

"Oh you want a fair one." Barker takes off his shirt.

"No! No fair one. Y'all please stop." Stacey begs. "Not this block. Boom please don't. They just kids."

"I'm eighteen yo. I ain't no kid. He want the fade. He can get five minutes. Come on nigga."

Another boys yells out, "Nah son. He gon' have to get five minutes wit' all of us.

The rest of the boys walk in to the street.

Stacey grabs China, "Do somethin' girl! Tell 'em to stop!"

"I can't do nothin' with them Ms. Stacey. They like that. They jump people. That's what they known for."

"Oh Lord! Then why you wit' 'em?"

"I don't know. I was following that girl. She wanted to hang out. She was with me at first at the rec, then before I knew it she was gone."

"How you know she in my house?"

"'Cause I know. She was with G next to me."

"Aight. But, how you know where I live at?" China cried profusely. "How you know China?" Stacey already knew the answer. "How many times you been here?"

"A lot." China cried, I'm sorry. "He said he loved me. Now he wit' her." Stacey consoled her. "Girl, you know how boys are. Damn it G."

Boom and the rambunctious pack where still arguing in the street when Chance pulled up sirens blasting. Lights flashing. He ran up between his friend and the motley crew. He shot his issued weapon in the air one time. Everybody froze.

"Enough. What is goin' on out here? Boom? Man what are you doin? These kids. These Lita's bad ass sons."

"We ain't doin' nothin' officer. We're just having a heated debate about football." the youth spat on the ground with eyes fixed on Barker.

"Boom. For real?"

Barker looked at Chance. Then he paned back to the group of goons. He too, spat on the ground. He picked up his shirt. He returned to the porch.

Stacey grabbed his arm, "You alright?"

He snatched away from her, "I told you to stay in the car. Don't touch me. Don't even speak to me again until you learn to respect me. I know I'm not your man. I am the father of your son. I've proclaimed my love enough. I've shown my concern for enough. You don't appreciate it. You keep embarrassing me. I ain't takin' no more off you Stacey. After I see about this boy, I'm done. Chance you can leave. We good here."

"Nah man. We boys. Imma stay. Make sure everything good inside. Let me just walk through with you. Then I'll bounce." The officer looked at Stacey. He shook his head. "And you'll be the one out here complainin' about where the real men at later on when you got one in your face. He ain't perfect but he's tryin'. That's some reality for you. Ain't nobody perfect out here Stacey. Stop givin' the brother a hard time. You ain't no angel yourself. We both know that." He whispered.

Barker politely asked Stacey, "May I have the key please?" She obliged him holding on to his finger. She snatched his hand away. "Stay out here please. Both of you. Thank you ladies."

Mrs. Amora comes out, "My baby. Come here mi amour. Let's get your friend fixed up. You get off of your feet my love. I will make some tea. Let the men be men. I was so worried. I heard a lot of noise coming from over there. I didn't mean to cause no problem for you baby."

"It's ok Mrs. A. You did the right thing. Thank you."

Chance knocked on Mrs. Amora's door, "Stacey, this time please listen. If you want to help. Pray. Don't interfere. Thank you ladies." Chance stepped into the house behind Barker. It was pitch black.

They heard rambling coming from the upstairs.

Boom yells up the staircase, "Yo! Yo! Gregory! That you boy. It's me."

Next they hear a bump and a woman's scream.

"Boom. I know this is your family but…"

"Yeah man, I know. I know. Do your thing. I'm behind you."

Chance knocks on the door bedroom door with his gun,
"Police. NPD...open up!"
They hear more moaning. "NPD. Open up or I'm coming in."

He turns the door knob. He pushes the door open slightly.
"Get up! Hands on your head! Right now!"

"What the....man who are you and why you in here?"

The young man snorts and laughs, "Chill son. Y'all on ten for
nothin B. I'm here wit my man."

"What man? A pregnant woman lives here."

"Nah Detective Peppers. It ain't even like that feel me? My
man G live here. This his spot."

"You got jokes? I'm supposed to believe you. You a white
boy, in a black neighborhood, in some black people's house,
in the black of night, wearing all black, with white powder
all over your nostrils, and I'm supposed find you credible?
Right? Hands behind your back. You goin' to jail."

"For what man? Chillin'?"

"Nah son. For the half ounce of coke in your possession and
the bag of dope in your pocket."

"Seriously? Yo! My father's a lawyer."

"Good then you won't mind calling him when you get to the
precinct. You gonna need him kid."

"Ok, ok. Wait, wait, wait..."

"What?"

"I remember his name now. His name is Grady or no...It's
Grant."

"Wrong baby powder. Let's go."

"Yo Gill! Yo! Man I just met him tonight. He hooked me up. He told me I can chill in here while he chill wit' dis exotic Zendaya lookin chick. C'mon man."

"Yo. I gotta go process this punk. You good chief?"

"Yeah Chance man, I'm good. I'll hit you up tomorrow."

"Do that."

Barker runs down stairs to check the basement and turn the lights on. He gets to the bottom of the stairs only to greet to his father. "Dad? Why you here?"

"I was driving past and I saw the door wide open so I came in to see if everything was ok. Is it? Where's Stacey?"

"It's handled. Everything's fine. She's around here somewhere destroying another man's manhood no doubt."

"Be easy boy. Grace and mercy. Love and forgiveness plus a little time. She's had a rough life. Be easy. Whatchu doin'?"

"A walk through. I and Chance heard some rumblings not too long ago. I just wanna make sure it's safe before Stacey comes back in here."

"You still care huh?"

"Dad don't start that. I do what I do for G. That's it. Whatever it was with her and I, is over. She's made that clear on more than one occasion. She hates me. I guess I'm gonna have to live with that."

"She doesn't hate you."

"I don't care ok. Let's just drop it please. Let's just move forward. Thank you."

Crash! "You heard that?"

"Yeah son, what do you think that is?"

"Sounds like glass. Coming from upstairs."

"Ok. Let's go check it out."

"Dad, dad, dad. Get behind me."

"You don't have to baby me boy. Remember, I used to change your diapers."

"I know." Barker whispered. "And one day I'll return the favor. I'm not babying you…I just know this house. Shh…I hear noises. Grab that bat and lock the door dad."

They sneak up the stairs.

"Shh…Boom…it's coming from in here."

Barker kicks the bedroom door open.

"Well damn! Wooooo! Fellas! Y'all almost got it. Thought y'all was that crazy white boy comin' in here all coked up. I was 'bout to smoke that fool." He said in a South Central accent. He laughed standing with his pants down to his ankles holding a 9mm.

"Gregory?"

"Yeah man. Who you thought it was gon' be huh? Who you lookin for?"

"G. Man what are you doin? Young lady get up. Get off of your knees. Gather yourself and get out!"

"You shouldn't do that Granddad. That's my company. Pretty ain't she? Wait down stairs. I'll take you home."

"G what the hell are you doing?"

"Ummmmm… being a gentlemen like you taught me. Ah man, I forgot to give her something to wipe her mouth with. Aye ma! It's some mouth wash in the bathroom if you need it. Keepin' her number on speed dial. Yessir!"

Barker pushes past Al. He grabs G by the throat. He pushes him up against the wall. "Boy I will kill you! You hear me! How dare you disrespect your mother's house like that? How dare you disrespect that young lady like that? And hold up… I know I don't smell weed up in here?!"

G laughs, "First of all…" he chokes.

"Come up off his neck like that Barker. Turn him loose fo' you kill him. Let him explain."

"Now like I was saying, first of all, this my house. My mother ain't never here. She live in Brooklyn. You late as usual. Like the rest of the churches. No disrespect Granddad."

"None taken son."

"Second, that chick down there, as you can clearly see, exhibit A, shows, she may be young, but a lady she is not." He pointed to the semen stained carpet. "She good though. She real good."

Barker lunged at his son again. Al pulled him back. Gregory pointed the gun at him, "…and you gon' do what?"

"Oh so you pointing a gun at me G? Your father? Really? What has gotten in to you?"

"The devil." said Al. He pulled Barker back. He walked over and took the gun from G. "You just being emotional. You can talk to him without this. He ain't no stick up kid in the street. This is your father. Y'all hash this out like men. I know you angry boy. But you don't do you father like that. Now this piece here… We gon' just pretend this never happened. I'll call Chance and have him turn it in tomorrow. Now, Imma move on back, you and ya dad talk."

"Dad? Whatever. Streets is talkin. I know how loose my mother was. How do I even know he is my dad? Pardon me, FATHER... You have to be there to be a dad."

"Boy did you just disrespect your mother again after I done told you..."

"WHAT?!" G rages. "YOU BEEN DOIN' IT FOR YEARS FROM WHAT I HEAR. AIN'T NOTHIN NEW UNDER THE SUN Y'ALL ALWAYS SAY, RIGHT?! HOW LONG Y'ALL THINK YALL WAS GON' BE ABLE TO KEEP ALL THESE SECRETS FROM ME, HUH? JUST SWEEP SHIT UNDER THE RUG RIGHT? CHRISTIANS!"

"Boy Imma ..."

"WHAT BOOM?! YOU GON' DO WHAT?! FIGHT ME LIKE A GROWN ASS MAN?! WE CAN TAKE IT TO THE MAT WHENEVER YO. ONE THING YOU AIN'T ABOUT TO DO IS THREATEN ME LIKE I'M SOME PUNK ASS KID! ANOTHER THING YOU AIN'T ABOUT TO DO IS WHOOP MY ASS!"

"G, I know you got some stuff goin' on. We probably need to talk. But if you yell at me one more time....if you cuss at me in front of your Grandfather one more time..."

"WHAT?! WHAT NIGGA WHAT?! I'M SICK OF YOU! I HATE YOU!" He punches his father in the face.

Barker goes to swing back at him. Al grabs him, "No you don't. No you don't. He ain't no little boy no more Boom. He's a man. You gotta let him get his frustrations out. Let him have his moment."

"Nah! Let me go. I'm not gon' let him tag me in the face like that. No!"

Al lets him go. They wrestle on the floor like bears in the wild. Ten minutes pass. Barker knowing he's the bigger and stronger of the two, looks over at his father near the top of the staircase. Al nods his head yes. Barker covers his face.

He balls up in a fetal position, allowing his son to take all of the body shots he wants. Through his fingers Al can hear him utter, "I love you. You can hate me. But I love you. You're my son. I know I messed up. But I always loved you. I'm sorry man. I'm sorry. G I'm so sorry."

G begins to punch harder yet slower. Tears run down his face. He punches as hard as he can. Barker still chanting his apology. Pleading his case. Twenty minutes go by. At last his son tires out. He falls on top of his father and wails like a man mourning the death of the love of his life. "I hate you. I hate you. I hate you."

Barker cries, "I know man. I know. I deserve it. I need to own my stuff. I'm sorry. I'm so sorry son. It's ok. No more secrets. I promise."

"I look crazy out here. You don't know. I don't even know who I am. People keep comin' up to me tellin' me stories. I don't know what to believe. I'm tired of lies man. I hate this family."

Al walks over. He kneels down, "Let's pray. We got a lot of issues. Lord help us. Let us pray."

Barker and Gregory rose to their knees to join the patriarch in prayer. Al began to pray, giving honor and glory to God first and foremost, when Heather tipped up the stairs bowing her head in shame.

"I'm sorry to interrupt. But I just wanted to apologize. I'm sorry y'all saw me like that. I didn't mean to disrespect your home. I promise." she cried and started back down the stairs.

The men looked at one another. Gregory got up, "Yo? You want prayer? You welcome to come up."

"No thank you. I know God don't wanna hear from me. I'm not a good person. I reject Him all of the time. It's ok."

Al crawled to the top of the staircase, "Yes He does. He loves you. Just as you are. Don't matter what you have done young lady. He's merciful and forgiving. There's a thing called grace you need to learn about. You are welcome to join us in prayer."

"Nah. I know y'all think a certain way about me. Its cool." tears gushed from her eyes.

G ran down the stairs, "Look man, can't nobody judge you aight. I was in there with you. We was together. I'm just as wrong. Maybe even more so because I know better. So if God mad at anybody, it's me, I promise. And I'm also sorry. I treated you like garbage. I wasn't raised like that. I don't know what came over me. Please forgive me. You deserve better."

"It's ok. I'll come up. But I don't know how to pray. What do I do?"

"You just talk with God. Talk to him. Wait for him to speak back. You ain't gotta be perfect. Just be honest. You know how we was talkin' just plain and simple, you being yourself, me being myself...you know just kickin' it at the event tonight?"

"Yeah."

"Well just talk to God like that. Just without the cussin'."

"Ok", she smiled.

Barker bellowed, "Wait. G go next door and get Mrs. A. The young lady don't need to be up here with a group of men by herself. Prayer or not, it just don't look right. Respect and order."

"Aight man. Wait right here. As a matter of fact, if you feel more comfortable, wait on the porch. I'm just going to get this nosey old Spanish lady for a minute."

All of the women come running over to the house. Stacey yells up the staircase, "Look at my baby's face Boom! Somebody gon' tell me what happened!"

Al whispered, "Calm down. Men was talking. That's all. A bunch of men working through their issues. You with child now, don't get yourself upset. As a matter of fact, don't even come up here. We'll come to y'all ladies."

China sat by Heather on the couch, "I'm pissed!"

Heather grabbed her hand, "Don't be. I'm sorry. I can't help it. I don't know why I'm like this."

China knew she was sincere. The way she grabbed her hand and sobbed.

"What happened to your nose?"

"I got attacked by a moose." she looked at Stacey.

Stacey shrugged her shoulders. "That's what mothers do. Sorry."

"Alright ladies settle down. The pastor is ready." Mrs. Amora chimed.

They gathered in a circle. They bowed their heads. Al began to pray, "Thank you heavenly Father for giving us this day. For your grace and mercy. Another chance to get it right. Thank you Lord for family and friends. This time together where we come to lay our burdens down. A happy place Father. Before your throne, at the foot of the cross. Oh yes. Yes! We come weary, ready to lay our burdens down.

Father, in your word it says where two or more are gathered, there you will be in the midst. With that we say thank you Lord. We humbly welcome your Holy Spirit to have His way this day."

"Holy Spirit have your way." Urged Mrs. Amora.

"We come to you as we are Father. Tattered and torn, beat and worn to lay our burdens down. Guilty of sin and thirsty within. We desire to lay…our burdens down. Thank you oh Sovereign God that you allow us to come before you, come one come all, to the foot of the cross, the door is open. The time is now for us to lay your burdens down.

Lord we thank you for all of these young people. For every soul in this house tonight. For every living soul period Lord. For we know, you know each and every one of us by name and by number. It's personal Father. We thank you. We thank you for sending your son, our Lord and Savior, Jesus the Christ to come, humbly, down from where you are; he relinquished His crown and laid it all down; deserted His home; forsook His throne to live and die all for the love of us, all of us, wretched sinners.

In your word Father, it says that whoever calls on the name of the Lord shall be saved. So with that being said, we, ask whosoever will, to come. Father we know it is not your will that any soul be lost. Jesus gave His precious life, that every soul be saved."

Stacey consented, "Every soul Lord."

Al maintained, "Yes Lord. At the foot of the cross. Come if you will. The Lord is calling you. There is room at the foot of the cross for everybody. Yesterday is old news. Tomorrow's headlines have yet to be published. That's if it even comes. Tomorrow is not promised. And if the Father bid the morrow to dawn, that, and everything it holds for us; good, bad and everything in between, is in His hands. Know now, that all we have is today. All we have is the God-given now. The present, a gift. A precious, fleeting moment that is fading even as we pray. Won't you make it count? Won't you come? Today."

Heather stared into space. She was frozen. Tears pouring from her eyes. She squeezed Stacey's and China's hands until they were sore. Stacey peeked over at Mrs. A, holding Al's hand while looking over at Heather. Mrs. Amora then nodded to Stacey. Stacey wept. She rejoiced. That's when they heard footsteps. Someone was crossing the threshold. Everyone lifted their heads and opened their eyes.

"Ah yes! The doors of the church are now open. Hey family! Sure is good to see y'all."

"Who is that?" China said.

Al couldn't believe his eyes.

"Who are you and why are you in my house?" Stacey said. Barker and Al stood in front of Gregory and the women.

"Can I help you man?" Barker asked.

Al gripped the gun placed in the back of his pants. His heart raced. He began to sweat. He stood in front of Barker. He said "G take the women to the kitchen."

"But Granddad..."

Al grit his teeth, "Just do it boy."

"The stranger said, "It's wise to listen son." He smiled at Gregory.

Barker looked at Gregory, "G, you know him?"

The stranger said smugly, "Why shouldn't he? We kin ain't we Al?"

Barker looked at Al, "What...who is this?"

Al walked over to the man, "Get out. You are not welcomed here."

The man laughed in Al's face, "I thought you just welcomed everybody to the foot of the cross pastor?"

Barker yelled impatiently, "Dad!"

The stranger said, "Yes son." he taunted Al.

"What the? Joker you better say somethin' and it better make sense or it's gonna get live in here."

"Well Al, shall I or would you like to do the honors? Time is money we both know that."

Barker says, "Dad?"

Gregory, "Pop?"

Again the man says, "Yes son."

Barker looks at Al. Al looks at the man. "This is Slick."

Barker goes, "Who?"

The man says, "How about a more formal introduction? My name is Reggie Benson."

"...and? How do you know my father? Better yet? How do you know my son?"

"Oh Al and I go way back. Carla and I went back even further. Ain't that right man of God?"

Al grabbed the man around the collar. He smiled, "Aww pastor. Now you know anger is not a fruit of the spirit."

Barker yelled, "WILL SOMEBODY PLEASE TELL ME WHAT IS GOING ON?!"

Al turned to his son, "I tried to tell you months ago. I never wanted you to find out this way."

The man straightens his tie, "I'd be happy to tell you. Luke, I am your father." He laughed with a dark chord. He clapped his hands, "Ha! Lay some burdens down indeed. Now where's that old rugged cross. Surely there's room for me. Right pastor? I mean you did say there was room for everybody right? What's one more amongst family and friends?

Stacey peeked over G's shoulder popping grapes into her mouth she enquired, "Who in the hell left the gate open?"

10 Brothers and sisters, my heart's desire and prayer to God for the Israelites is that they may be saved. ² For I can testify about them that they are zealous for God, but their zeal is not based on knowledge. ³ Since they did not know the righteousness of God and sought to establish their own, they did not submit to God's righteousness. ⁴ Christ is the culmination of the law so that there may be righteousness for everyone who believes.

⁵ Moses writes this about the righteousness that is by the law: "The person who does these things will live by them."[a] ⁶ But the righteousness that is by faith says: "Do not say in your heart, 'Who will ascend into heaven?'"[b] (that is, to bring Christ down) ⁷ "or 'Who will descend into the deep?'"[c] (that is, to bring Christ up from the dead). ⁸ But what does it say? "The word is near you; it is in your mouth and in your heart,"[d] that is, the message concerning faith that we proclaim: ⁹ If you declare with your mouth, "Jesus is Lord," and believe in your heart that God raised him from the dead, you will be saved. ¹⁰ For it is with your heart that you believe and are justified, and it is with your mouth that you profess your faith and are saved. ¹¹ As Scripture says, "Anyone who believes in him will never be put to shame."[e] ¹² For there is no difference between Jew and Gentile—the same Lord is Lord of all and richly blesses all who call on him, ¹³ for, "Everyone who calls on the name of the Lord will be saved."[f]

¹⁴ How, then, can they call on the one they have not believed in? And how can they believe in the one of whom they have not heard? And how can they hear without someone preaching to them? ¹⁵ And how can anyone

preach unless they are sent? As it is written: "How beautiful are the feet of those who bring good news!"[a]